Nightmare at 20,000 Feet

Also by Richard Matheson

Bid Time Return
Earthbound
Fury on Sunday
Hell House
I Am Legend
Journal of the Gun Years
Now You See It . . .
The Path
Ride the Nightmare
7 Steps to Midnight
The Incredible Shrinking Man
Someone Is Bleeding
Somewhere in Time
A Stir of Echoes
What Dreams May Come

Nightmare at 20,000 Feet

Horror Stories by

RICHARD MATHESON

TOR® A TOM DOHERTY ASSOCIATES BOOK / NEW YORK

NIGHTMARE AT 20,000 FEET

Copyright © 2002 by RXR, Inc.

A Tor Book
Published by Tom Doherty Associates, LLC
175 Fifth Avenue
New York, NY 10010

www.tor.com

Tor® is a registered trademark of Tom Doherty Associates, LLC.

ISBN 0-765-30411-2 (hardcover)

ISBN 0-312-87827-3 (trade paperback)

First Edition: January 2002

Printed in the United States of America

0 9 8 7 6 5 4 3 2 1

Bibliography:

Original Publications

"Nightmare at 20,000 Feet," *Alone by Night* (Michael & Don Congdon, ed.) Ballantine, NYC, 1962.

"Dress of White Silk," *Fantasy & Science Fiction*, October 1951.

"Blood Son" (as " 'Drink My Red Blood . . .' "), *Imagination*, April 1951.

"Through Channels," *Fantasy & Science Fiction*, April 1951.

"Witch War," *Startling Stories*, July 1951.

"Mad House," *Fantastic*, January/February 1953.

"Disappearing Act," *Fantasy & Science Fiction*, March 1953.

"Legion of Plotters," *Detective Story Magazine*, July 1953.

"Long Distance Call" (as "Sorry, Right Number"), *Beyond Fantasy Fiction*, November 1953.

"Slaughter House," *Weird Tales*, July 1953.

"Wet Straw," *Weird Tales*, January 1953.

"Dance of the Dead," *Star Science Fiction Stories* #3, (Frederik Pohl, ed.) Ballantine, NYC, 1954.

"The Children of Noah," *Alfred Hitchcock's Mystery Magazine*, March 1957.

"The Holiday Man," *Fantasy & Science Fiction*, July 1957.

"Old Haunts," *Fantasy & Science Fiction*, October 1957.

"The Distributor," *Playboy*, March 1958.

"Crickets," *Shock*, May 1960.

"First Anniversary," *Playboy*, July 1960.

"The Likeness of Julie" (under the pseudonym Logan Swanson), *Alone by Night* (Michael & Don Congdon, ed.) Ballantine, NYC, 1962.

"Prey," *Playboy*, April 1969.

To Stephen King,
with much admiration
for taking the ball
and running with it
all the way

Contents

10 Contents

Introduction

by Stephen King

To say that Richard Matheson invented the horror story would be as ridiculous as it would be to say that Elvis Presley invented rock and roll—what, the purist would scream, about Chuck Berry, Little Richard, Stick McGhee, The Robins, and a dozen others? The same is true in the horror genre, which is the literary equivalent of rock and roll—a quick hit to the head that bops your nerves and makes them hurt so good.

Before Matheson came dozens, going back to the author of the Grendel story, and Mary Shelley, and Horace Walpole, and Edgar Allan Poe, and Bram Stoker, and H. P. Lovecraft, and . . .

But like rock and roll, or any other genre that skates across the nerve-endings, horror must constantly regenerate and renew itself or die.

In the early 1950s, when *Weird Tales* was dying its slow death and Robert Bloch, horror's greatest writer at the time, had turned to psychological tales (and at this same time Fritz Leiber, easily Bloch's equal, had fallen oddly silent for a time) and the genre was languishing in the horse latitudes, Richard Matheson came like a bolt of pure ozone lightning.

He single-handedly regenerated a stagnant genre, rejecting the conventions of the pulps which were already dying, incorporating sexual impulses and images into his work as Theodore Sturgeon had already begun to do in his science fiction, and writing a series of gut-bucket short stories that were like shots of white lightning.

What do I remember about those stories?

I remember what they taught me; the same thing rock's most recent regenerator, Bruce Springsteen, articulates in one of his songs: No retreat, baby, no surrender. I remember that Matheson would never give ground. When you thought it *had* to be over, that your nerves couldn't stand any more, *that* was when Matheson turned on the afterburners and went into overdrive. He wouldn't quit. He was relentless. The baroque intonations of Lovecraft, the perfervid prose of the pulps, the sexual innuendoes were all absent. You were faced with so much pure drive that only re-readings showed Matheson's wit, cleverness, and control.

When people talk about the genre, I guess they mention my name first, but without Richard Matheson, I wouldn't be around. He is as much my father as Bessie Smith was Elvis Presley's mother. He came when he was needed, and these stories hold all their original hypnotic appeal.

Be warned: You are in the hands of a writer who asks no quarter and gives none. He will wring you dry . . . and when you close this volume he will leave you with the greatest gift a writer can give: He will leave you wanting more.

Nightmare at 20,000 Feet

S eat belt, please," said the stewardess cheerfully as she passed him.

Almost as she spoke, the sign above the archway which led to the forward compartment lit up—FASTEN SEAT BELT—with, below, its attendant caution—NO SMOKING. Drawing in a deep lungful, Wilson exhaled it in bursts, then pressed the cigarette into the armrest tray with irritable stabbing motions.

Outside, one of the engines coughed monstrously, spewing out a cloud of fume which fragmented into the night air. The fuselage began to shudder and Wilson, glancing through the window, saw the exhaust of flame jetting whitely from the engine's nacelle. The second engine coughed, then roared, its propeller instantly a blur of revolution. With a tense submissiveness, Wilson fastened the belt across his lap.

Now all the engines were running and Wilson's head throbbed in unison with the fuselage. He sat rigidly, staring at the seat ahead as the DC-7 taxied across the apron, heating the night with the thundering blast of its exhausts.

At the edge of the runway, it halted. Wilson looked out through the window at the leviathan glitter of the terminal. By late morning, he thought, showered and cleanly dressed, he would be sitting in the office of one more contact discussing one more specious deal the net result of which would not add one jot of meaning to the history of mankind. It was all so damned—

Wilson gasped as the engines began their warm-up race preparatory to takeoff. The sound, already loud, became deafening—waves of sound that crashed against Wilson's ears like club blows. He opened his mouth as if to let it drain. His eyes took on the glaze of a suffering man, his hands drew in like tensing claws.

He started, legs retracting, as he felt a touch on his arm. Jerking aside his head, he saw the stewardess who had met him at the door. She was smiling down at him.

"Are you all right?" he barely made out her words.

Wilson pressed his lips together and agitated his hand at her as if pushing her away. Her smile flared into excess brightness, then fell as she turned and moved away.

The plane began to move. At first lethargically, like some behemoth struggling to overthrow the pull of its own weight. Then with more speed, forcing off the drag of friction. Wilson, turning to the window, saw the dark runway rushing by faster and faster. On the wing edge, there was a mechanical whining as the flaps descended. Then, imperceptibly, the giant wheels lost contact with the ground, the earth began to fall away. Trees flashed underneath, buildings, the darting quicksilver of car lights. The DC-7 banked slowly to the right, pulling itself upward toward the frosty glitter of the stars.

Finally, it levelled off and the engines seemed to stop until Wilson's adjusting ear caught the murmur of their cruising speed. A moment of relief slackened his muscles, imparting a sense of well-being. Then it was gone. Wilson sat immobile, staring at the NO SMOKING sign until it winked out, then, quickly, lit a cigarette. Reaching into the seat-back pocket in front of him, he slid free his newspaper.

As usual, the world was in a state similar to his. Friction in diplomatic circles, earthquakes and gunfire, murder, rape, tornadoes and collisions, business conflicts, gangsterism. God's in his heaven, all's right with the world, thought Arthur Jeffrey Wilson.

Fifteen minutes later, he tossed the paper aside. His stomach felt awful. He glanced up at the signs beside the two lavatories. Both, illuminated, read OCCUPIED. He pressed out his third cigarette since takeoff and, turning off the overhead light, stared out through the window.

Along the cabin's length, people were already flicking out their lights and reclining their chairs for sleep. Wilson glanced at his watch. Eleven-twenty. He blew out tired breath. As he'd anticipated, the pills he'd taken before boarding hadn't done a bit of good.

He stood abruptly as the woman came out of the lavatory and, snatching up his bag, he started down the aisle.

His system, as expected, gave no cooperation. Wilson stood with a tired moan and adjusted his clothing. Having washed his hands and face, he removed the toilet kit from the bag and squeezed a filament of paste across his toothbrush.

As he brushed, one hand braced for support against the cold bulkhead, he looked out through the port. Feet away was the pale blue of the inboard propeller. Wilson visualized what would happen if it were to tear loose and, like a tri-bladed cleaver, come slicing in at him.

There was a sudden depression in his stomach. Wilson swallowed instinctively and got some paste-stained saliva down his throat. Gagging, he turned and spat into the sink, then, hastily, washed out his mouth and took a drink. Dear God, if only he could have gone by train; had his own compartment, taken a casual stroll to the club car, settled down in an easy chair with a drink and a magazine. But there was no such time or fortune in this world.

He was about to put the toilet kit away when his gaze caught on the oilskin envelope in the bag. He hesitated, then, setting the small briefcase on the sink, drew out the envelope and undid it on his lap.

He sat staring at the oil-glossed symmetry of the pistol. He'd carried it around with him for almost a year now. Originally, when he'd thought about it, it was in terms of money carried, protection from holdup, safety from teenage gangs in the cities he had to attend. Yet, far beneath, he'd always known there was no valid reason except one. A reason he thought more of every day. How simple it would be—here, now—

Wilson shut his eyes and swallowed quickly. He could still taste the toothpaste in his mouth, a faint nettling of peppermint on the buds. He sat heavily in the throbbing chill of the lavatory, the oily gun resting in his hands. Until, quite suddenly, he began to shiver without control. God, let me go! his mind cried out abruptly.

"Let me go, *let me go*." He barely recognized the whimpering in his ears.

Abruptly, Wilson sat erect. Lips pressed together, he rewrapped the pistol and thrust it into his bag, putting the briefcase on top of it, zipping the bag shut. Standing, he opened the door and stepped outside, hurrying to his seat and sitting down, sliding the overnight bag precisely into place. He indented the armrest button and pushed himself back. He was a business man and there was business to be conducted on the morrow. It was as simple as that. The body needed sleep, he would give it sleep.

Twenty minutes later, Wilson reached down slowly and depressed the button, sitting up with the chair, his face a mask of vanquished acceptance. Why fight it? he thought. It was obvious he was going to stay awake. So that was that.

He had finished half of the crossword puzzle before he let the paper drop to his lap. His eyes were too tired. Sitting up, he rotated his shoulders, stretching the muscles of his back. Now what? he thought. He didn't want to read, he couldn't sleep. And there were still—he checked his watch—seven to eight hours left before Los Angeles was reached. How was he to spend them? He looked along the cabin and saw that, except for a single passenger in the forward compartment, everyone was asleep.

A sudden, overwhelming fury filled him and he wanted to scream, to throw something, to hit somebody. Teeth jammed together so rabidly it hurt his jaws, Wilson shoved aside the curtains with a spastic hand and stared out murderously through the window.

Outside, he saw the wing lights blinking off and on, the lurid flashes of exhaust from the engine cowlings. Here he was, he thought; twenty-thousand feet above the earth, trapped in a howling shell of death, moving through polar night toward—

Wilson twitched as lightning bleached the sky, washing its false daylight across the wing. He swallowed. Was there going to be a storm? The thought of rain and heavy winds, of the plane a chip in the sea of sky was not a pleasant one. Wilson was a bad flyer. Excess motion always made him ill. Maybe he should have taken another few Dramamines to be on the safe side. And, naturally, his seat was next to the emergency door. He thought about it opening accidentally; about himself sucked from the plane, falling, screaming.

Wilson blinked and shook his head. There was a faint tingling at the back of his neck as he pressed close to the window and stared out. He sat there motionless, squinting. He could have sworn—

Suddenly, his stomach muscles jerked in violently and he felt his eyes strain forward. There was something crawling on the wing.

Wilson felt a sudden, nauseous tremor in his stomach. Dear God, had some dog or cat crawled onto the plane before takeoff and, in some way managed to hold on? It was a sickening thought. The poor animal would be deranged with terror. Yet, how, on the smooth, wind-blasted surface, could it possibly discover gripping places? Surely that was impossible. Perhaps, after all, it was only a bird or—

The lightning flared and Wilson saw that it was a man.

He couldn't move. Stupefied, he watched the black form crawling down the wing. *Impossible.* Somewhere, cased in layers of shock, a voice declared itself but Wilson did not hear. He was conscious of nothing but the titanic, almost muscle-tearing leap of his heart—and of the man outside.

Suddenly, like ice-filled water thrown across him, there was a reaction; his mind sprang for the shelter of explanation. A mechanic had, through some incredible oversight, been taken up with the ship and had managed to cling to it even though the wind had torn his clothes away, even though the air was thin and close to freezing.

Wilson gave himself no time for refutation. Jarring to his feet, he shouted: "Stewardess! Stewardess!" his voice a hollow, ringing sound in the cabin. He pushed the button for her with a jabbing finger.

"Stewardess!"

She came running down the aisle, her face tightened with alarm. When she saw the look on his face, she stiffened in her tracks.

"There's a man out there! A man!" cried Wilson.

"What?" Skin constricted on her cheeks, around her eyes.

"Look, *look!*" Hand shaking, Wilson dropped back into his seat and pointed out the window. "He's crawling on the—"

The words ended with a choking rattle in his throat. There was nothing on the wing.

Wilson sat there trembling. For a while, before he turned back, he looked at the reflection of the stewardess on the window. There was a blank expression on her face.

At last, he turned and looked up at her. He saw her red lips part as though she meant to speak but she said nothing, only placing the lips together again and swallowing. An attempted smile distended briefly at her features.

"I'm sorry," Wilson said. "It must have been a—"

He stopped as though the sentence were completed. Across the aisle a teenage girl was gaping at him with sleepy curiosity.

The stewardess cleared her throat. "Can I get you anything?" she asked.

"A glass of water," Wilson said.

The stewardess turned and moved back up the aisle.

Wilson sucked in a long breath of air and turned away from the young girl's scrutiny. He felt the same. That was the thing that shocked him most. Where were the visions, the cries, the pummelling of fists on temples, the tearing out of hair?

Abruptly he closed his eyes. There had been a man, he thought. There had, actually, been a man. That's why he felt the same. And yet, there couldn't have been. He knew that clearly.

Wilson sat with his eyes closed, wondering what Jacqueline would be doing now if she were in the seat beside him. Would she be silent, shocked beyond speaking? Or would she, in the more accepted manner, be fluttering around him, smiling, chattering, pretending that she hadn't seen? What would his sons think? Wilson felt a dry sob threatening in his chest. Oh, God—

"Here's your water, sir."

Twitching sharply, Wilson opened his eyes.

"Would you like a blanket?" inquired the stewardess.

"No." He shook his head. "Thank you," he added, wondering why he was being so polite.

"If you need anything, just ring," she said.

Wilson nodded.

Behind him, as he sat with the untouched cup of water in his hand, he heard the muted voices of the stewardess and one of the passengers. Wilson tightened with resentment. Abruptly, he reached down and, careful not to spill the water, pulled out the overnight bag. Unzipping it, he removed the box of sleeping capsules and washed two of them down. Crumpling the empty cup, he pushed it into the seat-pocket in front of him, then, not looking, slid the curtains shut. There—it was ended. One hallucination didn't make insanity.

Wilson turned onto his right side and tried to set himself against the fitful motion of the ship. He had to forget about this, that was the most important thing. He mustn't dwell on it. Unexpectedly, he found a wry smile forming on his lips. Well, by God, no one could accuse him of mundane hallucinations anyway. When he went at it, he did a royal job. A naked man crawling down a DC-7's wing at twenty-thousand feet—there was a chimera worthy of the noblest lunatic.

The humor faded quickly. Wilson felt chilled. It had been so clear, so vivid. How could the eyes see such a thing when it did not exist? How could what was in his mind make the physical act of seeing work to its purpose so completely? He hadn't been groggy, in a daze—nor had it been a shapeless, gauzy vision. It had been sharply three-dimensional, fully a part of the things he saw which he *knew* were real. That was the frightening part of it. It had not been dreamlike in the least. He had looked at the wing and—

Impulsively, Wilson drew aside the curtain.

He did not know, immediately, if he would survive. It seemed as if all the contents of his chest and stomach were bloating horribly, the excess pushing up into his throat and head, choking away breath, pressing out his eyes. Imprisoned in this swollen mass, his heart pulsed strickenly, threatening to burst its case as Wilson sat, paralyzed.

Only inches away, separated from him by the thickness of a piece of glass, the man was staring at him.

It was a hideously malignant face, a face not human. Its skin was grimy, of a wide-pored coarseness; its nose a squat, discolored lump; its lips misshapen, cracked, forced apart by teeth of a grotesque size and crookedness; its eyes recessed and small— unblinking. All framed by shaggy, tangled hair which sprouted, too, in furry tufts from the man's ears and nose, birdlike, down across his cheeks.

Wilson sat riven to his chair, incapable of response. Time stopped and lost its meaning. Function and analysis ceased. All were frozen in an ice of shock. Only the beat of heart went on—alone, a frantic leaping in the darkness. Wilson could not so much as blink. Dull-eyed, breathless, he returned the creature's vacant stare.

Abruptly then, he closed his eyes and his mind, rid of the sight, broke free. It isn't there, he thought. He pressed his teeth together, breath quavering in his nostrils. It isn't there, *it simply is not there.*

Clutching at the armrests with pale-knuckled fingers, Wilson braced himself. There is no man out there, he told himself. It was impossible that there should be a man out there crouching on the wing looking at him.

He opened his eyes—

—to shrink against the seat back with a gagging inhalation. Not only was the man still there but he was grinning. Wilson turned his fingers in and dug the nails into his palms until pain flared. He kept it there until there was no doubt in his mind that he was fully conscious.

Then, slowly, arm quivering and numb, Wilson reached up for the button which would summon the stewardess. He would not make the same mistake again—cry out, leap to his feet, alarm the creature into flight. He kept reaching upward, a tremor of aghast excitement in his muscles now because the man was watching him, the small eyes shifting with the movement of his arm.

He pressed the button carefully once, twice. Now come, he thought. Come with your objective eyes and see what I see—but *hurry*.

In the rear of the cabin, he heard a curtain being drawn aside and, suddenly, his body stiffened. The man had turned his caliban head to look in that direction. Paralyzed, Wilson stared at him. Hurry, he thought. For God's sake, hurry!

It was over in a second. The man's eyes shifted back to Wilson, across his lips a smile of monstrous cunning. Then with a leap, he was gone.

"Yes, sir?"

For a moment, Wilson suffered the fullest anguish of madness. His gaze kept jumping from the spot where the man had stood to the stewardess's questioning face, then back again. Back to the stewardess, to the wing, to the stewardess, his breath caught, his eyes stark with dismay.

"What *is* it?" asked the stewardess.

It was the look on her face that did it. Wilson closed a vise on his emotions. She couldn't possibly believe him. He realized it in an instant.

"I'm—I'm sorry," he faltered. He swallowed so dryly that it made a clicking noise in his throat. "It's nothing. I—apologize."

The stewardess obviously didn't know what to say. She kept leaning against the erratic yawing of the ship, one hand holding on to the back of the seat beside Wilson's, the other stirring limply along the seam of her skirt. Her lips were parted slightly as if she meant to speak but could not find the words.

"Well," she said finally and cleared her throat, "if you—need anything."

"Yes, yes. Thank you. Are we—going into a storm?"

The stewardess smiled hastily. "Just a small one," she said. "Nothing to worry about."

Wilson nodded with little twitching movements. Then, as the stewardess turned away, breathed in suddenly, his nostrils flaring. He felt certain that she already thought him mad but didn't know what to do about it because, in her course of training, there had been no instruction on the handling of passengers who thought they saw small men crouching on the wing.

Thought?

Wilson turned his head abruptly and looked outside. He stared at the dark rise of the wing, the spouting flare of the exhausts, the blinking lights. He'd *seen* the man—to that he'd swear. How could he be completely aware of everything around him—be, in all ways, sane and still imagine such a thing? Was it logical that the mind, in giving way, should, instead of distorting all reality, insert, within the still intact arrangement of details, one extraneous sight?

No, not logical at all.

Suddenly, Wilson thought about war, about the newspaper stories which recounted the alleged existence of creatures in the sky who plagued the Allied pilots in their duties. They called them gremlins, he remembered. Were there, actually, such beings? Did they, truly, exist up here, never falling, riding on the wind, apparently of bulk and weight, yet impervious to gravity?

He was thinking that when the man appeared again.

One second the wing was empty. The next, with an arcing descent, the man came jumping down to it. There seemed no impact. He landed almost fragilely, short, hairy arms outstretched as if for balance. Wilson tensed. Yes, there was knowledge in his look. The man—was he to think of it as a man?—somehow understood that he had tricked Wilson into calling the stewardess in vain. Wilson felt himself tremble with alarm. How could he prove the man's existence to others? He looked around desperately. That girl across the aisle. If he spoke to her softly, woke her up, would she be able to—

No, the man would jump away before she could see. Probably to the top of the fuselage where no one could see him, not even the pilots in their cockpit. Wilson felt a sudden burst of self-condemnation that he hadn't gotten that camera Walter had asked for. Dear Lord, he thought, to be able to take a picture of the man.

He leaned in close to the window. What was the man doing?

Abruptly, darkness seemed to leap away as the wing was chalked with lightning and Wilson saw. Like an inquisitive child, the man was squatted on the hitching wing edge, stretching out his right hand toward one of the whirling propellers.

As Wilson watched, fascinatedly appalled, the man's hand drew closer and closer to the blurring gyre until, suddenly, it jerked away and the man's lips twitched back in a soundless cry. He's lost a finger! Wilson thought, sickened. But, immediately, the man reached forward again, gnarled finger extended, the picture of some monstrous infant trying to capture the spin of a fan blade.

If it had not been so hideously out of place it would have been amusing for, objectively seen, the man, at that moment, was a comic sight—a fairy tale troll somehow come to life, wind whipping at the hair across his head and body, all of his attention centered on the turn of the propeller. How could this be madness? Wilson suddenly thought. What self-revelation could this farcical little horror possibly bestow on him?

Again and again, as Wilson watched, the man reached forward. Again and again jerked back his fingers, sometimes, actually, putting them in his mouth as if to cool them. And, always, apparently checking, he kept glancing back across at his shoulder looking at Wilson. *He knows*, thought Wilson. Knows that this is a game between us. If I am able to get someone else to see him, then he loses. If I am the only witness, then he wins. The sense of faint amusement was gone now. Wilson clenched his teeth. Why in hell didn't the pilots see!

Now the man, no longer interested in the propeller, was settling himself across the engine cowling like a man astride a bucking horse. Wilson stared at him. Abruptly a shudder plaited down his back. The little man was picking at the plates that sheathed the engine, trying to get his nails beneath them.

Impulsively, Wilson reached up and pushed the button for the stewardess. In the rear of the cabin, he heard her coming and, for a second, thought he'd fooled the man, who seemed absorbed with his efforts. At the last moment, however, just before the stewardess arrived, the man glanced over at Wilson. Then, like a marionette jerked upward from its stage by wires, he was flying up into the air.

"Yes?" She looked at him apprehensively.

"Will you—sit down, please?" he asked.

She hesitated. "Well, I—"

"Please."

She sat down gingerly on the seat beside his.

"What is it, Mr. Wilson?" she asked.

He braced himself.

"That man is still outside," he said.

The stewardess stared at him.

"The reason I'm telling you this," Wilson hurried on, "is that he's starting to tamper with one of the engines."

She turned her eyes instinctively toward the window.

"No, no, don't look," he told her. "He isn't there now." He cleared his throat viscidly. "He—jumps away whenever you come here."

A sudden nausea gripped him as he realized what she must be thinking. As he realized what he, himself, would think if someone told him such a story, a wave of dizziness seemed to pass across him and he thought—I *am* going mad!

"The point is this," he said, fighting off the thought. "If I'm not imagining this thing, the ship is in danger."

"Yes," she said.

"I know," he said. "You think I've lost my mind."

"Of course not," she said.

"All I ask is this," he said, struggling against the rise of anger. "Tell the pilots what I've said. Ask them to keep an eye on the wings. If they see nothing—all right. But if they do—"

The stewardess sat there quietly, looking at him. Wilson's hands curled into fists that trembled in his lap.

"*Well?*" he asked.

She pushed to her feet. "I'll tell them," she said.

Turning away, she moved along the aisle with a movement that was, to Wilson, poorly contrived—too fast to be normal yet, clearly, held back as if to reassure him that she wasn't fleeing. He felt his stomach churning as he looked out at the wing again.

Abruptly, the man appeared again, landing on the wing like some grotesque ballet dancer. Wilson watched him as he set to work again, straddling the engine casing with his thick, bare legs and picking at the plates.

Well, what was he so concerned about? thought Wilson. That miserable creature couldn't pry up rivets with his finger-nails. Actually, it didn't matter if the pilots saw him or not—at least as far as the safety of the plane was concerned. As for his own personal reasons—

It was at that moment that the man pried up one edge of a plate.

Wilson gasped. "Here, quickly!" he shouted, noticing, up ahead, the stewardess and the pilot coming through the cockpit doorway.

The pilot's eyes jerked up to look at Wilson, then abruptly, he was pushing past the stewardess and lurching up the aisle.

"*Hurry!*" Wilson cried. He glanced out the window in time to see the man go leaping upward. That didn't matter now. There would be evidence.

"What's going on?" the pilot asked, stopping breathlessly beside his seat.

"He's torn up one of the engine plates!" said Wilson in a shaking voice.

"He's what?"

"The man outside!" said Wilson. "I tell you he's—!"

"Mister Wilson, keep your voice down!" ordered the pilot. Wilson's jaw went slack.

"I don't know what's going on here," said the pilot, "but—"

"Will you look?!" shouted Wilson.

"Mister Wilson, I'm warning you."

"For God's sake!" Wilson swallowed quickly, trying to repress the blinding rage he felt. Abruptly, he pushed back against his seat and pointed at the window with a palsied hand. "Will you, for God's sake, *look*?" he asked.

Drawing in an agitated breath, the pilot bent over. In a moment, his gaze shifted coldly to Wilson's. "Well?" he asked.

Wilson jerked his head around. The plates were in their normal position.

"Oh, now wait," he said before the dread could come. "I saw him pry that plate up."

"Mister Wilson, if you don't—"

"I said I saw him pry it up," said Wilson.

The pilot stood there looking at him in the same withdrawn, almost aghast way as the stewardess had. Wilson shuddered violently.

"Listen, I *saw* him!" he cried. The sudden break in his voice appalled him.

In a second, the pilot was down beside him. "Mister Wilson, please," he said. "All right, you saw him. But remember there are other people aboard. We mustn't alarm them."

Wilson was too shaken to understand at first.

"You—mean you've *seen* him then?" he asked.

"Of course," the pilot said, "but we don't want to frighten the passengers. You can understand that."

"Of course, of course, I don't want to—"

Wilson felt a spastic coiling in his groin and lower stomach. Suddenly, he pressed his lips together and looked at the pilot with malevolent eyes.

"I understand," he said.

"The thing we have to remember—" began the pilot.

"We can stop now," Wilson said.

"Sir?"

Wilson shuddered. "Get out of here," he said.

"Mister Wilson, what—?"

"Will you stop?" Face whitening, Wilson turned from the pilot and stared out at the wing, eyes like stone.

He glared back suddenly.

"Rest assured I'd not say another word!" he snapped.

"Mr. Wilson, try to understand our—"

Wilson twisted away and stared out venomously at the engine. From a corner of his vision, he saw two passengers standing in the aisle looking at him. *Idiots!* his mind exploded. He felt his hands begin to tremble and, for a few seconds, was afraid that he was going to vomit. It's the motion, he told himself. The plane was bucking in the air now like a storm-tossed boat.

He realized that the pilot was still talking to him and, refocusing his eyes, he looked at the man's reflection in the window. Beside him, mutely somber, stood the stewardess. Blind idiots, both of them, thought Wilson. He did not indicate his notice of their departure. Reflected on the window, he saw them heading toward the rear of the cabin. They'll be discussing me now, he thought. Setting up plans in case I grow violent.

He wished now that the man would reappear, pull off the cowling plate and ruin the engine. It gave him a sense of vengeful pleasure to know that only he stood between catastrophe and the more than thirty people aboard. If he chose, he could allow that catastrophe to take place. Wilson smiled without humor. There would be a royal suicide, he thought.

The little man dropped down again and Wilson saw that what he'd thought was correct—the man had pressed the plate back into place before jumping away. For, now, he was prying it up again and it was raising easily, peeling back like skin excised by some grotesque surgeon. The motion of the wing was very broken but the man seemed to have no difficulty staying balanced.

Once more Wilson felt panic. What was he to do? No one believed him. If he tried to convince them any more they'd probably restrain him by force. If he asked the stewardess to sit by him it would be, at best, only a momentary reprieve. The second she departed or, remaining, fell asleep, the man would return. Even if she stayed awake beside him, what was to keep the man from tampering with the engines on the other wing? Wilson shuddered, a coldness of dread misting along his bones.

Dear God, there was nothing to be done.

He twitched as, across the window through which he watched the little man, the pilot's reflection passed. The insanity of the moment almost broke him—the man and the pilot within feet of each other, both seen by him yet not aware of one another. No, that was wrong. The little man had glanced across his shoulder as the pilot passed. As if he knew there was no need to leap off any more, that Wilson's capacity for interfering was at an end. Wilson suddenly trembled with mind-searing rage. I'll kill you! he thought! You filthy little animal, I'll *kill* you!

Outside, the engine faltered.

It lasted only for a second, but, in that second, it seemed to Wilson as if his heart had, also, stopped. He pressed against the window, staring. The man had bent the cowling plate far back and now was on his knees, poking a curious hand into the engine.

"Don't," Wilson heard the whimper of his own voice begging. *"Don't . . ."*

Again, the engine failed. Wilson looked around in horror. Was everyone deaf? He raised his hand to press the button for the stewardess, then jerked it back. No, they'd lock him up, restrain him somehow. And he was the only one who knew what was happening, the only one who could help.

"God . . ." Wilson bit his lower lip until the pain made him whimper. He twisted around again and jolted. The stewardess was hurrying down the rocking aisle. She'd heard it! He watched her fixedly and saw her glance at him as she passed his seat.

She stopped three seats down the aisle. Someone else had heard! Wilson watched the stewardess as she leaned over, talking to the unseen passenger. Outside, the engine coughed again. Wilson jerked his head around and looked out with horror-pinched eyes.

"*Damn you!*" he whined.

He turned again and saw the stewardess coming back up the aisle. She didn't look alarmed. Wilson stared at her with unbelieving eyes. It wasn't possible. He twisted around to follow her swaying movement and saw her turn in at the kitchen.

"*No.*" Wilson was shaking so badly now he couldn't stop. No one had heard.

No one knew.

Suddenly, Wilson bent over and slid his overnight bag out from under the seat. Unzipping it, he jerked out his briefcase and threw it on the carpeting. Then, reaching in again, he grabbed the oilskin envelope and straightened up. From the corners of his eyes, he saw the stewardess coming back and pushed the bag beneath the seat with his shoes, shoving the oilskin envelope beside himself. He sat there rigidly, breath quavering in his chest, as she went by.

Then he pulled the envelope into his lap and untied it. His movements were so feverish that he almost dropped the pistol.

He caught it by the barrel, then clutched at the stock with white-knuckled fingers and pushed off the safety catch. He glanced outside and felt himself grow cold.

The man was looking at him.

Wilson pressed his shaking lips together. It was impossible that the man knew what he intended. He swallowed and tried to catch his breath. He shifted his gaze to where the stewardess was handing some pills to the passenger ahead, then looked back at the wing. The man was turning to the engine once again, reaching in. Wilson's grip tightened on the pistol. He began to raise it.

Suddenly, he lowered it. The window was too thick. The bullet might be deflected and kill one of the passengers. He shuddered and stared out at the little man. Again the engine failed and Wilson saw an eruption of sparks cast light across the man's animal features. He braced himself. There was only one answer.

He looked down at the handle of the emergency door. There was a transparent cover over it. Wilson pulled it free and dropped it. He looked outside. The man was still there, crouched and probing at the engine with his hand. Wilson sucked in trembling breath. He put his left hand on the door handle and tested. It wouldn't move downward. Upward there was play.

Abruptly, Wilson let go and put the pistol in his lap. No time for argument, he told himself. With shaking hands, he buckled the belt across his thighs. When the door was opened, there would be a tremendous rushing out of air. For the safety of the ship, he must not go with it.

Now. Wilson picked the pistol up again, his heartbeat staggering. He'd have to be sudden, accurate. If he missed, the man might jump onto the other wing—worse, onto the tail assembly where, inviolate, he could rupture wires, mangle flaps, destroy the balance of the ship. No, this was the only way. He'd fire low and try to hit the man in the chest or stomach. Wilson filled his lungs with air. Now, he thought. *Now.*

The stewardess came up the aisle as Wilson started pulling at the handle. For a moment, frozen in her steps, she couldn't speak. A look of stupefied horror distended her features and she raised one hand as if imploring him. Then, suddenly, her voice was shrilling above the noise of the engines.

"Mr. Wilson, no!"

"Get back!" cried Wilson and he wrenched the handle up.

The door seemed to disappear. One second it was by him, in his grip. The next, with a hissing roar, it was gone.

In the same instant, Wilson felt himself enveloped by a monstrous suction which tried to tear him from his seat. His head and shoulders left the cabin and, suddenly, he was breathing tenuous, freezing air. For a moment, eardrums almost bursting from the thunder of the engines, eyes blinded by the arctic winds, he forgot the man. It seemed he heard a prick of screaming in the maelstrom that surrounded him, a distant shout.

Then Wilson saw the man.

He was walking across the wing, gnarled form leaning forward, talon-twisted hands outstretched in eagerness. Wilson flung his arm up, fired. The explosion was like a popping in the roaring violence of the air. The man staggered, lashed out and Wilson felt a streak of pain across his head. He fired again at immediate range and saw the man go flailing backward—then, suddenly, disappear with no more solidity than a paper doll swept in a gale. Wilson felt a bursting numbness in his brain. He felt the pistol torn from failing fingers.

Then all was lost in winter darkness.

———

He stirred and mumbled. There was a warmness trickling in his veins, his limbs felt wooden. In the darkness, he could hear a shuffling sound, a delicate swirl of voices. He was lying, face up, on something—moving, joggling. A cold wind sprinkled on his face, he felt the surface tilt beneath him.

He sighed. The plane was landed and he was being carried off on a stretcher. His head wound, likely, plus an injection to quiet him.

"Nuttiest way of tryin' to commit suicide *I* ever heard of," said a voice somewhere.

Wilson felt the pleasure of amusement. Whoever spoke was wrong, of course. As would be established soon enough when the engine was examined and they checked his wound more closely. Then they'd realize that he'd saved them all.

Wilson slept without dreams.

Dress of White Silk

Quiet is here and all in me.

Granma locked me in my room and wont let me out. Because its happened she says. I guess I was bad. Only it was the dress. Mommas dress I mean. She is gone away forever. Granma says your momma is in heaven. I dont know how. Can she go in heaven if shes dead?

Now I hear granma. She is in mommas room. She is putting mommas dress down the box. Why does she always? And locks it too. I wish she didnt. Its a pretty dress and smells sweet so. And warm. I love to touch it against my cheek. But I cant never again. I guess that is why granma is mad at me.

But I amnt sure. All day it was only like everyday. Mary Jane came over to my house. She lives across the street. Everyday she comes to my house and play. Today she was.

I have seven dolls and a fire truck. Today granma said play with your dolls and it. Dont you go inside your mommas room now she said. She always says it. She just means not mess up I think. Because she says it all the time. Dont go in your mommas room. Like that.

But its nice in mommas room. When it rains I go there. Or when granma is doing her nap I do. I dont make noise. I just sit on the bed and touch the white cover. Like when I was only small. The room smells like sweet.

I make believe momma is dressing and I am allowed in. I smell her white silk dress. Her going out for night dress. She called it that I dont remember when.

I hear it moving if I listen hard. I make believe to see her sitting at the dressing table. Like touching on perfume or something I mean. And see her dark eyes. I can remember.

Its so nice if it rains and I see eyes on the window. The rain sounds like a big giant outside. He says shushshush so every one will be quiet. I like to make believe that in mommas room.

What I like almost best is to sit at mommas dressing table. It is like pink and big and smells sweet too. The seat in front has a pillow sewed in it. There are bottles and bottles with bumps and have colored perfume in them. And you can see almost your whole self in the mirror.

When I sit there I make believe to be momma. I say be quiet mother I am going out and you can not stop me. It is something I say I dont know why like I hear it in me. And oh stop your sobbing mother they will not catch me I have my magic dress.

When I pretend I brush my hair long. But I only use my own brush from my room. I didnt never use mommas brush. I dont think granma is mad at me for that because I never use mommas brush. I wouldnt never.

Sometimes I did open the box up. Because I know where granma puts the key. I saw her once when she wouldnt know I saw her. She puts the key on the hook in mommas closet. Behind the door I mean.

I could open the box lots of times. Thats because I like to look at mommas dress. I like best to look at it. It is so pretty and feels soft and like silky. I could touch it for a million years.

I kneel on the rug with roses on it. I hold the dress in my arms and like breathe from it. I touch it against my cheek. I wish I could take it to sleep with me and hold it. I like to. Now I cant. Because granma says. And she says I should burn it up but I loved her so. And she cries about the dress.

I wasnt never bad with it. I put it back neat like it was never touched. Granma never knew. I laughed that she never knew before. But she knows now I did it I guess. And shell punish me. What did it hurt her? Wasnt it my mommas dress?

What I like real best in mommas room is look at the picture of momma. It has a gold thing around it. Frame is what granma says. It is on the wall on top the bureau.

Momma is pretty. Your momma was pretty granma says. Why does she? I see momma there smiling on me and she *is* pretty. For always.

Her hair is black. Like mine. Her eyes are even pretty like black. Her mouth is red so red. I like the dress and its the white one. It is all down on her shoulders. Her skin is white almost white like the dress. And so are her hands. She is so pretty. I love her even if she is gone away forever. I love her so much.

I guess I think thats what made me bad. I mean to Mary Jane.

Mary Jane came from lunch like she does. Granma went to do her nap. She said dont forget now no going to your mommas room. I told her no granma. And I was saying the truth but then Mary Jane and I was playing fire truck. Mary Jane said I bet you havent no mother I bet you made up it all she said.

I got mad at her. I have a momma I know. She made me mad at her to say I made up it all. She said Im a liar. I mean about the bed and the dressing table and the picture and the dress even and every thing.

I said well Ill show you smarty.

I looked into granmas room. She was doing her nap still. I went down and said Mary Jane to come on because granma wont know.

She wasnt so smart after then. She giggled like she does. Even she made a scaredy noise when she hit into the table in the hall upstairs. I said youre a scaredy cat to her. She said back well *my* house isnt so dark like this. Like that was so much.

We went in mommas room. It was more dark than you could see. I said this is my mommas room I suppose I made up it all.

She was by the door and she wasnt smart then either. She didnt say any word. She looked around the room. She jumped when I got her arm. Well come on I said.

I sat on the bed and said this is my mommas bed see how soft it is. She didnt say nothing. Scaredy cat I said. Am not she said like she does.

I said to sit down how can you tell if its soft if you dont sit down. She sat down by me. I said feel how soft it is. Smell how sweet it is.

I closed my eyes but funny it wasnt like always. Because Mary Jane was there. I told her to stop feeling the cover. You said to she said. Well stop it I said.

See I said and I pulled her up. Thats the dressing table. I took her and brought her there. She said let go. It was so quiet and like always. I started to feel bad. Because Mary Jane was there. Because it was in my mommas room and momma wouldnt like Mary Jane there.

But I had to show her the things because. I showed her the mirror. We looked at each other in it. She looked white. Mary Jane is a scaredy cat I said. Am not am not she said anyway nobodys house is so quiet and dark inside. Anyway she said it smells.

I got mad at her. No it doesnt smell I said. Does so she said you said it did. I got madder too. It smells like sugar she said. It smells like sick people in your mommas room.

Dont say my mommas room is like sick people I said to her.

Well you didnt show me no dress and youre lying she said there isnt no dress. I felt all warm inside so I pulled her hair. Ill show you I said youre going to see my mommas dress and youll better not call me a liar.

I made her stand still and I got the key off the hook. I kneeled down. I opened the box with the key.

Mary Jane said pew that smells like garbage.

I put my nails in her and she pulled away and got mad. Dont you pinch me she said and she was all red. Im telling my mother on you she said. And anyway its not a white dress its dirty and ugly she said.

Its not dirty I said. I said it so loud I wonder why granma didnt hear. I pulled out the dress from the box. I held it up to show her how its white. It fell open like the rain whispering and the bottom touched on the rug.

It is too white I said all white and clean and silky.

No she said she was so mad and red it has a hole in it. I got more madder. If my momma was here shed show you I said. You got no momma she said all ugly. I hate her.

I have. I said it way loud. I pointed my finger to mommas picture. Well who can see in this stupid dark room she said. I pushed her hard and she hit against the bureau. See then I said mean look at the picture. Thats my momma and shes the most beautiful lady in the world.

Shes ugly she has funny hands Mary Jane said. She hasnt I said shes the most beautiful lady in the world!

Not not she said *she has buck teeth.*

I dont remember then. I think the dress moved in my arms. Mary Jane screamed. I dont remember what. It got dark and the curtains were closed I think I couldnt see anyway. I couldnt hear nothing except buck teeth funny hands buck teeth funny hands even when no one was saying it.

There was something else because I think I heard some one call *dont let her say that*! I couldnt hold to the dress. And I had it on me I cant remember. Because I was grown up strong. But I was a little girl still I think I mean outside.

I think I was terrible bad then.

Granma took me away from there I guess. I dont know. She was screaming god help us its happened its happened. Over and over. I dont know why. She pulled me all the way here to my room and locked me in. She wont let me out. Well Im not so scared. Who cares if she locks me in a million billion years? She doesn't have to even give me supper. Im not hungry anyway.

Im full.

Blood Son

The people on the block decided definitely that Jules was crazy when they heard about his composition.

There had been suspicions for a long time.

He made people shiver with his blank stare. His coarse guttural tongue sounded unnatural in his frail body. The paleness of his skin upset many children. It seemed to hang loose around his flesh. He hated sunlight.

And his ideas were a little out of place for the people who lived on the block.

Jules wanted to be a vampire.

People declared it common knowledge that he was born on a night when winds uprooted trees. They said he was born with three teeth. They said he'd used them to fasten himself on his mother's breast drawing blood with the milk.

They said he used to cackle and bark in his crib after dark. They said he walked at two months and sat staring at the moon whenever it shone.

Those were things that people said.

His parents were always worried about him. An only child, they noticed his flaws quickly.

They thought he was blind until the doctor told them it was

just a vacuous stare. He told them that Jules, with his large head, might be a genius or an idiot. It turned out he was an idiot.

He never spoke a word until he was five. Then, one night coming up to supper, he sat down at the table and said "Death."

His parents were torn between delight and disgust. They finally settled for a place in between the two feelings. They decided that Jules couldn't have realized what the word meant.

But Jules did.

From that night on, he built up such a large vocabulary that everyone who knew him was astonished. He not only acquired every word spoken to him, words from signs, magazines, books; he made up his own words.

Like—*nightouch*. Or—*killove*. They were really several words that melted into each other. They said things Jules felt but couldn't explain with other words.

He used to sit on the porch while the other children played hopscotch, stickball and other games. He sat there and stared at the sidewalk and made up words.

Until he was twelve Jules kept pretty much out of trouble.

Of course there was the time they found him undressing Olive Jones in an alley. And another time he was discovered dissecting a kitten on his bed.

But there were many years in between. Those scandals were forgotten.

In general he went through childhood merely disgusting people.

He went to school but never studied. He spent about two or three terms in each grade. The teachers all knew him by his first name. In some subjects like reading and writing he was almost brilliant.

In others he was hopeless.

One Saturday when he was twelve, Jules went to the movies. He saw *Dracula*.

When the show was over he walked, a throbbing nerve mass, through the little girl and boy ranks.

He went home and locked himself in the bathroom for two hours.

His parents pounded on the door and threatened but he wouldn't come out.

Finally he unlocked the door and sat down at the supper table. He had a bandage on his thumb and a satisfied look on his face.

The morning after he went to the library. It was Sunday. He sat on the steps all day waiting for it to open. Finally he went home.

The next morning he came back instead of going to school.

He found *Dracula* on the shelves. He couldn't borrow it because he wasn't a member and to be a member he had to bring in one of his parents.

So he stuck the book down his pants and left the library and never brought it back.

He went to the park and sat down and read the book through. It was late evening before he finished.

He started at the beginning again, reading as he ran from street light to street light, all the way home.

He didn't hear a word of the scolding he got for missing lunch and supper. He ate, went in his room and read the book to the finish. They asked him where he got the book. He said he found it.

As the days passed Jules read the story over and over. He never went to school.

Late at night, when he had fallen into an exhausted slumber, his mother used to take the book into the living room and show it to her husband.

One night they noticed that Jules had underlined certain sentences with dark shaky pencil lines.

Like: "The lips were crimson with fresh blood and the stream had trickled over her chin and stained the purity of her lawn death robe."

Or: "When the blood began to spurt out, he took my hands in one of his, holding them tight and, with the other seized my neck and pressed my mouth to the wound . . ."

When his mother saw this, she threw the book down the garbage chute.

In the next morning when Jules found the book missing he screamed and twisted his mother's arm until she told him where the book was.

Then he ran down to the cellar and dug in the piles of garbage until he found the book.

Coffee grounds and egg yolk on his hands and wrists, he went to the park and read it again.

For a month he read the book avidly. Then he knew it so well he threw it away and just thought about it.

Absence notes were coming from school. His mother yelled. Jules decided to go back for a while.

He wanted to write a composition.

One day he wrote it in class. When everyone was finished writing, the teacher asked if anyone wanted to read their composition to the class.

Jules raised his hand.

The teacher was surprised. But she felt charity. She wanted to encourage him. She drew in her tiny jab of a chin and smiled.

"All right," she said. "Pay attention children. Jules is going to read us his composition."

Jules stood up. He was excited. The paper shook in his hands.

"My Ambition by . . ."

"Come to the front of the class, Jules, dear."

Jules went to the front of the class. The teacher smiled lov-
ingly. Jules started again.

"My Ambition by Jules Dracula."

The smile sagged.

"When I grow up I want to be a vampire."

The teacher's smiling lips jerked down and out. Her eyes
popped wide.

"I want to live forever and get even with everybody and
make all the girls vampires. I want to smell of death."

"Jules!"

"I want to have a foul breath that stinks of dead earth and
crypts and sweet coffins."

The teacher shuddered. Her hands twitched on her green blot-
ter. She couldn't believe her ears. She looked at the children. They
were gaping. Some of them were giggling. But not the girls.

"I want to be all cold and have rotten flesh with stolen blood
in the veins."

"That will . . . hrrumph!"

The teacher cleared her throat mightily.

"That will be all Jules," she said.

Jules talked louder and desperately.

"I want to sink my terrible white teeth in my victims' necks.
I want them to . . ."

"Jules! Go to your seat this instant!"

"I want them to slide like razors in the flesh and into the
veins," read Jules ferociously.

The teacher jolted to her feet. Children were shivering.
None of them were giggling.

"Then I want to draw my teeth out and let the blood flow
easy in my mouth and run hot in my throat and . . ."

The teacher grabbed his arm. Jules tore away and ran to a
corner. Barricaded behind a stool he yelled:

"And drip off my tongue and run out my lips down my victims' throats! I want to drink girls' blood!"

The teacher lunged for him. She dragged him out of the corner. He clawed at her and screamed all the way to the door and the principal's office.

"That is my ambition! That is my ambition! *That is my ambition!*"

It was grim.

Jules was locked in his room. The teacher and the principal sat with Jules's parents. They were talking in sepulchral voices.

They were recounting the scene.

All along the block parents were discussing it. Most of them didn't believe it at first. They thought their children made it up.

Then they thought what horrible children they'd raised if the children could make up such things.

So they believed it.

After that everyone watched Jules like a hawk. People avoided his touch and look. Parents pulled their children off the street when he approached. Everyone whispered tales of him.

There were more absence notes.

Jules told his mother he wasn't going to school anymore. Nothing would change his mind. He never went again.

When a truant officer came to the apartment Jules would run over the roofs until he was far away from there.

A year wasted by.

Jules wandered the streets searching for something; he didn't know what. He looked in alleys. He looked in garbage cans. He looked in lots. He looked on the east side and the west side and in the middle.

He couldn't find what he wanted.

He rarely slept. He never spoke. He stared down all the time. He forgot his special words.

Then.

One day in the park, Jules strolled through the zoo.

An electric shock passed through him when he saw the vampire bat.

His eyes grew wide and his discolored teeth shone dully in a wide smile.

From that day on, Jules went daily to the zoo and looked at the bat. He spoke to it and called it the Count. He felt in his heart it was really a man who had changed.

A rebirth of culture struck him.

He stole another book from the library. It told all about wild life.

He found the page on the vampire bat. He tore it out and threw the book away.

He learned the selection by heart.

He knew how the bat made its wound. How it lapped up the blood like a kitten drinking cream. How it walked on folded wing stalks and hind legs like a black furry spider. Why it took no nourishment but blood.

Month after month Jules stared at the bat and talked to it. It became the one comfort in his life. The one symbol of dreams come true.

One day Jules noticed that the bottom of the wire covering the cage had come loose.

He looked around, his black eyes shifting. He didn't see anyone looking. It was a cloudy day. Not many people were there.

Jules tugged at the wire.

It moved a little.

Then he saw a man come out of the monkey house. So he

pulled back his hand and strolled away whistling a song he had just made up.

Late at night, when he was supposed to be asleep he would walk barefoot past his parents' room. He would hear his father and mother snoring. He would hurry out, put on his shoes and run to the zoo.

Every time the watchman was not around, Jules would tug at the wiring.

He kept on pulling it loose.

When he was finished and had to run home, he pushed the wire in again. Then no one could tell.

All day Jules would stand in front of the cage and look at the Count and chuckle and tell him he'd soon be free again.

He told the Count all the things he knew. He told the Count he was going to practice climbing down walls head first.

He told the Count not to worry. He'd soon be out. Then, together, they could go all around and drink girls' blood.

One night Jules pulled the wire out and crawled under it into the cage.

It was very dark.

He crept on his knees to the little wooden house. He listened to see if he could hear the Count squeaking.

He stuck his arm in the black doorway. He kept whispering.

He jumped when he felt a needle jab in his finger.

With a look of great pleasure on his thin face, Jules drew the fluttering hairy bat to him.

He climbed down from the cage with it and ran out of the zoo; out of the park. He ran down the silent streets.

It was getting late in the morning. Light touched the dark skies with gray. He couldn't go home. He had to have a place.

He went down an alley and climbed over a fence. He held tight to the bat. It lapped at the dribble of blood from his finger.

He went across a yard and into a little deserted shack.

It was dark inside and damp. It was full of rubble and tin cans and soggy cardboard and excrement.

Jules made sure there was no way the bat could escape.

Then he pulled the door tight and put a stick through the metal loop.

He felt his heart beating hard and his limbs trembling. He let go of the bat. It flew to a dark corner and hung on the wood.

Jules feverishly tore off his shirt. His lips shook. He smiled a crazy smile.

He reached down into his pants pocket and took out a little pen knife he had stolen from his mother.

He opened it and ran a finger over the blade. It sliced through the flesh.

With shaking fingers he jabbed at his throat. He hacked. The blood ran through his fingers.

"Count! Count!" he cried in frenzied joy. "Drink my red blood! Drink me! Drink me!"

He stumbled over the tin cans and slipped and felt for the bat. It sprang from the wood and soared across the shack and fastened itself on the other side.

Tears ran down Jules's cheeks.

He gritted his teeth. The blood ran across his shoulders and across his thin hairless chest.

His body shook in fever. He staggered back toward the other side. He tripped and felt his side torn open on the sharp edge of a tin can.

His hands went out. They clutched the bat. He placed it against his throat. He sank on his back on the cool wet earth. He sighed.

He started to moan and clutch at his chest. His stomach heaved. The black bat on his neck silently lapped his blood.

Jules felt his life seeping away.

He thought of all the years past. The waiting. His parents. School. Dracula. Dreams. For this. This sudden glory.

Jules's eyes flickered open.

The inside of the reeking shack swam about him.

It was hard to breathe. He opened his mouth to gasp in the air. He sucked it in. It was foul. It made him cough. His skinny body lurched on the cold ground.

Mists crept away in his brain.

One by one like drawn veils.

Suddenly his mind was filled with terrible clarity.

He felt the aching pain in his side.

He knew he was lying half naked on garbage and letting a flying bat drink his blood.

With a strangled cry, he reached up and tore away the furry throbbing bat. He flung it away from him. It came back, fanning his face with its vibrating wings.

Jules staggered to his feet.

He felt for the door. He could hardly see. He tried to stop his throat from bleeding so.

He managed to get the door open.

Then, lurching into the dark yard, he fell on his face in the long grass blades.

He tried to call out for help.

But no sounds save a bubbling mockery of words came from his lips.

He heard the fluttering wings.

Then, suddenly they were gone.

Strong fingers lifted him gently. Through dying eyes Jules saw the tall dark man whose eyes shone like rubies.

"My son," the man said.

Through Channels

Click
   Swish swish swish
   All set, Sergeant?
   Set.
   Okay. This recording made on January fifteenth, nineteen fifty-four, twenty-third precinct police . . .
   Swish
   . . . in the presence of Detective James Taylor and, uh, Sergeant Louis Ferazzio.
   Swish swish
   Name, please.
   Huh?
   What's your name, son?
   My name?
   Come on, son, we're trying to help you.
   Swish
   L-Leo.
   Last name.
   I d-don't . . . Leo.
   What's your last name, son?
   Vo . . . Vo . . .

All right, son. Take it easy.

V–Vogel.

Leo Vogel. That it?

Yeah.

Address?

T–twenny two thirty, avena J.

Age?

I'm . . . almost. . . . Where's . . . my ma?

Swish swish

Turn it off a minute, Sergeant.

Right.

Click

C *lick*

    Swish

All right, son. Okay now?

Y–yeah. But where . . . ?

You're how old?

Fi–fifteen.

Now, uh, where were you last night from six o'clock till you went home?

I was . . . at . . . at the show. Ma give . . . give me the dough.

How come you didn't stay home to watch television with your parents?

'Cause. Because . . .

Yes?

The Le–Lenottis was comin' over to watch it with them.

They came often?

N–no. It was the first time they'd . . . ever come.

Uh-huh. So your mother sent you to the movies.

Y–yeah.

Sergeant, give the kid some of that coffee. And see if you can him find a blanket.

Right away, chief.

Now, uh, son. What time did you get out of the movies?

Time? I . . . don't know what time.

About nine-thirty, would you say?

I guess. I don't know . . . w-what time. All I . . .

Yes?

Nothin'.

Well, you saw the show only once, didn't you?

Swish

Huh?

You saw it only once. You didn't see any picture twice, did you?

No. No, I only seen it once.

Okay. That would make it, uh . . .

Swish

. . . roughly about nine-thirty, then, that you got out of the movies. You went home right away?

Yeah . . . I mean no.

Where did you stop?

I had a Coke at the . . . at the drugstore.

I see. Then you went home.

Ye—

Swish.

. . . yeah, then I went home.

The house was dark?

Yeah. But . . . they never used no lights when they watch-ed TV.

Uh-huh. You went in?

Y-yeah.

Take a sip of that coffee, son, before it gets cold. Take it easy, take it easy. Don't choke on it. There. Okay?

Yeah.

All right then. Now . . . oh, good. Put it over his shoulders, Sergeant. There we go. Better?

Mmmm

Okay. Let's get on with it. And believe me, son, this is no more fun for us than it is for you. We saw it too.

I want mama. I want her. Please, can I . . .

Oh. What did I . . . well, shut it off, Sergeant. Here kid. You don't have a handkerchief, do you? Here. Did you shut it off, Sergeant?

Oh. Right away.

Swish click

C lick

When you went in, was there anything . . . peculiar?

What?

You told us last night you smelled something.

Yeah. It . . . it. . . . There was a funny smell.

Anything you know?

Huh?

Did it smell like anything you ever smelled before?

No. It wasn't much. Not in the . . . hall.

All right. So you went into the living room.

No. No. I went . . . Ma. Can I . . .

Swish swish

Come on, son, snap out of it. We know you've had a bad time. But we're trying to help.

Swish swish swish

You, uh, didn't go in the living room. Didn't you think you should mention that smell?

I . . . h–heard the set on and . . .

Set?

The TV set. I thought—I figured they were still watchin'.

And?

And ma didn't like me to . . . b–bust in on them. So I went
up to my room so's I wouldn't . . . you know.

Bother them.

Y–yeah.

Okay. How long were you up there?

I was . . . I don't know how long. Maybe an hour.

And?

There . . . wasn't no sound downstairs.

Nothing at all?

No. There wasn't nothing at all.

Didn't that make you suspicious?

Yeah. Well, I figured . . . they'd . . . laugh at somethin' or
talk loud or . . .

Dead quiet.

Yeah. Dead quiet.

Did you go down then?

L–later I went. I was goin' to bed. I figured I . . .

You wanted to say goodnight.

Yeah. I . . .

Swish

You went down and opened the living room door?

Yeah, I . . . yeah.

What did you see?

I . . . I . . . . Oh, can't ya. . . . I want my ma. Lemme alone.
I want her!

Kid! Hold him, Sergeant. Take it easy!

Swish swish

I'm sorry, kid. Did it hurt? I had to calm you. I know . . .

how you feel, Leo. We saw it too. We feel sick and . . . awful too.

Swish

Just a few more questions and we'll take you to your aunt's. Now first. The television set. Was it on?

Yeah. It was on.

And you . . . smelled something?

Yeah. Like in the hall. Only worse. Only lots worse.

That smell.

That smell. Dead. A dead stink. Like a pile o' dead . . . dead. . . . I don't know. Garbage. Piles of it.

No one was talking?

No, there was nothin'. 'Cept the TV.

What was on it?

I already told ya.

I know, I know. Tell us again. For the record.

It was . . . like I said . . . just them letters. Great big letters.

What were they?

F . . . uh. . . . F-E-E-D.

F-E-E-D?

Y-yeah. Big crooked-like letters.

You'd seen them before?

Yeah. I told ya. They was on our set all the time. . . . Not all the time. Plenty though.

Your parents never wondered about it?

No. They said . . . they figured it was a sort of commercial. You know.

But the things you saw.

I don't know. Ma said . . . it was for kids. Some, I mean.

What did you see?

Swish swish swish

Sort of . . . mouths. Big ones. Wide. Open, all open. They wasn't p-people.

Swish

What did it look like? I mean, couldn't you tell what it was?

No. I mean . . . they was like . . . bugs, maybe, or maybe . . . w-worms. Big ones. All mouths. Wide open.

All right.

Swish

You, uh, said the letters flashed on, then off and you saw the . . . mouths, and then the letters again?

Yeah. Like that.

This happen every night?

Yeah.

Same time?

No. Different times.

Between programs?

No. Anytime.

Was it always on the same channel?

No. All different ones. No matter which one we had . . . we seen them.

And . . .

I wanna go. Can't I. . . . Ma! Where is she? I want her. I want her.

Swish click

C*lick*
    A few more questions, Leo, and that's it. Now, you said your parents never had the set checked.

No, I told you. They thought it was—

All right.

Swish

You went in the living room. You said something about slipping, didn't you?

Yeah. On that stuff.

What stuff?

I don't know. Greasy stuff. Like hot grease. It stunk awful.
And then you . . . you found . . .

Swish

I found them. Ma. And Pa. And the Lenottis. They was. . . .
Ohhh, I wanna . . .

Leo! What about the set, Leo? What about it?

Huh, what?

The picture on the set. You said something about it.

I, yeah . . . I . . .

It was the letters, wasn't it, Leo?

Yeah, yeah. Them letters. Them big crooked letters. They
was up there. On the set. I seen them. And . . . and . . .

What?

One of the E's. It kinda . . . faded. It went away. And . . .
and . . .

What, Leo?

The other letters. They come together. So . . . so there was
only three.

And it was a word.

Swish swish swish

Take him to his aunt, Sergeant.

And the tube went black . . .

All right, Leo. The sergeant'll take you ho—to your aunt's.

I turned on the lights.

All right, Leo.

I turned on the light! Ma! MAMA!

Click

Witch War

Seven pretty little girls sitting in a row. Outside, night, pouring rain—war weather. Inside, toasty warm. Seven overalled little girls chatting. Plaque on the wall saying: P.G. CENTER.

Sky clearing its throat with thunder, picking and dropping lint lightning from immeasurable shoulders. Rain hushing the world, bowing the trees, pocking earth. Square building, low, with one wall plastic.

Inside, the buzzing talk of seven pretty little girls.

"So I say to him—'Don't give me *that*, Mr. High and Mighty.' So he says, 'Oh yeah?' And I say, 'Yeah!' "

"Honest, will I ever be glad when this thing's over. I saw the cutest hat on my last furlough. Oh, *what* I wouldn't give to wear it!"

"You too? Don't I *know* it! You just can't get your hair right. Not in *this* weather. Why don't they let us get rid of it?"

"*Men!* They make me sick."

Seven gestures, seven postures, seven laughters ringing thin beneath thunder. Teeth showing in girl giggles. Hands tireless, painting pictures in the air.

P.G. Center. Girls. Seven of them. Pretty. Not one over sixteen. Curls. Pigtails. Bangs. Pouting little lips—smiling, frowning, shaping emotion on emotion. Sparkling young eyes—glittering, twinkling, narrowing, cold or warm.

Seven healthy young bodies restive on wooden chairs. Smooth adolescent limbs. Girls—pretty girls—seven of them.

An army of ugly shapeless men, stumbling in mud, struggling along the pitchblack muddy road.

Rain a torrent. Buckets of it thrown on each exhausted man. Sucking sound of great boots sinking into oozy yellow-brown mud, pulling loose. Mud dripping from heels and soles.

Plodding men—hundreds of them—soaked, miserable, depleted. Young men bent over like old men. Jaws hanging loosely, mouth gasping at black wet air, tongues lolling, sunken eyes looking at nothing, betraying nothing.

Rest.

Men sink down in the mud, fall on their packs. Heads thrown back, mouths open, rain splashing on yellow teeth. Hands immobile—scrawny heaps of flesh and bone. Legs without motion—khaki lengths of worm-eaten wood. Hundreds of useless limbs fixed to hundreds of useless trunks.

In back, ahead, beside, rumble trucks and tanks and tiny cars. Thick tires splattering mud. Fat treads sinking, tearing at mucky slime. Rain drumming wet fingers on metal and canvas.

Lightning flashbulbs without pictures. Momentary burst of light. The face of war seen for a second—made of rusty guns and turning wheels and faces staring.

Blackness. A night hand blotting out the brief storm glow. Windblown rain flitting over fields and roads, drenching trees and trucks. Rivulets of bubbly rain tearing scars from the earth. Thunder, lightning.

A whistle. Dead men resurrected. Boots in sucking mud

again—deeper, closer, nearer. Approach to a city that bars the way to a city that bars the way to a . . .

A n officer sat in the communication room of the P.G. Center. He peered at the operator, who sat hunched over the control board, phones over his ears, writing down a message.

The officer watched the operator. They are coming, he thought. Cold, wet and afraid they are marching at us. He shivered and shut his eyes.

He opened them quickly. Visions fill his darkened pupils—of curling smoke, flaming men, unimaginable horrors that shape themselves without words or pictures.

"Sir," said the operator, "from advance observation post. Enemy forces sighted."

The officer got up, walked over to the operator and took the message. He read it, face blank, mouth parenthesized. "Yes," he said.

He turned on his heel and went to the door. He opened it and went into the next room. The seven girls stopped talking. Silence breathed on the walls.

The officer stood with his back to the plastic window. "Enemies," he said, "two miles away. Right in front of you."

He turned and pointed out the window. "Right out there. Two miles away. Any questions?"

A girl giggled.

"Any vehicles?" another asked.

"Yes. Five trucks, five small command cars, two tanks."

"That's too easy," laughed the girl, slender fingers fussing with her hair.

"That's all," said the officer. He started from the room. "Go to it," he added and, under his breath, "Monsters!"

He left.

"Oh, me," sighed one of the girls, "here we go again."

"What a bore," said another. She opened her delicate mouth and plucked out chewing gum. She put it under her chair seat.

"At least it stopped raining," said a redhead, tying her shoelaces.

The seven girls looked around at each other. *Are you ready?* said their eyes. *I'm ready, I suppose.* They adjusted themselves on the chairs with girlish grunts and sighs. They hooked their feet around the legs of their chairs. All gum was placed in storage. Mouths were tightened into prudish fixity. The pretty little girls made ready for the game.

Finally they were silent on their chairs. One of them took a deep breath. So did another. They all tensed their milky flesh and clasped fragile fingers together. One quickly scratched her head to get it over with. Another sneezed prettily.

"Now," said a girl on the right end of the row.

Seven pairs of beady eyes shut. Seven innocent little minds began to picture, to visualize, to transport.

Lips rolled into thin gashes, faces drained of color, bodies shivered passionately. Their fingers twitching with concentration, seven pretty little girls fought a war.

The men were coming over the rise of a hill when the attack came. The leading men, feet poised for the next step, burst into flame.

There was no time to scream. Their rifles slapped down into the muck, their eyes were lost in fire. They stumbled a few steps and fell, hissing and charred, into the soft mud.

Men yelled. The ranks broke. They began to throw up their

weapons and fire at the night. More troops puffed incandescently, flared up, were dead.

"Spread out!" screamed an officer as his gesturing fingers sprouted flame and his face went up in licking yellow heat.

The men looked everywhere. Their dumb terrified eyes searched for an enemy. They fired into the fields and woods. They shot each other. They broke into flopping runs over the mud.

A truck was enveloped in fire. Its driver leaped out, a two-legged torch. The truck went bumping over the road, turned, wove crazily over the field, crashed into a tree, exploded and was eaten up in blazing light. Black shadows flitted in and out of the aura of light around the flames. Screams rent the night.

Man after man burst into flame, fell crashing on his face in the mud. Spots of searing light lashed the wet darkness—screams—running coals, sputtering, glowing, dying—incendiary ranks—trucks cremated—tanks blowing up.

A little blonde, her body tense with repressed excitement. Her lips twitch, a giggle hovers in her throat. Her nostrils dilate. She shudders in giddy fright. She imagines, imagines. . . .

A soldier runs headlong across a field, screaming, his eyes insane with horror. A gigantic boulder rushes at him from the black sky.

His body is driven into the earth, mangled. From the rock edge, fingertips protrude.

The boulder lifts from the ground, crashes down again, a shapeless trip hammer. A flaming truck is flattened. The boulder flies again to the black sky.

A pretty brunette, her face a feverish mask. Wild thoughts tumble through her virginal brain. Her scalp grows taut with ecstatic fear. Her lips draw back from clenching teeth. A gasp of terror hisses from her lips. She imagines, imagines. . . .

A soldier falls to his knees. His head jerks back. In the light of burning comrades, he stares dumbly at the white-foamed wave that towers over him.

It crashes down, sweeps his body over the muddy earth, fills his lungs with salt water. The tidal wave roars over the field, drowns a hundred flaming men, tosses their corpses in the air with thundering whitecaps.

Suddenly the water stops, flies into a million pieces and disintegrates.

A lovely little redhead, hands drawn under her chin in tight bloodless fists. Her lips tremble, a throb of delight expands her chest. Her white throat contracts, she gulps in a breath of air. Her nose wrinkles with dreadful joy. She imagines, imagines. . . .

A running soldier collides with a lion. He cannot see in the darkness. His hands strike wildly at the shaggy mane. He clubs with his rifle butt.

A scream. His face is torn off with one blow of thick claws. A jungle roar billows in the night.

A red-eyed elephant tramples wildly through the mud, picking up men in its thick trunk, hurling them through the air, mashing them under driving black columns.

Wolves bound from the darkness, spring, tear at throats. Gorillas scream and bounce in the mud, leap at falling soldiers.

A rhinoceros, leather skin glowing in the light of living torches, crashes into a burning tank, wheels, thunders into blackness, is gone.

Fangs—claws—ripping teeth—shrieks—trumpeting—roars. The sky rains snakes.

Silence. Vast brooding silence. Not a breeze, not a drop of rain, not a grumble of distant thunder. The battle is ended.

Gray morning mist rolls over the burned, the torn, the drowned, the crushed, the poisoned, the sprawling dead.

Motionless trucks—silent tanks, wisps of oily smoke still rising from their shattered hulks. Great death covering the field. Another battle in another war.

Victory—everyone is dead.

The girls stretched languidly. They extended their arms and rotated their round shoulders. Pink lips grew wide in pretty little yawns. They looked at each other and tittered in embarrassment. Some of them blushed. A few looked guilty.

Then they all laughed out loud. They opened more gum-packs, drew compacts from pockets, spoke intimately with schoolgirl whispers, with late-night dormitory whispers.

Muted giggles rose up fluttering in the warm room.

"Aren't we awful?" one of them said, powdering her pert nose.

Later they all went downstairs and had breakfast.

Mad House

He sits down at his desk. He picks up a long, yellow pencil and starts to write on a pad. The lead point breaks.

The ends of his lips turn down. The eye pupils grow small in the hard mask of his face. Quietly, mouth pressed into an ugly, lipless gash, he picks up the pencil sharpener.

He grinds off the shavings and tosses the sharpener back in the drawer. Once more he starts to write. As he does so, the point snaps again and the lead rolls across the paper.

Suddenly his face becomes livid. Wild rage clamps the muscles of his body. He yells at the pencil, curses it with a stream of outrage. He glares at it with actual hate. He breaks it in two with a brutal snap and flings it into the wastebasket with a triumphant, "There! See how you like it in *there*!"

He sits tensely on the chair, his eyes wide, his lips trembling. He shakes with a frenzied wrath; it sprays his insides with acid.

The pencil lies in the wastebasket, broken and still. It is wood, lead, metal, rubber; all dead, without appreciation of the burning fury it has caused.

And yet . . .

He is quietly standing by the window, peering out at the street. He is letting the tightness sough away. He does not hear the rustle in the wastebasket which ceases immediately.

Soon his body is normal again. He sits down. He uses a fountain pen.

He sits down before his typewriter.

He inserts a sheet of paper and begins tapping on the keys.

His fingers are large. He hits two keys at once. The two strikers are jammed together. They stand in the air, hovering impotently over the black ribbon.

He reaches over in disgust and slaps them back. They separate, flap back into their separate berths. He starts typing again.

He hits a wrong key. The start of a curse falls from his lips, unfinished. He snatches up the round eraser and rubs the unwanted letter from the sheet of paper.

He drops the eraser and starts to type again. The paper has shifted on the roller. The next sentences are on a level slightly above the original. He clenches a fist, ignores the mistake.

The machine sticks. His shoulders twitch, he slams a fist on the space bar with a loud curse. The carriage jumps, the bell tinkles. He shoves the carriage over and it crashes to a halt.

He types faster. Three keys stick together. He clenches his teeth and whines in helpless fury. He smacks the type arms. They will not come apart. He forces them to separate with bent, shaking fingers. They fall away. He sees that his fingers are smudged with ink. He curses out loud, trying to outrage the very air for revenge on the stupid machine.

Now he hits the keys brutally, fingers falling like the stiff claws of a derrick. Another mistake, he erases savagely. He types still faster. Four keys stick together.

He screams.

He slams his fist on the machine. He clutches at the paper and rips it from the machine in jagged pieces. He welds the fragments in his fist and hurls the crumpled ball across the room. He beats the carriage over and slams the cover down on the machine.

He jumps up and glares down.

"You fool!" he shouts with a bitter, revolted voice. "You stupid, idiotic, asinine *fool!*"

Scorn drips from his voice. He keeps talking, he drives himself into a craze.

"You're no damn good. You're no damn good at all. I'm going to break you in pieces. I'm going to crack you into splinters, melt you, *kill* you! You stupid, moronic, lousy goddamn machine!"

He quivers as he yells. And he wonders, deep in the self-isolated recesses of his mind whether he is killing himself with anger, whether he is destroying his system with fury.

He turns and stalks away. He is too outraged to notice the cover of the machine slip down and hear the slight whirring of metal such as he might hear if the keys trembled in their slots.

He is shaving. The razor will not cut. Or the razor is too sharp and cuts too much.

Both times a muffled curse billows through his lips. He hurls the razor on the floor and kicks it against the wall.

He is cleaning his teeth. He draws the fine silk floss between his teeth. It shreds off. A fuzzy bit remains in the gap. He tries to press another piece down to get that bit out. He cannot force the white thread down. It snaps in his fingers.

He screams. He screams at the man in the mirror and draws back his hand, throws the floss away violently. It hits the wall.

It hangs there and waves in the rush of angry breeze from the man.

He has torn another piece of floss from the container. He is giving the dental floss another chance. He is holding back his fury. If the floss knows what is good for it, it will plunge down between the teeth and draw out the shredded bit immediately.

It does. The man is mollified. The systematic juices leave off bubbling, the fires sink, the coals are scattered.

But the anger is still there, apart. Energy is never lost; a primal law.

He is eating.

His wife places a steak before him. He picks up the knife and fork and slices. The meat is tough, the blade is dull.

A spot of red puffs up in the flesh of his cheeks. His eyes narrow. He draws the knife through the meat. The blade will not sever the browned flesh.

His eyes widen. Withheld tempest tightens and shakes him. He saws at the meat as though to give it one last opportunity to yield.

The meat will not yield.

He howls. *"God damn it!"* White teeth jam together. The knife is hurled across the room.

The woman appears, alarm etching transient scars on her forehead. Her husband is beyond himself. Her husband is shooting poison through his arteries. Her husband is releasing another cloud of animal temper. It is mist that clings. It hangs over the furniture, drips from the walls.

It is alive.

So through the days and nights. His anger falling like frenzied axe blows in his house, on everything he owns. Sprays of teeth-grinding hysteria clouding his windows and falling to his floors. Oceans of wild, uncontrolled hate flooding through every room of his house; filling each iota of space with a shifting, throbbing life.

He lay on his back and stared at the sun-mottled ceiling.

The last day, he told himself. The phrase had been creeping in and out of his brain since he'd awakened.

In the bathroom he could hear the water running. He could hear the medicine cabinet being opened and then closed again. He could hear the sound of her slippers shuffling on the tile floor.

Sally, he thought, don't leave me.

"I'll take it easy if you stay," he promised the air in a whisper.

But he knew he couldn't take it easy. That was too hard. It was easier to fly off the handle, easier to scream and rant and attack.

He turned on his side and stared out into the hall at the bathroom door. He could see the line of light under the door. Sally is in there, he thought. Sally, my wife, whom I married many years ago when I was young and full of hope.

He closed his eyes suddenly and clenched his fists. It came on him again. The sickness that prevailed with more violence every time he contracted it. The sickness of despair, of lost ambition. It ruined everything. It cast a vapor of bitterness over all his comings and goings. It jaded appetite, ruined sleep, destroyed affection.

"Perhaps if we'd had children," he muttered and knew before he said it that it wasn't the answer.

Children. How happy they would be watching their wretched father sinking deeper into his pit of introspective fever each day.

All right, tortured his mind, let's have the facts. He gritted his teeth and tried to make his mind a blank. But, like a dull-eyed idiot, his mind repeated the words that he muttered often in his sleep through restless, tossing nights.

I'm forty years old. I teach English at Fort College. Once I had hoped to be a writer. I thought this would be a fine place to write. I would teach class part of the day and write with the rest of my time. I met Sally at school and married her. I thought everything would be just fine. I thought success was inevitable. Eighteen years ago.

Eighteen years.

How, he thought, did you mark the passing of almost two decades? The time seemed a shapeless lump of failing efforts, of nights spent in anguish; of the secret, the answer, the revelation always being withheld from him. Dangled overhead like cheese swinging in a maddening arc over the head of a berserk rat.

And resentment creeping. Days spent watching Sally buy food and clothing and pay rent with his meager salary. Watching her buy new curtains or new chair covers and feeling a stab of pain every time because he was that much farther removed from the point where he could devote his time to writing. Every penny she spent he felt like a blow at his aspirations.

He forced himself to think that way. He forced himself to believe that it was only the time he needed to do good writing.

But once a furious student had yelled at him, "You're just a third-rate talent hiding behind a desk!"

He remembered that. Oh, God, how he remembered that moment. Remembered the cold sickness that had convulsed him when those words hit his brain. Recalled the trembling and the shaky unreason of his voice.

He had failed the student for the semester despite good marks. There had been a great to-do about it. The student's father had come to the school. They had all gone before Dr. Ramsay, the head of the English Department.

He remembered that too; the scene could crowd out all other memories. Him, sitting on one side of the conference table, facing the irate father and son. Dr. Ramsay stroking his beard until he thought he'd hurl something at him. Dr. Ramsay had said—well let's see if we can't straighten out this matter.

They had consulted the record book and found the student was right. Dr. Ramsay had looked up at him in great surprise. Well, I can't see what . . . he had said and let his syrupy voice break off and looked probingly at him, waiting for an explanation.

And the explanation had been hopeless, a jumbled and pointless affair. Irresponsible attitude, he had said, flaunting of unpardonable behavior; morally a failure. And Dr. Ramsay, his thick neck getting red, telling him in no uncertain terms that morals were not subject to the grading system at Fort College.

There was more but he'd forgotten it. He'd made an effort to forget it. But he couldn't forget that it would be years before he made a professorship. Ramsay would hold it back. And his salary would go on being insufficient and bills would mount and he would never get his writing done.

He regained the present to find himself clutching the sheets with taut fingers. He found himself glaring in hate at the bathroom door. Go on!—his mind snapped vindictively—Go home to your precious mother. See if I care. Why just a trial separation? Make it permanent. Give me some peace. Maybe I can do some writing then.

Maybe I can do some writing then.

The phrase made him sick. It had no meaning anymore. Like a word that is repeated until it becomes gibberish that sentence, for him, had been used to extinction. It sounded silly; like some bit of cliché from a soap opera. Hero saying in dramatic tones— Now, by God, maybe I can do some writing. Senseless.

For a moment, though, he wondered if it was true. Now that she was leaving could he forget about her and really get some work done? Quit his job? Go somewhere and hole up in a cheap furnished room and write?

You have $123.89 in the bank, his mind informed him. He pretended it was the only thing that kept him from it. But, far back in his mind, he wondered if he could write anywhere. Often the question threw itself at him when he was least expecting it. You have four hours every morning, the statement would rise like a menacing wraith. You have time to write many thousands of words. Why don't you?

And the answer was always lost in a tangle of because and wells and endless reasons that he clung to like a drowning man at straws.

The bathroom door opened and she came out, dressed in her good red suit.

For no reason at all, it seemed, he suddenly realized that she'd been wearing that same outfit for more than three years and never a new one. The realization angered him even more. He closed his eyes and hoped she wasn't looking at him. I hate her, he thought. I hate her because she has destroyed my life.

He heard the rustle of her skirt as she sat at the dressing table and pulled out a drawer. He kept his eyes shut and listened to the venetian blinds tap lightly against the window frame as morning breeze touched them. He could smell her perfume floating lightly on the air.

And he tried to think of the house empty all the time. He tried to think of coming home from class and not finding Sally there waiting for him. The idea seemed, somehow, impossible. And that angered him. Yes, he thought, she's gotten to me. She's worked on me until I am so dependent of her for really unessential things that I suffer under the delusion that I cannot do without her.

He turned suddenly on the mattress and looked at her.

"So, you're really going," he said in a cold voice.

She turned briefly and looked at him. There was no anger on her face. She looked tired.

"Yes," she said. "I'm going."

Good riddance. The words tried to pass his lips. He cut them off.

"I suppose you have your reasons," he said.

Her shoulders twitched a moment in what he took for a shrug of weary amusement.

"I have no intention of arguing with you," he said. "Your life is your own."

"Thank you," she murmured.

She's waiting for apologies, he thought. Waiting to be told that he didn't hate her as he'd said. That he hadn't struck *her* but all his twisted and shattered hopes; the mocking spectacle of his own lost faith.

"And just how long is this *trial* separation going to last?" he said, his voice acidulous.

She shook her head.

"I don't know, Chris," she said quietly. "It's up to you."

"Up to me," he said. "It's always up to me, isn't it?"

"Oh, please darl—Chris. I don't want to argue anymore. I'm too tired to argue."

"It's easier to just pack and run away."

She turned and looked at him. Her eyes were very dark and unhappy.

"Run away?" she said. "After eighteen years you accuse me of that? Eighteen years of watching you destroy yourself. And me along with you. Oh, don't look surprised. I'm sure you know you've driven me half insane too."

She turned away and he saw her shoulders twitch. She brushed some tears from her eyes.

"It's n-not just because you hit me," she said. "You kept saying that last night when I said I was leaving. Do you think it would matter if . . ." She took a deep breath. "If it meant you were angry with *me*? If it was that I could be hit every day. But you didn't hit me. I'm nothing to you. I'm not wanted."

"Oh, stop being so . . ."

"No," she broke in. "That's why I'm going. Because I can't bear to watch you hate me more every day for something that . . . that isn't my fault."

"I suppose you . . ."

"Oh, don't say anymore," she said, getting up. She hurried out of the room and he heard her walk into the living room. He stared at the dressing table.

Don't say anymore?—his mind asked as though she were still there. Well, there's more to say; lots more. You don't seem to realize what I've lost. You don't seem to understand. I had hopes, oh God, what hopes I had. I was going to write prose to make the people sit up and gasp. I was going to tell them things they needed badly to know. I was going to tell them in so entertaining a way that they would never realize that the truth was getting to them. I was going to create immortal works.

Now when I die, I shall only be dead. I am trapped in this depressing village, entombed in a college of science where men gape at dust and do not even know that there are stars above their heads. And what can I do, what can . . . ?

The thoughts broke off. He looked miserably at her perfume bottles, at the powder box that tinkled "Always" when the cover was lifted off.

I'll remember you. Always.

With a heart that's true. Always.

The words are childish and comical, he thought. But his throat contracted and he felt himself shudder.

"Sally," he said. So quietly that he could hardly hear it himself.

After a while he got up and dressed.

While he was putting on his trousers a rug slid from under him and he had to grab the dresser for support. He glared down, heart pounding in the total fury he had learned to summon in the space of seconds.

"Damn you," he muttered.

He forgot Sally. He forgot everything. He just wanted to get even with the rug. He kicked it violently under the bed. The anger plunged down and disappeared. He shook his head. I'm sick, he thought. He thought of going in to her and telling her he was sick.

His mouth tightened as he went into the bathroom. I'm not sick, he thought. Not in body anyway. It's my mind that's ill and she only makes it worse.

The bathroom was still damply warm from her use of it. He opened the window a trifle and got a splinter in his finger. He cursed the window in a muffled voice. He looked up. Why so quiet? he asked. So *she* won't hear me?

"Damn you!" he snarled loudly at the window. And he picked at his finger until he had pulled out the sliver of wood.

He jerked at the cabinet door. It stuck. His face reddened. He pulled harder and the door flew open and cracked him on the wrist. He spun about and grabbed his wrist, threw back his head with a whining gasp.

He stood there, eyes clouded with pain, staring at the ceiling. He looked at the crack that ran in a crazy meandering line across the ceiling. Then he closed his eyes.

And began to sense something. Intangible. A sense of menace. He wondered about it. Why it's myself, of course, he answered then. It is the moral decrepitude of my own subconscious. It is bawling out to me, saying: You are to be punished for driving your poor wife away to her mother's arms. You are not a man. You are a—

"Oh, shut up," he said.

He washed his hands and face. He ran an inspecting finger over his chin. He needed a shave. He opened the cabinet door gingerly and took out his straight razor. He held it up and looked at it.

The handle has expanded. He told himself that quickly as the blade appeared to fall out of the handle willfully. It made him shiver to see it flop out like that and glitter in the light from the cabinet light fixture.

He stared in repelled fascination at the bright steel. He touched the blade edge. So sharp, he thought. The slightest touch would sever flesh. What a hideous thing it was.

"It's my hand."

He said it involuntarily and shut the razor suddenly. It *was* his hand, it had to be. It couldn't have been the razor moving by itself. That was sick imagination.

But he didn't shave. He put the razor back in the cabinet with a vague sense of forestalling doom.

Don't care if we *are* expected to shave every day, he muttered. I'm not taking a chance on my hand slipping. I'd better get a safety razor anyway. This kind isn't for me, I'm too nervous.

Suddenly, impelled by those words, the picture of him eighteen years before flew into his brain.

He remembered a date he'd had with Sally. He remembered telling her he was so calm it was akin to being dead. Nothing bothers me, he'd said. And it was true, at the time. He remembered too telling her he didn't like coffee, that one cup kept him awake at night. That he didn't smoke, didn't like the taste or smell. I like to stay healthy, he'd said. He remembered the exact words.

"And now," he muttered at his lean and worn reflection.

Now he drank gallons of coffee a day. Until it sloshed like a black pool in his stomach and he couldn't sleep any more than he could fly. Now he smoked endless strings of finger-yellowing cigarettes until his throat felt raw and clogged, until he couldn't write in pencil because his hand shook so much.

But all that stimulation didn't help his writing any. Paper still remained blank in the typewriter. Words never came, plots died on him. Characters eluded him, mocking him with laughter from behind the veil of their non-creation.

And time passed. It flew by faster and faster, seeming to single him out for highest punishment. He—a man who had begun to value time so neurotically that it overbalanced his life and made him sick to think of its passing.

As he brushed his teeth he tried to recall when this irrational temper had first begun to control him. But there was no way of tracing its course. Somewhere in mists that could not be pierced, it had started. With a word of petulance, an angry contraction of muscles. With a glare of unrecallable animosity.

And from there, like a swelling amoeba, it had gone its own perverted and downward course of evolution, reaching its present nadir in him; a taut embittered man who found his only solace in hating.

He spit out white froth and rinsed his mouth. As he put down the glass, it cracked and a barb of glass drove into his hand.

"Damn!" he yelled.

He spun on his heel and clenched his fist. It sprang open instantly as the sliver sank into his palm. He stood with tears on his cheeks, breathing heavily. He thought of Sally listening to him, hearing once more the audible evidence of his snapping nerves.

Stop it!—he ordered himself. You can never do anything until you rid yourself of this enervating temper.

He closed his eyes. For a moment he wondered why it seemed that everything was happening to him lately. As if some revenging power had taken roost in the house, pouring a savage life into inanimate things. Threatening him. But the thought was just a faceless, passing figure in the crushing horde of thoughts that mobbed past his mind's eye; seen but not appreciated.

He drew the glass sliver from his palm. He put on his dark tie.

Then he went into the dining room, consulting his watch. It was ten thirty already. More than half the morning was gone.

More than half the time for sitting and trying to write the prose that would make people sit up and gasp.

It happened that way more often now than he would even admit to himself. Sleeping late, making up errands, doing anything to forestall the terrible moment when he must sit down before his typewriter and try to wrench some harvest from the growing desert of his mind.

It was harder every time. And he grew more angry every time; and hated more. And never noticed until now, when it was too late, that Sally had grown desperate and could no longer stand his temper or his hate.

She was sitting at the kitchen table drinking dark coffee. She too drank more than she once had. Like him, she drank it black, without sugar. It jangled her nerves too. And she smoked now although she'd never smoked until a year before. She got no pleasure from it. She drew the fumes deep down into her lungs and then blew them out quickly. And her hands shook almost as badly as his did.

He poured himself a cup of coffee and sat down across from her. She started to get up.

"What's the matter? Can't you stand the sight of me?"

She sat back and took a deep pull on the cigarette in her hand. Then she stamped it out on the saucer.

He felt sick. He wanted to get out of the house suddenly. It felt alien and strange to him. He had the feeling that she had renounced all claim to it, that she had retreated from it. The touch of her fingers and the loving indulgences she had bestowed on every room; all these things were taken back. They had lost tangibility because she was leaving. She was deserting it and it was not their home anymore. He felt it strongly.

Sinking back against the chair he pushed away his cup and

stared at the yellow oilcloth on the table. He felt as if he and Sally were frozen in time; that seconds were drawn out like some fantastic taffy until each one seemed an eternity. The clock ticked slower. And the house was a different house.

"What train are you getting?" he asked, knowing before he spoke that there was only one morning train.

"Eleven forty-seven," she said.

When she said it, he felt as if his stomach were pulled back hard against his backbone. He gasped, so actual was the physical pain. She glanced up at him.

"Burned myself," he said hastily, and she got up and put her cup and saucer in the sink.

Why did I say that?—he thought. Why couldn't I say that I gasped because I was filled with terror at the thought of her leaving me? Why do I always say the things I don't mean to say? I'm not bad. But every time I speak I build higher the walls of hatred and bitterness around me until I cannot escape from them.

With words I have knit my shroud and will bury myself therein.

He looked at her back and a sad smile raised his lips. I can think of words when my wife is leaving me. It is very sad.

Sally had walked out of the kitchen. His mind reverted to its sullen attitude. This is a game we're playing. Follow the leader. You walk in one room, head high, the justified spouse, the injured party. I am supposed to follow, slope shouldered and contrite, pouring out apologetic hecatombs.

Once more conscious of himself, he sat tensely at the table, rage making his body tremble. Consciously he relaxed and pressed his left hand over his eyes. He sat there trying to lose his misery in silence and blackness.

It wouldn't work.

And then his cigarette really burned him and he sat erect. The cigarette hit the floor scattering ashes. He bent over and picked it up. He threw it at the wastecan and missed. To hell with it, he thought. He got up and dumped his cup and saucer in the sink. The saucer broke in half and nicked his right thumb. He let it bleed. He didn't care.

She was in the extra room finishing her packing.

The extra room. The words tortured him now. When had they stopped calling it "the nursery"? When had it begun to eat her insides out because she was so full of love and wanted children badly? When had he begun to replace this loss with nothing better than volcanic temper and days and nights of sheath-scraped nerves?

He stood in the doorway and watched her. He wanted to get out the typewriter and sit down and write reams of words. He wanted to glory in his coming freedom. Think of all the money he could save. Think of how soon he could go away and write all the things he'd always meant to write.

He stood in the doorway, sick.

Is all this possible?—his mind asked, incredulous. Possible that she was leaving? But she and he were man and wife. They had lived and loved in this house for more than eighteen years. Now she was leaving. Putting articles of clothing in her old black suitcase and leaving. He couldn't reconcile himself to that. He couldn't understand it or ally it with the functions of the day. Where did it fit into the pattern?—the pattern that was Sally right there cleaning and cooking and trying to make their home happy and warm.

He shivered and, turning abruptly, went back into the bedroom.

He slumped on the bed and stared at the delicately whirring electric clock on their bedside table.

Past eleven, he saw. In less than an hour I have to hold class for a group of idiot freshmen. And, on the desk in the living room, is a mountain of mid-term examinations with essays that I must suffer through, feeling my stomach turn at their paucity of intelligence, their adolescent phraseology.

And all that tripe, all those miles of hideous prose, had been wound into an eternal skein in his head. And there it sat unraveling into his own writing until he wondered if he could stand the thought of living anymore. I have digested the worst, he thought. Is it any wonder that I exude it piecemeal?

Temper began again, a low banking fire in him, gradually fanned by further thinking. I've done no writing this morning. Like every morning after every other morning as time passes. I do less and less. I write nothing. Or I write worthless material. I could write better when I was twenty than I can now.

I'll *never* write anything good!

He jolted to his feet and his head snapped around as he looked for something to strike at, something to break, something to hate with such hate that it would wither in the blast.

It seemed as though the room clouded. He felt a throbbing. His left leg banged against a corner of the bed.

He gasped in fury. He wept. Tears of hate and repentance and self commiseration. I'm lost, he thought. Lost. There is nothing.

He became very calm, icy calm. Drained of pity, of emotion. He put on his suit coat. He put on his hat and got his briefcase off the dresser.

He stopped before the door to the room where she still

fussed with her bag. So she will have something to occupy herself with now, he thought, so she won't have to look at me. He
felt his heart thudding like a heavy drum beat.

"Have a nice time at your mother's," he said dispassionately.

She looked up and saw the expression on his face. She turned
away and put a hand to her eyes. He felt a sudden need to run
to her and beg her forgiveness. Make everything right again.

Then he thought again of papers and years of writing undone. He turned away and walked across the living room. The
small rug slipped a little and it helped to focus the strength of
anger he needed. He kicked it aside and it fluttered against the
wall in a rumpled heap.

He slammed the door behind him.

His mind gibbered. Now, soap opera like, she has thrown
herself on the coverlet and is weeping tears of martyr-tinged
sorrow. Now she is digging nails into the pillow and moaning
my name and wishing she were dead.

His shoes clicked rapidly on the sidewalk. God help me, he
thought. God help all us poor wretches who would create and
find that we must lose our hearts for it because we cannot afford
to spend our time at it.

It was a beautiful day. His eyes saw that but his mind would
not attest to it. The trees were thick with green and the air
warm and fresh. Spring breezes flooded down the streets. He
felt them brush over him as he walked down the block, crossed
Main Street to the bus stop.

He stood there on the corner looking back at the house.

She is in there, his mind persisted in analysis. In there, the
house in which we've lived for more than eight years. She is
packing or crying or doing something. And soon she will call
the Campus Cab Company. A cab will come driving out. The
driver will honk the horn, Sally will put on her light spring coat

and take her suitcase out on the porch. She will lock the door behind her for the last time.

"*No—*"

He couldn't keep the word from strangling in his throat. He kept staring at the house. His head ached. He saw everything weaving. I'm sick, he thought.

"I'm *sick*!"

He shouted it. There was no one around to hear. He stood gazing at the house. She is going away forever, said his mind.

Very well then! I'll write, write, write. He let the words soak into his mind and displace all else.

A man had a choice, after all. He devoted his life to his work or to his wife and children and home. It could not be combined; not in this day and age. In this insane world where God was second to income and goodness to wealth.

He glanced aside as the green-striped bus topped the distant hill and approached. He put the briefcase under his arm and reached into his coat pocket for a token. There was a hole in the pocket. Sally had been meaning to sew it. Well, she would never sew it now. What did it matter anyway?

I would rather have my soul intact than the suit of clothes I wear.

Words, words, he thought, as the bus stopped before him. They flood through me now that she is leaving. Is that evidence that it is her presence that clogs the channels of thought?

He dropped the token in the coin box and weaved down the length of the bus. He passed a professor he knew and nodded to him distractedly. He slumped down on the back seat and stared at the grimy, rubberized floor boards.

This is a great life, his mind ranted. I am so pleased with this, my life and these, my great and noble accomplishments.

He opened the briefcase a moment and looked in at the

thick prospectus he had outlined with the aid of Dr. Ramsay.

First week—1. *Everyman*. Discussion of. Reading of selections from *Classic Readings For College Freshmen*. 2. *Beowulf*. Reading of. Class discussion. Twenty minute quotation quiz.

He shoved the sheaf of papers back into the briefcase. It sickens me, he thought. I hate these things. The classics have become anathema to me. I begin to loathe the very mention of them. Chaucer, the Elizabethan poets, Dryden, Pope, Shakespeare. What higher insult to a man than to grow to hate these names because he must share them by part with unappreciative clods? Because he must strain them thin and make them palatable for the dullards who should better be digging ditches.

He got off the bus downtown and started down the long slope of Ninth Street.

Walking, he felt as though he were a ship with its hawser cut, prey to a twisted network of currents. He felt apart from the city, the country, the world. If someone told me I were a ghost, he thought, I would be inclined to believe.

What is she doing now?

He wondered about it as the buildings floated past him. What is she thinking as I stand here and the town of Fort drifts by me like vaporous stage flats? What are her hands holding? What expression has she on her lovely face?

She is alone in the house, our house. What might have been our *home*. Now it is only a shell, a hollow box with sticks of wood and metal for furnishings. Nothing but inanimate dead matter.

No matter what John Morton said.

Him with his gold leaves parting and his test tubes and his God of the microscope. For all his erudite talk and his papers of slideruled figures; despite all that—it was simple witchcraft he professed. It was idiocy. The idiocy that prompted that ass Charles Fort to burden the world with his nebulous fancies. The idiocy that made that fool of a millionaire endow this place and from the arid soil erect these huge stone structures and house within a zoo of wild-eyed scientists always searching for some fashion of elixir while the rest of the clowns blew the world out from under them.

No, there is nothing right with the world, he thought as he plodded under the arch and onto the wide, green campus.

He looked across at the huge Physical Sciences Center, its granite face beaming in the late morning sun.

Now she is calling the cab. He consulted his watch. No. She is in the cab already. Riding through the silent streets. Past the houses and down into the shopping district. Past the red brick buildings spewing out yokels and students. Through the town that was a potpourri of the sophisticated and the rustic.

Now the cab was turning left on Tenth Street. Now it was pulling up the hill, topping it. Gliding down toward the railroad station. Now . . .

"Chris!"

His head snapped around and his body twitched in surprise. He looked toward the wide-doored entrance to the Mental Sciences Building. Dr. Morton was coming out.

We attended school together eighteen years ago, he thought. But I took only a small interest in science. I preferred wasting my time on the culture of the centuries. That's why I'm an associate and he's a doctor and the head of his department.

All this fled like racing winds through his mind as Dr. Morton approached, smiling. He clapped Chris on the shoulder.

"Hello there," he said. "How are things?"

"How are they ever?"

Dr. Morton's smile faded.

"What is it, Chris?" he asked.

I won't tell you about Sally, Chris thought. Not if I die first. You'll never know it from me.

"The usual," he said.

"Still on the outs with Ramsay?"

Chris shrugged. Morton looked over at the large clock on the face of the Mental Sciences Building.

"Say, look," he said. "Why are we standing here? Your class isn't for a half hour yet, is it?"

Chris didn't answer. He's going to invite me for coffee, he thought. He's going to regale me with more of his inane theories. He's going to use me as whipping boy for his mental merry-go-round.

"Let's get some coffee," Morton said, taking Chris's arm. They walked along in silence for a few steps.

"How's Sally?" Morton asked then.

"She's fine," he answered in an even voice.

"Good. Oh, incidentally. I'll probably drop by tomorrow or the next day for that book I left there last Thursday night."

"All right."

"What were you saying about Ramsay now?"

"I wasn't."

Morton skipped that. "Been thinking anymore about what I told you?" he asked.

"If you're referring to your fairy tale about my house—no. I haven't been giving it any more thought than it deserves—which is none."

They turned the corner of the building and walked toward Ninth Street.

"Chris, that's an indefensible attitude," Morton said. "You have no right to doubt when you don't know."

Chris felt like pulling his arm away, turning and leaving Morton standing there. He was sick of words and words and words. He wanted to be alone. He almost felt as if he could put a pistol to his head now, get it over with. Yes, I could—he thought. If someone handed it to me now it would be done in a moment.

They went up the stone steps to the sidewalk and crossed over to the Campus Cafe. Morton opened the door and ushered Chris in. Chris went in back and slid into a wooden booth.

Morton brought two coffees and sat across from him.

"Now listen," he said, stirring in sugar, "I'm your best friend. At least I regard myself as such. And I'm damned if I'll sit by like a mute and watch you kill yourself."

Chris felt his heart jump. He swallowed. He got rid of the thoughts as though they were visible to Morton.

"Forget it," he said. "I don't care what proofs you have. I don't believe any of it."

"What'll it take to convince you, damn it?" Morton said. "Do you have to lose your life first?"

"Look," Chris said pettishly. "I don't believe it. That's *it*. Forget it now, let it go."

"Listen, Chris, I can show you . . ."

"You can show me nothing!" Chris cut in.

Morton was patient. "It's a recognized phenomenon," he said.

Chris looked at him in disgust and shook his head.

"What dreams you white-frocked kiddies have in the sanctified cloister of your laboratories. You can make yourself believe anything after a while. As long as you can make up a measurement for it."

"Will you listen to me, Chris? How many times have you complained to me about splinters, about closet doors flying open, about rugs slipping? How many times?"

"Oh, for God's sake, don't start *that* again. I'll get up and walk out of here. I'm in no mood for your lectures. Save them for those poor idiots who pay tuition to hear them."

Morton looked at him with a shake of his head.

"I wish I could get to you," he said.

"Forget it."

"Forget it?" Morton squirmed. "Can't you see that you're in danger because of your temper?"

"I'm telling you, John . . ."

"Where do you think that temper of yours goes? Do you think it disappears? No. It doesn't. It goes into your rooms and into your furniture and into the air. It goes into Sally. It makes everything sick; including you. It crowds you out. It welds a link between animate and inanimate. *Psychobolie.* Oh, don't look so petulant; like a child who can't stand to hear the word *spinach.* Sit down, for God's sake. You're an adult; listen like one."

Chris lit a cigarette. He let Morton's voice drift into a non-intelligent hum. He glanced at the wall clock. Quarter to twelve. In two minutes, if the schedule was adhered to, she would be going. The train would move and the town of Fort would pass away from her.

"I've told you any number of times," Morton was saying. "No one knows what matter is made of. Atoms, electrons, pure energy—all words. Who knows where it will end? We guess, we theorize, we make up means of measurement. But we don't know.

"And that's for matter. Think of the human brain and its still unknown capacities. It's an uncharted continent, Chris. It may stay that way for a long time. And all that time the suspected powers will still be affecting us and, maybe, affecting matter, even if we *can't* measure it on a gauge.

"And I say you're poisoning your house. I say your temper

has become ingrained in the structure, in every article you touch. All of them influenced by you and your ungovernable rages. And I think too that if it weren't for Sally's presence acting as an abortive factor, well . . . you might actually be attacked by . . ."

Chris heard the last few sentences.

"Oh, stop this gibberish!" he snapped angrily. "You're talking like a juvenile after his first Tom Swift novel."

Morton sighed. He ran his fingers over the cup edge and shook his head sadly.

"Well," he said, "all I can do is hope that nothing breaks down. It's obvious to me that you're not going to listen."

"Congratulations on one statement I can agree with," said Chris. He looked at his watch. "And now if you'll excuse me I'll go and listen to saddle-shoed cretins stumble over passages they haven't the slightest ability to assimilate."

They got up.

"I'll take it," said Morton but Chris slapped a coin on the counter and walked out. Morton followed, putting his change into his pocket slowly.

In the street he patted Chris on the shoulder.

"Try to take it easy," he said. "Look, why don't you and Sally come out to the house tonight? We could have a few rounds of bridge."

"That's impossible," Chris said.

The students were reading a selection from *King Lear*. Their heads were bent over the books. He stared at them without seeing them.

I've got to resign myself to it, he told himself. I've got to forget her, that's all. She's gone. I'm not going to bewail the fact. I'm not going to hope against hope that she'll return. I don't *want* her back. I'm better off without her. Free and unfettered now.

His thoughts drained off. He felt empty and helpless. He felt as though he could never write another word for the rest of his life. Maybe, he thought, sullenly displeased with the idea, maybe it was only the upset of her leaving that enabled my brain to find words. For, after all, the words I thought of, the ideas that flourished, though briefly, were all to do with her—her going and my wretchedness because of it.

He caught himself short. No!—he cried in silent battle. I will not let it be that way. I'm strong. This feeling is only temporary, I'll very soon have learned to do without her. And then I'll do work. Such work as I have only dreamed of doing. After all, haven't I lived eighteen years more? Haven't those years filled me to overflowing with sights and sounds, ideals, impressions, interpretations?

He trembled with excitement.

Someone was waving a hand in his face. He focused his eyes and looked coldly at the girl.

"Well?" he said.

"Could you tell us when you're going to give back our midterm papers, Professor Neal?" she asked.

He stared at her, his right cheek twitching. He felt about to hurl every invective at his command into her face. His fists closed.

"You'll get them back when they're marked," he said tensely.

"Yes, but . . ."

"You heard me," he said.

His voice rose at the end of the sentence. The girl sat down.

As he lowered his head he noticed that she looked at the boy next to her and shrugged her shoulders, a look of disgust on her face.

"Miss . . ."

He fumbled with his record book and found her name.

"Miss Forbes!"

She looked up, her features drained of color, her red lips standing out sharply against her white skin. Painted alabaster idiot. The words clawed at him.

"You may get out of this room," he ordered sharply.

Confusion filled her face.

"Why?" she asked in a thin, plaintive voice.

"Perhaps you didn't hear me," he said, the fury rising. "I said get out of this room!"

"But . . ."

"Do you hear me!" he shouted.

Hurriedly she collected her books, her hands shaking, her face burning with embarrassment. She kept her eyes on the floor and her throat moved convulsively as she edged along the aisle and went out the doorway.

The door closed behind her. He sank back. He felt a terrible sickness in himself. Now, he thought, they will all turn against me in defense of an addle-witted little girl. Dr. Ramsay would have more fuel for his simple little fire.

And they were right.

He couldn't keep his mind from it. They *were* right. He knew it. In that far recess of mind which he could not cow with thoughtless passion, he knew he was a stupid fool. I have no right to teach others. I cannot even teach myself to be a human being. He wanted to cry out the words and weep confessions and throw himself from one of the open windows.

"The whispering will stop!" he demanded fiercely.

The room was quiet. He sat tensely, waiting for any signs of militance. I am your teacher, he told himself, I am to be obeyed, I am . . .

The concept died. He drifted away again. What were students or a girl asking about mid-term papers? What was anything?

He glanced at his watch. In a few minutes the train would pull into Centralia. She would change to the main line express to Indianapolis. Then up to Detroit and her mother. Gone.

Gone. He tried to visualize the word, put it into living terms. But the thought of the house without her was almost beyond his means. Because it wasn't the house without her; it was something else.

He began to think of what John had said.

Was it possible? He was in a mood to accept the incredible. It was incredible that she had left him. Why not extend the impossibilities that were happening to him?

All right then, he thought angrily. The house is alive. I've given it this life with deadly outpourings of wrath. I hope to God that when I get back there and enter the door, the roof collapses. I hope the walls buckle and I'm crushed to pulp by the crushing weight of plaster and wood and brick. That's what I want. Some agency to do away with me. I cannot drive myself to it. If only a gun would commit my suicide for me. Or gas blow its deadly fumes at me for the asking or a razor slice my flesh upon request.

The door opened. He glanced up. Dr. Ramsay stood there, face drawn into a mask of indignation. Behind him in the hall Chris could see the girl, her face streaked with tears.

"A moment, Neal," Ramsay said sharply and stepped back into the hall again.

Chris sat at the desk staring at the door. He felt suddenly

very tired, exhausted. He felt as if getting up and moving into the hall was more than he could possibly manage. He glanced at the class. A few of them were trying to repress smiles.

"For tomorrow you will finish the reading of *King Lear*," he said. Some of them groaned.

Ramsay appeared in the doorway again, his cheeks pink.

"Are you coming, Neal?" he asked loudly.

Chris felt himself tighten with anger as he walked across the room and out into the hall. The girl lowered her eyes. She stood beside Dr. Ramsay's portly frame.

"What's this I hear, Neal?" Ramsay asked.

That's right, Chris thought. Don't ever call me professor. I'll never be one, will I? You'll see to that, you bastard.

"I don't understand," he said, as coolly as possible.

"Miss Forbes here claims you ejected her from class for no reason at all."

"Then Miss Forbes is lying quite stupidly," he said. Let me hold this anger, he thought. Don't let it flood loose. He shook with holding it back.

The girl gasped and took out her handkerchief again. Ramsay turned and patted her shoulder.

"Go in my office, child. Wait for me."

She turned away slowly. Politician!—cried Neal's mind. How easy it is for you to be popular with them. You don't have to deal with their bungling minds.

Miss Forbes turned the corner and Ramsay looked back.

"Your explanation had better be good," he said. "I'm getting a little weary, Neal, of your behavior."

Chris didn't speak. Why am I standing here?—he suddenly wondered. Why, in all the world, am I standing in this dimlit hall and, voluntarily, listening to this pompous boor berate me?

"I'm waiting, Neal."

Chris tightened. "I told you she was lying," he said quietly.

"I choose to believe otherwise," said Dr. Ramsay, his voice trembling.

A shudder ran through Chris. His head moved forward and he spoke slowly, teeth clenched.

"You can believe anything you damn well please."

Ramsay's mouth twitched.

"I think it's time you appeared before the board," he muttered.

"Fine!" said Chris loudly. Ramsay made a move to close the classroom door. Chris gave it a kick and it banged against the wall. A girl gasped.

"What's the matter?" Chris yelled. "Don't you want your students to hear me tell you off? Don't you even want them to suspect that you're a dolt, a windbag, an ass!"

Ramsay raised shaking fists before his chest. His lips trembled violently.

"This will do, Neal!" he cried.

Chris reached out and shoved the heavy man aside, snarling, "Oh, *get* out of my way!"

He started away. The hall fled past him. He heard the bell ring. It sounded as though it rang in another existence. The building throbbed with life; students poured from classrooms.

"Neal!" called Dr. Ramsay.

He kept walking. Oh, God, let me out of here, I'm suffocating, he thought. My hat, my briefcase. Leave them. Get out of here. Dizzily he descended the stairs surrounded by milling students. They swirled about him like an unidentifiable tide. His brain was far from them.

Staring ahead dully he walked along the first floor hall. He turned and went out the door and down the porch steps to the campus sidewalk. He paid no attention to the students who stared at his ruffled blond hair, his mussed clothes. He kept walking. I've done it, he thought belligerently. I've made the break. I'm *free*!

I'm sick.

All the way down to Main Street and out on the bus he kept renewing his stores of anger. He went over those few moments in the hallway again and again. He summoned up the vision of Ramsay's stolid face, repeated his words. He kept himself taut and furious. I'm glad, he told himself forcibly. Everything is solved. Sally has left me. Good. My job is done. Good. Now I'm free to do as I like. A strained and angry joy pounded through him. He felt alone, a stranger in the world and glad of it.

At his stop, he got off the bus and walked determinedly toward the house pretending to ignore the pain he felt at approaching it. It's just an empty house, he thought. Nothing more. Despite all puerile theories, it is nothing but a house.

Then, when he went in, he found her sitting on the couch.

He almost staggered as if someone had struck him. He stood dumbly, staring at her. She had her hands tightly clasped. She was looking at him.

He swallowed.

"Well," he managed to say.

"I . . ." Her throat contracted. "Well . . ."

"Well *what*!" he said quickly and loudly to hide the shaking in his voice.

She stood up. "Chris, please. Won't you . . . ask me to stay?" She looked at him like a little girl, pleading.

The look enraged him. All his day dreams shattered; he saw the growing thing of new ideas ground under foot.

"Ask you to stay!" he yelled at her. "By God, I'll ask you nothing!"

"Chris! Don't!"

She's buckling, cried his mind. She's cracking. Get her now. Get her out of here. Drive her from these walls!

"Chris," she sobbed, "be kind. Please be kind."

"Kind!"

He almost choked on the word. He felt a wild heat coursing his body.

"Have *you* been kind? Driving me crazy, into a pit of despair. I can't get out. Do you understand? Never. Never! Do you understand that! I'll never write. I *can't* write! You drained it out of me! You killed it! Understand *that*? *Killed* it!"

She backed away toward the dining room. He followed her, hands shaking at his sides, feeling that she had driven him to this confession and hating her the more for it.

"Chris," she murmured in fright.

It seemed as if his rage grew cell-like, swelling him with fury until he was nothing of bone and blood but a hating accusation made flesh.

"I don't want you!" he yelled. "You're right, I don't want you! Get out of here!"

Her eyes were wide, her mouth an open wound. Suddenly she ran past him, eyes glistening with tears. She fled through the front doorway.

He went to the window and watched her running down the block, her dark brown hair streaming behind her.

Dizzy suddenly, he sank down on the couch and closed his eyes. He dug his nails into his palms. Oh God, I *am* sick, his mind churned.

He twitched and looked around stupidly. What was it? This feeling that he was sinking into the couch, into the floorboards, dissolving in the air, joining the molecules of the house. He whimpered softly, looking around. His head ached; he pressed a palm against his forehead.

"What?" he muttered. "What?"

He stood up. As though there were fumes he tried to smell them. As though it were a sound he tried to hear it. He turned around to see it. As though there were something with depth and length and width; something menacing.

He wavered, fell back on the couch. He stared around. There was nothing, all intangible. It might only be in the mind. The furniture lay as it did before. The sunlight filtered through the windows, piercing the gauzelike curtains, making gold patterns on the inlaid wooden floor. The walls were still creamy, the ceiling was as it was before. Yet there was this darkening, darkening . . .

What?

He pushed up and walked dizzily around the room. He forgot about Sally. He was in the dining room. He touched the table, he stared at the dark oak. He went into the kitchen. He stood by the sink and looked out the window.

Far up the block, he saw her walking, stumbling. She must have been waiting for the bus. Now she couldn't wait any longer and she was walking away from the house, away from him.

"I'll go after her," he muttered.

No, he thought. No, I won't go after her like a . . .

He forgot like what. He stared down at the sink. He felt drunk. Everything was fuzzy on the edges.

She's washed the cups. The broken saucer was thrown away.

He looked at the nick on his thumb. It was dried. He'd forgotten about it.

He looked around suddenly as if someone had sneaked behind him. He stared at the wall. Something was rising. He felt it. It's not me. But it had to be; it had to be imagination.

Imagination!

He slammed a fist on the sink. I'll write. Write, *write.* Sit down and drain it all away in words; this feeling of anguish and terror and loneliness. Write it out of my system.

He cried, "Yes!"

He ran from the kitchen. He refused to accept the instinctive fear in himself. He ignored the menace that seemed to thicken the very air.

A rug slipped. He kicked it aside. He sat down. The air hummed. He tore off the cover on the typewriter. He sat nervously, staring at the keyboard. The moment before attack. It was in the air. But it's *my* attack!—he thought triumphantly, my attack on stupidity and fear.

He rolled a sheet into the typewriter. He tried to collect his throbbing thoughts. Write, the word called in his mind. Write— *now.*

"Now!" he cried.

He felt the desk lurch against his shins.

The flaring pain knifed open his senses. He kicked the desk in automatic frenzy. More pain. He kicked again. The desk flung back at him. He screamed.

He'd seen it move.

He tried to back off, the anger torn from him. The typewriter keys moved under his hands. His eyes swept down. He couldn't tell whether he was moving the keys or whether they moved by themselves. He pulled hysterically, trying to dislodge his fingers but he couldn't. The keys were moving faster than his eye could see. They were a blur of motion. He felt them shredding his skin, peeling his fingers. They were raw. Blood started to ooze out.

He cried out and pulled. He managed to jerk away his fingers and jump back in the chair.

His belt buckle caught, the desk drawer came flying out. It slammed into his stomach. He yelled again. The pain was a black cloud pouring over his head.

He threw down a hand to shove in the drawer. He saw the yellow pencils lying there. They glared. His hand slipped, it banged into the drawer.

One of the pencils jabbed at him.

He always kept the points sharp. It was like the bite of a snake. He snapped back his hand with a gasp of pain. The point was jammed under a nail. It was imbedded in raw, tender flesh. He cried out in fury and pain. He pulled at the pencil with his other hand. The point flew out and jabbed into his palm. He couldn't get rid of the pencil, it kept dragging over his hand. He pulled at it and it made black, jagged lines on his skin. It tore the skin open.

He heaved the pencil across the room. It bounced on the wall. It seemed to jump as it fell on the eraser. It rolled over and was still.

He lost his balance. The chair fell back with a rush. His head banged sharply against the floorboards. His outclutched hand grabbed at the window sill. Tiny splinters flashed into his skin like invisible needles. He howled in deathly fear. He kicked his legs. The mid-term papers showered down over him like the beating wings of insane bird flocks.

The chair snapped up again on its springs. The heavy wheels rolled over his raw, bloody hands. He drew them back with a shriek. He reared a leg and kicked the chair over violently. It crashed on the side against the mantelpiece. The wheels spun and chattered like a swarm of furious insects.

He jumped up. He lost his balance and fell again, crashing against the window sill. The curtains fell on him like a python. The rods snapped. They flew down and struck him across the scalp. He felt warm blood trickle across his forehead. He thrashed about on the floor. The curtains seemed to writhe around him like serpents. He screamed again. He tore at them wildly. His eyes were terror-stricken.

He threw them off and lurched up suddenly, staggering around for balance. The pain in his hands assailed him. He looked at them. They were like raw butcher meat, skin hanging down in shreds. He had to bandage them. He turned toward the bathroom.

At his first step the rug slid from under him, the rug he had kicked aside. He felt himself rush through the air. He reached down his hands instinctively to block the fall.

The white pain made his body leap. One finger snapped. Splinters shot into his raw fingers, he felt a burning pain in one ankle.

He tried to scramble up but the floor was like ice under him. He was deadly silent. His heart thudded in his chest. He tried to rise again. He fell, hissing with pain.

The bookshelf loomed over him. He cried out and flung up an arm. The case came crashing down on him. The top shelf drove into his skull. Black waves dashed over him, a sharp blade of pain drove into his head. Books showered over him. He rolled on his side with a groan. He tried to crawl out from underneath. He shoved the books aside weakly and they fell open. He felt the page edges slicing into his fingers like razor blades.

The pain cleared his head. He sat up and hurled the books aside. He kicked the bookcase back against the wall. The back fell off it and it crashed down.

He rose up, the room spinning before his eyes. He staggered into the wall, tried to hold on. The wall shifted under his hands it seemed. He couldn't hold on. He slipped to his knees, pushed up again.

"Bandage myself," he muttered hoarsely.

The words filled his brain. He staggered up through the quivering dining room, into the bathroom.

He stopped. No! Get out of the house! He knew it was not his will that brought him in there.

He tried to turn but he slipped on the tiles and cracked his elbow against the edge of the bathtub. A shooting pain barbed into his upper arm. The arm went numb. He sprawled on the floor, writhing in pain. The walls clouded; they welled around him like a blank shroud.

He sat up, breath tearing at his throat. He pushed himself up with a gasp. His arm shot out, he pulled open the cabinet door. It flew open against his cheek, tearing a jagged rip in the soft flesh.

His head snapped back. The crack in the ceiling looked like a wide idiot smile on a blank, white face. He lowered his head, whimpering in fright. He tried to back away.

His hand reached out. For iodine, for gauze!—his mind cried.

His hand came out with the razor.

It flopped in his hand like a new caught fish. His other hand reached in. For iodine, for gauze!—shrieked his mind.

His hand came out with dental floss. It flooded out of the

tube like an endless white worm. It coiled around his throat and shoulders. It choked him.

The long shiny blade slipped from its sheath.

He could not stop his hand. It drew the razor heavily across his chest. It slit open the shirt. It sliced a valley through his chest. Blood spurted out.

He tried to hurl away the razor. It stuck to his hand. It slashed at him, at his arms and hands and legs and body.

At his throat.

A scream of utter horror flooded from his lips. He ran from the bathroom, staggering wildly into the living room.

"Sally!" he screamed, "Sally, Sally, Sally . . ."

The razor touched his throat. The room went black. Pain. Life ebbing away into the night. Silence over all the world.

The next day Dr. Morton came. He called the police. And later the coroner wrote in his report:

Died of self-inflicted wounds.

Disappearing Act

These entries are from a school notebook which was found two weeks ago in a Brooklyn candy store. Next to it on the counter was a half-finished cup of coffee. The owner of the store said no one had been there for three hours prior to the time he first noticed the book.

Saturday morning early:

I shouldn't be writing this. What if Mary found it? Then what? The end, that's what, five years out the window.

But I have to put it down. I've been writing too long. There's no peace unless I put things on paper. I have to get them out and simplify my mind. But it's so hard to make things simple and so easy to make them complicated.

Thinking back through the months.

Where did it start? An argument of course. There must have been a thousand of them since we married. And always the same one, that's the horror.

Money.

"It's not a question of confidence in your writing," Mary will say. "It's a question of bills and are we or aren't we going to pay them?"

"Bills for what?" I'll say. "For necessities? No. For things we don't even need."

"Don't need!" And off we go. God, how impossible life is without money. Nothing can overcome it, it's everything when it's anything. How can I write in peace with endless worries of money, money, money? The television set, the refrigerator, the washer—none of them paid for yet. And the bed she wants . . .

But despite all, I—I with wide-eyed idiocy—keep making it even worse.

Why did I have to storm out of the apartment that first time? We'd argued, sure, but we'd argued before. Vanity, that's all. After seven years—*seven!*—of writing I've made only $316 from it. And I'm still working nights at the lousy part-time typing job. And Mary has to keep working at the same place with me. Lord knows she has a perfect right to doubt. A perfect right to keep insisting I take that full-time job Jim keeps offering me on his magazine.

All up to me. An admission of lack, a right move and everything would be solved. No more night work. Mary could stay home the way she wants to, the way she should. The right move, that's all.

So, I've been making the wrong one. God, it makes me sick.

Me, going out with Mike. Both of us glassy-eyed imbeciles meeting Jean and Sally. For months now, pushing aside the obvious knowledge that we were being fools. Losing ourselves in a new experience. Playing the ass to perfection.

And, last night, both of us married men, going with them to their club apartment and . . .

Can't I say it? Am I afraid, too weak? Fool!

Adulterer.

How can things get so mixed up? I love Mary. Very much. And yet, even loving her, I did this thing.

And to make it all even more complicated, I enjoyed it. Jean is sweet and understanding, passionate, a sort of symbol of lost things. It was wonderful. I can't say it wasn't.

But how can wrong be wonderful? How can cruelty be exhilarating? It's all perverse, it's jumbled and confused and enraging.

Saturday afternoon:

She's forgiven me, thank God. I'll never see Jean again. Everything will be all right.

This morning I went and sat on the bed and Mary woke up. She stared up at me, then looked at the clock. She'd been crying.

"Where have you been?" she asked in that thin little girl's voice she gets when she's scared.

"With Mike," I told her. "We drank and talked all night."

She stared a second more. Then she took my hand slowly and pressed it against her cheek.

"I'm sorry," she said and tears came to her eyes.

I had to put my head next to hers so she wouldn't see my face. "Oh, Mary," I said. "I'm sorry too."

I'll never tell her. She means too much to me. I *can't* lose her.

Saturday night:

We went down to Mandel's Furniture Mart this afternoon and got a new bed.

"We can't afford it, honey," Mary said.

"Never mind," I said. "You know how lumpy the old one is. I want my baby to sleep in style."

She kissed my cheek happily. She bounced on the bed like an excited kid. "Oh, feel how soft!" she said.

Everything is all right. Everything except the new batch of bills in today's mail. Everything except for my latest story which won't get started. Everything except for my novel which has bounced five times. Burney House *has* to take it. They've held it long enough. I'm counting on it. Things are coming to a head with my writing. With everything. More and more I get the feeling that I'm a wound-up spring.

Well, Mary's all right.

S unday night:
  More trouble. Another argument. I don't even know what it was about. She's sulking. I'm burning. I can't write when I'm upset. She knows that.

I feel like calling Jean. At least *she* was interested in my writing. I feel like saying the hell with everything. Getting drunk, jumping off a bridge, something. No wonder babies are happy. Life is simple for them. Some hunger, some cold, a little fear of darkness. That's all. Why bother growing up? Life gets too complicated.

Mary just called me for supper. I don't feel like eating. I don't even feel like staying in the house. Maybe I'll call up Jean later. Just to say hello.

M onday morning:
  Damn, damn, damn!

Not only to hold the book for over three months. That's not bad enough, oh no! They had to spill coffee all over the manuscript and send me a *printed* rejection slip to boot. I could kill them! I wonder if they think they know what they're doing?

Mary saw the slip. "Well, what *now*?" she said disgustedly.

"Now?" I said. I tried not to explode.

"Still think you can write?" she said.

I exploded. "Oh, they're the last judge and jury, aren't they?" I raged. "They're the final word on my writing aren't they?"

"You've been writing seven years," she said. "Nothing's happened."

"And I'll write seven more," I said. "A hundred, a *thousand*!"

"You won't take that job on Jim's magazine?"

"No, I will not."

"You said you would if the book failed."

"I *have* a job," I said, "and you have a job and that's the way it is and that's the way it's going to stay."

"It's not the way *I'm* going to stay!" she snapped.

She may leave me. Who cares! I'm sick of it all anyway. Bills, bills. Writing, writing. Failures, failures, *failures*! And little old life dribbling on, building up its beautiful, brain-bursting complexities like an idiot with blocks.

You! Who run the world, who spin the universe. If there's anybody listening to me, make the world simpler! I don't believe in anything but I'd give . . . *anything*! If only . . .

Oh, what's the use? I don't care anymore.

I'm calling Jean tonight.

Monday afternoon:

I just went down to call up Jean about Saturday night. Mary is going to her sister's house that night. She hasn't mentioned me going with her so *I'm* certainly not going to mention it.

I called Jean last night but the switchboard operator at the

Club Stanley said she was out. I figured I'd be able to reach her today at her office.

So I went to the corner candy store to look up the number. I probably should have memorized it by now. I've called her enough. But somehow, I never bothered. What the hell, there are always telephone books.

She works for a magazine called *Design Handbook* or *Designer's Handbook* or something like that. Odd, I can't remember that either. Guess I never gave it much thought.

I do remember where the office is though. I called for her there a few months ago and took her to lunch. I think I told Mary I was going to the library that day.

Now, as I recall, the telephone number of Jean's office was in the upper right hand corner of the right page in the directory. I've looked it up dozens of times and that's where it always was.

Today it wasn't.

I found the word *Design* and different business names starting with that word. But they were in the lower left hand corner of the left page, just the opposite. And I couldn't seem to find any name that clicked. Usually as soon as I see the name of the magazine I think: *there it is*. Then I look up the number. Today it wasn't like that.

I looked and looked and thumbed around but I couldn't find anything like *Design Handbook*. Finally I settled for the number of *Design Magazine* but I had the feeling it wasn't the one I was searching for.

I . . . I'll have to finish this later. Mary just called me for lunch, dinner, what have you? The big meal of the day anyway since we both work at night.

Later:

It was a good meal. Mary can certainly cook. If only

there weren't those arguments. I wonder if Jean can cook.

At any rate the meal steadied me a little. I needed it. I was a little nervous about that telephone call.

I dialed the number. A woman answered.

"Design Magazine," she said.

"I'd like to talk to Miss Lane," I told her.

"Who?"

"Miss Lane."

"One moment," she said. And I knew it was the wrong number. Every other time I'd called the woman who answered had said, "All right" immediately and connected me with Jean.

"What was that name again?" she asked.

"Miss Lane. If you don't know her, I must have the wrong number."

"You might mean Mr. Payne."

"No, no. Before, the secretary who answered always knew right away who I wanted. I have the wrong number. Excuse me."

I hung up. I was pretty irritated. I've looked that number up so many times it isn't funny.

Now, I can't find it.

Of course I didn't let it get me at first. I thought maybe the phone book in the candy store was an old one. So I went down the street to the drugstore. It had the same book.

Well, I'll just have to call her from work tonight. But I wanted to get her this afternoon so I'd be sure she'd save Saturday night for me.

I just thought of something. That secretary. Her voice. It was the same one who used to answer for *Design Handbook.*

But . . . Oh, I'm dreaming.

———

Monday night:

I called the club while Mary was out of the office getting us some coffee.

I told the switchboard operator the same way I've told her dozens of times. "I'd like to speak to Miss Lane, please."

"Yes sir, one moment," she said.

There was silence a long time. I got impatient. Then the phone clicked again.

"What was that name?" the operator asked.

"Miss Lane, Miss *Lane*," I said. "I've called her any number of times."

"I'll look at the list again," she said.

I waited some more. Then I heard her voice again.

"I'm sorry. No one by that name is listed here."

"But I've called her any number of times there."

"Are you sure you have the right number?"

"Yes, yes, I'm sure. This is the Club Stanley, isn't it?"

"Yes, it is."

"Well, that's where I'm calling."

"I don't know what to say," she said. "All I can tell you is that I'm certain there isn't anyone by that name living here."

"But I just called *last night*! You said she wasn't in."

"I'm sorry, I don't remember."

"Are you sure? Absolutely sure?"

"Well, if you want, I'll look at the list again. But no one by that name is on it, I'm positive."

"And no one by that name moved out within the last few days?"

"We haven't had a vacancy for a year. Rooms are hard to get in New York, you know."

"I know," I said, and hung up.

I went back to my desk. Mary was back from the drugstore.

She told me my coffee was getting cold. I said I was calling Jim in regard to that job. That was an ill-chosen lie. Now she'll start in on that again.

I drank my coffee and typed a while. But I didn't know what I was doing. I was trying hard to settle my mind.

She has to be somewhere, I thought. I know I didn't dream all those moments together. I know I didn't imagine all the trouble I had keeping it a secret from Mary. And I know that Mike and Sally didn't . . .

Sally! Sally lived at the Club Stanley too.

I told Mary I had a headache and was going out for an aspirin. She said there must be some in the men's room. I told her they were a kind I didn't like. I get involved in the flimsiest lies!

I half ran to the nearby drugstore. Naturally I didn't want to use the phone at work again.

The same operator answered my ring.

"Is Miss Sally Norton there?" I asked.

"One moment please," she said, and I felt a sinking sensation in my stomach. She always knew the regular members right away. And Sally and Jean had been living there for at least *two* years.

"I'm sorry," she said. "No one by that name is listed here."

I groaned. "Oh my God."

"Is something wrong?" she asked.

"No Jean Lane and no Sally Norton live there?"

"Are you the same party who called a little while ago?"

"Yes."

"Now look. If this is a joke . . ."

"A joke! Last night I called you and you told me Miss Lane was out and would I like to leave a message. I said no. Then I call tonight and you tell me there's nobody there by that name."

"I'm sorry. I don't know what to say. I was on the board last night but I don't recall what you say. If you like I'll connect you with the house manager."

"No, never mind," I said and hung up.

Then I dialed Mike's number. But he wasn't home. His wife Gladys answered, told me Mike had gone bowling.

I was a little nervous or I wouldn't have slipped up.

"With the boys?" I asked her.

She sounded kind of slighted. "Well, I *hope* so," she said.

I'm getting scared.

Tuesday night:

I called Mike again tonight. I asked him about Sally.

"Who?"

"Sally."

"Sally who?" he asked.

"You know damn well Sally who, you hypocrite!"

"What is this, a gag?" he asked.

"Maybe it is," I said. "How about cutting it out?"

"Let's start all over," he said. "Who the hell is Sally?"

"You don't know Sally Norton?"

"No. Who is she?"

"You never went on a date with her and Jean Lane and me?"

"Jean Lane! What are you talking about?"

"You don't know Jean Lane either?"

"No, I *don't* and this is getting very unfunny. I don't know what you're trying to pull but cut it out. As two married men we . . ."

"Listen!" I almost shouted into the phone. "Where were you three weeks ago Saturday night?"

He was silent a moment.

"Wasn't that the night you and I bached while Mary and Glad went to see the fashion show at . . ."

"Bached! There was no one with us?"

"Who?"

"No girls? Sally? Jean?"

"Oh, here we go again," he groaned. "Look, pal, what's eating you? Anything I can do?"

I slumped against the wall of the telephone booth.

"No," I said weakly. "No."

"Are you sure you're all right? You sound upset as hell."

I hung up. I *am* upset. I have a feeling as though I'm starving and there isn't a scrap of food in the whole world to feed me.

What's wrong?

Wednesday afternoon:
        There was only one way to find out if Sally and Jean had really disappeared.

I had met Jean through a friend I knew at college. Her home is in Chicago and so is my friend Dave's. He was the one who gave me her New York address, the Club Stanley. Naturally I didn't tell Dave I was married.

So I'd looked up Jean and I went out with her and Mike went out with her friend Sally. That's the way it was, I *know* it happened.

So today I wrote a letter to Dave. I told him what had happened. I begged him to check up at her home and write quickly and tell me it was a joke or some amazing set of coincidences. Then I got out my address book.

Dave's name is gone from the book.

Am I really going crazy? I know perfectly well that the address was in there. I can remember the night, years ago, when

I carefully wrote it down because I didn't want to lose contact with him after we graduated from college. I can even remember the ink blot I made when I wrote it because my pen leaked.

The page is blank.

I remember his name, how he looked, how he talked, the things we did, the classes we took together.

I even had a letter of his he sent me one Easter vacation while I was at school. I remember Mike was over at my room. Since we lived in New York there wasn't time to get home because the vacation was only for a few days.

But Dave had gone home to Chicago and, from there, sent us a very funny letter, special delivery. I remember how he sealed it with wax and stamped it with his ring for a gag.

The letter is gone from the drawer where I always kept it.

And I had three pictures of Dave taken on graduation day. Two of them I kept in my picture album. They're still there . . .

But he's not on them.

They're just pictures of the campus with buildings in the background.

I'm afraid to go on looking. I could write the college or call them and ask if Dave ever went there.

But I'm afraid to try.

Thursday afternoon:

Today I went out to Hempstead to see Jim. I went to his office. He was surprised when I walked in. He wanted to know why I'd traveled so far just to see him.

"Don't tell me you've decided to take that job offer," he said.

I asked him, "Jim, did you ever hear me talking about a girl named Jean in New York?"

"Jean? No, I don't think so."

"Come on, Jim. I did mention her to you. Don't you re-member the last time you and I and Mike played poker? I told you about her then."

"I don't remember, Bob," he said. "What about her?"

"I can't find her. And I can't find the girl Mike went out with. And Mike denies that he ever knew either of them."

He looked confused so I told him again. Then he said, "What's this? Two old married men gallivanting around with . . ."

"They were just friends," I cut in. "I met them through a fellow I knew at college. Don't get any bright ideas."

"All right, all right, skip it. Where do I fit in?"

"I can't *find* them. They're gone. I can't even prove they existed."

He shrugged. "So what?" Then he asked me if Mary knew about it. I brushed that off.

"Didn't I mention Jean in any of my letters?" I asked him.

"Couldn't say. I never keep letters."

I left soon after that. He was getting too curious. I can see it now. He tells his wife, his wife tells Mary—fireworks.

When I rode to work late this afternoon I had the most awful feeling that I was something temporary. When I sat down it was like resting on air.

I guess I must be cracking. Because I bumped into an old man deliberately to find out if he saw me or felt me. He snarled and called me a clumsy idiot.

I was grateful for that.

Thursday night:

Tonight at work I called up Mike again to see if he remembered Dave from college.

The phone rang, then it clicked off. The operator cut in and asked, "What number are you calling, sir?"

A chill covered me. I gave her the number. She told me there wasn't any such number.

The phone fell out of my hand and clattered on the floor. Mary stood up at her desk and looked over. The operator was saying, "Hello, hello, hello . . ." I hurriedly put the phone back in the cradle.

"What happened?" Mary asked when I came back to my desk.

"I dropped the phone." I said.

I sat and worked and shivered with cold.

I'm afraid to tell Mary about Mike and his wife Gladys.

I'm afraid she'll say she never heard of them.

Friday:

Today I checked up on *Design Handbook*. Information told me there was no such publication listed. But I went over to the city anyway. Mary was angry about me going. But I had to go.

I went to the building. I looked at the directory in the lobby. And even though I knew I wouldn't find the magazine listed there, it was still a shock that made me feel sick and hollow.

I was dizzy as I rode up the elevator. I felt as if I were drifting away from everything.

I got off at the third floor at the exact spot where I'd called for Jean that afternoon.

There was a textile company there.

"There never was a magazine here?" I asked the receptionist.

"Not as long as I can remember," she said. "Of course I've only been here three years."

I went home. I told Mary I was sick and didn't want to go to work tonight. She said all right she wouldn't go either. I went into the bedroom to be alone. I stood in the place where we're going to put the new bed when it's delivered next week.

Mary came in. She stood in the doorway restively.

"Bob, what's the matter?" she asked. "Don't I have a right to know?"

"Nothing," I told her.

"Oh, please don't tell me that," she said. "I know there is."

I started toward her. Then I turned away.

"I . . . I have to write a letter," I said.

"Who to?"

I flared up. "That's my business," I said. Then I told her to Jim.

She turned away. "I wish I could believe you," she said.

"What does *that* mean?" I asked. She looked at me for a long moment and then turned away again.

"Give *Jim* my best," she said, and her voice shook. The way she said it made me shudder.

I sat down and wrote the letter to Jim. I decided he might help. Things were too desperate for secrecy. I told him that Mike was gone. I asked him if he remembered Mike.

Funny. My hand hardly shook at all. Maybe that's the way it is when you're almost gone.

S aturday:

Mary had to work on some special typing today. She left early.

After I had breakfast I got the bank book out of the metal box in the bedroom closet. I was going down to the bank to get the money for the bed.

At the bank I filled out a withdrawal slip for $97. Then I waited in line and finally handed the slip and the book to the teller.

He opened it and looked up with a frown.

"This supposed to be funny?" he asked.

"What do you mean, funny?"

He pushed the book across to me. "Next," he said.

I guess I shouted. "What's the matter with you!"

Out of the corner of my eye I saw one of the men at the front desks jump up and hurry over. A woman behind me said, "Let me at the window, if you please."

The man came fussing up.

"What seems to be the trouble, sir?" he asked me.

"The teller refuses to honor my bank book," I told him.

He asked for the book and I handed it to him. He opened it. Then he looked up in surprise. He spoke quietly.

"This book is blank," he said.

I grabbed it and stared at it, my heart pounding.

It was completely unused.

"Oh, my God," I moaned.

"Perhaps we can check on the number of the book," the man said. "Why don't you step over to my desk?"

But there wasn't any number on the book. I saw that. And I felt tears coming into my eyes.

"No," I said. "No." I walked past him and started toward the doorway.

"One moment, sir," he called after me.

I ran out and ran all the way home.

I waited in the front room for Mary to come home. I'm waiting now. I'm looking at the bank book. At the line where we both signed our names. At the spaces where we had made our deposits. Fifty dollars from her parents on our first anniversary. Two hundred and thirty dollars from my veteran's insurance dividend. Twenty dollars. Ten dollars.

All blank.

Everything is going. Jean. Sally. Mike. Names fluttering away and the people with them.

Now this. What's next?

L ater:

I know.

Mary hasn't come home.

I called up the office. I heard Sam answer and I asked him if Mary was there. He said I must have the wrong number, no Mary works there. I told him who I was. I asked him if *I* worked there.

"Stop the kidding around," he said. "See you Monday night."

I called up my cousin, my sister, her cousin, her sister, her parents. No answer. Not even ringing. None of the numbers work. Then they're all gone.

S unday:

I don't know what to do. All day I've been sitting in the living room looking out at the street. I've been watching to see if anybody I know comes by the house. But they don't. They're all strangers.

I'm afraid to leave the house. That's all there is left. Our furniture and our clothes.

I mean *my* clothes. Her closet is empty. I looked into it this morning when I woke up and there wasn't a scrap of clothing left. It's like a magic act, everything disappearing, it's like . . .

I just laughed. I must be . . .

I called the furniture store. It's open Sunday afternoons. They said they had no record of us buying a bed. Would I like to come in and check?

I hung up and looked out the window some more.

I thought of calling up my aunt in Detroit. But I can't remember the number. And it isn't in my address book any more. The entire book is blank. Except for my name on the cover stamped in gold.

My name. Only my name. What can I say? What can I do? Everything is so simple. There's *nothing* to do.

I've been looking at my photograph album. Almost all the pictures are different. There aren't any people on them.

Mary is gone and all of our friends and our relatives.

It's funny.

In the wedding picture I sit all by myself at a huge table covered with food. My left arm is out and bent as though I were embracing my bride. And all along the table are glasses floating in the air.

Toasting me.

Monday morning:

I just got back the letter I sent Jim. It has NO SUCH ADDRESS stamped on the envelope.

I tried to catch the mailman but I couldn't. He was gone before I woke up.

I went down to the grocer before. He knew me. But when I asked him about Mary he said stop kidding, I'd die a bachelor and we both knew it.

I have only one more idea. It's a risk, but I'll have to take it. I'll have to leave the house and go downtown to the Veteran's

Administration. I want to see if my records are there. If they are, they'll have something about my schooling and about my marriage and the people who were in my life.

I'm taking this book with me. I don't want to lose it. If I lost it, then I wouldn't have a thing in the world to remind me that I'm not insane.

Monday night:

The house is gone.

I'm sitting in the corner candy store.

When I got back from the V.A. I found an empty lot there. I asked some of the boys playing there if they knew me. They said they didn't. I asked them what happened to the house. They said they'd been playing in that empty lot since they were babies.

The V.A. didn't have any records about me. Not a thing.

That means I'm not even a person now. All I have is all I am, my body and the clothes on it. All the identification papers are gone from my wallet.

My watch is gone too. Just like that. From my wrist.

It had an inscription on the back. I remember it.

To my own darling with all my love. Mary.

I'm having a cup of cof

Legion of
Plotters

Then there was the man who sniffed interminably.

He sat next to Mr. Jasper on the bus. Every morning he would come grunting up the front step and weave along the aisle to plop himself down beside Mr. Jasper's slight form.

And—*sniff!* he would go as he perused his morning paper—*sniff, sniff!*

Mr. Jasper would writhe. And wonder why the man persisted in sitting next to him. There were other seats available, yet the man invariably dropped his lumpish frame beside Mr. Jasper and sniffed the miles away, winter and summer.

It wasn't as if it were cold out. Some Los Angeles mornings were coolish, granted. But they certainly did not warrant this endless sniffling as though pneumonia were creeping through the man's system.

And it gave Mr. Jasper the willies.

He made several attempts to remove himself from the man's sphere of sniffling. First of all, he moved back two seats from his usual location. The man followed him. I *see*, surmised a near-fuming Mr. Jasper, the man is in the habit of sitting by me and hasn't noticed that I've moved back two seats.

The following day Mr. Jasper sat on the other side of the

aisle. He sat with irascible eye watching the man weave his bulk up the aisle. Then his vitals petrified as the man's tweeded person plumped down by him. He glared an abominating glare out the window.

Sniff!—went the man—*Sa-niff!*—and Mr. Jasper's dental plates ground together in porcelain fury.

The next day he sat near the back of the bus. The man sat next to him. The next day he sat near the front of the bus. The man sat next to him. Mr. Jasper sat amidst his corroding patience for a mile and a third. Then, jaded beyond endurance, he turned to the man.

"Why are you following me?" he asked, his voice a trembling plaint.

The man was caught in mid-sniff. He gaped at Mr. Jasper with cowlike, uncomprehending eyes. Mr. Jasper stood and stumbled a bus length away from the man. There he stood swaying from the overhead bar, his eyes as stone. The way that sniffing fool had looked at him, he brooded. It was insufferable. As if, by heaven, *he* had done something offensive!

Well, at least, he was momentarily free of those diurnally dripping nostrils. Crouched muscles unflexed gratefully. He sighed with relief.

And the boy standing next to him whistled twenty-three choruses of "Dixie."

M r. Jasper sold neckties.

It was an employment ridden with vexations, an employment guaranteed to scrape away the lining of any but the most impassive of stomachs.

Mr. Jasper's stomach walls were of the most susceptive variety.

They were stormed daily by aggravation, by annoyance and by women. Women who lingered and felt of wool and cotton and silk and walked away with no purchase. Women who beleaguered Mr. Jasper's inflammable mind with interrogations and decrees and left no money but only a rigid Mr. Jasper, one jot nearer to inevitable detonation.

With every taxing customer, a gushing host of brilliantly nasty remarks would rise up in Mr. Jasper's mind, each one surpassing the one before. His mind would positively ache to set them free, to let them pour like torrents of acid across his tongue and, burning hot, spout directly into the women's faces.

But invariably close by was the menacing phantom of a floor-walker or store inspector. It flitted through his mind with ghostly dominion, shunting aside his yearning tongue, calcifying his bones with unspent wrath.

Then there were the women in the store cafeteria.

They talked while they ate and they smoked and blew clouds of nicotine into his lungs at the very moment he was trying to ingest a bowl of tomato soup into his ulcered stomach. *Poof!* went the ladies and waved their pretty hands to dispel the unwanted smoke.

Mr. Jasper got it all.

Eyes beginning to emboss, he would wave it back. The women returned it. Thus did the smoke circulate until thinned out or reinforced by new, yet more intense, exhalations. *Poof!* And between waving and ladling and swallowing, Mr. Jasper had spasms. The tannic acid of his tea hardly served to stem the course of burning in his stomach. He would pay his forty cents with oscillating fingers and return to work, a cracking man.

To face a full afternoon of complaints and queries and thumbing of merchandise and the topping of all by the girl who shared the counter with him and chewed gum as though she wanted the people in Arabia to hear her chewing. The smacking and the popping and the grinding made Mr. Jasper's insides do frenzied contortions, made him stand statuelike and disordered or else burst out with a hissing:

"Stop that disgusting sound!"

Life was full of irritations.

Then there were the neighbors, the people who lived upstairs and on the sides. The society of *them*, that ubiquitous brotherhood which always lived in the apartments around Mr. Jasper.

They were a unity, those people. There was a touchstone of attitude in their behavior, a distinct criterion of method.

It consisted of walking with extra weighty tread, of moving furniture with sustained regularity, of throwing wild and noisy parties every other night and inviting only those people who promised to wear hobnailed boots and dance the chicken reel. Of arguing about all subjects at top voice, of playing only cowboy and hillbilly music on a radio whose volume knob was irretrievably stuck at its farthest point. Of owning a set of lungs disguised as a two- to twelve-month-old child, which puffed out each morning to emit sounds reminiscent of the lament of air raid sirens.

Mr. Jasper's present nemesis was Albert Radenhausen, Junior, age seven months, possessor of one set of incredibly hardy lungs which did their best work between four and five in the morning.

Mr. Jasper would find himself rolling onto his thin back in the dark, furnished, two-room apartment. He would find himself staring at the ceiling and waiting for the sound. It got to a point where his brain dragged him from needed sleep exactly ten seconds before four each morning. If Albert Radenhausen, Junior, chose to slumber on, it did no good to Mr. Jasper. He just kept waiting for the cries.

He would try to sleep, but jangling concentration made him prey, if not to the expected wailing, then to the host of other sounds which beset his hypersensitive ears.

A car coughing past in the street. A rattle of venetian blind. A set of lone footsteps somewhere in the house. The drip of a faucet, the barking of a dog, the rubbing legs of crickets, the creaking of wood. Mr. Jasper could not control it all. Those sound makers he could not stuff, pad, twist off, adjust to—kept plaguing him. He would shut his eyes until they hurt, grip tight fists at his sides.

Sleep still eluded. He would jolt up, heaving aside the sheets and blankets, and sit there staring numbly into the blackness, waiting for Albert Radenhausen, Junior, to make his utterance so he could lie down again.

Analyzing in the blackness, his mind would click out progressions of thought. Unduly sensitive?—he would comment within. I deny this vociferously. I am aware, Mr. Jasper would self-claim. No more. I have ears. I can hear, can't I?

It was suspicious.

What morning in the litter of mornings that notion came, Mr. Jasper could not recall. But once it had come, it would not be dismissed. Though the definition of it was blunted by passing days, the core remained unremovable.

Sometimes in a moment of teeth-gritting duress, the idea would reoccur. Other times it would be only a vague current of impressions flowing beneath the surface.

But it stuck. All these things that happened to him. Were they subjective or objective, within or without? They seemed to pile up so often, each detail linking until the sum of provocations almost drove him mad. It almost seemed as though it were done with intent. As if. . . .

As if it were a plan.

Mr. Jasper experimented.

Initial equipment consisted of one white pad, lined, plus his ball-point pen. Primary approach consisted of jotting down various exasperations with the time of their occurrence, the location, the sex of the offender and the relative grossness of the annoyance; this last aspect gradated by numbers ranging from one to ten.

Example one, clumsily notated while still half asleep.

Baby crying, 4:52 a.m., next door to room, male, 7.

Following this entry, Mr. Jasper settled back on his flattened pillow with a sigh approximating satisfaction. The start was made. In a few days he would know with assurance if his unusual speculation was justified.

Before he left the house at eight-seventeen a.m., Mr. Jasper had accumulated three more entries; viz:

Loud thumping on floor, 6:33 a.m., upstairs from room, male (guess), 5.

Traffic noise, 7:00 a.m. on, outside of room, males, 6.

Radio on loud, 7:40 a.m. on, upstairs from room, female, 7.

One rather odd facet of Mr. Jasper's efforts came to his attention as he left his small apartment. This was, in short, that he had put down much of his temper through this simple expedient of written analysis. Not that the various noises had failed, at first, to set his teeth on edge and cause his hands to flex involuntarily at his sides. They had not. Yet the translation of amorphous vexation into words, the reduction of an aggravation to one succinct memorandum somehow helped. It was strange but pleasing.

The bus trip to work provided further notations.

The sniffing man drew one immediate and automatic entry.

But once that irritant was disposed of, Mr. Jasper was alarmed to note the rapid accumulation of four more. No matter where he moved on the bus there was fresh cause for drawing penpoint from scabbard and stabbing out more words.

Garlic breath, 8:27 a.m., bus, male, 7.

Heavy jostling, 8:28 a.m., bus, both sexes, 8.

Feet stepped on. No apology, 8:29 a.m., bus, woman, 9.

Driver telling me to go to back of bus, 8:33 a.m., bus, male, 9.

Then Mr. Jasper found himself standing again beside the man with the uncommon cold. He did not take the pad from his pocket but his eyes closed and his teeth clamped together bitterly. Later he erased the original grading for the man.

10! he wrote in a fury.

And at lunch, amidst usual antagonizations, Mr. Jasper, with a fierce and jaundiced eye, saw system to it all.

He seized on a blank pad page.

1. At least one irritation per five minutes. (Twelve per hour.) Not perfectly timed. Some occurring two in a minute. Clever. Trying to throw me off the track by breaking continuity.

2. Each of the 12 hourly irritations is worse than the one before. The last of the 12 almost makes me explode.

THEORY: By placing the irritations so that each one tops the preceding one, the final hourly addition is thus designed to provide maximum nerve impact: i.e.—Steering me into insanity!

He sat there, his soup getting cold, a wild, scientific luster to his eyes, investigatory heat churning up his system. Yes, by Heaven, yes, yes, *yes!*

But he must make sure.

He finished his lunch, ignoring smoke and chattering and unpalatable food. He slunk back to his counter. He spent a joyous afternoon scribbling down entries in his journal of convulsions.

The system held.

It stood firm before unbiased test. One irritation per five minutes. Some of them, naturally, were so subtle that only a man with Mr. Jasper's intuitive grasp, a man with a quest, could notice them. These aggravations were underplayed. And cleverly so!—realized Mr. Jasper. Underplayed and intended to dupe.

Well, he would not be duped.

Tie rack knocked over, 1:18 p.m., store, female, 7.

Fly walking on hand, 1:43 p.m., store, female (?), 8.

Faucet in washroom splashing clothes, 2:19 p.m., store, (sex?), 9.

Refusal to buy tie because torn, 2:38 p.m., store, WOMAN, 10.

These were typical entries for the afternoon.

They were jotted down with a bellicose satisfaction by a shaking Mr. Jasper. A Mr. Jasper whose incredible theory was being vindicated.

About three o'clock he decided to eliminate those numbers from one to five since no provocations were mild enough to be judged so leniently.

By four he had discarded every grading but nine and ten.

By five he was seriously considering a new system which began at ten and ranged up to twenty-five.

Mr. Jasper had planned to compile at least a week's annotations before preparing his case. But, somehow, the shocks of the day weakened him. His entries grew more heated, his penmanship less legible.

And, at eleven that night, as the people next door got their second wind and resumed their party with a great shout of laughter, Mr. Jasper hurled his pad against the wall with a choking oath and stood there trembling violently. It was definite.

They were out to get him.

———

Suppose, he thought, there was a secret legion in the world. And that their prime devotion was to drive him from his senses.

Wouldn't it be possible for them to do this insidious thing without another soul knowing it? Couldn't they arrange their maddening little intrusions on his sanity so cleverly that it might always seem as if *he* were at fault; that he was only a hypersensitive little man who saw malicious intent in every accidental irritation? Wasn't that possible?

Yes. His mind pounded out the acceptance over and over. It was conceivable, feasible, possible and, by heaven, he believed it!

Why not? Couldn't there be a great sinister legion of people who met in secret cellars by guttering candlelight? And sat there, beady eyes shining with nasty intent, as their leader spoke of more plans for driving Mr. Jasper straight to hell?

Sure! Agent X assigned to the row behind Mr. Jasper at a movie, there to talk during parts of the picture in which Mr. Jasper was most absorbed, there to rattle paper bags at regular intervals, there to masticate popcorn deafeningly until Mr. Jasper hunched up, blind-raging, into the aisle and stomped back to another seat.

Where Agent Y would take over with candy and crinkly wrappers and extra-moist sneezes.

Possible. More than possible. It could have been going on for years without his ever acquiring the slightest inkling of its existence. A subtle, diabolical intrigue, near impossible to detect. But now, at last, stripped of its concealing robes, shown in all its naked, awful reality.

Mr. Jasper lay abed, cogitating.

No, he thought with a scant remainder of rationality, it is silly. It is a point outlandishly taken.

Why should these people do these things? That was all one had to ask. What was their motive?

Wasn't it absurd to think that all these people were out to get him? Dead, Mr. Jasper was worth nothing. Certainly his two thousand dollar policy subdivided among a vast hidden legion would not amount to more than three or four cents a plotter. Even if he were to be coerced into naming them all as his beneficiaries.

Why, then, did Mr. Jasper find himself drifting helplessly into the kitchenette? Why, then, did he stand there so long, balancing the long carving knife in his hand? And why did he shake when he thought of his idea?

Unless it was true. Before he retired Mr. Jasper put the carving blade into its cardboard sheath. Then, almost automatically, he found himself sliding the knife into the inside pocket of his suit coat.

And, horizontal in the blackness, eyes open, his flat chest rising and falling with unsteady beat, he sent out his bleak ultimatum to the legion that might be:

"If you are there, I will take no more."

Then there was Albert Radenhausen, Junior, again at four in the morning. Jolting Mr. Jasper into waking state, touching one more match to his inflammable system. There were the footsteps, the car horns, the dogs barking, the blinds rattling, the faucet dripping, the blankets bunching, the pillow flattening, the pajamas twisting. And morning with its burning toast and bad coffee and broken cup and loud radio upstairs and broken shoelace.

And Mr. Jasper's body grew rigid with unspeakable fury and he whined and hissed and his muscles petrified and his hands shook and he almost wept. Forgotten was his pad and list, lost in violent temper. Only one thing remained. And that . . . was self-defense.

For Mr. Jasper knew then there *was* a legion of plotters and he knew also that the legion was redoubling its efforts because he *did* know and would fight back.

He fled the apartment and hurried down the street, his mind tormented. He must get control, he *must!* It was the crucial moment, the time of ferment. If he let the course of things go unimpeded, then madness *would* come and the legion would have its victim.

Self-defense!

He stood, white-jawed and quivering, at the bus stop, trying with utmost vigor to resist. Never mind that exploding exhaust! Forget that strident giggle of passing female agent. Ignore the rising, mounting crescendo of split nerves. They would not win! His mind a rigid, waiting spring, Mr. Jasper vowed victory.

On the bus, the man's nostrils drew mightily and people bumped into Mr. Jasper and he gasped and knew that any moment he was going to scream and it would happen.

Sniff, sniff! went the man—SNIFF!

Mr. Jasper moved away tensely. The man had never sniffed that loudly before. It was in the plan. Mr. Jasper's hand fluttered up to touch the hard length of knife beneath his coat.

He shoved through packed commuters. Someone stepped on his foot. He hissed. His shoelace broke again. He bent over to fix it, and someone's knee hit the side of his head. He straightened up dizzily in the lurching bus, a strangled curse almost prying through his pressed, white lips.

One last hope remaining. *Could* he escape? The question punched away his senses. A new apartment? He'd moved before. On what he could afford there was no way of finding anything better. He'd always have the same type of neighbors.

A car instead of bus travel? He couldn't afford it.

Leave his miserable job? All sales jobs were just as bad and it was all he knew and he was getting older.

And even if he changed everything—*everything!*—the legion would still pursue him, tracking him down ruthlessly from tension to tension until the inevitable breakdown.

He was trapped.

And, suddenly, standing there with all the people looking at him, Mr. Jasper saw the hours ahead, the days, the years—an agonizing, crushing heap of annoyances and irritations and mind-searing aggravations. His head snapped around as he looked at everybody.

And his hair almost stood on end because he realized that all the people in the bus were members of the legion too. And he was helpless in their midst, a pawn to be buffeted about by their vicious, inhuman presence, his rights and individual sanctities endlessly subject to their malevolent conspiracy.

"No!" He screamed it out at them.

And his hand flew in beneath his coat like an avenging bird. And the blade flashed and the legion backed away screaming as, with a frenzied lunge, Mr. Jasper fought his war for sanity.

MAN STABS SIX

IN CROWDED BUS;

SHOT BY POLICE

No Motive Found

For Wild Attack

Long Distance Call

Just before the telephone rang, storm winds toppled the tree outside her window and jolted Miss Keene from dreaming sleep. She flung herself up with a gasp, her frail hands crumpling twists of sheet in either palm. Beneath her fleshless chest the heart jerked taut, the sluggish blood spurted. She sat in rigid muteness, her eyes staring at the night.

In another second, the telephone rang.

Who on earth? The question shaped unwittingly in her brain. Her thin hand faltered in the darkness, the fingers searching a moment and then Miss Elva Keene drew the cool receiver to her ear.

"Hello," she said.

Outside a cannon of thunder shook the night, twitching Miss Keene's crippled legs. *I've missed the voice,* she thought, *the thunder has blotted out the voice.*

"Hello," she said again.

There was no sound. Miss Keene waited in expectant lethargy. Then she repeated. "Hel-*lo*," in a cracking voice. Outside the thunder crashed again.

Still no voice spoke, not even the sound of a phone being disconnected met her ears. Her wavering hand reached out and thumped down the receiver with an angry motion.

"Inconsideration," she muttered, thudding back on her pillow. Already her infirm back ached from the effort of sitting.

She forced out a weary breath. Now she'd have to suffer through the whole tormenting process of going to sleep again—the composing of jaded muscles, the ignoring of abrasive pain in her legs, the endless, frustrating struggle to turn off the faucet in her brain and keep unwanted thoughts from dripping. Oh, well, it had to be done; Nurse Phillips insisted on proper rest. Elva Keene breathed slowly and deeply, drew the covers to her chin and labored hopefully for sleep.

In vain.

Her eyes opened and, turning her face to the window, she watched the storm move off on lightning legs. *Why can't I sleep*, she fretted, *why must I always lie here awake like this?*

She knew the answer without effort. When a life was dull, the smallest element added seemed unnaturally intriguing. And life for Miss Keene was the sorry pattern of lying flat or being propped on pillows, reading books which Nurse Phillips brought from the town library, getting nourishment, rest, medication, listening to her tiny radio—and waiting, *waiting* for something different to happen.

Like the telephone call that wasn't a call.

There hadn't even been the sound of a receiver replaced in its cradle. Miss Keene didn't understand that. Why would anyone call her exchange and then listen silently while she said, "Hello," over and over again? *Had* it actually been anyone calling?

What she should have done, she realized then, was to keep listening until the other person tired of the joke and put down the receiver. What she should have done was to speak out forcefully about the inconsideration of a prankish call to a crippled maiden lady in the middle of a stormy night. Then, if there had been someone listening, whoever it was would have been properly chastened by her angry words and . . .

"Well, of course."

She said it aloud in the darkness, punctuating the sentence with a cluck of somewhat relieved disgust. Of course, the telephone was out of order. Someone had tried to contact her, perhaps Nurse Phillips to see if she was all right. But the other end of the line had broken down in some way, allowing her phone to ring but no verbal communication to be made. Well, of course, that was the case.

Miss Keene nodded once and closed her eyes gently. Now to sleep, she thought. Far away, beyond the county, the storm cleared its murky throat. *I hope no one is worrying*, Elva Keene thought, *that would be too bad*.

She was thinking that when the telephone rang again.

There, she thought, *they are trying to reach me again*. She reached out hurriedly in the darkness, fumbled until she felt the receiver, then pulled it to her ear.

"Hello," said Miss Keene.

Silence.

Her throat contracted. She knew what was wrong, of course, but she didn't like it, no, not at all.

"Hello?" she said tentatively, not yet certain that she was wasting breath.

There was no reply. She waited a moment, then spoke a third time, a little impatiently now, loudly, her shrill voice ringing in the dark bedroom. *"Hello!"*

Nothing. Miss Keene had the sudden urge to fling the receiver away. She forced down that curious instinct—no, she must wait; wait and listen to hear if anyone hung up the phone on the other end of the line.

So she waited.

The bedroom was very quiet now, but Elva Keene kept straining to hear; either the sound of a receiver going down or the buzz which usually follows. Her chest rose and fell in delicate lurches, she closed her eyes in concentration, then opened them again and blinked at the darkness. There was no sound from the telephone; not a click, not a buzz, not a sound of someone putting down a receiver.

"Hello!" she cried suddenly, then pushed away the receiver.

She missed her target. The receiver dropped and thumped once on the rug. Miss Keene nervously clicked on the lamp, wincing as the leprous bulb light filled her eyes. Quickly, she lay on her side and tried to reach the silent, voiceless telephone.

But she couldn't stretch far enough and crippled legs prevented her from rising. Her throat tightened. My God, must she leave it there all night, silent and mystifying?

Remembering then, she reached out abruptly and pressed the cradle arm. On the floor, the receiver clicked, then began to buzz normally. Elva Keene swallowed and drew in a shaking breath as she slumped back on her pillow.

She threw out hooks of reason then and pulled herself back from panic. *This is ridiculous*, she thought, *getting upset over such a trivial and easily explained incident. It was the storm, the night, the way in which I'd been shocked from sleep. (What was it that had awakened me?) All these things piled on the mountain of teeth-grinding monotony that's my life. Yes, it was bad, very bad.* But it wasn't the incident that was bad. It was her reaction to it.

Miss Elva Keene numbed herself to further premonitions. *I shall sleep now*, she ordered her body with a petulant shake. She lay very still and relaxed. From the floor she could hear the telephone buzzing like the drone of far-off bees. She ignored it.

E arly the next morning, after Nurse Phillips had taken away the breakfast dishes, Elva Keene called the telephone company.

"This is Miss Elva," she told the operator.

"Oh, yes, Miss Elva," said the operator, a Miss Finch. "Can I help you?"

"Last night my telephone rang twice," said Elva Keene. "But when I answered it, no one spoke. And I didn't hear any receiver drop. I didn't even hear a dial tone—just silence."

"Well, I'll tell you, Miss Elva," said the cheery voice of Miss Finch, "that storm last night just about ruined half our service. We're being flooded with calls about knocked down lines and bad connections. I'd say you're pretty lucky your phone is working at all."

"Then you think it was probably a bad connection," prompted Miss Keene, "caused by the storm?"

"Oh yes, Miss Elva, that's all."

"Do you think it will happen again?"

"Oh, it *may*," said Miss Finch. "It *may*. I really couldn't tell you, Miss Elva. But if it does happen again, you just call me and then I'll have one of our men check on it."

"All right," said Miss Elva. "Thank you, dear."

She lay on her pillows all morning in a relaxed torpor. *It gives one a satisfied feeling*, she thought, *to solve a mystery, slight as it is. It had been a terrible storm that caused the bad connection. And no wonder when it had even knocked down the ancient oak tree beside the house. That was the noise that had awakened me of course, and a pity it was that the dear tree had fallen. How it shaded the house in hot summer months. Oh, well, I suppose I should be grateful,* she thought, *that the tree fell across the road and not across the house.*

The day passed uneventfully, an amalgam of eating, reading Angela Thirkell and the mail (two throw-away advertisements and the light bill), plus brief chats with Nurse Phillips. Indeed, routine had set in so properly that when the telephone rang early that evening, she picked it up without even thinking.

"Hello," she said.

Silence.

It brought her back for a second. Then she called Nurse Phillips.

"What is it?" asked the portly woman as she trudged across the bedroom rug.

"This is what I was telling you about," said Elva Keene, holding out the receiver. "Listen."

Nurse Phillips took the receiver in her hand and pushed back gray locks with the earpiece. Her placid face remained placid. "There's nobody there," she observed.

"That's right," said Miss Keene. "That's right. Now you just listen and see if you can hear a receiver being put down. I'm sure you won't."

Nurse Phillips listened for a moment, then shook her head. "I don't hear anything," she said and hung up.

"Oh, wait!" Miss Keene said hurriedly. "Oh, well, it doesn't matter," she added, seeing it was already done. "If it happens too often, I'll just call Miss Finch and they'll have a repairman check on it."

"I see," Nurse Phillips said and went back to the living room.

Nurse Phillips left the house at eight, leaving on the bedside table, as usual, an apple, a cookie, a glass of water and the bottle of pills. She puffed up the pillows behind Miss Keene's fragile back, moved the radio and telephone a little closer to the bed, looked around complacently, then turned for the door, saying, "I'll see you tomorrow."

It was fifteen minutes later when the telephone rang. Miss Keene picked up the receiver quickly. She didn't bother saying hello this time—she just listened.

At first it was the same—an absolute silence. She listened a moment more, impatiently. Then, on the verge of replacing the receiver, she heard the sound. Her cheek twitched, she jerked the telephone back to her ear.

"Hello?" she asked tensely.

A murmuring, a dull humming, a rustling sound—what was it? Miss Keene shut her eyes tightly, listening hard, but she couldn't identify the sound; it was too soft, too undefined. It deviated from a sort of whining vibration . . . to an escape of air . . . to a bubbling sibilance. *It must be the sound of the connection*, she thought, *it must be the telephone itself making the noise. Perhaps a wire blowing in the wind somewhere, perhaps . . .*

She stopped thinking then. She stopped breathing. The sound had ceased. Once more, silence rang in her ears. She could feel the heartbeats stumbling in her chest again, the walls of her throat closing in. *Oh, this is ridiculous*, she told herself. *I've already been through this—it was the storm, the storm!*

She lay back on her pillows, the receiver pressed to her ear, nervous breaths faltering from her nostrils. She could feel unreasoning dread rise like a tide within her, despite all attempts at sane deduction. Her mind kept slipping off the glassy perch of reason; she kept falling deeper and deeper.

Now she shuddered violently as the sounds began again. They couldn't *possibly* be human sounds, she knew, and yet there was something about them, some inflection, some almost identifiable arrangement of . . .

Her lips shook and a whine began to hover in her throat. But she couldn't put down the telephone, she simply couldn't. The sounds held her hypnotized. Whether they were the rise and fall of the wind or the muttering of faulty mechanisms, she didn't know, but they would not let her go.

"Hello?" she murmured, shakily.

The sounds rose in volume. They rattled and shook in her brain.

"Hello!" she screamed.

"H-e-l-l-o," answered a voice on the telephone. Then Miss Keene fainted dead away.

A re you certain it was someone saying *hello*?" Miss Finch asked Miss Elva over the telephone. "It might have been the connection, you know."

"I tell you it was a *man*!" a shaking Elva Keene cried. "It was the same man who kept listening to me say hello over and over and over again without answering me back. The same one who made terrible noises over the telephone!"

Miss Finch cleared her throat politely. "Well, I'll have a man check your line, Miss Elva, as soon as he can. Of course, the men are very busy now with all the repairs on storm wreckage, but as soon as it's possible . . ."

"And what am I going to do if this—this *person* calls again?"

"You just hang up on him, Miss Elva."

"But he keeps calling!"

"Well." Miss Finch's affability wavered. "Why don't you find out who he is, Miss Elva? If you can do that, why, we can take immediate action, you see and . . ."

After she'd hung up, Miss Keene lay against the pillows tensely, listening to Nurse Phillips sing husky love songs over the breakfast dishes. Miss Finch didn't believe her story, that was apparent. Miss Finch thought she was a nervous old woman falling prey to imagination. Well, Miss Finch would find out differently.

"I'll just keep calling her and calling her until she *does*," she said irritably to Nurse Phillips just before afternoon nap.

"You just do that," said Nurse Phillips. "Now take your pill and lie down."

Miss Keene lay in grumpy silence, her vein-rutted hands knotted at her sides. It was ten after two and, except for the bubbling of Nurse Phillip's front-room snores, the house was silent in the October afternoon. *It makes me angry*, thought Elva Keene, *that no one will take this seriously. Well*—her thin lips pressed together—*the next time the telephone rings I'll make sure that Nurse Phillips listens until she does hear something.*

Exactly then the phone rang.

Miss Keene felt a cold tremor lace down her body. Even in the daylight with sunbeams speckling her flowered coverlet, the strident ringing frightened her. She dug porcelain teeth into her lower lip to steady it. *Shall I answer it?* the question came and then, before she could even think to answer, her hand picked up the receiver. A deep ragged breath; she drew the phone slowly to her ear. She said, "Hello?"

The voice answered back, "Hello?"—hollow and inanimate.

"Who is this?" Miss Keene asked, trying to keep her throat clear.

"Hello?"

"Who's calling, please?"

"Hello?"

"Is anyone there!"

"Hello?"

"Please . . . !"

"Hello?"

Miss Keene jammed down the receiver and lay on her bed trembling violently, unable to catch her breath. *What is it,* begged her mind, *what in God's name is it?*

"Margaret!" she cried. *"Margaret!"*

In the front room she heard Nurse Phillips grunt abruptly and then start coughing.

"Margaret, please . . . !"

Elva Keene heard the large-bodied woman rise to her feet and trudge across the living room floor. *I must compose myself,* she told herself, fluttering hands to her fevered cheeks. *I must tell her exactly what happened, exactly.*

"What is it?" grumbled the nurse. "Does your stomach ache?"

Miss Keene's throat drew in tautly as she swallowed. "He just called again," she whispered.

"Who?"

"That man!"

"What man?"

"The one who keeps calling!" Miss Keene cried. "He keeps saying hello over and over again. That's all he says—hello, hello, hel . . ."

"Now stop this," Nurse Phillips scolded stolidly. "Lie back and . . ."

"I don't *want* to lie back!" she said frenziedly. "I want to know who this terrible person is who keeps frightening me!"

"Now don't work yourself into a state," warned Nurse Phillips. "You know how upset your stomach gets."

Miss Keene began to sob bitterly. "I'm afraid. I'm afraid of him. Why does he keep calling me?"

Nurse Phillips stood by the bed looking down in bovine inertia. "Now, what did Miss Finch tell you?" she said softly.

Miss Keene's shaking lips could not frame the answer.

"Did she tell you it was the connection?" the nurse soothed. "Did she?"

"But it isn't! It's a man, a *man*!"

Nurse Phillips expelled a patient breath. "If it's a man," she said, "then just hang up. You don't have to talk to him. Just hang up. Is that so hard to do?"

Miss Keene shut tear-bright eyes and forced her lips into a twitching line. In her mind the man's subdued and listless voice kept echoing. Over and over, the inflection never altering, the question never deferring to her replies—just repeating itself end-lessly in doleful apathy. *Hello? Hello?* Making her shudder to the heart.

"Look," Nurse Phillips spoke.

She opened her eyes and saw the blurred image of the nurse putting the receiver down on the table.

"There," Nurse Phillips said, "nobody can call you now. You leave it that way. If you need anything all you have to do is dial. Now isn't that all right? Isn't it?"

Miss Keene looked bleakly at her nurse. Then, after a mo-ment, she nodded once. Grudgingly.

She lay in the dark bedroom, the sound of the dial tone humming in her ear; keeping her awake. *Or am I just telling myself that?* she thought. *Is it really keeping me awake? Didn't I sleep that first night with the receiver off the hook? No, it wasn't the sound, it was something else.*

She closed her eyes obdurately. *I won't listen*, she told herself, *I just won't listen to it.* She drew in trembling breaths of the night. But the darkness would not fill her brain and blot away the sound.

Miss Keene felt around the bed until she found her jacket. She draped it over the receiver, swathing its black smoothness in woolly turns. Then she sank back again, stern breathed and taut. *I will sleep,* she demanded, *I will sleep.*

She heard it still.

Her body grew rigid and, abruptly, she unfolded the receiver from its thick wrappings and slammed it down angrily on the cradle. Silence filled the room with a delicious peace. Miss Keene fell back on the pillow with a feeble groan. *Now to sleep,* she thought.

The telephone rang.

Her breath snuffed off. The ringing seemed to permeate the darkness, surrounding her in a cloud of ear-lancing vibration. She reached out to put the receiver on the table again, then jerked her hand back with a gasp, realizing she would hear the man's voice again.

Her throat pulsed nervously. *What I'll do,* she planned, *what I'll do is take off the receiver very quickly—very quickly—and put it down, then push down on the arm and cut off the line. Yes, that's what I'll do!*

She tensed herself and spread her hand out cautiously until the ringing phone was under it. Then, breath held, she followed her plan, slashed off the ring, reached quickly for the cradle arm . . .

And stopped, frozen, as the man's voice reached out through darkness to her ears. "Where are you?" he asked. "I want to talk to you."

Claws of ice clamped down on Miss Keene's shuddering chest. She lay petrified, unable to cut off the sound of the man's dull, expressionless voice, asking, "Where are you? I want to talk to you."

A sound from Miss Keene's throat, thin and fluttering.

And the man said, "Where are you? I want to talk to you."

"No, no," sobbed Miss Keene.

"Where are you? I want . . ."

She pressed the cradle arm with taut white fingers. She held it down for five minutes before letting it go.

tell you I won't have it!"

Miss Keene's voice was a frayed ribbon of sound. She sat inflexibly on the bed, straining her frightened anger through the mouthpiece vents.

"You say you hang up on this man and he still calls?" Miss Finch inquired.

"I've *explained* all that!" Elva Keene burst out. "I had to leave the receiver off the phone all night so he wouldn't call. And the buzzing kept me awake. I didn't get a *wink* of sleep! Now, I want this line checked, do you hear me? I want you to stop this terrible thing!"

Her eyes were like hard, dark beads. The phone almost slipped from her palsied fingers.

"All right, Miss Elva," said the operator. "I'll send a man out today."

"Thank you, dear, thank you," Miss Keene said. "Will you call me when . . ."

Her voice stopped abruptly as a clicking sound started on the telephone.

"The line is busy," she announced.

The clicking stopped and she went on. "To repeat, will you let me know when you find out who this terrible person is?"

"Surely, Miss Elva, surely. And I'll have a man check your telephone this afternoon. You're at 127 Mill Lane, aren't you?"

"That's right, dear. You will see to it, won't you?"

"I promise faithfully, Miss Elva. First thing today."

"Thank you, dear," Miss Keene said, drawing in relieved breath.

There were no calls from the man all that morning, none that afternoon. Her tightness slowly began to loosen. She played a game of cribbage with Nurse Phillips and even managed a little laughter. It was comforting to know that the telephone company was working on it now. They'd soon catch that awful man and bring back her peace of mind.

But when two o'clock came, then three o'clock—and still no repairman at her house—Miss Keene began worrying again.

"What's the *matter* with that girl?" she said pettishly. "She promised me faithfully that a man would come this afternoon."

"He'll be here," Nurse Phillips said. "Be patient."

Four o'clock arrived and no man. Miss Keene would not play cribbage, read her book or listen to her radio. What had begun to loosen was tightening again, increasing minute by minute until five o'clock, when the telephone rang, her hand spurted out rigidly from the flaring sleeve of her bed jacket and clamped down like a claw on the receiver. *If the man speaks*, raced her mind, *if he speaks I'll scream until my heart stops*.

She pulled the receiver to her ear. "Hello?"

"Miss Elva, this is Miss Finch."

Her eyes closed and breath fluttered through her lips. "Yes?" she said.

"About those calls you say you've been receiving."

"Yes?" In her mind, Miss Finch's words cutting—"those calls you *say* you've been receiving."

"We sent a man out to trace them," continued Miss Finch. "I have his report here."

Miss Keene caught her breath. "Yes?"

"He couldn't find anything."

Elva Keene didn't speak. Her gray head lay motionless on the pillow, the receiver pressed to her ear.

"He says he traced the—the difficulty to a fallen wire on the edge of town."

"Fallen—wire?"

"Yes, Miss Elva." Miss Finch did not sound happy.

"You're telling me I didn't hear anything?"

Miss Finch's voice was firm. "There's no way anyone could have phoned you from that location," she said.

"I tell you a *man* called me!"

Miss Finch was silent and Miss Keene's fingers tightened convulsively on the receiver.

"There must be a phone there," she insisted. "There must be *some* way that man was able to call me!"

"Miss Elva, there's no one out there."

"Out where, *where?*"

The operator said, "Miss Elva, it's the cemetery."

In the black silence of her bedroom, a crippled maiden lady lay waiting. Her nurse would not remain for the night; her nurse had patted her and scolded her and ignored her.

She was waiting for a telephone call.

She could have disconnected the phone, but she had not the will. She lay there waiting, waiting, thinking.

Of the silence—of ears that had not heard, seeking to hear again. Of sounds bubbling and muttering—the first stumbling attempts at speech by one who had not spoken—how long? Of—*hello? hello?*—first greeting by one long silent. Of—*where are you?* Of (that which made her lie so rigidly) the clicking and the operator speaking her address. Of—

The telephone ringing.

A pause. Ringing. The rustle of a nightgown in the dark.

The ringing stopped.

Listening.

And the telephone slipping from white fingers, the eyes staring, the thin heartbeats slowly pulsing.

Outside, the cricket-rattling night.

Inside, the words still sounding in her brain—giving terrible meaning to the heavy, choking silence.

"Hello, Miss Elva. I'll be right over."

Slaughter House

I submit for your consideration, the following manuscript which was mailed to this office some weeks ago. It is presented with neither evidence nor judgment as to its validity. This determination is for the reader to make.

Samuel D. Machildon, *Associate Secretary, Rand Society for Psychical Research*

I

This occurred many years ago. My brother Saul and I had taken a fancy to the old, tenantless Slaughter House. Since we were boys the yellow-edged pronouncement—FOR SALE—had hung lopsided in the grimy front window. We had vowed with boyish ambition that, when we were old enough, the sign must come down.

When we had attained our manhood, this aspiration somehow remained. We had a taste for the Victorian, Saul and I. His painting was akin to that roseate and buxom transcription of nature so endeared by the nineteenth-century artists. And my writing, though far from satisfactory realization, bore the definite stamp of prolixity, was marked by that meticulous sweep of ornate phrase which the modernists decry as dullness and artifice.

Thus, for the headquarters of our artistic labors, what better retreat than the Slaughter House, that structure which matched in cornice and frieze our intimate partialities? None, we decided, and acted readily on that decision.

The yearly endowment arranged by our deceased parents, albeit meager, we knew to suffice, since the house was in gross need of repair and, moreover, without electricity.

There was also, if hardly credited by us, a rumor of ghosts. Neighborhood children quite excelled each other in relating the harrowing experiences they had undergone with various of the more eminent specters. We smiled at their clever fancies, never once losing the conviction that purchase of the house would be wholly practical and satisfactory.

The real estate office bumbled with financial delight the day we took off their hands what they had long considered a lost cause, having even gone so far as to remove the house from their listings. Convenient arrangements were readily fashioned and, in a matter of hours, we had moved all belongings from our uncommodious flat to our new, relatively large house.

Several days were then spent in the most necessary task of cleaning. This presented itself as far more difficult a project than first anticipated. Dust lay heavy throughout the halls and rooms. Our energetic dusting would send clouds of it billowing expansively, filling the air with powdery ghosts of dirt. We noted in respect to that observation that many a spectral vision might thus be made explicable if the proper time were utilized in experiment.

In addition to dust on all places of lodgment, there was thick grime on glass surfaces ranging from downstairs windows to silver-scratched mirrors in the upstairs bath. There were loose banisters to repair, door locks to recondition, yards of thick rugging out of whose mat to beat decades of dust, and a multitude of other chores large and small to be performed before the house could be deemed livable.

Yet, even with grime and age admitted, that we had come by an obvious bargain was beyond dispute. The house was completely furnished, moreover furnished in the delightful mode of the early 1900s. Saul and I were thoroughly enchanted. Dusted, aired, scrubbed from top to bottom, the house proved indeed a fascinating purchase. The dark luxurious drapes, the patterned rugs, the graceful furniture, the yellow-keyed spinet; everything was complete to the last detail, that detail being the portrait of a rather lovely young woman which hung above the living room mantel.

When first we came upon it, Saul and I stood speechless before its artistic quality. Saul then spoke of the painter's technique and finally, in rapt adulation, discussed with me the various possibilities as to the identity of the model.

It was our final conjecture that she was the daughter or wife of the former tenant, whoever he had been, beyond having the name of Slaughter.

Several weeks passed by. Initial delight was slaked by full-time occupancy and intense creative effort.

We rose at nine, had our breakfast in the dining room, then proceeded to our work, I in my sleeping chamber, Saul in the solarium, which we had been able to improvise into a small studio. Each in our places, the morning passed quietly and effectively. We lunched at one, a small but nourishing meal and then resumed work for the afternoon.

We discontinued our labors about four to have tea and quiet conversation in our elegant front room. By this hour it was too

late to go on with our work, since darkness would be com-
mencing its surrounding pall on the city. We had chosen not to
install electricity both for reasons of monetary prudence and the
less sordid one of pure aesthetics.

We would not, for the world, have distorted the gentle
charm of the house by the addition of blatant, sterile electric
light. Indeed we preferred the flickering silence of candlelight
in which to play our nightly game of chess. We needed no
usurping of our silence by noxious radio bleatings, we ate our
bakery bread unsinged and found our wine quite adequately
cooled from the old icebox. Saul enjoyed the sense of living in
the past and so did I. We asked no more.

But then began the little things, the intangible things, the
things without reason.

Walking on the stairs, in the hallway, through the rooms, Saul
or I, singly or together, would stop and receive the strangest
impulse in our minds; of fleeting moment yet quite definite
while existent.

It is difficult to express the feeling with adequate clarity. It
was as if we heard something although there was no sound, as
though we saw something when there was nothing before the
eye. A sense of shifting presence, delicate and tenuous, hidden
from all physical senses and yet, somehow, perceived.

There was no explaining it. In point of fact we never spoke
of it together. It was too nebulous a feeling to discuss, incapable
of being materialized into words. Restless though it made us,
there was no mutual comparison of sensation nor could there
be. Even the most abstract of thought formation could not approach what we were experiencing.

Sometimes I would come upon Saul casting a hurried glance
over his shoulder, or surreptitiously reaching out to stroke empty
air as though he expected his fingers to touch some invisible

entity. Sometimes he would catch me doing the same. On occasion we would smile awkwardly, both of us appreciating the
moment without words.

But our smiles soon faded. I almost think we were afraid to
deride this unknown aegis for fear that it might prove itself
actual. Not that my brother or I were superstitious in the least
degree. The very fact that we purchased the house without paying the slightest feasance to the old wives' tales about its supposed anathema seems to belie the suggestion that we were, in
any manner, inclined toward mystic apprehensions. Yet the
house did seem, beyond question, to possess some strange po-
tency.

Often, late at night, I would lie awake, knowing somehow
that Saul was also awake in his room and that we both were
listening and waiting, consciously certain about our expectation
of some unknown arrival which was soon to be effected.

And effected it was.

II

It was perhaps a month and a half after we had moved into
Slaughter House that the first hint was shown as to the house's
occupants other than ourselves.

I was in the narrow kitchen cooking supper on the small gas
stove. Saul was in the dining alcove arranging the table for supper. He had spread a white cloth over the dark, glossy mahogany
and, on it, placed two plates with attendant silver. A candela-
brum of six candles glowed in the center of the table casting
shadows over the snowy cloth.

Saul was about to place the cups and saucers beside the plates
as I turned back to the stove. I twisted the knob a trifle to lower
the flame under the chops. Then, as I began to open the icebox

to get the wine, I heard Saul gasp loudly and, something thumped on the dining-room rug. I whirled and hurried out of the kitchen as fast as I could.

One of the cups had fallen to the floor, its handle snapping off. I hurriedly picked it up, my eyes on Saul.

He was standing with his back to the living room archway, his right hand pressed to his cheek, a look of speechless shock contorting his handsome features.

"What is it?" I asked, placing the cup on the table.

He looked at me without answering and I noticed how his slender fingers trembled on his whitening cheek.

"Saul, what *is* it?"

"A hand," he said. "A hand. *It touched my cheek.*"

I believe my mouth fell open in surprise. I had, deep within the inner passages of my mind, been expecting something like this to happen. So had Saul. Yet now that it had, a natural sense of oppressive impact was on both of our shoulders.

We stood there in silence. How can I express my feeling at that moment? It was as though something tangible, a tide of choking air, crept over us like some shapeless, lethargic serpent. I noticed how Saul's chest moved in convulsive leaps and depressions and my own mouth hung open as I gasped for breath.

Then, in an added moment, the breathless vacuum was gone, the mindless dread dissolved. I managed to speak, trusting to break this awesome spell with words.

"Are you sure?" I asked.

His slender throat contracted. He forced a smile to his lips, a smile more frightened than pleasant.

"I hope not," he replied.

He reinforced his smile with some effort.

"Can it really be?" he went on, his joviality failing noticeably.

"Can it really be that we've been duped into buying ourselves a haunted house?"

I maintained an effort to join in with his spirit of artificial gusto for the sake of our own minds. But it could not long last nor did I feel any abiding comfort in Saul's feigned composure. We were both exceptionally hypersensitive, had been ever since our births, mine some twenty-seven years before, his twenty-five. We both felt this bodiless premonition deep in our senses.

We spoke no more of it, whether from distaste or foreboding I cannot say. Following our unenjoyable meal, we spent the remainder of the evening at pitifully conducted card games. I suggested, in one unguarded moment of fear, that it might be worth our consideration to have electrical outlets installed in the house.

Saul scoffed at my apparent submission and seemed a little more content to retain the relative dimness of candlelight than the occurrence before dinner would have seemed to make possible in him. Notwithstanding that, I made no issue of it.

We retired to our rooms quite early as we usually do. Before we separated, however, Saul said something quite odd to my way of thinking. He was standing at the head of the stairs looking down, I was about to open the door to my room.

"Doesn't it all seem familiar?" he asked.

I turned to face him, hardly knowing what he was talking about.

"Familiar?" I asked of him.

"I mean," he tried to clarify, "as though we'd been here before. No, more than just been here. Actually *lived* here."

I looked at him with a disturbing sense of alarm gnawing at my mind. He lowered his eyes with a nervous smile as though he'd said something he was just realizing he should not have said. He stepped off quickly for his room, muttering a most uncordial good night to me.

I then retired to my own room, wondering about the unusual restlessness which had seemed to possess Saul throughout the evening manifesting itself not only in his words but in his impatient card play, his fidgety pose on the chair upon which he sat, the agitated flexing of his fingers, the roving of his beautiful dark eyes about the living room. As though he were looking for something.

In my room, I disrobed, effected my toilet and was soon in bed. I had lain there about an hour when I felt the house shake momentarily and the air seemed abruptly permeated with a weird, discordant humming that made my brain throb.

I pressed my hands over my ears and then seemed to wake up, my ears still covered. The house was still. I was not at all sure that it had not been a dream. It might have been a heavy truck passing the house, thus setting the dream into motion in my upset mind. I had no way of being absolutely certain.

I sat up and listened. For long minutes I sat stock still on my bed and tried to hear if there were any sounds in the house. A burglar perhaps or Saul prowling about in quest of a midnight snack. But there was nothing. Once, while I glanced at the window, I thought I saw, out of the corner of my eye, a momentary glare of bluish light shining underneath my door. But, when I quickly turned my head, my eyes saw only the deepest of blackness and, at length, I sank back on my pillow and fell into a fitful sleep.

III

The next day was Sunday. Frequent wakings during the night and light, troubled sleep had exhausted me. I remained in bed until ten-thirty although it was my general habit to rise promptly at nine each day, a habit I had acquired when quite young.

I dressed hastily and walked across the hall, but Saul was already up. I felt a slight vexation that he had not come in to speak to me as he sometimes did nor even looked in to tell me it was past rising time.

I found him in the living room eating breakfast from a small table he had placed in front of the mantelpiece. He was sitting in a chair that faced the portrait.

His head moved around quickly as I came in. He appeared nervous to me.

"Good morning," he said.

"Why didn't you wake me up?" I said. "You know I never sleep this late."

"I thought you were tired," he said. "What difference does it make?"

I sat down across from him, feeling rather peevish as I took a warm biscuit from beneath the napkin and broke it open.

"Did you notice the house shaking last night?" I asked.

"No. Did it?"

I made no reply to the flippant air of his counter-question. I took a bite from my biscuit and put it down.

"Coffee?" he said. I nodded curtly and he poured me a cup, apparently oblivious to my pique.

I looked around the table.

"Where is the sugar?" I asked.

"I never use it," he answered. "You know that."

"*I* use it," I said.

"Well, you weren't up, John," he replied with an antiseptic smile.

I rose abruptly and went into the kitchen. I opened up one

side of the cabinet and retrieved the sugar bowl with irritable fingers.

Then, as I passed it, about to leave the room, I tried to open the other side of the cabinet. It would not open. The door had been stuck quite fast since we moved in. Saul and I had decided in facetious keeping with neighborhood tradition that the cabinet contained shelf upon shelf of dehydrated ghosts.

At the moment, however, I was in little humor for droll fancies. I pulled at the door knob with rising anger. That I should suddenly insist on that moment to open the cabinet only reflected the ill-temper Saul's neglect could so easily create in me. I put down the sugar bowl and placed both hands on the knob.

"What on earth are you doing?" I heard Saul ask from the front room.

I made no answer to his question but pulled harder on the cabinet knob. But it was as if the door were imbedded solidly into the frame and I could not loosen it the least fraction of an inch.

"What were you doing?" Saul asked as I sat down.

"Nothing," I said and the matter ended. I sat eating with little if any appetite. I do not know whether I felt more anger than hurt. Perhaps it was more a sense of injury since Saul is usually keenly sensitive to my responses, but that day he seemed not the slightest particle receptive. And it was that blasé dispassion in him, so different from his usual disposition, that had so thoroughly upset me.

Once, during the meal, I glanced up at him to discover that his eyes were directed over my shoulder, focusing on something behind me. It caused a distinct chill to excite itself across my back.

"What are you looking at?" I asked of him.

His eyes refocused themselves on me and the slight smile he held was erased from his lips.

"Nothing," he replied.

Nonetheless I twisted about in my chair to look. But there was only the portrait over the mantel and nothing more.

"The portrait?" I asked.

He made no answer but stirred his coffee with deceptive composure.

I said, "Saul, I'm talking to you."

His dark eyes on me were mockingly cold. As though they meant to say, Well, so you are but that is hardly a concern of mine, is it?

When he would not speak I chose to attempt an alleviation of this inexplicable tension which had risen between us. I put down my cup.

"Did you sleep well?" I asked.

His gaze moved up to me quickly, almost, I could not avoid the realization, almost suspiciously.

"Why do you ask?" he spoke distrustingly.

"Is it such an odd question?"

Again he made no reply. Instead he patted his thin lips with his napkin and pushed back his chair as though to leave.

"Excuse me," he muttered, more from habit than politeness, I sensed.

"Why are you being so mysterious?" I asked with genuine concern.

He was on his feet, ready to move away, his face virtually blank.

"I'm not," he said. "You're imagining things."

I simply could not understand this sudden alteration in him

nor relate it to any equivalent cause. I stared incredulously at him as he turned away and began walking toward the hallway with short, impatient steps.

He turned left to pass through the archway and I heard his quick feet jumping up the carpeted steps. I sat there unable to move, looking at the spot from which he had just disappeared.

It was only after a long while that I turned once more to examine the portrait more carefully.

There seemed nothing unusual about it. My eyes moved over the well-formed shoulders to the slender, white throat, the chin, the cupid-bowed red lips, the delicately upturned nose, the frank green eyes. I had to shake my head. It was only the portrait of a woman and no more. How could this affect any man of sense? How could it affect Saul?

I could not finish my coffee but let it stand cold on the table. I rose, pushed back my chair and started upstairs. I went directly to my brother's room and turned the knob to enter, then felt a stiffening in my body as I realized he had locked himself in. I turned away from his door, tight-lipped and thoroughly annoyed, disturbed beyond control.

As I sat in my room most of the day, sporadically reading, I listened for his footsteps in the hall. I tried to reason out the situation in my mind, to resolve this alien transformation in his attitude towards me.

But there seemed no resolution save that of assuming headache, imperfect sleep or other equally dissatisfying explanations. They served not at all to decipher his uneasiness, the foreign way in which his eye regarded me, his marked disinclination to speak civilly.

It was then, against my will I must state clearly, that I began to suspect other than ordinary causes and to yield a momentary credence to local accounts of the house in which we lived. We had not spoken of that hand he had felt, but was it because we believed it was imagination or because we knew it wasn't?

Once during the afternoon, I stood in the hallway with closed eyes, listening intently as though I meant to capture some particular sound and ferret it out. In the deep quiet I stood wavering back and forth on the floor, the very stillness ringing in my ears.

I heard nothing. And the day passed with slow, lonely hours. Saul and I had a morose supper together during which he rejected all extended conversation and multiple offers of card games and chess during the later evening.

After he had finished his meal, he returned immediately to his room and I, after washing the dishes, returned to mine and soon retired.

The dream returned again, yet not in certainty a dream, I thought lying there in the early morning. And had it not been a dream only a hundred trucks could have made such a vibration as that which shook the house in my fancy. And the light which shone beneath the door was too bright for candlelight, a glaring blue lucency of illumination. And the footsteps I heard were very audible. Were they only in my dream however? I could not be sure.

IV

It was nearly nine-thirty before I rose and dressed, strongly irritated that my work schedule was being thus altered by concern. I completed my toilet quickly and went out into the hall, anxious to lose myself in occupation.

Then, as I looked automatically toward Saul's room I noticed that the door was slightly ajar. I immediately assumed he was already up and at work above in the solarium, so I did not stop to see. Instead, I hurried downstairs to make myself a hasty breakfast, noticing as I entered the kitchen that the room was just as I had left it the night before.

After a moderate breakfast I went upstairs again and entered Saul's room.

It was with some consternation that I found him still on his bed. I say "on" rather than "in" since the blankets and sheets had been, and violently so, it appeared, thrown aside and were hanging down in twisted swirls upon the wooden floor.

Saul lay on the bottom sheet, clad only in a pajama trousers, his chest, shoulders and face dewed with tiny drops of perspiration.

I bent over and shook him once, but he only mumbled in sleep-ridden lethargy. I shook him again with hardened fingers and he rolled over angrily.

"Leave me alone," he spoke in thickened irritability. "You know I've been . . ."

He stopped, as though, once more, he was about to speak of something he should not.

"You've been what?" I inquired, feeling a rising heat of aggravation in my system.

He said nothing but lay there on his stomach, his face buried in the white pillow.

I reached down and shook him again by the shoulder, this time more violently. At this he pushed up abruptly and almost screamed at me.

"Get out of here!"

"Are you going to paint?" I asked shaking nervously.

He rolled on his side and squirmed a little, preparatory to sleeping again. I turned away with a harsh breath of anger.

"You make your own breakfast," I said, feeling yet more fury at the senseless import of my words. As I pulled shut the door in leaving I thought I heard Saul laughing.

I went back to my room and started to work on my play though hardly with success. My brain could not grasp concentration. All I could think of was the uncommon way in which my pleasant life had been usurped.

Saul and I had always been exceptionally close to one another. Our lives had always been inseparable, our plans were always mutual plans, our affections invariably directed primarily upon each other. This had been so since our boyhood when in grade school other children laughingly called us The Twins in contraction of our fuller title—The Siamese Twins. And, even though I had been two years ahead of Saul in school we were always together, choosing our friends with a regard to each other's tastes and distastes, living, in short, with and for each other.

Now this; this enraging schism in our relationship. This harsh severance of comradely association, this abrupt, painful transmutation from intimacy to callous inattention.

The change was of such a gravity to me that almost immediately I began to look for the most grave of causes. And, although the implied solution seemed at the very least tenuous, I could not help but entertain it willingly. And, once more entertained, I could not remove myself from the notion.

In the quiet of my room, I pondered of ghosts.

Was it then possible that the house was haunted? Hastily I mulled over the various implications, the various intimations that the theory was verifiable.

Excluding the possibility that they were dream content, there were the heaving vibrations and the weird, high-pitched humming which had assailed my brain. There was the eerie blue light I had dreamed or actually seen beneath my door. And, finally, the most damning of evidence, there was Saul's statement that he had felt a hand on his cheek. *A cold, damp hand!*

Yet, despite all, it is a difficult thing to admit the existence of ghosts in a coldly factual world. One's very instincts rebel at the admission of such maddening possibility. For, once the initial step is made into the supernatural, there is no turning back, no knowing where the strange road leads except that it is quite unknown and quite terrible.

So actual were the premonitions I began to feel that I put aside my unused writing tablet and pen and rushed into the hall and to Saul's room as though something were awry there.

The ludicrous, unexpected sound of his snoring set me momentarily at ease. But my smile was short-lived, vanishing instantly when I saw the half-empty liquor bottle on his bedside table.

The shock of it made my flesh grow cold. And the thought came—he is corrupted, although I had no knowledge of its source.

As I stood there above his spread-eagled form, he groaned once and turned on his back. He had dressed, but his slept-in attire was now dishevelled and crumpled. His face, I noted, was unshaven and extremely haggard and the bloodshot gaze he directed at me was that of one stranger to another.

"What do you want?" he asked in hoarse, unnatural tones.

"Are you out of your mind?" I said. "What in God's name . . . ?"

"Get out of here," he said again to me, his brother.

I stared at his face and, although I knew it could be only the result of drink distorting his unshaven features, I could not dispel the apprehension that he was, somehow, coarse, and a shudder of strange revulsion ran through me.

I was about to take the bottle away from him when he swung at me, a wildly inaccurate flinging of the arm, his sense of direction blunted by a drink-thickened brain.

"I said, get *out* of here!" he shouted in a fury, streaks of mottled red leaping into his cheeks.

I backed away, almost in fright, then turned on my heel and hurried into the hall, trembling with the shock of my brother's unnatural behavior. I stood outside his door for a long time, listening to him toss restlessly on his bed, groaning. And I felt close to tears.

Then, without thought, I descended the darkening stairway, moved across the living room and dining alcove and entered the small kitchen. There, in the black silence, I held aloft a spluttering match and then lit the heavy candle I retrieved from the stove.

My footsteps, as I moved about the kitchen, seemed oddly muffled, as though I were hearing them through thick, cotton padding in my ears. And I began to get the most incongruous sensation that the very silence was drumming roughly in my ears.

As I passed the left hand side of the cabinet I found myself swaying heavily as though the dead, motionless air had suddenly become mobile and were buffeting me about. The silence was a roaring now and, suddenly, I clutched out for support and my twitching fingers knocked a dish onto the tile floor.

A positive shudder ran through me then because the sound of the breaking dish had been hollow and unreal, the sound of something greatly distant. If I had not seen the porcelain fragments lying on the dark tile I might have sworn the dish had not shattered at all.

With a sense of mounting restlessness I pushed my index fingers into my ears and twisted them around as if to ease what seemed an obstruction. Then I clenched my fist and struck the fastened cabinet door, almost desperate for the comfort of logical sound. But no matter how strong my blows, the sound came to my ears no louder than that of someone far away knocking at some door.

I turned hastily to the small icebox, very anxious now to make my sandwiches and coffee and be out of there, up in my room once more.

I put the bread on a tray, poured a cupful of the steaming black coffee and put the coffee pot down on its burner again. Then, with distinct trepidation, I bent over and blew out the candle.

The dining alcove and living room were oppressively dark now. My heart began to thud heavily as I moved across the rug, my footsteps muffled as I walked. I held the tray in stiff, unfeeling fingers, my gaze directed straight ahead. As I moved, my breath grew more harsh, bursting from my nostrils as I held my lips pressed tightly together lest they begin shaking with fright.

The blackness and the dead, utter silence seemed to crush in on me like solid walls. I held my throat stiff, my every muscle suspended by will for fear that relaxation would cause me to shake without control.

Halfway to the hall I heard it.

A soft, bubbling laughter which seemed to permeate the room like a cloud of sound.

A swamping wave of coldness covered my body and my footsteps halted abruptly as my legs and body stiffened.

The laughter did not cease. It continued, moving about me as if someone—or some *thing*—circled me on soundless tread, its eyes always on me. I began to tremble and, in the stillness, I could hear the rattling of the cup on my tray.

Then, suddenly, a damp, cold hand pressed against my cheek!

With a terrified howl of fear, I dropped the tray and ran wildly into the hall and up the stairs, my weakening legs propelling me forward in the blackness. As I ran there was another gush of liquid laughter behind me, like a thin trail of icy air in the stillness.

I locked the door to my room and hurled myself on the bed, pulling the bedspread over myself with shaking fingers. My eyes tightly shut, I lay there with heart pounding against the mattress. And, in my mind, the hideous cognition that all my fears were justified was a knife stabbing at delicate tissues.

It was all true.

As actually as if a living human hand had touched me, I had felt that cold and soggy hand on my cheek. But what living person was down there in the darkness?

For a short time I belied to tell myself it had been Saul executing a cruel and vicious joke. But I knew it had not been, for I would have heard his footsteps and I had heard none, either before or now.

The clock was chiming ten when I was at last able to summon the courage to throw off the spread, scrabble for the box of matches on my bedside table and light the candle.

At first the guttering light assuaged fear slightly. But then I saw how little it illuminated the silent darkness and I avoided, with a shudder, the sight of huge and shapeless walls. I cursed the old house for its lack of electricity. Fear might be eased in blazing lamplight. As it was, the imperfect flickering of that tiny flame did nothing to allay my fears.

I wanted to go across the hall and see if Saul were all right. But I was afraid to open my door, imagining hideous apparitions lurking there in the blackness, hearing once more in my mind the ugly, viscid laughter. I hoped that Saul was so hopelessly under alcoholic influence that nothing short of an earthquake could awaken him.

And, though I yearned to be near him even if he were treating me faithlessly, I felt no courage whatsoever. And, quickly undressing, I hastened to my bed and buried my head beneath the blankets again.

V

I woke suddenly, shivering and afraid. The bedclothes were gone from my body, the black silence as awful as it had been earlier in the night.

I reached for the blankets anxiously, my fingers groping for them. They had fallen from the edge of the bed. I rolled on my side hurriedly and reached down, my fingers recoiling as they came in contact with the icy floorboards.

Then, as I reached for the blankets, I saw the light beneath the door.

It remained in sight only the fragment of a second but I knew I had seen it. And, as it passed abruptly from my eyes, the throbbing began. My room seemed filled with the humming pulsations. I could feel the bed shaking beneath me and my skin growing taut and frigid; my teeth chattering together.

Then the light appeared again and I heard the sound of bare feet and knew it was Saul walking in the night.

Driven more by fear for his safety than by courage, I threw my legs over the side of the bed and padded to the door, shuddering at the iciness of the flooring beneath my soles.

Slowly I opened the door, my body held tight in anticipation of what I might see.

But the hall was pitch black and I walked out and over to the door of Saul's room, listening to see if I could hear the sound of his breathing. But before I could judge anything, the hall below was suddenly illumined with that unearthly blue glow and I turned and rushed, again instinctively, to the head of the stairs and stood there clutching the old banister, staring down.

Below, an aura of intense brilliant blue light was passing through the hall moving in the direction of the living room.

My heart leaped! Saul was following it, arms ahead of him in the familiar pose of the somnambulist, his eyes staring ahead and glittering in the shapeless blue effulgence.

I tried to call his name but found that my voice could make no utterance. I tried to move for the stairs to wrest my Saul away from this terror. But a wall, invisible in the blackness, held me back. It grew close and airless. I struggled violently but it was to no avail. My muscles were strengthless against the horrible, impossible power that clutched me.

Then, suddenly, my nostrils and brain were assaulted by a pungent, sickly odor that made my senses reel. My throat and stomach burned with almost tangible fire. The darkness grew more intense. It seemed to cling to me like hot, black mud, constricting my chest so that I could hardly breathe. It was like being buried alive in a black oven, my body bound and rebound with heavy grave wrappings. I trembled, sobbing and ineffectual.

Then, abruptly, it all passed and I stood there in the cold hallway soaked with perspiration, weak from my frantic efforts. I tried to move but could not, tried to remember Saul, but was incapable of preventing the thought of him from slipping from my numbed brain. I shivered and turned to go back to my room but, at the first step, my legs buckled and I pitched forward heavily on the floor. The icy surface of it pressed against my flesh and, my body wracked by shivering, I lost consciousness.

When my eyes opened again I still lay crumpled on the cold floor.

I rose to a sitting position, the hall before my eyes wavering in alternate tides of light and darkness. My chest felt tight and a remorseless chill gripped my body. I pulled myself up to a bent-over stance and staggered to Saul's room, a cough burning in my throat as I stumbled across the floor and against his bed.

He was there and looked emaciated. He was unshaved and the dark wiry beard on his skin seemed like some repugnant growth. His mouth was open and emitting sounds of exhausted slumber and his smooth, white chest rose and fell with shallow movements.

He made no motion as I tugged weakly at his shoulder. I spoke his name and was shocked at the hoarse, grating sound of my own voice. I spoke it again, and he stirred with a grumble and opened one eye to look at me.

"I'm sick," I muttered, "Saul, I'm sick."

He rolled on one side, turning on his back to me. A sob of anguish tore at my throat.

"Saul!"

He seemed to snap his body around insanely then, his hands clenched into bony, white fists at his sides.

"Get out of here!" he screamed. "Leave me alone or I'll kill you!"

The body-shaking impact of his words drove me back from the bed to where I stood dumbly staring at him, breath stabbing at my throat. I saw him toss his body back over as if he wanted to break it. And I heard him mutter to himself miserably, *"Why does the day have to last so long?"*

A spasm of coughing struck me then and, my chest aching

with fiery pains, I struggled back to my own room and got into bed with the movements of an old man. I fell back on the pillow and pulled up the blankets, then lay there shivering and helpless.

There I slept all day in spasmodic periods offset by waking moments of extreme pain. I was unable to rise to get myself food or water. All I could do was lie there, shaking and weeping. I felt beaten as much by Saul's cruelty to me as by the physical suffering. And the pain in my body was extremely severe. So much so that during one seizure of coughing it was so awful I began to cry like a child, hitting the mattress with weak, ineffective fists and kicking my legs deliriously.

Yet, even then, I think I wept for more than the pain. I wept for my only brother who loved me not.

It seemed that night came more swiftly than I had ever seen it come before. I lay alone in the darkness praying through mute lips that no harm should come to him.

I slept a while and then, abruptly, I was awake, staring at the light beneath the door, hearing the high-pitched humming in my ears. And I realized in that moment that Saul still loved me but that the house had corrupted his love.

And from this knowledge came resolution, from despair I gained amazing heart. I struggled to my feet and swayed there dizzily until the streaks before my eyes dispersed. Then I put on my robe and slippers, went to the door and threw it open.

What made things happen as they did I cannot say. Perhaps it was my feeling of courage that caused the black obstruction in the hall to melt before me. The house was trembling with the vibrations and the humming. Yet they seemed to lessen as I moved down the stairway and, all of a sudden, the blue light vanished from the living room and I heard loud and furious rumblings there.

When I entered, the room was in its usual order. A candle was burning on the mantel. But my eyes were riveted to the center of the floor.

Saul stood there, half naked and motionless, his body poised as though he were dancing, his eyes fastened to the portrait.

I spoke his name sharply. His eyes blinked and, slowly, his head turned to me. He didn't seem to comprehend my presence there for, suddenly, his glance flew about the room and he cried out in despairing tones:

"Come back! Come back!"

I called his name again and he stopped looking around but directed his gaze at me. His face was gaunt and cruelly lined in the flickering candlelight. It was the face of a lunatic. He gnashed his teeth together and started to move toward me.

"I'll kill you," he muttered in liquid tones. "I'll *kill* you."

I backed away.

"Saul, you're out of your mind. You don't . . ."

I could say no more for he rushed at me, his hands extended as if he would clutch at my throat. I tried to step aside but he grabbed hold of my robe and pulled me against him.

We began to struggle, I begging him to throw off this terrible spell he was under, he panting and gnashing his teeth. My head was being shaken from side to side and I saw our monstrous shadows heaving on the walls.

Saul's grip was not his own. I have always been stronger than he but, at that moment, his hands seemed like cold iron. I began to choke and his face blurred before my eyes. I lost balance and we both fell heavily to the floor. I felt the prickly rug against my cheek, his cold hands tightening on my throat.

Then my hand came in contact with something cold and hard. It was the tray I had dropped the night before, I realized. I gripped it and, realizing that he was out of his mind and meant

to kill me, I picked it up and drove it across his head with all
the power I had remaining.

It was a heavy metal tray and Saul sank to the floor as if
struck dead, his hands slipping from my bruised throat. I struggled up, gasping for breath, and looked at him.

Blood was running from a deep gash in his forehead where
the edge of the tray had struck.

"Saul!" I screamed, horrified at what I'd done.

Frantically I leaped up and rushed to the front door. As I
flung it open I saw a man walking by in the street. I ran to the
porch railing and called to him.

"Help!" I cried. "Call an ambulance!"

The man lurched and looked over at me with startled fright.

"For God's sake!" I beseeched him. "My brother has struck
his head! Please call an ambulance!"

For a long moment he stared at me, open-mouthed, then
broke into a nervous flight up the street. I called after him but
he would not stop to listen. I was certain he would not do as
I'd asked.

As I turned back, I saw my bloodless face in the hall mirror
and realized with a start that I must have frightened the wits out
of the man. I felt weak and afraid again, the momentary strength
sapped from me. My throat was dry and raw, my stomach on
edge. I was barely able to walk back to the living room on
trembling stalks of legs.

I tried to lift Saul to a couch but dead weight was too much
for me and I sank to my knees beside him. My body slumped
forward and, half crouched, half lay by the side of my brother.
The harsh sound of my breathing was the only sound I could
hear. My left hand stroked Saul's hair absently and quiet tears
flowed from my eyes.

I cannot say how long I had been there when the throbbing

began again; as if to show me that it hadn't really gone away.

I still crouched there like a dead thing, my brain almost in coma. I could feel my heart beating like some old clock in my chest, the dull-edged and muffled pendulum hitting against my ribs with a lifeless rhythm. All sound registered with similar force, the clock on the mantel, my heart and the endless throbbing; all blending into one horrible beat that became a part of me, that became *me*. I could sense myself sinking deeper and deeper as a drowning man slips helplessly beneath the silent waters.

Then I thought I heard a tapping of feet through the room, the rustling of skirts and, far off, a hollow laughter of women.

I raised my head abruptly, my skin tight and cold.

A figure in white stood in the doorway.

It began to move toward me and I rose with a strangled cry on my lips only to collapse into darkness.

VI

What I had seen had been not a ghost but an intern from the hospital. The man I had called in the street had, apparently, done what I'd asked. It will give some indication of the state I was in when I reveal that I heard neither the ringing of the front doorbell nor the pounding of the intern's fist on the half-open door. Indeed, had the door not been open, I am certain that I would be dead now.

They took Saul to the hospital to have his head cared for. There being nothing wrong with me but nervous exhaustion, I remained in the house. I had wanted to go with Saul, but was told that the hospital was overcrowded and I would do more good by staying home in bed.

I slept late the next morning, rising about eleven. I went

downstairs and had a substantial breakfast, then returned to my room and slept a few hours more. About two, I had some lunch. I planned to leave the house well before darkness to make sure nothing further happened to me. I could find a room in a hotel. It was clear that we would have to desert the place regardless of whether we sold it or not. I anticipated some trouble with Saul on that point but made up my mind to stand firm on my decision.

About five o'clock I dressed and left my room, carrying a small bag for the night. The day was almost gone and I hurried down the stairs, not wishing to remain in the house any longer. At the bottom of the staircase I stepped across the entry hall and closed my hand over the doorknob.

The door would not open.

At first I would not allow myself to believe this. I stood there tugging, trying to combat the cold numbness that was spreading itself over my body. Then I dropped my bag and pulled at the knob with both hands but to no avail. It was as securely fastened as the cabinet door in the kitchen.

Suddenly, I turned from the door and ran into the living room but all the windows were jammed fast into their frames. I looked around the room, whimpering like a child, feeling unspoken hate for myself for letting myself be trapped again. I cursed loudly and, as I did, a cold wind lifted the hat from my head and hurled it across the floor.

Abruptly, I placed my shaking hands over my eyes and stood there trembling violently, afraid of what might happen any second, my heart hammering against my chest. The room seemed to chill markedly and I heard that grotesque humming noise again that came as if from another world. It sounded like laughter to me, laughter that mocked me for my poor, feeble efforts to escape.

Then, with equal suddenness, I remembered Saul again, re-membered that he needed me and I pulled away my hands from my eyes and screamed aloud:

"Nothing in this house can harm me!"

Sudden cessation of the sound gave me added courage. If my will could successfully defy the ungodly powers of the place, then perhaps it could also destroy them. If I went upstairs, if I slept in Saul's bed, then I too would know what he had experienced and thus be enabled to help him.

I felt no lack of confidence in my will to resist, never once stopping to think that my ideas might not be my own.

Quickly, two steps at a time, I rushed up the stairs and into my brother's room. There I quickly removed my hat, overcoat and suitcoat, loosened my tie and collar and sat down on the bed. Then, after a moment, I lay down and looked up at the darkening ceiling. I tried to keep my eyes open but, still fatigued, I soon fell asleep.

It seemed only a moment before I was fully awake, my body tingling with sensations of not unpleasant character. I could not understand the strangeness of it. The darkness seemed alive. It shimmered under my gaze as I lay there, warm with a heat that betokened sensualism although there was hardly any apparent cause for such a feeling.

I whispered Saul's name without thinking. Then the thought of him was taken from my brain as if invisible fingers had plucked it away.

I remember rolling over and laughing to myself, behavior most extraordinary if not unseemly for a person of my steady inclinations. The pillow felt like silk against my face and my senses began to fade. The darkness crept over me like warm syrup, soothing my body and mind. I muttered senselessly to myself, feeling as if my muscles were sucked dry of all energy, heavy as rock and lethargic with a delicious exhaustion.

Then, when I had almost slipped away, I felt another presence in the room. To my incredulous realization, it was not only familiar to me but I had absolutely no fear of it. Only an inexplicable sense of langorous expectation.

Then she came to me, the girl in the portrait.

I stared at the blue haze about her for only a moment for this quickly faded and, in my arms, was a vibrantly warm body. I remember no one feature of her behavior for everything was lost in overall sensation, a sensation mixed of excitement and revulsion, a sense of hideous yet overpowering rapacity. I hung suspended in a cloud of ambivalence, my soul and body corroded with unnatural desire. And in my mind and echoing on my tongue I spoke a name over and over again.

The name *Clarissa*.

How can I judge the number of sick, erotic moments I spent there with her? Sense of time completely vanished from the scheme of things. A thick giddiness enveloped me. I tried to fight it but it was no use. I was consumed as my brother Saul had been consumed by this foul presence from the grave of night.

Then, in some inconceivable fashion, we were no longer on the bed but downstairs, whirling about in the living room dancing wildly and closely. There was no music, only that incessant, beating rhythm I had heard those nights before. Yet now it seemed like music to me as I spun about the floor holding in my arms the ghost of a dead woman, entranced by her stunning beauty yet, at the same time, repelled by my uncontrollable hunger for her.

Once I closed my eyes for a second and felt a terrible coldness crawling in my stomach. But when I opened them it was gone and I was happy once more. *Happy?* It seems hardly the word now. Say rather hypnotized, torpid, my brain a numbed vessel of flesh unable to remove me one iota from this clutching spell.

Dancing went on and on. The floor was filled with couples. I am sure of that and yet I recall no aspect of their dress or form. All I remember is their faces, white and glistening, their eyes dull and lifeless, their mouths hanging open like dark, bloodless wounds.

Around and around and then a man with a large tray standing in the hallway arch and sudden immersion in the dark; empty and still.

VII

I awoke with a sense of complete exhaustion.

I was soaked with perspiration, dressed only in my bottom undergarment. My clothes lay scattered across the floor, apparently thrown about in a frenzy. The bedclothes also lay in disordered heaps on the floor. From all appearances, I had gone insane the night before.

The light from the window annoyed me for some reason and, quickly, I shut my eyes, reluctant to believe it was morning again. I turned over onto my stomach and put my head beneath the pillow. I could still remember the enticing odor of her hair. The memory of it made my body shudder with odious craving.

Then a warmth began to cover my back and I raised myself up with a muttering frown. The sunlight was streaming through the windows onto my back. With a restless movement I pushed myself up, threw my legs over the side of the bed and got up to draw the shades.

It was a little better without the glare. I threw myself on the bed again, closed my eyes tightly and crowded the pillow over my head. I felt the light.

It sounds incredible, I know, but I felt it as surely as do certain creeper plants that climb towards the light without ever seeing it. And, in feeling light, I yearned all the more for darkness. I felt like some nocturnal creature somehow forced into brightness, repelled and pained by it.

I sat on the bed and looked around, a sound of unremitting complaint in my throat. I bit my lips, clenched and unclenched my hands, wanting to strike out violently at something, at anything. I found myself standing over an unlit candle, blowing sharply on it. I knew, even then, the senselessness of the act and yet I did it nevertheless, trying, inanely, to make an invisible flame go out so that night could return through its dark roads. Bringing back Clarissa.

Clarissa.

A clicking sound filled my throat and my body positively writhed. Not in pain or pleasure but in a combination of the two. I put my brother's robe over my body and wandered out into the silent hallway. There were no physical wants, no hunger, thirst, or other needs. I was a detached body, a comatose slave to the tyranny which had shackled me and now refused to let me go.

I stood at the head of the stairway, listening intently, trying to imagine her gliding up to meet me, warm and vibrant in her mist of blue. *Clarissa.* I closed my eyes quickly, my teeth grated together and, for a split second, I felt my body stiffen with fright. For a moment I was returned to myself.

But then, in another breath, I was enslaved again. I stood there, feeling myself a part of the house, as much a portion of it as the beams or the windows. I breathed its breath, felt its soundless heartbeat in my own. I became at one with an inanimate body, knowing its past life, sensing the dead hands that had curled their fingers on the arms of the chairs, on banisters, on doorknobs, hearing the labored tread of invisible footsteps moving through the house, the laughter of long-consumed humor.

If, in those moments, I lost my soul, it became a part of the emptiness and stillness that surrounded me, an emptiness I could not sense nor a stillness feel for being drugged. Drugged with the formless presence of the past. I was no longer a living person. I was dead in all but those bodily functions which kept me from complete satisfaction.

Quietly, and without passion, the thought of killing myself drifted through my mind. It was gone in a moment but its passage had stirred no more in me than apathetic recognition. My thoughts were on the life beyond life. And present existence was no more than a minor obstruction which I could tumble with the slightest touch of razored steel, the minutest drop of poison. I had become the master of life for I could view its destruction with the most complete apathy.

Night. Night! When would it come? I heard my voice, thin and hoarse, crying out in the silence.

"Why does the day have to last so long!"

The words shocked me back again, for Saul had spoken them. I blinked, looked around me as if just realizing where I was. What was this terrible power over me? I tried to break its hold but, in the very effort, slipped back again.

To find myself once more in that strange coma which suspends the mortally ill in that slender portion of existence between life and death. I was hanging on a thread over the pit of everything that was hidden to me before. Now I could see and hear and the power to cut the thread was in my hands. I could let myself hang until the strands parted one by one and lowered me slowly down. Or I could wait until driven beyond endurance, then end it suddenly, cut myself loose and plunge down into the darkness; that signal darkness where she and hers remained always. Then I would have her maddening warmth. Maybe it was her coldness. Her comfort then. I could pass eternal moments with her and laugh at the robot world.

I wondered if it would help to get dead drunk and lose all consciousness till night.

I descended the stairs on unfeeling legs and sat for a long time before the mantel looking up at her. I had no idea what time it was nor did I care. Time was relative, even forgotten. I neither knew of it nor cared about it. Had she smiled at me then? Yes, her eyes glowed, how they glowed in the dimness. That smell again. Not pleasant yet something excitingly musky and pungent about it.

What was Saul to me? The idea filled my mind. He was no relation of mine. He was a stranger from another society, another flesh, another life. I felt complete dispassion toward him. You hate him, said the voice in my mind.

That was when it all collapsed like a flimsy house of cards.

For those words caused such a rebellion in my innermost mind that, suddenly, my eyes were cleared as though scales had fallen from them. I looked about, my head snapping crazily. What in God's name was I doing, still here in the house?

With a shiver of angry fear I jumped to my feet and ran upstairs to dress. As I passed the hall clock I saw with a start that it was past three in the afternoon.

As I dressed, normal sensations returned one by one. I felt the cold floor beneath my bare feet, became aware of hunger and thirst, heard the deep silence of the house.

Everything flooded over me. I knew why Saul had wanted

to die, why he loathed the day and waited for the night with such angry impatience. I could explain it to him now and he would understand because I had been through it myself.

And, as I ran down the stairs, I thought about the dead of Slaughter House, so outraged at their own inexplicable curse that they tried to drag the living down into their endless hell.

Over, over!—exulted my mind as I locked the front door behind me and started through the misty rain to the hospital.

I did not see the shadow behind me, crouching on the porch.

VIII

When the woman at the hospital desk told me that Saul had been discharged two hours before my arrival, I was too stunned to speak. I clutched at the counter, staring at her, hearing myself tell her that she must be mistaken. My voice was hoarse, unnatural. The woman shook her head.

I sagged against the counter then, all the drive gone out of me. I felt very tired and afraid. A sob broke in my throat as I turned away and I saw people staring at me while I moved across the tile floor with unsteady motions. Everything seemed to swirl about me. I staggered, almost fell. Someone clutched my arm and asked me if I were all right. I muttered something in reply and pulled away from the person without even noting if it were a man or a woman.

I pushed out through the door and into the gray light. It was raining harder and I pulled up my coat collar. Where was he? The question burned in my mind and the answer to it came quickly, too quickly. Saul was back in the house. I felt sure of it.

The idea made me start running up the dark street toward the trolley-car tracks. I ran for endless blocks. All I remember is the rain driving against my face and the gray buildings floating by. There were no people in the streets and all the taxicabs were full. It was getting darker and darker.

My legs almost buckled and I was thrown against a lamppost and clung to it, afraid of falling into the streaming gutter.

An ugly clanging filled my ears. I looked up, then chased after the trolley car and caught it at the next block. I handed the conductor a dollar and had to be called back for my change. I stood hanging from a black strap, swaying back and forth with the motion of the car, my mind tormented by thoughts of Saul alone in that house of horror.

The warm, stale air of the car began to make me sick to the stomach. I could smell the raincoats and the wet clothes of the people caught in the rain as well as the smell of dripping umbrellas and packages soaked. I closed my eyes and stood there, teeth clenched, praying that I would get home before it was too late.

I got off the car at last and ran up the block as fast as I could. The rain sprayed over my face and ran into my eyes, almost blinding me. I slipped and went sprawling on the sidewalk, skinning my hands and knees. I pushed up with a whine, feeling the clothes soaked against me. I kept running wildly, only sensing the direction by instinct until I stopped and saw through the thick veil of rain, the house in front of me, high and dark.

It seemed to crawl over the ground toward me and clutch me to itself for I found myself standing and shivering on the wooden porch. I coughed and felt the chill through my flesh.

I tried the door. At first I could not believe it. It was still locked and Saul had no key! I almost cried in gratitude. I ran down from the porch. Where was he then? I had to find him. I started down the path.

Then, as surely as if I had been tapped on the shoulder I whirled about and stared up at the porch. A flash of lightning illuminated the darkness and I saw the broken, jagged-edged window. My breath caught and I stared at it, my heart pounding like a heavy piston in my chest.

He *was* in there. Had she come already? Was he lying upstairs in bed smiling to himself in the blackness, waiting for her luminous self to come and envelop him?

I had to save him. Without hesitation I ran up on the porch and unlocked the door, leaving it wide open so that we could escape.

I moved across the rug and onto the steps. The house was quiet. Even the storm seemed apart from it. The rushing sound of the rain seemed to grow less and less distinct. Then I turned with a gasp as the front door slammed shut behind me.

I was trapped. The thought drove barbs of fear into me and I almost ran down to try and escape. But I remembered Saul and fought to quicken resolution. I had conquered the house once and I could do it again. I had to. For him.

I started up the stairs again. Outside the flashes of lightning were like false neon trying to invade the austerity of the house. I held onto the banister tightly, muttering beneath my breath to keep attention from degrading into fright, afraid to let the spell of the house beset me again.

I reached the door to my brother's room. There I stopped and leaned against the wall, eyes closed. What if I found him dead? I knew the sight would unnerve me. The house might defeat me then, taking me in that moment of utter despair and twisting my soul from my grip.

I would not let myself conceive of it. I would not allow myself the realization that without Saul life was empty, a meaningless travesty. He *was* alive.

Nervously, my hands numbed with fright, I pushed open the door. The room was a stygian cave. My throat contracted and I took a deep breath. I clenched tight fists at my sides.

"Saul?" I called his name softly.

The thunder roared and my voice disappeared beneath the swell. A flash of lightning brought a split second of daylight into the room and I looked around quickly, hoping to see him. Then it was dark again and silent except for the endless rain falling on the windows and roof. I took another step across the rug, cautiously, my ears tense, trying to hear. Every sound made me start. I twitched and shuffled across the floor. Was he here? But he must be. If he were here in the house, this was the room he would be in.

"Saul?" I called, louder. "Saul, answer me."

I began to walk toward the bed.

Then the door slammed behind me and there was a rushing sound behind me in the darkness. I whirled to meet it. I felt his hand clamp on my arm.

"Saul!" I cried.

Lightning filled the room with hideous light and I saw his twisted white face, the candlestick held in his right hand.

Then he struck me a violent blow on the forehead, driving a wedge of agonizing pain into my brain. I felt his hand release me as I slumped to my knees and my face brushed against his bare leg as I fell forward. The last sound I heard before my mind fell into the darkness was laughing and laughing and laughing.

IX

I opened my eyes. I was still lying on the rug. Outside it was raining even harder. The sound of it was like the crashing of a waterfall. Thunder still rolled in the sky and flashes of lightning made the night brilliant.

In one flash I looked at the bed. The sight of the covers and sheets all thrown about insanely made me push up. Saul was downstairs with *her*!

I tried to get to my feet but the pain in my head drove me back to my knees. I shook my head feebly, running trembling hands over my cheeks, feeling the gouged wound in my forehead, the dried blood which had trickled down across one temple. I swayed back and forth on my knees, moaning. I seemed to be back in that void again, struggling to regain my hold on life. The power of the house surrounded me. The power which I knew was her power. A cruel and malignant vitality which tried to drink out the life force from me and draw me down into the pit.

Then, once more, I remembered Saul, my brother, and the remembrance brought me back the strength I needed.

"No!" I cried out as if the house had told me I was now its helpless captive. And I pushed to my feet, ignoring the dizziness, stumbling through a cloud of pain across the room, gasping for breath. The house was throbbing and humming, filled with that obnoxious smell.

I ran drunkenly for the door, found myself running into the bed. I drew back with almost a snarl at the numbing pain in my shins. I turned in the direction of the door and ran again. I did not even hold my arms ahead of me and had no chance to brace myself when I ran into the door dizzily.

The excruciating pain of my nose being near broken caused a howl of agony to pass my lips. Blood immediately began gushing down across my mouth and I had to keep wiping it away. I jerked open the door and ran into the hall, feeling myself on the border of insanity. The hot blood kept running down across my chin and I felt it dripping and soaking into my coat. My hat had fallen off but I still wore my raincoat over my suit.

I was too bereft of perception to notice that nothing held me back at the head of the stairs. I half ran, half slid down the stairs, goaded on by that humming, formless laughter which was music and mockery. The pain in my head was terrible. Every downward step made it feel as if someone drove one more nail into my brain.

"Saul, Saul!" I cried out, running into the living room, gagging as I tried to call his name a third time.

The living room was dark, permeated with that sickly odor. It made my head reel but I kept moving. It seemed to thicken as I moved for the kitchen. I ran into the small room and leaned against the wall, almost unable to breathe, pinpoints of light spinning before my eyes.

Then, as lightning illumined the room I saw the left cupboard door wide open and, inside, a large bowl filled with what looked like flour. As I stared at it, tears rolled down my cheeks and my tongue felt like dry cloth in my mouth.

I backed out of the kitchen choking for breath, feeling as if my strength were almost gone. I turned and ran into the living room, still looking for my brother.

Then, in another flash of lightning, I looked at her portrait. It was different and the difference froze me to the spot. Her face was no longer beautiful. Whether it was shadow that did it or actual change, her expression was one of vicious cruelty. The eyes glittered, there was an insane cast to her smile. Even her hands, once folded in repose, now seemed more like claws waiting to strike out and kill.

It was when I backed away from her that I stumbled and fell over the body of my brother.

I pushed up to my knees and stared down in the blackness. One flash of lightning after another showed me his white, dead face, the smile of hideous knowledge on his lips, the look of insane joy in his wide-open eyes. My mouth fell open and breath caught in me. It seemed as if my world was ending. I could not believe it was true. I clutched at my hair and whimpered, almost believing that in a moment, Mother would wake me from my nightmare and I would look across at Saul's bed, smile at his innocent sleep and lie down again secure with the memory of his dark hair on the white pillow.

But it did not end. The rain slapped frenziedly at the windows and thunder drove deafening fists against the earth.

I looked up at the portrait. I felt as dead as my brother. I did not hesitate. Calmly I stood and walked to the mantel. There were matches there. I picked up the box.

Instantly, she divined my thoughts for the box was torn from my fingers and hurled against the wall. I dove for it and was tripped by some invisible force. Those cold hands clutched at my throat. I felt no fright but tore them away with a snarl and dove for the matches again. Blood began running faster and I spat out some.

I picked up the box. It was torn away again, this time to burst and spray matches all over the rug. A great hum of anguish seemed to rock the house as I reached for a match. I was grabbed. I tore loose. I fell to my knees and slapped at the rug in the darkness as lightning ceased. My arms were held tightly. Something cold and wet ran around in my stomach.

With maniacal fury I pressed my teeth against a match I saw in the lightning and bit at the head. There was no rewarding flare. The house was trembling violently now and I heard rustlings about me as if she had called them all to fight me, to save their cursed existence.

I bit at another match. A white face stared at me from the rug and I spit blood at it. It disappeared. I tore one arm loose and grabbed a match. I jerked myself to the mantel and dragged the match across the rough wood. A speck of flame flared up in my fingers and I was released.

The throbbing seemed more violent now. But I knew it was

helpless against flame. I protected the flame with my hand though, lest that cold wind come again and try to blow it out. I held the match against a magazine that was lying on a chair and it flared up. I shook it and the pages puffed into flame. I threw it down on the rug.

I went around in that light striking one match after another, avoiding the sight of Saul lying there. She had destroyed him but now I would destroy her forever.

I ignited the curtains. I started the rug to smoldering. I set fire to the furniture. The house rocked and a whistling sigh rose and ebbed like the wind.

At last I stood erect in the flaming room, my eyes riveted on the portrait. I walked slowly toward it. She knew my intentions for the house rocked even harder and a shrieking began that seemed to come from the walls. And I knew then that the house was controlled by her and that her power was in that portrait.

I drew it down from the wall. It shook in my very hands as if it were alive. With a shudder of repugnance I threw it on the flames.

I almost fell while the floor shuddered almost as if an earthquake were striking the land. But then it stopped and the portrait was burning and the last effect of her was gone. I was alone in an old burning house.

I did not want anyone to know about my brother. I did not want anyone to see his face like that.

So I lifted him and put him on the couch. I do not understand to this day how I could lift him up when I felt so weak. It was a strength not my own.

I sat at his feet, stroking his hand until the flames grew too hot. Then I rose. I bent over him and kissed him on the lips for a last goodbye. And I walked from the house into the rain.

And I never came back. Because there was nothing to ever come back for.

This is the end of the manuscript. There seems no adequate evidence to ascribe the events recounted as true. But the following facts, taken from the city's police files, might prove of interest.

In 1901, the city was severely shocked by the most wholesale murder ever perpetrated in its history.

At the height of a party being held at the home of Mr. and Mrs. Marlin Slaughter and their daughter Clarissa, an unknown person poisoned the punch by placing a very large amount of arsenic in it. Everyone died. The case was never solved although various theories were put forth as to its solution. One thesis had it that the murderer was one of those who died.

As to the identity of this murderer, supposition had it that it was not a murderer but a murderess. Although nothing definite exists to go by, there are several testimonies which refer to "that poor child Clarissa" and indicate that the young woman had been suffering for some years from a severe mental aberration which her parents had tried to keep a secret from the neighbors and the authorities. The party in mention was supposed to have been planned to celebrate what her parents took for the recovery of her faculties.

As to the body of the young man later supposed to be in the wreckage, a thorough search has revealed nothing. It may be that the entire story is imagination, fabricated by the one brother in order to conceal the death of the other, said death probably being unnatural. Thus, the older brother knowing the story of the house tragedy may have used it for a fantastic evidence in his favor.

Whatever the truth, the older brother has never been heard of again either in this city or in any of the adjacent localities.

And that's the story. S.D.M.

Wet Straw

It began some months after his wife died.

He had moved into a boarding house. There he lived a sheltered life; sale of her bonds had provided money. A book a day, concerts, solitary meals, visits to the museum—these sufficed. He listened to his radio and napped and thought a good deal. Life was good enough.

One night he put down his book and undressed. He turned out the lights and opened the window. He sat down on the bed and stared a moment at the floor. His eyes ached a little. Then he lay down and put his arms behind his head. There was a cold draft from the window, so he pulled the covers over his head and closed his eyes.

It was very still. He could hear his own regular breathing. The warmth began to cover him. The heat fondled his body and soothed it. He sighed heavily and smiled.

In an instant, his eyes were open.

There was a thin breeze stroking his cheek, and he could smell something like wet straw. It was not to be mistaken.

Reaching out, he could touch the wall and feel the breeze from the window. Yet, under the covers, where there had been only warmth before, was another breeze. And a damp, chilling smell of wet straw.

He threw the covers from him and lay on the bed, breathing harshly.

Then he laughed in his mind. A dream, a nightmare. Too much reading. Bad food.

He pulled up the covers and closed his eyes. He kept his head outside the blankets and slept.

The next morning he forgot about it. He had breakfast and went to the museum. There he spent the morning. He visited all the rooms and looked at everything.

When he was about to leave, he felt a desire to go back and look at a painting he had only glanced at before.

He stopped in front of it.

It was a painting of a countryside. There was a big barn down in the valley.

He began to breathe heavily, and his fingers played on his tie. How ridiculous, he thought after a moment, that such a thing should make me nervous.

He turned away. At the door he looked back at the painting.

The barn had frightened him. Only a barn, he thought, a barn in a painting.

After dinner he returned to his room.

As soon as he opened the door he remembered the dream. He went to the bed. He drew up the blanket and the sheets and shook them.

There was no smell of wet straw. He felt like a fool.

That night, when he went to bed, he left the window closed. He turned out the lights and got in bed and pulled the covers over his head.

At first it was the same. Silent and breathless and the creeping warmth.

Then the breeze began again and he distinctly felt his hair ruffled by it. He could smell wet straw. He stared into the blackness and breathed through his mouth so he wouldn't have to smell the straw.

Somewhere in the dark, he saw a square of grayish light.

It's a window, he thought, suddenly.

He looked longer and his heart jumped as a sudden flash of light showed in the window. It was like lightning. He listened. He smelled the wet straw.

He heard it starting to rain.

He became frightened and pulled the covers off his head.

The warm room was around him. It was not raining. It was oppressively hot because the window was closed.

He stared at the ceiling and wondered why he was having this illusion.

Again he pulled up the blanket to make sure. He lay still and kept his eyes tightly closed.

The smell was in his nostrils again. The rain was beating violently on the window. He opened his eyes and watched it and made out sheets of rain in the flashes. Then, rain began to beat above him, too, on a wooden roof. He was in some place with a wooden roof and wet straw.

He was in a barn.

That was why the picture had frightened him. But why frightened?

He tried to touch the window, but he couldn't reach it. The breeze blew on his hand and arm. He wanted to touch the window. Maybe, he delighted in the thought, maybe open it and stick his head out in the rain and then pull down the covers quickly to see if his hair were wet.

He began to sense himself surrounded by space. There was no feeling of confinement in the bed. He felt the mattress, yet it was as though he lay on it in an open place. The breeze blew over his entire body. And the smell was more pronounced.

He listened. He heard a squeak and then a horse whinnying. He listened a while longer.

Then he realized he couldn't feel the whole mattress.

It felt as though he were lying on a cold wooden floor from his waist down.

He reached out his hands in alarm and felt the edge of the blankets. He pulled them down.

He was covered with sweat and his pajamas stuck to his body. He got out of bed and turned on the light. A refreshing breeze came through the window when he opened it.

His legs shook as he walked, and he had to grab at the dresser to keep from falling.

In the mirror he saw his face pale with fear. He held up his hand and watched it shake. His throat was dry.

He went to the bathroom and got a drink of water. Then he went to the room and looked down at his bed. Nothing there but the tangled blanket and sheets and the stain where he had perspired. He held up the blanket and the sheets. He shook them before the light and examined them minutely. There was nothing.

He took up a book and read for the rest of the night.

The next day he went to the museum again and looked at the picture.

He tried to remember if he had ever been in a barn. Had it been raining and had he stared out a window at the lightning?

He remembered.

It was on his honeymoon. They had gone for a walk and been caught in the rain and stayed in a barn until it stopped. There had been a horse down in the stall and mice running and wet straw.

But what did it mean? There was no reason to remember it now.

That night he was afraid to go to bed. He put it off. At last, when his eyes would not stay open, he lay down fully dressed and left the window closed. He didn't use a blanket.

He slept heavily and there was no dream.

Toward early morning, he woke up. It was just getting light. Without thinking, he pulled a blanket off the chair and threw it over himself.

There was no wait. He was suddenly in the barn.

There was no sound. It was not raining. There was a gray light in the window. Could it be that it was also morning in his imaginary barn?

He smiled drowsily. It was all too charming. He would have to try it in the afternoon to see if the barn were fully lighted.

He started to pull the blanket off his head, when there was a rustle by his side.

He caught his breath. His heart seemed to stop and there was a tingling in his scalp.

A soft sigh reached his ears.

Something warm and moist brushed over his hand.

With a scream, he flung off the blanket and jumped onto the floor.

He stood there staring at the bed and clutching the blanket in his hands. His heart struck with gigantic beats.

He sank down weakly on the bed. The sun was just rising.

———

For a week, he slept sitting up in a chair. At last, he had to have a good night's rest and lay down on the bed, fully dressed. He would never use a blanket again.

Sleep came, dreamless and black.

He didn't know what time it was when he woke up. A sob caught in his throat. *He was in the barn again.* Lightning flashed in the window and rain was pounding on the roof.

He felt around in dread, but there was no blanket anywhere. His hands slapped at the air, frenziedly.

Suddenly, he looked at the window. If he could open it, he might escape! He stretched out his hand as far as he could. Closer. Closer. He was almost there. Another inch and his fingers would touch it.

"John."

A sudden reflex made his hand plunge through the glass. He felt the rain spattering across the back of his hand and his wrist burned terribly. He jerked back his hand and stared in terror at where the voice had come from.

Something white stirred at his side and a warm hand caressed his arm.

"John," came the murmur. *"John."*

He couldn't speak. He reached around clutching agonizingly for his blanket. But only the breeze blew over his fingers. There was a cold wooden floor under him.

He whimpered in fright. His name was spoken again.

Then the lightning flashed and he saw his wife lying by him, smiling at him.

Suddenly, the edge of the blanket was in his hand, and pulling it down, he rolled off the bed onto the floor.

Something was running across his wrist; there was a dull ache in his arm.

He stood up and put on the light. The bright glare filled the room.

He saw his arm covered with blood. He picked a piece of glass from his wrist and dropped it on the floor in horror.

On his lower arm, the prints of her fingers were red.

He tore the sheet from the bed and ran down the hall to the bathroom. He washed the blood off and poured iodine into the thick gash and bandaged it. The burning made him dizzy. Drops of cold sweat ran into his eyes.

One of the boarders came in. John told him he had cut himself accidentally. When the man saw the blood running he ran and called a doctor on the telephone.

John sat on the edge of the bathtub and watched his blood dripping on the tiles.

The next day the cut was cleaned and bandaged.

The doctor was dubious about the explanation. John told him he did it with a knife; but there was no knife to be found, and there were thick patterns of blood all over the sheets and blanket.

He was told to stay in his room and keep his arm still.

He read most of the day and thought about how he had cut himself on a dream.

The thought of her excited him. She was still beautiful.

Memories became vivid.

They had lain in each other's arms in the straw and listened to the rain. He couldn't remember what they'd said.

He was not afraid she was coming back. His outlook on life was realistic. She was dead and buried.

It was some aberration of the mind. Some mental climax that had put itself off until now.

Then he looked at his wrist and saw the bandage.

It hadn't been her fault though. She didn't ask him to crash his hand through the glass.

Perhaps he could be with her in one existence and have her money in another.

Something held him from it. It *had* been frightening. The wet straw and the darkness, the mice and the rain, the bone-stiffening chill.

He made up his mind what he would do.

That night he turned out the lights early. He got on his knees beside the bed.

He put his head under the covers. If anything went wrong he had only to pull away quickly.

He waited.

Soon he smelled the straw and heard the rain and looked for her. He called her name softly.

There was a rustling. A warm hand caressed his cheek. He started at first. Then he smiled. Her face appeared and she put her cheek against his. The perfume of her hair intoxicated him.

Words filled his mind.

John. We are always one. Promise? Never part? If one of us dies the other will wait? If I die you'll wait and I'll find a way to come to you? I'll come to you and take you with me.

And now I have gone. You made me that drink and I died. And you opened the window so the breeze would come in. And now I am back.

He began to shake.

Her voice became harsher, he could hear her teeth grinding. Her breath was faster. Her fingers touched his face. They ran through his hair and fondled his neck.

He began to moan. He asked her to let go. There was no answer. She breathed faster still. He tried to pull away. He felt the floor of his room with his feet. He tried hard to pull his head from under the blanket. But her grasp was very strong.

She began to kiss his lips. Her mouth was cold, her eyes wide open. He stared into them while her breath mingled with his.

Then she threw back her head and she was laughing and lightning was bursting through the window. Rain was thundering on the roof and the mice shrieked and the horse stamped and made the barn shake. Her fingers clenched on his neck. He pulled with all his might and gritted his teeth and wrenched from her grasp. There was a sudden pain, and he rolled across the floor.

When the landlady came in two days later to clean, he was in the same position. His arms were sprawled in the dried puddle of blood and his body was taut and cold. His head was not to be found.

Dance of the Dead

I wanna RIDE!
with my Rota-Mota honey
by my SIDE!
As we whiz along the highway
We will HUG and
SNUGGLE
And we'll have a
little STRUGGLE!

STRUGGLE (strug´ 'l), n., act of promiscuous loveplay; usage
evolved during WW III.

Double beams spread buttery lamplight on the highway.
Rotor-Motors Convertible, Model C, 1997, rushed after
it. Light spurted ahead, yellow glowing. The car pursued with
a twelve-cylindered snarling pursuit. Night blotted in behind,
jet and still. The car sped on. ST. LOUIS—10.

"I wanna FLY!" they sang, "with the Rota-Mota apple of
my EYE!" they sang. "It's the only way of living. . . ."

The quartet singing:

Len, 23.

Bud, 24.

Barbara, 20.

Peggy, 18.

Len with Barbara, Bud with Peggy.

Bud at the wheel, snapping around tilted curves, roaring up black-shouldered hills, shooting the car across silent flatlands. At the top of three lungs (the fourth gentler), competing with wind that buffeted their heads, that whipped their hair to lashing threads—singing:

"You can have your walkin' under MOONLIGHT BEAMS!
At a hundred miles an hour let me DREAM my DREAMS!"

Needle quivering at 130, two 5-mph notches from gauge's end. *A sudden dip!* Their young frames jolted and the thrown-up laughter of three was windswept into night. Around a curve, darting up and down a hill, flashing across a leveled plain—an ebony bullet skimming earth.

"In my *ROTORY, MOTORY, FLOATERY*, drivin' machi-i-i-ine!"

"YOU'LL BE A FLOATER IN YOUR ROTOR-MOTOR."

In the back seat:

"Have a jab, Bab."

"Thanks, I had one after supper" (pushing away needle fixed to eye-dropper).

In the front seat:

"You meana tell me this is the first time you ever been t'Saint Loo!"

"But I just started school in September."

"Hey, you're a *frosh*?!"

Back seat joining front seat:

"Hey, *frosh*, have a mussle-tussle."

(Needle passed forward, eye bulb quivering amber juice.)

"*Live* it, girl!"

MUSSLE-TUSSLE (mus´ 'l-tus´ 'l), n., slang for the result of injecting a drug into a muscle; usage evolved during WW III.

Peggy's lips failed at smiling. Her fingers twitched.

"No, thanks, I'm not . . ."

"Come *on*, frosh!" Len leaning hard over the seat, white-browed under black blowing hair. Pushing the needle at her face. "Live it, girl! Grab a li'l mussle-tussle!"

"I'd rather not," said Peggy. "If you don't—"

"What's '*at*, frosh?" yelled Len and pressed his leg against the pressing leg of Barbara.

Peggy shook her head and golden hair flew across her cheeks and eyes. Underneath her yellow dress, underneath her white brassiere, underneath her young breast—a heart throbbed heavily. *Watch your step, darling, that's all we ask. Remember, you're all we have in the world now.* Mother words drumming at her; the needle making her draw back into the seat.

"*Come* on, frosh!"

The car groaned its shifting weight around a curve and centrifugal force pressed Peggy into Bud's lean hip. His hand dropped down and fingered at her leg. Underneath her yellow dress, underneath her sheer stocking—flesh crawled. Lips failed again; the smile was a twitch of red.

"Frosh, live it up!"

"Lay off, Len, jab your own dates."

"But we gotta teach frosh how to mussle-tussle!"

"Lay off, I said! She's my date!"

The black car roaring, chasing its own light. Peggy anchored down the feeling hand with hers. The wind whistled over them and grabbed down chilly fingers at their hair. She didn't want his hand there but she felt grateful to him.

Her vaguely frightened eyes watched the road lurch beneath the wheels. In back, a silent struggle began, taut hands rubbing, parted mouths clinging. Search for the sweet elusive at 120 miles-per-hour.

"Rota-Mota honey," Len moaned the moan between salivary kisses. In the front seat a young girl's heart beat unsteadily. ST. LOUIS—6.

"No kiddin', you never been to Saint Loo?"

"No, I . . ."

"Then you never saw the loopy's dance?"

Throat contracting suddenly. "No, I . . . is that what . . . we're going to—"

"Hey, frosh never saw the loopy's dance!" Bud yelled back.

Lips parted, slurping; skirt was adjusted with blasé aplomb. "No kiddin'!" Len fired up the words. "Girl, you haven't *lived!*"

"Oh, she's *got* to see *that*," said Barbara, buttoning a button.

"Let's go there then!" yelled Len. "Let's give frosh a thrill!"

"Good enough," said Bud and squeezed her leg. "Good enough up here, right, Peg?"

Peggy's throat moved in the dark and the wind clutched harshly at her hair. She'd heard of it, she'd read of it but never had she thought she'd—

Choose your school friends carefully, darling. Be very careful.

But when no one spoke to you for two whole months? When you were lonely and wanted to talk and laugh and be alive? And someone spoke to you finally and asked you to go out with them?

"I yam Popeye, the sailor man!" Bud sang.

In back, they crowed artificial delight. Bud was taking a course in Pre-War Comics and Cartoons—2. This week the class was studying Popeye. Bud had fallen in love with the one-eyed seaman and told Len and Barbara all about him; taught them dialogue and song.

"I yam Popeye, the sailor man! I like to go swimmin' with bowlegged women! I yam Popeye, the sailor man!"

Laughter. Peggy smiled falteringly. The hand left her leg as the car screeched around a curve and she was thrown against the door. Wind dashed blunt coldness in her eyes and forced her back, blinking. 110—115—120 miles-per-hour. ST. LOUIS— 3. *Be very careful, dear.*

Popeye cocked wicked eye.

"O, Olive Oyl, you is my sweet patootie."

Elbow nudging Peggy. "You be Olive Oyl—*you.*"

Peggy smiled nervously. "I can't."

"Sure!"

In the back seat, Wimpy came up for air to announce, "I will gladly pay you Tuesday for a hamburger today."

Three fierce voices and a faint fourth raged against the howl of wind. "I fights to the *fin*-ish 'cause I eats my *spin*-ach! I yam Popeye, the sailor man! *Toot! Toot!*"

"I yam what I yam," reiterated Popeye gravelly and put his hand on the yellow-skirted leg of Olive Oyl. In the back, two members of the quartet returned to feeling struggle.

ST. LOUIS—1. The black car roared through the darkened suburbs. "On with the nosies!" Bud sang out. They all took out their plasticate nose-and-mouth pieces and adjusted them.

Ance in your pants would be a pity!
Wear your nosies in the city!!

ANCE (anse), n., slang for anticivilian germs; usage evolved
during WW III.

"You'll like the loopy's dance!" Bud shouted to her over the
shriek of wind. "It's sen-*saysh!*"

Peggy felt a cold that wasn't of the night or of the wind.
*Remember, darling, there are terrible things in the world today. Things
you must aviod.*

"Couldn't we go somewhere else?" Peggy said but her voice
was inaudible. She heard Bud singing, "I like to go swimmin'
with bowlegged women!" She felt his hand on her leg again
while, in the back, was the silence of grinding passion without
kisses.

Dance of the dead. The words trickled ice across Peggy's brain.

ST. LOUIS.

The black car sped into the ruins.

I t was a place of smoke and blatant joys. Air resounded with
the bleating of revelers and there was a noise of sounding brass
spinning out a cloud of music—1997 music, a frenzy of twisted
dissonances. Dancers, shoe-horned into the tiny square of open
floor, ground pulsing bodies together. A network of bursting
sounds lanced through the mass of them; dancers singing:

"Hurt me! Bruise me! Squeeze me TIGHT!
Scorch my blood with hot DELIGHT!
Please abuse me every NIGHT!
LOVER, LOVER, LOVER, be a beast-to-
        me!"

Elements of explosion restrained within the dancing bounds—instead of fragmenting, quivering. "Oh, be a beast, beast, beast, *Beast*, BEAST to me!"

"How is *this*, Olive old goil?" Popeye inquired of the light of his eye as they struggled after the waiter. "Nothin' like this in Sykesville, eh?"

Peggy smiled but her hand in Bud's felt numb. As they passed by a murky lighted table, a hand she didn't see felt at her leg. She twitched and bumped against a hard knee across the narrow aisle. As she stumbled and lurched through the hot and smoky, thick-aired room, she felt a dozen eyes disrobing her, abusing her. Bud jerked her along and she felt her lips trembling.

"Hey, how about that!" Bud exulted as they sat. "Right by the stage!"

From cigarette mists, the waiter plunged and hovered, pencil poised, beside their table.

"What'll it be!" His questioning shout cut through cacophony.

"Whiskey-water!" Bud and Len paralleled orders, then turned to their dates. "What'll it be!" the waiter's request echoed from their lips.

"*Green Swamp!*" Barbara said and, "*Green Swamp* here!" Len passed it along. Gin, Invasion Blood (1997 Rum), lime juice, sugar, mint spray, splintered ice—a popular college girl drink.

"What about you, honey?" Bud asked his date.

Peggy smiled. "Just some ginger ale," she said, her voice a fluttering frailty in the massive clash and fog of smoke.

"What?" asked Bud and, "What's that, didn't hear!" the waiter shouted.

"Ginger ale."

"*What?*"

"Ginger ale!"

"GINGER ALE!" Len screamed it out and the drummer, behind the raging curtain of noise that was the band's music, almost heard it. Len banged down his fist. *One—Two—Three!*

> CHORUS: *Ginger Ale was only twelve years old!*
> *Went to church and was as good as gold.*
> *Till that day when—*

"Come *on*, come *on*!" the waiter squalled. "Let's have that order, kids! I'm busy!"

"Two whiskey-waters and two Green Swamps!" Len sang out and the waiter was gone into the swirling maniac mist.

Peggy felt her young heart flutter helplessly. *Above all, don't drink when you're out on a date. Promise us that, darling, you must promise us that.* She tried to push away instructions etched in brain.

"How you like this place, honey? *Loopy*, ain't it?" Bud fired the question at her; a red-faced, happy-faced Bud.

LOOPY (lōō´ pī), adj., common alter. of L.U.P.

She smiled at Bud, a smile of nervous politeness. Her eyes moved around, her face inclined and she was looking up at the stage. *Loopy.* The word scalpeled at her mind. *Loopy, loopy.*

The stage was five yards deep at the radius of its wooden semicircle. A waist-high rail girdled the circumference, two pale purple spotlights, unlit, hung at each rail end. Purple on white— the thought came. *Darling, isn't Sykesville Business College good enough? No! I don't want to take a business course, I want to major in art at the University!*

The drinks were brought and Peggy watched the disembodied waiter's arm thud down a high, green-looking glass before her. *Presto!*—the arm was gone. She looked into the murky green swamp depths and saw chipped ice bobbing.

"A toast! Pick up your glass, Peg!" Bud clarioned.

They all clinked glasses:

"To lust primordial!" Bud toasted.

"To beds intemperate!" Len added.

"To flesh insensate!" Barbara added a third link.

Their eyes zeroed in on Peggy's face, demanding. She didn't understand.

"Finish it!" Bud told her, plagued by freshman sluggishness.

"To . . . u-*us*," she faltered.

"How o-*ri*-ginal," stabbed Barbara and Peggy felt heat licking up her smooth cheeks. It passed unnoticed as three Youths of America with Whom the Future Rested gurgled down their liquor thirstily. Peggy fingered at her glass, a smile printed to lips that would not smile unaided.

"Come on, *drink*, girl!" Bud shouted to her across the vast distance of one foot. "Chuggalug!"

"Live it, girl," Len suggested abstractedly, fingers searching once more for soft leg. And finding, under the table, soft leg waiting.

Peggy didn't want to drink, she was afraid to drink. Mother words kept pounding—*never on a date, honey, never.* She raised the glass a little.

"Uncle Buddy will help, will help!"

Uncle Buddy leaning close, vapor of whiskey haloing his head. Uncle Buddy pushing cold glass to shaking young lips. "Come on, Olive Oyl, old goil! Down the hatch!"

Choking sprayed the bosom of her dress with green swamp droplets. Flaming liquid trickled into her stomach, sending off-shoots of fire into her veins.

Bangity boom crash smash POW!! The drummer applied the

coup de grâce to what had been, in ancient times, a lover's waltz. Lights dropped and Peggy sat coughing and tear-eyed in the smoky cellar club.

She felt Bud's hand clamp strongly on her shoulder and, in the murk, she felt herself pulled off balance and felt Bud's hot wet mouth pressing at her lips. She jerked away and then the purple spots went on and a mottle-faced Bud drew back, gurgling, "I fights to the finish," and reaching for his drink.

"Hey, the loopy now, the loopy!" Len said eagerly, releasing exploratory hands.

Peggy's heart jolted and she thought she was going to cry out and run thrashing through the dark, smoke-filled room. But a sophomore hand anchored her to the chair and she looked up in white-faced dread at the man who came out on the stage and faced the microphone which, like a metal spider, had swung down to meet him.

"May I have your attention, ladies and gentlemen," he said, a grimfaced, sepulchral-voiced man whose eyes moved out over them like flicks of doom. Peggy's breath was labored, she felt thin lines of green swamp water filtering hotly through her chest and stomach. It made her blink dizzily. *Mother.* The word escaped cells of the mind and trembled into conscious freedom. *Mother, take me home.*

"As you know, the act you are about to see is not for the faint of heart, the weak of will." The man plodded through the words like a cow enmired. "Let me caution those of you whose nerves are not what they ought to be—*leave now.* We make no guarantees of responsibility. We can't even afford to maintain a house doctor."

No laughter appreciative. "Cut the crap and get off stage," Len grumbled to himself. Peggy felt her fingers twitching.

"As you know," the man went on, his voice gilded with

learned sonority, "this is not an offering of mere sensation but an honest scientific demonstration."

"Loophole for Loopy's!" Bud and Len heaved up the words with the thoughtless reaction of hungry dogs salivating at a bell.

It was, in 1997, a comeback so rigidly standard it had assumed the status of a catechism answer. A crenel in the postwar law allowed the LUP performance if it was orally prefaced as an exposition of science. Through this legal chink had poured so much abusing of the law that few cared any longer. A feeble government was grateful to contain infractions of the law at all.

When hoots and shoutings had evaporated in the smoke-clogged air, the man, his arms upraised in patient benediction, spoke again.

Peggy watched the studied movement of his lips, her heart swelling, then contracting in slow, spasmodic beats. An iciness was creeping up her legs. She felt it rising toward the threadlike fires in her body and her fingers twitched around the chilly moisture of the glass. *I want to go, please take me home*—Willspent words were in her mind again.

"Ladies and gentlemen," the man concluded, "brace yourselves."

A gong sounded its hollow, shivering resonance, the man's voice thickened and slowed.

"The L.U. Phenomenon!"

The man was gone; the microphone had risen and was gone. Music began; a moaning brassiness, all muted. A jazzman's conception of *the palpable obscure*—mounted on a pulse of thumping drum. A dolor of saxophone, a menace of trombone, a harnessed bleating of trumpet—they raped the air with stridor.

Peggy felt a shudder plaiting down her back and her gaze dropped quickly to the murky whiteness of the table. Smoke and darkness, dissonance and heat surrounded her.

Without meaning to, but driven by an impulse of nervous fear, she raised the glass and drank. The glacial trickle in her throat sent another shudder rippling through her. Then further shoots of liquored heat budded in her veins and a numbness settled in her temples. Through parted lips, she forced out a shaking breath.

Now a restless, murmuring movement started through the room, the sound of it like willows in a soughing wind. Peggy dared not lift her gaze to the purpled silence of the stage. She stared down at the shifting glimmer of her drink, feeling muscle strands draw tightly in her stomach, feeling the hollow thumping of her heart. *I'd like to leave, please let's leave.*

The music labored toward a rasping dissonant climax, its brass components struggling, in vain, for unity.

A hand stroked once at Peggy's leg and it was the hand of Popeye, the sailor man, who muttered roupily, "Olive Oyl, you is my goil." She barely felt or heard. Automatonlike, she raised the cold and sweating glass again and felt the chilling in her throat and then the flaring network of warmth inside her.

SWISH!

The curtain swept open with such a rush, she almost dropped her glass. It thumped down heavily on the table, swamp water cascading up its sides and raining on her hand. The music exploded shrapnel of ear-cutting cacophony and her body jerked. On the tablecloth, her hands twitched white on white while claws of uncontrollable demand pulled up her frightened eyes.

The music fled, frothing behind a wake of swelling drum rolls.

The nightclub was a wordless crypt, all breathing checked.

Cobwebs of smoke drifted in the purple light across the stage.

No sound except the muffled, rolling drum.

Peggy's body was a petrifaction in its chair, smitten to rock around her leaping heart, while, through the wavering haze of smoke and liquored dizziness, she looked up in horror to where it stood.

It had been a woman.

Her hair was black, a framing of snarled ebony for the tallow mask that was her face. Her shadow-rimmed eyes were closed behind lids as smooth and white as ivory. Her mouth, a lipless and unmoving line, stood like a clotted sword wound beneath her nose. Her throat, her shoulders and her arms were white, were motionless. At her sides, protruding from the sleeve ends of the green transparency she wore, hung alabaster hands.

Across this marble statue, the spotlights coated purple shimmer.

Still paralyzed, Peggy stared up at its motionless features, her fingers knitted in a bloodless tangle on her lap. The pulse of drumbeats in the air seemed to fill her body, its rhythm altering her heartbeat.

In the black emptiness behind her, she heard Len muttering, "I love my wife but, oh, you corpse," and heard the wheeze of helpless snickers that escaped from Bud and Barbara. The cold still rose in her, a silent tidal dread.

Somewhere in the smoke-fogged darkness, a man cleared viscid nervousness from his throat and a murmur of appreciative relief strained through the audience.

Still no motion on the stage, no sound but the sluggish cadence of the drum, thumping at the silence like someone seeking entrance at a far-off door. The thing that was a nameless victim of the plague stood palely rigid while the distillation sluiced through its blood-clogged veins.

Now the drum throbs hastened like the pulsebeat of a rising panic. Peggy felt the chill begin to swallow her. Her throat started tightening, her breathing was a string of lip-parted gasps.

The loopy's eyelid twitched.

Abrupt, black, straining silence webbed the room. Even the breath choked off in Peggy's throat when she saw the pale eyes flutter open. Something creaked in the stillness; her body pressed back unconsciously against the chair. Her eyes were wide, unblinking circles that sucked into her brain the sight of the thing that had been a woman.

Music again; a brass-throated moaning from the dark, like some animal made of welded horns mewling its derangement in a midnight alley.

Suddenly, the right arm of the loopy jerked at its side, the tendons contracted. The left arm twitched alike, snapped out, then fell back and thudded in purple-white limpness against the thigh. The right arm out, the left arm out, the right, the left-right-left-right—like marionette arms twitching from an amateur's dangling strings.

The music caught the time, drum brushes scratching out a rhythm for the convulsions of the loopy's muscles. Peggy pressed back further, her body numbed and cold, her face a livid, staring mask in the fringes of the stage light.

The loopy's right foot moved now, jerking up inflexibly as the distillation constricted muscles in its leg. A second and a third contraction caused the leg to twitch, the left leg flung out in a violent spasm and then the woman's body lurched stiffly forward, filming the transparent silk to its light and shadow.

Peggy heard the sudden hiss of breath that passed the clenching teeth of Bud and Len and a wave of nausea sprayed foaming sickness up her stomach walls. Before her eyes, the stage abruptly undulated with a watery glitter and it seemed as if the flailing loopy was headed straight for her.

Gasping dizzily, she pressed back in horror, unable to take her eyes from its now agitated face.

She watched the mouth jerk to a gaping cavity, then a twisted scar that split into a wound again. She saw the dark nostrils twitching, saw writhing flesh beneath the ivory cheeks, saw furrows dug and undug in the purple whiteness of the forehead. She saw one lifeless eye wink monstrously and heard the gasp of startled laughter in the room.

While music blared into a fit of grating noise, the woman's arms and legs kept jerking with convulsive cramps that threw her body around the purpled stage like a full-sized rag doll given spastic life.

It was a nightmare in an endless sleep. Peggy shivered in helpless terror as she watched the loopy's twisting, leaping dance. The blood in her had turned to ice; there was no life in her but the endless, pounding stagger of her heart. Her eyes were frozen spheres staring at the woman's body writhing white and flaccid underneath the clinging silk.

Then, something went wrong.

Up till then, its muscular seizures had bound the loopy to an area of several yards before the amber flat which was the background for its paroxysmal dance. Now its erratic surging drove the loopy toward the stage-encircling rail.

Peggy heard the thump and creaking strain of wood as the loopy's hip collided with the rail. She cringed into a shuddering knot, her eyes still raised fixedly to the purple-splashed face whose every feature was deformed by throes of warping convulsion.

The loopy staggered back and Peggy saw and heard its leprous hands slapping with a fitful rhythm at its silk-scaled thighs.

Again it sprang forward like a maniac marionette and the woman's stomach thudded sickeningly into the railing wood. The dark mouth gaped, clamped shut and then the loopy twisted through a jerking revolution and crashed back against the rail again, almost above the table where Peggy sat.

Peggy couldn't breathe. She sat rooted to the chair, her lips a trembling circle of stricken dread, a pounding of blood at her temples as she watched the loopy spin again, its arms a blur of flailing white.

The lurid bleaching of its face dropped toward Peggy as the loopy crashed into the waist-high rail again and bent across its top. The mask of lavender-rained whiteness hung above her, dark eyes twitching open into a hideous stare.

Peggy felt the floor begin to move and the livid face was blurred with darkness, then reappeared in a burst of luminosity. Sound fled on brass-shoed feet, then plunged into her brain again—a smearing discord.

The loopy kept on jerking forward, driving itself against the rail as though it meant to scale it. With every spastic lurch, the diaphanous silk fluttered like a film about its body and every savage collision with the railing tautened the green transparency across its swollen flesh. Peggy looked up in rigid muteness at the loopy's fierce attack on the railing, her eyes unable to escape the wild distortion of the woman's face with its black frame of tangled, snapping hair.

What happened then happened in a blurring passage of seconds.

The grim-faced man came rushing across the purple-lighted stage; the thing that had been a woman went crashing, twitching, flailing at the rail, doubling over it, the spasmodic hitching flinging up its muscle-knotted legs.

A clawing fall.

Peggy lurched back in her chair and the scream that started in her throat was forced back into a strangled gag as the loopy came crashing down onto the table, its limbs a thrash of naked whiteness.

Barbara screamed, the audience gasped and Peggy saw, on the fringe of vision, Bud jumping up, his face a twist of stunned surprise.

The loopy flopped and twisted on the table like a new-caught fish. The music stopped, grinding into silence; a rush of agitated murmur filled the room and blackness swept in brain-submerging waves across Peggy's mind.

Then the cold white hand slapped across her mouth, the dark eyes stared at her in purple light and Peggy felt the darkness flooding.

The horror-smoked room went turning on its side.

onsciousness. It flickered in her brain like gauze-veiled candlelight. A murmuring of sound, a blur of shadow before her eyes.

Breath dripped like syrup from her mouth.

"Here, Peg."

She heard Bud's voice and felt the chilly metal of a flask neck pressed against lips. She swallowed, twisting slightly at the trickle of fire in her throat and stomach, then coughed and pushed away the flask with deadened fingers.

Behind her, a rustling movement. "Hey, she's *back*," Len said. "Ol' Olive Oyl is back."

"You feel all right?" asked Barbara.

She felt all right. Her heart was like a drum hanging from piano wire in her chest, slowly, slowly beaten. Her hands and feet were numb, not with cold but with a sultry torpor. Thoughts moved with a tranquil lethargy, her brain a leisurely machine imbedded in swaths of woolly packing.

She felt all right.

Peggy looked across the night with sleepy eyes. They were on a hilltop, the braked convertible crouching on a jutting edge. Far below, the country slept, a carpet of light and shadow beneath the chalky moon.

An arm snake moved around her waist. "Where are we?" she asked him in a languid voice.

"Few miles outside school," Bud said. "How d'ya feel, honey?"

She stretched, her body a delicious strain of muscles. She sagged back, limp, against his arm.

"Wonderful," she murmured with a dizzy smile and scratched the tiny itching bump on her left shoulder. Warmth radiated through her flesh; the night was sabled glow. There seemed—*somewhere*—to be a memory, but it crouched in secret behind folds of thick content.

"Woman, you were *out*," laughed Bud; and Barbara added and Len added, "*Were* you!" and "Olive Oyl went *plunko!*"

"Out?" Her casual murmur went unheard.

The flask went around and Peggy drank again, relaxing further as the liquor needled fire through her veins.

"Man, I never saw a loopy dance like that!" Len said.

A momentary chill across her back, then warmth again. "Oh," said Peggy, "that's right. I forgot."

She smiled.

"That was what I calls a grand finale!" Len said, dragging back his willing date, who murmured, "*Lenny* boy."

"LUP," Bud muttered, nuzzling at Peggy's hair. "Son of a gun." He reached out idly for the radio knob.

LUP (Lifeless Undead Phenomenon)—This freak of physiological abnormality was discovered during the war when, following certain germ-gas attacks, many of the dead troops were found erect and performing the spasmodic gyrations which, later, became known as the "loopy's" (LUP's) dance. The particular germ spray responsible was later distilled and is now used in carefully controlled experiments which are conducted only under the strictest of legal license and supervision.

Music surrounded them, its melancholy fingers touching at their hearts. Peggy leaned against her date and felt no need to curb exploring hands. Somewhere, deep within the jellied layers of her mind, there was something trying to escape. It fluttered like a frantic moth imprisoned in congealing wax, struggling wildly but only growing weaker in attempt as the chrysalis hardened.

Four voices sang softly in the night.

> "If the world is here tomorrow
> I'll be waiting, dear, for you
> If the stars are there tomorrow
> I'll be wishing on them too."

Four young voices singing, a murmur in immensity. Four bodies, two by two, slackly warm and drugged. A singing, an embracing—a wordless accepting.

> "Star light, star bright
> Let there be another night."

The singing ended but the song went on.
A young girl sighed.
"Isn't it romantic?" said Olive Oyl.

The Children of
Noah

It was just past three A.M. when Mr. Ketchum drove past the sign that read ZACHRY: POP. 67. He groaned. Another in an endless string of Maine seaside towns. He closed his eyes hard a second, then opened them again and pressed down on the accelerator. The Ford surged forward under him. Maybe, with luck, he'd reach a decent motel soon. It certainly wasn't likely there'd be one in Zachry: pop. 67.

Mr. Ketchum shifted his heavy frame on the seat and stretched his legs. It had been a sour vacation. Motoring through New England's historic beauty, communing with nature and nostalgia was what he'd planned. Instead, he'd found only boredom, exhaustion and over-expense.

Mr. Ketchum was not pleased.

The town seemed fast asleep as he drove along its Main Street. The only sound was that of the car's engine, the only sight that of his raised headbeams splaying out ahead, lighting up another sign. SPEED 15 LIMIT.

"Sure, sure," he muttered disgustedly, pressing down on the gas pedal. Three o'clock in the morning and the town fathers expected him to creep through their lousy hamlet. Mr. Ketchum watched the dark buildings rush past his window. Goodbye Zachry, he thought. Farewell, pop. 67.

Then the other car appeared in the rearview mirror. About half a block behind, a sedan with a turning red spotlight on its roof. He knew what kind of car it was. His foot curled off the accelerator and he felt his heartbeat quicken. Was it possible they hadn't noticed how fast he was going?

The question was answered as the dark car pulled up to the Ford and a man in a big hat leaned out of the front window. "Pull over!" he barked.

Swallowing dryly, Mr. Ketchum eased his car over to the curb. He drew up the emergency brake, turned the ignition key and the car was still. The police car nosed in toward the curb and stopped. The right front door opened.

The glare of Mr. Ketchum's headlights outlined the dark figure approaching. He felt around quickly with his left foot and stamped down on the knob, dimming the lights. He swallowed again. Damned nuisance this. Three a.m. in the middle of nowhere and a hick policeman picks him up for speeding. Mr. Ketchum gritted his teeth and waited.

The man in the dark uniform and wide-brimmed hat leaned over into the window. "License."

Mr. Ketchum slid a shaking hand into his inside pocket and drew out his billfold. He felt around for his license. He handed it over, noticed how expressionless the face of the policeman was. He sat there quietly while the policeman held a flashlight beam on the license.

"From New Jersey."

"Yes, that . . . that's right," said Mr. Ketchum.

The policeman kept staring at the license. Mr. Ketchum stirred restlessly on the seat and pressed his lips together. "It hasn't expired," he finally said.

He saw the dark head of the policeman lift. Then, he gasped as the narrow circle of flashlight blinded him. He twisted his head away.

The light was gone. Mr. Ketchum blinked his watering eyes.

"Don't they read traffic signs in New Jersey?" the policeman asked.

"Why, I . . . You mean the sign that said p-population sixty-seven?"

"No, I don't mean that sign," said the policeman.

"Oh." Mr. Ketchum cleared his throat. "Well, that's the only sign I saw," he said.

"You're a bad driver then."

"Well, I'm—"

"The sign said the speed limit is fifteen miles an hour. You were doing fifty."

"Oh. I . . . I'm afraid I didn't see it."

"The speed limit is fifteen miles an hour whether you see it or not."

"Well . . . at—at *this* hour of the morning?"

"Did you see a timetable on the sign?" the policeman asked.

"No, of course not. I mean, I didn't see the sign at all."

"*Didn't* you?"

Mr. Ketchum felt hair prickling along the nape of his neck. "Now, now see here," he began faintly, then stopped and stared at the policeman. "May I have my license back?" he finally asked when the policeman didn't speak.

The policeman said nothing. He stood on the street, motionless.

"May I—?" Mr. Ketchum started.

"Follow our car," said the officer abruptly and strode away.

Mr. Ketchum stared at him, dumbfounded. *Hey wait!* he almost yelled. The officer hadn't even given him back his license.

Mr. Ketchum felt a sudden coldness in his stomach.

"What *is* this?" he muttered as he watched the policeman getting back into his car. The police car pulled away from the curb, its roof light spinning again.

Mr. Ketchum followed.

"This is ridiculous," he said aloud. They had no right to do this. Was this the Middle Ages? His thick lips pressed into a jaded mouth line as he followed the police car along Main Street.

Two blocks up, the police car turned. Mr. Ketchum saw his headlights splash across a glass store front. HAND'S GROCERIES read the weather-worn letters.

There were no lamps on the street. It was like driving along an inky passage. Ahead were only the three red eyes of the police car's rear lights and spotlight; behind only impenetrable blackness. The end of a perfect day, thought Mr. Ketchum; picked up for speeding in Zachry, Maine. He shook his head and groaned. Why hadn't he just spent his vacation in Newark; slept late, gone to shows, eaten, watched television?

The police car turned right at the next corner, then, a block up, turned left again and stopped. Mr. Ketchum pulled up behind it as its lights went out. There was no sense in this. This was only cheap melodrama. They could just as easily have fined him on Main Street. It was the rustic mind. Debasing someone from a big city gave them a sense of vengeful eminence.

Mr. Ketchum waited. Well, he wasn't going to haggle. He'd pay his fine without a word and depart. He jerked up the hand brake. Suddenly he frowned, realizing that they could fine him anything they wanted. They could charge him $500 if they chose! The heavy man had heard stories about small town police, about the absolute authority they wielded. He cleared his throat viscidly. Well, this is absurd, he thought. What foolish imagination.

The policeman opened the door.

"Get out," he said.

There was no light in the street or in any building. Mr. Ketchum swallowed. All he could really see was the black figure of the policeman.

"Is this the—station?" he asked.

"Turn out your lights and come on," said the policeman.

Mr. Ketchum pushed in the chrome knob and got out. The policeman slammed the door. It made a loud, echoing noise; as if they were inside an unlighted warehouse instead of on a street. Mr. Ketchum glanced upward. The illusion was complete. There were neither stars nor moon. Sky and earth ran together blackly.

The policeman's hard fingers clamped on his arm. Mr. Ketchum lost balance a moment, then caught himself and fell into a quick stride beside the tall figure of the policeman.

"Dark here," he heard himself saying in a voice not entirely familiar.

The policeman said nothing. The other policeman fell into step on the other side of him. Mr. Ketchum told himself: These damned hick-town nazis were doing their best to intimidate him. Well, they wouldn't succeed.

Mr. Ketchum sucked in a breath of the damp, sea-smelling air and let it shudder out. A crumby town of sixty-seven and they have two policemen patrolling the streets at three in the morning. Ridiculous.

He almost tripped over the step when they reached it. The policeman on his left side caught him under the elbow.

"Thank you," Mr. Ketchum muttered automatically. The

policeman didn't reply. Mr. Ketchum licked his lips. Cordial oaf, he thought and managed a fleeting smile to himself. There, that was better. No point in letting this get to him.

He blinked as the door was pulled open and, despite himself, felt a sigh of relief filtering through him. It was a police station all right. There was the podiumed desk, there a bulletin board, there a black, pot-bellied stove unlit, there a scarred bench against the wall, there a door, there the floor covered with a cracked and grimy linoleum that had once been green.

"Sit down and wait," said the first policeman.

Mr. Ketchum looked at his lean, angled face, his swarthy skin. There was no division in his eyes between iris and pupil. It was all one darkness. He wore a dark uniform that fitted him loosely.

Mr. Ketchum didn't get to see the other policeman because both of them went into the next room. He stood watching the closed door a moment. Should he leave, drive away? No, they'd have his address on the license. Then again, they might actually want him to attempt to leave. You never knew what sort of warped minds these small town police had. They might even— shoot him down if he tried to leave.

Mr. Ketchum sat heavily on the bench. No, he was letting imagination run amuck. This was merely a small town on the Maine seacoast and they were merely going to fine him for—

Well; why didn't they fine him then? What was all this play-acting? The heavy man pressed his lips together. Very well, let them play it the way they chose. This was better than driving anyway. He closed his eyes. I'll just rest them, he thought.

After a few moments he opened them again. It was damned quiet. He looked around the dimly lit room. The walls were dirty and bare except for a clock and one picture that hung behind the desk. It was a painting—more likely a reproduction—of a bearded man. The hat he wore was a seaman's hat. Probably one of Zachry's ancient mariners. No; probably not even that. Probably a Sears, Roebuck print: *Bearded Seaman.*

Mr. Ketchum grunted to himself. Why a police station should have such a print was beyond him. Except, of course, that Zachry was on the Atlantic. Probably its main source of income was from fishing. Anyway, what did it matter? Mr. Ketchum lowered his gaze.

In the next room he could hear the muffled voices of the two policemen. He tried to hear what they were saying but he couldn't. He glared at the closed door. *Come on,* will you? he thought. He looked at the clock again. Three twenty-two. He checked it with his wristwatch. About right. The door opened and the two policemen came out.

One of them left. The remaining one—the one who had taken Mr. Ketchum's license—went over to the raised desk and switched on the gooseneck lamp over it, drew a big ledger out of the top drawer and started writing in it. *At last,* thought Mr. Ketchum.

A minute passed.

"I—" Mr. Ketchum cleared his throat. "I beg your—"

His voice broke off as the cold gaze of the policeman raised from the ledger and fixed on him.

"Are you . . . that is, am I to be—fined now?"

The policeman looked back at the ledger. "Wait," he said.

"But it's past three in the mor—" Mr. Ketchum caught himself. He tried to look coldly belligerent. "Very well," he said curtly. "Would you kindly tell me how long it will be?"

The policeman kept writing in the ledger. Mr. Ketchum sat there stiffly, looking at him. *Insufferable,* he thought. This was the last damned time he'd ever go within a hundred miles of this damned New England.

The policeman looked up. "Married?" he asked.

Mr. Ketchum stared at him.

"Are you married?"

"No, I—it's on the license," Mr. Ketchum blurted. He felt a tremor of pleasure at his retort and, at the same time, an impaling of strange dread at talking back to the man.

"Family in Jersey?" asked the policeman.

"Yes. I mean no. Just a sister in Wiscons—"

Mr. Ketchum didn't finish. He watched the policeman write it down. He wished he could rid himself of this queasy distress.

"Employed?" asked the policeman.

Mr. Ketchum swallowed. "Well," he said, "I—I have no one particular em—"

"Unemployed," said the policeman.

"Not at all; not at *all*," said Mr. Ketchum stiffly. "I'm a—a freelance salesman. I purchase stocks and lots from . . ." His voice faded as the policeman looked at him. Mr. Ketchum swallowed three times before the lump stayed down. He realized that he was sitting on the very edge of the bench as if poised to spring to the defense of his life. He forced himself to settle back. He drew in a deep breath. Relax, he told himself. Deliberately, he closed his eyes. There. He'd catch a few winks. May as well make the best of this, he thought.

The room was still except for the tinny, resonant ticking of the clock. Mr. Ketchum felt his heart pulsing with slow, dragging beats. He shifted his heavy frame uncomfortably on the hard bench. *Ridiculous*, he thought.

Mr. Ketchum opened his eyes and frowned. That damned picture. You could almost imagine that bearded seaman was looking at you.

————

U*h!"*

Mr. Ketchum's mouth snapped shut, his eyes jerked open, irises flaring. He started forward on the bench, then shrank back.

A swarthy-faced man was bent over him, hand on Mr. Ketchum's shoulder.

"Yes?" Mr. Ketchum asked, heart jolting.

The man smiled.

"Chief Shipley," he said. "Would you come into my office?"

"Oh," said Mr. Ketchum. "Yes. Yes."

He straightened up, grimacing at the stiffness in his back muscles. The man stepped back and Mr. Ketchum pushed up with a grunt, his eyes moving automatically to the wall clock. It was a few minutes past four.

"Look," he said, not yet awake enough to feel intimidated. "Why can't I pay my fine and leave?"

Shipley's smile was without warmth.

"We run things a little different here in Zachry," he said.

They entered a small, musty-smelling office.

"Sit down," said the chief, walking around the desk while Mr. Ketchum settled into a straight-backed chair that creaked.

"I don't understand why I can't pay my fine and leave."

"In due course," said Shipley.

"But—" Mr. Ketchum didn't finish. Shipley's smile gave the impression of being no more than a diplomatically veiled warning. Gritting his teeth, the heavy man cleared his throat and waited while the chief looked down at a sheet of paper on his desk. He noticed how poorly Shipley's suit fitted. Yokels, the heavy man thought, don't even know how to dress.

"I see you're not married," Shipley said.

Mr. Ketchum said nothing. Give them a taste of their own no-talk medicine he decided.

"Have you friends in Maine?" Shipley asked.

"Why?"

"Just routine questions, Mr. Ketchum," said the chief. "Your only family is a sister in Wisconsin?"

Mr. Ketchum looked at him without speaking. What had all this to do with a traffic violation?

"Sir?" asked Shipley.

"I already told you; that is, I told the officer. I don't see—"

"Here on business?"

Mr. Ketchum's mouth opened soundlessly.

"Why are you asking me all these questions?" he asked. *Stop shaking!* he ordered himself furiously.

"Routine. Are you here on business?"

"I'm on my vacation. And I don't see this at all! I've been patient up to now but, *blast it*, I demand to be fined and released!"

"I'm afraid that's impossible," said the chief.

Mr. Ketchum's mouth fell open. It was like waking up from a nightmare and discovering that the dream was still going on. "I—I don't understand," he said.

"You'll have to appear before the judge."

"But that's ridiculous."

"Is it?"

"Yes, it is. I'm a citizen of the United States. I demand my rights."

Chief Shipley's smile faded.

"You limited those rights when you broke our law," he said. "Now you have to pay for it as we declare."

Mr. Ketchum stared blankly at the man. He realized that he was completely in their hands. They could fine him anything they pleased or put him in jail indefinitely. All these questions he'd been asked; he didn't know why they'd asked them but he knew that his answers revealed him as almost rootless, with no one who cared if he lived or—

The room seemed to totter. Sweat broke out on his body.

"You can't *do* this," he said; but it was not an argument.

"You'll have to spend the night in jail," said the chief. "In the morning you'll see the judge."

"But this is ridiculous!" Mr. Ketchum burst out. *"Ridiculous!"*

He caught himself. "I'm entitled to one phone call," he said quickly. "I can make a telephone call. It's my legal right."

"It would be," said Shipley, "if there was any telephone service in Zachry."

When they took him to his cell, Mr. Ketchum saw a painting in the hall. It was of the same bearded seaman. Mr. Ketchum didn't notice if the eyes followed him or not.

Mr. Ketchum stirred. A look of confusion lined his sleep-numbed face. There was a clanking sound behind him; he reared up on his elbow.

A policeman came into the cell and set down a tray.

"Breakfast," he said. He was older than the other policemen, even older than Shipley. His hair was iron-gray, his cleanly shaved face seamed around the mouth and eyes. His uniform fitted him badly.

As the policeman started relocking the door, Mr. Ketchum asked, "When do I see the judge?"

The policeman looked at him a moment. "Don't know," he said and turned away.

"Wait!" Mr. Ketchum called out.

The receding footsteps of the policeman sounded hollowly on the cement floor. Mr. Ketchum kept staring at the spot where the policeman had been. Veils of sleep peeled from his mind.

He sat up, rubbed deadened fingers over his eyes and held up his wrist. Seven minutes past nine. The heavy man grimaced. By God, they were going to hear about this! His nostrils twitched. He sniffed, started to reach for the tray; then pulled back his hand.

"No," he muttered. He wouldn't eat their damned food. He sat there stiffly, doubled at the waist, glaring at his sock-covered feet.

His stomach grumbled uncooperatively.

"Well," he muttered after a minute. Swallowing, he reached over and lifted off the tray cover.

He couldn't check the *oh* of surprise that passed his lips.

The three eggs were fried in butter, bright yellow eyes focused straight on the ceiling, ringed about with long, crisp lengths of meaty, corrugated bacon. Next to them was a platter of four book-thick slices of toast spread with creamy butter swirls, a cup of jelly leaning on them. There was a tall glass of frothy orange juice, a dish of strawberries bleeding in alabaster cream. Finally, a tall pot from which wavered the pungent and unmistakable fragrance of freshly brewed coffee.

Mr. Ketchum picked up the glass of orange juice. He took a few drops in his mouth and rolled them experimentally over his tongue. The citric acid tingled deliciously on his warm tongue. He swallowed. If it was poisoned it was by a master's hand. Saliva tided in his mouth. He suddenly remembered that, just before he was picked up, he'd been meaning to stop at a cafe for food.

While he ate, warily but decidedly, Mr. Ketchum tried to figure out the motivation behind this magnificent breakfast.

It was the rural mind again. They regretted their blunder. It seemed a flimsy notion, but there it was. The food was superb. One thing you had to say for these New Englanders; they could cook like a son-of-a-gun. Breakfast for Mr. Ketchum was usually a sweet roll, heated, and coffee. Since he was a boy in his father's house he hadn't eaten a breakfast like this.

He was just putting down his third cup of well-creamed coffee when footsteps sounded in the hall. Mr. Ketchum smiled. Good timing, he thought. He stood.

Chief Shipley stopped outside the cell. "Had your breakfast?"

Mr. Ketchum nodded. If the chief expected thanks he was in for a sad surprise. Mr. Ketchum picked up his coat.

The chief didn't move.

"*Well . . . ?*" said Mr. Ketchum after a few minutes. He tried to put it coldly and authoritatively. It came out somewhat less.

Chief Shipley looked at him expressionlessly. Mr. Ketchum felt his breath faltering.

"May I inquire—?" he began.

"Judge isn't in yet," said Shipley.

"But . . ." Mr. Ketchum didn't know what to say.

"Just came in to tell you," said Shipley. He turned and was gone.

Mr. Ketchum was furious. He looked down at the remains of his breakfast as if they contained the answer to this situation. He drummed a fist against his thigh. *Insufferable!* What were they trying to do—intimidate him? Well, by God—

—they were succeeding.

Mr. Ketchum walked over to the bars. He looked up and down the empty hallway. There was a cold knot inside him. The food seemed to have turned to dry lead in his stomach. He banged the heel of his right hand once against the cold bar. By God! *By God!*

———

t was two o'clock in the afternoon when Chief Shipley and
the old policeman came to the cell door. Wordlessly the policeman opened it. Mr. Ketchum stepped into the hallway and
waited again, putting on his coat while the door was relocked.

He walked in short, inflexible strides between the two men,
not even glancing at the picture on the wall. "Where are we
going?" he asked.

"Judge is sick," said Shipley. "We're taking you out to his
house to pay your fine."

Mr. Ketchum sucked in his breath. He wouldn't argue with
them; he just wouldn't. "All right," he said. "If that's the way
you have to do it."

"Only way to do it," said the chief, looking ahead, his face
an expressionless mask.

Mr. Ketchum pressed down the corners of a slim smile. This
was better. It was almost over now. He'd pay his fine and clear
out.

It was foggy outside. Sea mist rolled across the street like
driven smoke. Mr. Ketchum pulled on his hat and shuddered.
The damp air seemed to filter through his flesh and drew itself
around his bones. Nasty day, he thought. He moved down the
steps, eyes searching for his Ford.

The old policeman opened the back door of the police car
and Shipley gestured toward the inside.

"What about *my* car?" Mr. Ketchum asked.

"We'll come back here after you see the judge," said Shipley.

"Oh. I . . ."

Mr. Ketchum hesitated. Then he bent over and squeezed
into the car, dropping down on the back seat. He shivered as
the cold leather pierced trouser wool. He edged over as the chief
got in.

The policeman slammed the door shut. Again that hollow

sound, like the slamming of a coffin lid on a crypt. Mr. Ketchum grimaced as the simile occurred to him.

The policeman got into the car and Mr. Ketchum heard the motor cough into liquid life. He sat there breathing slowly and deeply while the policeman out-choked warmth into the engine. He looked out the window at his left.

The fog was just like smoke. They might have been parked in a burning garage. Except for that bone-gripping dampness. Mr. Ketchum cleared his throat. He heard the chief shift on the seat beside him.

"Cold," Mr. Ketchum said automatically.

The chief said nothing.

Mr. Ketchum pressed back as the car pulled away from the curb, U-turned and started slowly down the fog-veiled street. He listened to the crisp sibilance of tires on wet paving, the rhythmic swish of the wipers as they cleared off circle segments on the misted windshield.

After a moment he looked at his watch. Almost three. Half a day shot in this blasted Zachry.

He looked out through the window again as the town ghosted past. He thought he saw brick buildings along the curb but he wasn't sure. He looked down at his white hands, then glanced over at Shipley. The chief was sitting stiffly upright on the seat, staring straight ahead. Mr. Ketchum swallowed. The air seemed stagnant in his lungs.

On Main Street the fog seemed thinner. Probably the sea breezes, Mr. Ketchum thought. He looked up and down the street. All the stores and offices looked closed. He glanced at the other side of the street. Same thing.

"Where is everybody?" he asked.

"What?"

"I said where *is* everybody?"

"Home," the chief said.

"But it's Wednesday," said Mr. Ketchum. "Aren't your— stores open?"

"Bad day," said Shipley. "Not worth it."

Mr. Ketchum glanced at the sallow-faced chief, then with-drew his look hastily. He felt cold premonition spidering in his stomach again. What in God's name *is* this? he asked himself. It had been bad enough in the cell. Here, tracking through this sea of mist, it was worse.

"That's right," he heard his nerve-sparked voice saying. "There are only sixty-seven people, aren't there?"

The chief said nothing.

"How . . . h-how old is Zachry?"

In the silence he heard the chief's finger joints crackle dryly.

"Hundred fifty years," said Shipley.

"That old," said Mr. Ketchum. He swallowed with effort. His throat hurt a little. Come *on*, he told himself. *Relax*.

"How come it's named Zachry?" The words spilled out, uncontrolled.

"Noah Zachry founded it," said the chief.

"Oh. Oh. I see. I guess that picture in the station . . . ?"

"That's right," said Shipley.

Mr. Ketchum blinked. So that was Noah Zachry, founder of this town they were driving through—

—*block after block after block*. There was a cold, heavy sinking in Mr. Ketchum's stomach as the idea came to him.

In a town so big, why were there only 67 people?

He opened his mouth to ask it, then couldn't. The answer might be wrong.

"Why are there only—?" The words came out anyway be-fore he could stop them. His body jolted at the shock of hearing them.

"What?"

"Nothing, nothing. That is—" Mr. Ketchum drew in a shaking breath. No help for it. He had to know.

"How come there are only sixty-seven?"

"They go away," said Shipley.

Mr. Ketchum blinked. The answer came as such an anticlimax. His brow furrowed. Well, what else? he asked himself defensively. Remote, antiquated, Zachry would have little attraction for its younger generations. Mass gravitation to more interesting places would be inevitable.

The heavy man settled back against the seat. Of course. Think how much *I* want to leave the dump, he thought, and I don't even live here.

His gaze slid forward through the windshield, caught by something. A banner across the street. BARBECUE TONIGHT. Celebration, he thought. They probably went berserk every fortnight and had themselves a rip-roaring taffy pull or fishnet-mending orgy.

"Who was Zachry anyway?" he asked. The silence was getting to him again.

"Sea captain," said the chief.

"Oh?"

"Whaled in the South Seas," said Shipley.

Abruptly, Main Street ended. The police car veered left onto a dirt road. Out of the window Mr. Ketchum watched shadowy bushes glide by. There was only the sound of the engine laboring in second and of gravelly dirt spitting out from under the tires. Where does the judge live, on a mountain top? He shifted his weight and grunted.

The fog began thinning now. Mr. Ketchum could see grass and trees, all with a grayish cast to them. The car turned and faced the ocean. Mr. Ketchum looked down at the opaque carpet of fog below. The car kept turning. It faced the crest of the hill again.

Mr. Ketchum coughed softly. "Is . . . uh, that the judge's house up there?" he asked.

"Yes," the chief answered.

"High," said Mr. Ketchum.

The car kept turning on the narrow, dirt road, now facing the ocean, now Zachry, now the bleak, hill-topping house. It was a grayish-white house, three stories high, at each end of it the crag of an attic tower. It looked as old as Zachry itself, thought Mr. Ketchum. The car turned. He was facing the fog-crusted ocean again.

Mr. Ketchum looked down at his hands. Was it a deception of the light or were they really shaking? He tried to swallow but there was no moisture in his throat and he coughed instead, rattlingly. This is so *stupid*, he thought; there's no reason in the world for this. He saw his hands clench together.

The car was moving up the final rise toward the house now. Mr. Ketchum felt his breaths shortening. *I don't want to go*, he heard someone saying in his mind. He felt a sudden urge to shove out the door and run. Muscles tensed emphatically.

He closed his eyes. For God's sake, *stop* it! he yelled at himself. There was nothing wrong about this but his distorted interpretation of it. These were modern times. Things had explanations and people had reasons. Zachry's people had a reason too; a narrow distrust of city dwellers. This was their socially acceptable revenge. That made sense. After all—

The car stopped. The chief pushed open the door on his side and got out. The policeman reached back and opened the other door for Mr. Ketchum. The heavy man found one of his legs and foot to be numb. He had to clutch at the top of the door for support. He stamped the foot on the ground.

"Went to sleep," he said.

Neither of the men answered. Mr. Ketchum glanced at the house; he squinted. Had he seen a dark green drape slip back into place? He winced and made a startled noise as his arm was touched and the chief gestured toward the house. The three men started toward it.

"I, uh . . . don't have much cash on me, I'm afraid," he said. "I hope a traveler's check will be all right."

"Yes," said the chief.

They went up the porch steps, stopped in front of the door. The policeman turned a big, brass key-head and Mr. Ketchum heard a bell ring tinnily inside. He stood looking through the door curtains. Inside, he could make out the skeletal form of a hat rack. He shifted weight and the boards creaked under him. The policeman rang the bell again.

"Maybe he's—too sick," Mr. Ketchum suggested faintly.

Neither of the men looked at him. Mr. Ketchum felt his muscles tensing. He glanced back over his shoulder. Could they catch him if he ran for it?

He looked back disgustedly. You pay your fine and you leave, he explained patiently to himself. That's all; you pay your fine and you leave.

Inside the house there was dark movement. Mr. Ketchum looked up, startled in spite of himself. A tall woman was approaching the door.

The door opened. The woman was thin, wearing an ankle-length black dress with a white oval pin at her throat. Her face was swarthy, seamed with threadlike lines. Mr. Ketchum slipped off his hat automatically.

"Come in," said the woman.

Mr. Ketchum stepped into the hall.

"You can leave your hat there," said the woman, pointing

toward the hat rack that looked like a tree ravaged by flame. Mr. Ketchum dropped his hat over one of the dark pegs. As he did, his eye was caught by a large painting near the foot of the staircase. He started to speak but the woman said, "This way."

They started down the hall. Mr. Ketchum stared at the painting as they passed it.

"Who's that woman," he asked, "standing next to Zachry?"

"His wife," said the chief.

"But she—"

Mr. Ketchum's voice broke off suddenly as he heard a whimper rising in his throat. Shocked, he drowned it out with a sudden clearing of the throat. He felt ashamed of himself. Still . . . Zachry's wife?

The woman opened a door. "Wait here," she said.

The heavy man walked in. He turned to say something to the chief. Just in time to see the door shut.

"Say, uh . . ." He walked to the door and put his hand on the knob. It didn't turn.

He frowned. He ignored the pile-driver beats of his heart. "Hey, what's going on?" Cheerily bluff, his voice echoed off the walls. Mr. Ketchum turned and looked around. The room was empty. It was a square, empty room.

He turned back to the door, lips moving as he sought the proper words.

"Okay," he said, abruptly, "it's very—" He twisted the knob sharply. "Okay, it's a very funny joke." By God, he was mad. "I've taken all I'm—"

He whirled at the sound, teeth bared.

There was nothing. The room was still empty. He looked around dizzily. What was that sound? A dull sound, like water rushing.

"Hey," he said automatically. He turned to the door. "Hey!"

he yelled, "cut it out! Who do you think you are anyway?"

He turned on weakening legs. The sound was louder. Mr. Ketchum ran a hand over his brow. It was covered with sweat. It was warm in there.

"Okay, okay," he said, "it's a fine joke but—"

Before he could go on, his voice had corkscrewed into an awful, wracking sob. Mr. Ketchum staggered a little. He stared at the room. He whirled and fell back against the door. His outflung hand touched the wall and jerked away.

It was hot.

"Huh?" he asked incredulously.

This was impossible. This was a joke. This was their deranged idea of a little joke. It was a game they played. Scare the City Slicker was the name of the game.

"Okay!" he yelled. "*Okay!* It's funny, it's very funny! Now let me out of here or there's going to be trouble!"

He pounded at the door. Suddenly he kicked it. The room was getting hotter. It was almost as hot as an—

Mr. Ketchum was petrified. His mouth sagged open.

The questions they'd asked him. The loose way the clothes fit everyone he'd met. The rich food they'd given him to eat. The empty streets. The savagelike swarthy coloring of the men, of the women. The way they'd all looked at him. And the woman in the painting, Noah Zachry's wife—*a native woman with her teeth filed to a point.*

BARBECUE TONIGHT.

Mr. Ketchum screamed. He kicked and pounded on the door. He threw his heavy body against it. He shrieked at the people outside.

"Let me out! *Let me out!* LET . . . ME . . . OUT!"

The worst part about it was, he just couldn't believe it was really happening.

The Holiday Man

Y ou'll be late," she said.

He leaned back tiredly in his chair.

"I know," he answered.

They were in the kitchen having breakfast. David hadn't eaten much. Mostly, he'd drunk black coffee and stared at the tablecloth. There were thin lines running through it that looked like intersecting highways.

"Well?" she said.

He shivered and took his eyes from the tablecloth.

"Yes," he said. "All right."

He kept sitting there.

"*David,*" she said.

"I know, I know," he said, "I'll be late." He wasn't angry. There was no anger left in him.

"You certainly will," she said, buttering her toast. She spread on thick raspberry jam, then bit off a piece and chewed it cracklingly.

David got up and walked across the kitchen. At the door he stopped and turned. He stared at the back of her head.

"Why couldn't I?" he asked again.

"Because you can't," she said. "That's all."

"But *why*?"

"Because they need you," she said. "Because they pay you well and you couldn't do anything else. Isn't it obvious?"

"They could find someone else."

"Oh, stop it," she said. "You know they couldn't."

He closed his hands into fists. "Why should I be the one?" he asked.

She didn't answer. She sat eating her toast.

"Jean?"

"There's nothing more to say," she said, chewing. She turned around. "Now, will you go?" she said. "You shouldn't be late today."

David felt a chill in his flesh.

"No," he said, "not today."

He walked out of the kitchen and went upstairs. There, he brushed his teeth, polished his shoes and put on a tie. Before eight he was down again. He went into the kitchen.

"Good-bye," he said.

She tilted up her cheek for him and he kissed it. "Bye, dear," she said. "Have a—" She stopped abruptly.

"—nice day?" he finished for her. "Thank you." He turned away. "I'll have a lovely day."

Long ago he had stopped driving a car. Mornings he walked to the railroad station. He didn't even like to ride with someone else or take a bus.

At the station he stood outside on the platform waiting for the train. He had no newspaper. He never bought them any more. He didn't like to read the papers.

"Mornin', Garret."

He turned and saw Henry Coulter who also worked in the city. Coulter patted him on the back.

"Good morning," David said.

"How's it goin'?" Coulter asked.

"Fine. Thank you."

"Good. Lookin' forward to the Fourth?"

David swallowed. "Well . . ." he began.

"Myself, I'm takin' the family to the woods," said Coulter. "No lousy fireworks for us. Pilin' into the old bus and headin' out till the fireworks are over."

"Driving," said David.

"Yes, sir," said Coulter. "Far as we can."

It began by itself. No, he thought; *not now.* He forced it back into its darkness.

"—tising business," Coulter finished.

"What?" he asked.

"Said I trust things are goin' well in the advertising business." David cleared his throat.

"Oh, yes," he said. "Fine." He always forgot about the lie he'd told Coulter.

When the train arrived he sat in the No Smoking car, knowing that Coulter always smoked a cigar en route. He didn't want to sit with Coulter. Not now.

All the way to the city he sat looking out the window. Mostly he watched road and highway traffic; but, once, while the train rattled over a bridge, he stared down at the mirrorlike surface of a lake. Once he put his head back and looked up at the sun.

He was actually to the elevator when he stopped.

"Up?" said the man in the maroon uniform. He looked

at David steadily. "Up?" he said. Then he closed the rolling doors.

David stood motionless. People began to cluster around him. In a moment, he turned and shouldered by them, pushing through the revolving door. As he came out, the oven heat of July surrounded him. He moved along the sidewalk like a man asleep. On the next block he entered a bar.

Inside, it was cold and dim. There were no customers. Not even the bartender was visible. David sank down in the shadow of a booth and took his hat off. He leaned his head back and closed his eyes.

He couldn't do it. He simply could not go up to his office. No matter what Jean said, no matter what anyone said. He clasped his hands on the table edge and squeezed them until the fingers were pressed dry of blood. He just *wouldn't.*

"Help you?" asked a voice.

David opened his eyes. The bartender was standing by the booth, looking down at him.

"Yes, uh . . . beer," he said. He hated beer but he knew he had to buy something for the privilege of sitting in the chilly silence undisturbed. He wouldn't drink it.

The bartender brought the beer and David paid for it. Then, when the bartender had gone, he began to turn the glass slowly on the table top. While he was doing this it began again. With a gasp, he pushed it away. No!—he told it, savagely.

In a while he got up and left the bar. It was past ten. That didn't matter of course. They knew he was always late. They knew he always tried to break away from it and never could.

is office was at the back of the suite, a small cubicle fur-nished only with a rug, sofa, and a small desk on which lay pencils and white paper. It was all he needed. Once, he'd had a secretary but he hadn't liked the idea of her sitting outside the door and listening to him scream.

No one saw him enter. He let himself in from the hall through a private door. Inside, he relocked the door, then took off his suitcoat and laid it across the desk. It was stuffy in the office so he walked across the floor and pulled up the window.

Far below, the city moved. He stood watching it. How many of them? he thought.

Sighing heavily, he turned. Well, he was here. There was no point in hesitating any longer. He was committed now. The best thing was to get it over and clear out.

He drew the blinds, walked over to the couch and lay down. He fussed a little with the pillow, then stretched once and was still. Almost immediately, he felt his limbs going numb.

It began.

He did not stop it now. It trickled on his brain like melted ice. It rushed like winter wind. It spun like blizzard vapor. It leaped and ran and billowed and exploded and his mind was filled with it. He grew rigid and began to gasp, his chest twitching with breath, the beating of his heart a violent stagger. His hands drew in like white talons, clutching and scratching at the couch. He shivered and groaned and writhed. Finally he screamed. He screamed for a very long while.

When it was done, he lay limp and motionless on the couch, his eyes like balls of frozen glass. When he could, he raised his arm and looked at his wristwatch. It was almost two.

He struggled to his feet. His bones felt sheathed with lead but he managed to stumble to his desk and sit before it.

There he wrote on a sheet of paper and, when he was finished, slumped across the desk and fell into exhausted sleep.

Later, he woke up and took the sheet of paper to his superior, who, looking it over, nodded.

"Four hundred eighty-six, huh?" the superior said. "You're sure of that?"

"I'm sure," said David, quietly. "I watched every one." He didn't mention that Coulter and his family were among them.

"All right," said his superior. "Let's see now. Four hundred fifty-two from traffic accidents, eighteen from drowning, seven from sunstroke, three from fireworks, six from miscellaneous causes."

Such as a little girl being burned to death, David thought. Such as a baby boy eating ant poison. Such as a woman being electrocuted; a man dying of snake bite.

"Well," his superior said, "let's make it—oh, four hundred and fifty. It's always impressive when more people die than we predict."

"Of course," David said.

The item was on the front page of all the newspapers that afternoon. While David was riding home the man in front of him turned to his neighbor and said, "What I'd like to know is—*how can they tell?*"

David got up and went back on the platform on the end of the car. Until he got off, he stood there listening to the train wheels and thinking about Labor Day.

Old Haunts

Originally he'd intended to spend the one night in town at the Hotel Tiger. But it had occurred to him that maybe his old room was available. It was summer session now and there might not be a student living there. It was certainly worth a try. He could think of nothing more pleasant than sleeping in his old room, in his old bed.

The house was the same. He moved up the cement steps, smiling at their still crumbled edges. Same old steps, he thought, still on the bum. As was the sagging screen door to the porch and the doorbell that had to be pushed in at an angle before connection was made. He shook his head, smiling, and wondered if Miss Smith were still alive.

It wasn't Miss Smith who answered the bell. His heart sank as, instead of her tottering old form, a husky middle-aged woman came bustling to the door.

"Yes?" she said, her voice a harsh, inhospitable sound.

"Is Miss Smith still here?" he asked, hoping, in spite of everything, that she was.

"No, Miss Ada's been dead for years."

It was like a slap on his face. He felt momentarily stunned as he nodded at the woman.

"I see," he said then. "I see. I used to room here while I was in college, you see, and I thought . . ."

Miss Smith dead.

"You going to school?" the woman asked.

He didn't know whether to take it as insult or praise.

"No, no," he said, "I'm just passing through on my way to Chicago. I graduated many years ago. I wondered if . . . anyone was living in the old room."

"The hall room, you mean?" the woman asked, regarding him clinically.

"That's right."

"Not till fall," she said.

"Could I . . . look at it?"

"Well, I . . ."

"I thought I might stay overnight," he said, hastily, "that is, if—"

"Oh, *that's* all right." The woman warmed her tone. "If that's what you want."

"I would," he said. "Sort of renew old acquaintanceship, you know."

He smiled self-consciously, wishing he hadn't said that.

"What would you want to pay?" asked the woman, more concerned with money than with memories.

"Well, I tell you," he said, impulsively, "I used to pay twenty dollars a month. Suppose I pay you that?"

"For one night?"

He felt foolish. But he couldn't back down now even though he felt that his offer had been a nostalgic blunder. No room was worth twenty dollars a night.

He caught himself. Why quibble? It was worth that much to relive old memories. Twenty dollars was nothing to him any-more. The past was.

"Glad to pay it," he said. "Well worth it to me."

He slid the bills from his wallet with awkward fingers and held them out to her.

He glanced at the bathroom as they walked down the dimlit hall. The familiar sight made him smile. There was something wonderful about returning. He couldn't help it; there just was.

"Yes, Miss Ada's been dead nigh onto five years," the woman said.

His smile faded.

When the woman opened the door to the room he wanted to stand there for a long moment looking at it before letting himself enter once more. But she stood waiting for him and he knew he'd feel ridiculous asking her to wait so he took a deep breath and went in.

Time travel. The phrase crossed his mind as he entered the room. Because it seemed as if he was suddenly back; the new student stepping into the room for the first time, suitcase in hand, at the beginning of a new adventure.

He stood there mutely, looking around the room, a sense of inexplicable fright taking hold of him. The room seemed to bring back everything. *Everything.* Mary and Norman and Spencer and David and classes and concerts and parties and dances and football games and beer-busts and all-night talks and everything. Memories crowded on him until it seemed that they would crush him.

"It's a little dusty but I'll clean it up when you go out to eat," the woman said. "I'll go get you some sheets."

He didn't hear her words or her footsteps moving down the hallway. He stood there possessed by the past.

He didn't know what it was that made him shudder and look around suddenly. It wasn't a sound or anything he saw. It was a feeling in his body and mind; a sense of unreasonable foreboding.

He jumped with a gasp as the door slammed violently shut.

"It's the wind does it," said the woman returning with sheets for his old bed.

B roadway. The traffic light turned red and he eased down the brake. His gaze moved across the store fronts.

There was the Crown Drug Store, still the same. Next to it, Flora Dame's Shoe Store. His eyes moved across the street. The Glendale Shop was still there. Barth's Clothes was still in its old location too.

Something in his mind seemed to loosen and he realized that he had been afraid of seeing the town changed. For when he'd turned the corner onto Broadway and seen that Mrs. Sloane's Book Shoppe and The College Grille were gone he'd felt almost a sense of betrayal. The town he remembered existed intact in his mind and it gave him a tense, restless feeling to see it partially changed. It was like meeting an old friend and discovering, with a shock, that one of his legs was gone.

But enough things were the same to bring the solemn smile back to his lips.

The College Theatre where he and his friends had gone to midnight shows on Saturday nights after a date or long hours of study. The Collegiate Bowling Alleys; upstairs from them, the pool room.

And downstairs . . .

Impulsively, he pulled the car to the curb and switched off the motor. He sat there looking, for a moment, at the entrance to the Golden Campus. Then he slid quickly from the car.

The same old awning hung over the doorway, its once gaudy colors worn conservative by time and weather. He moved forward, a smile playing on his lips.

Then a sense of overpowering depression struck him as he stood looking down the steep, narrow staircase. He caught hold of the railing with his fingers and, after hesitating, let himself down slowly. He hadn't remembered the stairway being *this* narrow.

Near the bottom of the stairs, a whirring sound reached his ears. Someone was waxing the small dance floor with rotary brushes. He moved down the last step and saw the small black man following the gently bucking machine around the floor. He saw and heard the metal nose of the polisher bump into one of the columns that marked the boundaries of the dance floor.

Another frown crossed his face. The place was so small, so dingy. Surely memory hadn't erred that badly. No, he hastily explained to himself. No, it was because the place was empty and there were no lights. It was because the jukebox wasn't frothing with colored bubbles and there were no couples dancing.

Unconsciously, he slid his hands into his trouser pockets, a pose he hadn't assumed more than once or twice since he'd left college eighteen years before. He moved closer to the dance floor, nodding once to the low, battered bandstand as one would to an old acquaintance.

He stood by the dance floor edge and thought of Mary.

How many times had they circled that tiny area, moving to the rhythms that pulsed from the glowing jukebox? Dancing slowly, their bodies intimately close, her warm hand idly stroking the back of his neck. How many times? Something tightened in his stomach. He could almost see her face again. He turned away quickly from the dance floor and looked at the dark wooden booths.

A forced smile raised his lips. Were they still there? He moved around the edge of a column and started for the back.

"You lookin' for somebody?" the old black man asked.

"No, no," he said. "I just want to look at something."

He moved down the rows of booths, trying to ignore the feeling of awkwardness. Which one is it? he asked himself. He couldn't remember; they all looked the same. He stopped, hands on hips, and looked at all the booths, shaking his head slowly. On the dance floor, the black man finished his polishing, pulled the plug out and drew the lumbering machine away. The place grew deathly still.

He found them in the third booth he looked at. Worn thin, the letters almost as dark as the surrounding wood but, most assuredly, there. He slid into the booth and looked at them.

B. J. Bill Johnson. And, under the initials, the year 1939.

He thought about all the nights he and Spence and Dave and Norm had sat in this booth dissecting the universe with the deft, assured scalpels of college seniors.

"We thought we had it all," he murmured. "Every darn bit of it."

Slowly, he took off his hat and set it down on the table. What he wished for now was a glass of the old beer: that thick, malty brew that filled your veins and pumped your heart, as Spence used to say.

He nodded his head in appreciation, toasting a quiet toast.

"To you," he whispered. "The unbeatable past."

As he said it, he looked up from the table and saw a young man standing far across the room at the shadowy foot of the stairway. Johnson looked at the young man, unable to see him sharply without his glasses on.

After a moment, the young man turned and went back up the stairs. Johnson smiled to himself. Come back at six, he thought. The place doesn't open till six.

That made him think again of all the nights he'd spent down here in the musty dimness, drinking beer, talking, dancing, spending his youth with the casual improvidence of a millionaire.

He sat silent in the semi-darkness, memories swirling about him like a restless tide, lapping at his mind, forcing him to keep his lips pressed together because he knew that all this was gone forever.

In the midst of it, the memory of her came again. Mary, he thought and he wondered what had ever become of Mary.

It started again as he walked under the archway that led to the campus. An uneasy feeling that past and present were blending, that he was tightrope-walking between the two of them, on the verge of falling into either one.

The feeling dogged his steps, chilling the sense of elation he felt at being back.

He'd look at a building, thinking of the classes he'd taken there, the people he'd known there. Then, almost in the same moment, he'd see his present life, the dull empty rounds of selling. The months and years of solitary driving around the country. Ending only in return to a home he disliked, a wife he did not love.

He kept thinking about Mary. What a fool he'd been to let her go. To think, with the thoughtless assurance of youth, that the world was replete with endless possibilities. He'd thought it a mistake to choose so early in life and embrace the present good. He'd been a great one for looking for greener pastures. He'd kept looking until all his pastures were brown with time.

That feeling again: a combination of sensations. A creeping dissatisfaction that gnawed at him and choked him—and a restless, pursued feeling. An inescapable urge to look over his shoulder and see who was following him. He couldn't dismiss it and it bothered and upset him.

Now he was walking along the east side of the campus, his suitcoat thrown over his right arm, his woven hat cocked back on his balding head. He could feel small sweat drops trickling down his back as he walked.

He wondered if he should stop and sit on the campus awhile. There were several students sprawled out under the trees, laughing and chatting.

But he was leery of speaking to students anymore. Just before he'd come onto the campus, he'd stopped at the Campus Cafe for a glass of iced tea. He'd sat next to a student there and tried to start a conversation.

The young man had treated him with insufferable deference. He hadn't said anything about it, of course, but it had been highly offensive.

Something else had happened too. While he was moving for the cashier's booth, a young man had walked by outside. Johnson had thought he knew him and had raised his arm to catch the student's attention.

Then he'd realized it was impossible that he knew any of the current students and he'd guiltily lowered his arm. He had paid his check, feeling very depressed.

The depression still clung to him as he walked up the steps of the Liberal Arts Building.

He turned at the head of the steps and looked back over the campus. In spite of deflated sentiment, it gave him a lift to see the campus still the same. It, at least, was unchanged and there was some sense of continuity in the world.

He smiled and turned, then turned again. *Was* there someone following him? The feeling was certainly strong enough. His worried gaze moved over the campus without seeing anything unusual. With an irritated shrug, he walked into the building.

It was still the same too and it made him feel good to walk on the dark tile floors again, beneath the ceiling murals, up the marble steps, through the soundproof, air-cooled halls.

He didn't notice the face of the student who walked by him even though their shoulders almost touched. He did seem to notice the student looking at him. But he wasn't sure and, when he looked over his shoulder, the student had turned a corner.

The afternoon passed slowly. He walked from building to building, entering each one religiously, looking at bulletin boards, glancing into classrooms and smiling carefully-timed smiles at everything.

But he was beginning to feel a desire to run away. He resented the fact that no one spoke to him. He thought of going to the alumni director and chatting with him but he decided against it. He didn't want to seem pretentious. He was just an ex-student quietly visiting the scenes of his college days. That was all. No point in making a show of it.

As he walked back to the room that evening after supper, he had the definite impression that someone was following him.

Yet, whenever he stopped with a suspicious frown and looked back, there was nothing. Only the sound of cars honking down on Broadway or the laughter of young men up in their rooms.

On the porch steps of the house he stopped and looked up the street, an uneasy chill running down his back. Probably perspired too much this afternoon, he thought. Now the cooling air was chilling him. After all, he wasn't as young as—

He shook his head, trying to rid his mind of the phrase. A man's as young as he feels, he told himself authoritatively and nodded once curtly to impress the fact on his mind.

The woman had left the front door unlocked. As he entered, he heard her talking on the telephone in Miss Smith's bedroom. Johnson nodded to himself. How many times had he spoken to Mary on that old phone? What was the number again? 4458.

That was it. He smiled proudly at being able to remember it.

How many times had he sat there in the old black rocker exchanging light conversation with her? His face fell. Where was she now? Was she married and did she have children? Did she—

He stopped, tensing, as a floor board creaked behind him. He waited a moment, expecting to hear the woman's voice. Then he looked back quickly.

The hallway was empty.

With a swallow, he entered his room and shut the door firmly. He fumbled for the light switch and finally found it.

He smiled again. This was more like it. He walked around his old room, running his hand over the top of the bureau, the student's desk, the mattress on the bed. He tossed down his hat and coat on the desk and settled down on the bed with a weary sigh. A grin lit his face as the old springs groaned. Same old springs, he thought.

He threw up his legs and fell back on the pillow. God, but it felt good. He ran his fingers over the bedspread, stroking it affectionately.

The house was very still. Johnson turned on his stomach and glanced out the window. There was the old alley, the big oak tree still towering over the house. He shook his head at the chest-filling sensation that thoughts of the past caused in him.

Then he started as the door thudded slightly in its frame. He looked quickly over his shoulder. *It's the wind does it*, the woman's words came to him.

He was certainly overwrought, he decided, but all these things were disturbing. Well, that was understandable. The day had been an emotional experience. To relive the past and regret the present was a full day's work for any man.

He was drowsy after the heavy meal he'd eaten at the Black

and Gold Inn. He pushed himself up and shuffled over to the light switch.

The room plunged into darkness and he felt his way cautiously back to the bed. He lay down with a satisfied grunt.

It was still a good old bed. How many nights had he slept there, his brain seething with the contents of books he'd been studying? He reached down and loosened his belt, pretending he didn't feel a twinge of remorse at the way his once slender body had thickened. He sighed as the pressure on his stomach was eased. Then he rolled on his side in the warm, airless room and closed his eyes.

He lay there for a few minutes listening to the sound of a car passing in the street. Then he rolled onto his back with a groan. He stretched out his legs, let them go slack. Then he sat up and, reaching down, untied his shoes and dropped them on the floor. He fell back on the pillow and turned on his side again with a sigh.

It came slowly.

At first he thought it was his stomach bothering him. Then he realized it wasn't just his stomach muscles but every muscle in his body. He felt bands of ligament drawing in and a shudder ran through his frame.

He opened his eyes and blinked in the darkness. What in God's name was wrong? He stared at the desk and saw the dark outline of his hat and coat. Again, he closed his eyes. He had to relax. There were some big customers coming up in Chicago.

It's *cold*, he thought irritably, fumbling around at his side and finally drawing the bedspread over his stout body. He felt his skin crawling. He found himself listening but there was no other sound than the harshness of his own breathing. He twisted uncomfortably, wondering how the room could have gotten so cold all of a sudden. He must have gotten a chill.

He rolled onto his back and opened his eyes.

In an instant, his body stiffened and all sound was paralyzed in his throat.

There, leaning over him, bare inches from him, was the whitest, the most hating face he had ever seen in his entire life.

He lay there, staring up in numb, open-mouthed horror at the face.

"Get out," said the face, its grating voice hoarse with malevolence. *"Get out. You can't come back."*

For a long time after the face had disappeared, Johnson lay there, barely able to breathe, his hands in rigid knots at his sides, his eyes wide and staring. He kept trying to think but the memory of the face and the words spoken petrified his mind.

He didn't stay. When strength had returned, he got up, and managed to sneak out without attracting the attention of the woman. He drove quickly from the town, his face pale, thinking only of what he'd seen.

Himself.

The face of himself when he was in college. His young self hating this coarsened interloper for intruding on what could never be his again. And the young man in the Golden Campus; that had been his younger self. The student passing the Campus Cafe had been himself as he once was. And the student in the hallway and the resentful presence that had followed him around the campus, hating him for coming back and pawing at the past—they had all been him.

He never went back and he never told anyone what had happened. And when, in rare moments, he spoke of his college days, it was always with a shrug and a cynical smile to show how little it had really meant to him.

The Distributor

Time to move.

He'd found a small, furnished house on Sylmar Street. The Saturday morning he moved in, he went around the neighborhood introducing himself.

"Good morning," he said to the old man pruning ivy next door. "My name is Theodore Gordon. I just moved in."

The old man straightened up and shook Theodore's hand. "How do," he said. His name was Joseph Alston.

A dog came shuffling from the porch to sniff Theodore's cuffs. "He's making up his mind about you," said the old man.

"Isn't that cute?" said Theodore.

Across the street lived Inez Ferrel. She answered the door in a housecoat, a thin woman in her late thirties. Theodore apologized for disturbing her.

"Oh, that's all right," she said. She had lots of time to herself when her husband was selling on the road.

"I hope we'll be good neighbors," said Theodore.

"I'm sure we will," said Inez Ferrel. She watched him through the window as he left.

Next door, directly across from his own house, he knocked quietly because there was a NIGHTWORKER SLEEPING sign. Dorothy Backus opened the door—a tiny, withdrawn woman in her middle thirties.

"I'm so glad to meet you," said Theodore.

Next door lived the Walter Mortons. As Theodore came up the walk, he heard Bianca Morton talking loudly to her son, Walter, Jr.

"You are not old enough to stay out till three o'clock in the morning!" she was saying. "Especially with a girl as young as Katherine McCann!"

Theodore knocked and Mr. Morton, fifty-two and bald, opened the door.

"I just moved in across the street," said Theodore, smiling at them.

Patty Jefferson let him in next door. As he talked to her Theodore could see, through the back window, her husband Arthur filling a rubber pool for their son and daughter.

"They just love that pool," said Patty, smiling.

"I bet they do," said Theodore. As he left, he noticed the vacant house next door.

Across the street from the Jeffersons lived the McCanns and their fourteen-year-old daughter Katherine. As Theodore approached the door he heard the voice of James McCann saying, "Aah, he's nuts. Why should I take his lawn edger? Just because I borrowed his lousy mower a couple of times."

"Darling, *please*," said Faye McCann. "I've got to finish these notes in time for the Council's next meeting."

"Just because Kathy goes out with his lousy son . . ." grumbled her husband.

Theodore knocked on the door and introduced himself. He chatted briefly with them, informing Mrs. McCann that he certainly would like to join the National Council for Christians and Jews. It was a worthy organization.

"What's your business, Gordon?" asked McCann.

"I'm in distribution," said Theodore.

Next door, two boys mowed and raked while their dog gamboled around them.

"Hello there," said Theodore. They grunted and watched him as he headed for the porch. The dog ignored him.

"I just *told* him." Henry Putnam's voice came through the living room window: "Put a coon in my department and I'm through. That's all."

"Yes, dear," said Mrs. Irma Putnam.

Theodore's knock was answered by the undershirted Mr. Putnam. His wife was lying on the sofa. Her heart, explained Mr. Putnam. "Oh, I'm sorry," Theodore said.

In the last house lived the Gorses.

"I just moved in next door," said Theodore. He shook Eleanor Gorse's lean hand and she told him that her father was at work.

"Is that him?" asked Theodore, pointing at the portrait of a stony-faced old man that hung above a mantel crowded with religious objects.

"Yes," said Eleanor, thirty-four and ugly.

"Well, I hope we'll be good neighbors," Theodore said.

That afternoon, he went to his new office and set up the darkroom.

JULY 23

That morning, before he left for the office, he checked the telephone directory and jotted down four numbers. He dialed the first.

"Would you please send a cab to 12057 Sylmar Street?" he said. "Thank you."

He dialed the second number. "Would you please send a repairman to my house," he said. "I don't get any picture. I live at 12070 Sylmar Street."

He dialed the third number: "I'd like to run this ad in Sunday's edition," he said. "1957 Ford. Perfect Condition. Seven-hundred eighty-nine dollars. That's right, seven-hundred eighty-nine. The number is DA-4-7408."

He made the fourth call and set up an afternoon appointment with Mr. Jeremiah Osborne. Then he stood by the living room window until the taxicab stopped in front of the Backus house.

As he was driving off, a television repair truck passed him. He looked back and saw it stop in front of Henry Putnam's house.

Dear sirs, he typed in the office later, *Please send me ten booklets for which I enclose one hundred dollars in payment.* He put down the name and address.

The envelope dropped into the OUT box.

JULY 27

When Inez Ferrel left her house that evening, Theodore followed in his car. Downtown, Mrs. Ferrel got off the bus and went into a bar called the Irish Lantern. Parking, Theodore entered the bar cautiously and slipped into a shadowy booth.

Inez Ferrel was at the back of the room perched on a bar stool. She'd taken off her jacket to reveal a clinging yellow sweater. Theodore ran his gaze across the studied exposition of her bust.

At length, a man accosted her and spoke and laughed and spent a modicum of time with her. Theodore watched them exit, arm in arm. Paying for his coffee, he followed. It was a short walk; Mrs. Ferrel and the man entered a hotel on the next block.

Theodore drove home, whistling.

The next morning, when Eleanor Gorse and her father had left with Mrs. Backus, Theodore followed.

He met them in the church lobby when the service was over. Wasn't it a wonderful coincidence, he said, that he, too, was a Baptist? And he shook the indurate hand of Donald Gorse.

As they walked into the sunshine, Theodore asked them if they wouldn't share his Sunday dinner with him. Mrs. Backus smiled faintly and murmured something about her husband. Donald Gorse looked doubtful.

"Oh, please," begged Theodore. "Make a lonely widower happy."

"Widower," tasted Mr. Gorse.

Theodore hung his head. "These many years," he said. "Pneumonia."

"Been a Baptist long?" asked Mr. Gorse.

"Since birth," said Theodore with fervor. "It's been my only solace."

For dinner he served lamb chops, peas, and baked potatoes. For dessert, apple cobbler and coffee.

"I'm so pleased you'd share my humble food," he said.

"This is, truly, loving thy neighbor as thyself." He smiled at Eleanor who returned it stiffly.

That evening, as darkness fell, Theodore took a stroll. As he passed the McCann house, he heard the telephone ringing, then James McCann shouting, "It's a *mistake*, damn it! Why in the lousy hell should I sell a '57 Ford for seven-hundred eighty-nine bucks!"

The phone slammed down. "God *damn!*" howled James McCann.

"Darling, please be *tolerant!*" begged his wife.

The telephone rang again.

Theodore moved on.

AUGUST 1

At exactly two-fifteen A.M. Theodore slipped outside, pulled up one of Joseph Alston's longest ivy plants and left it on the sidewalk.

In the morning, as he left the house, he saw Walter Morton, Jr., heading for the McCann house with a blanket, a towel and a portable radio. The old man was picking up his ivy.

"Was it pulled up?" asked Theodore.

Joseph Alston grunted.

"So *that* was it," said Theodore.

"What?" the old man looked up.

"Last night," said Theodore, "I heard some noise out here. I looked out and saw a couple of boys."

"You seen their faces?" asked Alston, his face hardening.

"No, it was too dark," said Theodore. "But I'd say they were—oh, about the age of the Putnam boys. Not that it was them, of course."

Joe Alston nodded slowly, looking up the street.

Theodore drove up to the boulevard and parked. Twenty minutes later, Walter Morton, Jr., and Katherine McCann boarded a bus.

At the beach, Theodore sat a few yards behind them.

"That Mack is a character," he heard Walter Morton say. "He gets the urge, he drives to Tijuana; just for kicks."

In a while Morton and the girl ran into the ocean, laughing. Theodore stood and walked to a telephone booth.

"I'd like to have a swimming pool installed in my backyard next week," he said. He gave the details.

Back on the beach he sat patiently until Walter Morton and the girl were lying in each other's arms. Then, at specific moments, he pressed a shutter hidden in his palm. This done, he returned to his car, buttoning his shirt front over the tiny lens. On his way to the office, he stopped at a hardware store to buy a brush and a can of black paint.

He spent the afternoon printing the pictures. He made them appear as if they had been taken at night and as if the young couple had been engaged in something else.

The envelope dropped softly into the OUT box.

AUGUST 5

The street was silent and deserted. Tennis shoes soundless on the paving, Theodore moved across the street.

He found the Morton's lawn mower in the backyard. Lifting it quietly, he carried it back across the street to the McCann garage. After carefully raising the door, he slid the mower behind the work bench. The envelope of photographs he put in a drawer behind a box of nails.

Returning to his house then, he phoned James McCann and, muffledly, asked if the Ford was still for sale.

In the morning, the mailman placed a bulky envelope on

the Gorses' porch. Eleanor Gorse emerged and opened it, sliding out one of the booklets. Theodore watched the furtive look she cast about, the rising of dark color in her cheeks.

As he was mowing the lawn that evening he saw Walter Morton, Sr., march across the street to where James McCann was trimming bushes. He heard them talking loudly. Finally, they went into McCann's garage from which Morton emerged pushing his lawn mower and making no reply to McCann's angry protests.

Across the street from McCann, Arthur Jefferson was just getting home from work. The two Putnam boys were riding their bicycles, their dog racing around them.

Now, across from where Theodore stood, a door slammed. He turned his head and watched Mr. Backus, in work clothes, storming to his car, muttering disgustedly, *"A swimming pool!"* Theodore looked to the next house and saw Inez Ferrel moving in her living room.

He smiled and mowed along the side of his house, glancing into Eleanor Gorse's bedroom. She was sitting with her back to him, reading something. When she heard the clatter of his mower she stood and left the bedroom, pushing the bulky envelope into a bureau drawer.

AUGUST 15

Henry Putnam answered the door.

"Good evening," said Theodore. "I hope I'm not intruding."

"Just chatting in the den with Irma's folks," said Putnam. "They're drivin' to New York in the mornin'."

"Oh? Well, I'll only be a moment." Theodore held out a pair of BB guns. "A plant I distribute for was getting rid of these," he said. "I thought your boys might like them."

"Well, *sure*," said Putnam. He started for the den to get his sons.

While the older man was gone, Theodore picked up a couple of matchbooks whose covers read *Putnam's Wines and Liquors*. He'd slipped them into his pocket before the boys were led in to thank him.

"Mighty nice of you, Gordon," said Putnam at the door. "Sure appreciate it."

"My pleasure," said Theodore.

Walking home, he set the clock-radio for three-fifteen and lay down. When the music began, he moved outside on silent feet and tore up forty-seven ivy plants, strewing them over Alston's sidewalk.

"Oh, *no*," he said to Alston in the morning. He shook his head, appalled.

Joseph Alston didn't speak. He glanced down the block with hating eyes.

"Here, let me help you," Theodore said. The old man shook his head but Theodore insisted. Driving to the nearest nursery he brought back two sacks of peat moss; then squatted by Alston's side to help him replant.

"You hear anything last night?" the old man asked.

"You think it was those boys again?" asked Theodore, open-mouthed.

"Ain't sayin'," Alston said.

Later, Theodore drove downtown and bought a dozen post-card photographs. He took them to the office.

Dear Walt, he printed crudely on the back of one, *Got these here in Tijuana. Hot enough for you?* In addressing the envelope, he failed to add *Jr.* to *Mr. Walter Morton.*

Into the OUT box.

AUGUST 23

"Mrs. Ferrel!"

She shuddered on the bar stool. "Why, Mister—"

"Gordon," he provided, smiling. "How nice to see you again."

"Yes." She pressed together lips that trembled.

"You come here often?" Theodore asked.

"Oh, no, *never*," Inez Ferrel blurted. "I'm—just supposed to meet a friend here tonight. A *girl* friend."

"Oh, I see," said Theodore. "Well, may a lonely widower keep you company until she comes?"

"Why . . ." Mrs. Ferrel shrugged. "I guess." Her lips were painted brightly red against the alabaster of her skin. The sweater clung adhesively to the hoisted jut of her breasts.

After a while, when Mrs. Ferrel's friend didn't show up, they slid into a darkened booth. There, Theodore used Mrs. Ferrel's powder room retreat to slip a pale and tasteless powder in her drink. On her return she swallowed this and, in minutes, grew stupefied. She smiled at Theodore.

"I like you Misser Gor'n," she confessed. The words crawled viscidly across her lolling tongue.

Shortly thereafter, he led her, stumbling and giggling, to his car and drove her to a motel. Inside the room, he helped her strip to stockings, garter belt and shoes and, while she posed with drugged complacency, Theodore took flashbulb pictures.

After she'd collapsed at two A.M. Theodore dressed her and

drove her home. He stretched her fully dressed across her bed. After that he went outside and poured concentrated weed killer on Alston's replanted ivy.

Back in the house he dialed the Jefferson's number.

"Yes," said Arthur Jefferson irritably.

"Get out of this neighborhood or you'll be sorry," whispered Theodore, then hung up.

In the morning he walked to Mrs. Ferrel's house and rang the bell.

"Hello," he said politely. "Are you feeling better?"

She stared at him blankly while he explained how she'd gotten violently ill the night before and he'd taken her home from the bar. "I do hope you're feeling better," he concluded.

"Yes," she said, confusedly, "I'm—all right."

As he left her house he saw a red-faced James McCann approaching the Morton house, an envelope in his hand. Beside him walked a distraught Mrs. McCann.

"We must be *tolerant*, Jim," Theodore heard her say.

AUGUST 3 I

At two-fifteen A.M. Theodore took the brush and the can of paint and went outside.

Walking to the Jefferson house he set the can down and painted, jaggedly, across the door—NIGGER!

Then he moved across the street allowing an occasional drip of paint. He left the can under Henry Putnam's back porch, accidentally upsetting the dog's plate. Fortunately, the Putnams' dog slept indoors.

Later, he put more weed killer on Joseph Alston's ivy.

In the morning, when Donald Gorse had gone to work, he

took a heavy envelope and went to see Eleanor Gorse. "Look at this," he said, sliding a pornographic booklet from the envelope. "I received this in the mail today. *Look* at it." He thrust it into her hands.

She held the booklet as if it were a spider.

"Isn't it hideous?" he said.

She made a face. *"Revolting,"* she said.

"I thought I'd check with you and several others before I phoned the police," said Theodore. "Have you received any of this filth?"

Eleanor Gorse bristled. "Why should I receive them?" she demanded.

Outside, Theodore found the old man squatting by his ivy. "How are they coming?" he asked.

"They're dyin'."

Theodore looked stricken. "How can this be?" he asked.

Alston shook his head.

"Oh, this is *horrible.*" Theodore turned away, clucking. As he walked to his house he saw, up the street, Arthur Jefferson cleaning off his door and, across the way, Henry Putnam watching carefully.

She was waiting on his porch.

"Mrs. McCann," said Theodore, surprised, "I'm so glad to see you."

"What I came to say may not make you so glad," she said unhappily.

"Oh?" said Theodore. They went into his house.

"There have been a lot of . . . *things* happening in this neighborhood since you moved in," said Mrs. McCann after they were seated in the living room.

"Things?" asked Theodore.

"I think you know what I mean," said Mrs. McCann.

"However, this—this *bigotry* on Mr. Jefferson's door is too much, Mr. Gordon, too much."

Theodore gestured helplessly. "I don't understand."

"Please don't make it difficult," she said. "I may have to call the authorities if these things don't stop, Mr. Gordon. I hate to think of doing such a thing but—"

"Authorities?" Theodore looked terrified.

"None of these things happened until you moved in, Mr. Gordon," she said. "Believe me, I hate what I'm saying but I simply have no choice. The fact that none of these things has happened to you—"

She broke off startledly as a sob wracked Theodore's chest. She stared at him. "Mr. Gordon—" she began uncertainly.

"I don't know what these things are you speak of," said Theodore in a shaking voice, "but I'd *kill* myself before I harmed another, Mrs. McCann."

He looked around as if to make sure they were alone.

"I'm going to tell you something I've never told a single soul," he said. He wiped away a tear. "My name isn't Gordon," he said. "It's Gottlieb. I'm a Jew. I spent a year at Dachau."

Mrs. McCann's lips moved but she said nothing. Her face was getting red.

"I came from there a broken man," said Theodore. "I haven't long to live, Mrs. McCann. My wife is dead, my three children are dead. I'm all alone. I only want to live in peace—in a little place like this—among people like you.

"To be a neighbor, a friend . . ."

"Mr.—*Gottlieb*," she said brokenly.

After she was gone, Theodore stood silent in the living room, hands clenched whitely at his sides. Then he went into the kitchen to discipline himself.

"Good morning, Mrs. Backus," he said an hour later when

the little woman answered the door, "I wonder if I might ask you some questions about our church?"

"Oh. Oh, yes." She stepped back feebly. "Won't you—come in?"

"I'll be very still so as not to wake your husband," Theodore whispered. He saw her looking at his bandaged hand. "I burned myself," he said. "Now, about the church. Oh, there's someone knocking at your back door."

"There is?"

When she'd gone into the kitchen, Theodore pulled open the hall closet door and dropped some photographs behind a pile of overshoes and garden tools. The door was shut when she returned.

"There wasn't anyone," she said.

"I could have sworn . . ." He smiled deprecatingly. He looked down at a circular bag on the floor. "Oh, does Mr. Backus bowl?"

"Wednesdays and Fridays when his shift is over," she said. "There's an all-night alley over on Western Avenue."

"I love to bowl," said Theodore.

He asked his questions about the church, then left. As he started down the path he heard loud voices from the Morton house.

"It wasn't bad enough about Katherine McCann and *those* awful pictures," shrieked Mrs. Morton. "Now this. . . . *filth!*"

"But, Mom!" cried Walter, Jr.

SEPTEMBER 14

Theodore awoke and turned the radio off. Standing, he put a small bottle of grayish powder in his pocket and slipped from the house. Reaching his destination, he sprinkled powder into the water bowl and stirred it with a finger until it dissolved.

Back in the house he scrawled four letters reading: *Arthur Jefferson is trying to pass the color line. He is my cousin and should admit he is black like the rest of us. I am doing this for his own good.*

He signed the letter *John Thomas Jefferson* and addressed three of the envelopes to Donald Gorse, the Mortons, and Mr. Henry Putnam.

This completed, he saw Mrs. Backus walking toward the boulevard and followed. "May I walk you?" he asked.

"Oh," she said. "All right."

"I missed your husband last night," he told her.

She glanced at him.

"I thought I'd join him bowling," Theodore said, "but I guess he was sick again."

"Sick?"

"I asked the man behind the counter at the alley and he said that Mr. Backus hadn't been coming in because he was sick."

"Oh," Mrs. Backus's voice was thinly stricken.

"Well, maybe next Friday," said Theodore.

Later, when he came back, he saw a panel truck in front of Henry Putnam's house. A man came out of the alley carrying a blanket-wrapped body which he laid in the truck. The Putnam boys were crying as they watched.

Arthur Jefferson answered the door. Theodore showed the letter to Jefferson and his wife. "It came this morning," he said.

"This is *monstrous!*" said Jefferson, reading it.

"Of *course* it is," said Theodore.

While they were talking, Jefferson looked through the window at the Putnam house across the street.

SEPTEMBER 15

Pale morning mist engulfed Sylmar Street. Theodore moved through it silently. Under the back porch of the Jeffersons' house he set fire to a box of damp papers. As it began to smolder he walked across the yard and, with a single knife stroke, slashed apart the rubber pool. He heard it pulsing water on the grass as he left. In the alley he dropped a book of matches that read *Putnam's Wines and Liquors.*

A little after six that morning he woke to the howl of sirens and felt the small house tremble at the heavy trucks passing by. Turning on his side, he yawned, and mumbled, "Goody."

SEPTEMBER 17

It was a paste-complexioned Dorothy Backus who answered Theodore's knock.

"May I drive you to church?" asked Theodore.

"I—I don't believe I—I'm not . . . feeling too well," stumbled Mrs. Backus.

"Oh, I'm sorry," Theodore said. He saw the edges of some photographs protruding from her apron pocket.

As he left he saw the Mortons getting in their car, Bianca wordless, both Walters ill at ease. Up the street, a police car was parked in front of Arthur Jefferson's house.

Theodore went to church with Donald Gorse who said that Eleanor was feeling ill.

"I'm so sorry," Theodore said.

That afternoon, he spent a while at the Jefferson house helping clear away the charred debris of their back porch. When he saw the slashed rubber pool he drove immediately to a drug store and bought another one.

"But they love that pool," said Theodore, when Patty Jefferson protested. "You told me so yourself."

He winked at Arthur Jefferson but Jefferson was not communicative that afternoon.

SEPTEMBER 23

Early in the evening Theodore saw Alston's dog walking in the street. He got his BB gun and, from the bedroom window, soundlessly, fired. The dog nipped fiercely at its side and spun around. Then, whimpering, it started home.

Several minutes later, Theodore went outside and started pulling up the door to the garage. He saw the old man hurrying down his alley, the dog in his arms.

"What's wrong?" asked Theodore.

"Don't know," said Alston in a breathless, frightened voice. "He's hurt."

"Quickly!" said Theodore. "Into my car!"

He rushed Alston and the dog to the nearest veterinary, passing three stop signs and groaning when the old man held his hand up, palsiedly, and whimpered, *"Blood!"*

For three hours Theodore sat in the veterinary's waiting room until the old man staggered forth, his face a grayish white.

"No," said Theodore, jumping to his feet.

He led the old man, weeping, to the car and drove him home. There, Alston said he'd rather be alone so Theodore left. Shortly afterward, the black and white police car rolled to a stop in front of Alston's house and the old man led the two officers past Theodore's house.

In a while, Theodore heard angry shouting up the street. It lasted quite a long time.

SEPTEMBER 27

"Good evening," said Theodore. He bowed.

Eleanor Gorse nodded stiffly.

"I've brought you and your father a casserole," said Theodore, smiling, holding up a towel-wrapped dish. When she told him that her father was gone for the night, Theodore clucked and sighed as if he hadn't seen the old man drive away that afternoon.

"Well then," he said, proffering the dish, "for *you*. With my sincerest compliments."

Stepping off the porch he saw Arthur Jefferson and Henry Putnam standing under a street lamp down the block. While he watched, Arthur Jefferson struck the other man and, suddenly, they were brawling in the gutter. Theodore broke into a hurried run.

"But this is *terrible!*" he gasped, pulling the men apart.

"Stay out of this!" warned Jefferson, then, to Putnam, challenged, "You better tell me how that paint can got under your porch! The police may believe it was an accident I found that matchbook in my alley but I don't!"

"I'll tell you nothing," Putnam said, contemptuously. "*Coon.*"

"Coon! Oh, of course! You'd be the first to believe that, you stupid—!"

Five times Theodore stood between them. It wasn't until Jefferson had, accidentally, struck him on the nose that tension faded. Curtly, Jefferson apologized; then, with a murderous look at Putnam, left.

"Sorry he hit you," Putnam sympathized. "Damned nigger."

"Oh, surely you're mistaken," Theodore said, daubing at his nostrils. "Mr. Jefferson told me how afraid he was of people believing this talk. Because of the value of his two houses, you know."

"Two?" asked Putnam.

"Yes, he owns the vacant house next door to his," said Theodore. "I assumed you knew."

"No," said Putnam warily.

"Well, you see," said Theodore, "if people think Mr. Jefferson is a Negro, the value of his houses will go down."

"So will the values of all of them," said Putnam, glaring across the street. "That dirty, son-of-a—"

Theodore patted his shoulder. "How are your wife's parents enjoying their stay in New York?" he asked as if changing the subject.

"They're on their way back," said Putnam.

"Good," said Theodore.

He went home and read the funny papers for an hour. Then he went out.

It was a florid-faced Eleanor Gorse who opened to his knock. Her bathrobe was disarrayed, her dark eyes feverish.

"May I get my dish?" asked Theodore politely.

She grunted, stepping back jerkily. His hand, in passing, brushed on hers. She twitched away as if he'd stabbed her.

"Ah, you've eaten it all," said Theodore, noticing the tiny residue of powder on the bottom of the dish. He turned. "When will your father return?" he asked.

Her body seemed to tense. "After midnight," she muttered.

Theodore stepped to the wall switch and cut off the light. He heard her gasp in the darkness. "No," she muttered.

"Is this what you want, Eleanor?" he asked, grabbing harshly.

Her embrace was a mindless, fiery swallow. There was nothing but ovening flesh beneath her robe.

Later, when she lay snoring satedly on the kitchen floor, Theodore retrieved the camera he'd left outside the door. Drawing down the shades, he arranged Eleanor's limbs and took twelve exposures. Then he went home and washed the dish.

Before retiring, he dialed the phone.

"Western Union," he said. "I have a message for Mrs. Irma Putnam of 12070 Sylmar Street."

"That's me," she said.

"Both parents killed in auto collision this afternoon," said Theodore. "Await word regarding disposition of bodies. Chief of Police, Tulsa, Okla—"

At the other end of the line there was a strangled gasp, a thud; then Henry Putnam's cry of "Irma!" Theodore hung up.

After the ambulance had come and gone, he went outside and tore up thirty-five of Joseph Alston's ivy plants. He left, in the debris, another matchbook reading *Putnam's Wines and Liquors.*

SEPTEMBER 28

In the morning, when Donald Gorse had gone to work, Theodore went over. Eleanor tried to shut the door on him but he pushed in.

"I want money," he said. "These are my collateral." He threw down copies of the photographs and Eleanor recoiled, gagging. "Your father will receive a set of these tonight," he said, "unless I get two hundred dollars."

"But I—!"

"Tonight."

He left and drove downtown to the Jeremiah Osborne Realty office where he signed over, to Mr. George Jackson, the vacant house at 12069 Sylmar Street. He shook Mr. Jackson's hand.

"Don't you worry now," he comforted. "The people next door are black too."

When he returned home, there was a police car in front of the Backus house.

"What happened?" he asked Joseph Alston who was sitting quietly on his porch.

"Mrs. Backus," said the old man lifelessly. "She tried to kill Mrs. Ferrel."

"Is that right?" said Theodore.

That night, in his office, he made his entries on page 700 of the book.

Mrs. Ferrel dying of knife wounds in local hospital. Mrs. Backus in jail; suspects husband of adultery. J. Alston accused of dog poisoning, probably more. Putnam boys accused of shooting Alston's dog, ruining his lawn. Mrs. Putnam dead of heart attack. Mr. Putnam being sued for property destruction. Jeffersons thought to be black. McCanns and Mortons deadly enemies. Katherine McCann believed to have had relations with Walter Morton, Jr. Morton, Jr. being sent to school in Washington. Eleanor Gorse has hanged herself. Job completed.

Time to move.

Crickets

After supper, they walked down to the lake and looked at its moon-reflecting surface.

"Pretty, isn't it?" she said.

"Mmm-hmm."

"It's been a nice vacation."

"Yes, it has," he said.

Behind them, the screen door on the hotel porch opened and shut. Someone started down the gravel path towards the lake. Jean glanced over her shoulder.

"Who is it?" asked Hal without turning.

"That man we saw in the dining room," she said.

In a few moments, the man stood nearby on the shoreline. He didn't speak or look at them. He stared across the lake at the distant woods.

"Should we talk to him?" whispered Jean.

"I don't know," he whispered back.

They looked at the lake again and Hal's arm slipped around her waist.

Suddenly the man asked:

"Do you hear them?"

"Sir?" said Hal.

The small man turned and looked at them. His eyes appeared to glitter in the moonlight.

"I asked if you heard them," he said.

There was a brief pause before Hal asked, "Who?"

"The crickets."

The two of them stood quietly. Then Jean cleared her throat. "Yes, they're nice," she said.

"*Nice?*" The man turned away. After a moment, he turned back and came walking over to them.

"My name is John Morgan," he said.

"Hal and Jean Galloway," Hal told him and then there was an awkward silence.

"It's a lovely night," Jean offered.

"It would be if it weren't for them," said Mr. Morgan. "The crickets."

"Why don't you like them?" asked Jean.

Mr. Morgan seemed to listen for a moment, his face rigid. His gaunt throat moved. Then he forced a smile.

"Allow me the pleasure of buying you a glass of wine," he said.

"Well—" Hal began.

"Please." There was a sudden urgency in Mr. Morgan's voice.

The dining hall was like a vast shadowy cavern. The only light came from the small lamp on their table which cast up formless shadows of them on the walls.

"Your health," said Mr. Morgan, raising his glass.

The wine was dry and tart. It trickled in chilly drops down Jean's throat, making her shiver.

"So what about the crickets?" asked Hal.

Mr. Morgan put his glass down.

"I don't know whether I should tell you," he said. He looked at them carefully. Jean felt restive under his surveillance and reached out to take a sip from her glass.

Suddenly, with a movement so brusque that it made her hand twitch and spill some wine, Mr. Morgan drew a small, black notebook from his coat pocket. He put it on the table carefully.

"There," he said.

"What is it?" asked Hal.

"A code book," said Mr. Morgan.

They watched him pour more wine into his glass, then set down the bottle and the bottle's shadow on the table cloth. He picked up the glass and rolled its stem between his fingers.

"It's the code of the crickets," he said.

Jean shuddered. She didn't know why. There was nothing terrible about the words. It was the way Mr. Morgan had spoken them.

Mr. Morgan leaned forward, his eyes glowing in the lamp-light.

"Listen," he said. "They aren't just making indiscriminate noises when they rub their wings together." He paused. *"They're sending messages,"* he said.

Jean felt as if she were a block of wood. The room seemed to shift balance around her, everything leaning towards her.

"Why are you telling us?" asked Hal.

"Because now I'm sure," said Mr. Morgan. He leaned in close. "Have you ever really listened to the crickets?" he asked. "I mean really? If you had you'd have heard a rhythm to their noises. A pace—a definite beat.

"I've listened," he said. "For seven years I've listened. And the more I listened the more I became convinced that their noise was a code; that they were sending messages in the night.

"Then—about a week ago—I suddenly heard the pattern. It's like a Morse code only, of course, the sounds are different."

Mr. Morgan stopped talking and looked at his black notebook.

"And there it is," he said. "After seven years of work, here it is. I've deciphered it."

His throat worked convulsively as he picked up his glass and emptied it with a swallow.

"Well—what are they saying?" Hal asked, awkwardly.

Mr. Morgan looked at him.

"Names," he said. "Look, I'll show you."

He reached into one of his pockets and drew out a stubby pencil. Tearing a blank page from his notebook, he started to write on it, muttering to himself.

"Pulse, pulse—silence—pulse, pulsepulse—silence—pulse—silence—"

Hal and Jean looked at each other. Hal tried to smile but couldn't. Then they were looking back at the small man bent over the table, listening to the crickets and writing.

Mr. Morgan put down the pencil. "It will give you some idea," he said, holding out the sheet to them. They looked at it.

MARIE CADMAN, it read. JOHN JOSEPH ALSTER. SAMUEL—

"You see," said Mr. Morgan. "Names."

"Whose?" Jean had to ask it even though she didn't want to.

Mr. Morgan held the book in a clenching hand.

"The names of the dead," he answered.

L ater that night, Jean climbed into bed with Hal and pressed close to him. "I'm cold," she murmured.

"You're scared."

"Aren't you?"

"Well," he said, "if I am, it isn't in the way you think."

"How's that?"

"I don't believe what he said. But he might be a dangerous man. That's what I'm afraid of."

"Where'd he get those names?"

"Maybe they're friends of his," he said. "Maybe he got them from tombstones. He might have just made them up." He grunted softly. "But I don't think the crickets told him," he said.

Jean snuggled against him.

"I'm glad you told him we were tired," she said. "I don't think I could have taken much more."

"Honey," he said, "here that nice little man was giving us the lowdown on crickets and you disparage him."

"Hal," she said, "I'll never be able to enjoy crickets for the rest of my life."

They lay close to each other and slept. And, outside in the still darkness, crickets rubbed their wings together until morning came.

Mr. Morgan came rapidly across the dining room and sat down at their table.

"I've been looking for you all day," he said. "You've got to help me."

Hal's mouth tightened. "Help you how?" he asked, putting down his fork.

"They know I'm on to them," said Mr. Morgan. "They're after me."

"Who, the crickets?" Hal asked, jadedly.

"I don't know," said Mr. Morgan. "Either them or—"

Jean held her knife and fork with rigid fingers. For some reason, she felt a chill creeping up her legs.

"Mr. Morgan." Hal was trying to sound patient.

"Understand me," Mr. Morgan pleaded. "The crickets are under the command of the dead. The dead send out these messages."

"Why?"

"They're compiling a list of all their names," said Mr. Morgan. "They keep sending the names through the crickets to let the others know."

"Why?" repeated Hal.

Mr. Morgan's hands trembled. "I don't know, I don't know," he said. "Maybe when there are enough names, when enough of them are ready, they'll—" His throat moved convulsively. *"They'll come back,"* he said.

After a moment, Hal asked, "What makes you think you're in any danger?"

"Because while I was writing down more names last night," said Mr. Morgan, *"they spelled out my name."*

Hal broke the heavy silence.

"What can we do?" he asked in a voice that bordered on uneasiness.

"Stay with me," said Mr. Morgan, "so they can't get me."

Jean looked nervously at Hal.

"I won't bother you," said Mr. Morgan. "I won't even sit here, I'll sit across the room. Just so I can see you."

He stood up quickly and took out his notebook.

"Will you watch this?" he asked.

Before they could say another word, he left their table and walked across the dining room, weaving in and out among the white-clothed tables. About fifty feet from them, he sat down, facing them. They saw him reach forward and turn on the table lamp.

"What do we do now?" asked Jean.

"We'll stay here a little while," said Hal. "Nurse the bottle along. When it's empty, we'll go to bed."

"Do we have to stay?"

"Honey, who knows what's going on in that mind of his? I don't want to take any chances."

Jean closed her eyes and exhaled wearily. "What a way to polish off a vacation," she said.

Hal reached over and picked up the notebook. As he did, he became conscious of the crickets rasping outside. He flipped through the pages. They were arranged in alphabetical order, on each page three letters with their pulse equivalents.

"He's watching us," said Jean.

"Forget him."

Jean leaned over and looked at the notebook with him. Her eyes moved over the arrangements of dots and dashes.

"You think there's anything to this?" she asked.

"Let's hope not," said Hal.

He tried to listen to the crickets' noise and find some point of comparison with the notes. He couldn't. After several minutes, he shut the book.

When the wine bottle was empty, Hal stood. "Beddy-bye," he said.

Before Jean was on her feet, Mr. Morgan was halfway to their table. "You're leaving?" he asked.

"Mr. Morgan, it's almost eleven," Hal said. "We're tired. I'm sorry but we have to go to bed."

The small man stood wordless, looking from one to the other with pleading, hopeless eyes. He seemed about to speak, then his narrow shoulders slumped and his gaze dropped to the floor. They heard him swallowing.

"You'll take care of the book?" he asked.

"Don't you want it?"

"No." Mr. Morgan turned away. After a few paces, he stopped and glanced back across his shoulder. "Could you leave your door open so I can—call?"

"All right, Mr. Morgan," he said.

A faint smile twitched Mr. Morgan's lips.

"Thank you," he said and walked away.

It was after four when the screaming woke them. Hal felt Jean's fingers clutching at his arm as they both jolted to a sitting position, staring into the darkness.

"What is it?" gasped Jean.

"I don't know." Hal threw off the covers and dropped his feet to the floor.

"Don't leave me!" said Jean.

"Come on then!"

The hall had a dim bulb burning overhead. Hal sprinted over the floorboards towards Mr. Morgan's room. The door to it was closed although it had been left open before. Hal banged his fist on it. "Mr. Morgan!" he called.

Inside the room, there was a sudden, rustling, crackling sound—like that of a million, wildly shaken tambourines. The noise made Hal's hand jerk back convulsively from the door knob.

"What's *that*?" Jean asked in a terrified whisper.

He didn't answer. They stood immobile, not knowing what to do. Then, inside, the noise stopped. Hal took a deep breath and pushed open the door.

The scream gagged in Jean's throat.

Lying in a pool of blood-splotched moonlight was Mr. Morgan, his skin raked open as if by a thousand tiny razor blades. There was a gaping hole in the window screen.

Jean stood paralyzed, a fist pressed against her mouth while Hal moved to Mr. Morgan's side. He knelt down beside the motionless man and felt at Mr. Morgan's chest where the pajama top had been sliced to ribbons. The faintest of heartbeats pulsed beneath his trembling fingers.

Mr. Morgan opened his eyes. Wide, staring eyes that recognized nothing, that looked right through Hal.

"P-H-I-L-I-P M-A-X-W-E-L-L." Mr. Morgan spelled out the name in a bubbling voice.

"M-A-R-Y G-A-B-R-I-E-L," spelled Mr. Morgan, eyes stark and glazed.

His chest lurched once. His eyes widened.

"J-O-H-N M-O-R-G-A-N," he spelled.

Then his eyes began focusing on Hal. There was a terrible rattling in his throat. As though the sounds were wrenched from him one by one by a power beyond his own, he spoke again.

"H-A-R-O-L-D G-A-L-L-O-W-A-Y," he spelled, "J-E-A-N G-A-L-L-O-W-A-Y."

Then they were alone with a dead man. And outside in the night, a million crickets rubbed their wings together.

First Anniversary

Just before he left the house on Thursday morning, Adeline asked him, "Do I still taste sour to you?"

Norman looked at her reproachfully.

"Well, do I?"

He slipped his arms around her waist and nibbled at her throat.

"Tell me now," said Adeline.

Norman looked submissive.

"Aren't you going to let me live it down?" he asked.

"Well, you *said* it, darling. And on our first anniversary too!"

He pressed his cheek to hers. "So I said it," he murmured. "Can't I be allowed a faux pas now and then?"

"You haven't answered me."

"Do you taste sour? Of course you don't." He held her close and breathed the fragrance of her hair. "Forgiven?"

She kissed the tip of his nose and smiled and, once more, he could only marvel at the fortune which had bestowed on him such a magnificent wife. Starting their second year of marriage, they were still like honeymooners.

Norman raised her face and kissed her.

"Be damned," he said.

"What's wrong? Am I sour again?"

"No." He looked confused. "Now I can't taste you at all."

Now you can't taste her at all," said Dr. Phillips.

Norman smiled. "I know it sounds ridiculous," he said.

"Well, it's unique, I'll give it that," said Phillips.

"More than you think," added Norman, his smile grown a trifle labored.

"How so?"

"I have no trouble tasting anything else."

Dr. Phillips peered at him awhile before he spoke. "Can you smell her?" he asked then.

"Yes."

"You're sure."

"*Yes*. What's that got to do with—" Norman stopped. "You mean that the senses of taste and smell go together," he said.

Phillips nodded. "If you can smell her, you should be able to taste her."

"I suppose," said Norman, "but I can't."

Dr. Phillips grunted wryly. "Quite a poser."

"No ideas?" asked Norman.

"Not offhand," said Phillips, "though I suspect it's allergy of some kind."

Norman looked disturbed.

"I hope I find out soon," he said.

Adeline looked up from her stirring as he came into the kitchen. "What did Dr. Phillips say?"

"That I'm allergic to you."

"He didn't say that," she scolded.

"Sure he did."

"Be serious now."

"He said I have to take some allergy tests."

"He doesn't think it's anything to worry about, does he?" asked Adeline.

"No."

"Oh, good." She looked relieved.

"Good, nothing," he grumbled. "The taste of you is one of the few pleasures I have in life."

"You stop that." She removed his hands and went on stirring. Norman slid his arm around her and rubbed his nose on the back of her neck. "Wish I could taste you," he said. "I like your flavor."

She reached up and caressed his cheek. "I love you," she said.

Norman twitched and made a startled noise.

"What's wrong?" she asked.

He sniffed. "What's that?" He looked around the kitchen. "Is the garbage out?" he asked.

She answered quietly. "Yes, Norman."

"Well, something sure as hell smells awful in here. Maybe—" He broke off, seeing the expression on her face. She pressed her lips together and, suddenly, it dawned on him. "Honey, you don't think I'm saying—"

"Well, *aren't* you?" Her voice was faint and trembling.

"Adeline, come on."

"First, I taste sour. Now—"

He stopped her with a lingering kiss.

"I love you," he said, "understand? I *love* you. Do you think I'd try to hurt you?"

She shivered in his arms. "You *do* hurt me," she whispered.

He held her close and stroked her hair. He kissed her gently on the lips, the cheeks, the eyes. He told her again and again how much he loved her.

He tried to ignore the smell.

nstantly, his eyes were open and he was listening. He stared up sightlessly into the darkness. Why had he woken up? He turned his head and reached across the mattress. As he touched her, Adeline stirred a little in her sleep.

Norman twisted over on his side and wriggled close to her. He pressed against the yielding warmth of her body, his hand slipping languidly across her hip. He lay his cheek against her back and started drifting downward into sleep again.

Suddenly, his eyes flared open. Aghast, he put his nostrils to her skin and sniffed. An icy barb of dread hooked at his brain; *my God, what's wrong?* He sniffed again, harder. He lay against her, motionless, trying not to panic.

If his senses of taste and smell were atrophying, he could understand, accept. They weren't, though. Even as he lay there, he could taste the acrid flavor of the coffee that he'd drunk that night. He could smell the faint odor of mashed-out cigarettes in the ashtray on his bedside table. With the least effort, he could smell the wool of the blanket over them.

Then *why*? She was the most important thing in his life. It was torture to him that, in bits and pieces, she was fading from his senses.

t had been a favorite restaurant since their days of courtship. They liked the food, the tranquil atmosphere, the small ensemble which played for dining and for dancing. Searching in his mind, Norman had chosen it as the place where they could best discuss this problem. Already, he was sorry that he had. There was no atmosphere that could relieve the tension he was feeling; and expressing.

"What *else* can it be?" he asked, unhappily. "It's nothing physical." He pushed aside his untouched supper. "It's got to be my mind."

"But why, Norman?"

"If I only knew," he answered.

She put her hand on his. "Please don't worry," she said.

"How can I help it?" he asked. "It's a nightmare. I've *lost* part of you, Adeline."

"Darling, don't," she begged, "I can't bear to see you un-happy."

"I *am* unhappy," he said. He rubbed a finger on the table-cloth. "And I've just about made up my mind to see an analyst." He looked up. "It's got to be my mind," he repeated. "And—damnit!—I resent it. I want to root it out."

He forced a smile, seeing the fear in her eyes.

"Oh, the hell with it," he said. "I'll go to an analyst; he'll fix me up. Come on, let's dance."

She managed to return his smile.

"Lady, you're just plain gorgeous," he told her as they came together on the dance floor.

"Oh, I love you so," she whispered.

It was in the middle of their dance that the feel of her began to change.

Norman held her tightly, his cheek forced close to hers so that she wouldn't see the sickened expression on his face.

A nd now it's gone?" finished Dr. Bernstrom.

Norman expelled a burst of smoke and jabbed out his

cigarette in the ashtray. "Correct," he said, angrily.

"When?"

"This morning," answered Norman. The skin grew taut across his cheeks. "No taste. No smell." He shuddered fitfully. "And now no sense of touch."

His voice broke. "What's wrong?" he pleaded. "What kind of breakdown *is* this?"

"Not an incomprehensible one," said Bernstrom.

Norman looked at him anxiously. "What then?" he asked. "Remember what I said: it has to do only with my wife. Outside of her—"

"I understand," said Bernstrom.

"Then what is it?"

"You've heard of hysterical blindness."

"Yes."

"Hysterical deafness."

"Yes, but—"

"Is there any reason, then, there couldn't be an hysterical restraint of the other senses as well?"

"All right, but why?"

Dr. Bernstrom smiled.

"That, I presume," he said, "is why you came to see me."

Sooner or later, the notion had to come. No amount of love could stay it. It came now as he sat alone in the living room, staring at the blur of letters on a newspaper page.

Look at the facts. Last Wednesday night, he'd kissed her and, frowning, said, "You taste sour, honey." She'd tightened, drawn away. At the time, he'd taken her reaction at its obvious value: she felt insulted. Now, he tried to summon up a detailed memory of her behavior afterward.

Because, on Thursday morning, he'd been unable to taste her at all.

Norman glanced guiltily toward the kitchen where Adeline was cleaning up. Except for the sound of her occasional footsteps, the house was silent.

Look at the facts, his mind persisted. He leaned back in the chair and started to review them.

Next, on Saturday, had come that dankly fetid stench. Granted, she should feel resentment if he'd accused her of being its source. But he hadn't; he was sure of it. He'd looked around the kitchen, asked her if she'd put the garbage out. Yet, instantly, she'd assumed that he was talking about her.

And, that night, when he'd woken up, he couldn't smell her.

Norman closed his eyes. His mind must really be in trouble if he could justify such thoughts. He loved Adeline; needed her. How could he allow himself to believe that *she* was, in any way, responsible for what had happened?

Then, in the restaurant, his mind went on, unbidden, while they were dancing, she'd, suddenly, felt cold to him. She'd suddenly felt—he could not evade the word—*pulpy*.

And, then, this morning—

Norman flung aside the paper. *Stop it!* Trembling, he stared across the room with angry, frightened eyes. It's me, he told himself, *me*! He wasn't going to let his mind destroy the most beautiful thing in his life. He wasn't going to let—

It was as if he'd turned to stone, lips parted, eyes widened, blank. Then, slowly—so slowly that he heard the delicate crackling of bones in his neck—he turned to look toward the kitchen. Adeline was moving around.

Only it wasn't footsteps he heard.

He was barely conscious of his body as he stood. Compelled, he drifted from the living room and across the dining alcove, slippers noiseless on the carpeting. He stopped outside the kitchen door, his face a mask of something like revulsion as he listened to the sounds she made in moving.

Silence then. Bracing himself, he pushed open the door. Adeline was standing at the opened refrigerator. She turned and smiled.

"I was just about to bring you—" She stopped and looked at him uncertainly. "Norman?" she said.

He couldn't speak. He stood frozen in the doorway, staring at her.

"Norman, what is it?" she asked.

He shivered violently.

Adeline put down the dish of chocolate pudding and hurried toward him. He couldn't help himself; he shrank back with a tremulous cry, his face twisted, stricken.

"Norman, what's the matter?"

"I don't know," he whimpered.

Again, she started for him, halting at his cry of terror. Suddenly, her face grew hard as if with angry understanding.

"What is it now?" she asked. "I want to know."

He could only shake his head.

"I want to know, Norman!"

"No." Faintly, frightenedly.

She pressed trembling lips together. "I can't take much more of this," she said. "I mean it, Norman."

He jerked aside as she passed him. Twisting around, he watched her going up the stairs, his expression one of horror as he listened to the noises that she made. Jamming palsied hands across his ears, he stood shivering uncontrollably. *It's me!* he told himself again, again; until the words began to lose their meaning—*me, it's me, it's me, it's me!*

Upstairs, the bedroom door slammed shut. Norman lowered

his hands and moved unevenly to the stairs. She had to know that he loved her, that he wanted to believe it was his mind. She had to understand.

Opening the bedroom door, he felt his way through the darkness and sat on the bed. He heard her turn and knew that she was looking at him.

"I'm sorry," he said, "I'm . . . sick."

"No," she said. Her voice was lifeless.

Norman stared at her. "What?"

"There's no problem with other people, our friends, tradesmen . . ." she said. "They don't see me enough. With you, it's different. We're together too often. The strain of hiding it from you hour after hour, day after day, for a whole year, is too much for me. I've lost the power to control your mind. All I can do is—blank away your senses one by one."

"You're not—"

"—telling you those things are real? I am. They're real. The taste, the smell, the—and what you heard tonight."

He sat immobile, staring at the dark form of her.

"I should have taken all your senses when it started," she said. "It would have been easy then. Now it's too late."

"What are you talking about?" He could barely speak.

"It isn't fair!" cried her voice. "I've been a good wife to you! Why should I have to go back? I *won't* go back! I'll find somebody else. I won't make the same mistake next time!"

Norman jerked away from her and stood on wavering legs, his fingers clutching for the lamp.

"Don't touch it!" ordered the voice.

The light flared blindingly into his eyes. He heard a thrashing on the bed and whirled. He couldn't even scream. Sound coagulated in his throat as he watched the shapeless mass rear upward, dripping decay.

"All right!" the words exploded in his brain with the illusion of sound. "All right, then *know* me!"

All his senses flooded back at once. The air was clotted with the smell of her. Norman recoiled, lost balance, fell. He saw the moldering bulk rise from the bed and start for him. Then his mind was swallowed in consuming blackness and it seemed as if he fled along a night-swept hall pursued by a suppliant voice which kept repeating endlessly, "Please! I don't want to go back! *None of us want to go back!* Love me, let me stay with you! love me, love me, love me . . ."

The Likeness of Julie

Eddy Foster had never noticed the girl in his English class until that day.

It wasn't because she sat behind him. Any number of times, he'd glanced around while Professor Euston was writing on the blackboard or reading to them from *College Literature*. Any number of times, he'd seen her as he left or entered the classroom. Occasionally, he'd passed her in the hallways or on the campus. Once, she'd even touched him on the shoulder during class and handed him a pencil which had fallen from his pocket.

Still, he'd never noticed her the way he noticed other girls. First of all, she had no figure—or if she did she kept it hidden under loose-fitting clothes. Second, she wasn't pretty and she looked too young. Third, her voice was faint and high-pitched.

Which made it curious that he should notice her that day. All through class, he'd been thinking about the redhead in the first row. In the theater of his mind he'd staged her—and himself—through an endless carnal play. He was just raising the curtain on another act when he heard the voice behind him.

"Professor?" it asked.

"Yes, Miss Eldridge."

Eddy glanced across his shoulder as Miss Eldridge asked a question about *Beowulf*. He saw the plainness of her little girl's face, heard her faltering voice, noticed the loose yellow sweater she was wearing. And, as he watched, the thought came suddenly to him.

Take her.

Eddy turned back quickly, his heartbeat jolting as if he'd spoken the words aloud. He repressed a grin. What a screwy idea that was. Take *her*? With no figure? With that kid's face of hers?

That was when he realized it was her face which had given him the idea. The very childishness of it seemed to needle him perversely.

There was a noise behind him. Eddy glanced back. The girl had dropped her pen and was bending down to get it. Eddy felt a crawling tingle in his flesh as he saw the strain of her bust against the tautening sweater. Maybe she had a figure after all. That was more exciting yet. A child afraid to show her ripening body. The notion struck dark fire in Eddy's mind.

ldridge, Julie, read the year book. *St. Louis, Arts & Sciences*. As he'd expected, she belonged to no sorority or organizations. He looked at her photograph and she seemed to spring alive in his imaginations—shy, withdrawn, existing in a shell of warped repressions.

He had to have her.

Why? He asked himself the question endlessly but no logical answer ever came. Still, visions of her were never long out of his mind—the two of them locked in a cabin at the *Hiway Motel*, the wall heater crowding their lungs with oven air while they rioted in each other's flesh; he and this degraded innocent.

The bell had rung and, as the students left the classroom, Julie dropped her books.

"Here, let me pick them up," said Eddy.

"Oh." She stood motionless while he collected them. From the corners of his eyes, he saw the ivory smoothness of her legs. He shuddered and stood with the books.

"Here," he said.

"Thank you." Her eyes lowered and the faintest of color touched her cheeks. She wasn't so bad-looking, Eddy thought. And she did have a figure. Not much of one but a figure.

"What is it we're supposed to read for tomorrow?" he heard himself asking.

"The—'Wife of Bath's Tale,' isn't it?" she asked.

"Oh, is that it?" Ask her for a date, he thought.

"Yes. I think so."

He nodded. Ask her now, he thought.

"Well," said Julie. She began to turn away.

Eddy smiled remotely at her and felt his stomach muscles trembling.

"Be seeing you," he said.

He stood in the darkness staring at her window. Inside the room, the light went on as Julie came back from the bathroom. She wore a terrycloth robe and was carrying a towel, a washcloth, and a plastic soap box. Eddy watched her put the washcloth and soap box on her bureau and sit down on the bed.

He stood there rigidly, watching her with eyes that did not blink. What was he doing here? he thought. If anybody caught him, he'd be arrested. He had to leave.

Julie stood. She undid the sash at her waist and the bathrobe slipped to the floor. Eddy froze. He parted his lips, sucking at the damp air. She had the body of a woman—full-hipped with breasts that both jutted and hung. And with that pretty child's face—

Eddy felt hot breath forcing out between his lips. He muttered, *"Julie, Julie, Julie—"*

Julie turned away to dress.

The idea was insane. He knew it but he couldn't get away from it. No matter how he tried to think of something else, it kept returning.

He'd invite her to a drive-in movie, drug her Coke there, take her to the *Hiway Motel*. To guarantee his safety afterward, he'd take photographs of her and threaten to send them to her parents if she said anything.

The idea was insane. He knew it but he couldn't fight it. He had to do it now—now when she was still a stranger to him; an unknown female with a child's face and a woman's body. That was what he wanted; not an individual.

No! It was insane! He cut his English class twice in succession. He drove home for the weekend. He saw a lot of movies. He read magazines and took long walks. He could beat this thing.

Miss Eldridge?"

Julie stopped. As she turned to face him, the sun made

ripples on her hair. She looked very pretty, Eddy thought.

"Can I walk with you?" he asked.

"All right," she said.

They walked along the campus path.

"I was wondering," said Eddy, "if you'd like to go to the drive-in movie Friday night." He was startled at the calmness of his voice.

"Oh," said Julie. She glanced at him shyly. "What's playing?" she asked.

He told her.

"That sounds very nice," she said.

Eddy swallowed. "Good," he answered. "What time shall I pick you up?"

He wondered, later, if it made her curious that he didn't ask her where she lived.

There was a light burning on the porch of the house she roomed in. Eddy pushed the bell and waited, watching two moths flutter around the light. After several moments, Julie opened the door. She looked almost beautiful, he thought. He'd never seen her dressed so well.

"Hello," she said.

"Hi," he answered. "Ready to go?"

"I'll get my coat." She went down the hall and into her room. In there, she'd stood naked that night, her body glowing in the light. Eddy pressed his teeth together. He'd be all right. She'd never tell anyone when she saw the photographs he was going to take.

Julie came back down the hallway and they went out to the car. Eddy opened the door for her.

"Thank you," she murmured. As she sat down, Eddy caught

a glimpse of stockinged knees before she pulled her skirt down. He slammed the door and walked around the car. His throat felt parched.

Ten minutes later, he nosed the car onto an empty ramp in the last row of the drive-in theater and cut the engine. He reached outside and lifted the speaker off its pole and hooked it over the window. There was a cartoon playing.

"You want some popcorn and Coke?" he asked, feeling a sudden bolt of dread that she might say no.

"Yes. Thank you," Julie said.

"I'll be right back." Eddy pushed out of the car and started for the snack bar. His legs were shaking.

He waited in the milling crowd of students, seeing only his thoughts. Again and again, he shut the cabin door and locked it, pulled the shades down, turned on all the lights, switched on the wall heater. Again and again, he walked over to where Julie lay stupefied and helpless on the bed.

"Yours?" said the attendant.

Eddy started. "Uh—two popcorns and a large and a small Coke," he said.

He felt himself begin to shiver convulsively. He couldn't do it. He might go to jail the rest of his life. He paid the man mechanically and moved off with the cardboard tray. The photographs, you idiot, he thought. They're your protection. He felt angry desire shudder through his body. Nothing was going to stop him. On the way back to the car, he emptied the contents of the packet into the small Coke.

Julie was sitting quietly when he opened the door and slid back in. The feature had begun.

"Here's your Coke," he said. He handed her the small cup with her box of popcorn.

"Thank you," said Julie.

Eddy sat watching the picture. He felt his heart thud slowly like a beaten drum. He felt bugs of perspiration running down his back and sides. The popcorn was dry and tasteless. He kept drinking Coke to wet his throat. Soon now, he thought. He pressed his lips together and stared at the screen. He heard Julie eating popcorn, he heard her drinking Coke.

The thoughts were coming faster now: the door locked, the shades drawn, the room a bright-lit oven as they twisted on the bed together. Now they were doing things that Eddy almost never thought of—wild, demented things. It was her face, he thought; that damned angel's face of hers. It made the mind seek out every black avenue it could find.

Eddy glanced over at Julie. He felt his hands retract so suddenly that he spilled Coke on his trousers. Her empty cup had fallen on the floor, the box of popcorn turned over on her lap. Her head was lying on the seat back and, for one hideous moment, Eddy thought she was dead.

Then she inhaled raspingly and turned her head towards him. He saw her tongue move, dark and sluggish, on her lips.

Suddenly, he was deadly calm again. He picked the speaker off the window and hung it up outside. He threw out the cups and boxes. He started the engine and backed out into the aisle. He turned on his parking lights and drove out of the theater.

Hiway Motel. The sign blinked off and on a quarter of a mile away. For a second, Eddy thought he read *No Vacancy* and he made a frightened sound. Then he saw that he was wrong. He was still trembling as he circled the car around the drive and parked to one side of the office.

Bracing himself, he went inside and rang the bell. He was very calm and the man didn't say a word to him. He had Eddy fill out the registration card and gave him the key.

Eddy pulled his car into the breezeway beside the cabin. He

put his camera in the room, then went out and looked around. There was no one in sight. He ran to the car and opened the door. He carried Julie to the cabin door, his shoes crunching quickly on the gravel. He carried her into the dark room and dropped her on the bed.

Then it was his dream coming true. The door was locked. He moved around the room on quivering legs, pulling down the shades. He turned on the wall heater. He found the light switch by the door and pushed it up. He turned on all the lamps and pulled their shades off. He dropped one of them and it rolled across the rug. He left it there. He went over to where Julie lay.

In falling to the bed, her skirt had pulled up to her thighs. He could see the tops of her stockings and the garter buttons fastened to them. Swallowing, Eddy sat down and drew her up into a sitting position. He took her sweater off. Shakily, he reached around her and unhooked her bra; her breasts slipped free. Quickly, he unzipped her skirt and pulled it down.

In seconds, she was naked. Eddy propped her against the pillows, posing her. *Dear God, the body on her.* Eddy closed his eyes and shuddered. *No,* he thought, this is the important part. First get the photographs and you'll be safe. She can't do anything to you then; she'll be too scared. He stood up, tensely, and got his camera. He set the dials. He got her centered on the viewer. Then he spoke.

"Open your eyes," he said.

Julie did.

He was at her house before six the next morning, moving up the alley cautiously and into the yard outside her window. He hadn't slept all night. His eyes felt dry and hot.

Julie was on her bed exactly as he'd placed her. He looked

at her a moment, his heartbeat slow and heavy. Then he raked a nail across the screen. "Julie," he said.

She murmured indistinctly and turned onto her side. She faced him now.

"Julie."

Her eyes fluttered open. She stared at him dazedly. "Who's that?" she asked.

"Eddy. Let me in."

"Eddy?"

Suddenly, she caught her breath and shrank back and he knew that she remembered.

"Let me in or you're in trouble," he muttered. He could feel his legs begin to shake.

Julie lay motionless a few seconds, eyes fixed on his. Then she pushed to her feet and weaved unsteadily towards the door. Eddy turned for the alley. He strode down it nervously and started up the porch steps as she came outside.

"What do you want?" she whispered. She looked exciting, half asleep, her clothes and hair all mussed.

"Inside," he said.

Julie stiffened. "No."

"All right, come on," he said, taking her hand roughly. "We'll talk in my car."

She walked with him to the car and, as he slid in beside her, he saw that she was shivering.

"I'll turn on the heater," he said. It sounded stupidly inane. He was here to threaten her, not comfort. Angrily, he started the engine and drove away from the curb.

"Where are we going?" Julie asked.

He didn't know at first. Then, suddenly, he thought of the place outside of town where dating students always parked. It would be deserted at this hour. Eddy felt a swollen tingling in his body and he pressed down on the accelerator. Sixteen minutes later, the car was standing in the silent woods. A pale mist hung across the ground and seemed to lap at the doors.

Julie wasn't shivering now; the inside of the car was hot.

"What is it?" she asked, faintly.

Impulsively, Eddy reached into his inside coat pocket and pulled out the photographs. He threw them on her lap.

Julie didn't make a sound. She just stared down at the photographs with frozen eyes, her fingers twitching as she held them.

"Just in c-ase you're thinking of calling the police," Eddy faltered. He clenched his teeth. *Tell her!* he thought savagely. In a dull, harsh voice, he told her everything he'd done the night before. Julie's face grew pale and rigid as she listened. Her hands pressed tautly at each other. Outside, the mist appeared to rise around the windows like a chalky fluid. It surrounded them.

"You want money?" Julie whispered.

"Take off your clothes," he said. It wasn't his voice, it occurred to him. The sound of it was too malignant, too inhuman.

Then Julie whimpered and Eddy felt a surge of blinding fury boil upward in him. He jerked his hand back, saw it flail out in a blur of movement, heard the sound of it striking her on the mouth, felt the sting across his knuckles.

"Take them off!" His voice was deafening in the stifling closeness of the car. Eddy blinked and gasped for breath. He stared dizzily at Julie as, sobbing, she began to take her clothes off. There was a thread of blood trickling from a corner of her mouth. *No, don't*, he heard a voice beg in his mind. *Don't do this.* It faded quickly as he reached for her with alien hands.

When he got home at ten that morning there was blood and skin under his nails. The sight of it made him violently ill. He lay trembling on his bed, lips quivering, eyes staring at the ceiling. I'm through, he thought. He had the photographs. He didn't have to see her any more. It would destroy him if he saw her any more. Already, his brain felt like rotting sponge, so bloated with corruption that the pressure of his skull caused endless overflow into his thoughts. Trying to sleep, he thought, instead, about the bruises on her lovely body, the ragged scratches, and the bite marks. He heard her screaming in his mind.

He would not see her any more.

DECEMBER

Julie opened her eyes and saw tiny falling shadows on the wall. She turned her head and looked out through the window. It was beginning to snow. The whiteness of it reminded her of the morning Eddy had first shown her the photographs.

The photographs. That was what had woken her. She closed her eyes and concentrated. They were burning. She could see the prints and negatives scattered on the bottom of a large enamel pan—the kind used for developing film. Bright flames crackled on them and the enamel was smudging.

Julie held her breath. She pushed her mental gaze further— to scan the room that was lit by the flaming enamel pan—until it came to rest upon the broken thing that dangled and swayed, suspended from the closet hook.

She sighed. It hadn't lasted very long. That was the trouble with a mind like Eddy's. The very weakness which made it vulnerable to her soon broke it down. Julie opened her eyes, her ugly child's face puckered in a smile. Well, there were others.

She stretched her scrawny body languidly. Posing at the window, the drugged Coke, the motel photographs—these were

getting dull by now although that place in the woods was wonderful. Especially in the early morning with the mist outside,
the car like an oven. That she'd keep for a while; and the
violence of course. The rest would have to go. She'd think of
something better next time.

Philip Harrison had never noticed the girl in his Physics class
until that day—

Prey

Amelia arrived at her apartment at six-fourteen. Hanging her coat in the hall closet, she carried the small package into the living room and sat on the sofa. She nudged off her shoes while she unwrapped the package on her lap. The wooden box resembled a casket. Amelia raised its lid and smiled. It was the ugliest doll she'd ever seen. Seven inches long and carved from wood, it had a skeletal body and an oversized head. Its expression was maniacally fierce, its pointed teeth completely bared, its glaring eyes protuberant. It clutched an eight-inch spear in its right hand. A length of fine, gold chain was wrapped around its body from the shoulders to the knees. A tiny scroll was wedged between the doll and the inside wall of its box. Amelia picked it up and unrolled it. There was handwriting on it. *This is He Who Kills*, it began. *He is a deadly hunter.* Amelia smiled as she read the rest of the words. Arthur would be pleased.

The thought of Arthur made her turn to look at the telephone on the table beside her. After a while, she sighed and set the wooden box on the sofa. Lifting the telephone to her lap, she picked up the receiver and dialed a number.

Her mother answered.

"Hello, Mom," Amelia said.

"Haven't you left yet?" her mother asked.

Amelia steeled herself. "Mom, I know it's Friday night—" she started.

She couldn't finish. There was silence on the line. Amelia closed her eyes. Mom, please, she thought. She swallowed. "There's this man," she said. "His name is Arthur Breslow. He's a high school teacher."

"You aren't coming," her mother said.

Amelia shivered. "It's his birthday," she said. She opened her eyes and looked at the doll. "I sort of promised him we'd . . . spend the evening together."

Her mother was silent. There aren't any good movies playing tonight, anyway, Amelia's mind continued. "We could go tomorrow night," she said.

Her mother was silent.

"Mom?"

"Now even Friday night's too much for you."

"Mom, I see you two, three nights a week."

"To *visit*," said her mother. "When you have your own room here."

"Mom, *let's not start on that again*," Amelia said. I'm not a child, she thought. Stop treating me as though I were a child!

"How long have you been seeing him?" her mother asked.

"A month or so."

"Without telling me," her mother said.

"I had every intention of telling you." Amelia's head was starting to throb. I will *not* get a headache, she told herself. She looked at the doll. It seemed to be glaring at her. "He's a nice man, Mom," she said.

Her mother didn't speak. Amelia felt her stomach muscles drawing taut. I won't be able to eat tonight, she thought.

She was conscious suddenly of huddling over the telephone.

She forced herself to sit erect. *I'm thirty-three years old*, she thought. Reaching out, she lifted the doll from its box. "You should see what I'm giving him for his birthday," she said. "I found it in a curio shop on Third Avenue. It's a genuine Zuni fetish doll, extremely rare. Arthur is a buff on anthropology. That's why I got it for him."

There was silence on the line. All right, *don't talk*, Amelia thought. "It's a hunting fetish," she continued, trying hard to sound untroubled. "It's supposed to have the spirit of a Zuni hunter trapped inside it. There's a golden chain around it to prevent the spirit from—" She couldn't think of the word; ran a shaking finger over the chain. "—escaping, I guess," she said. "His name is He Who Kills. You should see his face." She felt warm tears trickling down her cheeks.

"Have a good time," said her mother, hanging up.

Amelia stared at the receiver, listening to the dial tone. Why is it always like this? she thought. She dropped the receiver onto its cradle and set aside the telephone. The darkening room looked blurred to her. She stood the doll on the coffee-table edge and pushed to her feet. I'll take my bath now, she told herself. I'll meet him and we'll have a lovely time. She walked across the living room. A lovely time, her mind repeated emptily. She knew it wasn't possible. Oh, *Mom!* she thought. She clenched her fists in helpless fury as she went into the bedroom.

In the living room, the doll fell off the table edge. It landed head down and the spear point, sticking into the carpet, braced the doll's legs in the air.

The fine, gold chain began to slither downward.

t was almost dark when Amelia came back into the living room. She had taken off her clothes and was wearing her terrycloth robe. In the bathroom, water was running into the tub.

She sat on the sofa and placed the telephone on her lap. For several minutes, she stared at it. At last, with a heavy sigh, she lifted the receiver and dialed a number.

"Arthur?" she said when he answered.

"Yes?" Amelia knew the tone—pleasant but suspecting. She couldn't speak.

"Your mother," Arthur finally said.

That cold, heavy sinking in her stomach. "It's our night together," she explained. "Every Friday—" She stopped and waited. Arthur didn't speak. "I've mentioned it before," she said.

"I know you've mentioned it," he said.

Amelia rubbed at her temple.

"She's still running your life, isn't she?" he said.

Amelia tensed. "I just don't want to hurt her feelings anymore," she said. "My moving out was hard enough on her."

"I don't want to hurt her feelings either," Arthur said. "But how many birthdays a year do I have? We *planned* on this."

"I know." She felt her stomach muscles tightening again.

"Are you really going to let her do this to you?" Arthur asked. "One Friday night out of the whole year?"

Amelia closed her eyes. Her lips moved soundlessly. I just can't hurt her feelings anymore, she thought. She swallowed. "She's my mother," she said.

"Very well," he said. "I'm sorry. I was looking forward to it, but—" He paused. "I'm sorry," he said. He hung up quietly.

Amelia sat in silence for a long time, listening to the dial tone. She started when the recorded voice said loudly, "Please hang up." Putting the receiver down, she replaced the telephone on its table. So much for my birthday present, she thought. It would be pointless to give it to Arthur now. She reached out, switching on the table lamp. She'd take the doll back tomorrow.

The doll was not on the coffee table. Looking down, Amelia saw the gold chain lying on the carpet. She eased off the sofa edge onto her knees and picked it up, dropping it into the wooden box. The doll was not beneath the coffee table. Bending over, Amelia felt around underneath the sofa.

She cried out, jerking back her hand. Straightening up, she turned to the lamp and looked at her hand. There was something wedged beneath the index fingernail. She shivered as she plucked it out. It was the head of the doll's spear. She dropped it into the box and put the finger in her mouth. Bending over again, she felt around more cautiously beneath the sofa.

She couldn't find the doll. Standing with a weary groan, she started pulling one end of the sofa from the wall. It was terribly heavy. She recalled the night that she and her mother had shopped for the furniture. She'd wanted to furnish the apartment in Danish modern. Mother had insisted on this heavy, maple sofa; it had been on sale. Amelia grunted as she dragged it from the wall. She was conscious of the water running in the bathroom. She'd better turn it off soon.

She looked at the section of carpet she'd cleared, catching sight of the spear shaft. The doll was not beside it. Amelia picked it up and set it on the coffee table. The doll was caught beneath the sofa, she decided; when she'd moved the sofa, she had moved the doll as well.

She thought she heard a sound behind her—fragile, skittering. Amelia turned. The sound had stopped. She felt a chill move up the backs of her legs. "It's He Who Kills," she said with a smile. "He's taken off his chain and gone—"

She broke off suddenly. There had definitely been a noise inside the kitchen; a metallic, rasping sound. Amelia swallowed nervously. What's going on? she thought. She walked across the living room and reached into the kitchen, switching on the light. She peered inside. Everything looked normal. Her gaze moved falteringly across the stove, the pan of water on it, the table and chair, the drawers and cabinet doors all shut, the electric clock, the small refrigerator with the cookbook lying on top of it, the picture on the wall, the knife rack fastened to the cabinet side—

—its small knife missing.

Amelia stared at the knife rack. Don't be silly, she told herself. She'd put the knife in the drawer, that's all. Stepping into the kitchen, she pulled out the silverware drawer. The knife was not inside it.

Another sound made her look down quickly at the floor. She gasped in shock. For several moments, she could not react; then, stepping to the doorway, she looked into the living room, her heartbeat thudding. Had it been imagination? She was sure she'd seen a movement.

"Oh, come on," she said. She made a disparaging sound. She hadn't seen a thing.

Across the room, the lamp went out.

Amelia jumped so startledly, she rammed her right elbow against the doorjamb. Crying out, she clutched the elbow with her left hand, eyes closed momentarily, her face a mask of pain.

She opened her eyes and looked into the darkened living room. "Come on," she told herself in aggravation. Three sounds plus a burned-out bulb did not add up to anything as idiotic as—

She willed away the thought. She had to turn the water off. Leaving the kitchen, she started for the hall. She rubbed her elbow, grimacing.

There was another sound. Amelia froze. Something was coming across the carpet toward her. She looked down dumbly. No, she thought.

She saw it then—a rapid movement near the floor. There was a glint of metal, instantly, a stabbing pain in her right calf. Amelia gasped. She kicked out blindly. Pain again. She felt warm blood running down her skin. She turned and lunged into the hall. The throw rug slipped beneath her and she fell against the wall, hot pain lancing through her right ankle. She clutched at the wall to keep from falling, then went sprawling on her side. She thrashed around with a sob of fear.

More movement, dark on dark. Pain in her left calf, then her right again. Amelia cried out. Something brushed along her thigh. She scrabbled back, then lurched up blindly, almost falling again. She fought for balance, reaching out convulsively. The heel of her left hand rammed against the wall, supporting her. She twisted around and rushed into the darkened bedroom. Slamming the door, she fell against it, panting. Something banged against it on the other side, something small and near the floor.

Amelia listened, trying not to breathe so loudly. She pulled carefully at the knob to make sure the latch had caught. When there were no further sounds outside the door, she backed toward the bed. She started as she bumped against the mattress edge. Slumping down, she grabbed at the extension phone and pulled it to her lap. Whom could she call? The police? They'd think her mad. Mother? She was too far off.

She was dialing Arthur's number by the light from the bathroom when the doorknob started turning. Suddenly, her fingers couldn't move. She stared across the darkened room. The door latch clicked. The telephone slipped off her lap. She heard it thudding onto the carpet as the door swung open. Something dropped from the outside knob.

Amelia jerked back, pulling up her legs. A shadowy form was scurrying across the carpet toward the bed. She gaped at it.

It isn't true, she thought. She stiffened at the tugging on her bedspread. *It was climbing up to get her.* No, she thought; *it isn't true.* She couldn't move. She stared at the edge of the mattress.

Something that looked like a tiny head appeared. Amelia twisted around with a cry of shock, flung herself across the bed and jumped to the floor. Plunging into the bathroom, she spun around and slammed the door, gasping at the pain in her ankle. She had barely thumbed in the button on the doorknob when something banged against the bottom of the door. Amelia heard a noise like the scratching of a rat. Then it was still.

She turned and leaned across the tub. The level of the water was almost to the overflow drain. As she twisted shut the faucets, she saw drops of blood falling into the water. Straightening up, she turned to the medicine-cabinet mirror above the sink.

She caught her breath in horror as she saw the gash across her neck. She pressed a shaking hand against it. Abruptly, she became aware of pain in her legs and looked down. She'd been slashed along the calves of both legs. Blood was running down her ankles, dripping off the edges of her feet. Amelia started crying. Blood ran between the fingers of the hand against her neck. It trickled down her wrist. She looked at her reflection through a glaze of tears.

Something in her aroused her, a wretchedness, a look of terrified surrender. *No*, she thought. She reached out for the medicine-cabinet door. Opening it, she pulled out iodine, gauze and tape. She dropped the cover of the toilet seat and sank down gingerly. It was a struggle to remove the stopper of the iodine bottle. She had to rap it hard against the sink three times before it opened.

The burning of the antiseptic on her calves made her gasp. Amelia clenched her teeth as she wrapped gauze around her right leg.

A sound made her twist toward the door. She saw the knife blade being jabbed beneath it. It's trying to stab my feet, she thought; it thinks I'm standing there. She felt unreal to be considering its thoughts. *This is He Who Kills*; the scroll flashed suddenly across her mind. *He is a deadly hunter.* Amelia stared at the poking knife blade. God, she thought.

Hastily, she bandaged both her legs, then stood and, looking into the mirror, cleaned the blood from her neck with a washrag. She swabbed some iodine along the edges of the gash, hissing at the fiery pain.

She whirled at the new sound, heartbeat leaping. Stepping to the door, she leaned down, listening hard. There was a faint metallic noise inside the knob.

The doll was trying to unlock it.

Amelia backed off slowly, staring at the knob. She tried to visualize the doll. Was it hanging from the knob by one arm, using the other to probe inside the knob lock with the knife? The vision was insane. She felt an icy prickling on the back of her neck. *I mustn't let it in*, she thought.

A hoarse cry pulled her lips back as the doorknob button popped out. Reaching out impulsively, she dragged a bath towel off its rack. The doorknob turned, the latch clicked free. The door began to open.

Suddenly the doll came darting in. It moved so quickly that its figure blurred before Amelia's eyes. She swung the towel down hard, as though it were a huge bug rushing at her. The doll was knocked against the wall. Amelia heaved the towel on top of it and lurched across the floor, gasping at the pain in her ankle. Flinging open the door, she lunged into the bedroom.

She was almost to the hall door when her ankle gave. She pitched across the carpet with a cry of shock. There was a noise behind her. Twisting around, she saw the doll come through the bathroom doorway like a jumping spider. She saw the knife blade glinting in the light. Then the doll was in the shadows, coming at her fast. Amelia scrabbled back. She glanced over her shoulder, saw the closet and backed into its darkness, clawing for the doorknob.

Pain again, an icy slashing at her foot. Amelia screamed and heaved back. Reaching up, she yanked a topcoat down. It fell across the doll. She jerked down everything in reach. The doll was buried underneath a mound of blouses, skirts and dresses. Amelia pitched across the moving pile of clothes. She forced herself to stand and limped into the hall as quickly as she could. The sound of thrashing underneath the clothes faded from her hearing. She hobbled to the door. Unlocking it, she pulled the knob.

The door was held. Amelia reached up quickly to the bolt. It had been shot. She tried to pull it free. It wouldn't budge. She clawed at it with sudden terror. It was twisted out of shape. "No," she muttered. *She was trapped.* "Oh, God." She started pounding on the door. "Please help me! *Help* me!"

Sound in the bedroom. Amelia whirled and lurched across the living room. She dropped to her knees beside the sofa, feeling for the telephone, but her fingers trembled so much that she couldn't dial the numbers. She began to sob, then twisted around with a strangled cry. The doll was rushing at her from the hallway.

Amelia grabbed an ashtray from the coffee table and hurled it at the doll. She threw a vase, a wooden box, a figurine. She couldn't hit the doll. It reached her, started jabbing at her legs. Amelia reared up blindly and fell across the coffee table. Rolling to her knees, she stood again. She staggered toward the hall, shoving over furniture to stop the doll. She toppled a chair, a table. Picking up a lamp, she hurled it at the floor. She backed into the hall and, spinning, rushed into the closet, slammed the door shut.

She held the knob with rigid fingers. Waves of hot breath pulsed against her face. She cried out as the knife was jabbed beneath the door, its sharp point sticking into one of her toes. She shuffled back, shifting her grip on the knob. Her robe hung open. She could feel a trickle of blood between her breasts. Her legs felt numb with pain. She closed her eyes. Please, someone help, she thought.

She stiffened as the doorknob started turning in her grasp. Her flesh went cold. It couldn't be stronger than she: it *couldn't* be. Amelia tightened her grip. *Please*, she thought. The side of her head bumped against the front edge of her suitcase on the shelf.

The thought exploded in her mind. Holding the knob with her right hand, she reached up, fumbling, with her left. The suitcase clasps were open. With a sudden wrench, she turned the doorknob, shoving at the door as hard as possible. It rushed away from her. She heard it bang against the wall. The doll thumped down.

Amelia reached up, hauling down her suitcase. Yanking open the lid, she fell to her knees in the closet doorway, holding the suitcase like an open book. She braced herself, eyes wide, teeth clenched together. She felt the doll's weight as it banged against the suitcase bottom. Instantly, she slammed the lid and threw the suitcase flat. Falling across it, she held it shut until her shaking hands could fasten the clasps. The sound of them clicking into place made her sob with relief. She shoved away the suitcase. It slid across the hall and bumped against the wall. Amelia struggled to her feet, trying not to listen to the frenzied kicking and scratching inside the suitcase.

She switched on the hall light and tried to open the bolt. It was hopelessly wedged. She turned and limped across the living room, glancing at her legs. The bandages were hanging loose. Both legs were streaked with caking blood, some of the gashes still bleeding. She felt at her throat. The cut was still wet. Amelia pressed her shaking lips together. She'd get to a doctor soon now.

Removing the ice pick from its kitchen drawer, she returned to the hall. A cutting sound made her look toward the suitcase. She caught her breath. The knife blade was protruding from the suitcase wall, moving up and down with a sawing motion. Amelia stared at it. She felt as though her body had been turned to stone.

She limped to the suitcase and knelt beside it, looking, with revulsion at the sawing blade. It was smeared with blood. She tried to pinch it with the fingers of her left hand, pull it out. The blade was twisted, jerked down, and she cried out, snatching back her hand. There was a deep slice in her thumb. Blood ran down across her palm. Amelia pressed the finger to her robe. She felt as though her mind was going blank.

Pushing to her feet, she limped back to the door and started prying at the bolt. She couldn't get it loose. Her thumb began to ache. She pushed the ice pick underneath the bolt socket and tried to force it off the wall. The ice pick point broke off. Amelia slipped and almost fell. She pushed up, whimpering. There was no time, no time. She looked around in desperation.

The window! She could throw the suitcase out! She visualized it tumbling through the darkness. Hastily, she dropped the ice pick, turning toward the suitcase.

She froze. The doll had forced its head and shoulders through the rent in the suitcase wall. Amelia watched it struggling to get out. She felt paralyzed. The twisting doll was staring at her. No, she thought, it isn't true. The doll jerked free its legs and jumped to the floor.

Amelia jerked around and ran into the living room. Her right foot landed on a shard of broken crockery. She felt it cutting deep into her heel and lost her balance. Landing on her side, she thrashed around. The doll came leaping at her. She could see the knife blade glint. She kicked out wildly, knocking back the doll. Lunging to her feet, she reeled into the kitchen, whirled, and started pushing shut the door.

Something kept it from closing. Amelia thought she heard a screaming in her mind. Looking down, she saw the knife and a tiny wooden hand. The doll's arm was wedged between the door and the jamb! Amelia shoved against the door with all her might, aghast at the strength with which the door was pushed the other way. There was a cracking noise. A fierce smile pulled her lips back and she pushed berserkly at the door. The screaming in her mind grew louder, drowning out the sound of splintering wood.

The knife blade sagged. Amelia dropped to her knees and tugged at it. She pulled the knife into the kitchen, seeing the wooden hand and wrist fall from the handle of the knife. With a gagging noise, she struggled to her feet and dropped the knife into the sink. The door slammed hard against her side; the doll rushed in.

Amelia jerked away from it. Picking up the chair, she slung it toward the doll. It jumped aside, then ran around the fallen chair. Amelia snatched the pan of water off the stove and hurled it down. The pan clanged loudly off the floor, spraying water on the doll.

She stared at the doll. It wasn't coming after her. It was trying to climb the sink, leaping up and clutching at the counter side with one hand. It wants the knife, she thought. It has to have its weapon.

She knew abruptly what to do. Stepping over to the stove, she pulled down the broiler door and twisted the knob on all the way. She heard the puffing detonation of the gas as she turned to grab the doll.

She cried out as the doll began to kick and twist, its maddened thrashing flinging her from one side of the kitchen to the other. The screaming filled her mind again and suddenly she knew it was the spirit in the doll that screamed. She slid and crashed against the table, wrenched herself around and, dropping to her knees before the stove, flung the doll inside. She slammed the door and fell against it.

The door was almost driven out. Amelia pressed her shoulder, then her back against it, turning to brace her legs against the wall. She tried to ignore the pounding scrabble of the doll inside the broiler. She watched the red blood pulsing from her heel. The smell of burning wood began to reach her and she closed her eyes. The door was getting hot. She shifted carefully. The kicking and pounding filled her ears. The screaming flooded through her mind. She knew her back would get burned, but she didn't dare to move. The smell of burning wood grew worse. Her foot ached terribly.

Amelia looked up at the electric clock on the wall. It was four minutes to seven. She watched the red second hand revolving slowly. A minute passed. The screaming in her mind was fading now. She shifted uncomfortably, gritting her teeth against the burning heat on her back.

Another minute passed. The kicking and the pounding stopped. The screaming faded more and more. The smell of burning wood had filled the kitchen. There was a pall of gray smoke in the air. That they'll see, Amelia thought. Now that it's over, they'll come and help. That's the way it always is.

She started to ease herself away from the broiler door, ready to throw her weight back against it if she had to. She turned around and got on her knees. The reek of charred wood made her nauseated. She had to know, though. Reaching out, she pulled down the door.

Something dark and stifling rushed across her and she heard the screaming in her mind once more as hotness flooded over her and into her. It was a scream of victory now.

Amelia stood and turned off the broiler. She took a pair of ice tongs from its drawer and lifted out the blackened twist of wood. She dropped it into the sink and ran water over it until the smoke had stopped. Then she went into the bedroom, picked up the telephone and depressed its cradle. After a moment, she released the cradle and dialed her mother's number.

"This is Amelia, Mom," she said. "I'm sorry I acted the way I did. I want us to spend the evening together. It's a little late, though. Can you come by my place and we'll go from here?" She listened. "Good," she said. "I'll wait for you."

Hanging up, she walked into the kitchen, where she slid the longest carving knife from its place in the rack. She went to the front door and pushed back its bolt, which now moved freely. She carried the knife into the living room, took off her bathrobe and danced a dance of hunting, of the joy of hunting, of the joy of the impending kill.

Then she sat down, cross-legged, in the corner. He Who Kills sat, cross-legged, in the corner, in the darkness, waiting for the prey to come.

JACK KEROUAC

Jack Kerouac was born in Lowell, Massachusetts, in 1922, the youngest of three children in a Franco-American family. He attended local Catholic and public schools and won a football scholarship to Columbia University in New York City, where he met Neal Cassady, Allen Ginsberg, and William S. Burroughs. He quit school in his sophomore year and joined the Merchant Marine, beginning the restless wanderings that were to continue for the greater part of his life. His first novel, *The Town and the City*, appeared in 1950, but it was *On the Road*, first published in 1957 and memorializing his adventures with Neal Cassady, that epitomized to the world what became known as "the Beat generation" and made Kerouac one of the most controversial and best-known writers of his time. Publication of his many other books followed, among them *The Dharma Bums*, *The Subterraneans*, and *Big Sur*. Kerouac considered them all to be part of "one enormous comedy," which he called the Duluoz Legend. "In my old age," he wrote, "I intend to collect all my work and reinsert my pantheon of uniform names, leave the long shelf full of books there, and die happy." He died in St. Petersburg, Florida, in 1969, at the age of forty-seven.

Ann Charters is the author of *Kerouac: A Biography* and editor of *The Portable Beat Reader* and *Jack Kerouac: Selected Letters, 1940–1956*. She teaches at the University of Connecticut in Storrs, Connecticut.

Each volume in The Viking Portable Library either presents a representative selection from the works of a single outstanding writer or offers a comprehensive anthology on a special subject. Averaging 700 pages in length and designed for compactness and readability, these books fill a need not met by other compilations. All are edited by distinguished authorities, who have written introductory essays and included much other helpful material.

The Portable

JACK
KEROUAC

Edited by

Ann Charters

PENGUIN BOOKS

PENGUIN BOOKS

Published by the Penguin Group

Penguin Books USA Inc., 375 Hudson Street, New York, New York 10014, U.S.A.

Penguin Books Ltd, 27 Wrights Lane, London W8 5TZ, England

Penguin Books Australia Ltd, Ringwood, Victoria, Australia

Penguin Books Canada Ltd, 10 Alcorn Avenue, Toronto, Ontario, Canada M4V 3B2

Penguin Books (N.Z.) Ltd, 182–190 Wairau Road, Auckland 10, New Zealand

Penguin Books Ltd, Registered Offices: Harmondsworth, Middlesex, England

First published in the United States of America by Viking Penguin,
a division of Penguin Books USA Inc., 1995
Published in Penguin Books 1996

3   5   7   9   10   8   6   4   2

THE LIBRARY OF CONGRESS HAS CATALOGUED THE HARDCOVER AS FOLLOWS:
Kerouac, Jack, 1922–1969.
The portable Jack Kerouac/edited by Ann Charters.
p. cm.
Includes bibliographical references.
ISBN 0-670-84957-X (hc.)
ISBN 0 14 01.7819 8 (pbk.)
1. Beat generation—Literary collections.   I. Charters, Ann.
PS3521.E735A6 1995
813′.54—dc20   94–20120

Printed in the United States of America
Set in Sabon and Trajan

To the memory of

John Clellon Holmes

"A free man thinks of nothing less than of death, and his wisdom is a meditation not of death, but of life."
                    —Spinosa, *Ethics*

PREFACE

BECAUSE OF THE CIRCUMSTANCES, I can remember precisely when and where the idea for a Kerouac reader occurred to me. It was in 1975, two years after I had published my biography of Kerouac and soon after I'd started teaching at the University of Connecticut. It was also nearly a decade after the writer John Clellon Holmes and I had become friends. During a long conversation in the living room of his house in Old Saybrook, Connecticut, I proposed the idea of a Kerouac anthology to Holmes, saying that I thought Kerouac's writing was supremely suited to be presented in such a book and that I for one would love to read it. Holmes agreed immediately, and then he told me of the difficulties that had stopped him from realizing the plan ten years before.

As Kerouac's good friend and an avid supporter of his writing, Holmes first thought of the idea of a reader in 1965. He wrote a letter to Kerouac about it, and Kerouac enthusiastically endorsed the project, but the problem was that in the years between 1957 and 1965 he'd published fifteen books that had been issued by no less than nine different publishers. Trying to put together an anthology—as Holmes conceived it, that would "limn the larger shape" of Kerouac's work as a whole—he soon learned that Kerouac's various publishers refused to cooperate to release material they controlled for inclusion in a single volume.

Holmes and I put the idea on hold for another decade, until 1987, when he was undergoing chemotherapy for cancer of the jaw. This time, because of his limited energy, he proposed that we collaborate on the reader. Since I had compiled Kerouac's bibliography and written his first biography, Holmes thought that I had the more extensive knowledge of Jack's writing. We agreed that I would make the selections for the anthology and that Holmes would write the introduction.

But even in 1987 a Kerouac reader was still a book ahead of its time; when I couldn't get the necessary permissions, I had to tell Holmes that I couldn't compile the anthology. Holmes died the following year, and to my sorrow we never got to collaborate on the project.

What has changed since then are two essential conditions for going ahead with the reader: The Kerouac estate, which has controlled his literary property since his death in 1969, has given the green light; and the copyrights to Kerouac's books in print are now in the hands of fewer publishers, most of whom have cooperated in releasing material for this project. While assembling the book, I have sent my thoughts and confusions skyward to Holmes on many puzzling occasions, and I acknowledge his presence as my silent partner in this book.

My husband, Samuel Charters, has been my real partner. He has helped in more ways and on more occasions than I can remember. Here as in all my writing about Kerouac, Sam has steered me right on perilous roads, made both major and minor repairs to the transmission of the vehicle during the arduous journey, and provided refreshing rest stops when I felt myself spinning out of control. I take total responsibility for any shortcomings or errors in my selections and commentary on the material, but after our countless discussions about Kerouac over the past thirty years, it is fair to say that Sam has played a major role in provoking any insights that have surfaced in my study of Jack and his work.

A good friend who provided an important roadmap for my journey as a scholar through Kerouac country is Marshall Clements, who loved Kerouac's writing so much that he compiled, with his friend David Stivender, a photocopied anthology they called the "OVKU"—"One Volume Kerouac Uncollected"—made from their extensive searches in periodicals in which Kerouac's prose and poetry had appeared. In 1971 I was one of the select few who were fortunate enough to possess an edition about the size of the Manhattan telephone directory, hundreds of pages Clements and Stivender had copied and gathered into brown paper binders. Their informal anthology, later supplemented by reprints of the interviews Kerouac gave over the years, was a great asset to me when I assembled this volume.

More recently, other people have participated in the realization of the project. John Sampas, executor of the Kerouac estate, and Sterling Lord, Kerouac's literary agent, were solid supporters of the idea of a

Kerouac reader. My editor at Viking Penguin, David Stanford, and his assistant, Kristine Puopolo, have given me steady encouragement throughout the process of seeing the book through to completion.

Finally, I want to acknowledge the help of Donald Allen, whose ideas about how to anthologize Kerouac's shorter pieces were extremely astute, and Robert Gaspar, who was my reliable assistant in the physical preparation of the manuscript.

CONTENTS

INTRODUCTION

AS AN OPPORTUNITY to introduce readers to the larger dimensions of what Kerouac called the "world of raging action and folly and also of gentle sweetness seen through the keyhole of his eye," *The Portable Kerouac* features excerpts from most of the "true story novels" that he considered chapters in his Legend of Duluoz, the story of his lifetime. Readers familiar only with Kerouac's most popular books—*On the Road, The Subterraneans,* and *The Dharma Bums*—often miss the larger design in his work and tend to see him as the archetypal Beat author. This was a point of view that Kerouac himself energetically fostered in the early part of his career. He and his books did such a splendid job of it that in his later years he despaired of ever correcting his "beatnik" image.

In 1961, after publishing a dozen books, Kerouac wrote in *Big Sur* that his "work comprises one vast book." In this framework, his best-known book, *On the Road,* in which he appears as the narrator, "Sal Paradise," who tells the story of going on the road with his buddy "Dean Moriarty," is only one part of the larger whole. "Sal Paradise" is one of Kerouac's many pseudonyms, like "Jack Duluoz," his preferred name for himself. *On the Road* comes midway in the Duluoz chronology, which starts with the book *Visions of Gerard,* about Kerouac's childhood in Lowell, Massachusetts, in the 1920s. *Doctor Sax, Maggie Cassidy,* and *Vanity of Duluoz* make up the chronology before *On the Road,* which in turn is followed by the books *Lonesome Traveler, The Subterraneans, Tristessa, The Dharma Bums, Desolation Angels, Big*

Sur, and *Satori in Paris,* Kerouac's description of his trip to France four years before his death in 1969.

When I discussed Kerouac's work with him in 1966 while preparing his bibliography at his home in Hyannis, Massachusetts, he told me that he regarded the prose works making up the parts of the Duluoz Legend as episodic, picaresque narratives. Earlier he had explained in a letter to his friend John Clellon Holmes that he had "to cut the Duluoz Legend into suitable chronological lengths—I just couldnt pour the whole thing into one mould, if I did it would be a big round ball instead of figures. I suppose Lipschitz thought of this, one final big round ball sitting on a pedestal. But no, he divided his ball. Would Mozart blam all the 86 [sic] keys of the piano at once with his 86 fingers? or divide his ball into suitable symphonies, concerti, sonatas, serenatas, masses, dances, oratorios . . ."

The Portable Kerouac features representative selections from most of Kerouac's books written from 1951 to 1967, the period of his major work on the Duluoz Legend. Earlier fiction produced before he found his own voice as a writer—like his first published novel, *The Town and the City* (1950), or later books that could be considered "postscripts" to his legend, like *Satori in Paris* (1966) or *Pic* (1971)—are not included. In the first section of the anthology I've fashioned a chronology out of excerpts from the books describing the most significant events in Kerouac's life, interspersed with prose pieces that he shaped as shorter narratives that also tell important parts of his life story.

Since Kerouac typically structured his narrative into units composed of anywhere from one paragraph to several pages, his writing lends itself naturally to this format. He developed a literary style that he called "spontaneous prose" to enable him to write down his memories of what had happened in his past, shaped by his heightened emotional responses generated by the writing process itself. This blend of past memory combined with present dream and active reflection creates the allusive texture of his prose. Creating his reminiscences "on the run," he merged his past and his present on the pages of his manuscripts with a characteristic "Kerouacian" spin of heightened emotion and headlong narrative energy. His literary achievement can be savored in the selections contained in this anthology, but it is most fully appreciated when the reader turns from these excerpts to seek out Kerouac's books in their entirety.

Taken as "one vast book," the chapters of the Duluoz Legend in *The Portable Kerouac* suggest the dimensions of Kerouac's literary achievement and reflect the result of the years he spent primarily writing confessional picaresque memoirs. To an extent, the work of any writer forms "one vast book," but this concept is particularly appropriate for Kerouac. Attempting to be both James Boswell and Samuel Johnson in his lifetime, he was at once the dedicated chronicler of his own story as well as its most important participant. Gifted with an extraordinary memory that retained most of the details of what he saw, heard, tasted, and felt growing up an outsider in America, Kerouac was a true original, stubbornly going his own way as a writer to hew a path that paradoxically left him more committed to the act of creating literature out of his life than he was to living it.

The first section of this anthology, featuring Kerouac's achievement creating his Legend of Duluoz, is followed by several shorter sections, beginning with selections from Kerouac's poetry, suggesting his range as a writer. The poetry includes both long and short works, including excerpts from *San Francisco Blues,* a series of poems started in 1954 that was the first in a series of "blues" poems he wrote in different cities.

Kerouac's poetry is followed by prose pieces grouped by topics. First are his statements on his writing method of spontaneous prose. Then follow examples of how he practiced his method, beginning with relatively straightforward descriptions of a sporting event and a trip to Florida with photographer Robert Frank. This section continues with excerpts from the more experimental books *Visions of Cody, Book of Dreams,* and *Old Angel Midnight,* in which Kerouac totally abandoned conventional narrative.

The next section consists of essays on bop and the Beat Generation, the controversial term he invented in a conversation with Holmes in 1948, which later came back to haunt him. There are also articles written for magazines and newspapers, like his last published essay in 1969, "After Me, the Deluge." These items are followed by a section of writing influenced by Kerouac's study of Buddhism. For almost a decade this philosophy both challenged and comforted him, co-existing with the deeply felt Catholicism that, along with his first language, the French-Canadian dialect of "joual" (Québécois), were the most vital parts of the legacy of his French-Canadian heritage. The anthology ends with a section of Kerouac's letters, an early one furnishing a rare glimpse of the young Kerouac at twenty, burning with unquenchable desire to become a writer, as well as later letters to friends and associates suggesting the untold story or "backstage action" of his private life.

Creating works of fiction based on his real-life adventures, Kerouac used pseudonyms for himself and the "characters" in his books in order to avoid libel suits. In 1965, when he wrote to Holmes that he welcomed the idea of an anthology of his writing, he expected that the names of the people who appeared in his books as "fictional" characters closely modeled on his friends Neal Cassady, Allen Ginsberg, and William S. Burroughs, among others, would be changed to what he called "uniform pantheon names." Because of copyright restrictions this is still not possible, so *The Portable Kerouac* includes identity keys to the writers who were the models for the "fictional" characters in the Legend of Duluoz at the beginning of the sections of the narrative in which they appear; an identity key for the Duluoz Legend as a whole is included at the end of this reader.

CHRONOLOGY OF
JACK KEROUAC'S LIFE

1922   Jean-Louis Lebris de Kerouac born March 12 in Lowell, Massachusetts, third child of Gabrielle and Leo Kerouac, French-Canadian emigrants to New England

1939   Graduates from Lowell High School

1939–40   Attends Horace Mann Preparatory School in New York City

1940–41   Attends Columbia College

1942–43   Serves in Merchant Marine and U.S. Navy

1944   Meets Lucien Carr, William Burroughs, and Allen Ginsberg; marries first wife, Edith Parker

1946   Meets Neal Cassady

1946–48   Writes *The Town and the City* in New York City

1948   Meets John Clellon Holmes and invents the term "beat generation"

1947–50   First trips across country with Cassady; first attempts to write *On the Road*

1950   *The Town and the City* published; marries second wife, Joan Haverty

1951   Reads manuscripts of Burroughs's *Junkie* and Holmes's *Go* in January–March; in April writes roll manuscript of *On the Road* in three weeks in New York City; in October discovers his compositional method of "sketching" or "spontaneous prose" and begins to rewrite *On the Road* as the experimental book *Visions of Cody*

1951–52   Writes *Visions of Cody* in New York City and San Francisco

1952 Writes *Doctor Sax* in Mexico City; works as a student brakeman and writes "The Railroad Earth" in San Francisco; daughter, Jan Kerouac, born in Albany, New York

1953 Writes *Maggie Cassidy* and *The Subterraneans* in New York City

1954 Begins study of Buddhism in New York and California; writes *San Francisco Blues* in San Francisco, *Some of the Dharma* in New York and North Carolina

1955 Writes *Mexico City Blues,* begins *Tristessa* in Mexico City; attends "6 Poets at the 6 Gallery" reading in San Francisco

1956 Finishes *Tristessa* in Mexico City and writes *Visions of Gerard* in North Carolina; writes first part of *Desolation Angels* in Washington and Mexico City; Ginsberg's *Howl and Other Poems* published by City Lights in San Francisco

1957 *On the Road* published by the Viking Press in New York; writes *The Dharma Bums* in Florida

1958–60 Writes sketches in *Lonesome Traveler*

1959 Narrates film *Pull My Daisy* in New York

1961 Writes second half of *Desolation Angels* in Mexico City; writes *Big Sur* in Florida

1965 Writes *Satori in Paris* in Florida

1966 Marries third wife, Stella Sampas, and moves from Hyannis to Lowell, Massachusetts

1967 Writes *Vanity of Duluoz* in Lowell

1968 Neal Cassady dies in Mexico on February 4

1969 Jack Kerouac dies in St. Petersburg, Florida, on October 21

KEROUAC'S
INTRODUCTION

NAME Jack Kerouac

NATIONALITY Franco-American

PLACE OF BIRTH Lowell, Massachusetts

DATE OF BIRTH March 12, 1922

EDUCATION (*schools attended, special courses of study, degrees and years*)
Lowell (Mass.) High School; Horace Mann School for Boys; Columbia College (1940–42); New School for Social Research (1948–49). Liberal arts, no degrees (1936–1949). Got an A from Mark Van Doren in English at Columbia (Shakespeare course).—Flunked chemistry at Columbia.—Had a 92 average at Horace Mann School (1939–40). Played football on varsities. Also track, baseball, chess teams. . . .

SUMMARY OF PRINCIPAL OCCUPATIONS AND/OR JOBS
Everything: Let's elucidate: scullion on ships, gas station attendant, deckhand on ships, newspaper sportswriter (*Lowell Sun*), railroad brakeman, script synopsizer for 20th Century Fox in N.Y., soda jerk, railroad yardclerk, also railroad baggagehandler, cottonpicker, assistant furniture mover, sheet metal apprentice on the Pentagon in 1942, forest service fire lookout 1956, construction laborer (1941).

INTERESTS

HOBBIES I invented my own baseball game, on cards, extremely complicated, and am in the process of playing a whole 154-game season among eight clubs, with all the works, batting averages, E.R.A. averages, etc.

SPORTS Played all of them except tennis and lacrosse and skull.

SPECIAL Girls

PLEASE GIVE A BRIEF RESUME OF YOUR LIFE
Had beautiful childhood, my father a printer in Lowell, Mass., roamed fields and riverbanks day and night, wrote little novels in my room, first novel written at age 11, also kept extensive diaries and "newspapers" covering my own-invented horse-racing and baseball and football worlds (as recorded in novel *Doctor Sax*).—Had good early education from Jesuit brothers at St. Joseph's Parochial School in Lowell making me jump sixth grade in public school later on; as child traveled to Montreal, Quebec, with family; was given a horse at age 11 by mayor of Lawrence (Mass.), Billy White, gave rides to all kids in neighborhood; horse ran away. Took long walks under old trees of New England at night with my mother and aunt. Listened to their gossip attentively. Decided to become a writer at age 17 under influence of Sebastian Sampas, local young poet who later died on Anzio beach head; read the life of Jack London at 18 and decided to also be an adventurer, a lonesome traveler; early literary influences Saroyan and Hemingway; later Wolfe (after I had broken leg in Freshman football at Columbia read Tom [Thomas] Wolfe and roamed his New York on crutches).—Influenced by older brother Gerard Kerouac who died at age 9 in 1926 when I was 4, was great painter and drawer in childhood (he was)—(also said to be a saint by the nuns)—(recorded in novel *Visions of Gerard*).— My father was completely honest man full of gaiety; soured in last years over Roosevelt and World War II and died of cancer of the spleen.— Mother still living, I live with her a kind of monastic life that has enabled me to write as much as I did.—But also wrote on the road, as hobo, railroader, Mexican exile, Europe travel . . . One sister, Caroline, now married to Paul E. Blake Jr. of Henderson N.C., a government antimissile technician—she has one son, Paul Jr., my nephew, who calls me Uncle Jack and loves me.—My mother's name Gabrielle, learned all about natural story-telling from her long stories about Montreal and New Hampshire.—My people go back to Breton France, first North American ancestor Baron Alexandre Louis Lebris de Kérouac of Cornwall, Brittany, 1750 or so, was granted land along the Rivière du Loup after victory of Wolfe over Montcalm; his descendents married Indians

(Mohawk and Caughnawaga) and became potato farmers; first United States descendant my grandfather Jean-Baptiste Kérouac, carpenter, Nashua N.H.—My father's mother a Bernier related to explorer Bernier—all Bretons on father's side—My mother has a Norman name, L'Evesque.—

First formal novel *The Town and the City* written in tradition of long work and revision, from 1946 to 1948, three years, published by Harcourt Brace in 1950.—Then discovered "spontaneous" prose and wrote, say, *The Subterraneans* in 3 nights—wrote *On the Road* in 3 weeks—

Read and studied alone all my life.—Set a record at Columbia College cutting classes in order to stay in dormitory room to write a daily play and read, say, Louis Ferdinand Céline, instead of "classics" of the course.—

Had own mind.—Am known as "madman bum and angel" with "naked endless head" of "prose."—Also a verse poet, *Mexico City Blues* (Grove, 1959).—Always considered writing my duty on earth. Also the preachment of universal kindness, which hysterical critics have failed to notice beneath frenetic activity of my true-story novels about the "beat" generation.—Am actually not "beat" but strange solitary crazy Catholic mystic . . .

Final plans: hermitage in the woods, quiet writing of old age, mellow hopes of Paradise (which comes to everybody anyway). . . .

[Introduction to *LONESOME TRAVELER* (1960)]

THE LEGEND
OF DULUOZ

EDITOR'S INTRODUCTION

ON A SWELTERING DAY in July 1965, sitting at his desk in the air-conditioned "one-bathroom two-bedroom cottage" he shared with his mother in St. Petersburg, Florida, Jack Kerouac wrote to his friend John Clellon Holmes in Old Saybrook, Connecticut, about an idea that Holmes had proposed to him about compiling a "Jack Kerouac Reader."

Dear John,
Of course your idea is a dilly, just great, I just wonder why someone else didnt think of it a long time ago—For me to initiate such a "Kerouac Reader" (let's say) is a little unseemly—Five years ago when I saw the Viking Portable Steinbeck and the Viking Portable someone-or-other I forget who, I wondered in all honesty, what's wrong with me? . . .

Also, good idea not to call it an "Anthology" since this Pepsi generation of twisting illiterates dont even know what the word means. "Reader" I think just fine. . . .

Your plan for the "Reader" fits in with my need for making a living and also with my need to be understood, put in essence in one binder for anybody to carry around and read at leisure, and fits in with your own plans to make some money too and be read in the introduction in the context which is the classic context of a couple of the originators of the new literature which Ferlinghetti yelled about recently at the Spoleto festival, telling the European writers they all stunk and were dead, and bravo for him for telling the truth. . . .

You go right ahead with the whole plan, write Sterling [Lord], or call, and DEPEND ON ME to do anything that's necessary, you be the general and tell me what you want. From the fact that I furiously scribbled a whole novel only last week, you can tell how full my head is with many, many things, but now that my work is done for another year I'll have plenty time to ponder and study with you and correspond and if need be, go visit you and lay off the Scotch.

Now, as I say, I've thought of a "Reader" like this for a long time, and as I say it would've been unseemly for me to broach it myself, but now you have broached it . . . you, YOU my dear boy, go ahead and do this: I really dont know, in fact, how to go about it in all its facets.

And the idea of the uniform pantheon names of the Duluoz Legend is the idea I thought would only be broached in my old age, and really brought a kind of tear to my mind's eye when I read your letter.

You've got my cooperation and good wishes. In fact I think it's time you and I stop taking it on the chin from ignoramuses, and start belting them around for a change, give them some of their own medicine and more. If the publishers throw a stumbling block into this idea with their goddamn and myriad ephemeral rights to something they dont even own, I'll burn the houses down at midnight with an acetylene torch, plastic bombs, fourteen Malayan harpooners, Melville's ghost, seventeen strips of Saul Maloff tied to a TNT box as a fuse, and in court I'll put those publishers in a horseshoe for a horse to wear in the Battle of Chickamauga.

Jack

In 1965, when Kerouac wholeheartedly endorsed his friend John Clellon Holmes's proposal to compile a reader that would contain what Kerouac called the "essence" of his prose and poetry "in one binder for anybody to carry around and read at leisure," an anthology of his work in the form of a Viking Portable seemed ideal. For one thing, Kerouac understandably hoped to see his work placed in the company of such distinguished Viking Portable authors as John Steinbeck, Ernest Hemingway, F. Scott Fitzgerald, Thomas Wolfe, William Faulkner, and D. H. Lawrence. Their writing had been included in the many volumes making up the series, which originated as an idea to offer a representative body of an important author's work in a handy "portable" volume. For another, Kerouac's most popular novels, *On the Road* and *The Dharma Bums,* had been published by Viking, which seemed to be the logical publisher for an anthology of his work.

But Kerouac also had another reason for welcoming the idea of a reader. He felt that this format was ideally suited to revealing the larger design of his writing. Three years before, in the introduction to his novel *Big Sur,* he had stressed that all of his books formed a single entity:

My work comprises one vast book like Proust's except that my remembrances are written on the run instead of afterwards in a sick bed. Because of the objections of my early publishers I was not allowed to use the same personae names in each work. *On the Road, The Subterraneans, The Dharma Bums, Doctor Sax, Maggie Cassidy, Tristessa, Desolation Angels, Visions of Cody* and the others including this book *Big Sur* are just chapters in the whole work which I call *The Duluoz Legend*. In my old age I intend to collect all my work and re-insert my pantheon of uniform names, leave the long shelf full of books there, and die happy. The whole thing forms one enormous comedy, seen through the eyes of poor Ti Jean (me), otherwise known as Jack Duluoz, the world of raging action and folly and also of gentle sweetness seen through the keyhole of his eye.

Kerouac's statement that his "work comprises one vast book like Proust's except that my remembrances are written on the run instead of afterwards in a sick bed" is one of the most memorable descriptions of his writing that he ever made, but there are problems with this comparison of his work to Proust's *Remembrance of Things Past*. Taken literally, his words are a typical Kerouac boast: He admitted to his friend Philip Whalen that he was never able to finish reading Proust's monumental reminiscences. Perhaps it is poetic justice that few of Kerouac's readers can claim to have finished all the books making up his Duluoz Legend. As with Proust, there are just too many words: Who has the time to sit down and plow through the dozen books comprising Kerouac's saga?

To be fair to Kerouac, when he compared himself to great French authors he wasn't insisting on close similarities between their work and his own. Instead he was measuring himself on the grand scale of their ambition as writers and implying that, as a Franco-American author, he felt himself to be participating in their literary tradition. On another occasion he told one of his editors that he envisioned his Duluoz Chronology as including "hundreds of characters and events and levels interswirling and reappearing and becoming complete, somewhat à la Balzac and his *Comedie Humaine,* and Proust too. But each section of the Legend, that is, each novel, has to stand by itself as an individual story with a flavor of its own and a pivot of its own. Nevertheless they must all fit together on one shelf as a continuous tale. The whole thing complete forms a Mandala, the Wheel, the Circle, of an individual existence."

Kerouac enjoyed making large claims for what he was attempting to achieve in his Legend of Duluoz, but thinking about his writing in grandiose terms came naturally to him. He created his three-syllable pseudonym "Duluoz" in 1942, when he was barely twenty years old. This was a decade before he began writing the books that comprise the Legend of Duluoz. Kerouac invented his pseudonym after encountering the name "Stephen Dedalus," created by James Joyce for his protagonist in *Portrait of the Artist as a Young Man,* which Kerouac read after he dropped out of Columbia College and worked briefly as a sports reporter for his hometown newspaper. According to his journals and a poem in "Richmond Hill Blues" (1953), Kerouac noticed a story in the Lowell *Sun* about a local man named "Daoulas," and he later played around with several variations on it, like "Dalouas," "Dalous," and "Duouoz," before settling on "Duluoz."

As a merchant seaman during World War II, Kerouac read the novels forming the series in John Galsworthy's *Forsyte Saga.* The prose style of British authors Joyce and Galsworthy didn't make a deep impression on him, although Galsworthy's chronicle gave Kerouac the idea for a series of linked books about his own life. In 1950 he modeled his first published novel, *The Town and the City,* after the autobiographical fiction of the American writer Thomas Wolfe. Kerouac admired the scope of Wolfe's novels about the American experience, but during the composition of *The Town and the City* he became dissatisfied with what he considered Wolfe's conventional prose style.

Kerouac's search for a way to express his own voice ended in 1951, after he wrote *On the Road* and discovered what he called his "writing soul at last." This was the method he called sketching or spontaneous prose, which resulted in the "wild form" of his experimental work. It was only after he had used spontaneous prose to recast *On the Road* into another book—*Visions of Cody,* again about his friend Neal Cassady—that Kerouac deliberately began to write the series of books about his own life that would comprise the Legend of Duluoz. The first was *Doctor Sax,* written in 1952, about his early adolescence in his hometown of Lowell, Massachusetts.

Six months later he followed it with *Maggie Cassidy,* which became the next book in the Duluoz chronology, about his senior year in Lowell High School in 1938–1939. Kerouac planned another book about growing up in Lowell that he titled *Memory Babe,* but he never completed it. *Doctor Sax* wasn't meant to be the earliest book in the chronology, and Kerouac felt free to write about his recent experience as well as his past. Since he was only thirty when he began turning his life into a legend, he could hardly be faulted for not being able to predict the books he would write about his lifetime. As he said, he created them "on the run."

During the 1950s Kerouac's work on the books in his Duluoz saga reflected the turbulence in his own life. In the summer of 1953, for example, while living with his mother on Long Island and writing *Maggie Cassidy,* he had a love affair with an African-American woman in New York City. He felt he could never bring her home to meet his mother, but he described the affair and his wild life with his friends in Manhattan in the book he wrote in his mother's kitchen right after finishing his Lowell book, titling it *The Subterraneans.*

Kerouac's pattern of alternating books about the past and the present continued throughout his creation of the Duluoz series. In 1955 he began writing the book *Tristessa,* about a junky he was seeing in Mexico City. After completing the first part, he returned to his family and wrote *Visions of Gerard* in early 1956 about his older brother's sickness and death from rheumatic fever thirty years before. This became the earliest book in the Duluoz chronology, covering the years 1922–1926.

In the fall of 1956, Kerouac went back to Mexico City to complete *Tristessa* and start the book *Desolation Angels,* about his recent experiences as a firewatcher in the Cascade Mountains. Sixteen months later, in December 1957, he wrote *The Dharma Bums,* about adventures he'd had in California in 1955–1956. This book can be placed between *Tristessa* and *Desolation Angels* in the Duluoz chronology.

In 1961 Kerouac wrote the second half of *Desolation Angels* and a new book about his visit to California the previous year, titled *Big Sur.* Two more books were completed before his death in 1969: the last book in the Duluoz chronology, *Satori in Paris,* written right after a trip to France in 1965; and *Vanity of Duluoz,* written in 1967 to fill what he considered an important gap (the years 1940–1946) in the chronology between the end of *Maggie Cassidy* and the beginning of *On the Road.*

This summary of the dates of composition of important books in the Duluoz Legend makes it clear that Kerouac wrote them out of chronological sequence. It also accounts for the variety (some readers would say confusion) in their literary styles and narrative points of view. Kerouac was untroubled by such matters. He never fully explained what he was implying when he took the word "legend" to describe his life-time. As Ken Kesey later recognized, Kerouac wrote his books not so much to tell the truth as to *make* the truth. Kerouac could have meant by "legend" his belief in the transformational power of storytelling, because he told his friends that they could also translate their lives into legends by committing themselves to the act of writing about what had happened to them.

Kerouac's ambition in his "legend" wasn't to be a heroic figure in his own life story. He wanted to become a legendary American writer by virtue of taking on the heroic task of creating a completely written lifetime. As "Ti Jean" (his family's French-Canadian nickname for him) or "Jack Duluoz" or "Sal Paradise" or "Ray Smith"—he used different pseudonyms in different books—he appeared as a child in *Visions of Gerard* and *Doctor Sax,* as a teenager in *Maggie Cassidy,* as a young man in *Vanity of Duluoz* and *On the Road,* as a road-weary traveler in *Visions of Cody* and *Tristessa,* as a committed seeker after truth in *The Dharma Bums* and *Desolation Angels,* and as a man at the end of the road in *Big Sur* and *Satori in Paris.*

In Kerouac's books he not only recorded what happened to him by recalling or inventing a myriad of minute details dredged up out of the recesses of his apparently inexhaustible memory, but he also shaped these details on the pages of his manuscripts with the consciousness that they must be read as fiction in order to hold together as a coherent story. Although Kerouac insisted that, with his writing style of spontaneous prose, he had created a "new literature" that would make all previous fiction obsolete, he considered himself an old-fashioned story-teller. In his various books he presented his lifetime as a series of stories, relying on the power of narrative to weave the separate strands of his memories, dreams, and reflections into the golden cloth of his legend, each segment colored by his different emotional state at the time.

All of Kerouac's writing is autobiographical, but he fictionalized the stories about his direct experience by changing the names of the real-life characters he described and by altering the settings of his narrative if he or his publishers feared libel action would be taken by the people he was writing about. For example, although his affair with the girl he called "Mardou" in *The Subterraneans* actually took place in the East Village in New York City, Kerouac changed the locale to San Francisco. This means that books in the Legend of Duluoz are a unique blend of fact and fiction. Because they follow the details of his life so closely and yet are totally imagined entities, his books don't really fit into either traditional category of novel or autobiography.

Shelved in bookstores and libraries as fiction, they have been described by literary critics as inhabiting the murky territory of "fictionalized autobiography" or "autobiographical fiction," genres that are difficult to pin down. Certainly Kerouac never presented his work as "autobiography"; he called his books "true-story novels" and insisted that "narrative sections of one long life story is what my 'novels' are." The term "autobiographical fictions" suggests that Kerouac took a literal approach in his books ("autobiography") but combined it with his view of himself as a storyteller, free to change fact into fiction and use different narrative strategies in the various books ("fictions"). But this term is also unacceptable: Kerouac's approach to creating narratives solidly based on his direct experience is a world apart from Jorge Luis Borges's brilliantly imagined "fictions," and the term is indelibly linked to the South American writer's short narratives.

Kerouac himself stressed two essential qualities in the various books he wrote about his life: first, that they were picaresque narratives based on "true life" events; and second, that they were told in a confessional manner that heightened the emotional content of what he was saying —as if, like Augustine's *Confessions,* his books continued the Christian tradition of self-examination of the mysteries of his interior life. Perhaps the term "confessional picaresque memoirs" is the best description of his work, suggesting the originality of their form, which was as unconventional as his literary style of spontaneous prose.

While Kerouac's stubborn originality is evident in the shape and scope of his lifelong project, his presentation of himself using different narrative voices in his different books can create problems for readers expecting to find the integrated literary style of Proust or Balzac when they finish one section of the Duluoz series and move on to the next. These readers experience the macrocosm of Kerouac's universe as a series of abrupt transitions between the various books in the legend. On the microcosm of the individual page, the freedom of his language is another surprise. Kerouac's assertion that he wrote his remembrances "on the run" helps to explain what he was trying to accomplish.

On one level, Kerouac meant by the phrase that he turned the actual events of his life into fiction nearly as quickly as they happened to him, instead of reflecting on his impressions for years before writing them down and then revising them. The sections of the Legend literally written "on the run"—that is, within a year or two (or less) after they occurred in his life—include the last two parts of *On the Road* and much of *Visions of Cody,* as well as all of *The Subterraneans, Tristessa, Big Sur, Satori in Paris* and the first part of *Desolation Angels.*

But in a larger sense, all of Kerouac's books were written "on the run" after his discovery of his spontaneous prose method in October 1951. He told Holmes that the courage to write this way came to him while he "was listening to Lee Konitz take on 'I Remember April' from the middle of it somehow, the 'pithy middle eye,' and ripple and swim right out of it carrying it shining on his horn (all, all a long story), triumphant, the tune in his pocket, October night 1951. I swore in my notebook right there in the dim blue lights of Birdland, 'Blow as Deep as You Want to Blow.' "

Kerouac based his approach to writing on the performances of the jazz musicians he admired: Lester Young, Charlie Parker, Charlie Mingus, and Brew Moore, among others. He heard in their music the rhythms of language: Miles Davis is described in "The Beginning of Bop" as "leaning against the piano fingering his trumpet with a cigarette hand working making raw iron sound like wood speaking in long sentences like Marcel Proust." Trying to capture the emotional truth of his direct experience, Kerouac let the words pour out onto the page instead of editing them in the writing process. Listening to jazz, he learned to extend the line of his sentences and to follow the sounds of words, writing for the ear as much as for the printed page, as when he wrote in "The Railroad Earth" that in San Francisco

> It was the fantastic drowse and drum hum of lum mum afternoon nathin' to do, ole Frisco with end of land sadness—the people—the alley full of trucks and cars of businesses nearabouts and nobody knew or far from cared who I was all my life three thousand five hundred miles from birth-O opened up and at last belonged to me in Great America.

In spontaneous prose passages like this one, Kerouac wrote jazz, improvising on the page like Charlie Parker on the saxophone, believing, as the critic Warren Tallman understood, that "the truth is in the improvisation." Kerouac tirelessly chased melodies and practiced chord changes as he recorded the conversations he overheard moments after they happened and his observations in the little spiral notebooks he invariably kept tucked nearly out of sight in his shirt pocket. He wrote in *Desolation Angels* that "as an artist I need solitude and a kind of 'do-nothing' philosophy that does allow me to dream all day and work out chapters of forgotten reveries that emerge years later in story form."

As Henry Miller recognized when he praised *The Dharma Bums,* Kerouac had to write millions of words in order to describe what happened to him so freely. From his pocket notebooks he transcribed what he wanted to keep of his reportage and "reveries" into larger journals, so what he was going to say was partly on paper as well as in his head before he started writing one of his picaresque memoirs.

Kerouac felt that editors like Malcolm Cowley never tried to understand what he was trying to do as a writer, refusing to believe that he wasn't a conventional novelist and expecting him to write like what Kerouac called "1920s heroes. . . . I've nothing to do with Scott Fitzgerald and much to do with Joyce and Proust." He told his friend Holmes that "if critics say your work stinks it's because they want it to stink and they can make it stink by scaring you into conformity with their comfortable little standards, standards so low that they can no longer be considered 'dangerous' but set in place in their compartmental understandings."

Critics like Truman Capote said that what Kerouac did was typing, not writing; but creating books with the method of spontaneous prose wasn't a simple business. Kerouac wrote in concentrated sessions. As he told Holmes in 1965, he "furiously scribbled a whole novel [*Satori in Paris*] only last week." He relied on various drugs—including alcohol —to fuel the process, to not only enhance his physical stamina while he sat at his desk writing for hours but also to expand his memory and induce the characteristic sense of euphoria present in most of his narratives. He sought joy, or what he called "mental kicks," in his life, explaining in *Desolation Angels* that

> I was determined to be Glad!—Dostoevsky said "Give man his Utopia and he will deliberately destroy it with a grin" and I was determined with the same grin to disprove Dostoevsky!— I was also a notorious wino who exploded anywhere anytime he got drunk—My friends in San Francisco said I was a Zen Lunatic, at least a Drunken Lunatic, yet sat with me in moonlight fields drinking and singing. . . . I was an "Idealist" and I believed in "Life" and was going about it with my earnest scribblings—Strangely enough, these scribblings were the first of their kind in the world, I was originating (without knowing

it, you say?) a new way of writing about life, no fiction, no craft, no revising afterthoughts, the heartbreaking discipline of the veritable fire ordeal where you cant go back but have made the vow of "speak now or forever hold your tongue" and all of it innocent go-ahead confession, the discipline of making the mind the slave of the tongue with no chance to lie or re-elaborate (in keeping not only with the dictums of Dichtung Warheit [sic] Goethe but those of the Catholic Church my childhood).

By the time Kerouac died of alcoholism at the relatively young age of forty-seven he'd achieved what he'd wanted: He'd left the legend of his completed lifetime in the books on his shelves. Perhaps because he felt himself an outsider as the son of French-Canadian immigrants, his narratives dramatized his vision of America as the fabled land of promise, beginning with his birth in Lowell, Massachusetts, on March 12, 1922, as the third child of Gabrielle and Leo Kerouac.

Kerouac's parents had each emigrated separately from rural Quebec to milltowns in New England, lured by the promise of a better life in America. After their marriage, Leo ran a print shop in Lowell, managing to provide a comfortable life for his family by the time Jack was born. Four years later, when Jack's older brother died of rheumatic fever, their family tragedy introduced the dark, underlying theme in all of Kerouac's books: that all life is suffering, because we are born on earth only to die. In *Visions of Gerard,* Kerouac tapped his earliest memories of childhood:

> For the first four years of my life, while he lived, I was not Ti Jean Duluoz, I was Gerard, the world was his face, the flower of his face, the pale stooped disposition, the heartbreakingness and the holiness and his teachings of tenderness to me, and my mother constantly reminding me to pay attention to his goodness and advice.

The confessional style of *Visions of Gerard,* the earliest volume in the Duluoz saga, is a good introduction to Kerouac's writing, because in this book he tells his story with such eloquence that he sweeps the reader into the intensely lyrical world of his imagination. Kerouac's prose is studded with startlingly personal images and idiomatic speech rhythms, almost as if he were translating the *joual* French words in his head as he wrote about the earliest years of his childhood. The French-Canadian dialect of *joual* was Kerouac's first language; he didn't learn English until he went to grade school. When he described his family's conversation around the supper table in *Visions of Gerard,* he commented on their "semi-Iroquoian French-Canadian accent. . . . I can still hear the lugubrious sound of it and comfort-a-suppers of it, *M'ué'n pauss*. . . ."

Kerouac felt that the origin of his spontaneous prose method was in the confession box of the Catholic Church, and the world of *Visions of Gerard* is saturated with the rites and rituals of the Catholicism of his Franco-American childhood in Lowell. But the text is also infused with Buddhist references that reflect Kerouac's immersion in Buddhist studies at the time he wrote it. Past and present constantly intersect in Kerouac's prose, as his memory mixed with his dreams and reflections.

After *Visions of Gerard,* the Duluoz chronology continues with the more straightforward story "Home at Christmas," describing Kerouac's life in 1932–34, when his family lived on Phebe Avenue in Lowell. Its subject is a winter walk a few days before Christmas that Kerouac took as an eleven-year-old, trudging with his hockey stick through backyard fields and neighborhood streets drifted high with snow, to Dracut on the outskirts of town.

This is followed by the experimental *Doctor Sax,* where in Book Two, "A Gloomy Bookmovie," Kerouac presents twenty-five scenes of his life at home in Lowell with his mother and father, to be visualized in the reader's "bookmovie" imagination. These were based on his memories of being a thirteen-year-old boy in what he called "the gloomy special brown Technicolor interior of my house. . . . I'm a little kid with blue eyes, 13, I'm munching on a fresh cold mackintosh apple. . . ." Kerouac believed that he'd invented a new literary form with his "book-movie" idea, telling Holmes that "people would be able to look at my page and become the camera themselves and even see unphotographable moviettes within the movie. This is my most ambitious invention."

Next in the chronology, the action of the Duluoz saga fast-forwards a few years to the book *Maggie Cassidy,* with "Jackie Duluoz" as a high-school senior in Lowell. After Leo Kerouac suffered financial losses in his business, the family moved to a tenement apartment in the French-Canadian neighborhood of Pawtucketville. Gabrielle Kerouac helped to support her family by working a factory job, so Jack was dependent on a scholarship to go to college. A gifted student, he was also a promising track and football star, but in his senior year of high school in 1938–

39 he fell in love with a hometown Irish girl to whom he gave the pseudonym "Maggie Cassidy." Kerouac translated his memories of this period of his life into a story dramatizing the joys and torments of teenage love. Here the action moves swiftly as he gives a sense of his physical prowess and emotional vulnerability in what he remembered as his golden years.

After leaving Lowell to attend Columbia College on a scholarship, Kerouac's life nearly spun out of control. *Vanity of Duluoz* opens with his confused experiences as a student in 1940–41, when he broke his leg playing freshman football at Columbia and ran afoul of his coach, Lou Little, at the beginning of his sophomore year. Kerouac adopted a looser, chattier prose style in this book, saying that it was for his third wife, Stella Sampas. She was the sister of his Lowell friend Sebastian Sampas, who was very close to Kerouac during his college years and who encouraged him to become a writer. Sebastian died after being wounded on the Anzio beachhead in World War II; he was described as the character "Sabby" in *Vanity of Duluoz*.

Just as America entered the war Kerouac dropped out of college. Unable to take Navy discipline, he served in the merchant marine during World War II. During these tumultuous years he was married briefly to his first wife, Edie Parker. He also met William Burroughs and Allen Ginsberg in New York City. The period of Kerouac's life described in *Vanity of Duluoz* concluded in 1946, when he immersed himself in the writing of his first published novel after his father died of cancer.

The next period of Kerouac's life, "the part of my life you could call my life on the road," extended for nearly fifteen years, beginning when he met his friend Neal Cassady in New York City in the winter of 1947. Cassady got him on the road, but Kerouac described his own mishaps as a twenty-five-year-old hitchhiking west from New York for the first time to meet Cassady in part one of *On the Road*. Coming back from the West Coast on a bus just before Christmas in 1947, Kerouac met a girl he described in his story "The Mexican Girl," excerpted from his novel. The cross-country trip back to California in Cassady's new Hudson automobile in 1949 became part two of *On the Road*, in which Kerouac and Cassady visit Burroughs and his family in Louisiana before rushing on to San Francisco.

"Jazz of the Beat Generation," a description of his evenings spent listening to jazz with Cassady in San Francisco and Chicago clubs later in 1949, was a piece Kerouac refashioned from the pages of the unpublished manuscripts of *On the Road* and *Visions of Cody* and published separately. Its prose style reflects the influence of jazz on Kerouac's writing and serves as a transition to what he called the "wild form" of his experimental prose in "The Railroad Earth," *The Subterraneans,* and *Tristessa.* These are Kerouac's "meditations" on his life as a student brakeman on the railroad in San Francisco in 1952 and his account of two brief affairs a short time later. The section from *The Subterraneans* is his transcription of the story his lover "Mardou" told him about her emotional breakdown.

Kerouac's ride with the "Good Blonde" who picked him up on a California highway in the fall of 1955 fits into the narrative time frame of *The Dharma Bums,* the book in the Duluoz Legend that follows *Tristessa.* In *The Dharma Bums,* Kerouac modeled the most important character, "Japhy Ryder," on his West Coast friend, the poet Gary Snyder. As Cassady had been the inspiration for Kerouac's adventures on the road, so Snyder confirmed the spiritual dimension of Kerouac's vision of living as a "rucksack wanderer." Snyder and Philip Whalen, another Berkeley poet interested in Buddhism, helped Kerouac get a job as a firewatcher on Desolation Peak in Washington State during the summer of 1956. During his seventy days on the mountain, Kerouac kept a detailed journal, which became the basis of the first part of *Desolation Angels.* When he turned the journal into an extended narrative, he shaped the opening chapters carefully to form what he described to his agent, Sterling Lord, as a "mountain you walk down from, into, first, introspective narrative, and then into mundane narrative."

After leaving the Cascade Mountains, Kerouac traveled back to San Francisco and Mexico City before embarking on a trip to Tangiers to visit Burroughs. He described these events straightforwardly in *Desolation Angels.* He financed the trip to Tangiers early in 1957 by selling the manuscript of *On the Road* to Viking Press, six years after he'd written it. In Tangiers at the age of thirty-five, Kerouac finally wearied of being on the road. He gave little explanation for his change of heart, except to say that he might have taken too many drugs with Burroughs in Tangiers. Suddenly "all I wanted somehow now was Wheaties by a pine breeze kitchen window in America, that is, I guess a vision of my childhood in America."

When Kerouac returned from Europe, he tried to settle down and make a home for himself and his sixty-two-year-old mother in Berkeley, dragging her cross-country from Florida to California on a Greyhound bus. The last sections from *Desolation Angels* describe this futile attempt, which included an awkward moment when Kerouac's literary legend collided with his actual life. When his old friend Neal Cassady and a box of books from his publisher arrived simultaneously at his Berkeley apartment in 1957, Kerouac gave the first copy of his newly published *On the Road* to Cassady, the hero of the book. In *Desolation Angels* Kerouac wrote that when Cassady ["Cody"] said goodbye that day, "He for the first time in our lives failed to look me a goodbye in the eye but looked away shifty-like—I couldn't understand it and still dont—I knew something was bound to be wrong and it turned out very wrong."

Kerouac gave various explanations for Cassady's behavior, but his intuition that something was "shifty-like" was correct. The next book in the legend, *Big Sur,* describes Kerouac's last trip to California three years later. After the publication of *On the Road* he became a famous "beatnik" author badgered by his fans in Long Island and Florida and discovering, as he said, that he "had no guts" to tell them to leave him alone. In *Big Sur* Kerouac, not yet forty, wrote about what had happened to him in heightened prose that stripped bare the emotional cost of his way of life. For the first time in his books, he faced the extent of his alcoholism and admitted to his personal tragedy in relying on his friends' lives for the adventures that he turned into "true-story" novels to further his own career.

There is no darker moment in the Legend of Duluoz. Kerouac never resolved the unresolvable contradictions of his earthly vanity as a writer, and when he went on after *Big Sur* "to speak for things" in later books like *Vanity of Duluoz* and *Satori in Paris,* his tone reflected a new self-consciousness. The promises of his dreams and visions, captured on the pages of his manuscripts, were always more compelling to him than the reality of the life he actually lived when he wasn't writing about it.

There are certain risks attendant upon total immersion in the Duluoz Legend, rather than unsystematically dipping into the separate books one at a time. For example, readers might be unprepared for Kerouac's Buddhist references in *Visions of Gerard,* or his series of short "bookmovie" scenes in *Doctor Sax,* or his abrupt asides to his wife in *Vanity of Duluoz.* They might tire of his authorial reveries and the lack of straightforward narrative in "Railroad Earth" and *Tristessa,* or balk at the sprawling sections describing his mood swings in *Big Sur.*

Kerouac sometimes neglected to furnish a larger thematic framework for the events presented in books like *Desolation Angels,* expecting his readers to know about his background and furnish the motivation for his endless journeys from Seattle to San Francisco to

Mexico City to New York to Tangiers to London to New York to St. Petersburg to New Orleans to El Paso to Juarez to Los Angeles to Oakland to Berkeley ad infinitum. At the other extreme, he tended to recycle the same material about his boyhood in Lowell, indulging his fantasies about what would have happened if he'd married "Maggie Cassidy" and never left his hometown. Kerouac lived his life so intensely that he wanted to leave it whole and intact on the pages of the books he left behind him, but sometimes his alcoholism made him garrulous. Then he wrote as if he were listening in his inner ear to a faint recording only he could hear of Frank Sinatra singing the words to one of his favorite songs:

> . . . And when I'm gloomy,
> you've simply got to listen to me,
> until it's talked away. . . .

On the other hand, Kerouac's achievements in the Duluoz Legend are as prodigious as his excesses. Most of his readers have a list of their favorite moments, but all agree that as a storyteller Kerouac possessed an extraordinary prose energy that succeeded in both promising and delivering the irresistible appeal of the American open road. There is also what Allen Ginsberg calls Kerouac's "open heart," his sensitivity to the fact of our shared experience of a common mortality. Others are particularly susceptible to his sense of humor and pleasure in wordplay, or his ability to capture the speech rhythms of the people he heard on the road, like the Mexican girl's sweet refrain from a popular song, "If you can't boogie I know I show you how."

Another of Kerouac's achievements is what Snyder calls his "writerliness": He created unforgettable portraits of Burroughs, Snyder, and above all Cassady, who represents the American "cowboy crashing." Also, Kerouac's love of his family shines through his books about growing up in Lowell, and in celebrating the importance of the family he speaks for all immigrants and first-generation Americans—even if, after he left Lowell, he sometimes seemed naive in his portrayal of women, minorities, and those he called "fellaheen," Third World characters like Tristessa. His best books, *On the Road* and *Big Sur,* succeed because Kerouac was not overly sentimental; he was clear-eyed about how life treats characters who drop out like Cassady or who turn into alcoholics like himself.

Readers will decide for themselves whether the strengths on the pages of the Duluoz Legend outweigh the weaknesses. An anthology is no substitute for the individual books themselves, but its format eases the transitions between Kerouac's books when the authorial voice changes unexpectedly, as in the leap from the final paragraphs of *Doctor Sax* to the first pages of *Maggie Cassidy,* or from *Tristessa* to *The Dharma Bums.* The organization of this anthology also allows for inclusion of important segments of the Duluoz Legend published separately—like "Home at Christmas," "The Railroad Earth," and "Good Blonde"—now inserted into their place in the chronology.

The highlights are all here, as Kerouac envisioned, for anyone to "carry around and read at leisure." You can share Gerard's wonder at the miracle and unfairness of life, participate in young Duluoz's triumph at his high-school track meet, float along the California highways with Cassady behind the wheel of a brand new car, empathize with "Mardou's" emotional breakdown as a woman sexually exploited by her uncaring lovers, take a deep breath and run down a California mountaintop with a bunch of "zen lunatics," or go over the ragged edge with repentant Duluoz on his last trip to Bixby Canyon.

Kerouac's favorite definition of literature was that it was a "tale told for companionship and to teach something religious, of religious reverence, about real life, in this real world which literature should (and here does) reflect." Read the tales comprising his Legend of Duluoz and judge for yourself.

from
DOCTOR SAX
1922

It was in Centralville I was born, in Pawtucketville saw Doctor Sax. Across the wide basin to the hill—on Lupine Road, March 1922, at five o'clock in the afternoon of a red-all-over suppertime, as drowsily beers were tapped in Moody and Lakeview saloons and the river rushed with her cargoes of ice over reddened slick rocks, and on the shore the reeds swayed among mattresses and cast-off boots of Time, and lazily pieces of snow dropped plunk from bagging branches of black thorny oily pine in their thaw, and beneath the wet snows of the hillside receiving the sun's lost rays the melts of winter mixed with roars of Merrimack—I was born. Bloody rooftop. Strange deed. All eyes I came hearing the river's red; I remember that afternoon, I perceived it through beads hanging in a door and through lace curtains and glass of a universal sad lost redness of mortal damnation . . . the snow was melting. The snake was coiled in the hill not my heart.

Young Doctor Simpson who later became tragic tall and grayhaired and unloved, snapping his—"I think everything she is going to be alright, Angy," he said to my mother who'd given birth to her first two, Gerard and Catherine, in a hospital.

"Tank you Doctor Simpson, he's fat like a tub of butter—*mon ti n'ange* . . ." Golden birds hovered over her and me as she hugged me to her breast; angels and cherubs made a dance, and floated from the ceiling with upsidedown assholes and thick folds of fat, and there was a mist of butterflies, birds, moths and brownnesses hanging dull and stupid over pouting births.

* * *

One gray afternoon in Centralville when I was probably 1, 2 or 3 years old, I saw in my child self dream-seeing voids a cluttered dark French Canadian shoe repair shop all lost in gray bleak wings infolded on the shelf and clatter of the thing. Later on the porch of Rose Paquette's tenement (big fat woman friend of my mother's, with children) I realized the brokendown rainy dream shoeshop was just downstairs

. . . a thing I knew about the block. It was the day I learned to say door in English . . . door, door, *porte, porte*—this shoe repair shop is lost in the rain of my first memories and's connected to the Great Bathrobe Vision.

I'm sitting in my mother's arms in a brown aura of gloom sent up by her bathrobe—it has cords hanging, like the cords in movies, bellrope for Catherine Empress, but brown, hanging around the bathrobe belt —the bathrobe of the family, I saw it for 15 or 20 years—that people were sick in—old Christmas morning bathrobe with conventional diamonds or squares design, but the brown of the color of life, the color of the brain, the gray brown brain, and the first color I noticed after the rainy grays of my first views of the world in the spectrum from the crib so dumb. I'm in my mother's arms but somehow the chair is not on the floor, it's up in the air suspended in the voids of sawdust smelling mist blowing from Lajoie's wood yard, suspended over yard of grass at corner of West Sixth and Boisvert—that daguerreotype gray is all over, but my mother's robe sends auras of warm brown (the brown of my family)—so now when I bundle my chin in a warm scarf in a wet gale—I think on that comfort in the brown bathrobe—or as when a kitchen door is opened to winter allowing fresh ices of air to interfere with the warm billowy curtain of fragrant heat of cooking stove . . . say a vanilla pudding . . . I am the pudding, winter is the gray mist. A shudder of joy ran through me—when I read of Proust's teacup—all those saucers in a crumb—all of History by thumb—all of a city in a tasty crumb—I got all my boyhood in vanilla winter waves around the kitchen stove. It's exactly like cold milk on hot bread pudding, the meeting of hot and cold is a hollow hole between memories of childhood.

The brown that I saw in the bathrobe dream, and the gray in the shoeshop day, are connected with the browns and grays of Pawtucketville—the black of Doctor Sax came later.

• • •

The kids yelling in the tenement yards at night—I remember now and realize the special sound of it—mothers and families hear it in aftersupper windows. They're slaloming the iron posts, I'm walking through them in that spectral dream of revisiting Pawtucketville, quite often I get in from the hill, sometimes from Riverside. I've come wearying out of my pillow, I hear pots rattling in kitchens, complaints of an elder sister in the yard becoming a chant, which the littler ones accept, some with cat meows and sometimes actual cats do join in from their posts along the house and garbage cans—wrangles, African chatters at murky circles—moans of repliers, little coughs, mother-moans, pretty soon too late, go in and play no more, and with my what-woe trailing behind me like the Dragon Net of Bad Dreams I come sploopsing to a no-good end and wake up.

The children in the court pay no attention to me, either that or because I am a ghost they dont see me.

Pawtucketville rattles in my haunted head . . .

from
VISIONS OF GERARD
1922–1926

EDITOR'S NOTE
In this book Kerouac calls himself "Ti Jean Duluoz," his mother is "Ange Duluoz," his father is "Emil Alcide Duluoz," his older brother is "Gerard Duluoz," and his older sister is "Caroline 'Nin' Duluoz."

GERARD DULUOZ WAS BORN IN 1917 a sickly little kid with a rheumatic heart and many other complications that made him ill for the most part of his life which ended in July 1926, when he was 9, and the nuns of St. Louis de France Parochial School were at his bedside to take down his dying words because they'd heard his astonishing revelations of heaven delivered in catechism class on no more encouragement than that it was his turn to speak—Saintly Gerard, his pure and tranquil face, the mournful look of him, the piteousness of his little soft shroud of hair falling down his brow and swept aside by the hand over blue serious eyes—I would deliver no more obloquies and curse at my damned earth, but obsecrations only, could I resolve in me to keep his fixed-in-memory face free of running off from me—For the first four years of my life, while he lived, I was not Ti Jean Duluoz, I was Gerard, the world was his face, the flower of his face, the pale stooped disposition, the heartbreakingness and the holiness and his teachings of tenderness to me, and my mother constantly reminding me to pay attention to his goodness and advice—Summers he'd lain a-afternoons, on back, in yard, hand to eyes, gazing at the white clouds passing on by, those perfect Tao phantoms that materialize and then travel and then go, dematerialized, in one vast planet emptiness, like souls of people, like substantial fleshy people themselves, like your quite substantial redbrick smokestacks of the Lowell Mills along the river on sad red sun Sunday afternoons when big scowling Emil Pop Duluoz our father is in his shirtsleeves reading the funnies in the corner by the potted plant of time and home—Patting his sickly little Gerard on the head, "*Mon pauvre ti Loup,* me poor lil Wolf, you were born to suffer" (little dreaming how soon it would be his sufferings'd end, how soon the rain, incense and teary glooms of the funeral which would be held across the way in St. Louis de France's cellar-like basement church on Boisvert and West Sixth).

For me the first four years of my life are permeant and gray with the memory of a kindly serious face bending over me and being me and blessing me—The world a hatch of Duluoz Saintliness, and him the big chicken, Gerard, who warned me to be kind to little animals and took me by the hand on forgotten little walks.

• • •

Behold:—One day he found a mouse caught in Scoop's mousetrap outside the fish market on West Sixth Street—Faces more bleak than envenomed spiders, those who invented mousetraps, and had paths of bullgrained dullishness beaten to their bloodstained doors, and crowed in the sill—For that matter, on this gray morning, I can remember the faces of the Canucks of Lowell, the small tradesmen, butchers, butter and egg men, fishmen, barrelmakers, bums in benches (no benches but the oldtime sidewalk chair spitters by the dump, by banana peels steaming in the midday broil)—The hungjawed dull faces of grown adults who had no words to praise or please little trying-angels like Gerard working to save the mouse from the trap—But just stared or gawped on jawpipes and were silly in their prime—The little mouse, thrashing in the concrete, was released by Gerard—It went wobbling to the gutter with the fish-juice and spit, to die—He picked it tenderly and in his pocket sowed the goodness—Took it home and nursed it, actually bandaged it, held it, stroked it, prepared a little basket for it, as Ma watched amazed and men walked around in the streets "doin good for themselves" rounding up paper beyond their beans—Bums! all!—A thought smaller than a mouse's turd directed to the Sunday Service Mass necessity, and that usually tinged by inner countings how much they'll plap

in th'basket—I dont remember rationally but in my soul and mind Yes
there's a mouse, peeping, and Gerard, and the basket, and the kitchen
the scene of this heart-tender little hospital—"That big thing hurt you
when it fell on your little leg" (because Gerard could really feel empa-
thetically that pain, pain he'd had enough to not be apprentice at the
trade and pang)—He could feel the iron snap grinding his little imagined
birdy bones and squeezing and cracking and pressing harder unto
worse-than-death the bleak-in-life—For it's not innocent blank nature
made hills look sad and woe-y, it's men, with their awful minds—Their
ignorance, grossness, mean petty thwarthings, schemes, hypocrite tendencies, repenting over losses, gloating over gains—Pot-boys, bone-
carriers, funeral directors, glove-wearers, fog-breathers, shit-betiders,
pissers, befoulers, stenchers, fat calf converters, utter blots & scabs on
the face of it the earth—"Mouse? Who cares about a gad dam mouse
—God musta made em to fit our traps"—Typical thought—I'd as soon
drop a barrel of you-know-what on the roof of my own house, as walk
a mile in conversation about one of them—I dont count Gerard in that
seedy lot, that crew of bulls—The particular bleak gray jowled pale eyed
sneaky fearful French Canadian quality of man, with his black store,
his bags of produce, his bottomless mean and secret cellar, his herrings
in a barrel, his hidden gold rings, his wife and daughter jongling in
another dumb room, his dirty broom in the corner, his piousness, his
cold hands, his hot bowels, his well-used whip, his easy greeting and
hard opinion—Lay me down in sweet India or old Tahiti, I dont want
to be buried in *their* cemetery—In fact, cremate me and deliver me to
les Indes, I'm through—Wait till I get going on some of these other
blood-louts, for that matter—Yet not likely Gerard ever, if he'd have
lived, would have fattened as I to come and groan about peoples and
in plain print loud and foolish, but was a soft tenderhearted angel the
likes of which you'll never find again in science fictions of the future
with their bleeding plastic penis-rods and round hole-machines and worries about how to get from Pit to Pisspot which is one millionth of a
billionth of an inch further in endlessness of our gracious Lord than the
earth speck (which I'd spew) (if I were you) (Maha Meru)—Some afternoon, Gerard goes to school—It had been on a noontime errand
when sent to the store to buy smoked fish, that he'd found the mouse
—Now, smiling, I see him from my overstuffed glooms in the parlor
corner walking up Beaulieu Street to school with his strapped books
and long black stockings and that peculiar gloomy sweetness of his
person that was all things to me, I saw nothing else—Happy because

his mouse was fed and repaired and safe in her little basket—Innocent enough comes our cat in the mid drowses of day, and eats, and leaves but the tail, enough to make all Lowell Laugh, but when Gerard comes home at 4 to see his tail-let in the bottom of the poor little basket he'd so laboriously contrived, he cried—I cried too.

My mother tried to explain that it wasnt the cat's fault and no-body's fault and such was life.

He knew it wasnt the cat's fault but he took Nanny and sat her on the rocking chair and held her jowls and delivered her an exhortation no less:

"*Méchante!* Bad girl! Dont you understand what you've done? When will you understand? We dont disturb little animals and little things! We leave them alone! We'll never go to heaven if we go on eating each other and destroying each other like that all the time!—without thinking, without knowing!—wake up, foolish girl!—realize what you've done!—Be ashamed! shame! crazy face! stop wiggling your ears! Understand what I'm tellin you! It's got to stop some fine day! There wont always be time!—Bad girl! Go on! Go in your corner! Think it over well!"

I had never seen Gerard angry.

I was amazed and scared in the corner, as one might have felt seeing Christ in the temple bashing the moneychanger tables everywhichaway and scourging them with his seldom whip.

· · ·

When my father comes home from his printing shop and undoes his tie and removes 1920's vest and sits himself down at hamburger and boiled potatoes and bread and butter of the prime with the kiddies and the good wife, the proposition is put up to him why men be so cruel and mice betrayed and cats devour the rest—Why we were made to suffer and be harsh in return, one the other, and drop turds of iron on brows of hope, and mop up sick yards and sad—"I'll tell you, Ti Gerard, little one, in life it's a jungle, man eats man either you eat or get eaten—The cat eats the mouse, the mouse eats the worm, the worm eats the cheese, the cheese turns and eats the man—So to speak—It's like that, life—Dont cry and dont bother your sweet lil head over these things—All right, we're all born to die, it's the same story for everybody, see? We eat the cow and the cow gives us milk, dont ask me why."

"Yes, why—why do men make traps for little mice?"

"Because they eat their grain."

"Their old grain."

"It's grain that's in our bread—Look here, you eat it your bread? I dont see you throw it on the floor! and you dont make *passes* with the dust in the corner!"—*Passes* were the name Gerard had invented for when you run your bread over gravy, my mother'd do the soaking and throw the *passes* all around the table, even to me in my miffles and bibs at the little child flaptable—But because of our semi-Iroquoian French-Canadian accent *passe* was pronounced *PAUSS* so I can still hear the lugubrious sound of it and comfort-a-suppers of it, *M'ué'n pauss*, as you'd expect Bardolph to remember his cockwalloping heigho's of Eastcheap—My father is in the kitchen, young and primey, shirtsleeves, chomping up his supper, grease on his chin, bemused, explaining moralities to his angels—They'll grow 12 feet tall in the grave ere the monstrance that contains the solution to the problem be held up to shine and make true belief to shine, there's no explaining your way out of the evil of existence—"In any case, eat or be eaten—We eat now, later on the worms eat us."

Truer words were not spoken from any vantage point on this packet of earth.

"Why? *Pourquoi?*" cries lil Gerard with his brows forming woe and inabilities—"I dont want it to be like this, me."

"Though you want or not, it is."

"I dont care."

"What you gonna do?"

He pouts; he'll go to heaven, that's what; enough of this beastliness and compromising gluttony and compensating muck—Life, another word for mud.

"Come, come, little Gerard, maybe there's something you know that *we* dont know"—My father always did concede, Gerard had a deep mind and deep things to think that didnt find nook in insurance policies and printer's bills—They'd never write Gerard a policy but in eternity, he knew we were here a short while, and pathetic like the mouse, and O patheticker like the cat, and O worse! like the father-cant-explain!

"Awright," he'll go to bed and sleep it off, he'll tuck me in too, and kiss Ti Nin goodnight and the mouse be no lesser for her moment in his hands at noon—Together we pray for the Mouse. "Dear Lord, take care of the little mouse"—"Take care of the cat," we add to pray, since that's where the Lord'll have to do his work.

Ah, and the winds are cold and blow forlorner dust than they'll ever be able to invent in hell, in Northern Earth here, where people's hopes though warm fail to conceal the draft, the little draft that works all night moving curtains over radiator heat and sneaks around your blanket, and would bring you outdoors where russet dawn-men with cold-chapped ham-hands saw and pound at wood and work and steam with horses and curse the Satan in the air that made all Russias, Siberias, Americas bare to the blasts of infinity.

Gerard and I huddle in the warm gleeful bed of morning, afraid to get out—It's like remembering before you were born and your hap was at hand and Karma forced you out to start the story.

"Where is she the little mouse now?"

"This morning. The cat has shat her in the woods (*Le chat l'a shiez dans l'champ*)—with the little pipi yellow you see in the snow down there, see it?"

"*Oui.*"

"*Voilà* your fly of last summer, she's dead too—"

We think it over in motionless trance, as Ma prepares Pa's breakfast in the fragrant kitchen below.

"Angie," says Dad at the stove, "that kid'll break my heart yet—it hurt him so much to lose his little mouse."

"He's all heart."

"With his sickness inside—Ah, it busts my head—Eat or get eaten—not men?—Hah!—There's a gang downtown would, if their guts were big enough."

Gerard's feeling of the holiness of life extended into the realm of romance.

A drunkard under an ample tent was never more adamant concerning how his little sister should behave—"Mama, look what Ti Nin's doing she's going to school with her overshoes flopping and throwing her behind around like a flapper!" he yelled one morning looking out the window—It was one of those days when he was suffering a rheumatic fever relapse and had to stay in bed, weeks sometimes, some days worse than others—"Aw look at her!—" He was horrified—He refused to let her do it, when she came home at noon he had a speech worked out for her—"I'm telling you Gerard, you'll be a priest some day!" my mother'd say.

Meanwhile the kids at church did the sign of the cross some of them with the following words:

> "Au nom du père
> Ma tante Cafière
> Pistalette de bois
> Ainsi soit-il"

Meaning

> "In the name of the Father
> My Aunt Cafière
> Pistolet of wood
> Amen"

There's my pa—Emil Alcide Duluoz, at that time, 1925 a hale young printer of 36, dark complexioned, frowning, serious, hardjawed but soft in the gut (tho he had a gut so hard when he oomfed it and dared us kids butt our heads in it or punch fists off it and it felt like punching a powerful basketball)—5:7, Bretonsquat, blue eyed—He had a habit I cant forget, even now I just imitated it, lighting a small fire in the ashtray, out of cigarette pack paper or tobacco wrapping—Sitting in his chair he'd watch the little Nirvana fire consume the paper and render it black crisp void, and understand, mayhap, the bigger kindling of the 3,000 Chillicosms—That which would devour and digest to safety—A little matter of time, for him, for me, for you.

Too, he'd take fresh crisp MacIntosh apples of the Fall and sit in his easy chair and peel em with his pocket knife, making long tassels around and around the fruitglobe so perfect you could have hung them like tassels' canopies from chandelier to chandelier in the Hall Tolstoy, the which we'd take and sling around and I'd eat em in like great tapeworms and they'd end up flung out in the garbage can like coils of electric wire around and around—After which he'd eat his peeled apple at the gisty whitemeat cut-surface with great slobbering juicy bites that had all the world watering—"Imitate the roar of a lion! Imitate a tiger cat! Imitate an elephant!"—Which he'd do, in his chair, for us, evenings in New England, Gerard on one knee, me on the other, Nin on his lap—That is, when ever there was no poker game to speak of downtown.

"And you my little Gerard, why do you look so pensive tonight? What's goin on in that little head?" he'd say, hugging his Gerard to him, cheek against soft hair, as Nin and I watched rave lip't and rapt in the happiness of our childhood, little dreaming what quick work the winds of outside winter would do against the timbers and tendons of his poor house.

In the name of the father, the son, and the Holy Ghost, amen.

• • •

Would I were divinest punner and tell how the cold winds blow with one stroke of my quick head in this harsh unhospitable hospital called the earth, where "thou owest God a death"—Time for me to get on my own horse—

The Kat is up on the sink actually fascinated by the drip drip of the faucet, there he is with his paws under him and his tail curling down and his ruminative quickglancing face bending and earpricking to the phenomena, as tho he was trying to figure out, or pass the time, or make fun of us—But Mama has a headache, it's a cold windy night in Old February and Pa is out late at work (playing poker backstage B.F.Keiths maybe with W.C.Fields for all I know with my drawn yawp masque)—The winds belabor at the windows of the kitchen, Ma is on the couch on the newspapers where she's flopped in despair, it's about 9:30, supper dishes have been put away (tenderly by her own hands) and now she lies there head back on a kewpie cushion with an ice pack on her head—The woodstove roars—Gerard and I are at the stove rocker, warming our feet, Nin is at the table doing her "*devoir*" (homework)—

"Mama you're sick," demurs Gerard with the gods, with his piteous voice, "what are we going to do."

"Aw it'll go away."

He goes over and lays his head against hers and waits to hear her cure—

"If I had some aspirins."

"I'll go get you some—at drugstore!"

"It's too late."

"It's only 9:30—I'm not afraid."

"Poor Lil Gerard it's too cold tonight and it's too late."

"No mama! I'll dress up good! My hat my rubbers!"

"Run. Go to Old Man Bruneau, ask him for a bottle of aspirin— the money is in my pocketbook."

Together Gerard and I peer and probe into the mysterious pocketbook for the mysterious nickles and dimes that are always there intermingled with rosaries and gum and powder puffs—

Little Gerard runs and puts his muffcap and draws it over his ears and draws on his rubbers with that tragic bent over motion no angels who never lived on earth could know—A cold key in a tight lock, our situation, the skin so warm, thin, the night of Winter so broad and cool—So Saskatchewan'd with advantage—

"Hurry up my golden, Mama'll be afraid—"

"I'll go get your medicine and you'll be all right, just watch!"

Gleefully he goes off, the door admits Spectre into the kitchen an instant and he slams it—I watch him tumble off.

Beaulieu Street going down towards West Sixth, 4 houses, to the Fire House, is swept by dusts—The lamp on the corner only serves to accentuate by contrast the lightlessness in the general air—The stars above are no help, they twinkle in a vain freeze—The cold sweeps down Gerard's neck, he tries to bundle in—He hurries around the corner and down West Sixth, towards the lights of the big corner at Aiken and Lilley and West Sixth where bleak graypaint tenements stand with dull brown kitchen lights under the hard stars—Not a soul in sight, a few cruds of old snow stuck in the gutters—A fine world for icebergs and stones—A world not made for men—A world, if made for anything, made for something dead to sympathy—Since sympathizing there'll not be in it ever—He runs to warm up—

Down at Aiken the wind from the river hits him full-blast with a roar, around the corner, bringing with it the odor of cold rocks in the river's ice, and the savor of rust—

"God doesnt look like he made the world for people" he guesses all by himself as it occurs in his chilled bones the hopeless sensation— No help in sight, the utter helpless-ness up, down, around—The stars, rooftops, dusty swirls, streetlamps, cold storefronts, vistas at street-ends where you know the earthflat just continues on and on into a round February the roundness of which and warm ball of which wont be vouchsafed us Slav-level fools as but flat—Flat as a tin pan—So for winds to swail across, a man oughta lie down on his back on a cold night and miss those winds—No thought, no hope of the mind can dispel, nay no millions in the bank, can break, the truth of the Winter night and that we are not made for this world—Stones yes, grass and trees for all their green return I'd say no to judge from their dead brown-ness tonight—A million may buy a hearth, but a hearth wont buy rich safety—

Gerard divines that all of this is pure division, a grief of separation, the cold is cold because there are two to know it, the cold and he who is en-colded—"If it wasn't for that, like in Heaven, . . ."

"And Mama has a headache, aw God why'd you do all this this suffering?"

En route back with the aspirins he hears a forlorn rumble in Ennell Street, it's the old junkman coming back from some over extended work somewhere in windswept junk-slopes, his horse is steaming, his steel-on-wood-wheels are grinding grit on grit and stone on stone and wind swirls dust about his burlaps, as he smiles that tooth-smile of the cold between embittered lips, you see the suffering of his mitts and the weeping in his beard, the woe—Going home to some leaky rafter—To count his rusty corsets and by-your-leaves and tornpaper accounts and pile-alls—To die on his heap of mistakes, finally, and what was gained in emptiness you'll never find debited or credited in any account—What the preachers say not excepted—"Poor old man, he hasnt got a nice warm kitchen, he hasnt got a mother, he hasnt got a little sister and little brother and Papa, he's alone under the hole under the open stars —If it was all together in one ball of wool—!—" The horse's hooves strike sparks, the wheels labor to turn into West Sixth, the whole she-bang sorrows out of sight—Gerard approaches our house, our golden kitchen lights and pauses on the cold porch for one last look up—The stars have nothing to do with anything.

In some other way, he hopes.

"There, your little hands are cold—thank you my child—bring me a glass of water—I'll be all right—Mama's sick tonight—"

"Mama—why is it so cold?"

"Dont ask me."

"Why did God leave us sick and cold? Why didnt he leave us in Heaven."

"You're sure we were there?"

"Yes, I'm sure."

"How are you sure?"

"Because it cant be like it is."

"*Oui*"—Ma in her rare moments when thinking seriously she doesnt admit anything that doesnt ring all the way her bell of mind—"but it is."

"I dont like it. I wanta go to Heaven. I wish we were all in Heaven."

"Me too I wish."

"Why cant we have what we want?" but as soon as he says that the tears appear in his eyes, as he knows the selfish demand—

"Aw Mama, I dont understand."

"Come come we'll make some nice hot chocolate!—"

"Hot chocolate! (*Du coco!*)" cries Ti Nin, and I echo it:

"Klo Klo!"

The big cocoa deal boils and bubbles chocolating on the stove and soon Gerard forgets—

If his mortality be the witness of Gerard's sin, as Augustine Page One immediately announced, then his sin must have been a great deal greater than the sin of mortals who enjoy, millionaires in yachts a-sailing in the South Seas with blondes and secretaries and flasks and engineers and endless hormone pills and Tom Collins Moons and peaceful deaths—The sins of the junkman on Ennell Street, they were vast almost as mine and brother's—

In bed that night he lies awake, Gerard, listening to the moan of wind, the flap of shutters—From where he lies he can just see one cold sparkle star—The fences have no hope.

Like, the protection you'd get tonight huddling against an underpass.

But Gerard had his holidays, they bruited before his wan smile—New Year's Eve we're all in bed upstairs under the wall-papered eaves listening to the racket horns and rattlers below and out the window the dingdong bells and sad horizon hush of all Lowell and towards Kearney Square where we see the red glow embrowned and aura'd in the new (1925) sky and we think: "A new year"—A new year with a new number and a new little boy with candlelight and *kitchimise* standing radiant in the eternities, as the old, some old termagant with beard and scythe, goes wandering down the darkness field, and on the sofa arms of the parlor chairs even now the fairies are dancing—Gerard and Nin and I are sitting up in the one bed of conclave, with a happy smile he's trying to explain to us what's really happening but by and by the drunks come upstairs with wild hats to kiss us—Some sorrow involved in the crinkly ends of pages of old newspapers bound in old readingroom files so that you turn and see the news of that bygone New Year's day, the advertisements with top hats, the crowds in Hail streets, the snow—The little boy under the quilt who will have X's in his eyes when the rubber lamppost ushers in his latter New Years Eves, one scythe after another lopping off his freshness juices till he comes to bebibbling them from corny necks of bottles—And the swarm in the darkness, of an ethereal kind, where nobody ever looks, as if if they did look the swarms ethereal

would wink off, winking, to wink on again when no one's watching—
Gerard's bright explanations about dark time, and cowbells—Then we
had our Easter.

Which came with lilies in April, and you had white doves in the
fields, and we went seesawing thru Palm Sunday and we'd stare at those
pictures of Jesus meek on the little *azno* entering the city and the palm
multitudes, "The Lord has found that nice little animal there and he got
up on his back and they rode into the city"—"Look, the people are all
glad"—A few chocolate rabbits one way or the other was not the impress of our palmy lily-like Easter, our garland of roses, our muddy-
earth Spring sigh when all in new shoes we squeaked to the church and
outside you could smell the fragrant cigarettes and see men spit and
inside the church was all dormant and adamant like wine with white
white flowers everywhere—

We had our Fourth of July, some firecrackers, some fence sitting
spitting of sparks, warm trees of night, boys throwing torpedoes against
fences, general wars, oola-oo-ah popworks at the Common with the big
bomb was the finale, and popcorn and Ah Lemonade—

And Halloween: the Halloween of 1925, when Ma dressed me up
as a little Chinaman with a queu and a white robe and Gerard as a
Pirate and Nin as a Vamp and old Papa took us by the hand and paraded us down to the corner at Lilley and Aiken, ice cream sodas,
swarms of eyes on the sidewalks—

All the little children of the world keep quickly coming and going
to the holidays that only slowly change, but the quality of the brightness
of their eyes monotonously reverts—Seeds, seeds, the seed sown everywhere blossoming the fruit of our loom, living-but-to-die—There's
just no fun in holidays when you know.

All the living and dying creatures of the endless future wont even
wanta be forewarned—wherefore, I should shut up and close up shop
and bang shutters and broom my own dark and nasty nest.

At this time my father had gotten sick and moved part of his printing
business in the basement of the house where he had his press, and upstairs in an unused bedroom where he had some racks of type—He had
rheumatism too, and lay in white sheets groaned and saying *"La
marde!"* and looking at his type racks in the next room where his helper
Manuel was doing his best in an inkstained apron.

It was later on, about the time Gerard got really sick (long-sick,
year-sick, his last illness) that this paraphernalia was moved back to the

rented shop on Merrimack Street in an alley in back of the Royal Theater, an alley which I visited just last year to find unchanged and the
old graywood Colonial one storey building where Pa's pure hopeshop
rutted, a boarded up ghost-hovel not even fit for bums—And forlorner
winds never did blow ragspaper around useless rubbish piles, than those
that blow there tonight in that forgotten alley of the world which is no
more forgotten than the heartbreaking and piteous way Gerard had of
holding his head to the side whenever he was interested or bemused in
something, and as if to say, "Ay-you, world, what are our images but
dust?—and our shops,"—sad.

Nonetheless, lots of porkchops and beans came to me via my old man's
efforts in the world of business which for all the fact that 't is only the
world of adult playball, procures tightwad bread from hidden cellars
the locks of which are guarded by usurping charlatans who know how
easy it is to enslave people with a crust of bread withheld—He, Emil,
went bustling and bursting in his neckties to find the money to pay rents,
coalbills (for to vaunt off that selfsame winter night and I'd be ingrat
to make light of it whenever trucks come early morning and dump their
black and dusty coal roar down a chute of steel into our under bins)—
Ashes in the bottom of the furnace, that Ma herself shoveled out and
into pails, and struggled to the ashcan with, were ashes representative
of Poppa's efforts and tho their heating faculties were in Nirvana now
'twould be loss of fealty to deny—I curse and rant nowaday because I
dont want to have to work to make a living and do childish work for
other men (any lout can move a board from hither to yonder) but'd
rather sleep all day and stay it up all night scrubbling these visions of
the world which is only an ethereal flower of a world, the coal, the
chute, the fire and the ashes all, imaginary blossoms, nonetheless,
"somebody's got to do the work-a the world"—Artist or no artist, I
cant pass up a piece of fried chicken when I see it, compassion or no
compassion for the fowl—Arguments that raged later between my father and myself about my refusal to go to work—"I wanta *write*—I'm
an *artist*"—"Artist shmartist, ya cant be supported all ya life—"
     And I wonder what Gerard would have done had he lived, sickly,
artistic—But by my good Jesus, with that holy face they'd have stumbled over one another to come and give him bread and breath—He left
me his heart but not his tender countenance and sorrowful patience and
kindly lights—
     "Me when I'm big, I'm gonna be a painter of beautiful pictures and

I'm gonna build beautiful bridges"—He never lived to come and face the humble problem, but he would have done it with that *noblesse tendresse* I never in my bones and dead man heart could ever show.

It's a bright cold morning in December 1925, just before Christmas, Gerard is setting out to school—Aunt Marie has him by the hand, she's visiting us for a week and she wants to take a morning constitutional, and take deep breaths and show Gerard how to do likewise, for his health—Aunt Marie is my father's favorite sister (and my favorite aunt), a talkative openhearted, teary bleary lovely with red lipstick always and gushy kisses and a black ribbon pendant from her specs—While my father has been abed with rheumatism she's helped somewhat with the housework—Crippled, on crutches, a modiste—Never married but many boyfriends helped her—The spittin image of Emil and the lover of Gerard's little soul as no one else, unless it be the cold eyed but warm hearted Aunt Anna from up in Maine—"Ti Gerard, for your health always do this, take big clacks of air in your lungs, hold it a long time, look" pounding her furpieced breast, "see?"—

"*Oui*, Matante Marie—"

"Do you love your Matante?"

"My Matante Marie I love her so big!" he cries affectionately as they hug and limp around the corner, to the school, where the kids are, in the yard, and the nuns, who now stare curiously at Gerard's distinguished aunt—Aunt Marie take her leave and drops in the church for a quick prayer—It's the Christmas season and everyone feels devout.

The kids bumble into their seats in the classroom.

"This morning," says the nun up front, "we're going to study the next chapter of the catechism—" and the kids turn the pages and stare at the illustrations done by old French engravers like Boucher and others always done with the same lamby gray strangeness, the curlicue of it, the reeds of Moses' bed-basket I remember the careful way they were drawn and divided and the astonished faces of women by the riverbank—It's Gerard's turn to read after Picou'll be done—He dozes in his seat from a bad night's rest during which his breathing was difficult, he doesnt know it but a new and serious attack on his heart is forming—Suddenly Gerard is asleep, head on arms, but because of the angle of the boy's back in front of him the nun doesnt see.

Gerard dreams that he is sitting in a yard, on some house steps with me, his little brother, in the dream he's thinking sorrowfully: "Since the beginning of time I've been charged to take care of this little brother, my Ti Jean, my poor Ti Jean who cries he's afraid—" and he is about to stroke me on the head, as I sit there drawing a stick around in the sand, when suddenly he gets up and goes to another part of the yard, nearby, trees and bushes and something strange and gray and suddenly the ground ends and there's just air and supported there at the earth's gray edge of immateriality, is a great White Virgin Mary with a flowing robe ballooning partly in the wind and partly tucked in at the edges and held aloft by swarms, countless swarms of grave bluebirds with white downy bellies and necks—On her breast, a crucifix of gold, in her hand a rosary of gold, on her head a star of gold—Beauteous beyond bounds and belief, like snow, she speaks to Gerard:

"Well my goodness Ti Gerard, we've been looking for you all morning—where were you?"

He turns to explain that he was with . . . that he was on . . . that he was . . . that . . . —He cant remember what it is that it was, he cant remember why he forgot where he was, or why the time, the morning-time, was shortened, or lengthened—The Virgin Mary reads it in his perplexed eyes. "Look," pointing to the red sun, "it's still early, I wont be mad at you, you were only gone less than a morning—Come on—"

"Where?"

"Well, dont you remember? We were going—come on—"

"How'm I gonna follow you?"

"Well your wagon is there" and Oh yes, he snaps his finger and looks to remember and there it is, the snow-white cart drawn by two lambs, and as he sits in it two white pigeons settle on each of his shoulders; as prearranged, he bliss-remembers all of it now, and they start, tho one perplexing frown shows in his thoughts where he's still trying to remember what he was and what he was doing before, or during, his absence, so brief—And as the little wagon of snow ascends to Heaven, Heaven itself becomes vague and in his arm with head bent Gerard is contemplating the perfect ecstasy when his arm is rudely jolted by Sister Marie and he wakes to find himself in a classroom with the sad window-opening pole leaning in the corner and the erasers on the ledges of the blackboards and the surly marks of woe smudged thereon and the Sister's eyes astonished down on his:

"Well what are you doing Gerard! you're sleeping!"

"Well I was in Heaven."

"What?"

"Yes Sister Marie, I've arrived in Heaven!"

He jumps up and looks at her straight to tell her the news.

"It's your turn to read the catechism!"

"Where?"

"There—the chapter—at the end—"

Automatically he reads the words to please her; while pausing, he looks around at the children; Lo! all the beings involved! And look at the strange sad desks, the wood of them, and the carved marks on them, initials, and the little boy Ouellette (suddenly re-remembered) as usual with the same tranquil unconcern (outwardly) whistling soundlessly into his eraser, and the sun streaming in the high windows showing motes of room-dust—The whole pitiful world is still there! and nobody knows it! the different appearances of the same emptiness everywhere! the ethereal flower of the world!

"My sister, I saw the Virgin Mary."

The nun is stunned: "Where?"

"There—in a dream, when I slept."

She does the sign of the cross.

"Aw Gerard, you gave me a start!"

"She told me come on—and there was a pretty little white wagon with two little lambs to pull it and we started out and we were going to Heaven."

"Mon Seigneur!"

"A little white wagon!" echo several children with excitement.

"Yes—and two white pigeons on my shoulder—doves—and she asked me 'Where were you Gerard, we've been waiting for you all morning' "—

Sister Marie's mouth is open—"Did you see all this in a dream? —? here now?—in the room."

"Yes my good sister—dont be afraid my good sister, we're all in Heaven—but we dont know it!"—"Oh," he laughs, *"we dont know it!"*

"For the love of God!"

"God fixed all this a long time ago."

The bell is ringing announcing the end of the hour, some of the children are already poised to scamper on a word, Sister Marie is so stunned everyone is motionless—Gerard sits again and suddenly over him falls the tight overpowering drowsiness around his heart, as before, and his legs ache and a fever breaks on his brow—He remains in his seat in a trance, hand to brow, looking up minutes later to an empty room save for Soeur Marie and the elder Soeur Caroline who has been summoned—They are staring at him with tenderest respect.

"Will you repeat what you told me to Sister Caroline?"

"Yes—but I dont feel good."

"What's the matter, Gerard?"

"I'm starting to be sick again I guess."

"We'll have to send him home—"

"They'll put him to bed like they did last year, like before—He hasnt got much strength, the little one."

"He saw Heaven."

"Ah"—shrugging, Sister Caroline—"that"—nodding her head—

Slowly, at 9:30 o'clock that morning, my mother who's in the yard with clothespins in her mouth sees him coming down the empty school-time street, alone, with that lassitude and dragfoot that makes a chill in her heart—

"Gerard is sick—"

For the last time coming home from school.

When Christmas Eve comes a few days later he's in bed, in the side room downstairs—His legs swell up, his breathing is difficult and painful—The house is chilled. Aunt Louise sits at the kitchen table shaking her head—"*La peine, la peine,* pain, pain, always pain for the Duluozes—I knew it when he was born—his father, his aunt, all his uncles, all invalids—all in pain—Suffering and pain—I tell you, Emil, we havent been blessed by Chance."

The old man sighs and plops the table with his open hand. "That goes without saying."

Tears bubbling from her eyes, Aunt Louise, shifting one hand quickly to catch a falling crutch, "Look, it's Christmas already, he's got his tree, his toys are all bought and he's lying there on his back like a corpse—it's not *fair* to hurt little children like that that arent old enough to know—Ah Emil, Emil, Emil, what's going to happen, what's going to happen to *all* of us!"

And her crying and sobbing gets me crying and sobbing and soon Uncle Mike comes in, with wife and the boys, partly for the holidays, partly to see little Gerard and offer him some toys, and he too, Mike, cries, a great huge tormented tearful man with bald head and blue eyes, asthmatic thunderous efforts in his throat as he draws each breath to expostulate long woes: "My poor Emil, my poor little brother Emil, you have so much trouble!" followed by crashing coughs and in the kitchen the other aunt is saying to my mother:

"I told you to take care of him, that child—he was never strong, you know—you've always got to send him warmly dressed" and et cetera as tho my mother had somehow been to blame so she cries too and in the sickroom Gerard, waking up and hearing them, realizes with compassion heavy in his heart that it is only an ethereal sorrow and too will fade when heaven reveals her white.

"*Mon Seigneur*," he thinks, "bless them all"—

He pictures them all entering the belly of the lamb—Even as he stares at the wood of the windowframe and the plaster of the ceiling with its little cobwebs moving to the heat.

Hearken, amigos, to the olden message: it's neither what you think it is, nor what you think it isnt, but an elder matter, uncompounded and clear—Pigs may rut in field, come running to the Soo-Call, full of sowy glee; people may count themselves higher than pigs, and walk proudly down country roads; geniuses may look out of windows and count themselves higher than louts; tics in the pine needles may be inferior to the swan; but whether any of these and the stone know it, it's still the same truth: none of it is even there, it's a mind movie, *believe* this if you will and you'll be saved in the solvent solution of salvation and Gerard knew it well in his dying bed in his way, in his way—And who handed us down the knowledge here of the Diamond Light? Messengers unnumberable from the Ethereal Awakened Diamond Light. And why?—because is, is—and was, was—and will be, will be—t'will!

Christmas Eve of 1925 Ti Nin and I gayly rushed out with our sleds to a new snow layer in Beaulieu street, forgetting our brother in his sack, tho it was he sent us out with injunctions to play good and slide far—

"Look at the pretty snow outside, go play!" he cried like a kindly mother, and we bundled up and went out—

I still remember the quality of that sky, that very evening, tho I was only 3 years old—

Over the roofs, which held their white and would hold them all night now that the sun was casting himself cold and wan-pink over the final birches of griefstricken westward Dracut—Over the roofs was that blue, magic Lowell blue, that keen winter northern knifeblade blue of winter dusks so unforgettable and so cold and dry, like dry ice, flint, sparks, like powdery snow that ss'ses at under doorsills—Perfect for the silhouetting of birds heading darkward down their appointed lane, hushed—Perfect for the silhouetting presentations of church steeples and of rooftops and of the whole Lowell general, and always yon poor smoke putting from the human chimneys like prayer—The whole town aglow with the final russet adventures of the day staining windowpanes and sending pirates to the east and bringing other sabers of purple and of saffron scarlot harlot rage across the gashes and might ironworks of incomprehensible moveless cloud wars frowned and befronting one another on horizon Shrewsburies—Up there where instead of thickening, plots thinned and leaked and warrior groups pulled wan expiring acts on the monstrous rugs of sky areas with names in purple, and dull boom cannons, and maw-mouth awwp up-clouds far far away where the children say "There's an old man sleeping in the north with a big white mouth that's open and a round nose"—These mighty skies bending over Lowell and over Gerard as he lay knowing in his deathbed, rosaries in his hands, pans on papers by the bed, pillows under his feet—The sides and portion wedges of which sky he can barely see thru the window shade and frame, outside is December's big parley with night and it's Christmas Eve and his heart breaks to realize that it will be his last Christmas on our innocent mistaken earth—"Ah yes—if I could tell them what I knew—but when I start it stops coming, it's gone, it's not to talk about—but now I *know* it—just like my dream—poor people with their houses and their chimnies and their Christmases and their children—listen to them yelling in the street, listen to their sleds—they run, they throw themselves on the snow, the little sled takes them a little ways and then that's all—that's all—And me, big nut, I cant explain them what they're dying to know—It's because God doesnt wanta—"

God made us for His glory, not our own.

Nin and I have our sleds and mufflers and we have wrangled dramas with the other kids over the little dispositions of activity among snowbanks and slide-lanes, it all goes on endlessly this world in its big and little facets with no change in it.

• • •

I dont remember how Gerard died, but (in my memory, which is limited and mundane) here I am running pellmell out of the house about 4 o'clock in the afternoon and down the sidewalk of Beaulieu Street yelling to my father whom I've seen coming around the corner woeful and slow with strawhat back and coat over arms in the summer heat, gleefully I'm yelling *"Gerard est mort!"* (Gerard is dead!) as tho it was some great event that would make a change that would make everything better, which it actually was, which granted it actually was.

But I thought it had something to do with some holy transformation that would make him greater and more Gerard like—He would reap-

pear, following his "death," so huge and all powerful and renewed—
The dizzy brain of the four-year-old, with its visions and infold
mysticisms—I grabbed Pa and tugged his hand and glee'd to see the
expression of likewise gladness on his face, so when he wearily just said
"I know, Ti Pousse, I know" I had that same feeling that I have today
when I would rush and tell people the good news that Nirvana, Heaven,
Our Salvation is *Here* and *Now*, that gloomy reaction of theirs, which
I can only attribute to pitiful and so-to-be-loved Ignorance of mortal
brains.

"I know, my little wolf, I know," and sadly he drags himself into
the house as I dance after.

The undertakers presumably carry the little no-more-body of no-more-
pain-and-swelled-legs away, in a tidy basket, to prepare him for his
lying-in-state in our front parlor, and that night all the Duluozes do
drive up from Nashua in tragic blackflap cars and come to crying and
jawing in the brown kitchen of eternity as suddenly in my mind, as tho
it was only a dream, a vision in the mind, which it is, I see the whole
house and woe open up from within its every molecule and become
instead of contours of walls and ceilings and absence-holes of doors and
windows and there-yawps of voices and lamentings and wherewillgo-
beings of personality and name, Aunt Clementine, Uncle Mike, cousins
Roland and Edgar, Aunt Marie, Pa and Ma and Nin at the lot, just
suddenly a great swarming mass of roe-like fiery whitenesses, as if a
curtain had opened, and innumerably revealed the scene behind the
scene ("the scene behind the scene is always more interesting than the
show," says J. R. Williams the *Out Our Way* cartoonist), shows itself
compounded be, of emptiness, of pure light, of imagination, of mind,
mind-only, madness, mental woe, the strivings of mind pain, the
working-at-thinking which is all this imagined death & false life,
phantasmal beings, phantoms finagling in the gloom, goopy poor figures
haranguing and failing with lack-hands in a fallen-angel world of shadows and glore, the central entire essence of which is dazzling radiant
blissful ecstasy unending, the unbelievable Truth that cracks open in my
head like an oyster and I see it, the house disappears in her Swarm of
Snow, Gerard is dead and the soul is dead and the world is dead and
dead is dead.

I've since dreamed it a million times, down the corridors of Seeming
eternity where there are a million mirrored figures sitting thus and each

the same, the house on Beaulieu Street the night Gerard died and the assembled Duluozes wailing with green faces of death for fear of death in time, and Time's consumed it all already, it's a dream already a long time ended and they dont know it and I try to tell them, they wanta slap me in the kisser I'm so gleeful, they send me upstairs to bed—An old dream too I've had of me glooping, that night, in the parlor, by Gerard's coffin, I dont see him in the coffin but he's there, his ghost, brown ghost, and I'm grown sick in my papers (my writing papers, my bloody 'literary career' ladies and gentlemen) and the whole reason why I ever wrote at all and drew breath to bite in vain with pen of ink, great gad with indefensible Usable pencil, because of Gerard, the idealism, Gerard the religious hero—"*Write in honor of his death*" (*Écrivez pour l'amour de son mort*) (as one would say, write for the love of God)—for by his pain, the birds were saved, and the cats and mice, and the poor relatives crying, and my mother losing all her teeth in the six terrible weeks prior to his death during which time she stayed up all night every night and grew such a mess of nerves in her stomach that her teeth began falling one by one, might sight funny to some hunters of conceit, but this wit has had it.

Lord bless it, an Ethereal Flower, I saw it all blossom—they packed me to bed. They raved in the kitchen and had it their way.

There's the rocking chair, Uncle Mike's wife had it, the peculiar dreary voice she had, fast way she talked, things I cant utter but I'd roll and broil in butter, the gurgle in their throats—I could recount the dreary yellings and give you all the details—It's all in the same woods —It's all one flesh, and the pieces of it will come and go, alien hats and coats not to the contrary—Uncle Mike had a greenish face: he had barrelsful of pickles in Nashua, a sawdust oldtime store, meat-hacks and hung hams and baskets of produce on the sidewalk: fish in boxes, salted.—Emil's brother,—"So *vain*, so full of ego, people—shut your mouth you" he finally says to his wife, "I'm talkin tonight—in the great silence of our father we'll find the reasons for our prides, our avarices, our dollars—It's better any way, now that he's dead his belly doesnt hurt any more and his heart and his legs, it's better"—

"Have it your way," says my father listlessly.

"Ah Emil Emil dont you remember when we were children and we slept together and Papa built his house with his own hands and all the times I helped you—we too we'll die, Emil, and when we're dead will there be someone, *one person* for the love of God, who'll be able to look at us in our coffins and say 'It's all over, the *marde,* the fret, the force, the strength'?—more's the strength in the belly than anywhere else—finished, bought, sold, washed, brought to the great heaven! Emil dont cry, dont be discouraged, your little boy is better—remember you well what Papa used to say in back of his stove—"

"With his bottle on Sunday mornings, aw sure that one was a smart one!" (the wife).

"Shut your mouth I said!—All men die—And when they die as child, even better—they're *pure* for heaven—Emil, Emil,—poor young Emil, my little brother!"

They shake their heads violently the same way, thinking.

"Ah"—they bite their lips the same way, their bulgey eyes are on the floor.

"It ends like it ends"—

My mother's upstairs sobbing, lost all her control now—The aunts are cleaning out the death bed, there's a great to do of sheets and an end to sheets, a Spring cleaning.

"I brought him on earth, in my womb, the Virgin Mary help me! —in my womb, with pain—I gave him his milk!—I took care of him —I stood at his bedside—I bought him presents on Christmas, I made him little costumes Halloween—I'd make his nice oatmeal he loves so much in the mornings!—I'd listen to his little stories, I examined his little pictures he drew—I did everything in my power to make his little life contented—inside me, outside me, *and returned to the earth!*" wails my mother realizing the utter hopeless loss of life and death, the completely defeated conditionality and partiality of it, the pure mess it entails, yet people go on hoping and hoping—"I did everything," she sobs with handkerchief to face, in the bedroom, as the Bradleys, Aunt Pauline, her sister, come in, from New Hampshire, "and it didnt work— *he died anyhow*—They took him off to Heaven!—They didnt leave him with me!—Gerard, my little Gerard!"

"Calm yourself, poor Ange, you've suffered so."

"I havent suffered like he did, that's what *breaks* my heart!" and she yells that and they all know she really means it, she's had her fill of the injustice of it, a little lame boy dying without hope—"It's *that* that's tearing my heart out and breaking my head in two!"

"Ange, Ange, poor sensitive heart!" weeps gentle Aunt Marie at her shoulder.

Nin and I are sobbing horribly in bed side by side to hear these pitiful wracks of clack talk coming from our own human mother, the softness of her arms all gashed now in the steely proposition Death—

"I'll never be able to wipe that from my memory!"—"Not as long as I live!"—"He died *without* a chance!"

"We all die—"

"Good, damn it, good!" she cries, and this sends chills thru all of us man and child and the house is One Woe this night.

Meanwhile, insanely, our cousins Edgar and Roland have sneaked off with the firecrackers to the backyard, and like leering devils, which they arent really, but as much as like satyrs and Mockers and be-striders of misfortune, there they are setting off all our precious firecrackers, Nin's and mine and Gerard's, at midnight, callously, a veritable burning of the books of the Duluozes, Ker plack, whack, c a ka ta r a k sht boom!

"*Les mauva, les mauva,*" (mean! mean!) Ti Nin and I scream in pillows—

The Bradleys are going to drive us to Nashua for the night and bring us back for the funeral in 48 hours—With Gerard and the firecrackers all gone, and Ma crying on the very floor, we had better be driven somewhere—

When Ti Nin and I were little.

HOME AT CHRISTMAS
1932

IT'S A SUNDAY AFTERNOON in New England just three days before Christmas—Ma's making the roast in the kitchen range, also tapioca pudding so when Sister Nin comes in from outdoors with the shovel she's been wielding in the blizzard there are cold waves of snowy air mixing with the heat steams of tapioca over the stove and in my mouth I can taste whipped cream cold from the icebox on the hot pudding tonight.

While Ma cooks she also sits at the round kitchen table reading the *Boston American*—Pa's in the parlor playing the Gospel Singers of Sunday cigar-smoke funnies time—I'm getting ready to take my big blizzard walk into the Massachusetts Shroud begins just down the end of dirt road Phebe Avenue, I'm rummaging in the closet for my hockey stick which will be my walking-stick and feeling-stick to find where puddles and creeklets have disappeared under two feet of snow this day.

"Where you goin'?"

"Take my walk."

"Be careful don't fall in the ice—You're goin' to your Pine Brook?—Oh you're crazy you!" (exasperation)

I start out, down the porch steps, overshoes, woolcap, coat, corduroy pants, mittens—There are Christmas wreaths in all the windows of sweet Phebe—No sign of G.J. or Billy with the kids sliding on the park slope, no sign of them on their porch except G.J.'s sister in her coat all wrapped communing with the plicking fall of vast snows in a silence of her own, girl-like, watching it pile on the porch rail, the little rills, sadnesses, mysteries—She waves—I plod down off our Sis-shoveled walk into Mrs. Quinn's unshoveled walk where the going is deep, profound, happy—No shoveled walks all the way to Billy's where bigbrother sixfoot Jack has worked, in muffler with pink cheeks and white teeth, laughing—Black birds in the black cherry tree, and in the new snow breadcrumbs, bird tweak tracks, a little dot of kitty yellow, a star blob of plopsnow ball against Old MacArthur's wreathy front door—O the clean porches of New England in the holy dry snow that's drifting across new painted planks to pile in corners over rubber doormats, sleds, overshoes—The steam in the windows, the frost, the faces looking out—And over the sandbank now and down on semi-snow-plowed Phebe comes the great fwoosh of hard stormwind from the river cracking leafless shrubs in stick-unison, throwing swirls of coldsifted power, pure, the freezing freshness everywhere, the sand frozen solid underneath—

Down at the end of Phebe I'm in the middle of the road now preparing my big Arab strides for the real business of crossing miles of field and forest to my wanted Brook which in summer's a rendezvous of swimmers crossing gold and greenleaf day, bees of bugs, hay, haze, but now the gigantic Snow King has laid his drape upon the world, locked it in new silence, all you hear is the profound higher-than-human-ear screaming of snow radios bedazzling and electrifying the air like orgones and spermatazoas in a Universe Dance—They start black specks from heaven, swirl to avoid my gaze, fall white and ploppy on my nose—I turn my face up to the sweet soft kiss of Heaven—My feet are getting cold, I hurry on—Always with a smile of my numb cheeks and pinked lips I think (remembering movies) how really comfortable it would be to lie down and go to sleep in the soft thick snow, head rested—I plod, the hockey stick trails after—I go through the sandbank draw and rise to survey the sand field bordered on the other side by a cut of earth with saplings and boulders—I cluck up my horse and off we gallop in a snowbound Westerner to the scene, deep, the sand field is all milky creamy waves of smooth level snow, my blasphemous impertinence tracks make a sad plod in the smoothness—I jump up the cut, stand to survey further vast fields stretching a mile to the wall of pines, the forest of Pine Brook in the unbelievable riot murk beyond, the momentous swing of other swirlstorms.

One last look at Phebe, turning, I see the sweet rooftops of life, of man, of mother and father and children, my heart aches to go back home, I see the dear smokewhip of chimneys, the innocent fall of snow from roofs, the bedangled icicles, the little piteous fences outlined in all that numb null white, the tracks of people, the gleeful steplets of humans twinkling and twittering across the snow and already again over the sandbank ridge a great pall of wind and snow sweeping to fill holes with soft new outline—The mystery—Tears in my eyes from cold and wonder I turn and strike across the plain—The grief of birch that's bent and wintering, the strange mist—Far off the white story frame house in the pine woods stands proud, families are in there furying, living—

The left field of our baseball field is lost—Where the spring bubbles from short right I can see just snow and just one hint of blackening snow where waters below have formed a slush and darking ice—Behind me now I can see my footsteps in silence and sadness of white distance filling, forming, growing vaguer, returning to the macrocosms of even snow from the microcosms of my striving—and far back of that and now by distance seeable where before by nearness not, the vague un-believable hardly-discernible caped gray smoke stacks of the mills across the river and the dim smoke urging to rise from their warm Dickensian interiors of grime, labor, personal involvements among dye vats to the universe of the blizzard oversweeping all—

I reach the end of the plain, go up the wagon path past the backstop homeplate pines, the rocks, past the Greek farm on the left now stilled from Cretan ripple olive peace of summers to frost squat Winter—The top of the hill, the view of the woods, the descent into the woods—The pond at the bottom of the hill, the star beneath the ice in the bottom of the pond, the ice skaters thronging by, an old La Salle with a mattress in the back clonking by and sloshing in the snowplow's flat—I circle the pond, the houses, the French Canadian *paisans* are stomping their feet on still-screened porches, Christmas trees on their backs—Merry

Christmas zings in the air—It darkens, dusk's about to come, I've got to hurry, the first heartbreaking Christmas light comes on red and blue in a little farm window across the locked pond—My nose snuffles, my hands the back of em are like thronged red leather—Off the road and into the country path, the fear of shrouded woods ahead—No more houses now, just bushes and pines and boulders and occasional clearings, occasional woodpiles beautifully wreathed with a snow crown— The jump over the little property wire fence, the old tree base where black rocks of Indian Summer kid fires show stark dark through iced snowtops, remnant pieces of charred wood, the pine fronds gray as dead birds—Somewhere above, the coalblack crow is yawking, cr-a-a-a-ck, c-r-a-a-ck, I see the flop of raven twit limbs battering onward through treetop twigs of aerial white to a hole in the heart of the forest, to the central pine and pain of my aching desire, the real Christmas is hiding somewhere from me and it is still, it is holy, it is dark, it is insane, the crow broods there, some Nativity darker than Christianity, with Wise Men from underground, a Virgin Mary of the ice and snow, a Joseph of the trees, a Jesus like a star—a Bethlehem of pinecones, rocks, snakes—Stonewalls, eyes—

But dark gray is the nightfall reality now, I plow my hockey stick in front of me, sometimes it sinks three feet in culverts, holes—I jump and stagger and grind—Now a solid wall of pine is overhead, through the dark skinny limbs I can see loured gloomy night is overshadowing the blizzard's white shadow—Darker, deeper, the forest densens like a room—Numbbuzzing silences ring my ears, I pause to listen, I hear stars—I hear one dog, one farmer-door slam a mile away—I hear a hoot of sledders, a keen shrill of littlegirl—I hear the tick of snowflake on snow, on limb—Ice is forming on my eyebrows—I come haunting, emerging from the forest, go down the hill to the brook, the stonewall has crystal icing in the heavy winter dim—Black bleak lines in the sky —my mouth is awed open, vapors puff out, it's stopped snowing and I've begun to sense a blue scene in the new night—Soon I see one star above—I reach the brook, it flows under jagged ice caps black as ink, gurgly, silver at the ice rim, cold steaming between blanketwhite banks to its destinations and rivers down—I follow in the gloom—Our diving board's all white, alone, unsupple, stiffwooded in wintertime—Our trapeze hangs looping, dull, iceroped—

"Aaooo!" I yell in the one-room world—My stick penetrates no bottom, I've found a traphole, I walk around cautiously, follow the river bank—Suddenly there's an orange feeling in the air, the sun somewhere has pirouetted protruding limbs into the mass of brass and iron blizzards, silver's being rouged by the blast-works of the real hidden tropic sky—An Arabian Nights blue spreads blue-icing in the West, the Evestar sparks and shivers in the blanket, one lank icicle suddenly stabs from its center to the earth, dissolves—Cold. No more snowfalls, now the faint howl winds of the New England bring Alaskan shivers from the other hill, down my collar—

I leave the black brook, see the first and last touch of orange on the deepwaters, I know it's beautiful now and everything is good, I hurry back to my city—The path follows the brook, turns off in tangled tragic brushwood, goes deep across a cornfield—I hurry in a semi circling road back across my pond jumping path to the top of Moody Street where again the snowplow's work is piled in double rumps each side, my liberated feet moving in snowshoe flopping jingling gladness—There stands the white Colonial house, on the iron lawn the Christmas-glittering spruce, the noble snowy porch, fresh beginnings of a cocktail party inside—I've reached the top of the hill overlooking all Lowell.

And there she is in the keen blue winternight, be-starred above, the round brown sadface of the City Hall clock in her granite tower a mile and a half away, the speechless throat of throbbing red neons against distant redbrick of bowling alleys, business, Squares, Chinese restaurants—the giant river scything white and black around, from wilderness of hoar to wilderness of hoar and sea—The thunder and the rumble everywhere in the roundandround horizon phantom night, the distant snake of a hundred-car freight (Boston & Maine), the clean snow smoke in the new snow plain, the red glow of the locomotive's boilers, the distant two-long-one-short-one-long howl at a countryroad crossing, the lone wee caboose at the rear drawn to other worlds, to deeper night—The blue mill eternity windows, sighing froth of falls, reflections of the city actual sad in river's ice—And the one long thoroughfare Moody Street from my feet ribboning clear down Pawtucketville suburb and over the river and down the dense fantastic humaned Little Canada to the downtown thrill—Clear. Cold. Immortal.

I start home down the middle of the plowed street, joyous cries on all sides of sliding kids, the run, the thap of feet, the slap of the sled down, the crumpy ride of the runners over nostalgic snow, rock scrapes, sparks like stars—The scarved bundled gleechildren of New England screeching, the black and white fantasy of their turmoil—Sister Marie is yelling irritably at her brother Ray down the level ice wood of the tenement "Yes, I'm going, yes I'm going. I told you a hundred times!"

The wash hangs stiff and frozen, long underwear stands by itself hanged, brown porchlights are on where the mother is packing the frozen wash in fragrant piles—Little tiny nameless infant bundled-to-the-ears sits brooding in the snow like Shakespeare's bird, the wreathed window's golden with Christmas behind him, he's looking and wondering: "Where was I born and what is my name? Roland Lambert? Roland Lambert? Who is that, Roland Lambert? Who are you Roland? Hello Mister that passes—" I wave my hand, my footsteps squeak and squidge in the tightpacked snow—I come down deeper in the joy of people.

Past Mr. Vernon, the white houses, the spruce, the lost parochial white yard of night, the concrete wall, the first grocery store—Screams, snow slush, traffic ahead of me—Oilstove heat rushes down dim hallways, out the raw door—There's Al Roberts throwing a snowball at Joe Plouffe, another one, crazy crisscrossing snowballs, hoots, whoopees—The boys are ducking into the brown scarred door of the club for a brew—There's Jim with his Christmas tree, his rubbers are too low, the snow spills into his shoes, against his silk socks, he yells: "Last damn time I'm gonna buy a Christmas tree!" Mrs. T. is yelling to Mrs. H. across the wash rope of the court: "What time ya goin?"— Doors slam, buses ball by, cars race motors in drifts sending blue exhaust in the blue purity—Keen. That same star shudders exploding on the roof of the church where candles flicker—There go the old ladies of the parish to their evening vespers, bundled in black coats, white faced, gray brushed-back hair, their poor little fragile hands hidden in muffs of indoor prayer—Golden light spills from Blezan's store onto the scuffled sidewalk where the gang stands wrangling, I go in to buy my Old Nick and Clark's, browse at my usual comic books and pulp magazines—The wood stove is red hot in the back, there's the smell of heated overshoes, snow wet floors, infolded night, smoke—I hurry down Gershom, past the snowball fights, the yoo-hoos, the proud adults in big coats bundling off to social evenings, adjusting scarves, opening garage doors, guffawing—The rosy faced girls are hurrying to the bus, the show, the dance—Sad is the long fence of the long yard and the great high white frozen tree where the sick boy lives—I see him in the window, watching—Little narrow Sarah Avenue hasn't got a window that's not red or green or blue, not one sidewalk unmusical with shovels—Wearily I come to the corner, turn up Phebe, my three mile circle's complete, come to my house on slow wet sodden feet, glad—

Everything is saved. There's heat and warm joy in my house. I linger at the window looking in. My heart breaks to see they're moving so slowly, with such dear innocence within, they don't realize time and death will catch them—not now. Ma moves to lift the pot with such a bemused and serious hardly-knowing goodness and sadness—My father's huge still presence, his thighs in the chair, the absent-minded dark-in-thought face, so wordless, unexplainable, sad—My sister bending over her adolescent fingernails so preoccupied, ravenously attentive in the dream—When I open the door they look up blandly, with blue eyes—I stand facing them all red-faced and frozen—

"Well—it's about time! You missed your supper!—The roast is in the oven, it's not as hot any more—Your mashed potatoes are almost cold—Sit down, crazy!"

I sit at the sparkling table in the bright warm light, ready. She brings me a big helping, glass of milk, bread, butter, tapioca pudding with whipped cream.

"When you're finished eating we're going to go get the Christmas tree and put it up, ah?"

"Yes!"

"Eat, honey, after your big walk you must be hungry."

That night in bed I can still see the great bulging star white as ice beating in the dark field of heaven among the lesser glittering arrays, I can see its reflection in an icicle that depends from an eave above my window, I can hear my winter apple tree cracking black limbs in frost, see the Milky Way all far and cold and cragdeep in Time—I smell the softcoal heat of the furnace in the cellar—Soon dawn, the rosy spread over pure snowfields, the witless winter bird with his muffly feathers inward—My sleep is deep in New England wintertime night.

from

DOCTOR SAX

1936

EDITOR'S NOTE

In this book Kerouac calls himself "Ti Jean Duluoz," his mother is "Mama Angelique," and his father is "Emil Duluoz."

BOOK TWO
A GLOOMY BOOKMOVIE

SCENE 1   Two o'clock—strange—thunder and the yellow walls of my mother's kitchen with the green electric clock, the round table in the middle, the stove, the great twenties castiron stove now only used to put things on next to the modern thirties green gas stove upon which so many succulent meals and flaky huge gentle apple pies have been hot, whee—(Sarah Avenue house).

SCENE 2   I'm at the window in the parlor facing Sarah Avenue and its white sands dripping in the shower, from thick hot itchy stuffed furniture huge and bearlike for a reason they liked then but now call 'overstuffed'—looking at Sarah Avenue through the lace curtains and beaded windows, in the dank gloom by the vast blackness of the square-back piano and dark easy chairs and maw sofa and the brown painting on wall depicting angels playing around a brown Virgin Mary and Child in a Brown Eternity of the Brown Saints—

SCENE 3   With the cherubs (look closeup) all gloomy in their little sad disports among clouds and vague butterflies of themselves and somehow quite inhuman and cherub-like ("I have a cherub tells me," says Hamlet to the Rosencranz and Guildenstern track team hotfooting back to Engla-terre)—(I'm rushing around with a wild pail in the winters in that now-raining street, I have a scheme to build bridges in the snow and let the gutter hollow canyons under . . . in the backyard of springtime baseball mud, I in the winter dig great steep Wall Streets in the snow and cut along giving them Alaskan names and avenues which is a game I'd still like to play—and when Ma's wash is icy stiff on the line I march it down piece-meal on a side dredge into the drifts of the porch and shovel Mexican gloriettas around the washline merrygoround pole).

SCENE 4   The brown picture on the wall was done by some old Italian who has long since faded from my parochial school textbooks with his brown un-Goudt inks and inkydinky lambs about to be slaughtered by stern Jewish businesslike Mose with his lateral nose, won't listen to his own little son's wails, would rather—the picture is still around, many like it— But see close, my face now in the window of the Sarah Avenue house, six little houses in the entire dirt street, one big tree, my face looking out through dew-drops of the rain from within, the gloomy special brown Technicolor interior of my house where also lurks a pisspot gloom of family closets in the Graw North—I'm wearing corduroy pants, brown ones, smooth and easy, and some sneakers, and a black sweater over a brown shirt open at collar (I wore no Dick Tracy badges ever, I was a proud professional of the Shades with my Shadow & Sax)— I'm a little kid with blue eyes, 13, I'm munching on a fresh cold mackintosh apple my father bought last Sunday on the Sundaydriving road in Groton or in Chelmsford, the juice just pops and flies out of my teeth when I cool these apples. And I munch, and chaw, and look out the window at the rain.

SCENE 5   Look up, the huge tree of Sarah Avenue, belonged to Mrs. Flooflap whose name I forget but sprung God-like Emer Hammerthong from the blue earth of her gigantic grassy yard (it ran clear to long white concrete garage) and mushroomed into the sky with limb-spreads that o'ertopped many roofs in the neighborhood and did so without particularly touching any of em, now huge and grooking vegetable peotl Nature in the gray slash rain of New England mid-April—the tree drips down huge drops, it rears up and away in an eternity of trees, in its own flambastic sky—

SCENE 6   This tree fell down in the Hurricane finally, in 1938, but now it only bends and sinews with a mighty woodlimb groan, we see where the boughs tear at their green, the juncture point of tree-trunk with arm-trunk, tossing of wild forms upside down flailing in the wind,— the sharp tragic crack of a smaller limb stricken from the tree by stormhound—

SCENE 7   Along the splashing puddles of grassyard, at worm level, that fallen branch looks enormous and demented on its arms in the hail—

SCENE 8   My little boy blue eyes shine in the window. I'm drawing crude swastikas in the steamy window, it was one of my favorite signs long before I heard of Hitler or the Nazis—behind me suddenly you see my mother smiling,—"*Tiens*," she's saying, "*je tlai dit qu'eta bonne les pommes* (There, I told you they were good the apples!)"—leaning over me to look out the window too. "*Tiens, regard, l'eau est deu pieds creu dans la rue* (There, look, the water's two feet deep in the street)—*Une grosse tempête* (a big storm)— *Je tlai dit pas allez école aujourdhui* (I told you not to go to school today)—*Wé tu? comme qui mouille?* (See? how it rains?) *Je suis tu dumb?* (Am I dumb?)"

SCENE 9   Both our faces peer fondly out the window at the rain, it made it possible for us to spend a pleasant afternoon together, you can tell how the rain pelts the side of the house and the window—we don't budge an inch, just fondly look on—like a Madonna and son in the Pittsburgh milltown window—only this is New England, half like rainy Welsh mining towns, half the Irish kid sunny Saturday Skippy morning, with rose vines—(Bold Venture, when May came and it stopped raining, I played marbles in the mudholes with Fatso, they piled up with blossoms overnight, we had to dig em out for every day's game, blossoms from trees raining, Bold Venture won the Derby that Saturday)—My mother behind me in the window is oval faced, dark haired, large blue eyes, smiling, nice, wearing a cotton dress of the thirties that she'd wear in the house with an apron—upon which there was always flour and water from the work with the condiments and pastries she was doing in the kitchen—

SCENE 10   There in the kitchen she stands, wiping her hands as I taste one of her cup cakes with fresh icing (pink, chocolate, vanilla, in little cups) she says, "All them movies with the old grandmaw in the West slappin her leetle frontiers boy and smackin him 'Stay away from dem cookies,' Ah? la old Mama Angelique don't do that to you, ah?" "No Ma, boy," I say, "*si tu sera comme ça jara toujours faim* (No Ma, boy if you was like that I'd always be hungry)" "*Tiens—assay un beau blanc d'vanilla, c'est bon pour tué* (There, try a nice white one of vanilla, it's good for you.)" "Oh boy, *blanc sucre!* ("......") (Oh boy, white sugar!)" "*Bon*," she says firmly, turning away, "*asteur faut serrez mon lavage, je lai rentrez jusquavant quil mouille* (Good, now I've got to put away my wash, I got it in just before it rained)"—(as on the radio thirties broadcasts of old gray soap operas and news from Boston about finnan haddie and the prices, East Port to Sandy Hook, gloomy serials, static, thunder of the old America that thundered on the plain)—As she walks away from the stove I say, from under my little black warm sweater, "*Moi's shfué's fini mes race dans ma chambre* (Me I's got to finish my races in my room)"—"*Amuse toi* (amuse yourself)"—she calls back— you can see the walls of the kitchen, the green clock, the table, now also the sewing machine on the right, near the porch door, the rubbers and overshoes always piled in the door, a rocking chair facing the oil heat stove—coats and raincoats hanging on hooks in corners of the kitchen, brownwood waxed panelling on the cupboards and wainscots all around—a wooden porch outside, glistening from rain—gloom—things boiling on the stove—(when I was a very little kid I used to read the funnies on my belly, listen on the floor to boiling waters of stove, with a feeling of indescribable peace and burble, suppertime, funnies time, potato time, warm home time) (the second hand of the green electric clock turning relentlessly, delicately through wars of dust)—(I watched that too)—(Wash Tubbs in the ancient funnypage)—

SCENE 11   Thunder again, now you see my room, my bedroom with the green desk, bed and chair—and the other strange pieces of furniture, the Victrola already to go with *Dardanella* and crank hangs ready, stack of sad thirties thick records, among them Fred Astaire's *Cheek to Cheek, Parade of the Wooden Soldiers* by John Philip Sousa— You hear my footsteps unmistakably pounding up the stairs on the run, pleup plop ploop pleep plip and I'm rushing in the room and closing the door behind me and pick up my mop and with foot heavy pressed on it mop a thin strip from wall near door to wall near window—I'm mopping the race track ready—the wallpaper shows great goober lines of rose-bushes in a dull vague plaster, and a picture on the wall shows a horse, cut from a newspaper page (*Morning Telegraph*) and tacked, also a picture of Jesus on the Cross in a horrible oldprint darkness shining through the celluloid—(if you got close up you could see the lines of bloody black tears coursing down his tragic cheek, O the horrors of the darkness and clouds, no people, around the stormy tempest of his rock is void—you look for waves—He walked in the waves with silver rai-ment feet, Peter was a Fisherman but he never fished that deep—the Lord spoke to dark assemblies about gloomy fish—the bread was bro-ken . . . a miracle swept around the encampment like a flowing cape and everybody ate fish . . . dig your mystics in another Arabia . . .). The mop I am mopping the thin line with is just an old broomhandle with a frowsy drymop head, like old ladies' hair at the hair stylists—now I am getting down briskly on my knees to sweep away with my fingertips, feeling for spots of sand or glass, looking at the fingertips with a careful blow,—10 seconds pass as I prepare my floor, which is the first thing I do after slapping the door behind me— You saw first my one side of the room, when I come in, then left to my window and the gloomy rain splattering across it—rising from my knees, wiping fingers on pants, I turn slowly and raising fist to mouth I go "Ta-ta-ta-tra-tra-tra-etc."—the racetrack call to the post by the bugler, in a clear, well modulated voice actually singing in an intelligent voice-imitation of a trumpet (or bugle). And in the damp room the notes resound sadly— I look goopy with self-administered amazement as I listen to the last sad note and the silence of the house and the rain click and now the clearly sounding whistle of Boott Mills or Goop Mills coming loud and mournful from across the river and the rain outside where Doctor Sax even now is preparing for the night with his dark damp cape, in mists— My thin trail for the races began at a cardboard inclined on books—a Parchesi board,—folded, to the Domino side to keep the Parchesi side from fading (precursor to the now Monopoly board with checkers on other side)—no wait, the Parchesi board had a black blank side, down the huck of this all solid and round raced my marbles when I let them slip down from under the ruler— Lined on the bed are the eight gladiators of the race, it's the fifth race, the handicap of the day.

SCENE 12   "And now," I'm sayin, as I bend low at the bed, "and now the Fifth Race, handicap, four year olds and up etc."—"and now the Fifth Race of the gong, come on *Ti Jean arrete de jouer* and get on with the—they're headed for the post, the horses are headed for the post"— and I hear it echoing as I say it, hands upraised before the lined up horses on the blanket, I look around me like a racing fan asking himself, "Say, it shore is gonna rain soon, they're headed for the post?"— which I do—"Well son, better bet five on Flying Ebony the old gal'll make it, she didn't do too bad against Kransleet last week." "Okay Pa!"—striking new pose—"but I see Mate winning this race." "Old Mate? Nah!"

SCENE 13   I rush to the phonograph, turn on *Dardanella* with the push hook.

SCENE 14   Briskly I'm kneeled at the race-start barrier, horses in left hand, ruler barrier clamped down at starting line in right hand, *Dardanella*'s going da-daradera-da, I have my mouth open breathing in and out raspily to make racetrack crowd noises—the marbles pop into place with great fanfare, I straighten em around, "Woops," I say, "look— out—l-o-o-k-o-u-t no—NOPE! Mate broke from the starter's helper— back he goes—Jockey Jack Lewis exasperated on his back—set em up straight now—'the horses are at the post!'—Oh that old fool we know that"—"They're off!" *"What?"* *"They're off!*—hoff!" crowd sigh— boom! they're off— "You made me miss my start with that talk of yours—*and it's Mate taking an early lead!*" And off I rush following the marbles with my eyes.

SCENE 15   Next scene, I'm crawling along all stridey and careful following my marbles, and I'm calling em fast "Mate by two lengths"—

SCENE 16   POW flash shot of Mate the marble two inches ahead of big limping Don Pablo with his chipholes (regularly I held titanic marble-smashing ceremonies and "trainings" and some of the racers came out chipped and hobbled, great Don Pablo had been a great champion of the Turf, in spite of an original crooked slant in his round—but now chipped beyond repair—an uncommon tender fore hock, crock, wooden fenders of gloomy mainsmiths smashing up the horn in the horse's hoof on gray afternoons on Salem Street when still a little horseshit perfumed the Ah Afternoons of Lowell—tragic migs frantic in a raw bloom of the floor, of the flowery linoleum carpet just drymopped and curried by the racetrack trucks— "Don Pablo second!" I'm calling in the same low Doctor Sax crouch—"and Flying Ebony coming up fast from a slow start in the rear—Time Supply" (red stripes on white), (no one else will ever name them), blam, no more time, I'm already leaning over with my arm extended to lean falling on the wall over the finish line and hang my face tragically over the pit of the wood homestretch in entryway with wide amazement and speechless—just manage, wide-eyed, to say—"—s-a-a-a-,"—

SCENE 17   The marbles crashing into wall.

SCENE 18   "—Don Pablo rolled over and crashed in—gee, chipped, he's so heavy! *Don Pablo-o!*" with hands to my head in the great catastrophe of the "fans" in the grandstand. (One morning in that room there had been such glooms, no school, the first official day of racing, way back in the beginning, the dismal rainy 1934's when I used to keep history of myself—started that long before Scotty and I kept baseball history of our souls, in red ink, averages, P. Boldieu, p., .382 bat, .986 field—the day Mate became the first great winner of the Turf, capturing a coveted misty prize of lost afternoons (the Graw Futurity) beyond the hills of Mohican Springs racetrack "in Western Massachusetts" in the "Mohawk Trail country"—(it was only years later I turned from this to the stupidities and quiddities of H. G. Wells and Mososaurs—in these parentheses sections, so (-), the air is free, do what you will, I can—

why? whoo?—) the gray dismal rains I remember, the tragic damp on my windowpane, the flood of heat pouring up through the transom near the closet, my closet itself, the gloom of it, the doom of it, the hanging balloons of it, the papers, boxes, smatterdurgalia like William Allen White's closet in Wichita when he was 14—my yearning for peanut butter and Ritz crackers in the late afternoon, the gloom around my room at that hour, I'm eating my Ritz and gulping my milk by the wreckage of the day— The losses, the torn tickets, the chagrined footsteps disappearing out the ramp, the last faint glimmer of the toteboards in the rain, a torn paper rolling dismally in the wet ramps, my face long and anxious surveying this scene of gloomy jonquils in the floor-frat— that first bookkeeping graymorning when Mate won the Stakes and from the maw-mouth of the Victrola the electric yoigle yurgle little thirties crooners wound too fast with a slam-bash Chinese restaurant orchestry we fly into the latest 1931 hit, ukeleles, ro-bo-bos, hey now, smash-ah! *hah!* atch a *tcha!* but usually it was just, "Dow-dow-dow, tadoodle-lump!"—"Gee I like hot jyazz"—
Snazzz!
—but in that room all converted into something dark, cold, incredible gloomy, my room on rainy days and all in it was a saturation of the gray Yoik of Bleak Heaven when the sides of the rainbow mouth of God hang disfurdled in a bloomy rue—no color . . . the smell of thought and silence, "Don't hang around in that stuffy old room all the time," my mother had said to me when Mike came for our Dracut Fields Buck Jones appointment and instead I was busy running off the Mohican Futurity and digging back into earlier records of my antiquity for background material for the little newspaper story announcing the race . . . printed by hand on gloomy gray-green sheets of Time.

EIGHTH RACE: Claiming $1500, for 4 year olds and up. Six
                         furlongs
Post: 5:43 TIME 1:12 4-5
             CAW CAW (Lewis)   **$18.60** 7.40   3.80
             FLYING HOME (Stout)   2.40   2.30
             SUNDOWN LAD (Renick)   11.10
ALSO RAN: Flying Doodad, Saint Nazaire, a-Rink, Mynah, a-Remonade Girl, Gray Law, Rownomore, Going Home. Scratched: Happy Jack, Truckee. a-Jack Lewis entry.

—or my newspapers would have headlines:

REPULSION ARRIVES FOR BIG 'CAP

Lewis Predicts Third Straight

VICTORY FOR THE KING

APRIL 4, 1936—Mighty Repulsion arrived today by van from his resting-place at Lewis Farms; accompanying him were Jack Lewis, owner and jockey, trainer Ben Smith and his trusty Derby-cups and assistants.

TIPS BY LEWIS
TODAY
S Springs, 3rd
CARMAK

Bright skies and a fast track preceded the arrival of these tremendous luminaries upon the scene of a great week's end of racing with a thousand dollars pouring from individual pockets of wild jockey club bets, while less swanky Turf fans (like me and Paw from Arkansas) hang on the rail, railbirds, steely-eyed, far-seeing, thin, from Kentucky, brothers in the blood on the score of hosses and father and son in a tragic Southern family left destitute only with two horses that sometimes I'd actually rig races by putting solid champion types in 'workouts' among less luminous luminary marbles, and call the winner on my 'Tips' corner for that honor and also for hardboot father-and-son who need the money and have followed my, Lewis', advice— I was Jack Lewis and I owned the greatest horse, Repulsion, solid ballbearing a half inch thick, it rolled off the Parchesi board and into the linoleum as smooth, and soundless but as heavy as a rumbling ball of steel all tooled smooth, sometimes kicked poor aluminum-marbles out of sight and off the track at the hump bump of the rampbottom—sometimes kicked a winner in, too— but usually rolled smoothly off the plank and mashed any little glass or dust on the floor (while smallest marbles jiggled in the infinitesimal lilliputian microcosmos of the linoleum and World)—and zoomed swiftly all shiny silver across the race-course to its appointed homestretch in the rockly wood where it just assumed a new rumbling power and deep hum of floorboards and hooked up with the finish line with a forward slam of momentum—a tremendous bull-like rush in the stretch, like Whirlaway or Man O War or Citation—other marbles couldn't compete with this massive power, they all came tagging after, Repulsion was absolute king of the Turf till I lost him slapping him out of my yard into the Phebe Avenue yard a block away—a fabulous homerun as I say, turned my world upside down like the Atombomb—Jack

Lewis, I, owned that great Repulsion, also personally rode the beast, and trained him, and found him, and revered him, but I also ran the Turf, was Commissioner, Track Handicapper, President of the Racing Association, Secretary of the Treasury—Jack Lewis had nothing lacking, while he lived—his newspapers flourished—he wrote editorials against the Shade, he was not afraid of Black Thieves—The Turf was so complicated it went on forever. And in a gloom of ecstasy. —There I am, clutching my head, the fans in the grandstand go wild. Don Pablo at 18-1 upset the applecart, nobody expected he'd even make it to the wall with his half gait and great huge chips, he'd a been 28-1 if it wasn't for his old reputation as a battered veteran before he was chipped— *"He went and done it!"* I'm saying to myself in astonishment—boom!

SCENE 19   I'm at the Victrola putting in a new record, swiftly, it's *The Parade of the Wooden Soldiers,* everybody's leaving the racetrack—

SCENE 20   You see me marching up and down where I stand, moving slowly around the room, the races are over, I'm marching out of the grandstand but also shaking my head quizzically from side to side like a disgruntled bettor, tearing up my tickets, a poor child pantomime of what sometimes I'd seen my father do after the races at Narragansett or Suffolk Downs or Rockingham— On my little green desk the papers are all spread, my pencil, my editorial desk running the Turf. On the back of that desk still were chalkmarks Gerard had made when he was alive in the green desk—this desk rattled in my dreams because of Gerard's ghost in it—(I dream of it now on rainy nights turned almost vegetable by the open window, luridly green, as a tomato, as the rain falls in the block-hollow void outside all dank, adrip and dark . . . hateful walls of the Cave of Eternity suddenly appearing in a brown dream and when you slow the drape, fish the shroud, shape your mouth of mow and maw in this huge glissen tank called Rainy,—you can see the void now). —Pushed against the corner by the Victrola, my little pool table—it was a folding pool table, with velvet green, little holes and leather pockets and little cues with leather tips you could cue-chalk with blue chalk from my father's pool table at the bowling alley— It was a very important table because I played The Shadow at it— The Shadow was the name I gave to a tall, thin, hawknosed fellow called St. Louis who came into the Pawtucketville Social Club and shot pool sometimes with the proprietor my father . . . the greatest poolshark you ever saw, huge, enormous hands with fingers seemingly ten inches long

laid out spread-claw on the green to make his cue-rest, his little finger
alone sprouted and shot from his handmountain to a distance of six
inches you'd say, clean, neat, he slipped the cue right through a tiny
orifice between his thumb and forefinger, and slid on all woodsy shiny
to connect with that cue-ball at cue-kiss—he'd smack shots in with no
two cents about it, fwap, the ball would cluck in the leather hole basket
like a dead thing— So tall, shroudy, he bent long and distant and lean
for his shots, momentarily rewarding his audience with a view of his
enormous gravity head and great noble and mysterious hawk nose and
inscrutable never-saying eyes— The Shadow—We'd see him coming in
the club from the street—

SCENE 21   And in fact this is what we see now, The Shadow St. Louis
is coming into the Social Club to shoot pool, wearing hat and long coat,
somehow shadowy as he comes along the long plywood wall painted
gray, light, but's coming into an ordinary bowling alley four of which
you see to the left of The Shadow, with only two alleys going and two
pinboys at work (Gene Plouffe and Scotty Boldieu, Scotty wasn't a regular like Gene but because he was the pitcher on our team my father
let him make a few extra pennies spotting at the alleys)— A low ceiling
cellar is what the joint is, you see plumbing pipes,— We are watching
The Shadow come in and up the plywood walls from our seats at the
head of the alleys, Coca Colas, scoresheet boards that you stand at, by
the rack, and the duckpin balls in the rack and the duckpins set up
down the alley squat and shiny with a red band in their goldwood—
rainy Friday 6:30 P.M. in the P.S.C. alleys, we see smoke shroudens even
the shroudy Shadow as he moves up, we hear murmurs and hubbubs
and echo-roars of the hall, click of pool games, laughter, talk . . .

SCENE 22   My father's in the little cage office at the rear near the Gershom street-door, smoking a cigar behind the glass counter, it rises from
him in a cloud, he is frowning angrily at a piece of paper in his hand.
"Jesus Christ now where did *this* thing come from?—" (looking at
another)—"is that a?—" and he falls into scowling meditation with
himself over these two little pieces of paper, the other fellows in the
office are talking . . . there's Joe Plouffe, Vauriselle, and Sonny
Alberge—everything's jumping— We are only looking in at the door,
can't see the entire office, in fact we are looking in at the office from
about six feet up in the door a foot from it on a stone step level with
the office floor, we are just about as high as The Shadow's nose as we

look in with The Shadow whose hawk visage slants from us in a Huge. My father never looks up, except briefly, coldly, to see who it is, then a mere look of the eye signifying greeting—in fact no greeting at all, he just looks up and down again with that bemused perused expression my father always had, as though something was reading him and eating him inside and he all wrap't and silent in it. So St. Louis, his face doesn't budge anyway, just addresses the three—"*Ca vas?* (it goes?)"—"*Tiens, St. Louis! Ta pas faite ton 350 l'autre soir—ta mal au cul* (you didn't make your 350 t'other night, you got a sore ass)." This being said by Vauriselle, a tall, unpleasant fellow that my father didn't like—no answer from St. Louis who has just a fixed hawklike grin. Now Sonny Alberge, tall and athletic and handsome, became Boston Braves shortstop in a few years, with a big clean-teeth smile, a real bumpkin boy in his prime at home, his father was a little sad shrivelly man who adored him, Sonny responded to his father like an Ozark hero grave and Billy-the-Kid tender, but with French Canadian stern gravity that knows what's coming to everybody in Heaven later on inside Time—it's ever been so in the bottom of my soul, the stars are crying down the sides of Heaven—Sonny says to St. Louis—"*Une game?*" St. Louis' grin though moveless gains significance, and he opens his blue hawklike lips to say with sudden surprising young man voice "*Oui*"—and they look at one another the challenge and cut out to bowl—Vauriselle and Joe Plouffe (always a short solid wry listener and chieftain among the heroes of Pawtucketville) follow—my father's left alone in the office with his papers, looks up, checks the time, slaps cigar in mouth and cuts out following the boys in a thing-to-do of his own, fiddling for keys, bemused, as someone yells out at him in the next view

SCENE 23   (as he steps down from office with fat busy proprietor key look at chain from pocket), from the auras of smoke and pooltable glow a dark shaded man with a cuestick in the pissy background of cans and wood is calling "Hey, Emil, *il mouille dans ton pissoir* (it's raining in your toilet)—*a tu que chose comme un plat pour mettre entours?* (got anything like a pan to put under?)" There's another poolshark in the dark green background of blue rain evening in the golden club with its dank stone floor and shiny black bowling balls—In smoke—shouts (as Emil my father is muttering and nodding yes) (and St. Louis, Joe, Sonny, Vauriselle cross the scene in file, like Indians, Shadow's removing his coat)—"*Pauvre Emil commence a avoir des trou dans son pissoir, cosse wui va arrivez asteur, whew!—foura quon use le livre pour bouchez les trous* (Poor Emil's starting to have holes in his pissery, what's gonna happen now, whew! we'll have to use the book to block the holes!!!)" "*Hey la tu deja vu slivre la*—(Hey didja ever see that book?)" a pool-shark in the light, young Leo Martin saying to LeNoire who lived directly across the street from the club, on Gershom, adjoining Blezan's store, in a house that always seemed to me haunted by sad flowerpots of linoleum eternity in a sunny void also darkened by an inner almost idiot gloom French Canadian homes seem to have (as if a kid with water on the head was hiding in the closet somewhere)—LeNoire a cool little cat, I knew his kidbrother and exchanged marbles with him, they were related to some dim past relation I'd been told about—ladies with great white hair periwigs sewing in the Lowell rooms, wow— LeNoire: (we're watching from the end of the plywood wall, but almost on alley Number One at this spreadout smoky scene and talk) "*Quoi?—Non. Jaime ra ca, squi est?* (what, no, I'd like that, where's it?)" LeNoire says this from a crouch over his cueball— He was a very good bowler too, St. Louis had trouble beating him bowling—faintly we see brown folding chairs along the Gershom wall, with secret dark sitters but very close up to the table and listening to every word—a Fellaheen poolhall if there ever was one— The door opens quickly and out of the rain and in comes I, silent, swift, gliding in like The Shadow—sidling to the corner of the scene to watch, removing not coat nor budging, I'm already hung up on the scene's awe.

SCENE 24   "*Tiens, Ti Jean, donne ce plat la a Shammy,*" my father is saying to me, turning from the open storage room door with a white tin pan. "Here, Ti Jean, give this pan to Shammy." My father is standing with a peculiar French Canadian bowleggedness half up from a crouch with the pan outheld, waiting for me to take it, anxious till I do so, almost saying with his big frowning amazed face "Well my little son what are we doing in the penigillar, this strange abode, this house of life without roof be-hung on a Friday evening with a tin pan in my hand in the gloom and you in your raincoats—" "*Il commence a tombez de la neige,*" someone is shouting in the background, coming in from the door ("Snow's startin to fall")—my father and I stand in that immobile instant communicating telepathic thought-paralysis, suspended in the void together, understanding something that's always already happened, wondering where we were now, joint reveries in a dumb stun in the cellar of men and smoke . . . as profound as Hell . . . as red as Hell.— I take the pan; behind him, the clutter and tragedy of old cellars and

storage with its dank message of despair—mops, dolorous mops, clat-
tering tear-stricken pails, fancy sprawfs to suck soap suds from a glass,
garden drip cans—rakes leaning on meaty rock—and piles of paper and
official Club equipments— It now occurs to me my father spent most
of his time when I was 13 the winter of 1936, thinking about a hundred
details to be done in the Club alone not to mention home and business
shop—the energy of our fathers, they raised us to sit on nails— While
I sat around all the time with my little diary, my Turf, my hockey games,
Sunday afternoon tragic football games on the toy pooltable white
chalkmarked . . . father and son on separate toys, the toys get less
friendly when you grow up—my football games occupied me with the
same seriousness of the angels—we had little time to talk to each other.
In the fall of 1934 we took a grim voyage south in the rain to Rhode
Island to see Time Supply win the Narragansett Special—with Old Das-
lin we was . . . a grim voyage, through exciting cities of great neons,
Providence, the mist at the dim walls of great hotels, no Turkeys in the
raw fog, no Roger Williams, just a trolley track gleaming in the gray
rain— We drove, auguring solemnly over past performance charts, past
deserted shell-like Ice Cream Dutchland Farms stands in the dank of
rainy Nov.—bloop, it was the time on the road, black tar glisten-road
of thirties, over foggy trees and distances, suddenly a crossroads, or just
a side-in road, a house, or barn, a vista gray tearful mists over some
half-in cornfield with distances of Rhode Island in the marshy ways
across and the secret scent of oysters from the sea—but something dark
and rog-like.—*I had seen it before* . . . Ah weary flesh, burdened with
a light . . . that gray dark Inn on the Narragansett Road . . . this is the
vision in my brain as I take the pan from my father and take it to
Shammy, moving out of the way for LeNoire and Leo Martin to pass
on the way to the office to see the book my father had (a health book
with syphilitic backs)—

SCENE 25   Someone ripped the pooltable cloth that night, tore it with
a cue, I ran back and got my mother and she lay on it half-on-floor like
a great poolshark about to take a shot under a hundred eyes only she's
got a thread in her mouth and's sewing with the same sweet grave face
you first saw in the window over my shoulder in that rain of a late
Lowell afternoon.

   God bless the children of this picture, this bookmovie.

   I'm going on into the Shade.

from
MAGGIE CASSIDY
1938–1939

EDITOR'S NOTE
*In this book Kerouac calls himself "Jack Duluoz," nicknamed "Zagg"
by his friends and "Ti Jean" by his family.*

THE CONCORD RIVER flows by her house, in July evening the ladies of
Massachusetts Street are sitting on wooden doorsteps with newspapers
for fans, on the river the starlight shines. The fireflies, the moths, the
bugs of New England summer rattlebang on screens, the moon looms
huge and brown over Mrs. McInerney's tree. Little Buster O'Day is
coming up the road with his wagon, torn knees, punching it through
holes in the unpaved ground, the streetlamp dropping a brown vast halo
bugswept on his little homeward figure. Still, and soft, the stars on the
river run.

The Concord River, scene of sand embankments, railroad bridges,
reeds, bullfrogs, dye mills—copses of birch, vales, in winter the dreaming white—but now in July midsummer the stars roll vast and shiny
over its downward flow to the Merrimack. The railroad train crashes
over the bridges; the children beneath, among the tar poles, are swimming naked. The engine's fire glow is red as it goes over, flares of deep
hell are thrown on the little figures. Maggie is there, the dogs are there,
little fires . . .

The Cassidys live on Massachusetts Street at No. 31—it's a wood
house, seven rooms, apple tree in back; chimney; porch, with screen,
and swing; no sidewalk; rickety fence against which in June tall sun-
flowers lean at noon for wild and tender hallucinations of little infants
playing there with wagons. The father James Cassidy is an Irishman,
brakeman on the Boston and Maine; soon conductor; the mother, a
former O'Shaughnessy with dove's eyes still in her long-lost face of love
now face of life.

The river comes between lovely shores narrowing. Bungalows scat-
ter the landscape. The tannery's over to the west. Little grocery stores
with wood fences and dusty paths, grass, some drying-out wood at
noon, the ring ding of the little bell, kids buying Bostons or penny

Bolsters at lunch noon; or milk early Saturday morning when all is so blue and sweet for the day of the play. Cherry trees drop blossoms in May. The funny gladness of the cat rubbing against the porch steps in the drowsy two o'clock when Mrs. Cassidy with her littlest daughter returns from shopping at Kresge's downtown, gets off the bus at the junction, walks seven houses down Massachusetts Street with her bundles, the ladies see her, call out "What'd you buy Mrs. Cassidy? Is that fire sale still on at Giant store?"

"Radio says it is . . ." another greeter.

"Wasnt you on the Strand program on the sidewalk interviews?— Tom Wilson asked the silliest questions—Hee hee hee!"

Then among themselves "That little girl must have rickets the way she walks—"

"Those cakes she gave me yesterday I just had to throw them away—"

And the sun beams gladly on the woman at the gate of her house. "Now where can Maggie be? I told her a dozen times I wanted that wash hung out before I got back even if it was eleven o'clock—"

And at night the river flows, it bears pale stars on the holy water, some sink like veils, some show like fish, the great moon that once was rose now high like a blazing milk flails its white reflection vertical and deep in the dark surgey mass wall river's grinding bed push. As in a sad dream, under the streetlamp, by pocky unpaved holes in dirt, the father James Cassidy comes home with lunchpail and lantern, limping, redfaced, and turns in for supper and sleep.

Now a door slams. The kids have rushed out for the last play, the mothers are planning and slamming in kitchens, you can hear it out in swish leaf orchards, on popcorn swings, in the million-foliaged sweet wafted night of sighs, songs, shushes. A thousand things up and down the street, deep, lovely, dangerous, aureating, breathing, throbbing like stars; a whistle, a faint yell; the flow of Lowell over rooftops beyond; the bark on the river, the wild goose of the night yakking, ducking in the sand and sparkle; the ululating lap and purl and lovely mystery on the shore, dark, always dark the river's cunning unseen lips murmuring kisses, eating night, stealing sand, sneaky.

"Mag-gie!" the kids are calling under the railroad bridge where they've been swimming. The freight train still rumbles over a hundred cars long, the engine threw the flare on little white bathers, little Picasso horses of the night as dense and tragic in the gloom comes my soul

looking for what was there that disappeared and left, lost, down a
path—the gloom of love. Maggie, the girl I loved.

7

In winter night Massachusetts Street is dismal, the ground's frozen cold,
the ruts and pock holes have ice, thin snow slides over the jagged black
cracks. The river is frozen to stolidity, waits; hung on a shore with
remnant show-off boughs of June— Ice skaters, Swedes, Irish girls, yellers and singers—they throng on the white ice beneath the crinkly stars
that have no altar moon, no voice, but down heavy tragic space make
halyards of Heaven on in deep, to where the figures fantastic amassed
by scientists cream in a cold mass; the veil of Heaven on tiaras and
diadems of a great Eternity Brunette called night.

Among these skaters Maggie performed; in her sweet white skates,
white muff, you see the flash of her eye in their pools of darkness all
the more strikingly: the pinkness of her cheek, her hair, the crown of
her eyes corona'd by God's own bent wing— For all I knew as I toasted
my skated feet at Concord River fires in the February Lowell, Maggie
could have been the mother or the daughter of God—

Dirty snow piled in the gutters of Massachusetts Street, something
forlorn hid in little pits of dirt, dark—the mute companions of my midnight walks from the overpowering lavish of her kisses.

She gave me a kiss upsidedown in the chair, it was a winter night
not long after I'd met her, I was in the dark room with the big radio
with its throbbish big brown dial that Vinny also had in his house and
I'm rocking in the chair, Mrs. Cassidy her mother is in her own kitchen
the way my mother three miles across town was—same old big old good
old Lowell lady in her eternity wiping the dishes putting them away in
the clean cupboards with that little feminate neatness and orderly ideas
of how to go about things—Maggie's on the porch goofing in the icy
night a minute with Bessy Jones her chum from the bungalow across
the street, a big fat red-haired goodnatured girl with freckles and whose
inconceivably feeble little brother sometimes delivered me notes from
Maggie written the night before school in some brown light of her bedroom or in the morning at pipe keen frost, to hand to him, over the
crackly fence, and he in his usual round of days trudged to school two
miles away or took the bus and as he rheumy-eyedly weepingly came
into his Spanish class which was every morning the second and impos-

sibly dull he handed me the note sometimes with a feeble little joke—
just a little kid, for some reason they'd shoved him on to high school
through red morning cold parochials where he skipped grades and
missed the sixth, or fifth, or both, and here he was a little kid with a
hunting rag cap with a Scottish haggle tassel and we believed him to be
like our age. Maggie would plant the note in his thin freckly hand,
Bessy'd be giggling from behind the open kitchen window, she's taking
advantage of the window being open and also putting the empty milk-
bottles out. Little Massachusetts Street in the cold mornings of rosy
snow sun in January is alive with the fragrant whip of blacksmoke from
all the cottage chimneys; on the white frozen cap of the Concord River
we see last night's bonfire a charred ruinous black spot near the thin
bare reddish reeds of the other shore; the whistle of the Boston and
Maine engine sounds across the trees, you shudder and pull your coat
tighter to hear it. Bessy Jones . . . sometimes she'd write notes to me
too, giving instructions on how to win Maggie, that Maggie'd also read.
I accepted everything.

"Maggie loves you," etc., "she's madder about you than I can ever
remember her being mad about anybody else" and in effect she'd say
"Maggie loves you, but dont try her patience—tell her you want to
marry her or sumptin." Young girls—giggly—on the porch—as I sit in
the living-room dark waiting for Maggie to come back on the chair
with me. My tired track team legs are beneath me, folded. I hear other
voices on the Cassidy porch, some boys, that Art Swenson I heard
about—I feel jealousy but it's only the bare beginning of all the jealousy
that came later. I'm waiting for Maggie to come and kiss me, make it
official. While waiting I have ample time to review our love affair; how
the first night she'd meant nothing to me when we danced, I held her,
she seemed small, thin, dark, unsubstantial, not important enough—
Just her strange rare sadness coming from the other side of something
made me barely notice she was there: her pretty looks . . . all girls had
pretty looks, even G.J. hadnt mentioned her. . . . The profundity wave
of her womanhood had not yet settled over me. That was New Year's
Eve—after the dance we'd walked home in the cold night, the snow
was over, just tight and soft on the implacable frozen ground, we passed
long construction oil flares like avenues and parades on our way down
to South Lowell and the banks of the Concord—the silent frost on the
rooftops in the starlight, ten degrees above zero. "Sit on the porch
awhile anyway—" There were little children-whimpering understandings between us that we would join our lips and kiss even if we had to

do it outdoors—The thought of it had begun to excite me even then. But now, waiting in the chair, and why worry about time, the meaning of her *kissed* had become all things to me. In the variety of the tone of her words, moods, hugs, kisses, brushes of the lips, and this night the upside-down kiss over the back of the chair with her dark eyes heavy hanging and her blushing cheeks full of sweet blood and sudden tenderness brooding like a hawk over the boy over the back, holding the chair on both sides, just an instant, the startling sudden sweet fall of all her hair over my face and the soft downward brush of her lips, a moment's penetration of sweet lip flesh, a moment's drowned in thinking and kissing in it and praying and hoping and in the mouth of life when life is young to burn cool skin eye-blinking joy—I held her captured upside down, also for just a second, and savored the kiss which first had surprised me like blind man's bluff so I didnt know really who was kissing me for the very first instant but now I knew and knew everything more than ever, as, grace-wise, she descended to me from the upper dark where I'd thought only cold could be and with all her heavy lips and breast in my neck and on my head and sudden fragrance of the night brought with her from the porch, of some 5 & 10 cheap perfumes of herself the little hungry scent of perspiration warm in her flesh like preciousness.

I held her a long time, even when she struggled to fall back. I realized she'd done it for a mood. She loved me. Also I think we were both frightened later when we'd hold a kiss for 35 minutes until the muscles of our lips would get cramps and it was painful to go on—but somehow we were supposed to do this, and what everybody said, the other kids, Maggie and all the others "necking" at skate and post office parties and on porches after dances had learned this was the thing—and did it in spite of how they felt about it personally—the fear of the world, the children clinging in what they think is a mature, secure kiss (challenging and grown-up)—not understanding joy and personal reverence— It's only later you learn to lean your head in the lap of God, and rest in love. Some gigantic sexual drive was behind these futile long smooches, sometimes our teeth'd grind, our mouths burn from interchanged spittle, our lips blister, bleed, chap— We were scared.

I lay there on my side with my arm around her neck, my hand gripped on her rib, and I ate her lips and she mine. There were interesting crises. . . . No way to go further without fighting. After that we'd just sit and gab in the black of the parlor while the family slept and the radio played low. One night I heard her father come in the kitchen door—I had no idea then of the great fogs rolling over fields by the sea in Nova Scotia and the poor little cottages in lost storms, sad work, wintry work in the bottom of life, the sad men with pails who walk in fields—the new form of the sun every morning— Ah I loved my Maggie, I wanted to eat her, bring her home, hide her in the heart of my life the rest of my days. I prayed in Sainte Jeanne d'Arc church for the grace of her love; I'd almost forgotten . . .

Let me sing the beauty of my Maggie. Legs:—the knees attached to the thighs, knees shiny, thighs like milk. Arms:—the levers of my content, the serpents of my joy. Back:—the sight of that in a strange street of dreams in the middle of Heaven would make me fall sitting from glad recognition. Ribs?—she had some melted and round like a well formed apple, from her thigh bones to waist I saw the earth roll. In her neck I hid myself like a lost snow goose of Australia, seeking the perfume of her breast. . . . She didnt let me, she was a good girl. The poor big alley cat with her, though almost a year younger, had black ideas about her legs that he hid from himself, also in his prayers didnt mention . . . the dog. Across the big world darkness I've come, in boat, in bus, in airplane, in train standing my shadow immense traversing the fields and the redness of engine boilers behind me making me omnipotent upon the earth of the night, like God—but I have never made love with a little finger that has won me since. I gnawed her face with my eyes; she loved that; and that was bastardly I didnt know she loved me—I didnt understand.

"Jack—," after we'd had all our conversations about the kids she fiddled with all day, while I was at school and since I'd last seen her, the gossip, things of high school kids talking about others their age, the stories, rumors, news of the dance, of marriage . . . "Jack, marry me some day."

"Yes, yes, always—nobody else."

"You sure there's nobody else?"

"Well *who* could be?" I didnt love the girl Maggie was jealous of, Pauline, who'd found me standing in the gang of football players one night in autumn at a dance where I'd gone because there was a banquet for the players and a basketball game we wanted to see, boy stuff—I was waiting in the corner for the dance to end, the idea of dancing with a girl was impossible but I had it concealed— She picked me out of a corner like young men dream. She said, "Hey I like you!—you're bashful, I like bashful people!" and drew me tremblingly excitingly to the floor, great eyes in mine, and pulled my body and hers and squeezed me interestingly and made me "dance" to talk, to get acquainted—the smell of her hair was killing me! In her door at home she was looking at me with the moon in her eyes, saying, "If you wont kiss me I'll kiss you" and opened the screendoor I'd just closed and gave me a cool kiss— We had talked about kisses looking at each other's mouths all night; we had said we werent interested in such things—"I'm a good girl, I believe in h-hmmm—kissing"—flutter—"but I mean I wouldnt allow anything beyond that to happen"—like in New England the girls—"but you've got bedroom eyes, hey. Did I tell ya about the guy I didnt know who put his arm around me at the Girl Officers' Ball?" She was a Girl Officer.

"What?"

"Dont you want to know if I asked him to take his hands off me—?"

"Yeah?"

"Dont be silly, I dont talk to strangers."

Pauline, brown hair, blue eyes, the great glistening stars in her lips— She too lived near a river, the Merrimack, but near the highway, the big bridge, the big carnival and football field—you could see the factories across the river. I spent many afternoons there conversing with her in the snow, about kisses, before meeting Maggie. All of a sudden one night she opens the damned door and kisses me—big stuff! The first night I met her all I could do was smell her hair in my bed, in my hair—told this to Lousy, I smelt her in his hair too. It interested Lousy. When I told him we'd finally kissed the night before (sitting with him on my bed with the gang G.J. Scotty Iddyboy sitting in chairs of my bedroom after supper talking about the team my mother doing the dishes my father at the radio) Lousy wanted me to kiss him like I had kissed Pauline. We did it, too; the others didnt even stop talking about the team. But now Maggie was another matter—her kisses, an expensive wine, we dont have much, nor often—hidden in the earth—limited, like Napoleon brandy—pretty soon no more. Marry, love somebody else? Impossible. "I love only you, Maggie," I tried to say, no more success than with G.J. the little boy loves of puberty. I tried to assure her that she would never have cause for jealousy, truly. Enough of singing— I'll sing later—the story of Maggie—the beginning of my jealousy, the things that happened.

The mortality in my heart is heavy, they're going to throw me in a hole already eaten by the dogs of dolor like a sick Pope who's played with too many young girls the black tears flowing from his skeleton-hole eyes.

Ah life, God—we wont find them any more the Nova Scotias of flowers! No more saved afternoons! The shadows, the ancestors, they've all walked in the dust of 1900 seeking the new toys of the twentieth century just as Céline says—but it's still love has found us out, and in the stalls was nothing, eyes of drunken wolves was all. Ask the guys at the war.

8

I see her head bowed in thinking of me, by the river, her beautiful eyes searching inside for the proper famous thought of me she loved. Ah my angel—my new angel, black, follows me now—I exchanged the angel of life for the other. Before the crucifix of Jesus in the house I stood attentively, sure of many things, I was going to see the tears of God and already I saw them in that countenance elongated white in plaster that gave life—gave life bitten, finished, droop-eyed, the hands nailed, the poor feet also nailed, folded, like winter cold feet of the poor Mexican worker you see in the street waiting for the guys to come with the barrels to empty the rags the crap and keeps one foot on the other to keep warm— Ah— The head bent, like the moon, like my picture of Maggie, mine and God's; the dolors of a Dante, at sixteen, when we dont know conscience or what we're doing.

When I was younger, ten, I'd pray at the crucifix for the love of my Ernie Malo, a little boy in parochial school, son of a judge, who because he was like my dead brother Gerard I loved with as sublime a love—with the strangeness of childhood in it, for instance I'd pray at the picture of my brother Gerard, dead at nine when I was four, to insure the friendship, respect and grace of Ernie Malo—I wanted little Ernie to give me his hand, simply, and say to me, "Ti Jean, you you're nice!" And—"Ti Jean, we'll be friends always, we'll go hunting together in Africa when we finish school ha?" I found him as beautiful as seven times the pick because his rosy cheeks and white teeth and the eyes of a woman dreaming, of an angel maybe, bit my heart; children love each other like lovers, we dont look at their little dramas in the course of our adult days. The picture—, also at the crucifix I prayed. Every day at school it was one ruse after another to make me loved by my boy; I watched him when we all stood in line in the schoolyard, the Brother up front was delivering his speech, his prayer in the cold zero, redness of Heaven behind him, the big steam and balloon and ballturd of horses in the little alley that crossed the school property (Saint Joseph's Parochial), the ragmen were coming at the same time we were marching to class. Dont think we werent afraid! They had greasy hats, they grinned in dirty holes on top of tenements. . . . I was crazy then, my head ran fantastic ideas from seven morning till ten night like a little Rimbaud in his racks cracked. Ah the poetry I'd written at ten—letters to Maggie—afternoons walking to school I'd imagine movie cameras turned on me, the Complete Life of a Parochial School Boy, his thoughts, way he jumps against fences. —Voila, at sixteen, Maggie—the crucifix—there, God knew I had love troubles that were big and real now with his plastic statued head just neckbroke leaned over as sad as ever, more sad than ever. "You found yourself your little darknesses?" said God to me, silently, with his statue head, before it my hands clasped waiting. "Grew up with your little *gidigne?*" (dingdong). At the age of seven a priest had asked me in the confessional "And you played with your little *gidigne?*"

"Yes *mon père*."

"Well therefore, if you played with your little *gidigne* say a whole rosary and after that do ten *Notre Pères* and ten *Salut Marie's* in front of the altar and after that you can go." The Church carried me from one Saviour to another; who's done that for me since?—why the tears?—God spoke to me from the crucifix:—"Now it is morning and the good people are talking next door and the light comes in through the shade—my child, you find yourself in the world of mystery and pain not understandable—I know, angel—it is for your good, we shall save you, because we find your soul as important as the soul of the others in the world—but you must suffer for that, in effect my child, you must die, you must die in pain, with cries, frights, despairs—the ambiguities! the terrors!—the lights, heavy, breakable, the fatigues, ah—"

I listened in the silence of my mother's house to divine how God was going to arrange the success of my love with Maggie. Now I could see her tears too. Something there was, that was not, nothing, just the consciousness that God awaits us.

"Mixing up in the affairs of the world isnt for God," I told myself hurrying to school, ready for another day.

9

Here was a typical day, I'd get up in the morning, seven, my mother'd call, I'd smell the breakfast of toast and gruel, the windows were frozen an inch of snowy ice the whole glass illuminated rose by the transformations of the ocean of winter outside. I'd jump out of the sheets so warm soft, I wanted to stay buried all day with Maggie and maybe also just the darkness and the death of *no time;* I'd jump into my incontestable clothes; inescapable cold shoes, cold socks that I threw on the oil stove to warm. Why did people stop wearing long underwear?—it's a bitch to put on little undershirts in the morning—I'd throw my warm pajamas on the bed— My room was lit by the morning the color of a rose coal a half-hour dropped from the grate, my things all there like the Victrola, the toy pool table, the toy green desk, the linoleum all raised one side and sitting on books to make banks for the pool balls and raced track meets when I had time but I didnt any more— My tragic closet, my jacket hung in a dampness like powder from fresh plaster lost locked like adobe closets Casbah roof civilizations; the papers covered with my printed handwritings, on the floor, among shoes, bats, gloves, sorrows of pasts. . . . My cat who'd slept with me all night and was now thrown awake in the empty semi-warm bed was trying to hide himself in near the pillow and sleep a little more but smelled the bacon and hurried to begin his day, to the floor, plap, disappearing like a sound with little swift feet; sometimes he was gone when seven o'clock woke me, already out making crazy little tracks in the new snow and little yellow balls of pipi and shivering his teeth to see the birds in trees as cold as iron. "Peeteepeet!" the birds said; I look outside briefly before leaving my room, in a window hole, the roofs are pure, white, the trees frozen mad, the cold houses smoking thinly, docile-eyed in winter.

You have to put up with life.

10

In the tenement it was high, you could see downstairs the roofs of Gardner Street and the big field and the trail people used gray rose dawns five o'clock January to go flatulate in church. There were old women of the block who went to church every dawn, and late afternoon; and sometimes again evening; old, prayery, understanding of something that little children dont understand and in their tragedy so close you'd think to the tomb that you saw already their profiles sitting in rose satin the color of their rose-morns of life and expectoration but the scent of other things rising from the hearts of flowers that die at the end of autumn and we've thrown them on the fence. It was the women of interminable novenas, lovers of funerals, when somebody died they knew it right away and hurried to church, to the house of death and to the priest possibly; when they themselves died the other old women did the same thing, it was the cups of sugar in eternity— There's the trail; and winter important morning opening stores and people *hallo!* and I go ready to go to school. It's a *méli-mélon* of morning everywhere.

11

I'd have breakfast.

My father was usually away on his out-of-town job running a lino-type for some printer—Andover, near the little crewcuts there who had no idea of the darkness inherent in the earth if they didnt see that sad big man crossing the night to go make his 40-hour week—so he was not at our kitchen table, usually just my mother, cooking, and my sister, getting ready for her job at So and So's or *The Citizen,* she was a bookbinder—Grave facts of worklife were explained to me but I was too proud in purple love to listen— Ahead of me, nothing but the New York *Times,* Maggie, and the great world night and morning of the shrouds on twig and leaf, by lakes—"Ti Jean!" they called me—I was a big lout, ate enormous breakfasts, suppers, afternoon snacks (milk, one quart: peanut butter and crackers, ½ pound). "Ti Jean!"—when my father was home, *"Ti Pousse!"* he called me, chuckling (Little Thumb). Now oatmeal breakfasts in the rosiness—

"Well how's your love affair with Maggie Cassidy coming along?" my sister'd ask, grinning from behind a sandwich, "or did she give you the air because of Moe Cole!"

"You mean Pauline? Why Pauline?"

"You dont know how jealous women get—that's all they think about— You'll see—"

"I dont see anything."

"Tiens," my mother's saying, "here's some bacon with toast I made a big batch this morning because yesterday you finished em all up and you was fightin at the end for the last time like you used to do over Kremel, never mind the jealous girls and the tennis courts, it's gonna be awright if you just stick to your guns there like a real French Canadian boy the way I brought you up to respect decency—listen, Ti Jean, you'll

never be sorry if you always follow a clean life. You dont have to believe me, you know." And she'd sit and we'd all eat. At the last minute I'd stand undecided in my room, looking at the little radio I just got and in which I'd just started listening to Glenn Miller and Jimmy Dorsey and romantic songs that tore my heart out . . . *My Reverie, Heart and Soul,* Bob Eberle, Ray Eberle, all the blue sighing America was racked up behind me in the night that was all mine and the glory of the tenderness of the trembling kiss of Maggie and all love as only teenagers know it and like perfect blue ballrooms. I wrung my hands Shakespeareanly at my closet door; crossing the bathroom to grab a towel my eyes misted from sudden romantic notions of myself sweeping Maggie off a pink dancefloor onto a pier with a moon shining, into a slick convertible, a close kiss long and sincere (just a little to the right).

I'd just started shaving; one night my sister had surprised me combing my hair making a little tuck in my crown for a wave—"Oh boy, look at the Romeo!" It was surprising; two months before I'd been a boy, coming home from fall football practice in iron dusks wrapped in my jacket and earmuff cap, bent, offnights I'd spot pins at the alley with twelve-year-old boys, at three cents a string—20 strings, 60 cents, usually I made that or a buck— Just a boy, I'd only recently cried because I lost my hat while playing in a WPA League basketball game won at the last second by a sensational toss by Billy Artaud almost rivaling the time at the Boys' Club tie-score with one second to go against a Greek team tigrishly named I made a one-hand last-whistle jump shot out of the scrambling pack from about the foul line and the ball hung in the basket a horrid second for everybody to see, bagged, the game over, Zagg and his tricks—an inborn showman—everlasting hero. The hat now forgotten.

"By Ma," kissing my mother on the cheek, starting off for school, she herself worked part time in the shoe factory with her grave sense of life sitting grim and tireless at the skiving machine holding stubborn shoe leathers to a blade, her fingertips blackened, years on end of it from fourteen on, other girls like her up and down the machines—the whole family working, 1939 was a tail-end Depression year about to be overshadowed by events in Poland.

I got my lunch, prepared the night before by Ma, slices of bread and butter; nothing was more delicious than these slices at noon after four hours almost interesting sunny classroom absorbed in personalities of teachers like Joe Maple with his eloquent statements in English 3 or old Mrs. McGillicuddy the astronomy (inseparable)—bread and butter

and delicious, hot mashed potatoes, nothing else, at the roaring basement tables my lunch cost 10¢ a day— The pièce de résistance was my
magnificent chocolate-covered ice cream stick, everyone in school 95%
licked on them greedily every noon, on benches, in the huge cellar halls,
on the sidewalks—recess—I'd sometimes in my grace like the grace that
got me Maggie get thick ice cream almost an inch wide, by some mistake
in the ice cream factory with rich unbelievable thick chocolate layer that
also by mistake was larded and curled right on—by same industrial
perchance, I'd get feeble anemic sticks a half-inch, already half melted,
paper-thin chocolate falling on the sidewalk of Kirk Street as we'd Harry
McCarthy, Lousy, Bill Artaud and me lick our sticks ceremoniously
greedy in the winter sun my mind a million miles from romance— So
I'd bring my bread and butter lunch, to be stuffed quickly in my homeroom desk—kiss Mother—and take off, on foot, to stride as fast as I
could, like everybody else, down Moody past the posts of Textile to the
great bridge to Moody tenements and down the hill into the city, gray,
prosperous, puffing in the morn. And along the way the soldiers'd fall
in, G.J. off Riverside going to his business course in Lowell High where
he learned typing and bookkeeping and made fantasies around the luscious girls who were going to be sexy secretaries, he'd begun wearing
necktie and suit, he'd say "Zagg that Miss Gordon is going to take that
expression of cool indifference off her face one of these days and let her
panties slip on the floor for me, mark my words—and it'll be in one of
those empty rooms one of these afternoons"—but instead of actual sexual conquests he'd wind up at two in the afternoon with his books in
the Rialto B movie—alone, faced by the reality of Franchot Tone and
Bruce Cabot and Alice Faye and Don Ameche grinning smiling at Tyrone etc. and old men and old women living on relief wide-eyed in the
show. Too, Lousy'd come angling to my walk from Riverside; then,
incredibly, Billy Artaud'd overtake us all from the rear striding madly
down from the upper outskirt hill of Moody and just as we reached the
canal downtown we'd see all of us that Iddyboy was way ahead and
was already leaning out of his freshman homeroom window dutifully
obeying the teacher's request to open window—"Eeediboy!" he'd yell,
and disappear in, he was the most willing student in LHS and had the
lowest marks and otherwise he would have been able to play football
and would have killed everybody broken Malden guards in half with
one clip of his granite elbow—Open homeroom window in Lowell, rose
morn and birds upon the Boott Mill canal— Later it was going to be
the open window morn at Columbia University the pigeonshit on the

sill of Mark Van Doren and the Shakespeare of drunken sleeps under an Avon apple tree, ah—

Down Moody we'd sweep, primish, young, mad. Crossing us like a streamlet were the Bartlett Junior High School kids taking the riverbank route to the White Bridge and Wannalancitt Street which'd been our route for "How many years Mouse? Remember the winter it was so cold they had frostbites in the Principal's office with doctors?—"

"And the time we had that snowball war on Wannalancitt—"

"The crazy guys come to school with bikes, no kiddin Louse they had more trouble going up that hill from side to side than if they'd walk—"

"I used to walk home every noon me and Eddy Desmond wrapped in each other's arms falling on the ground—he was the laziest guy in the world, he didnt want to go to school in the afternoon, he wanted me to throw him in the river, I had to carry him—sleepy, he was like my cat, crazy—"

"Ah the old days!" Mouse'd pout black and brooding. "All I ask is a chance in this ga-dam world to earn a decent living and support my mother and see that all her needs are answered—"

"Where's Scotty workin now?"

"Didnt you hear?—out in Chelmsford, they're building a big war airplane base, Scotty and all the old WPA bums go out and dig up trees and cut em down and clear the ground—he's making a million dollars a week—he gets up at four o'clock in the morning—Fuggen Scotcho— I love Scotcho— Dont catch *him* going to no high school and no business school courses, Kid Faro wants his money *now*—"

We came to the bridge. The winter trickle between the jagged canyons of rock below, the pools of ice formed, rosy matin on the froth of little rapids, cold—far off, the bungalows of Centreville, and the snowy hump meadow, and hints of New Hampshire forests deep in where big men in mackinaws now with axes and boots and cigarettes and laughs drove old Reos through rutted dirt strips among pinestumps, to the house, the shack, the dream of wild New England in our hearts—

"You're quiet, Zagg—that damn Maggie Cassidy's got you boy, s'got you boy!"

"Dont let no broad get you, Zagg—love aint worth it—what's love, *nothin.*" G.J. was against it. Not Lousy.

"No, love is *great* Mouse—something to think about—go to church and pray Zagg You Babe! Marry her! Screw her! Zeet? Have a good one for me!"

"Zagg," advised Gus seriously, "screw her then leave her take it from an old seadog,—women are no good, forever 'tis written in the stars— Ah!" turning away, black—"Kick em in the pants, put em in their place—There's enough misery in this world, laugh, cry, sing, tomorrow is nothing— Dont let her get you down, Zagguth."

"I wont, Mouso."

"Zeet! Look here comes Billy Artaud—already for another day rubbing his hands together—" Sure enough Billy Artaud who lived with his mother and every morning didnt rise from his bed but leaped out grinning came up rubbing his hands, you could hear the cold wiry sound of his zeal across the street.

"Hey, you guys, wait up— Let the chess champion walk!"

"*You're* the chess champion? Ho Ho."

"What?—"

"With my bombarding tactics I can beat you all—"

"Zeet? Look at his books!"

—Wrangling, goofing, we stride without physical pause to school past Saint Jean Baptiste Church ponderous Chartres Cathedral of the slums, past gas stations, tenements, Vinny Bergeracs—("Fuggen Vinny's still sleepin . . . they wouldnt even take him in vocational school . . . all this morning he'll read Thrilling True Love stories and eat them Drake's Devil Cakes with the white cream in the middle . . . he never eats food, he lives on cakes. . . . Ah ga-dammit I know we played hooky yesterday but my soul cries out for Vinny this gray sad morning."

"We better be careful—two days in a row?"

"Did you hear him yestiddy?—he said he was going to get sexmad now and stick his head in the toilet bowl!")—past the City Hall, the library in back with already some old bums gathering smoking butts at the door of the newspaper room waiting for nine o'clock opening time—past Prince Street ("Zowie, only last summer think of the games we had there, Zagg, the homeruns, the triples, the great Scotch pitching shutouts—life is so *big!*")—("life my dear Lousy is immerelensum!")— past the YWCA, the canal bridge, the entrance street to the great cotton mills with all up down the morning-rosy cobbles the tight serried Colonial doors of a mid-nineteenth-century housing block for textile workers celebrated in some of Dickens' memoirs, the sad crapulous look of old redbrick sagging doorfronts and almost a century of work in the mills, gloom in the night.

And we came then mixing into the hundreds of students milling around the high school sidewalks and lawns waiting for the first bell which would be not heard outside but announced from within in a rumbling desperate-faced flying rumor so that sometimes when I was nightmarishly late I hurried all alone across the great deserted spaces only minutes ago scene of hundredfold grabbings now mopped out clean all the principals cubby-holed inside the silent high school windows in the morning's first classes, a mortifying great space of guilts, many times dreamed, sidewalk, grass. "I'm going back to school," dreams the old invalid in his innocent pillow, blind of time.

• • •

20

I went to the indoor racetrack that Saturday evening, Pa was with me, rode the bus down jabbing blah blah blah "Well so I said to so and so"—

"Hey Pa, *t'en rappelle tu quand qu'on faisa les lions*—Hey Pa remember when we made the lions, I was four years old, on Bridge Street, and you'd sit me on your knees imitating the noises of animals! Remember? and Ti Nin?"

"*Pauvre* Ti Nin," said my father; talk to him, it would start him, gather in him, "it's a damn shame the way that poor little girl has found troubles—!"

"—and we'd listen together, you made lions."

"It was fun, I was amusing myself with my little kids," he'd say way off brooding darkly, over lost youth, mistaken rooms, weird troubles and strange gossipy rumors and stiff unpleasant unhappiness of bleary people in parlors, remembering himself with pride and pity. The bus went downtown.

I explained my track to him, so he'd understand the night's races better; he understood that 3.7 was my best time and that night there was a Negro on the Worcester North team who was supposed to be like a lightning eagle in the sprints; I was afraid I was going to be beaten in my city that night by a Negro, just like the young boxers around the corner at the Crescent and the Rex Ballroom when they put the chairs and the ring in the floor of the cold dancers. My father said— "Go as fast as you can, beat the bastard: they're supposed to run like damn streaks! antelopes of Africa!"

"Hey Pa—and Pauline Cole's gonna be there."

"Oh— That's your other girl? Little Pauline, yeh, I like that little

one me— Too bad you dont get along with her, she must be just as good
as your little Maggie Papoopy there the other side of the river—"

"They're different!"

"Aw, well you're already startin to have trouble with women!"

"Well, what do you want me to do."

Hand up. "Don't ask *me!* Ask your mother—ask the old curé—
ask the askers—*I* dont know—I dont pretend to know—I'm just trying
to get along in the world— You'll all have to work with me. You'll see
that it's gonna be pretty damn bad, *Comprends?*" loud, in French, like
an uncle calling the idiot from the corner making clear to me meanings
that can never be recorded in the English language.

Together, heads bent forward with the bus, we rode downtown.
He wore a felt hat, I had an earmuff hunting cap; it was a cold
night.

The crowd was swarming around the dark street outside the brilliantly lit Annex, it was like some great church service suddenly let out
and they were all coming to the track meet, an old church a block away,
huge trees, redbrick factory annexes, the back of a bank, the glow of
midtown Kearney Square red and vague over the backs of tar roofs and
neon signs beyond. The football coach from some little suburban town
would be there, talking in the door with the owner of a sporting goods
store, or old soda-fountain habitué with long memories of track records
from 1915 (like in German Europe); my father and I, bashful, would
push through the crowds; my father'd be looking everywhere to see
somebody he knew, grinning, and wouldnt see anybody. The mysterious
inside, with people standing around the great door to the Annex and
the track, beyond them were the boards of the banked turns, like circus
props huge and dusty. Ticket takers. Little nameless kids jumping
around. "I'll go sit in the stands while I can still get a seat," Pop said.
"I'll wave at you when you come out."

"I'll *see you*—" But Pop thinks I said "be seeing you" and is already
waddling off through the crowds inside, he walks around the banks,
onto the floor, to his plank seat; others are standing in the middle of
the track in topcoats jawing. Young kids have already started running
around in shorts, when they get older than fourteen or fifteen they'll be
getting big hood suits with long running ski pants with the school's
colors on them; the older boys are inside leisurely changing. The great
mysterious Negro flyer is hidden in the opponents' showers somewhere—like a great lion beast I can feel his stalking presence—like a
thonged whip the surly tawny tail is flashing at the level floor, the growl,

the teeth, no greeting in the V's and W's of his Vow—the rumbling roar of other lions even further down below— My imagination had been fed on circuses and unclean magazines; I looked everywhere like a goof as I hurried to my track shoes.

Others were there—Johnny Lisle—Dibbick who ran so funny, the track team captain—smells of liniment, towels—

"Hey there Jack waddayasay boy?" Johnny Lisle out of the corner of his mouth. "Think we'll win the 300 tonight?"

"Hope I dont have to run it." It was like the railroad local, it was hard work.

"Melis'll run it tonight—and Mickey Maguire—and Kazarakis."

"Krise, they cant be beat."

"Joe was asking me to run it second man but I dont know that route—you know, I'm a 1000-yard runner, I dont wanta wear myself out and get my *#:! shins all cracked out—"

"I knew I'd have to run it," I said out loud, really complaining, but Johnny didnt hear me as just then a panic seized us all and we knew there was no more time to talk, in twenty seconds we were all bundling in our running hoods and parka pants and stepping out mincingly on little tiny toe-dancer sneakers with hard rubber bottoms to catch the wood of the indoor planks—nail shoes were for moderner high schools with all-cork tracks. In these tight sneakers you could really streak, they were light.

I saw Pauline at the door. She never looked more glamorous, great moist eyes of grueling blue were mooning right at me like swimming seas, at her age it had all the men turning quick furtive felt hats to see her twice. All I had to do was stand there like a post and let her go. She leaned on the wall wriggling before me, with hands back clasped, I just smiled, she made love speeches.

"Hey I bet you'll be watching for me behind the forty-yard line, huh? I'll wave. You wave back at me."

"Okay."

"Dont say that I didnt come here to see you because I dont love ya, see?"—in closer.

"What?"

"I didnt think you'd catch it the first time—I'll get even with you if you grrr with me." She was clenching her teeth and fists at me. All the time she never took her eyes off me; she was in love with something, probably me, probably love. I grieved inside that I had to give up her for Maggie. But I couldnt have Mary and Magdalene both so I had to decide my mind. And I didnt want to be a boor and do the wrong thing hurting Pauline—if boor is strong enough, gross enough. So I looked solemnly at her and said nothing and started out to my race. Her sympathies were with me. "What a funny rat!" she also must have thought—"Never comes and admits nothing." Like Faust.

21

The Worcester men were out, jogging the banks in blue run suits that looked ominous and alien among our red and gray homey suits—and suddenly there he was, the Negro Flyer, long and thin floating on ghost feet in the far corner of the Annex, picking up, laying down his delicate feet with experimental restraint as though when he'd be ready he'd fly like an arrow and all you'd see is the flashing white socks, the reptilian head stuck out forward to the run. Hurdles was his specialty. I was a sunk ghost of a trackman. But, for all his great streaking in wild track meets of indoor New England brightlight night he wasnt going to reckon Jack the white boy, sixteen, hands clasped behind him in a newspaper photo with white kid trunks and white undershirt when early at fifteen I was too young to get a regular track suit, ears sticking out, raw, hair piled inky mass on square Keltic head, neck line ramrod holding head up, broad pillared neck with base in collarbone muscles and on each side slope-muscled shoulders down to big arms, legs piano thick just above the white socks—Eyes hard and steely in a sentimental Mona Lisaing face—jawbone iron new. Like Mickey Mantle at nineteen. Another kind of speed and need.

The first event was the 30-yard dash. I saw with satisfaction the Negro star wasnt in my heat, which I won from a bunch of kids, breezy. In his heat I saw him win by yards, fast and low and light on his feet, when he reached he clawed for the finish line and not just dull air. The big moment of the final heat came. We didnt even look at each other at the starting line, he too bashful for me, I too bewildered for him, it was like warriors of two nations. In his eyes there was a sure glow of venom tiger eyes in an honest rockboned face, so your exotic is just a farmer, he goes to church as well as you, has fathers, brothers as well as you—honesties—The Canuck Fellaheen Indian and the Fallaheen Negro face to face in a battle of spears before they hit the long grass, contesting territories that howl around. Pauline was watching very closely, I could see her leaning elbows on knee in the stands with an intent smile digging the whole drama of the track meet and everybody there. In the middle of the track were the officials, with watches, switch lists, we were making our moves by the clock right on schedule with the Lowell *Sun* reporter's written list of events:

30-YARD DASH—*1st Heat (Time: 3.8)—Duluoz (Lowell).*
         Smith (WC)
         2nd Heat (Time: 3.7)—Lewis (WC).
         Kazarakis (Lowell)
         Final Heat   —

This was coming up, he had done 3.7 in his heat, I 3.8 in mine, which meant the difference of a yard, there was no doubt of his tremendous speed. His hands and arms hung loosely and muscular with great black veins. He was going to play beating drums to my wild alto.

We got down on the line, shivering in a sudden cold gust of air from the street; we tested our spit in the planks, kicked at it with dug-in sneakers, stuck the sneaker in and got down like to crawl but on thumb and forefingers level. Bent testing knees, teetered and balanced to feel. Spectators saw the madness of racers—human runners like Greeks of Sparta—the Socratic silences falling over the crowd as the starter raises his gun in the air. To my utter amazement I saw out of the corner of my eye the colored boy laid out almost flat on the floor in a low slung fantastic starting position, something impossibly modern and submarining and subterranean like bop, like the new gesture of a generation. It was in imitation of the great Ben Johnson who ran 60 yards in 6 seconds flat, this kid from the slums of Worcester was mad to imitate him who'd inconceivably broken the world's record by 2/10ths of a second, fabulous ghost streak Negro of Columbia in the late Thirties. Later on in life I'd see American Negro boys imitating Charley Parker and calling themselves Bird on street corners and it would be the same thing, and son to, this gesture of the early bop generation as I immeasurably understood it seeing it the first time. We teetered on thoughtful fingers just on the verge of exploding into fact, bang, the crash from the thought of running to the running itself, the kick-off to the dash. My friend—whose name was some forgotten-by-me Negro name of inconceivable anonymity and humility—John Henry Lewis was his name—he shot off ahead of the gun and we all flew off in a false start and held up when the gun cracked us to return, he ahead—We reorganized ourselves for the mental anguish of another start. I got down, saw him on my left low and lightly-hung to fly off the floor—

and just as I predicted in my own mind the absolute certainty that the starter would shoot he shot but I was already gone. I was flying, luckily legally just barely beat the gun—no one knew but myself and the starter and the starter was Joe Garrity who knew a jump-the-gun when it was illegal and was inflexible (wouldnt cheat) in his knowledge, pity, and sense of duty. I flew ahead of my Negro, my Jim, eyes half closed so as not to see the horror of his black skin at my breast, and hit the tape well ahead but just barely beginning to sense his catch-up as he too late gathered a stunned momentum and knew that he was beaten anyway and by the mind. The others were not altogether out—John Kazarakis who was just coming into his own in realization of what a great athlete he really was hung on John Lewis' shirt behind by some half-inch behind me by a foot and also closing in. But my muscular headlong rush beat the thin speed demons just the same and by sheer will. It was like the way I'd once seen Billy Carr run so fast he stumbled in his run and kept somehow in the air and regained his feet and literally threw himself across the air against the finish-line tape all muscles and white power, 3.5, beating great college sprinters in his high school years . . . Billy Carr that went to Notre Dame, whose glamour in Lowell was some rich and hidden thing in the dense tree mansions of Andover Street in the winter night of golden home lights, lovely girls of summer and finishing schools strolling under laceries of branch in streetlamp sorrows by bushes, driveways, iron fences, bandana under pouting lip . . .

My win over John Lewis was received with applause and by myself with awe—as I bounced off the mattress against the wall I looked furtively at John and caught his whites of eye conceding me the race. He even shook his head and said something to me himself like "Man you" or "Damn" and we laughed together as we walked back.

They were putting up the hurdles for the 35, bustles, talk, the reporters typed their results:

30-YARD DASH—Final Heat *(Time: 3.7)—Duluoz (Lowell),*
Lewis (WC), Kazarakis (Lowell)

Pauline waved; Pa gave me the okay sign. I'd overcome the ghost. "Ah," I thought, "Ma's gonna be glad—she'll see that I run and work hard and I'm getting to my hand. She'll say to herself, 'Bon, Ti Jean's doing his business, his homework too.'— I'll be able to sit home in the chair not sayin a word all day Sunday— It's at home we win." And I saw my father with joy. "Look at his big happy smile—he's talkin to the men near him— The enemies of my father!—they're far, not near tonight—their mystery doesnt tear my teeth out tonight—the fact that we dont know their face, their place, the savage extent of their indifference to us— We'll bury em a deep one before midnight." My thoughts ran like fallen stars. I saw in my eye in the middle of all the world the dark corners on the floor in my house where my cats, my migs hid, where I'd put my crazy face in rainy afternoons of no-school when I really dreamed immortality, the health of my blood and family, the frightening mystery too. I believed in the planks of the little corner; I knew that the earth, the streets, the floors and shadows of life were holy—like a Host—gray, dirty Host of interesting reality (like the bridge at Orleans) of great smoke of men and things, where I'd find myself an honor so great that my father with his old coats, humble hat, would look at me in another heavened life like you look at a man and we'd speak rare things—"Ti Nin'll read it in the paper, my sister— she'll show it to her friends— Lousy'll read it tomorrow morning when he gets up to go to church—Scotty—G.J.—Vinny—"

"And Maggie—"

"I beat the speedy *Neigre* from Worcester—and him, he'll go back to Worcester—maybe if not to tell to *know* that in Lowell the guys from the alleys and rock streets run like demons, let the name of Lowell make a noise in their hearts after this—that in the world where the name is Lowell the boys brothers and mad hurl themselves howling in this mortal ocean . . . brothers, boys, wolves of the North." (These thoughts were all in French, almost untranslatable.)

I could see all the rooftops of Lowell and Worcester in my victory, my ideas, sensations. They'd put a poet in my craw. I was ecstatically insane in my innocence. I knew joys not by name but that they crossed my clotting breast of hot blood and disappeared unnamed, unknown, uncommunicated with the thoughts of others but arranged in the same manner and therefore like the thoughts of the Negro, intent, normal. It was later they dropped us radar machines in the sky to derange the senses. Let's hear no more about the excesses of Rimbaud! I cried remembering the beautiful faces of life that night.

The 35-yard hurdles I also won flying at the start ahead of Lewis by that whiteflashing split second—I skimmed over the hurdles in a mad anxiety, level with the race I dug floors away, aimed down the line. I was more surprised than anybody and John Henry Lewis. And for the first time I hit 4.6. I even began to wonder if I'd suddenly become a really great runner.

22

The track floor was being laid out with broad-jump mats, high-jump poles, the big shotputters are standing around agreeing and determining the layout of the jump area so they can start warming up right away—Ernie Sanderman who later became a round-the-world magician seaman on luxurious passenger ships of the blue sea was our best broad-jumper—stood, on his takeoff board, and swung his arms back together and wailed out heaving his tortured neck into the annexvoid-athema of the wild Annex, reaching for his landing place of both feet he'd jump ten feet, clear across a narrow livingroom, with big feet flapping to the mark. I also participated in this event, jumped 9 feet and 5, 6 or 7 inches, made points for the team, but always losing to Ernie and usually the visiting champ too and finishing third—

The last event I led off, Kazarakis anchor, the 300-yard hated relay, with bull-necked Fullback Melis and Irish curly locks Mickey Maguire from Belvedere, zooming around the track like streamliners and the Worcester men in their blue regalia flying a half-foot behind in close-packed races of serious interest, when I was off and underway nothing gave me a bigger boot than the 300-yard run, it was frantic, you had to kill yourself, the guys were screaming on all sides, in the Annex, "Run!" and we'd be hollowy echoing with hard feet on wood bank board turns making a roar coming off just on the inside on the smooth basketball floor into the inside line without now any further booming noise, just cat feet sprinting, all the mothers of Lowell should have come to see their sons show their fathers how they can run—into the woods, into the thieveries and wood piles, into the hysterical idiot streakfoot madness of mankind—

I took off frightened, the guy with me was a white boy from Worcester, I let him shoulder me out of the first turn as we raced with the relay sticks—this was a courtesy on my part. We boomed around the boards—came off, both of us, sleekly, skinly, padding up our court, interested audiences watching interested racers, the whole corps of newspapermen now alert with heads up from their typewriters or from the sidelines, a few dull, immediate cries of opening-lap audiences. "Bang!" the gun had said, the gunpowder was just spreading in the air—we was off.

My Pop was standing at his bench plank, just bent to watch, tense, his whole huge body toned to hold up watchful on the quivering hard legs with which he used to play basketball in YMCAs of pre-World War I—

"Okay Jean"—under his breath—"Go on!" He was afraid because I'd given the kid the first bank I'd given up my show. No. I leisurely followed him around the far turn, and as we came into the homestretch of the first of two laps I just passed him with a sneaky quiet sprint he hardly heard and flew ahead of him bent for that first turn again, for the tilt of the boards, and flashed by the line of watchers, the kid was heard to curse, he pictures himself taking off after me—I was already boastfully in the back stretch and halfway along it and had done my booming and my soft off-step and all things of that nature and was in a straight line for the last turn, no sound, streaking across the kitchen, bent for the last boards—ghosting in—turning with the world on the revolving banks like a funhouse barrel and now very tired and hurting all over and my heart dying from so much pain in lungs, legs—The kid from Worcester overtook nothing, but lost spaces of breeze between us, hopelessly mawkfaced lost and discouraged, almost embarrassed to shame. I run up and assume the handout pose with the relay stick and give it to Melis with a 10-yard lead and he's off running his two laps while the next Worcester kid still waits, mincing nervously on a hot potato—Maguire and Kazarakis complete the race like invisible bullets and it's a farce, no contest, and relays are always sad.

—Won races, leaving other boys embarrassed to shame—Shame . . . that key to immortality in the Lord's grave . . . that key to courage . . . that key heart. "Lord, Lord, *Mon Doux, Mon Doux*" (Canadian boy's pronunciation of *Mon Dieu,* My God) I'm saying to myself. "What's gonna happen!"—won races, was applauded, laurel-wreathed, smiled, patted, understood, taken in—took showers, shouted—combed—was young, youthful, was the key—"Hey McKeever!" echoing now loud bang in the locker room glooms. "Hee hee hee didja take a big ass plunge off that 600 fight! Hee hyah ha—whatta batt-ed . . . Jee-heever, ole Jeeheever sure missed tonight!"

"Kelly? I told Kelly, stop throwing it will ya?"

"Oodja see Smack make that line?"

"Hey, know what happened tonight—"

"Where?"

"Keith's—"

"What?"

"Basketball game—they took on Lowell—"

"What score?"

"63–64."

"Jeez!"

"You shoulda seen Tsotakos—you know, Steve's brother—

"You mean Samaras?"

"No!—not Odysseus, the guy with the red-shirt brother!"

"Spaneas?"

"No!"

"Oh yeah!"

"He's the greatest—they never had a basketball player like him—Nobody talks about him"—(some little kid with thin hands falling under the sleeves of his coat weighing 98 pounds and a class officer and sometime team manager and only fourteen years old bringing back reports from other parts of Lowell in the eventful exciting Saturday night). My father's standing there laughing and getting his kicks from all these funny children and looking around fondly to find me. I'm just putting on my shirt, comb in my hand, making a Hitler mustache at Jimmy Jeeheever with it.

"A great night!" yells an enthusiast from that world-packed Lowell door. "Jimmy Foxx never hit more homers than you guys tonight!"

"Joe Garrity," announces somebody, and here comes our track coach in a shabby sad overcoat sad glinting Harry Truman eyes behind glasses and hands hopelessly folded into his coatpockets and says "Well boys, you did pretty well, you did pretty well. . . . We scored 55 points. . . ." He wants to tell us a thousand things but he's waiting for the reporters and enthusiasts to leave, Joe is very secretive about his track team and his quiet matter-of-fact grave relations with each of his boys and all of them in group. "I'm glad about that win, Johnny. I think you're going to make your name in Boston Garden before spring." Half grin, half joke, kids laughing—

"Gee coach, thanks"—Johnny Lisle, who was liked by Joe particularly because he was an Irish boy and close to his heart. Melis—Kazarakis—Duluoz—Sanderman—Hetka—Norbert—Marviles—Malesnik—Morin—Maraski—and seven Irishmen Joyce McDuff Dibbick Lisle Goulding Maguire, he had international national problems to deal with. My father, far from rushing up to the coach to be seen with him, hides in a corner wearing an appreciative smile as he secretly digs Joe the Coach in his real soul and mentally pictures him in City Hall and realizes what Joe is like—and likes him—

"Yah—I can see him at his old desk—like my Uncle Bob who was that railyard clerk in *Nashué* (Nashua)—trying to get along with things as best he can— No different than me— Didnt I know some brother of his a long time ago on the old *Citizen?* or was it Dowd's out on Memorial Road—Wal— And whattaya know, Jacky went and beat that *Neigre*—ha ha ha—when I saw him there I was sure he was too fast for him, but he did it! he did it! Ha ha ha, little tyke, I remember him when he was three feet high and used to crawl on the floor pushing up boxes to me and bringing me toys—two feet high—*Ti Pousse!* Ha ha — Say, that *Neigre* was built, he was sleek—I was damn glad to see my boy beat *him*—that proves he's an athlete—those *Neigres* are the fastest runners in the world—in the jungles of Africa even right now they're running like mad after wild pigs, with spears—You see it in the Olympics, the great Negro athletes there that Jesse not Jesse James Jesse Jones that Jesse Owens flying—the international flavor of the world—"

Pauline is waiting for me at the door, Pa joins her as soon as he finds her.

"Well by God—Pauline—I didnt know *where* you were—I'da sat with you!"

"Why didnt that damn Jack tell me you were here—Hey!" They loved each other, she always had a joke for him, he for her— Their eyes shined as I rushed out of the showers to join them. It was social, provincial, glad, sad; it was ecstasy in the heart. We felt vibrations of love laughing and yelling in the laughing yelling crowds pouring out and milling around; Saturday night is dense and tragic in all America from Rocky Mount on up, San Luis on over, Killdeer on down, Lowell on in.

"Jack! There you are! Dad," whispering in his ear, "tell that lout we's got a date of our own and we dont want him around tonight."

"Okay keed," my father'd say, puffing on the cigar in a strenuous acting pose, "we'll see if we cant fix him up with Cleopatra next week and make up to him for it." In his jests serious.

"All right, Mark Antony. Or wasnt your name Mark Antonio and you came rovin over here to steal this British baron from my castle?"

"Nah!—we'll shoot him tonight in the stagecoach— Dont worry about nothing keed. Let's go to Paige's and have an ice cream soda."

And off we fly, into the bright dry night, stars above the redbrick snows are keen and clear, knives drop from them—the big sinewy trees with their claws deep under the pavements are stuck so high in the sky they are like lost silver in the Up, people walk among streetlamps passing massive trunk bases of something living and never pay it a thought—We join the flow of the sidewalks leading downtown—to the

Lobster Cot—Merrimack Street—the Strand—the whole dense almost riotous inwards of the city aglow for the Saturday night in that time only fifteen years ago when not everybody had cars and people walked to shop and from buses to shows, not everything was locked-in strange behind tin walls with anxious eyes looking out to deserted sidewalks of modern America now— Pauline, Pa and I could not have laughed and experienced excitement and jumped so joyously as we did that night if we'd been in some automobile grimly buried three in a front seat haggling over traffics in the window of the television set of Time—instead we loped on foot over snowbanks, to dry shoveled sidewalks of downtown, to busy revolving doors of wild midnight sodas.

"Come on Jack, you're falling behind. Let's have some fun tonight!" Pauline was yelling in the street, punching me, playing with me.

"Okay."

Whispering in my ear: "Hey, did I enjoy your legs tonight! I didnt know you had legs like that! Gee, can I come and visit you when you have a bachelor apartment? Hey!"

"Say," my father an idea, "how 'bout a nice snack in Chin Lee's? —some chop suey or something?"

"No let's just have ice cream!"

"Where? In the B.C. or Paige's?"

"Oh anywhere— Gee, I dont wanta get fat Mister Duluoz."

"Aw wont hurt ya—I been fat for thirty years and I'm still here— Wont bother ya."

"Look at Mrs. Madison and her son— You know them Jack, they live next door to me. That little kid always peeking at us?"

"And the dog in the yard with the gray fence?"

"Say"—my Pop—"you two little kids sound to me like you'd make a fine little couple— Why is it ya dont step out together"—laughing in his sleeve—secretly serious.

Pauline "Oh we *used* to go steady Mr. Duluoz." Her eyes misting suddenly.

"Well why dont you now? Just because *Ti Pousse* is supposed to have some sweetie in another part of the county?—pay no attention to him, listen to his old man, psst," whispering in her ear, out of which they explode laughing, and the joke's on me but I tingle all over with joy to be known and loved by them and agree with my father.

Yet suddenly I remember Maggie. She's at the Rex, a stone's throw for me over the neons of Kearney Square and all the dark heads of night and there she is, dancing, with Bloodworth, in the inexpressibly sad musical rose of sunset and moonlight serenades, all I have to do is walk over there, sweep aside the curtain, see all the dancers, look for her form, all I have to do is look—

But I cant leave Pa and Pauline except under some pretext, pretense. We go to the soda fountain, people from the meet are there, also people from the show at Keith's Strand or Merrimack Square, people from events of social importance to be mentioned in the next day, you can see their expensive cars out on the Square, and sometimes right on it (pre-1942)— My Pa is shabby, crack-toothed, dark and humble in his big coat, he looks around and sees a few people he remembers, sneers, or laughs, according to his feelings—Pauline and I delicately eat our sundaes—because of the tremendous suppressed excitement to fall down on them devouring with big spoons— Just a little hometown scene on a Saturday night—in Kinston on Queen Street they're driving up and down sadly the Southerners, or walking, looking in at bleak hardware hay and grain stores, out at the colored section there's a mob chattering in front of chickenshacks and taxi stands— In Watsonville California it's the gloomy mad field and section hands of Mexico strolling, arms sometimes around each other, father and son or friend and friend, in the sad California night of white raw fog, the Filipino poolhalls, the town green at the bank—In Dickinson North Dakota on Saturday night in the winter it's the howling blizzard, the stalled buses out of town, the wild warm food and pool tables in great restaurant-lunchrooms of the night with pictures of old lost ranchers and outlaws decorating all the walls— The Arctic loneliness snowdust swirling on a rill of sage—outside town, the lost lean fence, the snow moon's fury— Lowell, the soda fountain, the girl, the father, the boy—the local yokels all around the local yokels—

"Okay keed," says my father, "and say, do you want to go home alone with Pauline now or are you coming home or what?"

"I'll go with her—" I have my big Maggie schemes—I wink at my father, false. He finds it amusing.

"See you tomorrow keed. Hey, say there goes Gene Plouffe anyway—I'll go along with him in the bus home."

Then, later, I also get rid of Pauline on some other pretense, concerning time, I hardly have room in my raining heart to see and hear what I have to—I'm lost, bumping in the Square crowds. We mill at the bus, I see her "home" to her home bus in front of Brockelman's— Then, in a dream, I rush to the Rex.

It's midnight. The last dance is playing. It's the lights-out dance.

Nobody at the ticket office. I rush in, look. It's dark. I see Bessy Jones, I hear mournful saxophones, the feet are shuffling. Last, late sitters in brooding overcoats up in the balcony.

"Hey Bess!"

"What?"

"Where's Maggie?"

"She left at eleven— Bloodworth's still here— She got peeved and went home—alone—"

"She's not here?" I cry hearing the anguish of my own voice.

"No—she left!"

"Oh"—and I cant dance with her, I cant surmount the mountain dream of this night, I'll have to go to bed with the leftover pain of another day. "Maggie, Maggie," I think— It only faintly dawns on me that she got mad at Bloodworth—

And when Bessy Jones yells "Jack, it's because she loves you," I know that. It's something else is wrong, and sad and sick— "Where's my Maggie?" I cry with myself. "I'll walk out there now. But she'll never let me in. Three miles. She wont care. Cold. What'll I do? Night."

The music is so beautiful and sad I droop to hear it standing thinking lost in my Saturday night tragedy—Around me all the faint blue angels of romance are flying with the polkadot spotlight, the music is heartbroken and yearns for young close hearts, lips of girls in their teens, lost impossible chorus girls of eternity dancing slowly in our minds to the mad ruined tambourine of love and hope—I see I want to hug my Greatshadow Maggie to myself for all time. Love's all lost. I walk out, to the music, to discouraged sidewalks, disaffected doors, unfriendly winds, growling buses, harsh eyes, indifferent lights, phantom griefs of Life in the Lowell streets. I go home again—I have no way of crying, or of asking.

Meanwhile Maggie's across town crying in her bed, everything is totally unhappy in the grave of things.

I go to bed with horror on my wings. In my pillow is sad comforts. Like my mother says, *"On essaye a s'y prendre, pi sa travaille pas* (We try to manage, and it turns out shit)."

from
VANITY OF DULUOZ
1940–1946

EDITOR'S NOTE
*In this book Kerouac calls himself "Jack Duluoz," Allen Ginsberg is
"Irwin Garden," William Burroughs is "Will Hubbard," his common-
law wife, Joan, is "June," Kerouac's first wife, Edith Parker, is "Johnnie," and his Lowell friend Sebastian Sampas is "Sabby Savakis."*

BUT NOW SOME OLD BUDDIES, the Ladeau brothers, proposed to drive
me to New York for my school year because they were going to see the
World's Fair at Flushing Meadows and might as well take me along for
the ride and I could help with the gas instead of taking a bus. And who
comes along, riding in the rumbleseat in back of the old 1935 coupe,
hair blowing in the wind, singing, "Whoooeee, here we come New
York!" if it wasn't my old Pop himself, Emil? Me and 350 pounds of
Pop and baggage in a rumbleseat, all the way with the car veering here,
veering there. I guess from the unsuitable disposition of weight in the
back, all the way to Manhattan, 116th Street, Columbia campus, where
me and Pa got out with my gear and went into my dormitory, Hartley
Hall.

What dreams you get when you think you're going to go to college!
Here we stood in this sort of drear room overlooking Amsterdam Avenue, a wooden desk, bed, chairs, bare walls, and one huge cockroach
suddenly rushing off. Furthermore in walks a little kid with glasses
wearing a blue skullcap and announces he will be my roommate for the
year and that he is a pledge with the Wi Delta Woowoo fraternity and
that's the skullcap. "When they rush you you'll have to wear one too."
But I was already devising means of changing my room on account of
that cockroach and others I saw later, bigger.

Pa and I then went out on the town, to the World's Fair too, restaurants, the usual, and when he left he said, as usual: "Now study,
play good ball, pay attention to what the coach and the profs tell you
and see if you cant make your old man proud and maybe be an all-
America." Fat chance, with the war a year away and England already
under blitz.

It seems I had chosen football and come to the brim of the top of it just at that time when it would no longer matter to anybody or his uncle.

There were always tears in my Pa's eyes when he said goodbye to me, always tears in his eyes those latter years, he was, as my mother often said, "*Un vrai Duluoz, ils font ainque braillez pi's lamentez* (A real Duluoz, all they do is cry and lament)." And rage too, b'God, as you'll see later when my Pa finally got to meet Coach Lu Libble of Columbia.

Because from the start I saw that the same old boloney was going to be pulled on me as in Lowell High School. In the freshman backfield there was a good blocking boy called Humphrey Wheeler, but slow, and a slow plodding fullback called Runstedt, and that's about it. Absolutely nobody of any real ability and nothing like the gang at HM.[1] In fact one of the boys was small, slow, weak, nothing at all in particular, and yet they started him instead of me and later on I talk to him and discover he's the son of the police chief of Scranton. Never in my life have I ever seen such a bum team. The freshman coach was Rolfe Firney who had made his mark at Columbia as a very good back who'd made a sensational run against Navy that won the game in 1934 or so. He was a good man, I liked Rolfe, but he seemed to keep warning me about something all the time and whenever the big coach, famous Lu Libble went by, all sartorial in one of his 100 suits, he never even gave me the once-over.

The fact of the matter is, Lu Libble was very famous because in his very first year as coach at Columbia, using a system of his own devised at his alma mater, Georgetown, he won the bloody Rose Bowl against Stanford. It was such a sensational smash in the eye all over football America nobody ever got over it, but that was 1934, and here it was 1940 and he hadnt done anything noteworthy since with his team and went clear into the 1950's doing nothing further either. I think it was that bunch of players he had in 1934 who carried him over: Cliff Montgomery, Al Barabas, *et al.*, and the surprise of that crazy KT-79 play of his that took everybody a year to understand. It was simply . . . well I had to run it, anyway, and you'll understand it when we run it.

So here I am out with the Columbia freshman team and I see I'm not going to be a starter. Will admit one thing, I wasnt being encouraged, as I'd been by Coach Ump Mayhew at HM, and psychologically

1. Horace Mann Prep School

this made me feel lackadaisical and my punting, for instance, fell off. I couldnt get off a good kick anymore and they didn't believe in the quick kick. I guess they didnt believe in touchdowns either. We practiced at Baker Field in the one field in back. At dusk you could see the lights of New York across the Harlem River, it was right smack in the middle of New York City, even tugboats went by in the Harlem River, a great bridge crossed it full of cars, I couldnt understand what had gone wrong.

One great move I made was to switch my dormitory room from Hartley Hall to Livingston Hall where there were no cockroaches and where b'God I had a room all to myself, on the second floor, overlooking the beautiful trees and walkways of the campus and overlooking, to my greatest delight, besides the Van Am Quadrangle, the library itself, the new one, with its stone frieze running around entire with the names engraved in stone forever: "Goethe . . . Voltaire . . . Shakespeare . . . Molière . . . Dante." That was more like it. Lighting my fragrant pipe at 8 P.M., I'd open the pages of my homework, turn on station WQXR for the continual classical music, and sit there, in the golden glow of my lamp, in a sweater, sigh and say "Well now I'm a collegian at last."

V

Only trouble is, the first week of school my job began as a dishwasher in the diningroom cafeteria sinks: this was to pay for my meals. Secondly, classes. Thirdly, homework: *i.e.*, read Homer's *Iliad* in three days and then the *Odyssey* in three more. Finally, go to football practice at four in the afternoon and return to my room at eight, eating voracious suppers right after at the training table in John Jay Hall upstairs. (Plenty of milk, plenty of meat, dry toast, that was good.)

But who on earth in his right mind can think that anybody can do all these things in one week? And get some sleep? And rest war-torn muscles? "Well," said they, "this is the Ivy League son, this is no college or group of colleges where you get a Cadillac and some money just because you play football, and remember you're on a Columbia University Club scholarship and you've got to get good marks. They cant feed you free, it's against the Ivy League rules against preference for athletes." In fact, tho, the entire Columbia football gang, both varsity and freshmen, had B averages. It was true. We had to work like Trojans to get our education and the old white-haired trainer used to intone, "All for glory, me boys, all for glory."

It was the work in the cafeteria that bothered me: because on Sundays it was closed and nobody who worked got to eat anything. I s'pose in this case we were s'posed to eat at the homes of friends in New York City or New Jersey or get food money from home. Some scholarship.

I did get invited to dinner, formally with a big formal card, by the dean of Columbia College, old Dean Hawkes, in the house on Morningside Drive or thereabouts right near the house of Nicholas Murray Butler, the president of Columbia. Here, all dressed up in Ma's best McQuade-Lowell-selected sports coat, with white shirt and tie and pressed slacks (the cleaner was on Amsterdam across the street), I sat and ate my soup by gently lifting the saucer away from me, spooning away from me, smiled politely, hair perfectly combed, showed suave interest in jokes and awe in the dean's serious moments. The entree was meat but I cut it delicately. I had the best table manners in those days because my sister Ti Nin had trained me back in Lowell for these past several years; she was a fan of Emily Post's. When, after dinner, the dean got up and showed me (and the three other special lads) his prized Dinosaur Egg I registered actual amazement; whoever thought I'd get to see a billion-year-old egg in the house of an old distinguished dean? I say house, it was a sumptuous apartment. He thereupon wrote a note to my mother saying: "Your son, John L. Duluoz, may I say with pride, Mrs. Duluoz, has absolutely the best and most charming table manners it has ever been my pleasure to enjoy at my dinner table." (Something like that.) She never forgot that. She told Pa. He said "Good boy," tho when Pa and I used to eat late-night snacks in Lowell it was eggs this way, butter that way, hell be damned, up on the ceiling, EAT.

But I loved Dean Hawkes, everybody did, he was an old, short bespectacled old fud with glee in his eyes. Him and his egg . . .

VI

The opening game of the season the freshman team traveled to New Brunswick N.J. for a game against Rutgers' freshmen. This was Saturday Oct. 12, 1940, and as our varsity defeated Dartmouth 20-6, we went down there and I sat on the bench and we lost 18-7. The little daily paper of the college said: FRESHMEN DROP GRID OPENER TO RUTGERS YEARLINGS BY 18-7 COUNT. It doesnt mention that I only got in the game in the second half, just like at Lowell High, and the article concludes with: "The Morningsiders showed a fairly good running attack at times with Jack Duluoz showing up well. . . . Outstanding in the backfield for the Columbia Frosh were Marsden [police chief's son], Runstedt and Duluoz, who was probably the best back on the field."

So that in the following game, against St. Benedict's Prep, okay, now they started me.

But you remember what I boasted about how, to beat St. John's, you gotta have old St. John on the team. Well I have a medal, as you know, over my backyard door. It's the medal of St. Benedict. An Irish girl once told me: "Whenever you move into a new house two things you must do according to your blood as an ancient Gael: you buy a new broom, and you pins a St. Benedict medal over the kitchen door." That's not the reason why I've got that medal now but here's what happened:

After the Rutgers game, and Coach Libble'd heard about my running, and now his backfield coach Cliff Battles was interested, everybody came down to Baker Field to see the new nut run. Cliff Battles was one of the greatest football players who ever lived, in a class with Red Grange and the others, one of the greatest runners anyway. I remember as a kid, when I was nine, Pa saying suddenly one Sunday "Come on Angie, Ti Nin, Ti Jean, let's all get in the car and drive down to Boston and watch the Boston Redskins play pro football, the great Cliff Battles is running today." Because of traffic we never made it, or we were waylaid by ice cream and apples in Chelmsford, Dunstable or someplace and wound up in New Hampshire visiting Grandmère Jean. And in those days I kept elaborate clippings of all sports and pasted them carefully, among my own sports writings, in my notebooks, and I knew very well about Cliff Battles. Now here all of a sudden the night before the game with St. Benedict and we freshmen are practicing, here comes Cliff Battles and up to me and says "So you're the great Dulouse that ran so good at Rutgers. Let's see how fast you can go."

"What do you mean?"

"I'll race you to the showers; practice is over." He stood there, 6 foot 3, smiling, in his coach pants and cleated shoes and sweat jacket.

"Okay," says I and I take off like a little bird. By God I've got him by 5 yards as we head for the sidelines at the end of the field, but here he comes with his long antelope legs behind me and just passes me under the goalposts and goes ahead 5 yards and stops at the shower doors, arms akimbo, saying:

"Well cant you run?"

"Ah heck your legs are longer than mine."

"You'll do allright kid," he says, pats me, and goes off laughing. "See you tomorrow," he throws back.

This made me happier than anything that had happened so far at Columbia, because also I certainly wasn't happy that I hadnt yet read the *Iliad* or the *Odyssey,* John Stuart Mill, Aeschylus, Plato, Horace and everything else they were throwing at us with the dishes.

VII

Comes the St. Benedict game, and what a big bunch of lugs you never saw, they reminded me of that awful Blair team a year ago, and the Malden team in high school, big, mean-looking, with grease under their eyes to shield the glare of the sun, wearing mean-looking brown-red uniforms against our sort of silly-looking (if you ask me) light-blue uniforms with dark-blue numerals. ("Sans Souci" is the name of the Columbia alma mater song, means "without care," humph.) (And the football rallying song is "Roar Lion Roar," sounds more like it.) Here we go, lined up on the field, on the sidelines I see that Coach Lu Libble is finally there to give me the personal once-over. He's heard about the Rutgers game naturally and he's got to think of next year's backfield. He'd heard, I s'pose, that I was a kind of nutty French kid from Massachusetts with no particular football savvy like his great Italian favorites from Manhattan that were now starring on the varsity (Lu Libble's real name is Guido Pistola, he's from Massachusetts).

St. Benedict was to kick off. They lined up, I went deep into safety near the goal line as ordered, and said to myself "Screw, I'm going to show these bums how a French boy from Lowell runs, Cliff Battles and the whole bunch, and who's that old bum standing next to him? Hey Runstedt, who's that guy in the coat next to Cliff Battles there near the water can?"

"They tell me that's the coach of Army, Earl Blaik, he's just whiling away an afternoon."

Whistle blows and St. Benedict kicks off. The ball comes wobbling over and over in the air into my arms. I got it secure and head straight down the field in the direction an arrow takes, no dodging, no looking, no head down either but just straight ahead at everybody. They're all converging there in midfield in smashing blocks and pushings so they can get through one way or the other. A few of the red Benedicts get through and are coming straight at me from three angles but the angles are narrow because I've made sure of that by coming in straight as an arrow down the very middle of the field. So that by the time I reach midfield where I'm going to be clobbered and smothered by eleven giants I give them no look at all, still, but head right into them: they gather up arms to smother me: it's psychological. They never dream I'm really roosting up in my head the plan to suddenly (as I do) dart, or jack off, bang to the right, leaving them all there bumbling for air. I run as fast as I can, which I could do very well with a heavy football uniform, as I say, because of thick legs, and had trackman speed, and before you know it I'm going down the sidelines all alone with the whole twenty-one other guys of the ball game all befuddling around in midfield and turning to follow me. I hear whoops from the sidelines. I go and I go. I'm down to the 30, the 20, the 10, I hear huffing and puffing behind me, I look behind me and there's that selfsame old longlegged end catchin up on me, like Cliff Battles done, like the guy last year, like the guy in the Nashua game, and by the time I'm over the 5 he lays a big hand on the scruff of my neck and lays me down on the ground. A 90-yard runback.

I see Lu Libble and Cliff Battles, and Rolfe Firney our coach too, rubbing their hands with zeal and dancing little Hitler dances on the sidelines. But St. John ain't got a chance against St. Benedict, it appears, because anyway naturally by now I'm out of breath and that dopey quarterback wants me to make my own touchdown. I just can't make it. I want to controvert his order, but you're not supposed to. I puff into the line and get buried on the 5. Then he, Runstedt, tries it, and the big St. Ben's line buries him, and then we miss the last down too and are down on the 3 and have to fall back for the St. Benedict punt.

By now I've got my wind again and I'm ready for another go. But the punt that's sent to me is so high, spirally, perfect, I see it's going to take an hour for it to fall down in my arms and I should really raise my arm for a fair catch and touch it down to the ground and start our team from there. But no, vain Jack, even tho I hear the huffing and puffing of the two downfield men practically on my toes I catch the ball free catch and practically say "Alley Oop" as I feel their four big hands squeeze like vises around my ankles, two on each, and puffing with pride I do the complete vicious twist of my whole body so that I can undo their grip and move on. But their St. Benedict grips have me rooted to where I am as if I was a tree, or an iron pole stuck to the ground, I do the complete turnaround twist and hear a loud crack and it's my leg breaking. They let me fall back deposited gently on the turf and look at me and say to each other "The only way to get *him,* don't *miss*" (more or less).

I'm helped off the field limping.

I go into the showers and undress and the trainer massages my right calf and says "O a little sprain wont hurt you, next week it's Princeton and we'll give them the old one-two again Jacky boy."

VIII

But, Wifey, it was a broken leg, a cracked tibia, like if you cracked a bone about the size of a pencil and the pencil was still stuck together except for that hairline crack, meaning if you wanted you could just break the pencil in half with a twist of two fingers. But nobody knew this. That entire week they told me I was a softy and to get going and run around and stop limping. They had liniments, this and that, I tried to run, I ran and practiced and ran but the limp got worse. Finally they sent me off to Columbia Medical Center, took X rays, and found out I had broken my tibia in right leg and that I had been spending a week running on a broken leg.

I'm not bitter about that, wifey, so much as that it was Coach Lu Libble who kept insisting I was putting it on and told the freshman coaches not to listen to my "lamentings" and make me "run it off." You just can't run off a broken leg. I saw right then that Lu for some reason I'll never understand had some kind of bug against me. He was always hinting I was a no-good and with those big legs he ought to put me in the line and make "a watch charm guard" out of me.

Yet (I guess I know now why) it was only that summer, I forgot to mention, Francis Fahey had me come out to Boston College field to give me a tryout for once and for all. He said "You really must come to B.C., we've got a system here, the Notre Dame system, where we take a back like you and with a good line play spring him loose down the field. Over at Columbia with Lu Libble they'll have you come around from the wing, you'll have to run a good twenty yards before you get back to the line of scrimmage with that silly KT-79 reverse type play of his and you'll only at best manage to evade maybe the end but the secondary'll be up on yours in no time. With us, it's *boom,* right through tackle, guard, or right or left end sweep." Then Fahey'd had me put on a uniform, got his backfield coach MacLuhan and said: "Find out about him." Alone in the field with Mac, facing him, Mac held the ball and said:

"Now, Jack, I'm going to throw this ball at you in the way a center does; when you get it you're off like a halfback on any kinda run you wanta try. If I touch you you're out, so to speak, and you know darn well I'm going to touch you because I used to be one of the fastest backs in the east."

"Phooey you are," I thought, and said "Okay, throw it." He centered it to me, direct, facing me, and I took off out of his sight, he had to turn his head to watch me pass around his left, and that's no Harvard lie.

"Well," he conceded, "you're not faster than I am but by God where'd you get that sudden takeoff? Track?"

"Yep." So in the showers of B.C. afterward, I'm wiping up, I hear Fahey and Mac discussing me in the coaches' showers and I hear Mac say to Fahey:

"Fran, that's the best halfback I ever saw. You've got to get him to B.C."

But I went to Columbia because I wanted to dig New York and become a big journalist in the big city beat. But what right had Lu Libble to say I was a no-good runner. And, wifey, listen to this, what about the night the winter before, at HM, when Francis Fahey had me meet him on Times Square and took me to William Saroyan's play *My Heart's in the Highlands,* and in the intermission when we went down to the toilet I'm sure I saw Rolfe Firney the Columbia man watching from behind the crowd of men? On top of which they then sent Joe Callahan to New York to take me out on the town too, to further persuade me about Boston College, and eventually Notre Dame, but here I was at Columbia, Pa had lost his job, and the coach thought I was so no-good he didnt even believe I'd broken my leg in earnest.

Years later I published a poem about this on the sports page of *Newsday,* the Long Island newspaper: fits pretty good: because it also involves the later fight my father had with Lu about his not playing me enough and some arrangement that went sour whereby Lu was s'posed to help him get a linotypist job in New York and nothing came of it:

TO LU LIBBLE

Lu, my father thought you put him down
    and said he didnt like you

He thought he was too shabby for your
    office; his coat had got so

And his hair he'd comb and come
    into an employment office with me

And have me speak alone with the man
    for the two of us, then sigh

And repented we home, to Lowell; where
    sweet mother put out the pie
        anywye.

In my first game I ran like mad
    at Rutgers, Cliff wasnt there;

He didnt believe what he read
    in the *Spectator* "Who's that Jack"

So I come in on the St. Benedicts game
    not willing to be caught by them bums

I took off the kickoff right straight at
    the gang, and lalooza'd around

To the pastafazoola five yard line,
    you were there, you remember

We didnt make first down; and I
    took the punt and broke my leg

And never said anything, and ate hot
    fudge sundaes & steaks in the
        Lion's Den.

Because that's one good thing that came of it, with my broken leg in a cast, and with two crutches under my good armpits, I hobbled every night to the Lion's Den, the Columbia fireplace-and-mahogany type restaurant, sat right in front of the fire in the place of honor, watched the boys and girls dance, ordered every blessed night the same rare filet mignon, ate it at leisure with my crutches athwart the table, then two hot fudge sundaes for dessert, that whole blessed sweet autumn.

And I never did say anything, so as to say, I never sued or made a fuss, I enjoyed the leisure, the steaks, the ice cream, the honor, and for the first time in my life at Columbia began to study at my own behest the complete awed wide-eyed world of Thomas Wolfe (not to mention the curricular work too).

For years afterward, however, Columbia still kept sending me the bill for the food I ate at training table.

I never paid it.

Why should I? My leg still hurts on damp days. Phooey.

Ivy League indeed.

If you dont say what you want, what's the sense of writing?

• • •

BOOK FIVE

I

Late that spring, just about when my freshman year was over and the sophomore year was on the way, I was coming out of a subway turnstile with Pa after we'd seen a French movie on Times Square and here comes Chad Stone the other way, with a bunch of Columbia footballers. Chad was destined to become captain of the Columbia varsity, later a doctor, later to die at age thirty-eight of an overworked heart, goodlooking big fellow from Leominster Mass. by the way, and he says to me: "Well Jack, you've been elected vice-president of the sophomore class."

"What? Me?"

"By one vote, you rat, by one vote over ME." And it was true. My father immediately took my picture in a ratty Times Square booth but little did he dream what was about to happen to my dingblasted old sophomore year, it was now May 1941 and events were brewing indeed in the world. But this sophomore vice-president baloney has no effect on my chemistry professor, Dr. So-and-So, who, puffing on his pipe, informed me that I had failed chemistry and had to make it up that summer at home in Lowell or lose my scholarship.

Thing about chemistry was, the first day I'd gone to class, or lab, that fall of 1940, and saw all those goddamned tubes and stinking pipes and saw these maniacs in aprons fiddling around with sulfur and molasses, I said to myself "Ugh, I'm never going to attend this class again." Dont know why, couldnt stand it. Funny too, because in my later years as more or less of a "drug" expert I sure did get to know a lot about chemistry and the chemical balances necessary for certain advantageous elations of the mind. But no, an F in chemistry, first time I'd ever flunked a course in my life and the professor was serious. I wasnt about to plead with him. He told me where to get the necessary books and tubes and Faustian whatnots to take home for the summer.

It was a nutty summer at home, therefore, where I absolutely refused to study my chemistry. I missed my Negro friend Joey James who'd tried to bone me all year, as I say.

I went home that summer, and instead I played around with swimming, drinking beer, making huge hamburger sandwiches for me and Lousy ("Ye old Zaggo Special" he called them because they were nothing but hamburg fried in lots of real butter and put on fresh bread with ketchup), and when late August came around I still hadnt made anything up in particular. But by now they were ready to let me try the course over again, as according to Lu Libble's plan, and other friends, because now we had a football team to contend upon and anyway I was probably smart enough to make it all up. Oddly, I didn't want to.

That summer Sabbas became a regular in my old boyhood gang of G.J., Lousy, Scotcho *et al.* and we even took a crazy trip to Vermont in an old jalopy to get drunk on whiskey for the first time in the woods, at a granite quarry swimming hole. At this swimming hole I took a deep breath, drunk, and went way down about 20 feet and stayed there grinning in the goggly dark. Poor Sabbas thought I had drowned, whipped off all his clothes and dove in after me. I popped up laughing. He cried on the bank. (St. Sabbas was the founder of a sixth-century monastery, Greek Orthodox, now buried in Holy Sepulcher Church in Jerusalem under the officiation of Patriarch Benedictos in 1965.) I took another shot of whiskey and grabbed a little tree about 5 feet tall, wrapped it around my bare back, and tried to rip it up by the roots from the earth. G.J. says he'll never forget it: he says I tried to pull all Vermont up from the roots. From then on he called me "Power Mad." As we drank the whiskey further I saw the Green Mountains move, to paraphrase Hemingway in his sleeping sack. We drove back to Lowell drunk and sick, me sleeping on Sabby's lap all the way, as he cried, then dozed, all night.

Later me and Sabby hitchhiked to Boston several times to go see movies, lounge in Boston Common watching the people go by, occasionally Sabby leaping up to make big Leninist speeches at the soapbox area where pigeons hung around watching the argufyings. There's Sabby in his blazing white shirtsleeves and with wild black curly hair haranguing everybody about the Brotherhood of Man. It was great. In those days we were all pro-Lenin, or pro-whatever, Communists, it was before we found out that Henry Fonda in *Blockade* was not such a great anti-Fascist idealist at all, just the reverse of the coin of Fascism, *i.e.*, what the hell's the difference between Fascist Hitler and anti-Fascist Stalin, or, as today, Fascist Lincoln Rockwell and anti-Fascist Ernesto Guevaro, or name your own? Besides, may I remark here in a sober mood, what did Columbia College offer me to study in the way of a course of theirs called Contemporary Civilization but the works of Marx, Engels, Lenin, Russell and other assorted blueprintings that look good on blue paper and all the time the architect is that invisible monster known as Living Man?

Also, I hitchhiked to Boston a couple of times with Dicky Hampshire to prowl the waterfront to see if we could hop a ship for Hong Kong and become big Victor McLaglen adventurers. On Fourth of July we all went to Boston and wandered around Scollay Square looking for quiff that wasnt there. I spend most of my Friday nights singing every show tune in the books under an apple tree in Centreville, Lowell, with Moe Cole: and boy could we sing: and later she sang with Benny Goodman's band awhile. She once came to see me in broad afternoon summer wearing a tightfitting fire engine red dress and high heels, whee. (I'm not mentioning love affairs much in this book because I think acquiescing to the lovin whims of girls was the least of my Vanity.)

But the summer wore on and I never got my chemistry figured out and then came the time when my father, who'd been working out of town as linotypist, sometimes at Andover Mass., sometimes Boston, sometimes Meriden Conn., now had a steady job lined up at New Haven Conn. and it was decided we move there. My sister by now was married. As we were packing, I went about and nighted the Pawtucketville stars of trees and wrote sad songs about "picking up my stakes and rolling." But that wasn't the point.

One night my cousin Blanche came to the house and sat in the kitchen talking to Ma among the packing boxes. I sat on the porch outside and leaned way back with feet on rail and gazed at the stars for the first time in my life. A clear August night, the stars, the Milky Way, the whole works clear. I stared and stared till they stared back at me. Where the hell was I and what was all this?

I went into the parlor and sat down in my father's old deep easy chair and fell into the wildest daydream of my life. This is important and this is the key to the story, wifey dear:

As Ma and Cousin talked in the kitchen, I daydreamed that I was now going to go back to Columbia for my sophomore year, with home in New Haven, maybe near Yale campus, with soft light in room and rain on the sill, mist on the pane, and go all the way in football and studies. I was going to be such a sensational runner that we'd win every game, against Dartmouth, Yale, Princeton, Harvard, Georgia U., Michigan U., Cornell, the bloody lot, and wind up in the Rose Bowl. In the Rose Bowl, worse even than Cliff Montgomery, I was going to run wild. Uncle Lu Libble for the first time in his life would throw his arms around me and weep. Even his wife would do so. The boys on the team would raise me up in Rose Bowl's Pasadena Stadium and march me to the showers singing. On returning to Columbia campus in January, having passed chemistry with an A, I would then idly turn my attention to winter indoor track and decide on the mile and run it in under 4 flat (that was fast in those days). So fast, indeed, that I'd be in the big meets at Madison Square Garden and beat the current great milers in final fantastic sprints bringing my time down to 3:50 flat. By this time everybody in the world is crying Duluoz! Duluoz! But, unsatisfied, I idly go out in the spring for the Columbia baseball team and bat homeruns clear over the Harlem River, one or two a game, including fast breaks from the bag to steal from first to second, from second to third, and finally, in the climactic game, from third to home, zip, slide, dust, boom. Now the New York Yankees are after me. They want me to be their next Joe DiMaggio. I idly turn that down because I want Columbia to go to the Rose Bowl again in 1943. (Hah!) But then I also, in mad midnight musings over a Faustian skull, after drawing circles in the earth, talking to God in the tower of the Gothic high steeple of Riverside Church, meeting Jesus on the Brooklyn Bridge, getting Sabby a part on Broadway as Hamlet (playing King Lear myself across the street) I become the greatest writer that ever lived and write a book so golden and so purchased with magic that everybody smacks their brows on Madison Avenue. Even Professor Claire is chasing after me on his crutches on the Columbia campus. Mike Hennessey, his father's hand in hand, comes screaming up the dorm steps to find me. All the kids of HM are singing in the field. Bravo, bravo, author, they're yelling for me in the theater where I've also presented my newest idle work, a play rivaling Eugene O'Neill and Maxwell Anderson and making Strindberg spin. Finally, a delegation of cigar-chewing guys come and get me and want to know if I want to train for the world's heavyweight boxing championship fight with Joe Louis. Okay, I train idly in the Catskills, come down on a June night, face big tall Joe as the referee gives us instructions, and then when the bell rings I rush out real fast and just pepper him real fast and so hard that he actually goes back bouncing over the ropes and into the third row and lays there knocked out.

I'm the world's heavyweight boxing champion, the greatest writer, the world's champ miler, Rose Bowl and (pro-bound with New York Giants football non pareil) now offered every job on every paper in New York, and what else? Tennis anyone?

I woke up from this daydream suddenly realizing that all I had to do was go back on the porch and look at the stars again, which I did, and still they just stared at me blankly.

In other words I suddenly realized that all my ambitions, no matter how they came out, and of course as you can see from the preceding narrative, they just came out fairly ordinary, it wouldnt matter anyway in the intervening space between human breathings and the "sigh of the happy stars," so to speak, to quote Thoreau again.

It just didnt matter what I did, anytime, anywhere, with anyone; life is funny like I said.

I suddenly realized we were all crazy and had nothing to work for except the next meal and the next good sleep.

O God in the Heavens, what a fumbling, hand-hanging, goof world it is, that people actually think they can gain anything from either this, or that, or thissa, or thatta, and in so doing, corrupt their sacred graves in the name of sacred-grave corruption.

Chemistry shemistry . . . football, shmootball . . . the war must have been getting in my bones.

When I looked up from that crazy reverie, at the stars, heard my mother and cousin still yakking in the kitchen about tea leaves, heard in fact my father yelling across the street in the bowling alley, I realized either I was crazy or the world was crazy: and I picked on the world.

And of course I was right.

II

In any case my father had gone ahead to New Haven, started working on the job in West Haven it was, and idly, or let someone else do it, had an "apartment" found for us in the Negro Ghetto district of New Haven. It wasn't so much that my mother or father or myself minded Negroes, God bless em, but broken glass and crap on the floor, broken windows, bottles, ruined plaster, the works. Ma and I traveled from Lowell, following the moving truck, on the New Haven Railroad, got there at dawn, a musty fust of pluck mist over the railyards at sunrise, and we walk in the hotting streets to this third story crapulous "apartment." "Is that man crazy?" says Ma. Already, after having done all the packing and arrangements, and after even running downstairs after poor Ti Gris our cat and falling down the stairs after it (on Gershom Avenue) and hurting her hip and leg, here she is, hopefully perfumed, tho worn out from the all-night train from Lowell with its interminable silly stops in Worcester or someplace of all places, here she finds a place not even the cheapest landlord in Lowell or Tashkent would rent to the milkiest Kurd or horsiest Khan in Outer Twangolia, let alone French Canadians used to polished-floor tenements and Christmas cheer based on elbow grease and Hope.

So we call up Pa, he says he didn't know any better, he says he'll call a French Canadian realtor and mover of New Haven and see what we can find. Ends up, Fromage the French Canadian mover has a little cottage by the sea at West Haven not far from Savin Rock Park. Our furniture by now is in the warehouse in New Haven. My little kitty Ti Gris has jumped out of his box somewhere along the route when the truckers stopped for chow and is gone forever in the woods of New England. In the warehouse as they're shoving around I see one of Ma's dresser drawers yaw open and inside I see her bloomers, crucifixes, rosaries, rubber bands, toys; it suddenly occurs to me people are lost when they leave their homes and convey themselves to the hands of brigands good or bad as they may be. But the French Canadian man, old fellow about sixty, has that wonderful French Canadian accent on Hope and says "Come on, cheer up, *là bas* ["there"] let's get the stuff on the truck, rain or no rain"—it's raining cats and dogs—"and let's go to your new cottage by the sea. I'll rent it to you for sixty dollars a month, is that so bad?" We even buy a bottle to nip us along and all go on the truck, the man, then Pa, then me all huddled up against the door, and Ma between Pa and me. Off we go in the rain. We drive out to the seacoast of Long Island Sound and there's the cottage.

They park the truck, the other French Canadian movers show up, and boom, they're unloading everything and rushing into the cottage with it. It's a two-story affair with three bedrooms upstairs, kitchen, parlor, heating arrangement, what else do you want? In the glee of the situation, and a little high on the bottle, I put on my swim trunks and ran across the mud toward the strand in a lashing gale from the Sound. Ah that menace of monstrous rolling waves of gray water and spray, put me in the mind of something past and something future.

Because you know, wifey, the first time I saw the sea? I was three years old and somebody took me to Salisbury Beach, I guess, or Hampton, I remember somebody offering me five dollars if I'd get into my bathing suit and I refused. In those days I used to lock myself in the toilet. Nobody was going to see me part naked in those days. But I stood there and put my little three-year-old hands to my brow and looked deep into the horizon of the sea out there, and it seems I saw what it was like, the actual waving gray, the Noah's Ark inevitably floating on it, popping up and down, the groan and creak of it, the lash of rigs winging, the very centerfoam splowsh and lick: I said to myself then: "Ah soliloquizer, what royal wake out there, what heave boom smack . . . etc. What pain in salt and door?"

As my poor mother huddled in the parlor of her new cottage she watched me walk right out into the sea and begin to swim. I rose high up with the crest of the waves and then sank way down into their valleys below, I tasted the salty spray, I smashed my face and eyes onward into the great sea, I could see it coming, I laughed aloud, I plowed on, bobbed up and down, got dizzy with the rise and fall of it, saw the horizon in the gray rainy distance, lost it in a monster wave, put out for a boat which was anchored there and said "We're Here."

Begod and BeJesus we were. I got on the boat and bobbed there awhile, side, side, stern, stern, looked back, saw my Ma waving, laughed, and jumped into the sea. Underneath I deliberately stared deepward to see the darker gray there. . . . Great day in the morning dont ever do it, during a rainstorm dont ever get down to the bottom of the sea and see what it looks like further in toward Neptune's unhappy *clous* ("nails").

Three silver nails in a blue field.

III

And the next day, to add to the woes of my mother and father, who are trying in one way or another to be happily unpacking, it's sunny, I put on my swimming trunks again and go out swimming straight a mile toward the nearest sandbar. I get out on the sandbar (having swum the Merrimack up and down along the Boulevard many times for practice), and one afternoon swam pine drunken Pine Brook about a hundred times up and down, a few miles or so, for practice, come to the sandbar and take a nap in the early September sun. Come dusk the water's lapping at me toes. I get up and swim back toward our cottage, which I can see a mile away. Slow, slow, always swim slow and let your head lean in the waves like in a pillow. There's my poor Paw out there on the seawall hands to eyes looking for his drowned son. He sees me coming. "Whoopee!" he yells to Angie my Ma. "Here he comes!"

"What?"

"There he is! That's him. Coming real slow!" And I pull up and go in the house and wonder what they were scared about. "It's time tomorrow for you to go to Columbia and start your sophomore year, now stop fooling around. Go down to the corner, it's only a mile, buy the evening paper, some ice cream, cigarettes, cigars, here's the money . . ."

"We're going to have a good time here," says Ma.

"When there's storms the sea'll be looking for your parlor," I shoulda warned her.

It was just a summer resort, empty in fall and winter, and really that Sound can kick up in December to March. A big mansion along the rocks a half mile down the beach was the home of Helen Twelvetrees the old actress. My Ma actually talked to her later on.

Bill Keresky you remember from HM, and Gene Mackstoll, and another guy came in a sports car to fetch me to take me to New York for the new year. To pack my suitcase I went up in the attic to fetch certain things and my both feet fell down thru the phony ceiling and I landed my crotch right on a beam and cried. I got over it in a half hour. We got in the car, kissed the folks goodbye, and went to the City.

They drove me straight to Baker Field, the Columbia U. training house, and there was Lu Libble working over his plays at the blackboard in the diningroom, the footballers sitting around watching and listening, everybody giving me dirty looks because I was a day late. Upstairs, bunks. Morning, breakfasts, saltpeter so we wouldnt get horny, showers, taping, aching muscles, hot September sun tacklings of silly dummies held by assistant coaches and idiots with cameras taking our pictures dodging this way or that.

What were the chances of Columbia this year? Nothing, as far as I could see, since the only real football player on the team, Hank Full our quarterback, had joined the Marines just a day ago and was leaving. Thackeray Carr wasnt bad. Big Turk Tadzic of Pennsy was ready but they had to make contact lenses for him, an end. Big Ben Kurowsky got sore at me after scrimmage because I evaded his attempted tackle and picked me up in the showers and held me up sky high at arm's length saying "You lil bastart." Then he glowered at Chad Stone who was too big to pick up. It was Chad's job and mine to take out Kurowsky on what is called the "high-low," that is, "you hit him high and I'll hit him low," I hit Kurowsky low and Chad hit him high. Chad was 6 foot 3. I was 5:8½. We got Kurowsky out of there some of the time. He was 6 foot 4 and weighed 240.

They could have had a good team but the war was coming up.

And then in practice I began to see that good old Lu Libble wasnt going to start me in the starting lineup but let me sit on the bench while Liam McDiarmid and Spider Barth, who were seniors, wore out their seniority. Now they were shifty and nifty runners but not as fast or strong as I was. That didnt matter to Lu Libble. He insulted me in front of everybody again by saying "You're not such a hot runner, you cant handle the KT-79 reverse deception"—as if I'd joined football for "deception" for God's sake—"first thing you know, you with your big legs"—they werent that big—"I'm going to make you a lineman.

"Now run and do that reverse."

With my eyes I said "I cant run any faster these first two days, my legs are sore."

Never mind, he said with his eyes, putting me in mind of the time he made me run on a broken leg for a week.

At night, after those meaningless big suppers of steak and milk and dry toast, I began to realize this: "Lu Libble wont let you start this year, not even in the Army game against your great enemy Art Janur (who pushed me out of the showers when I was a kid in Lowell High but got his come-uppance from Orestes Gringas), and not even maybe next year as a junior, he wants to make a big hero out of his Italian Mike Romanino, well Mike is certainly a great passer but he runs like Pietryka like an old cow. And Hank Full's leaving. The hell with it. What'll I do?"

I stared into the darkness of the bunkrooms thinking what to do.

"Ah shucks, go into the American night, the Thomas Wolfe darkness, the hell with these bigshot gangster football coaches, go after being an American writer, tell the truth, dont be pushed around by them or anybody else or any of their goons. . . . The Ivy League is just an excuse to get football players for nothing and get them to be American cornballs enough to make America sick for a thousand years. You shoulda stuck to Francis Fahey. . . ."

Well I cant remember what I was thinking altogether but all I know is that the next night, after dinner, I packed all my gear in my suitcase and sauntered down the steps right in front of Lu Libble's table where he was sitting with his assistant coaches figuring out plays. My bones were rasping against my muscles from the overtraining, I limped. "Where you going Dulouse?"

"Going over to my grandmother's house in Brooklyn and dump some of these clothes."

"It's Saturday night. Be back by tomorrow at eight. You gonna sleep there?"

"Yeh."

"Be back by eight. We're going to have a light calisthenics, you know the part where you get on your back and turn your skull to the grass and roll around so you wont get your fool neck broken in a game?"

"Yes sir."

"Be back at eight. What you got in there?"

"Junk. Presents from home, dirty laundry. . . ."

"We got a laundry here."

"There's presents, letters, stuff, Coach."

"Okay, back at eight."

And I went out and took the subway down to Brooklyn with all my gear, whipped out a few dollars from the suitcase, said goodbye to Uncle Nick saying I was going back to Baker Field, walked down the hot September streets of Brooklyn hearing Franklin Delano Roosevelt's speech about "I hate war" coming out of every barbershop in Brooklyn, took the subway to the Eighth Avenue Greyhound bus station, and bought a ticket to the South.

I wanted to see the Southland and start my career as an American careener.

* * *

BOOK SEVEN

I

Now that I look back on it, if Sabby could have got his Coast Guard papers on time and sailed on that ship with me he might have lived thru the war. It was now June 1942, with a little black bag containing rags and a collection of classical literature weighing several ounces in small print, I'd walked by a white fence near my mother's house on my way to the North Pole, to hitchhike to Boston with Timmy Clancy (later District Attorney of Essex County Massachusetts). It was, really, like Melville packing his little black bag and setting off to New Bedford to go a-whaling. If Sabby had come on board with me he might have signed off the *Dorchester* after this, her next-to-last trip, and come with me thence to Liverpool etc. But as I saw the flowers of death in the eyes of most of my shipmates I had seen the flowers of death in his eyes too. He got into the Army a few months later. Flowers of death, as Baudelaire well knew from his leaning balcony in sighin Paree, are everywhere and for all time for every-body.

We have destroyers too watching far out as we leave Boston Harbor and move north out of those waters toward the Maine waters and out to the Banks of Newfoundland where we're swallowed in fog, and the water in the scuppers, supped up from the sea to wash our buckets with, gets a-colder and a-colder. We're not in a convoy, it's only 1942, no Allied and British arrangement, just the S.S. *Dorchester* and her sister ship the S.S. *Chatham* going up north, with a freighter called the U.S. *Alcoa Pilot,* and surrounded by corvettes and cutters and destroyers and destroyer escorts and led by, my you better mind me now, the old wooden ice-cuttin ship of Admiral Byrd (the *North Star*). Five hundred civilian construction workers, carpenters, electricians, bulldoze cat men, laborers, all in Alaska boomtown wool shirts, and tho all life is but a skullbone and a rack of ribs through which we keep passing food and fuel just so's we can burn so furious (tho not so beautiful), here we went on a voyage to Greenland, "life's delicate children" on one sea, Saturday, July 18, oil-burning transport, out Merchant Miners dock, Boston, some of the crew going about with sheathed knives and daggers more of a semiromantic fancy than a necessity, poop decks, reading the funnies on poop decks, powder and ammunition in the afterdeck storeroom not 10 feet from the foc'sle where we'uns slept, up ahead foaming main and clouds. . . .

Let's get seamenlike. A bonus for sleeping on top of a powder magazine, does that sound like Captain Blah? AGWI Lines people, own this ship, ah bright and winedark sea. Anchor tied we pull out between those two lighthouses in Boston Harbor, only the *Chatham* follows us, an hour later we perceive a destroyer off our port and a light cruiser (that's right) off our starboard. A plane. Calm sea. July. Morning, a brisk sea. Off the coast of Maine. Heavy fog in the morning, misty in the afternoon. Log. All eyes peeled for the periscope. Wonderful evening spent before with the (not Navy, excuse me) Army gun crew near the big gun, playing popular records on the phonograph, the Army fellas seem much more sincere than the hardened cynical dockrats. Here's a few notes from my own personal log: "There are a few acceptable men here and there, like Don Gary, the new scullion, a sensible and friendly fellow. He has a wife in Scotland, joined the Merchant Marine to get back to Scotland, in fact. I met one of the passengers, or construction workers, an Arnold Gershon, an earnest youth from Brooklyn. And another fellow who works in the butcher shop. Outside of these, my acquaintances have so far been fruitless, almost foolish. I am trying hard to be sincere but the crew prefers, I suppose, embittered cursing and bawdry foolishness. Well, at least, being misunderstood is being like the hero in the movies." (Can you imagine such crap written in a scullion's diary?) "Sunday July 26: A beautiful day! Clear and windy, with a choppy sea that looks like a marine painting . . . long flecked billows of blue water, with the wake of our ship like a bright green road . . . Nova Scotia to larboard. We have now passed through the Cabot Straits." (Who's Cabot? A Breton?) (Pronounced Ca-boh.) "Up we go, to northern seas. Ah there you'll find that shrouded Arctic." (That wash of pronounced seatalk, that parturient snowmad ice mountain plain, that bloody Genghis Khan plain of seaweed talk broken only by uprisings of foam.)

Yessir, boy, the earth is an Indian thing but the waves are Chinese. Know what that means? Ask the guys who drew those old scrolls, or ask the old Fishermen of Cathay, and what Indian ever dared to sail to Europe or Hawaii from the salmon-tumbling streams of North America? When I say Indian, I mean Ogallag.

"As I write, tonight, we are passing thru the most dangerous phase of our journey to that mysterious northern land . . . we are steaming ahead in a choppy sea past the mouth of the St. Lawrence River in a crystal clear Moonglow." (Good enough for a Duluoz, descendant of the Gaspé and the Cape Breton.) "This is the region where many sinkings have occurred of late." (Keeping up with the news in New York's P.M. newspaper, I had been.) "Death hovers over my pencil. How do I feel? I feel nothing but dim acceptance." (O Eugene O'Neill!) "A sort of patience that is more dreamlike than real. The great card games, the tremendous card games and crap games go on in the diningroom, Pop is there with his cigarette holder, chef's cap, mad rich rakish laugh, some of the base workers mixed in the games, the scene seasoned with impossible characters, shit language, rich warm light, all kinds of men gambling their shore pay away in a dare at Neptune . . . Sums of money changing hands with death nearby. What an immense gambling ship this is . . . and our sister ship, the *Chatham,* off our stern, same thing of course. The stake is money and the stake is life. At dusk, with long lavender sashes hovering over distant Nova Scotia, a Negro baker conducted a religious sermon on the afterdeck. He had us kneel while he prayed. He spoke of God ('We howled'), and he prayed to God for a safe journey. Then I went to the bow and spent my usual hour staring the face of the mounting northern gales. We should be off the coast of Labrador tomorrow. As I was writing just now, I heard a hissing outside my porthole, the sea is heavy, the ship just rocks and rocks real deep, and I thought: 'Torpedo!' I waited for one long second. Death! Death!" (Think of your death scenes and death trips, LSD users!) "I tell you," sez confident young Jack London in his bunk, "I tell you, it is NOT hard to face death"—no, sirree—"I am patient, I shall now turn over to sleep. And the sea washes on, immense, endless, everlasting, my sweet brother [?], and sentencer [!]. In the moonlight tonight in these dangerous waters, one can see the two Navy ships that are convoying us, two tawny seacats, alert and lowslung" (O gee) . . .

Homeless waters in the North, the Aryan-Nordic up against his chappy sea-net hands.

II

But my hands werent sea-netted and chapped by rope and wire, as later the next year as deckhand, at present time I was a scullion. I'd vaguely heard of Shakespeare yelling about that, he who washes pots and scours out giant pans, with greasy apron, hair hanging in face like idiot, face splashed by dishwater, scouring not with a "scourer" as you understand it but with a goddamned Slave chain, grouped in fist as chain, s c r a t c h, s c r o u t c h, and the whole galley heaving slowly.

Oh the pots and pans the racket of their fear, the kitchen of the sea, the Neptunes down here, the herds of sea cows wanta milk us, the sea poem I aint finished with, the fear of the Scottish laird rowing out with a nape of another fox' neck in the leeward shirsh of S H A O W yon Irish Sea! The sea of her lip! The brattle of her Boney! The crack of Noah's Ark timbers built by Mosaic Schwarts in the unconditional night of Universal death.

Short chapter.

III

None of the adolescent scribblings of that time I kept in journals'll do us now.

Here now yon breaker awash the bowsprit, "Night aint fit for man nor dog," and what dog, O Burns, O Hardy, O Hawkins, would go to sea except for a bone with meat on it?

In our case it meant five hundred dollars if we got back safe free and that was a lot of money in nineteen forty two-ee.

The barefooted Indian deckhand toured every foc'sle at dusk to make sure the portholes were closed and secured.

He had a dagger in his belt.

Two Negro cooks had a big fight in the galley at midnight over gambling, that I didnt see, where they swung huge butcher knives at each other.

A little Moro chieftain turned third cook, with small neck, swiveled and shriveled when he turned to see.

He had the biggest knife of them all in his belt, a first-degree Swamee machete from old Mindanao.

The pastry cook was advertised as gay and they said he belted off his gun into the mixings for all of us to enjoy.

In the steward's linen department a veteran of the Spanish Civil War, member of the Abraham Lincoln leftwing anti-Fascist Brigade, tried to make a Communist out of me.

The chief steward had no more use for me than a piece of foam of the sea hath use for him or me or anybody.

The captain, Kendrick, was hardly seen, as he was so high on the bridge and this was a big ship.

The chief cook of my galley was Old Glory.

He was 6 foot 6 and 300 pounds of Negro glory.

He said "Everybody's puttin down a hype." He was the one who used to pray on the poop deck at dusk . . . the real prayer.

He liked me.

Frankie Fay the Farter slept with me in the foc'sle and kept farting. Another young kid from Charlestown Mass. with curly hair tried to make fun of me 'cause I was reading books all the time. The third guy in our foc'sle said nothing, was a tall lost junky I guess.

Some ship.

Pretty soon the liquor ran out and the real drunks went down to the barbershop to get their hair cut but really only wanted a bottle of bay rum aftershave lotion.

The clever punks in the galley sent me down to the engine room to ask the chief engineer for a "left-handed monkey wrench." The chief yelled at me over the booming pistons that were turning the shaft of the rear screw "There's no such-a-thing as a left-handed monkey wrench you dumbhead!"

Then they threw me a special honorary dinner and gave me the ass-hole of a duck, with yams and potatoes and asparagrass. I ate it and pronounced it delicious.

They said maybe I was a fancypants football player, and a college-educated boy, but I didnt know there was no such thing as a left-handed monkey wrench or that the ass of a duck was the ass of a duck. Good enough, I could use either.

I pleased the pastry cook who gave me a brown leather jacket that hung over my wrists. He was the poop deck preacher.

I observed icebergs in my diary; the diary is really very good and I should record it here: Like, "Incidentally, one of our two new convoy ships, a small-sized freighter converted into a sort of sub chaser and raider, carries a heroic legend. She has sunk every submarine she's found in these cold waters. She's a valiant little bitch: hits the waves briskly and carries a torpedo seaplane as well as a load of depth charges and shells." And here's the old Aryan complaining (before we got to those ice-bergs): "Fog, the *Chatham* looms astern, lowing like a mournful cow . . ."

IV

Icebergs are vast mountains of ice that float about in the North Atlantic and show themselves to be one-tenth of their whole bulk, which, hid beneath the waves, can stave a ship's hull in faster'n a black-eyed Spartan can do you in, in a Spartan provocation, only this here iceberg is white, icy, cold, dont care, and's bigger than five West St. Louis Police and Fire Departments. O Budweiser, pay homage and notice.

And you see them a mile away, white ice cubes, with waves crashing against their bowsprits like in slowmotion Dinosaur movies. S p l o w s h, slow, the gigantic sight of great waters against a cliff, of ice in this case (not a Kern), going P L O W. You know what the name of the Cornish Celtic language is? Kernuak.

So what's Kerouac? "Kern" being Cairn, and "uak" language of;

then, Ker, house, ouac, language of, THIS IS THE LANGUAGE OF THE HOUSE SPEAKING TO YOU IN PURE SEAMAN TONES.

Nobody on this ship of mine is going to hit an iceberg, not on your life, not with Cap'n Kendrick, and besides, we've got pork chops for supper.

V

D'jever see the eyes of the captain in the wheelroom? Did anybody bend over charts as much as that first mate? That second mate, did he have blue eyes? And the third, sharp? No ship as big as the *Dorchester* can hit disaster unless it hits into a genius.

The genius, Von Dönitz, hid under the waves in Belle Isle Strait, and we looked for his signs of foam or periscopey proppery, aye we did. Altho Hitler counseled his Naval youth to be wise and athletic you never saw better sailors than I saw in the United States Sea. Service. Na, no Dönitz can escape the mark of a Canadian.

The usual real Canadian has blue eyes and an eye for the sea and the cove too, a real pirate, tell that to the High Command of any Navy. He licks his lips in anticipation of any sight of breakage in the wave, whether it's a football, a turd, a dead gull, a floating happy albatross (if near enough Poles) or wavelet or sea sparrow or, really, the osprey, that do-do bird, that non go-go bird, that bird who floateth on the waves and sayeth to thee and I "Go saileth yourselfth, I am bird what floateth on water." Okay. Always found near land.

What land we got here? Irish Sea? Ju sea it?

VI

So I'm frying the bacon for one thousand men, that is, two thousand strips of bacon, on a vast black range, while Glory and the other assistant cooks are doing the scrambled eggs. I'm wearing a life jacket, O Baldwin apples. I hear "Boom boom" outside. Glory is wearing a life jacket too. Boom boom. The bacon sizzles. Glory looks at me and says "They're layin down a hipe out there."

"Yeh."

"Get that bacon crisp and put it in the pan, boy."

"Yowsah," says I, "boss." 'Cause he was my boss, and you buy that. "What's goin on out there Glory?"

"There's a bunch of Canadian corvettes and American destroyer escorts layin down depth charges against a German submarine attack."

"We're being attacked?"

"That aint no Memphis lie."

"S-n—ucc—Q—z," as I sneezed, "what time is it?"

"What you wearin your life jacket for?"

"You told me to wear it, you and the chief steward."

"Well you're makin bacon."

"Well sure I'm makin bacon," I said, "but I'm thinking of that kid on that German submarine who's also makin the bacon. And who is now chokin to death in drowning. Buy that, Glory."

"I aint layin down no hipe, you're right," said Glory, who was real big and blues singer too but I coulda licked him in any fight because he woulda let me.

That's your American Negro man, so dont talk to me about it.

VII

The sea speaketh. Remember, why'm I a wave? Three silver nails in a blue field, turned gray by sea. Jesus, it is a Polish sea. What, Djansk? Every nobleman in Russia wore furs and gelted everybody in sight. Djanks. Skoll. Aryans.

Slaves they dared to call us.

VIII

Slaves indeed, why when you looked at the bodyguards of Khrushchev or any other regular-lookin Russian you saw some guy sellin cows in North Carolina fields at 9 A.M. . . . Aryans . . . The look where you believe that God will forgive you in Heaven . . . 'T'sa look make the whores of Amsterdam not only quake but give up their knitting . . . Ah High Germanic Nordic Aryans you brutes of my heart! . . . Kill me! . . . Crucify me! . . . Go ahead, I've got Persian friends.

And what will my Persian friends do, grow mustaches and ride jets? . . . Do you know what Jesus meant when he cried out on the cross "Father, Father, why hast thou forsaken me?" . . . He was only quoting a Psalm of David like a poet remembering by heart: He did not repudiate His own kingdom, it's a crock to believe so, throw the Shield of David in the garbage can with the Cross of Jesus if that's what you think, let me prove it to you: Jesus was only quoting the first line of David's Psalm 22 with which he was familiar as a child even (not to mention that the sight of the Roman soldiers casting ballots for his garment reminded him of the line in the same Psalm "They cast lots upon my vesture," and add this too "They pierced my hands and my feet"). PSALM 22 OF DAVID (in part): *"My God, my God, why hast thou forsaken me? Loudly I call, but my prayer cannot reach thee. Thou dost not answer, my God, when I cry out. . . . I am a by-word to all, the laughing-stock of the rabble. All those who catch sight of me fall to mocking; mouthing out insults, while they toss their heads in scorn 'He committed himself to the Lord, why does not the Lord come to his rescue, and set his favourite free?' . . . I am spent as spilt water, all my bones out of joint . . . parched is my throat, like clay in the baking, and my tongue sticks fast in my mouth. . . . They have torn holes in my hands and feet . . . and they stand there watching me. . . . They divide my spoils among them, cast lots for my garments. . . ."*

He was just like a poet remembering lines of the prophecy of David.

Therefore I believe in Jesus. Tell you why if you dont know already: Jacob wrestled with his angel because he defied his own Guardian Angel. Typical.

Michael stands in my corner, 7 feet tall.

Look.

There go us.

. . .

BOOK ELEVEN

VII

. . . A very strange screw of events began to turn in early 1944.

To get to it, I'll just preamble by saying that in the month of May 1944 I did take a bus to New Orleans, went down to the N.M.U. hall to sign on for a ship, had no luck, hung around the seaman's club, at one point got drunk with a drunken seaman who used to be the Governor of the State of Florida (we drank under rotating ceiling fans) and walked up and down Magazine Street trying to make a lunchcart waitress, wrote notes to Johnnie telling her I was starving and send money, wrote home, became completely disgusted and decided to go back to New York to ship out from there as usual, or Boston. It was just a nutty subliminal desire to see New Orleans and the South, Mississippi and

Alabama and all that, which I saw out the window, the cottonpickin shacks miles and miles of em across those flats. I also got drunk in Asheville North Carolina with Tom Wolfe's drunken older brother right there in the parlor of Tom Wolfe's Asheville home with the picture of Tom and of his brother "Ben" right there on top of the squareback piano, and spent that night mooning around with a recalcitrant or miscreant miss on a porch in the Smokies foothill night right there by the Broad River mists. (French Broad, that is.) And skirmishes with women in Raleigh, etc., and another trip in Washington D.C. and same parks, etc., but the main point is, the whole trip was foolish and I came back real quick and took off my black leather jacket in Johnnie's bedroom while she was still at art class studying with the famous George Grosz, and just went to bed. When she got home she whooped when she saw my jacket on the back of the chair.

She hadnt ever read Ovid but she sure knew all his advice about riding that pony. (Ovid, *Art of Love,* Bk. III.)

And then sad nights, rain drumming on the roof, six flights up, on 118th Street and Amsterdam just about, and in start coming the new characters of my future "life."

VIII

There was this kid from New Orleans called Claude de Maubris who was born in England of a French viscount now in the consular service, and of an English mother, and who now lived with his grandmother in a Louisiana estate whenever he was there, which was seldom, blond, eighteen, of fantastic male beauty like a blond Tyrone Power with slanted green eyes and the same look, voice, words and build, I mean by words he expressed his words with the same forcefulness, a little more like Alan Ladd actually, actually like Oscar Wilde's model male heroes I s'pose but anyway he showed up on the Columbia campus at this time followed by a tall man of 6 foot 3 with a huge flowing red beard who looked like Swinburne.

I forgot to mention that during the winter of 1943 and 1944 I had worked at odd jobs for extry money, including of all things a job as switchboard operator in the little local campus hotels, then later as script synopsizer for Columbia Pictures on Seventh Avenue downtown, so on my return trip from New Orleans I was planning to get one of these jobs back while waiting for a ship. It so happened that this Claude got a room in Dalton Hall, small campus hotel, so did Swinburne, I knew the management there, and that was to be the focal point of most of these events.

Well, turns out Claude arrives on the campus one warm afternoon for the second semester as freshman at Columbia and immediately runs into the library so he can play some Brahms records free in the listening booth. Swinburne's right behind him but Angel Boy tells him to wait outside so he can listen to the music undisturbed with his earphones and think. Very intelligent kid of an order you'll see later. But point is, the professor of French Classics at Columbia University at the time, Ronald Mugwump I guess he was, a little fud of some kind I never saw, or cared to look at, ran into the booth where Claude was and said something like "Where did you come from, you marvelous boy?" You can see what was happening to this kid. And the scene.

Because talk about your Folies Bergère late 1890's *fin de siècle* dray-mas, this was the yellow pages of not only Tristan de Per- adventure (whoever he was or will be) but the very yellow decadence of Beardsley, Dowson, Aleister Crowley and the rest. I knew nothing of this at the time. It just turned out that my Johnnie's apartment became the focal point of meetings for the wild *outré* gang of Columbia campus. First she tells me there's this wild new young kid hanging around the West End Bar called Claude who is blond and beautiful and strong and intelligent and comes over to her place to take showers but doesnt try to make her. Strangely, I believe her, and turns out it's true. He's just chased so much he has to hide somewhere, and being a Southern "scion" of rich family, as she is, and needing the hearty companionship of a good gal protector, he comes there. He fi- nally starts bringing around his girl the rich girl from Westport, Cecily. Finally I first see him in the West End Bar after waking up from my long nap.

"There he is, there's that marvelous Claude."

"Looks to me like a mischievous little prick," I said to Johnnie, and I still think so. But he was okay. He wanted to ship out again, had been a seaman out of New Orleans, maybe ship out with me. He was no fairy and he was strong and wiry and that first night we got really drunk and I dont know whether it was that first night or not, it was, when he told me to get into an empty barrel and then proceeded to roll the barrel down the sidewalks of upper Broadway. A few nights later I do remem- ber we sat in puddles of rain together in a crashing downpour and poured black ink over our hair . . . yelling folk songs and all kindsa songs. I got to like him more and more.

IX

Also, as he's interested in symbolistic art, Surrealism not so much but, say, Modigliani, the French Impressionists, all that darkness of my night-sea life seems to disappear and in the spring sunshine it seems that colors are being splashed over my soul. (Now *that* sounds like Swinburne!)

Anyway, one afternoon he and Johnnie are off to study nude models with George Grosz, they'd asked me to try it one afternoon, I went there and sat there as all the kids sketched and George Grosz talked, and there she was, a naked brunette looking me right in the eye and I had to leave and say to Claude at the door: "What do you think I am?"

"What's that, a voyeur old boy?" And so they're out doing that and I've taken a shower and the door of Johnnie's apartment knocks and I open it and there's a tall thin fella in a seersucker jacket, with Franz Swinburne behind him. I say "What?" Swinburne, already talked to me in the bar with Claude, says:

"This is the Will Hubbard they were telling you about, from out west?"

"Well."

"He's spent a lot of time in New Orleans too, in other words, old friend of mine and Claude's. Just wants to ask you about how to ship out in the Merchant Marine."

"Not in the service?"

"Oh no," says Will looking around with a toothpick in his mouth, and removing it to give me the once-over, "just 4-F, phnunk." "Phnunk" is where he blows out of his nose a kind of sinus condition, and also English lord expression, as his name is very old.

X

Someday, in fact, I'll write a book about Will just by himself, so ever onward the Faustian soul, so especially about Wilson Holmes Hubbard I dont have to wait till he dies to complete his story, he above all's best left marching on with that aggressive swing of his arms thru the Medinas of the world . . . well, a long story, wait.

But in this case he's come to see me about Claude, but saying it's about the Merchant Marine. "But what was your last job?" I ask.

"Bartender in Newark."

"Before that?"

"Exterminator in Chicago. Of bedbugs, that is.

"Just came to see ya," he says, "to find out about how to get papers, to ship out." But when I had heard about "Will Hubbard" I had pictured a stocky dark-haired person of peculiar intensity because of the reports about him, the peculiar directedness of his actions, but here he had come walking into my pad tall and bespectacled and thin in a seersucker suit as tho he's just returned from a compound in Equatorial Africa where he'd sat at dusk with a martini discussing the peculiarities . . . Tall, 6 foot 1, strange, inscrutable because ordinary-looking (scrutable), like a shy bank clerk with a partrician thinlipped cold bluelipped face, blue eyes saying nothing behind steel rims and glass, sandy hair, a little wispy, a little of the wistful German Nazi youth as his soft hair fluffles in the breeze— So unobtrusive as he sat on the hassock in the middle of Johnnie's livingroom and asking me dull questions about how to get sea papers . . . Now there's my first secret intuitive vision about Will, that he had come to see me not because I was a principal character now in the general drama of that summer but because I was a seaman and thus a seaman type to whom one asked about shipping out as a preliminary means of digging the character of said seaman type. He didn't come to me expecting a jungle of organic depths, or a jumble of souls, which b'God on every level level I was as you can see, dear wifey and dear reader, he pictured a merchant seaman who would belong in the merchant seaman category and show blue eyes beyond that and a few choice involuntary remarks, and execute a few original acts and go away into endless space a flat, planed "merchant seaman"— And being queer, as he was, but didnt admit in those days, and never bothered me, he expected a little more on the same general level of shallowness. Thus, on that fateful afternoon in July of 1944 in New York City, as he sat on the hassock questioning me about sea papers (Franz smiling behind him), and as I, fresh from that shower, sat in the easy chair in just my pants, answering, began a relationship which, if he thought it was to remain a flat plane of an "interesting blue-eyed dark-haired goodlooking seaman who knows Claude," wasnt destined to remain so (a point of pride with me in that I've worked harder at this legend business than they have)—Okay, joke . . . Tho, on that afternoon, he had no reason to surmise anything otherwise than shoptalk from your aunt to mine, "Yes, you've got to go now and get your Coast Guard pass first, down near the Battery . . ."

XI

The fascination of Hubbard at first was based on the fact that he was a key member of this here new "New Orleans School" and thus this was nothing more than this handful of rich sharp spirits from that town led by Claude, their falling star Lucifer angel boy demon genius, and Franz the champeen cynical hero, and Will as observer weighted with more irony than the lot of em, and others like Will's caustic charming buddy Kyles Elgins who with him at Harvard had "collaborated on an ode" to 'orror which showed the *Titanic* sinking and the ship's captain (Franz) shooting a woman in a kimono to put on her said kimono and get on a life boat with the women and children and when heroic spray-ey men shout "Madame will you take this fourteen-year-old boy on your lap?" (Claude) Captain Franz smirks "Why of course" and mean-while Kyles' paranoid uncle who lisps is hacking away at the gunwales with a Peruvian machete as reaching hands rise from the waters "Ya buntha bathadts!" and a Negro orchestra is playing the *Star-Spangled Banner* on the sinking ship . . . a story they wrote together at Harvard, which, when I first saw it, gave me to realize that this here New Orleans clique was the most evil and intelligent buncha bastards and shits in America but had to admire in my admiring youth. Their style was dry, new to me, mine had been the misty-nebulous New England Idealist style tho (as I say) my saving grace in their eyes (Will's, Claude's es-pecially) was the materialistic Canuck taciturn cold skepticism all the picked-up Idealism in the world of books couldnt hide . . . "Duluoz is a shit posing as an angel." . . . "Duluoz is very funny."—Kyles I didnt get to meet till years later, doesnt matter here, but that Virginia gentry-man did say (Clancy by name): "Everybody who comes from New Or-leans in that group is marked with tragedy." Which I found to be true.

XII

The second time I saw Will he was sitting around talking with Claude and Franz in his apartment in the Village with that terrible intelligence and style of theirs, Claude chewing his beerglass and spitting out slivers, Franz following suit with I s'pose storebought teeth, and Hubbard long and lean in his summer seersucker suit emerging from the kitchen with a plate of razor blades and lightbulbs says, "I've something real nice in the way of delicacies my mother sent me this week, hmf hmf hmf" (when he laughs with compressed lips hugging his belly), I sit there with peasant frown getting my first glimpse of the Real Devil (the three of em together).

But I could see that Hubbard vaguely admired me.

But what was this with me with a thousand things to do?

But I bite my lips when I hear the word "marvel" and I shudder with excitement when I hear Will say "marvelous" because when he says it, it really's bound to be truly marvelous. "I just saw a *marvelous* scene in a movie this afternoon," with his face all flushed, exalted, rosy, fresh from wind or rain where he walked, his glasses a little wet or smoky from the heat of his enthused eyeballs, "this character in this awful beat movie about sex downtown, you see him with a great horse serum injector giving himself a big bang of dope then he rushes up and grabs this blonde in his arms and lifts her up and goes rushing off into a dark field goin 'Yip Yip Yipp ee!' " But I have to ask a thousand questions to know why Will is so glad:

"A dark field?"

"Well it's one of those dreary movies, real old and full of snaps in the screen, you can hear the rolls clank and blank up in the projection booth so it's some kind of evening or dusk or somethin, a great endless horizon you see him growin smaller and smaller as he rushes off with his girl, Yip Yip Yippeeee, finally you just dont hear him anymore . . ."

"He's gone way across that field?" asks I, looking for mines and touchdowns and Galsworthy and the Book of Job . . . and I'm amazed by Will's way of saying "Yip Yip Yip Pee" which he does with a cracky falsetto voice and never can say without bending over to hold his belly and compress his lips and go "Hm hm hm," the high suppressed surprised thoroughly gleeful laugh he has, or at least laughy. One afternoon probably when he'd arrived from Harvard for the summer, 1935 or so, with Kyles downtown kicked a few hours around with a sex movie in a cheap joint around Canal Street, these two great American sophisticates you might say sitting well up front (expensively dressed as always, like Loeb and Leopold) in a half-empty movie full of bums and early Thirties tea heads from the gutters of New Orleans, laughing in that way of theirs (actually Kyles' laugh, which Will had imitated since their childhood together?) and finally the great scene where the mad dope addict picks up the monstrous syringe and gives himself a big smack of H, and grabs the girl (who is some dumb moveless Zombie of the story and walks hands at her sides), he wild-haired and screaming with rain in the plip-plip of the ruined old film rushes off, her legs and hair dangling like Fay Wray in the arms of King Kong, across that mysterious dark endless Faustian horizon of Will's vision, happy like an Australian jackrabbit, his feet and heels flashing snow: Yip Yip, Yip eee, till, as Will says, his "Yips" get dimmer and dimmer as distance diminishes his eager all-fructified final goal-joy, for what would be greater than that, Will thinks, than to have your arms full of joy and a good shot in you and off you run into eternal gloom to flip all you want in infinity, that vision he must've had of that movie that day in that manse of his seat, legs crossed demurely, and so I picture him and Kyles sprawled then in laughter, broken up, on the floor, in tweed coats or something, unwrist-watchable, 1935, laughing Haw haw haw and even repeating Yip Yip Yippeeeee after the scene has long passed but they cant forget it (a classic even greater than their *Titanic* short story). Then it is I see Will Hubbard that night after dinner at home in New Orleans with in-laws and walking under the trees and lawn lights of suburbia, going, prob-ably, to see some clever friend, or even Claude, or Franz, "I just saw a marvelous scene in a movie today, God, Yip Yip Yippee!"

Here I say "And what did the guy look like?"

"Wild, bushy hair . . ."

"And he said Yip Yip Yippee as he rushed off?"

"With a girl in his arms."

"Across the dark field?"

"Some kinda field—"

"What was this field?"

"My *Gawd*—we're getting literary yet, don't bother me with such idiotic questions, a *field*"—he says "field" with an angry or impatient shrieking choke—"like it's a FIELD"—calming down—"a field . . . for God's sake you see him rushing off into the dark horizon—"

"Yip Yip Yippee," I say, hoping Will will say it again.

"Yip Yip Yippee," he says, just for me, and so this is Will, tho at first I really paid less attention to him than he did to me, which is a strange thing to reconsider because he always said "Jack, you're really very funny." But in those days this truly tender and curious soul looked on me (after that flat seaman phase) as some kind of intensity truth-guy with pride, owing to that scene one night the later week when we were all sitting on a park bench on Amsterdam Avenue, hot July night, Will, Franz, Claude, his girl Cecily, me, Johnnie, and Will says to me "Well why don't you wear a merchant seaman uniform man like you said you wore in London for your visit there, and get a lot of soft entries into things, it's wartime, isn't it, and here you go around in T-shirt and chino pints, or paints, or pants, and nobody knows you're a serviceman proud, should we say?" and I answered: " 'Tsa finkish thing to do" which he remembered and apparently took to be a great proud statement coming straight from the saloon's mouth, as he, a timid (at the time) middleclass kid with rich parents had always yearned to get away from his family's dull "suburban" life (in Chicago) into the real rich America of saloons and George Raft and Runyon characters, virile, sad, factual America of his dreams, tho he took my statement as an opportunity to say, in reply:

"It's a finkish world."

Harbinger of the day when we'd become fast friends and he'd hand me the full two-volume edition of Spengler's *Decline of the West* and say "EEE di fy your mind, my boy, with the grand actuality of Fact." When he would become my great teacher in the night. But in those early days, and at this about our third meeting, hearing me say, " 'Tsa finkish thing to do" (which for me was just an ordinary statement at the time based on the way seamen and my wife and I looked proudly and defiantly on the world of un-like-us "finks," a disgusting thing in itself granted, but that's what it was), hearing me say that, Will apparently marveled secretly, whether he remembers it now or not, and with timid and tender curiosity on top of that, his pale eyes behind the spectacles looking mildly startled. I think it was about then he rather vaguely began to admire me, either for virile independent thinking, or "rough trade" (whatever they think), or charm, or maybe broody melancholy philosophic Celtic unexpected depth, or simple ragged shiny frankness, or hank of hair, or reluctance in the revelation of interesting despair, but he remembered it well (we discussed it years later in Africa) and it was years later that I marveled over that, wishing we would turn time back and I could amaze him again with such unconscious simplicity, as our forefathers gradually unfolded and he began to realize I was really one, one, of Briton blood, and especially, after all, one kind of a funny imbecilic saint. With what maternal care he brooded over my way of saying it, looking away, down, frowning, " 'Tsa finkish thing to do," in that now (to me) "New Orleans way of Claude's," snively, learned, pronouncing the consonants with force and the vowels with that slight "eu" or "eow" also you hear spoken in that curious dialect they speak in Washington D.C. (I am trying to describe completely indescribable materials) but you say "deu" or "deuo" and you say "f" as tho it was being spat from your lazy lips. So Will sits by me on the bench in that irrecoverable night with mild amazement going "hm hm hm" and "It's a finkish world" and he's instructing me seriously, looking with blank and blink interested eyes for the first time into mine. And only because he knew little about me then, amazed, as "familiarity breeds contempt" and bread on the waters there's a lotta fish after it.

Where is he tonight? Where am I? Where are you?

XIII

O Will Hubbard in the night! A great writer today he is, he is a shadow hovering over western literature, and no great writer ever lived without that soft and tender curiosity, verging on maternal care, about what others think and say, no great writer ever packed off from this scene on earth without amazement like the amazement he felt because I was myself.

Tall strange "Old Bull" in his gray seersucker suit sitting around with us on a hot summernight in old lost New York of 1944, the grit in the sidewalk shining the same sad way in 'tween lights as I would see it years later when I would travel across oceans to see him just and just that same sad hopeless grit and my mouth like grit and myself trying to explain it to him: "Will, why get excited about anything, the grit is the same everywhere?"

"The grit is the same everywhere? What on EARTH are you talkin about, Jack, really you're awfully funny, hm h mf hmf?" holding his belly to laugh. "Whoever heard of such a thing?"

"I mean I saw the grit where we sat years ago, to me it's a symbol of your life."

"My LIFE? My dear fellow my life is perfectly free of grit, dearie. Let us relegate this subject to the I-Dont-Wanta-Hear-About-It Department. And order another drink . . . *Really.*"

"It blows in dreary winds outside the bars where you believe and believingly bend your head with the gray light to explain something to someone . . . it blows in the endless dusts of atomic space."

"My G A W D, I'm not going to buy you another drink if you get L I T E R A R Y!"

• • •

BOOK TWELVE

I

Anyway meanwhile there's this fantastic Claude rushing across the campus followed by at least twelve eager students, among them Irwin Garden, Lombard Crepnicz, Joe Amsterdam, I think Arnie Jewel, all famous writers today, he's hurling back epigrammatical epithets at them and jumping over bushes to get away from them, and way back in the ivied corners of the quadrangle you might see poor Franz Mueller slowly taking up the rear in his long meditative strides. He might even be carrying a new book for Claude to read, see the myth of Philoctetes and Neoptolemus, which he will tell Claude reminds him so much of their own relationship, the healthy young god and the sick old warrior, and all such twaddle. I tell you it was awful, I have notes about everything that was going on, Claude kept yelling stuff about a "New Vision" which he'd gleaned out of Rimbaud, Nietzsche, Yeats, Rilke, Alyosha Karamazov, anything. Irwin Garden was his closest student friend.

I was sitting in Johnnie's apartment one day when the door opened and in walks this spindly Jewish kid with horn-rimmed glasses and tremendous ears sticking out, seventeen years old, burning black eyes, a strangely deep mature voice, looks at me, says "Discretion is the better part of valor."

"Aw where's my food!" I yelled at Johnnie, because that's precisely all I had on my mind at the moment he walked in. Turns out it took years for Irwin to get over a certain fear of the "brooding football artist yelling for his supper in big daddy chair" or some such. I didn't like him anyway. One look at him, a few days of knowing him to avouch my private claim, and I came to the conclusion he was a lecher who wanted everybody in the world to take a bath in the same huge bathtub which would give him a chance to feel legs under the dirty water. This is precisely the image I had of him on first meeting. Johnnie also felt he was repugnant in this sense. Claude liked him, always has, and was amused, entertained, they wrote poems together, manifestoes of the "New Vision," rushed around with books, had bull sessions in Claude's Dalton Hall room where he hardly ever slept, took Johnnie and Cecily out to ballets and stuff downtown when I was out in Long Island visiting my folks. They tell me that Claude started a commotion in the ballet balcony, the ushers were coming with flashing lights, he led "the gang" out thru some strange door and they found themselves in the labyrinths underneath the Metropolitan Opera House running into dressing rooms some of them occupied, out again, around, back and forth and triumphantly emerged somewhere on Seventh Avenue and got away. That on the way home, in the crowded subway all four of them laughing and gay, Claude suddenly yelled out over everybody's heads: "WHEN THEY PUT CATTLE IN CARS THEY COPULATE!" All such Joe College stuff. Not bad style. In that same light Claude sorta looked at me as some kind of lout which was true.

Franz Mueller was jealous of Irwin, of me, of anybody Claude had anything to do with, especially of the blond college girl Cecily ("a bourgeois kitten" Claude called her) and one lilac dusk when we were all exhausted and asleep in the mad pad on the sixth floor, Will Hubbard and Franz came in quietly, saw Claude on the couch in Cecily's arms, and Mueller said: "Doesnt he look pale, as tho he were being sucked dry by a vampire?"

One night the same two came in, but found an empty apartment, so to amuse himself that no-good pederast Mueller took my little cat, wrapped Hubbard's tie around its neck, and tried to hang it from the lamp: a little kitty. Will Hubbard immediately took it down, undamaged and just slightly hurt I guess in the neck, I don't know, I wasnt there, I would have thrown that man out the window. It was only told to me much later on.

• • •

V

And in New York, I went straight to the Columbia campus, occupied a room on the sixth floor of Dalton Hall, called Cecily, held her in my arms (still a tease, she), yelled at her, then when she left settled out my new notebooks and embarked on a career as literary artist.

I lighted a candle, cut a little into my finger, dripped blood, and wrote "The Blood of the Poet" on a little calling card, with ink, then the big word "BLOOD" over it, and hung that up on the wall as reminder of my new calling. "Blood" writ in blood.

From Irwin I got all of the books I wanted, Rimbaud, Yeats, Huxley, Nietzsche, Maldoror, and I wrote all kinds of inanities that are really silly when you think of me, like, "Creative pregnancy justifies anything I do short of criminality. Why should I live a moral life and inconvenience pre-disinterested emotions towards it?" And the answer came in red ink: "If you dont, your creation will not be sound. Sound creation is moral in temper. Goethe proved that." I reopened the wound and tourniqueted more blood out of it to make a cross of blood and a "J.D." and a dash over the inked words of Nietzsche and Rimbaud:

"NIETZSCHE: Art is the highest task and the proper metaphysical activity of this life."

"RIMBAUD: *Quand irons-nous, par delà les grèves et les monts, saluer la naissance du travail nouveau, la sagesse nouvelle, la fuite des tyrans, et des démons, la fin de la superstition, adorer . . . les premiers! . . . Noël sur la terre?*" Translated it goes: "When shall we go, over there by the shores and mountains, to salute the birth of new work, the new wisdom, the flight of tyrans, and of demons, the end of superstition, to adore . . . the first ones! . . . Christmas on Earth?"

And this I pinned up on my wall.

I was completely alone, my wife and my family thought I was at sea, nobody knew I was there except Irwin, I was going to embark on an even deeper solitary room writing than I had done in Hartford Conn. with the little short stories. Now it was all Symbolism, all kinds of silly junk, the repertory of modern ideas, "neo-dogmatism à la Claudel," "the neo-Aeschylus, the realization of the need for correlation of introspective visionaryism and romanticist eclecticism."

Now I only mention these few quotes to show the reader what I was reading and How (and How!) I was absorbing it and how serious I was. In fact I had endless things lined up some of which might just about cover the tone of the period I was undergoing:

They went:

"(1) The Huxleyan (?) idea of ceaseless growth (also Goethean). *Élan vital.* The course in conversation (polemicism), reading, writing, and *experiencing* must never cease. *Becoming*.

"(2) Sexual neo-Platonism and the sexual understanding of a *grande dame* of the eighteenth century as a modern trend.

"(3) Political liberalism in the critical throes of adolescence (post-Marxian, pre-Socialistic). Bloody modern Europe. Materialism has picked up a bludgeon.

"(4) The conflict between modern bourgeois culture and artistic culture in Thomas Mann, in Rolland, in Wolfe, in Yeats, Joyce.

"(5) The new aspect, or the new vision—in Rimbaud, in Lautréamont (Maldoror), or as in Claudel.

"(6) Nietzscheanism—'Nothing is true, everything is allowed.' Superman. Neo-mysticism as exemplified in Zarathustra. An ethical revolution.

"(7) The decline of the Western church—Hardy's crass casuality in the same instant made subject to the fortitude of Jude.

"(8) Freud's mechanistics in practically the same instant made subject to emotions (as in Koestler) or to a new morality (as in Heard's vague sense).

"(9) From the humanism of H. G. Wells, from the naturalism of Shaw and Hauptmann and Lewisohn, immediately to the neo-Aeschylus Stephen Dedalus (*Bous Stephanoumenos*) and to universal Earwicker himself.

"(10) Spengler and Pareto—a resultant return, as in Louÿs or Rimbaud, to the East. (Malraux.) Why do the French return to the South? (Those Marseilles decadents in the mahogany tropics of Alfredo Segró.) Anglo-Catholicism and classicism of Eliot. 'Fine sentiment,' comments the Kensington Garden intellectual in Royal Albert Hall.

"(11) Music . . . toward conflict and discordance. The prophecy in end of third movement of Beethoven's Ninth. Shostakovich, Stravinsky, Schoenberg. Freud's ego-concept has risen to the surface and is now *heard* conflicting. *Seen* in painting as in the Impressionists, in Picasso, in Dali, *et al.*

"(12) Santayana's grandee mysticism . . . De Boeldieu and his white gloves in *Les Grandes Illusions*. High-consciousness.

"(13) Francis Thompson's lesson of the impalpability of human life. Melville: 'I seek that inscrutable thing!' Also Wolfe, Thompson, like the latter is haunted by the *truth of loneliness* until he is forced to accept it (!).

"(14) Gideanism . . . *acte gratuite* as abandonment of reason and return to impulse. But now our impulses exist in a society civilized by Christianity. Gideanism is richness in contradiction's Proteanism, immorality . . . is, in essence, the Dionysian overflow of the artistic morality." Etc.

VI

Artistic morality, that was the point, because then I devised the idea of burning most of what I wrote so that my art would not appear (to myself as well as to others) to be done for ulterior, or practical motives, but just as a function, a daily duty, a daily scatalogical "heap" for the sake of purgation. So I'd burn what I wrote, with the candle flame, and watch the paper curl up and squirm, and smile madly. The way writers are born, I guess. A holy idea, I called it "self ultimacy," or, S.U.

Also, to show you, the intellectualism that Claude and Irwin had now influenced over me. But the word "intellectualism" just made Hubbard snuff down his nose when he showed up early that December after much candle-writing and bleeding on my part, "My God, Jack, stop this nonsense and let's go out and have a drink."

"I've been eating potato soup out of the same bowl with Irwin in the West End."

"What about your shipping out and stuff?"

"I jumped the ship in Norfolk thinking I was coming back here for a big love affair with Cecily but she doesn't care."

"Oh you're a card. Let's go have dinner, then go see Jean Cocteau's movie *The Blood of the Poet* if that's in your line these days, then we'll repair to my apartment on Riverside Drive, me boy, and have a bang of morphine. That oughta give you some new visions."

This may make him sound sinister but he wasnt sinister at all, morphine came my way from other directions and I turned it down anyhow. Why, old Will in that time, he just awaited the next monstrous production from the pen of his young friend, me, and when I brought them in he pursed his lips in an attitude of amused inquiry and read. Having read what I offered up, he nodded his head and returned the production to the hands of the maker. Me, I sat there, perched on a stool somewhat near this man's feet, either in my room or in his apartment on Riverside Drive, in a conscious attitude of adoring expectation, and, finding my work returned to me with no more comment than a nod of the head, said, almost blushingly "You've read it, what you think?"

The man Hubbard nodded his head, like a Buddha, having come to ghastly life from out of Nirvana what else was he s'posed to do? He joined his fingertips resignedly. Peering over the arch of his hands he answered "Good, good."

"But what do you specifically think of it?"

"Why . . ." pursing his lips and looking away toward a sympathetic and equally amused wall, "why, I dont specifically *think* of it. I just rather like it, is all." (Only a few years before he'd been with Isherwood and Auden in Berlin, had known Freud in Vienna, and visited the Pierre Louÿs locales in North Africa.)

I returned the work to my inner pocket, again blushed, said "Well at any rate, it was fun writing it."

"I daresay," he'd murmur. "And now tell me, how is your family?"

But, you see, late that night he'd, alone, with fingers counterpoised under the glare of the lamp, with legs crossed and eyes heavy lidded in patience and waiting, remember again that tomorrow the young man would return with the records of his imagination . . . and ill-advised and importunate tho he might consider them . . . he, yes, waited for more. Elsewhere there was only established fact and ruinous retreat.

VII

So just about the whole next year I spent hungering to go see him, to be handed books by him, Spengler, even Shakespeare, Pope, a whole year of drug-taking and talking with him and meeting characters of the underworld he'd started to study as an *acte gratuite* of some kind.

Because around Christmas of 1944 Johnnie came back to me from Detroit, we lived and loved briefly in Dalton Hall, then moved in with her old girlfriend June up on 117th Street now and then persuaded Hubbard to move in too, in the empty room, and he later married June (Johnnie and I knew they would like each other).

But it was a year of low, evil decadence. Not only the drugs, the morphine, the marijuana, the horrible Benzedrine we used to take in those days by breaking open Benzedrine inhalers and removing the soaked paper and rolling it into poisonous little balls that made you sweat and suffer (lost thirty pounds in three days the first time I tried it on an overdose), but the characters we got to know, Times Square actual thieves who'd come in and stash stolen gumball machines from the subway, finally stashing guns, borrowing Will's own gun, or his blackjack, and worst of all, on June's huge doublebed with the Oriental drapecover on it we had ample room for sometimes six of us to sprawl with coffee cups and ashtrays and discuss the decadence of the "bourgeoisie" for days on end.

I'd come home to Ozone Park from these endless debauches looking like a pale skin-and-bones of my former self and my father would say "O that Hubbard and that Irwin Garden are going to destroy you someday." To add to everything my father had begun to develop Banti's disease, his belly would swell up every two or three weeks and have to be drained. He soon couldnt work anymore and was about to come home and die. Cancer.

I ran with horror from home to "them" and then from "them" to home but both equally dark and inhospitable places of guilt, sin, sorrow, lamentation, despair. It wasnt so much the darkness of the night that bothered me but the horrible lights men had invented to illuminate their darkness with . . . I mean the very streetlamp down at the end of the street . . .

It was a year when I completely gave up trying to keep my body in condition and a photo of myself on the beach at the time shows soft and flabby body. My hair had begun to recede from the sides. I wandered in Benzedrine depression hallucinations. A 6-foot redhead applied pancake makeup to my face and we went in the subway like that: she was the one who gave me the overdose: she was a gun moll. We met furtive awful characters at certain subway stops, some of them were subway "lush workers" (rolling subway drunks), we hung out in the evil bar on 8th Avenue around the corner from 42d Street. I myself took no part in any crime but I knew personally of many indeed. For Hubbard it was a jaded study of how awful people can be, but in his vacuity, how "alert" they could also be in a "dead" society, for me it was a romantic self-torture like the blood business in my Self Ultimacy writing garret the fall before. For Irwin, now a shipyard worker, and occasional merchant seaman coastwise to Texas, *et al.,* a new kind of material for his new Hart Crane poetry kick.

One of our "friends" who came in to stash a gun one day turned out, after he hanged himself in the Tombs some months later, to have been the "Mad Killer of Times Square," tho I didnt know about that: he'd walk right into a liquor store and shoot the proprietor dead: it was afterward confessed to me by another thief who couldnt hold the secret he said because he hurted from holding it.

VIII

My poor father had to see me, while dying of cancer, come down to all of this from that beginning on the sandlot football field of Dracut Tigers Lowell when the ambition was to make good in football and school, go to college, and become a "success." It was part of the war, really, and of the cold war to come. I can never forget how June's present husband, Harry Evans, suddenly came clomping down the hall of her apartment in his Army boots, fresh from the German front, around September 1945, and was appalled to see us, six fullgrown people, all high on Benny sprawled and sitting and cat-legged on that vast double-double-bed of "skepticism" and "decadence," discussing the nothingness of values, pale-faced, weak bodies, Gad the poor guy said: "This is what I fought for?" His wife told him to come down from his "character heights" or some such. He divorced her awhile later. Of course we know the same thing was going on in Paris and Berlin of the same month and year, now that we've read Günther Grass and Uwe Johnson and Sartre and even, of course, Auden and his *Age of Anxiety*.

But this didnt jibe with my dying father's continuing notion that people "should make the best of it, look hopefully to tomorrow, work, do well, make an effort, shake a leg," all the old 1930's expressions that were so stirring, like cranberry sauce, when we thought Prosperity was right around the corner and it sure was.

I myself, as you can see from this whole insane tirade of prose called a book, had been thru so much junk anyway you can hardly blame me for joining in with the despairists of my time.

Still, there were guys coming home from the war and getting married and going to school on the G.I. Bill who had no taste for such negativism and who would have punched me on the nose if they knew about how low I'd fallen from the time, maybe, when they had a beer with me in 1940. But I had goofed throughout entire wartime and this is my confession.

(At this time also, I let Johnnie my wife handle the annulment papers in Detroit, I was of no more use to her as a husband, I sent her home.)

IX

I took so much benzedrine that year out of those cracked tubes, I finally made myself real sick, developed thrombophlebitis, and by December had to go to the Queens General Hospital (on the V.A.) to lie there with my legs up on pillows swathed in hot compresses. There was talk at first of surgery, even. And even there I'd look out the window at the darkness of the Queens night and feel a nauseating gulp to see those poor streetlamps stretching out into the murmurous city like a string of woes.

Yet a little bunch of kids, twelve and thirteen, who were patients there, actually came to the foot of my bed and serenaded me with guitars one evening.

And my nurse, big fat gal, loved me.

They could see in my eyes what had been there in 1939, 38, nay 22.

In fact I began to bethink myself in that hospital. I began to understand that the city intellectuals of the world were divorced from the folkbody blood of the land and were just rootless fools, tho permissible fools, who really didnt know how to go on living. I began to get a new vision of my own of a truer darkness which just overshadowed all this overlaid mental garbage of "existentialism" and "hipsterism" and "bourgeois decadence" and whatever names you want to give it.

In the purity of my hospital bed, weeks on end, I, staring at the dim ceiling while the poor men snored, saw that life is a brute creation, beautiful and cruel, that when you see a springtime bud covered with rain dew, how can you believe it's beautiful when you know the moisture is just there to encourage the bud to flower out just so's it can fall off sere dead dry in the fall? All the contemporary LSD acid heads (of 1967) see the cruel beauty of the brute creation just by closing their eyes: I've seen it too since: a maniacal Mandala circle all mosaic and dense with millions of cruel things and beautiful scenes goin on, like say, swiftly on one side I saw one night a choirmaster of some sort in "Heaven" slowly going "Ooo" with his mouth in awe at the beauty of what they were singing, but right next to him is a pig being fed to an alligator by cruel attendants on a pier and people walking by unconcerned. Just an example. Or that horrible Mother Kali of ancient India and its wisdom aeons with all her arms bejeweled, legs and belly too, gyrating insanely to eat back thru the only part of her that's not jeweled, her yoni, or yin, everything she's given birth to. Ha ha ha ha she's laughing as she dances on the dead she gave birth to. Mother Nature giving you birth and eating you back.

And I say wars and social catastrophes arise from the cruel nature of bestial creation, and not from "society," which after all has good intentions or it wouldn't be called "society" would it?

It is, face it, a mean heartless creation emanated by a God of Wrath, Jehovah, Yaweh, No-Name, who will pat you kindly on the head and say "Now you're being good" when you pray, but when you're begging for mercy anyway say like a soldier hung by one leg from a tree trunk in today's Vietnam, when Yaweh's really got you out in back of the barn even in ordinary torture of fatal illness like my Pa's then, he wont listen, he will whack away at your lil behind with the long stick of what they called "Original Sin" in the Theological Christian dogmatic sects but what I call "Original Sacrifice."

That's not even worse, for God's sake, than watching your own human father Pop die in real life, when you really realize "Father, Father, why hast thou forsaken me?" for real, the man who gave you hopeful birth is copping out right before your eyes and leaves you flat with the whole problem and burden (your self) of his own foolishness in ever believing that "life" was worth anything but what it smells like down in the Bellevue Morgue when I had to identify Franz' body. Your human father sits there in death before you almost satisfied. That's what's so sad and horrible about the "God is Dead" movement in contemporary religion, it's the most tearful and forlorn philosophical idea of all time.

• • •

XIII

So, partially well, I went home and, in the general vanity of Duluoz, I decided to become a writer, write a huge novel explaining everything to everybody, try to keep my father alive and happy, while Ma worked in the shoe factory, the year 1946 now, and make a "go" at it.

But slowly he withered before my eyes. Every two weeks his belly became a big bag of water and the poor Jewish doctor had to come to the house, wince with compassion, and stick a long stabbing tube right into his belly in the kitchen (away from mother and son) to let the water pour out into a kitchen pail. My father never yelled out in pain, he just winced and groaned and wept softly, O good man of my heart. Then, one morning after we had an argument about how to brew coffee, and the doctor came again to "drain" him (O Nature go drain yourself you evil bitch!) he just died in his chair right in front of my eyes and I looked at his face in pouting repose and thought "You have forsaken me, my father. You have left me alone to take care of the 'rest' whatever the rest is." He'd said: "Take care of your mother whatever you do. Promise me." I promised I would, and have.

So the undertakers come and dump him in a basket and we have him hearsed up to the cemetery in New Hampshire in the town where he was born and little idiot birds are singing on the branch. At one point the bluejay mother throws the weakling out of the nest and he falls to the foot of the tree and thrashes there dying and starving. A priest tries to console me. I walk with my Uncle Vincent Duluoz after the funeral through the little streets of Nashua and understand, from his silence, why he was always considered the "mean" and "uncommunicative" Duluoz. He was the honest one. He said "Your father was a good boy but he was too ambitious and proud and crazy. I guess you're the same."

"I don't know."

"Well, in between. I never disliked Emil. But there you have it, and him, and I'm dying myself, and you'll die someday, and all this, poof, *ça s'en vas* (all this, poof, it goes). He made a Breton Gallic shrug at the empty blue sky above.

Of Uncle Vincent you could not say that he was a victim of the vanity of Duluoz.

XIV

But I still was a victim, went back to Ozone Park with Ma, she did her spring housecleaning (the old man gone, clean the house, drive the Celtic ghosts out) and I settled down to write, in solitude, in pain, writing hymns and prayers even at dawn, thinking "When this book is finished, which is going to be the sum and substance and crap of everything I've been thru throughout this whole gaddam life, I shall be redeemed."

But, wifey, I did it all, I wrote the book, I stalked the streets of life, of Manhattan, of Long Island, stalked thru 1,183 pages of my first novel, sold the book, got an advance, whooped, hallelujah'd, went on, did everything you're supposed to do in life.

But nothing ever came of it.

No "generation" is "new." There's "nothing new under the sun." "All is vanity."

from
ON THE ROAD
1947

EDITOR'S NOTE
In this book Kerouac calls himself "Sal Paradise," Neal Cassady is "Dean Moriarty," Allen Ginsberg is "Carlo Marx," William Burroughs is "Old Bull Lee," his common-law wife, June, is "Jane Lee," Herbert Huncke is "Elmer Hassel," and Carolyn Cassady is "Camille."

PART ONE

1

I FIRST MET DEAN not long after my wife and I split up. I had just gotten over a serious illness that I won't bother to talk about, except that it had something to do with the miserably weary split-up and my feeling that everything was dead. With the coming of Dean Moriarty began the part of my life you could call my life on the road. Before that I'd often dreamed of going West to see the country, always vaguely planning and never taking off. Dean is the perfect guy for the road because he actually was born on the road, when his parents were passing through Salt Lake City in 1926, in a jalopy, on their way to Los Angeles. First reports of him came to me through Chad King, who'd shown me a few letters from him written in a New Mexico reform school. I was tremendously interested in the letters because they so naïvely and sweetly asked Chad to teach him all about Nietzsche and all the wonderful intellectual things that Chad knew. At one point Carlo and I talked about the letters and wondered if we would ever meet the strange Dean Moriarty. This is all far back, when Dean was not the way he is today, when he was a young jailkid shrouded in mystery. Then news came that Dean was out of reform school and was coming to New York for the first time; also there was talk that he had just married a girl called Marylou.

One day I was hanging around the campus and Chad and Tim Gray told me Dean was staying in a cold-water pad in East Harlem, the Spanish Harlem. Dean had arrived the night before, the first time in New York, with his beautiful little sharp chick Marylou; they got off the Greyhound bus at 50th Street and cut around the corner looking for a place to eat and went right in Hector's, and since then Hector's cafeteria has always been a big symbol of New York for Dean. They spent money on beautiful big glazed cakes and creampuffs.

All this time Dean was telling Marylou things like this: "Now, darling, here we are in New York and although I haven't quite told you everything that I was thinking about when we crossed Missouri and especially at the point when we pass the Booneville reformatory which reminded me of my jail problem, it is absolutely necessary now to postpone all those leftover things concerning our personal lovethings and at once begin thinking of specific worklife plans . . ." and so on in the way that he had in those early days.

I went to the cold-water flat with the boys, and Dean came to the door in his shorts. Marylou was jumping off the couch; Dean had dispatched the occupant of the apartment to the kitchen, probably to make coffee, while he proceeded with his loveproblems, for to him sex was the one and only holy and important thing in life, although he had to sweat and curse to make a living and so on. You saw that in the way he stood bobbing his head, always looking down, nodding, like a young boxer to instructions, to make you think he was listening to every word, throwing in a thousand "Yeses" and "That's rights." My first impression of Dean was of a young Gene Autry—trim, thin-hipped, blue-eyed, with a real Oklahoma accent—a sideburned hero of the snowy West. In fact he'd just been working on a ranch, Ed Wall's in Colorado, before marrying Marylou and coming East. Marylou was a pretty blonde with immense ringlets of hair like a sea of golden tresses; she sat there on the edge of the couch with her hands hanging in her lap and her smoky blue country eyes fixed in a wide stare because she was in an evil gray New York pad that she'd heard about back West, and waiting like a longbodied emaciated Modigliani surrealist woman in a serious room. But, outside of being a sweet little girl, she was awfully dumb and capable of doing horrible things. That night we all drank beer and pulled wrists and talked till dawn, and in the morning, while we sat around dumbly smoking butts from ashtrays in the gray light of a gloomy day, Dean got up nervously, paced around, thinking, and decided the thing to do was to have Marylou make breakfast and sweep the floor. "In other words we've go to get on the ball, darling, what I'm saying, otherwise it'll be fluctuating and lack true knowledge or crystallization of our plans." Then I went away.

During the following week he confided in Chad King that he absolutely had to learn how to write from him; Chad said I was a writer and he should come to me for advice. Meanwhile Dean had gotten a job in a parking lot, had a fight with Marylou in their Hoboken apartment—God knows why they went there—and she was so mad and so down deep vindictive that she reported to the police some false trumped-up hysterical crazy charge, and Dean had to lam from Hoboken. So he had no place to live. He came right out to Paterson, New Jersey, where I was living with my aunt, and one night while I was studying there was a knock on the door, and there was Dean, bowing, shuffling obsequiously in the dark of the hall, and saying, "Hel-lo, you remember me—Dean Moriarty? I've come to ask you to show me how to write."

"And where's Marylou?" I asked, and Dean said she'd apparently

whored a few dollars together and gone back to Denver—"the whore!"
So we went out to have a few beers because we couldn't talk like we
wanted to talk in front of my aunt, who sat in the living room reading
her paper. She took one look at Dean and decided that he was a
madman.

In the bar I told Dean, "Hell, man, I know very well you didn't
come to me only to want to become a writer, and after all what do I
really know about it except you've got to stick to it with the energy of
a benny addict." And he said, "Yes, of course, I know exactly what you
mean and in fact all those problems have occurred to me, but the thing
that I want is the realization of those factors that should one depend
on Schopenhauer's dichotomy for any inwardly realized . . ." and so on
in that way, things I understood not a bit and he himself didn't. In those
days he really didn't know what he was talking about; that is to say,
he was a young jailkid all hung-up on the wonderful possibilities of
becoming a real intellectual, and he liked to talk in the tone and using
the words, but in a jumbled way, that he had heard from "real
intellectuals"—although, mind you, he wasn't so naïve as that in all
other things, and it took him just a few months with Carlo Marx to
become completely *in there* with all the terms and jargon. Nonetheless
we understood each other on other levels of madness, and I agreed that
he could stay at my house till he found a job and furthermore we agreed
to go out West sometime. That was the winter of 1947.

One night when Dean ate supper at my house—he already had the
parking-lot job in New York—he leaned over my shoulders as I typed
rapidly away and said, "Come on man, those girls won't wait, make it
fast."

I said, "Hold on just a minute, I'll be right with you soon as I finish
this chapter," and it was one of the best chapters in the book. Then I
dressed and off we flew to New York to meet some girls. As we rode
in the bus in the weird phosphorescent void of the Lincoln Tunnel we
leaned on each other with fingers waving and yelled and talked excitedly, and I was beginning to get the bug like Dean. He was simply a
youth tremendously excited with life, and though he was a con-man, he
was only conning because he wanted so much to live and to get involved
with people who would otherwise pay no attention to him. He was
conning me and I knew it (for room and board and "how-to-write,"
etc.), and he knew I knew (this has been the basis of our relationship),
but I didn't care and we got along fine—no pestering, no catering; we
tiptoed around each other like heartbreaking new friends. I began to

learn from him as much as he probably learned from me. As far as my work was concerned he said, "Go ahead, everything you do is great." He watched over my shoulder as I wrote stories, yelling, "Yes! That's right! Wow! Man!" and "Phew!" and wiped his face with his handkerchief. "Man, wow, there's so many thing to do, so many things to write! How to even *begin* to get it all down and without modified restraints and all hung-up on like literary inhibitions and grammatical fears . . ."

"That's right, man, now you're talking." And a kind of holy lightning I saw flashing from his excitement and his visions, which he described so torrentially that people in buses looked around to see the "overexcited nut." In the West he'd spent a third of his time in the poolhall, a third in jail, and a third in the public library. They'd seen him rushing eagerly down the winter streets, bareheaded, carrying books to the poolhall, or climbing trees to get into the attics of buddies where he spent days reading or hiding from the law.

We went to New York—I forget what the situation was, two colored girls—there were no girls there; they were supposed to meet him in a diner and didn't show up. We went to his parking lot where he had a few things to do—change his clothes in the shack in back and spruce up a bit in front of a cracked mirror and so on, and then we took off. And that was the night Dean met Carlo Marx. A tremendous thing happened when Dean met Carlo Marx. Two keen minds that they are, they took to each other at the drop of a hat. Two piercing eyes glanced into the two piercing eyes—the holy con-man with the shining mind, and the sorrowful poetic con-man with the dark mind that is Carlo Marx. From that moment on I saw very little of Dean, and I was a little sorry too. Their energies met head-on, I was a lout compared, I couldn't keep up with them. The whole mad swirl of everything that was to come began then; it would mix up all my friends and all I had left of my family in a big dust cloud over the American Night. Carlo told him of Old Bull Lee, Elmer Hassel, Jane: Lee in Texas growing weed, Hassel on Riker's Island, Jane wandering on Times Square in a benzedrine hallucination, with her baby girl in her arms and ending up in Bellevue. And Dean told Carlo of unknown people in the West like Tommy Snark, the clubfooted poolhall rotation shark and cardplayer and queer saint. He told him of Roy Johnson, Big Ed Dunkel, his boyhood buddies, his street buddies, his innumerable girls and sex-parties and pornographic pictures, his heroes, heroines, adventures. They rushed down the street together, digging everything in the early way they had, which later became so much sadder and perceptive and blank.

But then they danced down the streets like dingledodies, and I shambled after as I've been doing all my life after people who interest me, because the only people for me are the mad ones, the ones who are mad to live, mad to talk, mad to be saved, desirous of everything at the same time, the ones who never yawn or say a commonplace thing, but burn, burn, burn like fabulous yellow roman candles exploding like spiders across the stars and in the middle you see the blue centerlight pop and everybody goes "Awww!" What did they call such young people in Goethe's Germany? Wanting dearly to learn how to write like Carlo, the first thing you know, Dean was attacking him with a great amorous soul such as only a con-man can have. "Now, Carlo, let *me* speak—here's what *I'm* saying . . ." I didn't see them for about two weeks, during which time they cemented their relationship to fiendish allday-allnight-talk proportions.

Then came spring, the great time of traveling, and everybody in the scattered gang was getting ready to make one trip or another. I was busily at work on my novel and when I came to the halfway mark, after a trip down South with my aunt to visit my brother Rocco, I got ready to travel West for the very first time.

Dean had already left. Carlo and I saw him off at the 34th Street Greyhound station. Upstairs they had a place where you could make pictures for a quarter. Carlo took off his glasses and looked sinister. Dean made a profile shot and looked coyly around. I took a straight picture that made me look like a thirty-year-old Italian who'd kill anybody who said anything against his mother. This picture Carlo and Dean nearly cut down the middle with a razor and saved a half each in their wallets. Dean was wearing a real Western business suit for his big trip back to Denver; he'd finished his first fling in New York. I say fling, but he only worked like a dog in parking lots. The most fantastic parking-lot attendant in the world, he can back a car forty miles an hour into a tight squeeze and stop at the wall, jump out, race among fenders, leap into another car, circle it fifty miles an hour in a narrow space, back swiftly into tight spot, *hump,* snap the car with the emergency so that you see it bounce as he flies out; then clear to the ticket shack, sprinting like a track star, hand a ticket, leap into a newly arrived car before the owner's half out, leap literally under him as he steps out, start the car with the door flapping, and roar off to the next available spot, arc, pop in, brake, out, run; working like that without pause eight hours a night, evening rush hours and after-theater rush hours, in greasy wino pants with a frayed fur-lined jacket and beat shoes that flap. Now he'd bought a new suit to go back in; blue with pencil stripes, vest and all—eleven dollars on Third Avenue, with a watch and watch chain, and a portable typewriter with which he was going to start writing in a Denver rooming house as soon as he got a job there. We had a farewell meal of franks and beans in a Seventh Avenue Riker's and then Dean got on the bus and said Chicago and roared off into the night. There went our wrangler. I promised myself to go the same way when spring really bloomed and opened up the land.

And this was really the way that my whole road experience began, and the things that were to come are too fantastic not to tell.

Yes, and it wasn't only because I was a writer and needed new experiences that I wanted to know Dean more, and because my life hanging around the campus had reached the completion of its cycle and was stultified, but because, somehow, in spite of our difference in character, he reminded me of some long-lost brother; the sight of his suffering bony face with the long sideburns and his straining muscular sweating neck made me remember my boyhood in those dye-dumps and swim-holes and riversides of Paterson and the Passaic. His dirty workclothes clung to him so gracefully, as though you couldn't buy a better fit from a custom tailor but only earn it from the Natural Tailor of Natural Joy, as Dean had, in his stresses. And in his excited way of speaking I heard again the voices of old companions and brothers under the bridge, among the motorcycles, along the wash-lined neighborhood and drowsy doorsteps of afternoon where boys played guitars while their older brothers worked in the mills. All my other current friends were "intellectuals"—Chad the Nietzchean anthropologist, Carlo Marx and his nutty surrealist low-voiced serious staring talk, Old Bull Lee and his critical anti-everything drawl—or else they were slinking criminals like Elmer Hassel, with that hip sneer; Jane Lee the same, sprawled on the Oriental cover of her couch, sniffing at the *New Yorker*. But Dean's intelligence was every bit as formal and shining and complete, without the tedious intellectualness. And his "criminality" was not something that sulked and sneered; it was a wild yea-saying overburst of American joy; it was Western, the west wind, an ode from the Plains, something new, long prophesied, long a-coming (he only stole cars for joy rides). Besides, all my New York friends were in the negative, nightmare position of putting down society and giving their tired bookish or political or psychoanalytical reasons, but Dean just raced in society, eager for bread and love; he didn't care one way or the other, "so long's I can get that lil ole gal with that lil sumpin down there tween her legs, boy," and "so long's we can *eat,* son, y'ear me? I'm *hungry,* I'm *starving,* let's *eat right now!*"—and off we'd rush to *eat,* whereof, as saith Ecclesiastes, "It is your portion under the sun."

A western kinsman of the sun, Dean. Although my aunt warned me that he would get me in trouble, I could hear a new call and see a new horizon, and believe it at my young age; and a little bit of trouble or even Dean's eventual rejection of me as a buddy, putting me down, as he would later, on starving sidewalks and sickbeds—what did it matter? I was a young writer and I wanted to take off.

Somewhere along the line I knew there'd be girls, visions, everything; somewhere along the line the pearl would be handed to me.

2

In the month of July 1947, having saved about fifty dollars from old veteran benefits, I was ready to go to the West Coast. My friend Remi Boncoeur had written me a letter from San Francisco, saying I should come and ship out with him on an around-the-world liner. He swore he could get me into the engine room. I wrote back and said I'd be satisfied with any old freighter so long as I could take a few long Pacific trips and come back with enough money to support myself in my aunt's house while I finished my book. He said he had a shack in Mill City and I would have all the time in the world to write there while we went through the rigmarole of getting the ship. He was living with a girl called Lee Ann; he said she was a marvelous cook and everything would jump. Remi was an old prep-school friend, a Frenchman brought up in Paris and a really mad guy—I didn't know how mad at this time. So he expected me to arrive in ten days. My aunt was all in accord with my trip to the West; she said it would do me good, I'd been working so hard all winter and staying in too much; she even didn't complain when I told her I'd have to hitchhike some. All she wanted was for me to come back in one piece. So, leaving my big half-manuscript sitting on top of my desk, and folding back my comfortable home sheets for the last time one morning, I left with my canvas bag in which a few fundamental things were packed and took off for the Pacific Ocean with the fifty dollars in my pocket.

I'd been poring over maps of the United States in Paterson for months, even reading books about the pioneers and savoring names like Platte and Cimarron and so on, and on the road-map was one long red line called Route 6 that led from the tip of Cape Cod clear to Ely, Nevada, and there dipped down to Los Angeles. I'll just stay on 6 all the way to Ely, I said to myself and confidently started. To get to 6 I had to go up to Bear Mountain. Filled with dreams of what I'd do in Chicago, in Denver, and then finally in San Fran, I took the Seventh Avenue subway to the end of the line at 242nd Street, and there took a trolley into Yonkers; in downtown Yonkers I transferred to an outgoing trolley and went to the city limits on the east bank of the Hudson River. If you drop a rose in the Hudson River at its mysterious source in the Adirondacks, think of all the places it journeys by as it goes to sea forever—think of that wonderful Hudson Valley. I started hitching up the thing. Five scattered rides took me to the desired Bear Mountain Bridge, where Route 6 arched in from New England. It began to rain in torrents when I was let off there. It was mountainous. Route 6 came over the river, wound around a traffic circle, and disappeared into the wilderness. Not only was there no traffic but the rain came down in buckets and I had no shelter. I had to run under some pines to take cover; this did no good; I began crying and swearing and socking myself on the head for being such a damn fool. I was forty miles north of New York; all the way up I'd been worried about the fact that on this, my big opening day, I was only moving north instead of the so-longed-for west. Now I was stuck on my northernmost hangup. I ran a quarter-mile to an abandoned cute English-style filling station and stood under the dripping eaves. High up over my head the great hairy Bear Mountain sent down thunderclaps that put the fear of God in me. All I could see were smoky trees and dismal wilderness rising to the skies. "What the hell am I doing up here?" I cursed, I cried for Chicago. "Even now they're all having a big time, they're doing this, I'm not there, when will I get there!"—and so on. Finally a car stopped at the empty filling station; the man and the two women in it wanted to study a map. I stepped right up and gestured in the rain; they consulted; I looked like a maniac, of course, with my hair all wet, my shoes sopping. My shoes, damn fool that I am, were Mexican huaraches, plantlike sieves not fit for the rainy night of America and the raw road night. But the people let me in and rode me *back* to Newburgh, which I accepted as a better alternative than being trapped in the Bear Mountain wilderness all night. "Besides," said the man, "there's no traffic passes through 6. If you want to go to Chicago you'd do better going across the Holland Tunnel in New York and head for Pittsburgh," and I knew he was right.

It was my dream that screwed up, the stupid hearthside idea that it would be wonderful to follow one great red line across America instead of trying various roads and routes.

In Newburgh it had stopped raining. I walked down to the river, and I had to ride back to New York in a bus with a delegation of schoolteachers coming back from a weekend in the mountains—chatter-chatter blah-blah, and me swearing for all the time and the money I'd wasted, and telling myself, I wanted to go west and here I've been all day and into the night going up and down, north and south, like something that can't get started. And I swore I'd be in Chicago tomorrow, and made sure of that, taking a bus to Chicago, spending most of my money, and didn't give a damn, just as long as I'd be in Chicago tomorrow.

3

It was an ordinary bus trip with crying babies and hot sun, and coun-tryfolk getting on at one Penn town after another, till we got on the plain of Ohio and really rolled, up by Ashtabula and straight across Indiana in the night. I arrived in Chi quite early in the morning, got a room in the Y, and went to bed with a very few dollars in my pocket. I dug Chicago after a good day's sleep.

The wind from Lake Michigan, bop at the Loop, long walks around South Halsted and North Clark, and one long walk after midnight into the jungles, where a cruising car followed me as a suspicious character. At this time, 1947, bop was going like mad all over America. The fel-lows at the Loop blew, but with a tired air, because bop was somewhere between its Charlie Parker Ornithology period and another period that began with Miles Davis. And as I sat there listening to that sound of the night which bop has come to represent for all of us, I thought of all my friends from one end of the country to the other and how they were really all in the same vast backyard doing something so frantic and rushing-about. And for the first time in my life, the following af-ternoon, I went into the West. It was a warm and beautiful day for hitchhiking. To get out of the impossible complexities of Chicago traffic I took a bus to Joliet, Illinois, went by the Joliet pen, stationed myself just outside town after a walk through its leafy rickety streets behind, and pointed my way. All the way from New York to Joliet by bus, and I had spent more than half my money.

My first ride was a dynamite truck with a red flag, about thirty miles into great green Illinois, the truckdriver pointing out the place where Route 6, which we were on, intersects Route 66 before they both shoot west for incredible distances. Along about three in the afternoon, after an apple pie and ice cream in a roadside stand, a woman stopped for me in a little coupe. I had a twinge of hard joy as I ran after the car. But she was a middle-aged woman, actually the mother of sons my age, and wanted somebody to help her drive to Iowa. I was all for it. Iowa! Not so far from Denver, and once I got to Denver I could relax. She drove the first few hours, at one point insisted on visiting an old church somewhere, as if we were tourists, and then I took over the wheel and, though I'm not much of a driver, drove clear through the rest of Illinois to Davenport, Iowa, via Rock Island. And here for the first time in my life I saw my beloved Mississippi River, dry in the summer haze, low water, with its big rank smell that smells like the raw body of America itself because it washes it up. Rock Island—railroad tracks, shacks, small downtown section; and over the bridge to Davenport, same kind of town, all smelling of sawdust in the warm midwest sun. Here the lady had to go on to her Iowa hometown by another route, and I got out.

The sun was going down, I walked, after a few cold beers, to the edge of town, and it was a long walk. All the men were driving home from work, wearing railroad hats, baseball hats, all kinds of hats, just like after work in any town anywhere. One of them gave me a ride up the hill and left me at a lonely crossroads on the edge of the prairie. It was beautiful there. The only cars that came by were farmer-cars; they gave me suspicious looks, they clanked along, the cows were coming home. Not a truck. A few cars zipped by. A hotrod kid came by with his scarf flying. The sun went all the way down and I was standing in the purple darkness. Now I was scared. There weren't even any lights in the Iowa countryside; in a minute nobody would be able to see me. Luckily a man going back to Davenport gave me a lift downtown. But I was right where I started from.

I went to sit in the bus station and think this over. I ate another apple pie and ice cream; that's practically all I ate all the way across the country, I knew it was nutritious and it was delicious, of course. I decided to gamble. I took a bus in downtown Davenport, after spending a half-hour watching a waitress in the bus-station café, and rode to the city limits, but this time near the gas stations. Here the big trucks roared, wham, and inside two minutes one of them cranked to a stop for me. I ran for it with my soul whoopeeing. And what a driver—a great big tough truckdriver with popping eyes and a hoarse raspy voice who just slammed and kicked at everything and got his rig under way and paid hardly any attention to me. So I could rest my tired soul a little, for one of the biggest troubles hitchhiking is having to talk to innumerable people, make them feel that they didn't make a mistake picking you up, even entertain them almost, all of which is a great strain when you're going all the way and don't plan to sleep in hotels. The guy just yelled above the roar, and all I had to do was yell back, and we relaxed. And he balled that thing clear to Iowa City and yelled me the funniest stories about how he got around the law in every town that had an unfair speed limit, saying over and over again, "Them goddamn cops can't put no flies on *my* ass!" Just as we rolled into Iowa City he saw another truck coming behind us, and because he had to turn off at Iowa City he blinked his tail lights at the other guy and slowed down for me to jump out, which I did with my bag, and the other truck, acknowledging this exchange, stopped for me, and once again, in the twink of nothing, I was in another big high cab, all set to go hundreds of miles across the night, and was I happy! And the new truckdriver was as crazy as the other and yelled just as much, and all I had to do was lean back and roll on. Now I could see Denver looming ahead of me like the Promised Land, way out there beneath the stars, across the prairie of Iowa and the plains of Nebraska, and I could see the greater vision of San Francisco beyond, like jewels in the night. He balled the jack and told stories for a couple of hours, then, at a town in Iowa where years later Dean and I were stopped on suspicion in what looked like a stolen Cadillac, he slept a few hours in the seat. I slept too, and took one little walk along the lonely brick walls illuminated by one lamp, with the prairie brooding at the end of each little street and the smell of the corn like dew in the night.

He woke up with a start at dawn. Off we roared, and an hour later the smoke of Des Moines appeared ahead over the green cornfields. He had to eat his breakfast now and wanted to take it easy, so I went right on into Des Moines, about four miles, hitching a ride with two boys from the University of Iowa; and it was strange sitting in their brand-new comfortable car and hearing them talk of exams as we zoomed smoothly into town. Now I wanted to sleep a whole day. So I went to the Y to get a room; they didn't have any, and by instinct I wandered down to the railroad tracks—and there're a lot of them in Des Moines—and wound up in a gloomy old Plains inn of a hotel by the locomotive roundhouse, and spent a long day sleeping on a big clean hard white bed with dirty remarks carved in the wall beside my pillow and the beat yellow windowshades pulled over the smoky scene of the railyards. I woke up as the sun was reddening; and that was the one distinct time in my life, the strangest moment of all, when I didn't know who I was—I was far away from home, haunted and tired with travel, in a cheap hotel room I'd never seen, hearing the hiss of steam outside, and the creak of the old wood of the hotel, and footsteps upstairs, and all the sad sounds, and I looked at the cracked high ceiling and really didn't know who I was for about fifteen strange seconds. I wasn't scared; I was just somebody else, some stranger, and my whole life was a haunted life, the life of a ghost. I was halfway across America, at the dividing line between the East of my youth and the West of my future, and maybe that's why it happened right there and then, that strange red afternoon.

But I had to get going and stop moaning, so I picked up my bag, said so long to the old hotelkeeper sitting by his spittoon, and went to eat. I ate apple pie and ice cream—it was getting better as I got deper into Iowa, the pie bigger, the ice cream richer. There were the most beautiful bevies of girls everywhere I looked in Des Moines that afternoon—they were coming home from high school—but I had no time now for thoughts like that and promised myself a ball in Denver. Carlo Marx was already in Denver; Dean was there; Chad King and Tim Gray were there, it was their hometown; Marylou was there; and there was mention of a mighty gang including Ray Rawlins and his beautiful blond sister Babe Rawlins; two waitresses Dean knew, the Bettencourt sisters; and even Roland Major, my old college writing buddy, was there. I looked forward to all of them with joy and anticipation. So I rushed past the pretty girls, and the prettiest girls in the world live in Des Moines.

A guy with a kind of toolshack on wheels, a truck full of tools that he drove standing up like a modern milkman, gave me a ride up the long hill, where I immediately got a ride from a farmer and his son heading out for Adel in Iowa. In this town, under a big elm tree near a gas station, I made the acquaintance of another hitchhiker, a typical New Yorker, an Irishman who'd been driving a truck for the post office most of his work years and was now headed for a girl in Denver and a new life. I think he was running away from something in New York, the law most likely. He was a real rednose young drunk of thirty and would have bored me ordinarily, except that my senses were sharp for any kind of human friendship. He wore a beat sweater and baggy pants and had nothing with him in the way of a bag—just a toothbrush and handkerchiefs. He said we ought to hitch together. I should have said no, because he looked pretty awful on the road. But we stuck together and got a ride with a taciturn man to Stuart, Iowa, a town in which we were really stranded. We stood in front of the railroad-ticket shack in Stuart, waiting for the westbound traffic till the sun went down, a good five hours, dawdling away the time, at first telling about ourselves, then he told dirty stories, then we just kicked pebbles and made goofy noises of one kind and another. We got bored. I decided to spend a buck on beer; we went to an old saloon in Stuart and had a few. There he got as drunk as he ever did in his Ninth Avenue night back home, and yelled joyously in my ear all the sordid dreams of his life. I kind of liked him; not because he was a good sort, as he later proved to be, but because he was enthusiastic about things. We got back on the road in the darkness, and of course nobody stopped and nobody came by much. That went on till three o'clock in the morning. We spent some time trying to sleep on the bench at the railroad ticket office, but the telegraph clicked all night and we couldn't sleep, and big freights were slamming around outside. We didn't know how to hop a proper chain gang; we'd never done it before; we didn't know whether they were going east or west or how to find out or what boxcars and flats and de-iced reefers to pick, and so on. So when the Omaha bus came through just before dawn we hopped on it and joined the sleeping passengers—I paid for his fare as well as mine. His name was Eddie. He reminded me of my cousin-in-law from the Bronx. That was why I stuck with him. It was like having an old friend along, a smiling good-natured sort to goof along with.

We arrived at Council Bluffs at dawn; I looked out. All winter I'd been reading of the great wagon parties that held council there before hitting the Oregon and Santa Fe trails; and of course now it was only cute suburban cottages of one damn kind and another, all laid out in the dismal gray dawn. Then Omaha, and, by God, the first cowboy I saw, walking along the bleak walls of the wholesale meat warehouses in a ten-gallon hat and Texas boots, looked like any beat character of the brickwall dawns of the East except for the getup. We got off the bus and walked clear up the hill, the long hill formed over the millenniums by the mighty Missouri, alongside of which Omaha is built, and got out to the country and stuck our thumbs out. We got a brief ride from a wealthy rancher in a ten-gallon hat, who said the valley of the Platte was as great as the Nile Valley of Egypt, and as he said so I saw the great trees in that distance that snaked with the riverbed and the great verdant fields around it, and almost agreed with him. Then as we were standing at another crossroads and it was starting to get cloudy another cowboy, this one six feet tall in a modest half-gallon hat, called us over and wanted to know if either one of us could drive. Of course Eddie could drive, and he had a license and I didn't. Cowboy had two cars with him that he was driving back to Montana. His wife was at Grand Island, and he wanted us to drive one of the cars there, where she'd take over. At that point he was going north, and that would be the limit of our ride with him. But it was a good hundred miles into Nebraska, and of course we jumped for it. Eddie drove alone, the cowboy and myself following, and no sooner were we out of town than Eddie started to ball that jack ninety miles an hour out of sheer exuberance. "Damn me, what's that boy doing!" the cowboy shouted, and took off after him. It began to be like a race. For a minute I thought Eddie was trying to get away with the car—and for all I know that's what he meant to do. But the cowboy stuck to him and caught up with him and tooted the horn. Eddie slowed down. The cowboy tooted to stop. "Damn, boy, you're liable to get a flat going that speed. Can't you drive a little slower?"

"Well, I'll be damned, was I really going ninety?" said Eddie. "I didn't realize it on this smooth road."

"Just take it a little easy and we'll all get to Grand Island in one piece."

"Sure thing." And we resumed our journey. Eddie had calmed down and probably even got sleepy. So we drove a hundred miles across Nebraska, following the winding Platte with its verdant fields.

"During the depression," said the cowboy to me, "I used to hop freights at least once a month. In those days you'd see hundreds of men riding a flatcar or in a boxcar, and they weren't just bums, they were all kinds of men out of work and going from one place to another and some of them just wandering. It was like that all over the West. Brakemen never bothered you in those days. I don't know about today. Nebraska I ain't got no use for. Why in the middle nineteen thirties this place wasn't nothing but a big dustcloud as far as the eye could see. You couldn't breathe. The ground was black. I was here in those days. They can give Nebraska back to the Indians far as I'm concerned. I hate this damn place more than any place in the world. Montana's my home now—Missoula. You come up there sometime and see God's country." Later in the afternoon I slept when he got tired talking—he was an interesting talker.

We stopped along the road for a bite to eat. The cowboy went off to have a spare tire patched, and Eddie and I sat down in a kind of homemade diner. I heard a great laugh, the greatest laugh in the world, and here came this rawhide old-timer Nebraska farmer with a bunch of other boys into the diner; you could hear his raspy cries clear across the plains, across the whole gray world of them that day. Everybody else laughed with him. He didn't have a care in the world and had the hugest regard for everybody. I said to myself, Wham, listen to that man laugh. That's the West, here I am in the West. He came booming into the diner, calling Maw's name, and she made the sweetest cherry pie in Nebraska, and I had some with a mountainous scoop of ice cream on top. "Maw, rustle me up some grub before I have to start eatin myself raw or some damn silly idee like that." And he threw himself on a stool and went hyaw hyaw hyaw hyaw. "And throw some beans in it." It was the spirit of the West sitting right next to me. I wished I knew his whole raw life and what the hell he'd been doing all these years besides laughing and yelling like that. Whooee, I told my soul, and the cowboy came back and off we went to Grand Island.

We got there in no time flat. He went to fetch his wife and off to whatever fate awaited him, and Eddie and I resumed on the road. We got a ride from a couple of young fellows—wranglers, teenagers, country boys in a put-together jalopy—and were left off somewhere up the line in a thin drizzle of rain. Then an old man who said nothing—and God knows why he picked us up—took us to Shelton. Here Eddie stood forlornly in the road in front of a staring bunch of short, squat Omaha Indians who had nowhere to go and nothing to do. Across the road was the railroad track and the watertank saying SHELTON. "Damn me," said Eddie with amazement, "I've been in this town before. It was years ago, during the war, at night, late at night when everybody was sleeping. I went out on the platform to smoke, and there we was in the middle of nowhere and black as hell, and I look up and see that name Shelton written on the watertank. Bound for the Pacific, everybody snoring, every damn dumb sucker, and we only stayed a few minutes, stoking up or something, and off we went. Damn me, this Shelton! I hated this place ever since!" And we were stuck in Shelton. As in Davenport, Iowa, somehow all the cars were farmer-cars, and once in a while a tourist car, which is worse, with old men driving and their wives pointing out the sights or poring over maps, and sitting back looking at everything with suspicious faces.

The drizzle increased and Eddie got cold; he had very little clothing. I fished a wool plaid shirt from my canvas bag and he put it on. He felt a little better. I had a cold. I bought cough drops in a rickety Indian store of some kind. I went to the little two-by-four post office and wrote my aunt a penny postcard. We went back to the gray road. There she was in front of us, Shelton, written on the watertank. The Rock Island balled by. We saw the faces of Pullman passengers go by in a blur. The train howled off across the plains in the direction of our desires. It started to rain harder.

A tall, lanky fellow in a gallon hat stopped his car on the wrong side of the road and came over to us; he looked like a sheriff. We prepared our stories secretly. He took his time coming over. "You boys going to get somewhere, or just going?" We didn't understand his question, and it was a damned good question.

"Why?" we said.

"Well, I own a little carnival that's pitched a few mile down the road and I'm looking for some old boys willing to work and make a buck for themselves. I've got a roulette concession and a wooden-ring concession, you know, the kind you throw around dolls and take your luck. You boys want to work for me, you can get thirty per cent of the take."

"Room and board?"

"You can get a bed but no food. You'll have to eat in town. We travel some." We thought it over. "It's a good opportunity," he said, and waited patiently for us to make up our minds. We felt silly and didn't know what to say, and I for one didn't want to get hung-up with a carnival. I was in such a bloody hurry to get to the gang in Denver.

I said, "I don't know, I'm going as fast as I can and I don't think I have the time." Eddie said the same thing, and the old man waved his hand and casually sauntered back to his car and drove off. And that was that. We laughed about it awhile and speculated about what it would have been like. I had visions of a dark and dusty night on the plains, and the faces of Nebraska families wandering by, with their rosy children looking at everything with awe, and I know I would have felt like the devil himself rooking them with all those cheap carnival tricks. And the Ferris wheel revolving in the flatlands darkness, and, Godalmighty, the sad music of the merry-go-round and me wanting to get on to my goal—and sleeping in some gilt wagon on a bed of burlap.

Eddie turned out to be a pretty absent-minded pal of the road. A funny old contraption rolled by, driven by an old man; it was made of some kind of aluminum, square as a box—a trailer, no doubt, but a weird, crazy Nebraska homemade trailer. He was going very slow and stopped. We rushed up; he said he could only take one; without a word Eddie jumped in and slowly rattled from my sight, and wearing my wool plaid shirt. Well, alackaday, I kissed the shirt good-by; it had only sentimental value in any case. I waited in our personal godawful Shelton for a long, long time, several hours, and I kept thinking it was getting night; actually it was only early afternoon, but dark. Denver, Denver, how would I ever get to Denver? I was just about giving up and planning to sit over coffee when a fairly new car stopped, driven by a young guy. I ran like mad.

"Where you going?"

"Denver."

"Well, I can take you a hundred miles up the line."

"Grand, grand, you saved my life."

"I used to hitchhike myself, that's why I always pick up a fellow."

"I would too if I had a car." And so we talked, and he told me about his life, which wasn't very interesting, and I started to sleep some and woke up right outside the town of Gothenburg, where he let me off.

4

The greatest ride in my life was about to come up, a truck, with a flatboard at the back, with about six or seven boys sprawled out on it, and the drivers, two young blond farmers from Minnesota, were picking up every single soul they found on that road—the most smiling, cheerful couple of handsome bumpkins you could ever wish to see, both wearing cotton shirts and overalls, nothing else; both thick-wristed and earnest, with broad howareyou smiles for anybody and anything that came across their path. I ran up, said "Is there room?" They said, "Sure, hop on, 'sroom for everybody."

I wasn't on the flatboard before the truck roared off; I lurched, a rider grabbed me, and I sat down. Somebody passed a bottle of rotgut, the bottom of it. I took a big swig in the wild, lyrical, drizzling air of Nebraska. "Whooee, here we go!" yelled a kid in a baseball cap, and they gunned up the truck to seventy and passed everybody on the road. "We been riding this sonofabitch since Des Moines. These guys never stop. Every now and then you have to yell for pisscall, otherwise you have to piss off the air, and hang on, brother, hang on."

I looked at the company. There were two young farmer boys from North Dakota in red baseball caps, which is the standard North Dakota farmer-boy hat, and they were headed for the harvests; their old men had given them leave to hit the road for a summer. There were two young city boys from Columbus, Ohio, high-school football players, chewing gum, winking, singing in the breeze, and they said they were hitchhiking around the United States for the summer. "We're going to LA!" they yelled.

"What are you going to do there?"

"Hell, we don't know. Who cares?"

Then there was a tall slim fellow who had a sneaky look. "Where you from?" I asked. I was lying next to him on the platform; you couldn't sit without bouncing off, it had no rails. And he turned slowly to me, opened his mouth, and said, "Mon-ta-na."

Finally there were Mississippi Gene and his charge. Mississippi Gene was a little dark guy who rode freight trains around the country, a thirty-year-old hobo but with a youthful look so you couldn't tell exactly what age he was. And he sat on the boards crosslegged, looking out over the fields without saying anything for hundreds of miles, and finally at one point he turned to me and said, "Where *you* headed?"

I said Denver.

"I got a sister there but I ain't seed her for several couple years." His language was melodious and slow. He was patient. His charge was a sixteen-year-old tall blond kid, also in hobo rags; that is to say, they wore old clothes that had been turned black by the soot of railroads and the dirt of boxcars and sleeping on the ground. The blond kid was also quiet and he seemed to be running away from something, and it figured to be the law the way he looked straight ahead and wet his lips in worried thought. Montana Slim spoke to them occasionally with a sardonic and insinuating smile. They paid no attention to him. Slim was all insinuation. I was afraid of his long goofy grin that he opened up straight in your face and held there half-moronically.

"You got any money?" he said to me.

"Hell no, maybe enough for a pint of whisky till I get to Denver. What about you?"

"I know where I can get some."

"Where?"

"Anywhere. You can always folly a man down an alley, can't you?"

"Yeah, I guess you can."

"I ain't beyond doing it when I really need some dough. Headed up to Montana to see my father. I'll have to get off this rig at Cheyenne and move up some other way. These crazy boys are going to Los Angeles."

"Straight?"

"All the way—if you want to go to LA you got a ride."

I mulled this over; the thought of zooming all night across Nebraska, Wyoming, and the Utah desert in the morning, and then most likely the Nevada desert in the afternoon, and actually arriving in Los Angeles within a foreseeable space of time almost made me change my plans. But I had to go to Denver. I'd have to get off at Cheyenne too, and hitch south ninety miles to Denver.

I was glad when the two Minnesota farmboys who owned the truck decided to stop in North Platte and eat; I wanted to have a look at them. They came out of the cab and smiled at all of us. "Pisscall!" said one. "Time to eat!" said the other. But they were the only ones in the party who had money to buy food. We all shambled after them to a restaurant run by a bunch of women, and sat around over hamburgers and coffee while they wrapped away enormous meals just as if they were back in their mother's kitchen. They were brothers; they were transporting farm machinery from Los Angeles to Minnesota and making good money at it. So on their trip to the Coast empty they picked up everybody on the road. They'd done this about five times now; they were having a hell of a time. They liked everything. They never stopped smiling. I tried to talk to them—a kind of dumb attempt on my part to befriend the captains of our ship—and the only responses I got were two sunny smiles and large white cornfed teeth.

Everybody had joined them in the restaurant except the two hobo kids, Gene and his boy. When we all got back they were still sitting in the truck, forlorn and disconsolate. Now the darkness was falling. The drivers had a smoke; I jumped at the chance to go buy a bottle of whisky to keep warm in the rushing cold air of night. They smiled when I told them. "Go ahead, hurry up."

"You can have a couple shots!" I reassured them.

"Oh no, we never drink, go ahead."

Montana Slim and the two high-school boys wandered the streets of North Platte with me till I found a whisky store. They chipped in some, and Slim some, and I bought a fifth. Tall, sullen men watched us go by from false-front buildings; the main street was lined with square box-houses. There were immense vistas of the plains beyond every sad street. I felt something different in the air in North Platte, I didn't know what is was. In five minutes I did. We got back on the truck and roared off. It got dark quickly. We all had a shot, and suddenly I looked, and the verdant farmfields of the Platte began to disappear and in their stead, so far you couldn't see to the end, appeared long flat wastelands of sand and sagebrush. I was astounded.

"What in the hell is this?" I cried out to Slim.

"This is the beginning of the rangelands, boy. Hand me another drink."

"Whoopee!" yelled the high-school boys. "Columbus, so long! What would Sparkie and the boys say if they was here. Yow!"

The drivers had switched up front; the fresh brother was gunning the truck to the limit. The road changed too: humpy in the middle, with soft shoulders and a ditch on both sides about four feet deep, so that the truck bounced and teetered from one side of the road to the other —miraculously only when there were no cars coming the opposite way—and I thought we'd all take a somersault. But they were tremendous drivers. How that truck disposed of the Nebraska nub—the nub that sticks out over Colorado! And soon I realized I was actually at last over Colorado, though not officially in it, but looking southwest toward Denver itself a few hundred miles away. I yelled for joy. We passed the bottle. The great blazing stars came out, the far-receding sand hills got dim. I felt like an arrow that could shoot out all the way.

And suddenly Mississippi Gene turned to me from his crosslegged, patient reverie, and opened his mouth, and leaned close, and said, "These plains put me in the mind of Texas."

"Are you from Texas?"

"No sir, I'm from Green-vell Muzz-sippy." And that was the way he said it.

"Where's that kid from?"

"He got into some kind of trouble back in Mississippi, so I offered to help him out. Boy's never been out on his own. I take care of him best as I can, he's only a child." Although Gene was white there was something of the wise and tired old Negro in him, and something very much like Elmer Hassel, the New York dope addict, in him, but a railroad Hassel, a traveling epic Hassel, crossing and recrossing the country every year, south in the winter and north in the summer, and only because he had no place he could stay in without getting tired of it and because there was nowhere to go but everywhere, keep rolling under the stars, generally the Western stars.

"I been to Og-den a couple times. If you want to ride on to Ogden I got some friends there we could hole up with."

"I'm going to Denver from Cheyenne."

"Hell, go right straight thu, you don't get a ride like this every day."

This too was a tempting offer. What was in Ogden? "What's Ogden?" I said.

"It's the place where most of the boys pass thu and always meet there; you're liable to see anybody there."

In my earlier days I'd been to sea with a tall rawboned fellow from Louisiana called Big Slim Hazard, William Holmes Hazard, who was hobo by choice. As a little boy he'd seen a hobo come up to ask his mother for a piece of pie, and she had given it to him, and when the hobo went off down the road the little boy had said, "Ma, what is that fellow?" "Why, that's a ho-bo." "Ma, I want to be a ho-bo someday." "Shet your mouth, that's not for the like of the Hazards." But he never forgot that day, and when he grew up, after a short spell playing football at LSU, he did become a hobo. Big Slim and I spent many nights telling stories and spitting tobacco juice in paper containers. There was something so indubitably reminiscent of Big Slim Hazard in Mississippi Gene's demeanor that I said, "Do you happen to have met a fellow called Big Slim Hazard somewhere?"

And he said, "You mean the tall fellow with the big laugh?"

"Well, that sounds like him. He came from Ruston, Louisiana."

"That's right. Louisiana Slim he's sometimes called. Yessir, I shore have met Big Slim."

"And he used to work in the East Texas oil fields?"

"East Texas is right. And now he's punching cows."

And that was exactly right; and still I couldn't believe Gene could have really known Slim, whom I'd been looking for, more or less, for years. "And he used to work in tugboats in New York?"

"Well now, I don't know about that."

"I guess you only knew him in the West."

"I reckon. I ain't never been to New York."

"Well, damn me, I'm amazed you know him. This is a big country. Yet I knew you must have known him."

"Yessir, I know Big Slim pretty well. Always generous with his money when he's got some. Mean, tough fellow, too; I seen him flatten a policeman in the yards at Cheyenne, one punch." That sounded like Big Slim; he was always practicing that one punch in the air; he looked like Jack Dempsey, but a young Jack Dempsey who drank.

"Damn!" I yelled into the wind, and I had another shot, and by now I was feeling pretty good. Every shot was wiped away by the rushing wind of the open truck, wiped away of its bad effects, and the good effect sank in my stomach. "Cheyenne, here I come!" I sang. "Denver, look out for your boy."

Montana Slim turned to me, pointed at my shoes, and commented, "You reckon if you put them things in the ground something'll grow up?"—without cracking a smile, of course, and the other boys heard him and laughed. And they were the silliest shoes in America; I brought them along specifically because I didn't want my feet to sweat in the hot road, and except for the rain in Bear Mountain they proved to be the best possible shoes for my journey. So I laughed with them. And the shoes were pretty ragged by now, the bits of colored leather sticking up like pieces of fresh pineapple and my toes showing through. Well, we had another shot and laughed. As in a dream we zoomed through small crossroads towns smack out of the darkness, and passed long lines of lounging harvest hands and cowboys in the night. They watched us pass in one motion of the head, and we saw them slap their thighs from the continuing dark the other side of town—we were a funny-looking crew.

A lot of men were in this country at that time of the year; it was harvest time. The Dakota boys were fidgeting. "I think we'll get off at the next pisscall; seems like there's a lot of work around here."

"All you got to do is move north when it's over here," counseled Montana Slim, "and jes follow the harvest till you get to Canada." The boys nodded vaguely; they didn't take much stock in his advice.

Meanwhile the blond young fugitive sat the same way; every now and then Gene leaned out of his Buddhistic trance over the rushing dark plains and said something tenderly in the boy's ear. The boy nodded. Gene was taking care of him, of his moods and his fears. I wondered where the hell they would go and what they would do. They had no cigarettes. I squandered my pack on them, I loved them so. They were grateful and gracious. They never asked, I kept offering. Montana Slim had his own but never passed the pack. We zoomed through another crossroads town, passed another line of tall lanky men in jeans clustered in the dim light like moths on the desert, and returned to the tremendous darkness, and the stars overhead were pure and bright because of the increasingly thin air as we mounted the high hill of the western plateau, about a foot a mile, so they say, and no trees obstructing any low-leveled stars anywhere. And once I saw a moody whitefaced cow in the sage by the road as we flitted by. It was like riding a railroad train, just as steady and just as straight.

By and by we came to a town, slowed down, and Montana Slim said, "Ah, pisscall," but the Minnesotans didn't stop and went right on through. "Damn, I gotta go," said Slim.

"Go over the side," said somebody.

"Well, I *will*," he said, and slowly, as we all watched, he inched to the back of the platform on his haunch, holding on as best he could, till his legs dangled over. Somebody knocked on the window of the cab to bring this to the attention of the brothers. Their great smiles broke as they turned. And just as Slim was ready to proceed, precarious as it was already, they began zigzagging the truck at seventy miles an hour. He fell back a moment; we saw a whale's spout in the air; he struggled back to a sitting position. They swung the truck. Wham, over he went on his side, watering all over himself. In the roar we could hear him faintly cursing, like the whine of a man far across the hills. "Damn . . . damn . . ." He never knew we were doing this deliberately; he just struggled, as grim as Job. When he was finished, as such, he was wringing wet, and now he had to edge and shimmy his way back, and with a most woebegone look, and everybody laughing, except the sad blond boy, and the Minnesotans roaring in the cab. I handed him the bottle to make up for it.

"What the hail," he said, "was they doing that on purpose?"

"They sure were."

"Well, damn me, I didn't know that. I know I tried it back in Nebraska and didn't have half so much trouble."

We came suddenly into the town of Ogallala, and here the fellows in the cab called out, "*Pisscall!*" and with great good delight. Slim stood sullenly by the truck, ruing a lost opportunity. The two Dakota boys said good-by to everybody and figured they'd start harvesting here. We watched them disappear in the night toward the shacks at the end of town where lights were burning, where a watcher of the night in jeans said the employment men would be. I had to buy more cigarettes. Gene and the blond boy followed me to stretch their legs. I walked into the least likely place in the world, a kind of lonely Plains soda fountain for the local teenage girls and boys. They were dancing, a few of them, to the music on the jukebox. There was a lull when we came in. Gene and Blondey just stood there, looking at nobody; all they wanted was cigarettes. There were some pretty girls, too. And one of them made eyes at Blondey and he never saw it, and if he had he wouldn't have cared, he was so sad and gone.

I bought a pack each for them; they thanked me. The truck was ready to go. It was getting on midnight now, and cold. Gene, who'd been around the country more times than he could count on his fingers and toes, said the best thing to do now was for all of us to bundle up under the big tarpaulin or we'd freeze. In this manner, and with the rest of the bottle, we kept warm as the air grew ice-cold and pinged our ears. The stars seemed to get brighter the more we climbed the High Plains. We were in Wyoming now. Flat on my back, I stared straight up at the magnificent firmament, glorying in the time I was making, in how far I had come from sad Bear Mountain after all, and tingling with kicks at the thought of what lay ahead of me in Denver—whatever, whatever it would be. And Mississippi Gene began to sing a song. He sang it in a melodious, quiet voice, with a river accent, and it was simple, just "I got a purty little girl, she's sweet six-teen, she's the purtiest thing you ever seen," repeating it with other lines thrown in, all concerning how far he'd been and how he wished he could go back to her but he done lost her.

I said, "Gene, that's the prettiest song."

"It's the sweetest I know," he said with a smile.

"I hope you get where you're going, and be happy when you do."

"I always make out and move along one way or the other."

Montana Slim was asleep. He woke up and said to me, "Hey, Blackie, how about you and me investigatin' Cheyenne together tonight before you go to Denver?"

"Sure thing." I was drunk enough to go for anything.

As the truck reached the outskirts of Cheyenne, we saw the high red lights of the local radio station, and suddenly we were bucking through a great crowd of people that poured along both sidewalks. "Hell's bells, it's Wild West Week," said Slim. Big crowds of businessmen, fat businessmen in boots and ten-gallon hats, with their hefty wives in cowgirl attire, bustled and whooped on the wooden sidewalks of old Cheyenne; farther down were the long stringy boulevard lights of new downtown Cheyenne, but the celebration was focusing on Oldtown. Blank guns went off. The saloons were crowded to the sidewalk. I was amazed, and at the same time I felt it was ridiculous: in my first shot at the West I was seeing to what absurd devices it had fallen to keep its proud tradition. We had to jump off the truck and say good-by; the Minnesotans weren't interested in hanging around. It was sad to see them go, and I realized that I would never see any of them again, but that's the way it was. "You'll freeze your ass tonight," I warned. "Then you'll burn 'em in the desert tomorrow afternoon."

"That's all right with me long's as we get out of this cold night," said Gene. And the truck left, threading its way through the crowds, and nobody paying attention to the strangeness of the kids inside the tarpaulin, staring at the town like babes from a coverlet. I watched it disappear into the night.

5

I was with Montana Slim and we started hitting the bars. I had about seven dollars, five of which I foolishly squandered that night. First we milled with all the cowboy-dudded tourists and oilmen and ranchers, at bars, in doorways, on the sidewalk; then for a while I shook Slim, who was wandering a little slaphappy in the street from all the whisky and beer: he was that kind of drinker; his eyes got glazed, and in a minute he'd be telling an absolute stranger about things. I went into a chili joint and the waitress was Mexican and beautiful. I ate, and then I wrote her a little love note on the back of the bill. The chili joint was deserted; everybody was somewhere else, drinking. I told her to turn the bill over. She read it and laughed. It was a little poem about how I wanted her to come and see the night with me.

"I'd love to, Chiquito, but I have a date with my boy friend."

"Can't you shake him?"

"No, no, I don't," she said sadly, and I loved the way she said it.

"Some other time I'll come by here," I said, and she said, "Any time, kid." Still I hung around, just to look at her, and had another cup of coffee. Her boy friend came in sullenly and wanted to know when she was off. She bustled around to close the place quick. I had to get out. I gave her a smile when I left. Things were going on as wild as ever outside, except that the fat burpers were getting drunker and whooping up louder. It was funny. There were Indian chiefs wandering around in big headdresses and really solemn among the flushed drunken faces. I saw Slim tottering along and joined him.

He said, "I just wrote a postcard to my Paw in Montana. You reckon you can find a mailbox and put it in?" It was a strange request; he gave me the postcard and tottered through the swinging doors of a saloon. I took the card, went to the box, and took a quick look at it. "Dear Paw, I'll be home Wednesday. Everything's all right with me and I hope the same is with you. Richard." It gave me a different idea of him; how tenderly polite he was with his father. I went in the bar and joined him. We picked up two girls, a pretty young blonde and a fat brunette. They were dumb and sullen, but we wanted to make them. We took them to a rickety nightclub that was already closing, and there I spent all but two dollars on Scotches for them and beer for us. I was getting drunk and didn't care; everything was fine. My whole being and purpose was pointed at the little blonde. I wanted to go in there with all my strength. I hugged her and wanted to tell her. The nightclub closed and we all wandered out in the rickety dusty streets. I looked up at the sky; the pure, wonderful stars were still there, burning. The girls wanted to go to the bus station, so we all went, but they apparently wanted to meet some sailor who was there waiting for them, a cousin of the fat girl's, and the sailor had friends with him. I said to the blonde, "What's up?" She said she wanted to go home, in Colorado just over the line south of Cheyenne. "I'll take you in a bus," I said.

"No, the bus stops on the highway and I have to walk across that damn prairie all by myself. I spend all afternoon looking at the damn thing and I don't aim to walk over it tonight."

"Ah, listen, we'll take a nice walk in the prairie flowers."

"There ain't no flowers there," she said. "I want to go to New York. I'm sick and tired of this. Ain't no place to go but Cheyenne, and ain't nothin in Cheyenne."

"Ain't nothin in New York."

"Hell there ain't," she said with a curl of her lips.

The bus station was crowded to the doors. All kinds of people were waiting for buses or just standing around; there were a lot of Indians, who watched everything with their stony eyes. The girl disengaged herself from my talk and joined the sailor and the others. Slim was dozing on a bench. I sat down. The floors of bus stations are the same all over the country, always covered with butts and spit and they give a feeling of sadness that only bus stations have. For a moment it was no different from being in Newark, except for the great hugeness outside that I loved so much. I rued the way I had broken up the purity of my entire trip, not saving every dime, and dawdling and not really making time, fooling around with this sullen girl and spending all my money. It made me sick. I hadn't slept in so long I got too tired to curse and fuss and went off to sleep; I curled up on the seat with my canvas bag for a pillow, and slept till eight o'clock in the morning among the dreamy murmurs and noises of the station and of hundreds of people passing.

I woke up with a big headache. Slim was gone—to Montana, I guess. I went outside. And there in the blue air I saw for the first time, far off, the great snowy tops of the Rocky Mountains. I took a deep breath. I had to get to Denver at once. First I ate a breakfast, a modest one of toast and coffee and one egg, and then I cut out of town to the highway. The Wild West festival was still going on; there was a rodeo, and the whooping and jumping were about to start all over again. I left it behind me. I wanted to see my gang in Denver. I crossed a railroad overpass and reached a bunch of shacks where two highways forked off, both for Denver. I took the one nearest the mountains so I could look at them, and pointed myself that way. I got a ride right off from a young fellow from Connecticut who was driving around the country in his jalopy, painting; he was the son of an editor in the East. He talked and talked; I was sick from drinking and from the altitude. At one point I almost had to stick my head out the window. But by the time he let me off at Longmont, Colorado, I was feeling normal again and had even started telling him about the state of my own travels. He wished me luck.

It was beautiful in Longmont. Under a tremendous old tree was a bed of green lawn-grass belonging to a gas station. I asked the attendant if I could sleep there, and he said sure; so I stretched out a wool shirt, laid my face flat on it, with an elbow out, and with one eye cocked at the snowy Rockies in the hot sun for just a moment. I fell asleep for two delicious hours, the only discomfort being an occasional Colorado ant. And here I am in Colorado! I kept thinking gleefully. Damn! damn! damn! I'm making it! And after a refreshing sleep filled with cobwebby dreams of my past life in the East I got up, washed in the station men's room, and strode off, fit and slick as a fiddle, and got me a rich thick milkshake at the roadhouse to put some freeze in my hot, tormented stomach.

Incidentally, a very beautiful Colorado gal shook me that cream; she was all smiles too; I was grateful, it made up for last night. I said to myself, Wow! What'll *Denver* be like! I got on that hot road, and off I went in a brand-new car driven by a Denver businessman of about thirty-five. He went seventy. I tingled all over; I counted minutes and subtracted miles. Just ahead, over the rolling wheatfields all golden beneath the distant snows of Estes, I'd be seeing old Denver at last. I pictured myself in a Denver bar that night, with all the gang, and in their eyes I would be strange and ragged and like the Prophet who has walked across the land to bring the dark Word, and the only Word I had was "Wow!" The man and I had a long, warm conversation about our respective schemes in life, and before I knew it we were going over the wholesale fruitmarkets outside Denver; there were smokestacks, smoke railyards, red-brick buildings, and the distant downtown gray-stone buildings, and here I was in Denver. He let me off at Larimer Street. I stumbled along with the most wicked grin of joy in the world, among the old bums and beat cowboys of Larimer Street.

• • •

7

The following ten days were, as W. C. Fields said, "fraught with eminent peril"—and mad. I moved in with Roland Major in the really swank apartment that belonged to Tim Gray's folks. We each had a bedroom, and there was a kitchenette with food in the icebox, and a huge living room where Major sat in his silk dressing gown composing his latest Hemingwayan short story—a choleric, red-faced, pudgy hater of everything, who could turn on the warmest and most charming smile in the world when real life confronted him sweetly in the night. He sat like that at his desk, and I jumped around over the thick soft rug, wearing only my chino pants. He'd just written a story about a guy who comes to Denver for the first time. His name is Phil. His traveling companion is a mysterious and quiet fellow called Sam. Phil goes out to dig Denver and gets hung-up with arty types. He comes back to the hotel room. Lugubriously he says, "Sam, they're here too." And Sam is just looking out the window sadly. "Yes," says Sam, "I know." And the point was that Sam didn't have to go and look to know this. The arty types were all over America, sucking up its blood. Major and I were great pals; he thought I was the farthest thing from an arty type. Major liked good wines, just like Hemingway. He reminisced about his recent trip to France. "Ah, Sal, if you could sit with me high in the Basque country with a cool bottle of Poignon Dix-neuf, then you'd know there are other things besides boxcars."

"I know that. It's just that I love boxcars and I love to read the names on them like Missouri Pacific, Great Northern, Rock Island Line. By Gad, Major, if I could tell you everything that happened to me hitching here."

The Rawlinses lived a few blocks away. This was a delightful family—a youngish mother, part owner of a decrepit, ghost-town hotel, with five sons and two daughters. The wild son was Ray Rawlins, Tim Gray's boyhood buddy. Ray came roaring in to get me and we took to each other right away. We went off and drank in the Colfax bars. One of Ray's sisters was a beautiful blonde called Babe—a tennis-playing, surf-riding doll of the West. She was Tim Gray's girl. And Major, who was only passing through Denver and doing so in real style in the apartment, was going out with Tim's Gray's sister Betty. I was the only guy without a girl. I asked everybody, "Where's Dean?" They made smiling negative answers.

Then finally it happened. The phone rang, and it was Carlo Marx. He gave me the address of his basement apartment. I said, "What are you doing in Denver? I mean what are you *doing*? What's going on?"

"Oh, wait till I tell you."

I rushed over to meet him. He was working in May's department store nights; crazy Ray Rawlins called him up there from a bar, getting janitors to run after Carlo with a story that somebody had died. Carlo immediately thought it was me who had died. And Rawlins said over the phone, "Sal's in Denver," and gave him my addres and phone.

"And where is Dean?"

"Dean is in Denver. Let me tell you." And he told me that Dean was making love to two girls at the same time, they being Marylou, his first wife, who waited for him in a hotel room, and Camille, a new girl, who waited for him in a hotel room. "Between the two of them he rushes to me for our own unfinished business."

"And what business is that?"

"Dean and I are embarked on a tremendous season together. We're trying to communicate with absolute honesty and absolute completeness everything on our minds. We've had to take benzedrine. We sit on the bed crosslegged, facing each other. I have finally taught Dean that he can do anything he wants, become mayor of Denver, marry a million-airess, or become the greatest poet since Rimbaud. But he keeps rushing out to see the midget auto races. I go with him. He jumps and yells, excited. You know, Sal, Dean is really hung-up on things like that." Marx said "Hmm" in his soul and thought about this.

"What's the schedule?" I said. There was always a schedule in Dean's life.

"The schedule is this: I came off work a half-hour ago. In that time Dean is balling Marylou at the hotel and gives me time to change and dress. At one sharp he rushes from Marylou to Camille—of course neither one of them knows what's going on—and bangs her once, giving me time to arrive at one-thirty. Then he comes out with me—first he has to beg with Camille, who's already started hating me—and we come here to talk till six in the morning. We usually spend more time than that, but it's getting awfully complicated and he's pressed for time. Then at six he goes back to Marylou—and he's going to spend all day. tomorrow running around to get the necessary papers for their divorce. Marylou's all for it, but she insists on banging in the interim. She says she loves him—so does Camille."

Then he told me how Dean had met Camille. Roy Johnson, the poolhall boy, had found her in a bar and took her to a hotel; pride taking over his sense, he invited the whole gang to come up and see her. Everybody sat around talking with Camille. Dean did nothing but look out the window. Then when everybody left, Dean merely looked at Camille, pointed at his wrist, made a sign "four" (meaning he'd be back at four), and went out. At three the door was locked to Roy Johnson. At four it was opened to Dean. I wanted to go right out and see the madman. Also he had promised to fix me up; he knew all the girls in Denver.

Carlo and I went through rickety streets in the Denver night. The air was soft, the stars so fine, the promise of every cobbled alley so great, that I thought I was in a dream. We came to the rooming house where Dean haggled with Camille. It was an old red-brick building surrounded by wooden garages and old trees that stuck up from behind fences. We went up carpeted stairs. Carlo knocked; then he darted to the back to hide; he didn't want Camille to see him. I stood in the door. Dean opened it stark naked. I saw a brunette on the bed, one beautiful creamy thigh covered with black lace, look up with mild wonder.

"Why, Sa-a-al!" said Dean. "Well now—ah—ahem—yes, of course, you've arrived—you old sonumbitch you finally got on that old road. Well, now, look here—we must—yes, yes, at once—we must, we really must! Now Camille—" And he swirled on her. "Sal is here, this is my old buddy from New Yor-r-k, this is his first night in Denver and it's absolutely necessary for me to take him out and fix him up with a girl."

"But what time will you be back?"

"It is now" (looking at his watch) "exactly one-fourteen. I shall be back at exactly *three*-fourteen, for our hour of reverie together, real sweet reverie, darling, and then, as you know, as I told you and as we agreed, I have to go and see the one-legged lawyer about those papers —in the middle of the night, strange as it seems and as I tho-ro-ly explained." (This was a coverup for his rendezvous with Carlo, who was still hiding.) "So now in this exact minute I must dress, put on my pants, go back to life, that is to outside life, streets and what not, as we agreed, it is now one-*fifteen* and time's running, running—"

"Well, all right, Dean, but please be sure and be back at three."

"Just as I said, darling, and remember not three but three-fourteen. Are we straight in the deepest and most wonderful depths of our souls, dear darling?" And he went over and kissed her several times. On the wall was a nude drawing of Dean, enormous dangle and all, done by Camille. I was amazed. Everything was so crazy.

Off we rushed into the night; Carlo joined us in an alley. And we proceeded down the narrowest, strangest, and most crooked little city street I've ever seen, deep in the heart of Denver Mexican-town. We talked in loud voices in the sleeping stillness. "Sal," said Dean, "I have just the girl waiting for you at this very minute—if she's off duty" (looking at his watch). "A waitress, Rita Bettencourt, find chick, slightly hung-up on a few sexual difficulties which I've tried to straighten up and I think you can manage, you fine gone daddy you. So we'll go there at once—we must bring beer, no, they have some themselves, and damn!" he said socking his palm. "I've just got to get into her sister Mary tonight."

"What?" said Carlo. "I thought we were going to talk."

"Yes, yes, after."

"Oh, these Denver doldrums!" yelled Carlo to the sky.

"Isn't he the finest sweetest fel-low in the world?" said Dean, punching me in the ribs. "Look at him. *Look* at him!" And Carlo began his monkey dance in the streets of life as I'd seen him do many times everywhere in New York.

And all I could say was, "Well, what the hell are we doing in Denver?"

"Tomorrow, Sal, I know where I can find you a job," said Dean, reverting to businesslike tones. "So I'll call on you, soon as I have an hour off from Marylou, and cut right into that apartment of yours, say hello to Major, and take you on a trolley (damn, I've no car) to the

Camargo markets, where you can begin working at once and collect a paycheck come Friday. We're really all of us bottomly broke. I haven't had time to work in weeks. Friday night beyond all doubts the three of us—the old threesome of Carlo, Dean, and Sal—must go to the midget auto races, and for that I can get us a ride from a guy downtown I know. . . ." And on and on into the night.

We got to the house where the waitress sisters lived. The one for me was still working; the sister that Dean wanted was in. We sat down on her couch. I was scheduled at this time to call Ray Rawlins. I did. He came over at once. Coming into the door, he took off his shirt and undershirt and began hugging the absolute stranger, Mary Bettencourt. Bottles rolled on the floor. Three o'clock came. Dean rushed off for his hour of reverie with Camille. He was back on time. The other sister showed up. We all needed a car now, and we were making too much noise. Ray Rawlins called up a buddy with a car. He came. We all piled in; Carlo was trying to conduct his scheduled talk with Dean in the back seat, but there was too much confusion. "Let's all go to my apartment!" I shouted. We did; the moment the car stopped there I jumped out and stood on my head in the grass. All my keys fell out; I never found them. We ran, shouting, into the building. Roland Major stood barring our way in his silk dressing gown.

"I'll have no goings-on like this in Tim Gray's apartment!"

"What?" we all shouted. There was confusion. Rawlins was rolling in the grass with one of the waitresses. Major wouldn't let us in. We swore to call Tim Gray and confirm the party and also invite him. Instead we all rushed back to the Denver downtown hangouts. I suddenly found myself alone in the street with no money. My last dollar was gone.

I walked five miles up Colfax to my comfortable bed in the apartment. Major had to let me in. I wondered if Dean and Carlo were having their heart-to-heart. I would find out later. The nights in Denver are cool, and I slept like a log.

• • •

12

In Oakland I had a beer among the bums of a saloon with a wagon wheel in front of it, and I was on the road again. I walked clear across Oakland to get to the Fresno road. Two rides took me to Bakersfield, four hundred miles south. The first was the mad one, with a burly blond kid in a souped-up rod. "See that toe?" he said as he gunned the heap to eighty and passed everybody on the road. "Look at it." It was swathed in bandages. "I just had it amputated this morning. The bastards wanted me to stay in the hospital. I packed my bag and left. What's a toe?" Yes, indeed, I said to myself, look out now, and I hung on. You never saw a driving fool like that. He made Tracy in no time. Tracy is a railroad town; brakemen eat surly meals in diners by the tracks. Trains howl away across the valley. The sun goes down long and red. All the magic names of the valley unrolled—Manteca, Madera, all the rest. Soon it got dusk, a grapy dusk, a purple dusk over tangerine groves and long melon fields; the sun the color of pressed grapes, slashed with burgundy red, the fields the color of love and Spanish mysteries. I stuck my head out the window and took deep breaths of the fragrant air. It was the most beautiful of all moments. The madman was a breakman with the Southern Pacific and he lived in Fresno; his father was also a brakeman. He lost his toe in the Oakland yards, switching, I didn't quite understand how. He drove me into buzzing Fresno and let me off by the south side of town. I went for a quick Coke in a little grocery by the tracks, and here came a melancholy Armenian youth along the red boxcars, and just at that moment a locomotive howled, and I said to myself, Yes, yes, Saroyan's town.

I had to go south; I got on the road. A man in a brand-new pickup truck picked me up. He was from Lubbock, Texas, and was in the trailer business. "You want to buy a trailer?" he asked me. "Any time, look me up." He told stories about his father in Lubbock. "One night my old man left the day's receipts settin on top of the safe, plumb forgot. What happened—a thief came in the night, acetylene torch and all, broke open the safe, riffled up the papers, kicked over a few chairs, and left. And that thousand dollars was settin right there on top of the safe, what do you know about that?"

He let me off south of Bakersfield, and then my adventure began. It grew cold. I put on the flimsy Army raincoat I'd bought in Oakland for three dollars and shuddered in the road. I was standing in front of an ornate Spanish-type motel that was lit like a jewel. The cars rushed by, LA-bound. I gestured frantically. It was too cold. I stood there till midnight, two hours straight, and cursed and cursed. It was just like Stuart, Iowa, again. There was nothing to do but spend a little over two dollars for a bus the remaining miles to Los Angeles. I walked back along the highway to Bakersfield and into that station, and sat down on a bench.

THE MEXICAN GIRL
1947

I HAD BOUGHT MY TICKET and was waiting for the L.A. bus when all of a sudden I saw the cutest little Mexican girl in slacks come cutting across my sight. She was in one of the buses that had just pulled in with a big sigh of airbrakes and was discharging passengers for a rest stop. Her breasts stuck out straight; her little thighs looked delicious; her hair was long and lustrous black; and her eyes were great blue windows with timidities inside. I wished I was on her bus. A pain stabbed my heart, as it did every time I saw a girl I loved who was going the opposite direction in this too big world. "Los Angeles coach now loading in door two," says the announcer and I get on. I saw her sitting alone. I dropped right opposite her on the other window and began scheming right off. I was so lonely, so sad, so tired, so quivering, so broken, so beat that I got up my courage, the courage necessary to approach a strange girl, and acted. Even then I had to spend five minutes beating my thighs in the dark as the bus rolled down the road. "You gotta, you gotta or you'll die! Damn fool talk to her! What's wrong with you? Aren't you tired enough of yourself by now?" And before I knew what I was doing I leaned across the aisle to her (she was trying to sleep on the seat). "Miss, would you like to use my raincoat for a pillow?" She looked up with a smile and said, "No, thank you very much." I sat back trembling; I lit a butt. I waited till she looked at me, with a sad little sidelook of love, and I got right up and leaned over her. "May I sit with you, Miss?"

"If you wish."

And this I did. "Where going?"

"L.A." I loved the way she said L.A.; I love the way everybody says L.A. on the Coast; it's their one and only golden town when all is said and done.

"That's where I'm going too!" I cried. "I'm very glad you let me sit with you, I was very lonely and I've been traveling a hell of a long time." And we settled down to telling our stories. Her story was this; she had a husband and child. The husband beat her so she left him, back at Sabinal south of Fresno, and was going to L.A. to live with her sister awhile. She left her little son with her family, who were grape pickers and lived in a shack in the vineyards. She had nothing to do but brood and get mad. I felt like putting my arms around her right away. We talked and talked. She said she loved to talk with me. Pretty soon she was saying she wished she could go to New York too. "Maybe we could!" I laughed. The bus groaned up Grapevine Pass and then we were coming down into the great sprawls of light. Without coming to any particular agreement we began holding hands, and in the same way it was mutely and beautifully and purely decided that when I got my hotel room in L.A. she would be beside me. I ached all over for her; I leaned my face in her beautiful hair. Her little shoulders drove me mad, I hugged her and hugged her. And she loved it.

"I love love," she said closing her eyes. I promised her beautiful love. I gloated over her. Our stories were told, we subsided into silence and sweet anticipatory thoughts. It was as simple as that. You could have all your Peaches and Vi's and Ruth Glenarms and Marylous and Eleanors and Carmens in this world, this was my girl and my kind of girlsoul, and I told her that. She confessed she saw me watching from the bus station bench. "I thought you was a nice college boy."

"Oh I'm a college boy!" I assured her. The bus arrived in Hollywood. In the gray dirty dawn, like the dawn Joel McCrea met Veronica Lake in the diner in the picture *Sullivan's Travels,* she slept in my lap. I looked greedily out the window; stucco houses and palms and drive-ins, the whole mad thing, the ragged promised land, the fantastic end of America. We got off the bus at Main Street which was no different than where you get off a bus in Kansas City or Chicago or Boston, redbrick, dirty, characters drifting by, trolleys grating in the hopeless dawn, the whorey smell of a big city.

And here my mind went haywire, I don't know why. I began getting foolish paranoiac visions that Teresa, or Terry, her name, was a common little hustler who worked the buses for a guy's bucks by making regular appointments like ours in L.A. where she brought the sucker first to a breakfast place, where her boy waited, and then to a certain hotel to which he had access with his gun or his whatever. I never confessed this to her. We ate breakfast and a pimp kept watching us; I fancied Terry was making secret eyes at him. I was tired and felt strange and lost in a faraway, disgusting place. The goof of terror took over my thoughts and made me act petty and cheap. "Do you know that guy?" I said.

"What guy you mean, ho-ney?" I let it drop. She was slow and hung up in everything she did; it took her a long time to eat, she chewed slowly and stared into space, and smoked a cigarette slowly, and kept talking, and I was like a haggard ghost suspicioning every move she made, thinking she was stalling for time. This was all a fit of sickness. I was sweating as we went down the street hand in hand. Fellows kept turning and looking at us. The first hotel we hit had a vacant room and before I knew it I was locking the door behind me and she was sitting on the bed taking off her shoes. I kissed her meekly. Better she'd never know. To relax our nerves I knew we needed whiskey, especially me. I ran out and fiddled all over for twelve blocks hurrying till I found a pint of whiskey for sale at a newsstand. I ran back all energy. Terry was in the bathroom fixing her face. I poured one big drink in a waterglass and we had slugs. Oh it was sweet and delicious and worth my whole life and lugubrious voyage. I stood behind her at the mirror and we danced in the bathroom that way. I began talking about my friends back East. I said, "You oughta meet a great girl I know called Dorie. She's a sixfoot redhead. If you came to New York she'd show you where to get work."

"Who is this sixfoot redhead?" she demanded suspiciously. "Why do you tell me about her?" In her simple soul she couldn't fathom my kind of glad nervous talk. I let it drop. She began to get drunk in the bathroom.

"Come on to bed!" I kept saying.

"Sixfoot redhead, hey? And I thought you was a nice college boy, I saw you in your nice sweater and I said to myself, 'Hmm ain't he nice'—No! And no! And no! You have to be a goddam pimp like all of them!"

"What in the hell are you talking about?"

"Don't stand there and tell me that sixfoot redhead ain't a madam, 'cause I know a madam when I hear about one, and you, you're just a pimp like all the rest of 'em I meet, everybody's a pimp."

"Listen Terry, I am not a pimp. I swear to you on the Bible I am not a pimp. Why should I be a pimp. My only interest is you."

"All the time I thought I met a nice boy. I was so glad, I hugged myself and said, 'Hmm a real nice boy instead of a damn pimp!' "

"Terry," I pleaded with all my soul, "please listen to me and understand. I'm not a pimp, I'm just Sal Paradise, look at my wallet." And an hour ago I thought *she* was a hustler. How sad it was. Our minds with their store of madness had diverged. O gruesome life how I moaned and pleaded and then I got mad and realized I was pleading with a dumb little Mexican wench and I told her so; and before I knew it I picked up her red pumps and threw them at the bathroom door and told her to get out. "Go on, beat it!" I'd sleep and forget it; I had my own life; my own sad and ragged life forever. There was a dead silence in the bathroom. I took my clothes off and went to bed. Terry came out with tears of sorriness in her eyes. In her simple and funny little mind had been decided the fact that a pimp does not throw a woman's shoes against the door and does not tell her to get out. In reverent and sweet silence she took her things off and slipped her tiny body into the sheets with me. It was brown as grapes. Her hips were so narrow she couldn't bear a child without getting gashed open; a Caesarian scar crossed her poor belly. Her legs were like little sticks. She was only four-foot-ten. I made love to her in the sweetness of the weary morning. Then, two tired angels of some kind, hung up forlornly in an L.A. shelf, having found the closest and most delicious thing in life together, we fell asleep and slept till late afternoon.

For the next fifteen days we were together for better or worse. We decided to hitchhike to New York together; she was going to be my girl in town. I envisioned wild complexities, a season, a new season. First we had to work and earn enough money for the trip. Terry was all for starting at once with my twenty dollars. I didn't like it. And like a damnfool I considered the problem for two days reading the want ads of wild new L.A. papers I'd never seen before in my life, in cafeterias and bars, until my twenty'd dwindled to twelve. The situation was growing. We were happy as kids in our little hotel room. In the middle of the night I got up because I couldn't sleep, pulled the cover over baby's bare brown shoulder, and examined the L.A. night. What brutal, hot, siren-whining nights they are! Right across the street there was trouble. An old rickety rundown roominghouse was the scene of some kind of tragedy. The cruiser was pulled up below and the cops were questioning an old man with gray hair. Sobbings came from within. I could hear everything, together with the hum of my hotel neon. I never felt sadder in my life. L.A. is the loneliest and most brutal of American cities; New York gets godawful cold in the winter but there's a feeling of whacky comradeship somewhere in some streets. L.A. is a jungle.

South Main Street, where Terry and I took strolls with hotdogs, was a fantastic carnival of lights and wildness. Booted cops frisked people on practically every corner. The beatest characters in the country swarmed on the sidewalks—all of it under those soft Southern California stars that are lost in the brown halo of the huge desert encampment L.A. really is. You could smell tea, weed, I mean marijuana floating in the air, together with the chili beans and beer. That grand wild sound of bop floated from beerparlor jukes, Dizzy and Bird and Bags and early Miles; it mixed medleys with every kind of cowboy and boogiewoogie in the American night. Everybody looked like Hunkey. Wild Negroes with bop caps and goatees came laughing by; then longhaired broken-down hipsters straight off Route 66 from New York, then old desert rats carrying packs and heading for a park bench at the Plaza, then Methodist ministers with raveled sleeves, and an occasional Nature Boy saint in beard and sandals. I wanted to meet them all, talk to everybody, but Terry hurried along, we were busy trying to get a buck together, like everybody else.

We went to Hollywood to try to work in the drugstore at Sunset and Vine. The questions that were asked of us in upstairs offices to determine our fitness for the slime of the sodafountain greaseracks were so sinister that I had to laugh. It turned my gut. Sunset and Vine!— what a corner! Now there's a corner! Great families off jalopies from the hinterlands stood around the sidewalk gaping for sight of some movie star and the movie star never showed up. When a limousine passed they rushed eagerly to the curb and ducked to look: some character in dark glasses sat inside with a bejeweled blonde. "Don Ameche! Don Ameche!" "No George Murphy! George Murphy!" They milled around looking at one another. Luscious little girls by the thousands rushed around with drive-in trays; they'd come to Hollywood to be movie stars and instead got all involved in everybody's garbage, including Darryl Zanuck's. Handsome queer boys who had come to Hollywood to be cowboys walked around wetting their eyebrows with hincty fingertip. Those beautiful little gone gals cut by in slacks in a continuous unbelievable stream; you thought you were in heaven but it was only Purgatory and everybody was about to be pardoned, paroled, powdered and put down; the girls came to be starlets; they up-ended in drive-ins with pouts and goosepimples on their bare legs. Terry and I tried to find work at the drive-ins. It was no soap anywhere, thank God. Hollywood Boulevard was a great screaming frenzy of cars; there were minor accidents at least once a minute; everybody was rushing off toward the farthest palm . . . and beyond that was the desert and nothingness.

So they thought. You don't expect everybody to know that you can find water in a kopash cactus, or sweet taffy in your old mesquite. Hollywood Sams stood in front of swank restaurants arguing exactly, loudly and showoff the same way Broadway Sams argue on Jacobs Beach sidewalks, New York, only here they wore lightweight suits and their talk was even more dreary and unutterably cornier. Tall cadaverous preachers shuddered by. Seventy-year-old World Rosicrucian ladies with tiaras in their hair stood under palms signifying nothing. Fat screaming women ran across the Boulevard to get in line for the quiz shows. I saw Jerry Colonna buying a car at Buick Motors; he was inside the vast plateglass window fingering his mustachio, incredible, real, like seeing the Three Stooges seriously ashen-faced in a real room. Terry and I ate in a cafeteria downtown which was decorated to look like a grotto, with metal tits spurting everywhere and great impersonal stone buttoxes belonging to deities of fish and soapy Neptune. People ate lugubrious meals around the waterfalls, their faces green with marine sorrow. All the cops in L.A. looked like handsome gigolos; obviously, they'd come to L.A. to make the movies. Everybody had come to make the movies, even me. Terry and I were finally reduced to trying to get jobs on South Main Street among the beat countermen and dishgirls who made no bones about their beatness and even there it was no go. We still had twelve dollars.

"Man, I'm going to get my clothes from Sis and we'll hitchhike to New York," said Terry. "Come on man. Let's do it. If you can't boogie I know I'll show you how." That last part was a song of hers she kept singing, after a famous record. We hurried to her sister's house in the sliverous Mexican shacks somewhere beyond Alameda Avenue. I waited in a dark alley behind Mexican kitchens because her sister wasn't supposed to see me and like it. Dogs ran by. There were little lamps illuminating the little rat alleys. I stood there swigging from the bottle of wine and eying the stars and digging the sounds of the neighborhood. I could hear Terry and her sister arguing in the soft warm night. I was ready for anything. Terry came out and led me by the hand to Central Avenue, which is the colored main drag of L.A. And what a wild place it is, with chicken-shacks barely big enough to house a jukebox and the jukebox blowing nothing but blues, bop and jump. We went up dirty tenement stairs and came to the room of Terry's friend, Margarina, a colored girl apparently named by her loving mother after the spelling on an oleo wrapper. Margarina, a lovely mulatto, owed Terry a skirt and a pair of shoes; her husband was black as spades and kindly. He went right out and bought a pint of whiskey to host me proper. I tried to pay part of it but he said no. They had two little children. The kids bounced on the bed, it was their play-place. They put their arms around me and looked at me with wonder. The wild humming night of Central Avenue, the night of Hamp's *Central Avenue Breakdown,* howled and boomed along outside. They were singing in the halls, singing from their windows, just hell be damned and lookout. Terry got her clothes and we said goodbye. We went down to a chickenshack and played records on the jukebox. Yakking with our beer we decided what to do: we decided to hitch to New York with our remaining monies. She had five dollars coming from her sister; we rushed back to the shacks. So before the daily room rent was due again we packed up and took off on a red car to Arcadia, California, where Santa Anita racetrack is located under snowcapped mountains as I well knew from boyhood pastings of horse-race pictures in sad old notebooks showing Azucar winning in 1935 the great $100,000 'Cap and you see dim snows heaped over the back-stretch mountains. Route 66. It was night. We were pointed toward that enormity which is the American continent. Holding hands we walked several miles down the dark road to get out of the populated district. It was a Saturday night. We stood under a roadlamp thumbing when suddenly cars full of young kids roared by with streamers flying. "Yaah! yaah! we won! we won!" they all shouted. Then they yoo-hooed us and got great glee out of seeing a guy and a girl on the road. Dozens of them passed in successive jalopies, young faces and "throaty young voices" as the saying goes. I hated every one of them. Who did they think they were yaahing at somebody on the road because they were little high school punks and their parents carved the roast beef on Sunday afternoons. Nor did we get a ride. We had to walk back to town and worst of all we needed coffee and had the misfortune of going into the same gaudy wood-laced place with old soda johns with beerfountain mustaches out front. The same kids were there but we were still minding our own business. Terry and I sipped our coffee and cocoa. We had battered bags and all the world before us . . . all that ground out there, that desert dirt and rat tat tat. We looked like a couple of sullen Indians in a Navajo Springs sodafountain, black bent heads at a table. The schoolkids saw now that Terry was a Mexican, a Pachuco wildcat; and that her boy was worse than that. With her pretty nose in the air she cut out of there and we wandered together in the dark up along the ditches of highways. I carried the bags and wanted to carry more. We made tracks and cut along and were breathing fogs in the cold night air. I didn't want to go on another minute without a warm night's rest in a warm sack together. Morning be damned, let's hide from the world another night. I wanted to fold her up in my system of limbs under no light but stars in the window. We went to a motel court and asked if they had a cabin. Yes. We bought a comfortable little suite for four dollars. I was spending my money anyhow. Shower, bath towels, wall radio and all, just for one more night. We held each other tight. We had long serious talks and took baths and discussed things on the pillow with light on and then with light out. Something was being proved, I was convincing her of something, which she accepted, and we concluded the pact in the dark, breathless. Then pleased, like little lambs.

In the morning we boldly struck out on our new plan. Terry wore her dark glasses with authority. Her pretty little severe face beneath, with the noble nose, almost hawk-like Indian nose, but with upswerved cute hollow cheekbones to make an oval and a prettywoman blush, with red ruby full lips and Aunt Jemima skirt teeth, mud nowhere on her but was imprinted in the pigment of the Mongol skin. We were going to take a bus to Bakersfield with the last eight dollars and work picking grapes. "See instead of going to New York now we're all set to work awhile and get what we need, then we'll go, in a bus, we won't have to hitchhike, you see how no good it is . . ."

We arrived in Bakersfield in late afternoon, with our plan to hit every fruit wholesaler in town. Terry said we could live in tents on the job. The thought of me lying there in a tent, and picking grapes in the cool California mornings after nights of guitar music and wine with dipped grapes, hit me right. "Don't worry about a thing."

But there were no jobs to be had and much confusion with everybody giving confused Indian information and innumerable tips ("Go out to County Road you'll find Sacano") and no job materialized. So we went to a Chinese restaurant and had a dollar's worth of chow mein among the sad Saturday afternoon families, digging them, and set out with reinforced bodies. We went across the Southern Pacific tracks to Mexican town. Terry jabbered with her brethren asking for jobs. It was night now, we had a few dollars left, and the little Mextown street was one blazing bulb of lights: movie marquees, fruit stands, penny arcades, Five and Tens and hundreds of rickety trucks and mudspattered jalopies parked all over. Whole Mexican fruitpicking families wandered around eating popcorn. Terry talked to everybody. I was beginning to despair. What I needed, what Terry needed too, was a drink so we bought a quart of California port wine for 35 cents and went to the railyards to drink. We found a place where hoboes had drawn up crates to sit over fires. We sat there and drank the wine. On our left were the freight cars, sad and sooty red beneath the moon; straight ahead the lights and air-port pokers of Bakersfield proper; to our right a tremendous aluminum Quonset warehouse. I remembered it later in passing. Ah it was a fine night, a warm night, a wine-drinking night, a moony night, and a night to hug your girl and talk and spit and be heavengoing. This we did. She was a drinking little fool and kept up with me and passed me and went right on talking till midnight. We never moved from those crates. Oc-casionally bums passed, Mexican mothers passed with children, and the prowl car came by and the cop got out to leak but most of the time we were alone and mixing up our souls more and ever more till it would be terribly hard to say goodbye. At midnight we got up and goofed toward the highway.

Terry had a new idea. We would hitch to Sabinal, her hometown up the San Joaquin Valley, and live in her brother's garage. Anything was all right to me, especially a nice garage. On the road I made Terry sit down on my bag to make her look like a woman in distress and right off a truck stopped and we ran for it all glee-giggles. The man was a good man, his truck was poor. He roared and crawled on up the Valley. We got to Sabinal in the wee hours of the morning not until after that tired sleepy beau' pushed his old rattle rig from Indian Ponce de Leon Springs of down-valley up the screaming cricket fields of grape and lemon four hours, to let us off, with a cheerful "So long pard," and here we were with the wine finished (I, while she slept in the truck). Now I'm stoned. The sky is gray in the east. "Wake, for morning in the bowl of night . . ." There was a quiet leafy square, we walked around it, past sleeping sodafountains and barber shops, looking for some garage. There was no garage. Ghostly white houses. A whistle stop on the S.P. A California town of old goldbottle times. She couldn't find her brother's garage but now we were going to find her brother's buddy, who would know. Nobody home. It all went on in rickety alleys of little Mextown Sabinal, wrong side of the tracks. As dawn began to break I lay flat on my back in the lawn of the town square, and I'd done that once before when they thought I was drowned in an eastern resort, and I kept saying over and over, "You won't tell what he done up in Weed will you? What'd he do up in Weed? You won't tell will you? What'd he do up in Weed?" This was from the picture *Of Mice and Men* with Burgess Meredith talking to the big foreman of the ranch; I thought we were near Weed. Terry giggled. Anything I did was all right with her. I could lay there and go on saying "What'd he do up in Weed?" till the ladies come out for church and she wouldn't care.

Because her brother was in these parts I figured we'd be all set soon and I took her to an old hotel by the tracks and we went to bed comfortably. Five dollars left. It was all smelling of fresh paint in there, and old mahogany mirrors and creaky. In the bright sunny morning Terry got up early and went to find her brother. I slept till noon; when I looked out the window I suddenly saw an S.P. freight going by with hundreds of hoboes reclining on the flatcars and in gons and rolling merrily along with packs for pillows and funny papers before their noses and some munching on good California grapes picked up by the watertank. "Damn!" I yelled. "Hooee! It *is* the promised land." They were all coming from Frisco; in a week they'd all be going back in the same grand style.

Terry arrived with her brother, his buddy, and her child. Her brother was a wildbuck Mexican hotcat with a hunger for booze, a great good kid. His buddy was a big flabby Mexican who spoke English without much accent and was anxious to please and overconcerned to prove something. I could see he had always had eyes for Terry. Her little boy was Raymond, seven years old, darkeyed and sweet. Well there we were, and another wild day began.

Her brother's name was Freddy. He had a '38 Chevvy. We piled into that and took off to parts unknown. "Where we going?" I asked. The buddy did the explaining, Ponzo, that's what everybody called him. He stank. I found out why. His business was selling manure to farmers, he had a truck. We were going to check on that. Freddy always had three or four dollars in his pocket and was happygolucky about things. He always said "That's right man, there you go—dah you go, dah you go!" And he went. He drove 70 miles an hour in the old heap and we went to Madera beyond Fresno, throwing dust back of our tires, and saw farmers about manure. Their voices drawled to us from the hot sun open. Freddy had a bottle. "Today we drink, tomorrow we work. Dah you go man—take a shot." Terry sat in back with her baby; I looked back at her and saw a flush of homecoming joy on her face. She'd been driving around like this for years. The beautiful green countryside of October in California reeled by madly. I was guts and juice again and ready to go.

"Where do we go now man?"

"We go find a farmer with some manure layin around—tomorrow

we drive back in the truck and pick up. Man we'll make a lot of money. Don't worry about nothing."

"We're all in this together!" yelled Ponzo, who wouldn't have got the manure by himself. I saw this was so—everywhere I went everybody was in it together. We raced through the crazy streets of Fresno and on up the Valley to some farmers in certain backroads. Ponzo got out of the car and conducted confused conversations with old Mexicans; nothing of course came of it.

"What we need is a drink!" yelled Freddy and off we went to a crossroads saloon. Americans are always drinking in crossroads saloons on Sunday afternoon; they bring their kids; there are piles of manure outside the screendoor; they gabble and brawl over brews and grow haggly baggly and you hear harsh laughter rising from routs and song, nobody's really having any fun but faces get redder and time flies fading faster. But everything's fine. Come nightfall the kids come crying and the parents are drunk. Around the jukebox they go weaving back to the house. Everywhere in America I've been in crossroads saloons drinking with whole families. The kids eat popcorn and chips and play in back or sneak stale beers for all I know. Freddy and I and Ponzo and Terry sat there drinking and shouting. Vociferous types. The sun got red. Nothing had been accomplished. What was there to accomplish? "Mañana," said Freddy, "mañana, man, we make it; have another beer, man, dah you go, DAH YOU GO!" We staggered out and got in the car; off we went to a highway bar. This one had blue neons and pink lights. Ponzo was a big loud vociferous type who knew everybody in San Joaquin Valley apparently from the way every time we clomped into a joint he'd let out loud Ho-Yo's. Now I had a few bucks left and ruefully counted them. Festooned all over my brain were the ideas of going back home to New York at once with this handful of change, hitching as I'd been doing at Bakersfield that night, leave Terry with her wild brothers and mad Mexican manure piles and mañanas of crazy beer. But I was having a hell of a time. From the highway bar I went with Ponzo alone in the car to find some certain farmer; instead we wound up in Madera Mextown digging the girls and trying to pick up a few for him and Freddy; and then, as purple dusk descended over the grape country, I found myself sitting dumbly in the car as he argued with some old farmer at the kitchen door about the price of a watermelon the old man grew in the backyard. We had a watermelon, ate it on the spot and threw the rinds on the old Mexican's dirt sidewalk. All kinds of pretty little girls were cutting down the darkening street. I said "Where the hell are we?"

"Don't worry man," said big Ponzo, "tomorrow we make a lot of money, tonight we don't worry." We went back and picked up Terry and the others and wailed to Fresno in the highway lights of night. We were all raving hungry. We bounced over the railroad tracks and hit the wild streets of Fresno Mextown. Strange Chinamen hung out of windows digging the Sunday night streets; groups of Mex chicks swaggered around in slacks; mambo blasted from jukeboxes; the lights were festooned around like Halloween. We went into a restaurant and had tacos and mashed pinto beans rolled in tortillas; it was delicious. I whipped out my last shining four dollars and change which stood between me and the Atlantic shore and paid for the lot. Now I had three bucks. Terry and I looked at each other. "Where we going to sleep tonight baby?"

"I don't know." Freddy was drunk; now all he was saying was "Dah you go man—dah you go man" in a tender and tired voice. It had been a long day. None of us knew what was going on, or what the Good Lord appointed. Poor little Raymond fell asleep against my arm. We drove back to Sabinal. On the way we pulled up sharp at a roadhouse on the highway, 99, because Freddy wanted one last beer. In back were trailers and tents and a few rickety motel-style rooms. I inquired about the price and it was two bucks for a cabin. I asked Terry how about that and she said great, because we had the kid on our hands now and had to make him comfortable. So after a few beers in the saloon, where sullen Okies reeled to the music of a cowboy band and sprawled drawling at sticky tables where they'd been swiggling brew since one o'clock in the afternoon and here it was twelve hours later and all the stars out and long sleepy, Terry and I and Raymond went into a cabin and got ready to hit the sack. Ponzo kept hanging around, talking to us in the starry door; he had no place to sleep. Freddy slept at his father's house in the vineyard shack. "Where do you live, Ponzo?" I asked.

"Nowhere, man. I'm supposed to live with Big Rosey but she threw me out last night. I'm goin to get my truck and sleep in it tonight." Guitars tinkled. Terry and I gazed at the stars together from the tiny bathroom window and took a shower and dried each other.

"Mañana," she said, "everything'll be all right tomorrow, don't you think so Sal-honey man?"

"Sure baby, mañana." It was always mañana. For the next week that was all I heard, Mañana, a lovely word and one that probably means heaven. Little Raymond jumped in bed, clothes and all and went to sleep; sand spilled out of his shoes, Madera sand. Terry and I had to get up in the middle of the night and brush it off the sheets. In the morning I got up, washed and took a walk around the place. Sweet dew was making me breathe that human fog. We were five miles out of Sabinal in the cotton fields and grape vineyards along highway 99. I asked the big fat woman who owned the camp if any field tents were vacant. The cheapest one, a dollar a day, was vacant. I fished up that last dollar and moved into it. There was a bed, a stove and a cracked mirror hanging from a pole; it was delightful. I had to stoop to get in, and when I did there was my baby and my baby-boy. We waited for Freddy and Ponzo to arrive with the truck. They arrived with beer and started to get drunk in the tent. "Great tent!"

"How about the manure?"

"Too late today—tomorrow man we make a lot of money, today we have a few beers. What do you say, beer?" I didn't have to be prodded. "Dah you go—DAH YOU GO!" yelled Freddy. I began to see that our plans for making money with the manure truck would never materialize. The truck was parked outside the tent. It smelled like Ponzo. That night Terry and I went to sleep in the sweet night air and made sweet old love. I was just getting ready go to sleep when she said, "You want to love me now?"

I said, "What about Raymond?"

"He don't mind. He's asleep." But Raymond wasn't asleep and he said nothing.

The boys came back the next day with the manure truck and drove off to find whiskey; they came back and had a big time in the tent. Talking about the great old times when they were kids here and when they were kids in Calexico and their eccentric old uncles from Old Mexico and the fabulous characters out of the past I missed. "You tink I'm crazy!" yelled Freddy wildeyed, his hair over his eyes. That night Ponzo said it was too cold and slept on the ground in our tent wrapped in a big tarpaulin smelling of cowflaps. Terry hated him; she said he hung around her brother just to be close to her. He was probably in love with her. I didn't blame him.

Nothing was going to happen except starvation for Terry and me, I had a dime left, so in the morning I walked around the countryside asking for cottonpicking work. Everybody told me to go to a farm across the highway from the camp. I went; the farmer was in the kitchen with his women. He came out, listened to my story, and warned me he was only paying so much per hundred pound of picked cotton. I pictured myself picking at least three hundred pounds a day and took the job. He fished out some old long canvas bags from the barn and told me the picking started at dawn. I rushed back to Terry all glee. On the way a grapetruck went over a bump in the road and threw off great bunches of grapes on the hot tar. I picked it up and took it home. Terry was glad. "Raymond and me'll come with you and help."

"Pshaw!" I said. "No such thing!"

"You see, you see, it's very hard picking cotton. If you can't boogie I know I show you how." We ate the grapes and in the evening Freddy showed up with a loaf of bread and a pound of hamburg and we had a picnic. In a larger tent next to ours lived a whole family of Okie cottonpickers; the grandfather sat in a chair all day long, he was too old to work; the son and daughter, and their children, filed every dawn across the highway to my farmer's field and went to work. At dawn the next day I went with them. They said the cotton was heavier at dawn because of the dew and you could make more money than in the afternoon. Nevertheless they worked all day from dawn to sundown. The grandfather had come from Nebraska during the great plague of the thirties, that old selfsame dustcloud, with the entire family in a jalopy truck. They had been in California ever since. They loved to work. In the ten years the old man's son had increased his children to the number of four, some of whom were old enough now to pick cotton. And in that time they had progressed from ragged poverty in Simon Legree fields to a kind of smiling respectability in better tents, and that was all. They were extremely proud of their tent. "Ever going back to Nebraska?"

"Pshaw, there's nothing back there. What we want to do is buy a trailer." We bent down and began picking cotton. It was beautiful. Across the field were the tents, and beyond them the sere brown cottonfields that stretched out of sight, and over that the brown arroyo foothills and then as in a dream the snowcapped Sierras in the blue morning air. This was so much better than washing dishes on South Main Street. But I knew nothing about cottonpicking. I spent too much time disengaging the white ball from its crackly bed; the others did it in one flick. Moreover my fingertips began to bleed; I needed gloves, or more experience. There was an old Negro couple in the field with us. They picked cotton with the same Godblessed patience their grandfathers had practised in pre-war Alabama: they moved right along their rows, bent and blue, and their bags increased. My back began to ache. But it was beautiful kneeling and hiding in that earth; if I felt like resting I just lay down with my face on the pillow of brown moist earth. Birds sang an accompaniment. I thought I had found my life's work. Terry and Raymond came waving at me across the field in the hot lullal noon and pitched in with me. Damn if he wasn't faster than I was!!—a child. And of course Terry was twice as fast. They worked ahead of me and left me piles of clean cotton to add to my bag, my long lugubrious nightmare bag that dragged after me like some serpent or some bedraggled buttoned dragon in a Kafkean dream and worse. My mouth drops just to think of that deep bag. Terry left workmanlike piles, Raymond little childly piles. I stuck them in with sorrow. What kind of an old man was I that I couldn't support my own can let alone theirs. They spent all afternoon with me; the earth is an Indian thing. When the sun got red we trudged back together. At the end of the field I unloaded my burden on a scale, to my surprise it weighed a pound and a half only, and I got a buck fifty. Then I borrowed one of the Okie boys' bicycles and rode down 99 to a crossroads grocery where I bought cans of spaghetti and meatballs, bread, butter, coffee and five-cent cakes, and came back with the bag on the handlebars. L.A.-bound traffic zoomed by; Fresno-bound harassed my tail. I swore and swore. I looked up at the dark sky and prayed to God for a better break in life and a better chance to do something for the little people I loved. Nobody was paying any attention to me up there. I should have known better. It was Terry who brought my soul back; on the tent stove she warmed up the food and it was one of the greatest meals of my life I was so hungry and tired. Sighing like an old Negro cottonpicker, I reclined on the bed and smoked a cigarette. Dogs barked in the cool night. Freddy and Ponzo had given up calling in the evenings. I was satisfied with that. Terry curled up beside me, Raymond sat on my chest, and they drew pictures of animals in my notebook. The light of our tent burned on the frightful plain. The cowboy music twanged in the roadhouse and carried across the fields all sadness. It was all right with me. I kissed my baby and we put out the lights.

In the morning the dew made the tent sag; I got up with my towel and toothbrush and went to the general motel toilet to wash; then I came back, put on my pants, which were all torn from kneeling in the earth and had been sewed by Terry in the evening; put on my ragged strawhat, which had originally been Raymond's toy hat; and went across the highway with my canvas cottonbag. The cotton was wet and heavy. The sun was red on moist earth.

Every day I earned approximately a dollar and a half. It was just enough to buy groceries in the evening on the bicycle. The days rolled by. I forgot all about the East and the ravings of the bloody road. Raymond and I played all the time: he liked me to throw him up in the air and down on the bed. Terry sat mending clothes. I was a man of the earth precisely as I had dreamed I would be in New York. There was talk that Terry's husband was back in Sabinal and out for me; I was ready for him. One night the Okies went berserk in the roadhouse and tied a man to a tree and beat him with two-by-fours. I was asleep at the time and only heard about it. From then on I carried a big stick with me in the tent in case they got the idea we Mexicans were fouling up their trailer camp. They thought I was a Mexican, of course; and I am.

But now it was getting on in October and getting much colder in the nights. The Okie family had a woodstove and planned to stay for the winter. We had no stove, and besides the rent for the tent was due. Terry and I bitterly decided we'd have to leave and try something else. "Go back to your family," I gnashed. "For God's sake you can't be batting around tents with a baby like Raymond; the poor little tyke is cold." Terry cried because I was criticizing her motherly instincts; I meant no such thing. When Ponzo came in the truck one gray afternoon we decided to see her family about the situation. But I mustn't be seen and would have to hide in the vineyard. "Tell your mother you'll get a job and help with the groceries. Anything's better than this."

"But you're going, I can hear you talk."

"Well I got to go *some*time—"

"What do you mean, sometime. You said we'd stick together and go to New York together. Freddy wants to go to New York too! Now! We'll all go."

"I dunno, Terry, goddamit I dunno—"

We got in the truck and Ponzo started for Sabinal; the truck broke down in some backroad and simultaneously it started to rain wildly. We sat in the old truck cursing. Ponzo got out and toiled in the rain in his torn white shirt. He was a good old guy after all. We promised each other one big more bat. Off we went to a rickety bar in Sabinal Mextown and spent an hour sopping up the cerveza as the rain drove past the door and the jukebox boomed those brokenhearted campo lovesongs from old Mexico, sad, incredibly sad like clouds going over the horizon like dogs on their hind legs, the singer breaking out his wild Ya Ya Henna like the sound of a coyote crying, broken, half laughter, half tears. I was through with my chores in the cottonfield, I could feel it as the beer ran through me like wildfire. We screamed happily our insane conversations. We'd do it, we'd do everything! I could feel the pull of my own whole life calling me back. I needed fifty dollars to get back to New York. While Terry and Ponzo drank I ran in the rain to the post-office and scrawled a penny postcard request for $50 and sent it to my aunt; she'd do it. I was as good as saved; lazy butt was saved again. It was a secret from Terry.

The rain stopped and we drove to Terry's family shack. It was situated on an old road that ran between the vineyards. It was dark when we got there finally. They let me off a quarter-mile up the road and drove to the door. Light poured out of the door; Terry's six other brothers were playing their guitars and singing all together like a professional recording and beautiful. ". . . si tu corazón . . ." The old man was drinking wine. I heard shouts and arguments above the singing. They called her a whore because she'd left her no good husband and gone to L.A. and left Raymond with them. At intervals the brothers stopped singing to regroup their choruses. The old man was yelling. But the sad fat brown mother prevailed, as she always does among the great Fellaheen peoples of the world, and Terry was allowed to come back home. The brothers began to sing gay songs, fast. I huddled in the cold rainy wind and watched everything across the sad vineyards of October in the Valley. My mind was filled with that great song "Lover Man" as Billie Holiday sings it; I had my own concert in the bushes. "Someday we'll meet, and you'll dry all my tears, and whisper sweet little words in my ear, hugging and akissing, Oh what we've been missing, Lover Man Oh where can you be . . ." It's not the words so much as the great harmonic tune and the way Billie sings it, like a woman stroking her man's hair in soft lamplight. The winds howled. I got cold. Terry and Ponzo came back and we rattled off in the old truck to meet Freddy, who was now living with Ponzo's woman Big Rosey; we tooted the horn for him in woodfence alleys. Big Rosey threw him out, we heard yelling and saw Freddy running out with his head ducking. Everything was collapsing. Everybody was laughing. That night Terry held me tight, of course, and told me not to leave. She said she'd work picking grapes and make enough money for both of us; meanwhile I could live in Farmer Heffelfinger's barn down the road from her family. I'd have nothing to do but sit in the grass all day and eat grapes. "You like that?"

I rubbed my jaw. In the morning her cousins came to the tent to get us in the truck. These were also singers. I suddenly realized thousands of Mexicans all over the countryside knew about Terry and I and that it must have been a juicy romantic topic for them. The cousins were very polite and in fact charming. I stood on the truck platform with them as we rattlebanged into town, hanging on to the rail and smiling pleasantries, talking about where we were in the war and what the pitch was. There were five cousins in all and every one of them was nice. They seemed to belong to the side of Terry's family that didn't act up like her brother Freddy. But I loved that wild Freddy. He swore he was coming to New York and join me. I pictured him in New York putting off everything till mañana. He was drunk in a field someplace today.

I got off the truck at the crossroads and the cousins drove Terry and Raymond home. They gave me the high-sign from the front of the house: the father and mother weren't home. So I had the run of the house for the afternoon, digging it and Terry's three giggling fat sisters and the crazy children sitting in the middle of the road with tortillas in their hands. It was a four-room shack; I couldn't imagine how the whole family managed to live in there, find room. Flies flew over the sink. There were no screens, just like in the song: "The window she is broken and the rain she's coming in . . ." Terry was at home now and puttering around pots. The sisters giggled over True Love magazines in Spanish showing daguerreotype brown covers of lovers in great, somehow darker more passionate throes, with long sideburns and huge worries and burning secret eyes. The little children screamed in the road, roosters ran around. When the sun came out red through the clouds of my last Valley afternoon Terry led me to Farmer Heffelfinger's barn. Farmer Heffelfinger had a prosperous farm up the road. We put crates together, she brought blankets from the house, and I was all set except for a great hairy tarantula that lurked at the pinpoint top of the barnroof. Terry said it wouldn't harm me if I didn't bother it. I lay on my back and stared at it. I went out to the cemetery and climbed a tree. In the tree I sang "Blue Skies." Terry and Raymond sat in the grass; we had grapes. In California you chew the juice out of the grapes and spit the skin and pits away, the gist of the grape is always wine. Nightfall came. Terry went home for supper and came to the barn at nine o'clock with my secret supper of delicious tortillas and mashed beans. I lit a woodfire on the cement floor of the barn to make light. We made love on the crates. Terry got up and cut right back to the shack. Her father was yelling at her, I could hear him from the barn. "Where have you been? What you doing running around at night in the fields?" Words to that effect. She'd left me a cape to keep warm, some old Spanish garment, I threw it over my shoulder and skulked through the moonlit vineyard to see what was going on. I crept to the end of a row and kneeled in the warm dirt. Her five brothers were singing melodious songs in Spanish. The stars bent over the little roof; smoke poked from the stovepipe chimney. I smelled mashed beans and chili. The old man growled. The brothers kept right on singing. The mother was silent. Raymond and the kids were giggling on one vast bed in the bedroom. A California home; I hid in the grapevines digging it all. I felt like a million dollars; I was adventuring in the crazy American night. Terry came out slamming the door behind her. I accosted her on the dark road. "What's the matter?"

"Oh we fight all the time. He wants me to go to work tomorrow. He says he don't want me fooling around with boys. Sallie-boy I want to go to New York with you."

"But how?"

"I don't know honey. I'll miss you. I love you."

"But I can't stay here."

"You say what you like, I know what you mean. Yes yes, we lay down one more time then you leave." We went back to the barn; I made love to her under the tarantula. What was the tarantula doing? We slept awhile on the crates as the fire died. She went back at midnight; her father was drunk; I could hear him roaring; then there was silence as he fell asleep. The stars folded over the sleeping countryside.

In the morning Father Heffelfinger stuck his head through the horse gate and said, "How you doing young fella?"

"Fine. I hope it's all right my staying here."

"Sure. You going with that little Mexican floozie?"

"She's a very nice girl."

"Pretty too. S'got blue eyes. I think the bull jumped the fence there . . ." We talked about his farm.

Terry brought my breakfast. I had my handbag all packed and ready to go back East, as soon as I picked up my money in Sabinal. I knew it was waiting there for me. I told Terry I was leaving. She had been thinking about it all night and was resigned to it. Emotionlessly she kissed me in the vineyards and walked off down the row. We turned at a dozen paces, for love is a duel, and looked at each other for the last time. "See you in New York, Terry," I said. She was supposed to drive to New York in a month with her brother. But we both knew she wouldn't make it somehow. At a hundred feet I turned to look at her. She just walked on back to the shack, carrying my breakfast plate in one hand. I bowed my head and watched her. Well lackadaddy, I was on the road again. I walked down the highway to Sabinal eating black walnuts from the walnut tree, then on the railroad track balancing on the rail.

from
ON THE ROAD
1949

PART TWO

6

It was drizzling and mysterious at the beginning of our journey. I could see that it was all going to be one big saga of the mist. "Whooee!" yelled Dean. "Here we go!" And he hunched over the wheel and gunned her; he was back in his element, everybody could see that. We were all delighted, we all realized we were leaving confusion and nonsense behind and performing our one and noble function of the time, *move.* And we moved! We flashed past the mysterious white signs in the night somewhere in New Jersey that say SOUTH (with an arrow) and WEST (with an arrow) and took the south one. New Orleans! It burned in our brains. From the dirty snows of "frosty fagtown New York," as Dean called it, all the way to the greeneries and river smells of old New Orleans at the washed-out bottom of America; then west. Ed was in the back seat; Marylou and Dean and I sat in front and had the warmest talk about the goodness and joy of life. Dean suddenly became tender. "Now dammit, look here, all of you, we all must admit that everything is fine and there's no need in the world to worry, and in fact we should realize what it would mean to us to UNDERSTAND that we're not REALLY worried about ANYTHING. Am I right?" We all agreed. "Here we go, we're all together . . . What did we do in New York? Let's forgive." We all had our spats back there. "That's behind us, merely by miles and inclinations. Now we're heading down to New Orleans to dig Old Bull Lee and ain't that going to be kicks and listen will you to this old tenorman blow his top"—he shot up the radio volume till the car shuddered—"and listen to him tell the story and put down true relaxation and knowledge."

We all jumped to the music and agreed. The purity of the road. The white line in the middle of the highway unrolled and hugged our left front tire as if glued to our groove. Dean hunched his muscular neck, T-shirted in the winter night, and blasted the car along. He insisted I drive through Baltimore for traffic practice; that was all right, except he and Marylou insisted on steering while they kissed and fooled around. It was crazy; the radio was on full blast. Dean beat drums on the dashboard till a great sag developed in it; I did too. The poor Hudson—the slow boat to China—was receiving her beating.

"Oh man, what kicks!" yelled Dean. "Now Marylou, listen really, honey, you know that I'm hotrock capable of everything at the same time and I have unlimited energy—now in San Francisco we must go on living together. I know just the place for you—at the end of the regular chain-gang run—I'll be home just a cut-hair less than every two days and for twelve hours at a stretch, and *man,* you know what we can do in twelve hours, darling. Meanwhile I'll go right on living at Camille's like nothin, see, she won't know. We can work it, we've done it before." It was all right with Marylou, she was really out for Camille's scalp. The understanding had been that Marylou would switch to me in Frisco, but I now began to see they were going to stick and I was going to be left alone on my butt at the other end of the continent. But why think about that when all the golden land's ahead of you and all kinds of unforeseen events wait lurking to surprise you and make you glad you're alive to see?

We arrived in Washington at dawn. It was the day of Harry Truman's inauguration for his second term. Great displays of war might were lined along Pennsylvania Avenue as we rolled by in our battered boat. There were B-29s, PT boats, artillery, all kinds of war material that looked murderous in the snowy grass; the last thing was a regular small ordinary lifeboat that looked pitiful and foolish. Dean slowed down to look at it. He kept shaking his head in awe. "What are these people up to? Harry's sleeping somewhere in this town. . . . Good old Harry. . . . Man from Missouri, as I am. . . . That must be his own boat."

Dean went to sleep in the back seat and Dunkel drove. We gave him specific instructions to take it easy. No sooner were we snoring than he gunned the car up to eighty, bad bearings and all, and not only that but he made a triple pass at a spot where a cop was arguing with a motorist—he was in the fourth lane of a four-lane highway, going the wrong way. Naturally the cop took after us with his siren whining. We were stopped. He told us to follow him to the station house. There was a mean cop in there who took an immediate dislike to Dean; he could smell jail all over him. He sent his cohort outdoors to question Marylou and me privately. They wanted to know how old Marylou was, they were trying to whip up a Mann Act idea. But she had her marriage certificate. Then they took me aside alone and wanted to know who was sleeping with Marylou. "Her husband," I said quite simply. They were curious. Something was fishy. They tried some amateur Sherlocking by asking the same questions twice, expecting us to make a slip. I said, "Those two fellows are going back to work on the railroad in California, this is the short one's wife, and I'm a friend on a two-week vacation from college."

The cop smiled and said, "Yeah? Is this really your own wallet?"

Finally the mean one inside fined Dean twenty-five dollars. We told them we only had forty to go all the way to the Coast; they said that made no difference to them. When Dean protested, the mean cop threatened to take him back to Pennsylvania and slap a special charge on him.

"What charge?"

"Never mind what charge. Don't worry about *that*, wise guy."

We had to give them the twenty-five. But first Ed Dunkel, that culprit, offered to go to jail. Dean considered it. The cop was infuriated; he said, "If you let your partner go to jail I'm taking you back to Pennsylvania right now. You hear that?" All we wanted to do was go. "Another speeding ticket in Virginia and you lose your car," said the mean cop as a parting volley. Dean was red in the face. We drove off silently. It was just like an invitation to steal to take our trip-money away from us. They knew we were broke and had no relatives on the road or to wire to for money. The American police are involved in psychological warfare against those Americans who don't frighten them with imposing papers and threats. It's a Victorian police force; it peers out of musty windows and wants to inquire about everything, and can make crimes if the crimes don't exist to its satisfaction. "Nine lines of crime, one of boredom," said Louis-Ferdinand Céline. Dean was so mad he wanted to come back to Virginia and shoot the cop as soon as he had a gun.

"Pennsylvania!" he scoffed. "I wish I knew what that charge was! Vag, probably; take all my money and charge me vag. Those guys have it so damn easy. They'll out and shoot you if you complain, too." There was nothing to do but get happy with ourselves again and forget about it. When we got through Richmond we began forgetting about it, and soon everything was okay.

Now we had fifteen dollars to go all the way. We'd have to pick up hitchhikers and bum quarters off them for gas. In the Virginia wilderness suddenly we saw a man walking on the road. Dean zoomed to a stop. I looked back and said he was only a bum and probably didn't have a cent.

"We'll just pick him up for kicks!" Dean laughed. The man was a ragged, bespectacled mad type, walking along reading a paperbacked muddy book he'd found in a culvert by the road. He got in the car and went right on reading; he was incredibly filthy and covered with scabs. He said his name was Hyman Solomon and that he walked all over the USA, knocking and sometimes kicking at Jewish doors and demanding money: "Give me money to eat, I am a Jew."

He said it worked very well and that it was coming to him. We asked him what he was reading. He didn't know. He didn't bother to look at the title page. He was only looking at the words, as though he had found the real Torah where it belonged, in the wilderness.

"See? See? See?" cackled Dean, poking my ribs. "I told you it was kicks. Everybody's kicks, man!" We carried Solomon all the way to Testament. My brother by now was in his new house on the other side of town. Here we were back on the long, bleak street with the railroad track running down the middle and the sad, sullen Southerners loping in front of hardware stores and five-and-tens.

Solomon said, "I see you people need a little money to continue your journey. You wait for me and I'll go hustle up a few dollars at a Jewish home and I'll go along with you as far as Alabama." Dean was all beside himself with happiness; he and I rushed off to buy bread and cheese spread for a lunch in the car. Marylou and Ed waited in the car. We spent two hours in Testament waiting for Hyman Solomon to show up; he was hustling for his bread somewhere in town, but we couldn't see him. The sun began to grow red and late.

)mon never showed up so we roared out of Testament. "Now you see, Sal, God does exist, because we keep getting hung-up with this town, no matter what we try to do, and you'll notice the strange Biblical name of it, and that strange Biblical character who made us stop here once more, and all things tied together all over like rain connecting everybody the world over by chain touch. . . ." Dean rattled on like this; he was overjoyed and exuberant. He and I suddenly saw the whole country like an oyster for us to open; and the pearl was there, the pearl was there. Off we roared south. We picked up another hitchhiker. This was a sad young kid who said he had an aunt who owned a grocery store in Dunn, North Carolina, right outside Fayetteville. "When we get there can you bum a buck off her? Right! Fine! Let's go!" We were in Dunn in an hour, at dusk. We drove to where the kid said his aunt had the grocery store. It was a sad little street that dead-ended at a factory wall. There was a grocery store but there was no aunt. We wondered what the kid was talking about. We asked him how far he was going; he didn't know. It was a big hoax; once upon a time, in some lost back-alley adventure, he had seen the grocery store in Dunn, and it was the first story that popped into his disordered, feverish mind. We bought him a hot dog, but Dean said we couldn't take him along because we needed room to sleep and room for hitchhikers who could buy a little gas. This was sad but true. We left him in Dunn at nightfall.

I drove through South Carolina and beyond Macon, Georgia, as Dean, Marylou, and Ed slept. All alone in the night I had my own thoughts and held the car to the white line in the holy road. What was I doing? Where was I going? I'd soon find out. I got dog-tired beyond Macon and woke up Dean to resume. We got out of the car for air and suddenly both of us were stoned with joy to realize that in the darkness all around us was fragrant green grass and the smell of fresh manure and warm waters. "We're in the South! We've left the winter!" Faint daybreak illuminated green shoots by the side of the road. I took a deep breath; a locomotive howled across the darkness, Mobile-bound. So were we. I took off my shirt and exulted. Ten miles down the road Dean drove into a filling station with the motor off, noticed that the attendant was fast asleep at the desk, jumped out, quietly filled the gas tank, saw to it the bell didn't ring, and rolled off like an Arab with a five-dollar tankful of gas for our pilgrimage.

I slept and woke up to the crazy exultant sounds of music and Dean and Marylou talking and the great green land rolling by. "Where are we?"

"Just passed the tip of Florida, man—Flomaton, it's called." Florida! We were rolling down to the coastal plain and Mobile; up ahead were great soaring clouds of the Gulf of Mexico. It was only thirty-two hours since we'd said good-by to everybody in the dirty snows of the North. We stopped at a gas station, and there Dean and Marylou played piggyback around the tanks and Dunkel went inside and stole three packs of cigarettes without trying. We were fresh out. Rolling into Mobile over the long tidal highway, we all took our winter clothes off and enjoyed the Southern temperature. This was when Dean started telling his life story and when, beyond Mobile, he came upon an obstruction of wrangling cars at a crossroads and instead of slipping around them just balled right through the driveway of a gas station and went right on without relaxing his steady continental seventy. We left gaping faces behind us. He went right on with his tale. "I tell you it's true, I started at nine, with a girl called Milly Mayfair in back of Rod's garage on Grant Street—same street Carlo lived on in Denver. That's when my father was still working at the smithy's a bit. I remember my aunt yelling out the window, 'What are you doing down there in back of the garage?' Oh honey Marylou, if I'd only known you then! Wow! How sweet you musta been at nine." He tittered maniacally; he stuck his finger in her mouth and licked it; he took her hand and rubbed it over himself. She just sat there, smiling serenely.

Big long Ed Dunkel sat looking out the window, talking to himself. "Yes sir, I thought I was a ghost that night." He was also wondering what Galatea Dunkel would say to him in New Orleans.

Dean went on. "One time I rode a freight from New Mexico clear to LA—I was eleven years old, lost my father at a siding, we were all in a hobo jungle, I was with a man called Big Red, my father was out drunk in a boxcar—it started to roll—Big Red and I missed it—I didn't see my father for months. I rode a long freight all the way to California, really flying, first-class freight, a desert Zipper. All the way I rode over the couplings—you can imagine how dangerous, I was only a kid, I didn't know—clutching a loaf of bread under one arm and the other hooked around the brake bar. This is no story, this is true. When I got to LA I was so starved for milk and cream I got a job in a dairy and the first thing I did I drank two quarts of heavy cream and puked."

"Poor Dean," said Marylou, and she kissed him. He stared ahead proudly. He loved her.

We were suddenly driving along the blue waters of the Gulf, and at the same time a momentous mad thing began on the radio; it was the Chicken Jazz'n Gumbo disk-jockey show from New Orleans, all mad jazz records, colored records, with the disk jockey saying, "Don't worry 'bout *nothing!*" We saw New Orleans in the night ahead of us with joy. Dean rubbed his hands over the wheel. "Now we're going to get our kicks!" At dusk we were coming into the humming streets of New Orleans. "Oh, smell the people!" yelled Dean with his face out the window, sniffing. "Ah! God! Life!" He swung around a trolley. "Yes!" He darted the car and looked in every direction for girls. "Look at *her!*" The air was so sweet in New Orleans it seemed to come in soft bandannas; and you could smell the river and really smell the people, and mud, and molasses, and every kind of tropical exhalation with your nose suddenly removed from the dry ices of a Northern winter. We bounced in our seats. "And dig her!" yelled Dean, pointing at another woman. "Oh, I love, love, love women! I think women are wonderful! I love women!" He spat out the window; he groaned; he clutched his head. Great beads of sweat fell from his forehead from pure excitement and exhaustion.

We bounced the car up on the Algiers ferry and found ourselves crossing the Mississippi River by boat. "Now we must all get out and dig the river and the people and smell the world," said Dean, bustling with his sunglasses and cigarettes and leaping out of the car like a jack-in-the-box. We followed. On rails we leaned and looked at the great brown father of waters rolling down from mid-America like the torrent of broken souls—bearing Montana logs and Dakota muds and Iowa vales and things that had drowned in Three Forks, where the secret began in ice. Smoky New Orleans receded on one side; old, sleepy Algiers with its warped woodsides bumped us on the other. Negroes were working in the hot afternoon, stoking the ferry furnaces that burned red and made our tires smell. Dean dug them, hopping up and down in the heat. He rushed around the deck and upstairs with his baggy pants hanging halfway down his belly. Suddenly I saw him eagering on the flying bridge. I expected him to take off on wings. I heard his mad laugh all over the boat—"Hee-hee-hee-hee-hee!" Marylou was with him. He covered everything in a jiffy, came back with the full story, jumped in the car just as everybody was tooting to go, and we slipped off, passing two or three cars in a narrow space, and found ourselves darting through Algiers.

"Where? Where?" Dean was yelling.

We decided first to clean up at a gas station and inquire for Bull's whereabouts. Little children were playing in the drowsy river sunset; girls were going by with bandannas and cotton blouses and bare legs. Dean ran up the street to see everything. He looked around; he nodded; he rubbed his belly. Big Ed sat back in the car with his hat over his eyes, smiling at Dean. I sat on the fender. Marylou was in the women's john. From bushy shores where infinitesimal men fished with sticks, and from delta sleeps that stretched up along the reddening land, the big humpbacked river with its mainstream leaping came coiling around Algiers like a snake, with a nameless rumble. Drowsy, peninsular Algiers with all her bees and shanties was like to be washed away someday. The sun slanted, bugs flip-flopped, the awful waters groaned.

We went to Old Bull Lee's house outside town near the river levee. It was on a road that ran across a swampy field. The house was a dilapidated old heap with sagging porches running around and weeping willows in the yard; the grass was a yard high, old fences leaned, old barns collapsed. There was no one in sight. We pulled right into the yard and saw washtubs on the back porch. I got out and went to the screen door. Jane Lee was standing in it with her eyes cupped toward the sun. "Jane," I said. "It's me. It's us."

She knew that. "Yes, I know. Bull isn't here now. Isn't that a fire or something over there?" We both looked toward the sun.

"You mean the sun?"

"Of course I don't mean the sun—I heard sirens that way. Don't you know a peculiar glow?" It was toward New Orleans; the clouds were strange.

"I don't see anything," I said.

Jane snuffed down her nose. "Same old Paradise."

That was the way we greeted each other after four years; Jane used to live with my wife and me in New York. "And is Galatea Dunkel here?" I asked. Jane was still looking for her fire; in those days she ate three tubes of benzedrine paper a day. Her face, once plump and Germanic and pretty, had become stony and red and gaunt. She had caught polio in New Orleans and limped a little. Sheepishly Dean and the gang came out of the car and more or less made themselves at home. Galatea Dunkel came out of her stately retirement in the back of the house to meet her tormentor. Galatea was a serious girl. She was pale and looked like tears all over. Big Ed passed his hand through his hair and said hello. She looked at him steadily.

"Where have you been? Why did you do this to me?" And she gave

Dean a dirty look; she knew the score. Dean paid absolutely no attention; what he wanted now was food; he asked Jane if there was anything. The confusion began right there.

Poor Bull came home in his Texas Chevy and found his house in-
vaded by maniacs; but he greeted me with a nice warmth I hadn't seen
in him for a long time. He had bought this house in New Orleans with
some money he had made growing black-eyed peas in Texas with an
old college schoolmate whose father, a mad paretic, had died and left
a fortune. Bull himself only got fifty dollars a week from his own family,
which wasn't too bad except that he spent almost that much per week
on his drug habit—and his wife was also expensive, gobbling up about
ten dollars' worth of benny tubes a week. Their food bill was the lowest
in the country; they hardly ever ate; nor did the children—they didn't
seem to care. They had two wonderful children: Dodie, eight years old;
and little Ray, one year. Ray ran around stark naked in the yard, a little
blond child of the rainbow. Bull called him "the Little Beast," after
W. C. Fields. Bull came driving into the yard and unrolled himself from
the car bone by bone, and came over wearily, wearing glasses, felt hat,
shabby suit, long, lean, strange, and laconic, saying, "Why, Sal, you
finally got here; let's go in the house and have a drink."

It would take all night to tell about Old Bull Lee; let's just say now,
he was a teacher, and it may be said that he had every right to teach
because he spent all his time learning; and the things he learned were
what he considered to be and called "the facts of life," which he learned
not only out of necessity but because he wanted to. He dragged his
long, thin body around the entire United States and most of Europe and
North Africa in his time, only to see what was going on; he married a
White Russian countess in Yugoslavia to get her away from the Nazis
in the thirties; there are pictures of him with the international cocaine
set of the thirties—gangs with wild hair, leaning on one another; there
are other pictures of him in a Panama hat, surveying the streets of Algiers; he never saw the White Russian countess again. He was an exterminator in Chicago, a bartender in New York, a summons-server in
Newark. In Paris he sat at café tables, watching the sullen French faces
go by. In Athens he looked up from his *ouzo* at what he called the
ugliest people in the world. In Istanbul he threaded his way through
crowds of opium addicts and rug-sellers, looking for the facts. In English
hotels he read Spengler and the Marquis de Sade. In Chicago he planned
to hold up a Turkish bath, hesitated just for two minutes too long for
a drink, and wound up with two dollars and had to make a run for it.

He did all these things merely for the experience. Now the final study was the drug habit. He was now in New Orleans, slipping along the streets with shady characters and haunting connection bars.

There is a strange story about his college days that illustrates something else about him: he had friends for cocktails in his well-appointed rooms one afternoon when suddenly his pet ferret rushed out and bit an elegant teacup queer on the ankle and everybody hightailed it out the door, screaming. Old Bull leaped up and grabbed his shotgun and said, "He smells that old rat again," and shot a hole in the wall big enough for fifty rats. On the wall hung a picture of an ugly old Cape Cod house. His friends said, "Why do you have that ugly thing hanging there?" and Bull said, "I like it because it's ugly." All his life was in that line. Once I knocked on his door in the 60th Street slums of New York and he opened it wearing a derby hat, a vest with nothing underneath, and long striped sharpster pants; in his hands he had a cookpot, birdseed in the pot, and was trying to mash the seed to roll in cigarettes. He also experimented in boiling codeine cough syrup down to a black mash—that didn't work too well. He spent long hours with Shakespeare—the "Immortal Bard," he called him—on his lap. In New Orleans he had begun to spend long hours with the Mayan Codices on his lap, and, although he went on talking, the book lay open all the time. I said once, "What's going to happen to us when we die?" and he said, "When you die you're just dead, that's all." He had a set of chains in his room that he said he used with his psychoanalyst; they were experimenting with narcoanalysis and found that Old Bull had seven separate personalities, each growing worse and worse on the way down, till finally he was a raving idiot and had to be restrained with chains. The top personality was an English lord, the bottom the idiot. Halfway he was an old Negro who stood in line, waiting with everyone else, and said, "Some's bastards, some's ain't, that's the score."

Bull had a sentimental streak about the old days in America, especially 1910, when you could get morphine in a drugstore without prescription and Chinese smoked opium in their evening windows and the country was wild and brawling and free, with abundance and any kind of freedom for everyone. His chief hate was Washington bureaucracy; second to that, liberals; then cops. He spent all his time talking and teaching others. Jane sat at his feet; so did I; so did Dean; and so had Carlo Marx. We'd all learned from him. He was a gray, nondescript-looking fellow you wouldn't notice on the street, unless you looked closer and saw his mad, bony skull with its strange youthfulness—a Kansas minister with exotic, phenomenal fires and mysteries. He had studied medicine in Vienna; had studied anthropology, read everything; and now he was settling to his life's work, which was the study of things themselves in the streets of life and the night. He sat in his chair; Jane brought drinks, martinis. The shades by his chair were always drawn, day and night; it was his corner of the house. On his lap were the Mayan Codices and an air gun which he occasionally raised to pop benzedrine tubes across the room. I kept rushing around, putting up new ones. We all took shots and meanwhile we talked. Bull was curious to know the reason for this trip. He peered at us and snuffed down his nose, *thfump,* like a sound in a dry tank.

"Now, Dean, I want you to sit quiet a minute and tell me what you're doing crossing the country like this."

Dean could only blush and say, "Ah well, you know how it is."

"Sal, what are you going to the Coast for?"

"Only for a few days. I'm coming back to school."

"What's the score with this Ed Dunkel? What kind of character is he?" At that moment Ed was making up to Galatea in the bedroom; it didn't take him long. We didn't know what to tell Bull about Ed Dunkel. Seeing that we didn't know anything about ourselves, he whipped out three sticks of tea and said to go ahead, supper'd be ready soon.

"Ain't nothing better in the world to give you an appetite. I once ate a horrible lunchcart hamburg on tea and it seemed like the most delicious thing in the world. I just got back from Houston last week, went to see Dale about our black-eyed peas. I was sleeping in a motel one morning when all of a sudden I was blasted out of bed. This damn fool had just shot his wife in the room next to mine. Everybody stood around confused, and the guy just got in his car and drove off, left the shotgun on the floor for the sheriff. They finally caught him in Houma, drunk as a lord. Man ain't safe going around this country any more without a gun." He pulled back his coat and showed us his revolver. Then he opened the drawer and showed us the rest of his arsenal. In New York he once had a sub-machine-gun under his bed. "I got something better than that now—a German Scheintoth gas gun; look at this beauty, only got one shell. I could knock out a hundred men with this gun and have plenty of time to make a getaway. Only thing wrong, I only got one shell."

"I hope I'm not around when you try it," said Jane from the kitchen. "How do *you* know it's a gas shell?" Bull snuffed; he never paid any attention to her sallies but he heard them. His relation with his wife was one of the strangest: they talked till late at night; Bull liked to hold the floor, he went right on in his dreary monotonous voice, she tried to break in, she never could; at dawn he got tired and then Jane talked and he listened, snuffing and going *thfump* down his nose. She loved that man madly, but in a delirious way of some kind; there was never any mooching and mincing around, just talk and a very deep companionship that none of us would ever be able to fathom. Something curiously unsympathetic and cold between them was really a form of humor by which they communicated their own set of subtle vibrations. Love is all; Jane was never more than ten feet away from Bull and never missed a word he said, and he spoke in a very low voice, too.

Dean and I were yelling about a big night in New Orleans and wanted Bull to show us around. He threw a damper on this. "New Orleans is a very dull town. It's against the law to go to the colored section. The bars are insufferably dreary."

I said, "There must be some ideal bars in town."

"The ideal bar doesn't exist in America. An ideal bar is something that's gone beyond our ken. In nineteen ten a bar was a place where men went to meet during or after work, and all there was was a long counter, brass rails, spittoons, player piano for music, a few mirrors, and barrels of whisky at ten cents a shot together with barrels of beer at five cents a mug. Now all you get is chromium, drunken women, fags, hostile bartenders, anxious owners who hover around the door, worried about their leather seats and the law; just a lot of screaming at the wrong time and deadly silence when a stranger walks in."

We argued about bars. "All right," he said, "I'll take you to New Orleans tonight and show you what I mean." And he deliberately took us to the dullest bars. We left Jane with the children; supper was over; she was reading the want ads of the New Orleans *Times-Picayune*. I asked her if she was looking for a job; she only said it was the most interesting part of the paper. Bull rode into town with us and went right on talking. "Take it easy, Dean, we'll get there, I hope; hup, there's the ferry, you don't have to drive us clear into the river." He held on. Dean had gotten worse, he confided in me. "He seems to me to be headed for his ideal fate, which is compulsive psychosis dashed with a jigger of psychopathic irresponsibility and violence." He looked at Dean out of the corner of his eye. "If you go to California with this madman you'll never make it. Why don't you stay in New Orleans with me? We'll play the horses over to Graetna and relax in my yard. I've got a nice set of knives and I'm building a target. Some pretty juicy dolls downtown, too, if that's in your line these days." He snuffed. We were on the ferry and Dean had leaped out to lean over the rail. I followed, but Bull sat on in the car, snuffing, *thfump*. There was a mystic wraith of fog over the brown waters that night, together with dark driftwoods; and across the way New Orleans glowed orange-bright, with a few dark ships at her hem, ghostly fogbound Cereno ships with Spanish balconies and ornamental poops, till you got up close and saw they were just old freighters from Sweden and Panama. The ferry fires glowed in the night; the same Negroes plied the shovel and sang. Old Big Slim Hazard had once worked on the Algiers ferry as a deckhand; this made me think of Mississippi Gene too; and as the river poured down from mid-America by starlight I knew, I knew like mad that everything I had ever known and would ever know was One. Strange to say, too, that night we crossed the ferry with Bull Lee a girl committed suicide off the deck; either just before or just after us; we saw it in the paper the next day.

We hit all the dull bars in the French Quarter with Old Bull and went back home at midnight. That night Marylou took everything in the books; she took tea, goofballs, benny, liquor, and even asked Old Bull for a shot of M, which of course he didn't give her; he did give her a martini. She was so saturated with elements of all kinds that she came to a standstill and stood goofy on the porch with me. It was a wonderful porch Bull had. It ran clear around the house; by moonlight with the willows it looked like an old Southern mansion that had seen better days. In the house Jane sat reading the want ads in the living room; Bull was in the bathroom taking his fix, clutching his old black necktie in his teeth for a tourniquet and jabbing with the needle into his woesome arm with the thousand holes; Ed Dunkel was sprawled out with Galatea in the massive master bed that Old Bull and Jane never used; Dean was rolling tea; and Marylou and I imitated Southern aristocracy.

"Why, Miss Lou, you look lovely and most fetching tonight."

"Why, thank you, Crawford, I sure do appreciate the nice things you do say."

Doors kept opening around the crooked porch, and members of our sad drama in the American night kept popping out to find out where everybody was. Finally I took a walk alone to the levee. I wanted to sit on the muddy bank and dig the Mississippi River; instead of that I had to look at it with my nose against a wire fence. When you start separating the people from their rivers what have you got? "Bureaucracy!" says Old Bull; he sits with Kafka on his lap, the lamp burns above him, he snuffs, *thfump*. His old house creaks. And the Montana log rolls by in the big black river of the night. " 'Tain't nothin but bureaucracy. And unions! Especially unions!" But dark laughter would come again.

7

It was there in the morning when I got up bright and early and found Old Bull and Dean in the back yard. Dean was wearing his gas-station coveralls and helping Bull. Bull had found a great big piece of thick rotten wood and was desperately yanking with a hammerhook at little nails imbedded in it. We stared at the nails; there were millions of them; they were like worms.

"When I get all these nails out of this I'm going to build me a shelf that'll last a *thousand years!*" said Bull, every bone shuddering with boyish excitement. "Why, Sal, do you realize the shelves they build these days crack under the weight of knickknacks after six months or generally collapse? Same with houses, same with clothes. These bastards have invented plastics by which they could make houses that last *forever*. And tires. Americans are killing themselves by the millions every year with defective rubber tires that get hot on the road and blow up. They could make tires that never blow up. Same with tooth powder. There's a certain gum they've invented and they won't show it to anybody that if you chew it as a kid you'll never get a cavity for the rest of your born days. Same with clothes. They can make clothes that last forever. They prefer making cheap goods so's everybody'll have to go on working and punching timeclocks and organizing themselves in sullen unions and floundering around while the big grab goes on in Washington and Moscow." He raised his big piece of rotten wood. "Don't you think this'll make a splendid shelf?"

It was early in the morning; his energy was at its peak. The poor fellow took so much junk into his system he could only weather the greater proportion of his day in that chair with the lamp burning at noon, but in the morning he was magnificent. We began throwing knives at the target. He said he'd seen an Arab in Tunis who could stick a man's eye from forty feet. This got him going on his aunt, who went to the Casbah in the thirties. "She was with a party of tourists led by a guide. She had a diamond ring on her little finger. She leaned on a wall to rest a minute and an Ay-rab rushed up and appropriated her ring finger before she could let out a cry, my dear. She suddenly realized she had no little finger. Hi-hi-hi-hi-hi!" When he laughed he compressed his lips together and made it come out from his belly, from far away, and doubled up to lean on his knees. He laughed a long time. "Hey Jane!" he yelled gleefully. "I was just telling Dean and Sal about my aunt in the Casbah!"

"I heard you," she said across the lovely warm Gulf morning from the kitchen door. Great beautiful clouds floated overhead, valley clouds that made you feel the vastness of old tumbledown holy America from mouth to mouth and tip to tip. All pep and juices was Bull. "Say, did I ever tell you about Dale's father? He was the funniest old man you ever saw in your life. He had paresis, which eats away the forepart of your brain and you get so's you're not responsible for anything that comes into your mind. He had a house in Texas and had carpenters working twenty-four hours a day putting on new wings. He'd leap up in the middle of the night and say, 'I don't want that goddam wing; put it over there.' The carpenters had to take everything down and start all over again. Come dawn you'd see them hammering away at the new wing. Then the old man'd get bored with that and say, 'Goddammit, I wanta go to Maine!' And he'd get into his car and drive off a hundred miles an hour—great showers of chicken feathers followed his track for hundreds of miles. He'd stop his car in the middle of a Texas town just to get out and buy some whisky. Traffic would honk all around him and he'd come rushing out of the store, yelling, 'Thet your goddam noith, you bunth of bathats!' He lisped; when you have paresis you lips, I mean you lisps. One night he came to my house in Cincinnati and tooted the horn and said, 'Come on out and let's go to Texas to see Dale.' He was going back from Maine. He claimed he bought a house —oh, we wrote a story about him at college, where you see this horrible shipwreck and people in the water clutching at the sides of the lifeboat, and the old man is there with a machete, hackin at their fingers. 'Get away, ya bunth a bathats, thith my cottham boath!' Oh, he was horrible. I could tell you stories about him all day. Say, ain't this a nice day?"

And it sure was. The softest breezes blew in from the levee; it was worth the whole trip. We went into the house after Bull to measure the wall for a shelf. He showed us the dining-room table he built. It was made of wood six inches thick. "This is a table that'll last a thousand years!" said Bull, leaning his long thin face at us maniacally. He banged on it.

In the evenings he sat at this table, picking at his food and throwing the bones to the cats. He had seven cats. "I love cats. I especially like the ones that squeal when I hold 'em over the bathtub." He insisted on demonstrating; someone was in the bathroom. "Well," he said, "we can't do that now. Say, I been having a fight with the neighbors next door." He told us about the neighbors; they were a vast crew with sassy children who threw stones over the rickety fence at Dodie and Ray and sometimes at Old Bull. He told them to cut it out; the old man rushed out and yelled something in Portuguese. Bull went in the house and came back with his shotgun, upon which he leaned demurely; the incredible simper on his face beneath the long hatbrim, his whole body writhing coyly and snakily as he waited, a grotesque, lank, lonely clown beneath the clouds. The sight of him the Portuguese must have thought something out of an old evil dream.

We scoured the yard for things to do. There was a tremendous fence Bull had been working on to separate him from the obnoxious neighbors; it would never be finished, the task was too much. He rocked it back and forth to show how solid it was. Suddenly he grew tired and quiet and went in the house and disappeared in the bathroom for his pre-lunch fix. He came out glassy-eyed and calm, and sat down under his burning lamp. The sunlight poked feebly behind the drawn shade. "Say, why don't you fellows try my orgone accumulator? Put some juice in your bones. I always rush up and take off ninety miles an hour for the nearest whorehouse, hor-hor-hor!" This was his "laugh" laugh—when he wasn't really laughing. The orgone accumulator is an ordinary box big enough for a man to sit inside on a chair: a layer of wood, a layer of metal, and another layer of wood gather in orgones from the atmosphere and hold them captive long enough for the human body to absorb more than a usual share. According to Reich, orgones are vibratory atmospheric atoms of the life-principle. People get cancer because they run out of orgones. Old Bull thought his orgone accumulator would be improved if the wood he used was as organic as possible, so he tied bushy bayou leaves and twigs to his mystical outhouse. It stood there in the hot, flat yard, an exfoliate machine clustered and bedecked with maniacal contrivances. Old Bull slipped off his clothes and went in to sit and moon over his navel. "Say, Sal, after lunch let's you and me go play the horses over to the bookie joint in Graetna." He was magnificent. He took a nap after lunch in his chair, the air gun on his lap and little Ray curled around his neck, sleeping. It was a pretty sight, father and son, a father who would certainly never bore his son when it came to finding things to do and talk about. He woke up with a start and stared at me. It took him a minute to recognize who I was. "What are you going to the Coast for, Sal?" he asked, and went back to sleep in a moment.

In the afternoon we went to Graetna, just Bull and me. We drove in his old Chevy. Dean's Hudson was low and sleek; Bull's Chevy was high and rattly. It was just like 1910. The bookie joint was located near the waterfront in a big chromium-leather bar that opened up in the back to a tremendous hall where entries and numbers were posted on the wall. Louisiana characters lounged around with *Racing Form*s. Bull and I had a beer, and casually Bull went over to the slot machine and threw a half-dollar piece in. The counters clicked "Jackpot"—"Jackpot"—"Jackpot"—and the last "Jackpot" hung for just a moment and slipped back to "Cherry." He had lost a hundred dollars or more just by a hair. "Damn!" yelled Bull. "They got these things adjusted. You could see it right then. I had the jackpot and the mechanism clicked it back. Well, what you gonna do." We examined the *Racing Form*. I hadn't played the horses in years and was bemused with all the new names. There was one horse called Big Pop that sent me into a temporary trance thinking of my father, who used to play the horses with me. I was just about to mention it to Old Bull when he said, "Well I think I'll try this Ebony Corsair here."

Then I finally said it. "Big Pop reminds me of my father."

He mused for just a second, his clear blue eyes fixed on mine hypnotically so that I couldn't tell what he was thinking or where he was. Then he went over and bet on Ebony Corsair. Big Pop won and paid fifty to one.

"Damn!" said Bull. "I should have known better, I've had experience with this before. Oh, when will we ever learn?"

"What do you mean?"

"Big Pop is what I mean. You had a vision, boy, a *vision*. Only damn fools pay no attention to visions. How do you know your father, who was an old horseplayer, just didn't momentarily communicate to you that Big Pop was going to win the race? The name brought the feeling up in you, he took advantage of the name to communicate. That's what I was thinking about when you mentioned it. My cousin in Missouri once bet on a horse that had a name that reminded him of his mother, and it won and paid a big price. The same thing happened this afternoon." He shook his head. "Ah, let's go. This is the last time I'll ever play the horses with you around; all these visions drive me to distraction." In the car as we drove back to his old house he said,

"Mankind will someday realize that we are actually in contact with the dead and with the other world, whatever it is; right now we could predict, if we only exerted enough mental will, what is going to happen within the next hundred years and be able to take steps to avoid all kinds of catastrophes. When a man dies he undergoes a mutation in his brain that we know nothing about now but which will be very clear someday if scientists get on the ball. The bastards right now are only interested in seeing if they can blow up the world."

We told Jane about it. She sniffed. "It sounds silly to me." She plied the broom around the kitchen. Bull went in the bathroom for his afternoon fix.

Out on the road Dean and Ed Dunkel were playing basketball with Dodie's ball and a bucket nailed on a lamppost. I joined in. Then we turned to feats of athletic prowess. Dean completely amazed me. He had Ed and me hold a bar of iron up to our waists, and just standing there he popped right over it, holding his heels. "Go ahead, raise it." We kept raising it till it was chest-high. Still he jumped over it with ease. Then he tried the running broad jump and did at least twenty feet and more. Then I raced him down the road. I can do the hundred in 10:5. He passed me like the wind. As we ran I had a mad vision of Dean running through all of life just like that—his bony face outthrust to life, his arms pumping, his brow sweating, his legs twinkling like Groucho Marx, yelling, "Yes! Yes, man, you sure can go!" But nobody could go as fast as he could, and that's the truth. Then Bull came out with a couple of knives and started showing us how to disarm a would-be shivver in a dark alley. I for my part showed him a very good trick, which is falling on the ground in front of your adversary and gripping him with your ankles and flipping him over on his hands and grabbing his wrists in full nelson. He said it was pretty good. He demonstrated some jujitsu. Little Dodie called her mother to the porch and said, "Look at the silly men." She was such a cute sassy little thing that Dean couldn't take his eyes off her.

"Wow. Wait till *she* grows up! Can you see *her* cuttin down Canal Street with her cute eyes. Ah! Oh!" He hissed through his teeth.

We spent a mad day in downtown New Orleans walking around with the Dunkels. Dean was out of his mind that day. When he saw the T & NO freight trains in the yard he wanted to show me everything at once. "You'll be brakeman 'fore I'm through with ya!" He and I and Ed Dunkel ran across the tracks and hopped a freight at three individual points; Marylou and Galatea were waiting in the car. We rode the train a half-mile into the piers, waving at switchmen and flagmen. They showed me the proper way to get off a moving car; the back foot first and let the train go away from you and come around and place the other foot down. They showed me the refrigerator cars, the ice compartments, good for a ride on any winter night in a string of empties. "Remember what I told you about New Mexico to LA?" cried Dean. "This was the way I hung on . . ."

We got back to the girls an hour late and of course they were mad. Ed and Galatea had decided to get a room in New Orleans and stay there and work. This was okay with Bull, who was getting sick and tired of the whole mob. The invitation, originally, was for me to come alone. In the front room, where Dean and Marylou slept, there were jam and coffee stains and empty benny tubes all over the floor; what's more it was Bull's workroom and he couldn't get on with his shelves. Poor Jane was driven to distraction by the continual jumping and running around on the part of Dean. We were waiting for my next GI check to come through; my aunt was forwarding it. Then we were off, the three of us—Dean, Marylou, me. When the check came I realized I hated to leave Bull's wonderful house so suddenly, but Dean was all energies and ready to do.

In a sad red dusk we were finally seated in the car and Jane, Dodie, little boy Ray, Bull, Ed, and Galatea stood around in the high grass, smiling. It was good-by. At the last moment Dean and Bull had a misunderstanding over money; Dean had wanted to borrow; Bull said it was out of the question. The feeling reached back to Texas days. Con-man Dean was antagonizing people away from him by degrees. He giggled maniacally and didn't care; he rubbed his fly, stuck his finger in Marylou's dress, slurped up her knee, frothed at the mouth, and said, "Darling, you know and I know that everything is straight between us at last beyond the furthest abstract definition in metaphysical terms or any terms you want to specify or sweetly impose or harken back . . ." and so on, and zoom went the car and we were off again for California.

8

What is that feeling when you're driving away from people and they recede on the plain till you see their specks dispersing?—it's the too-huge world vaulting us, and it's good-by. But we lean forward to the next crazy venture beneath the skies.

We wheeled through the sultry old light of Algiers, back on the ferry, back toward the mud-splashed, crabbed old ships across the river, back on Canal, and out; on a two-lane highway to Baton Rouge in purple darkness; swung west there, crossed the Mississippi at a place called Port Allen. Port Allen—where the river's all rain and roses in a misty pinpoint darkness and where we swung around a circular drive in yellow foglight and suddenly saw the great black body below a bridge and crossed eternity again. What is the Mississippi River?—a washed clod in the rainy night, a soft plopping from drooping Missouri banks, a dissolving, a riding of the tide down the eternal waterbed, a contribution to brown foams, a voyaging past endless vales and trees and levees, down along, down along, by Memphis, Greenville, Eudora, Vicksburg, Natchez, Port Allen, and Port Orleans and Port of the Deltas, by Potash, Venice, and the Night's Great Gulf, and out.

With the radio on to a mystery program, and as I looked out the window and saw a sign that said USE COOPER'S PAINT and I said, "Okay, I will," we rolled across the hoodwink night of the Louisiana plains— Lawtell, Eunice, Kinder, and De Quincy, western rickety towns becoming more bayou-like as we reached the Sabine. In Old Opelousas I went into a grocery store to buy bread and cheese while Dean saw to gas and oil. It was just a shack; I could hear the family eating supper in the back. I waited a minute; they went on talking. I took bread and cheese and slipped out the door. We had barely enough money to make Frisco. Meanwhile Dean took a carton of cigarettes from the gas station and we were stocked for the voyage—gas, oil, cigarettes, and food. Crooks don't know. He pointed the car straight down the road.

Somewhere near Starks we saw a great red glow in the sky ahead; we wondered what it was; in a moment we were passing it. It was a fire beyond the trees; there were many cars parked on the highway. It must have been some kind of fish-fry, and on the other hand it might have been anything. The country turned strange and dark near Deweyville. Suddenly we were in the swamps.

"Man, do you imagine what it would be like if we found a jazzjoint in these swamps, with great big black fellas moanin guitar blues and drinkin snakejuice and makin signs at us?"

"Yes!"

There were mysteries around here. The car was going over a dirt road elevated off the swamps that dropped on both sides and drooped with vines. We passed an apparition; it was a Negro man in a white shirt walking along with his arms upspread to the inky firmament. He must have been praying or calling down a curse. We zoomed right by;

I looked out the back window to see his white eyes. "Whoo!" said Dean. "Look out. We better not stop in this here country." At one point we got stuck at a crossroads and stopped the car anyway. Dean turned off the headlamps. We were surrounded by a great forest of viny trees in which we could almost hear the slither of a million copperheads. The only thing we could see was the red ampere button on the Hudson dashboard. Marylou squealed with fright. We began laughing maniac laughs to scare her. We were scared too. We wanted to get out of this mansion of the snake, this mireful drooping dark, and zoom on back to familiar American ground and cowtowns. There was a smell of oil and dead water in the air. This was a manuscript of the night we couldn't read. An owl hooted. We took a chance on one of the dirt roads, and pretty soon we were crossing the evil old Sabine River that is responsible for all these swamps. With amazement we saw great structures of light ahead of us. "Texas! It's Texas! Beaumont oil town!" Huge oil tanks and refineries loomed like cities in the oily fragrant air.

"I'm glad we got out of there," said Marylou. "Let's play some more mystery programs now."

We zoomed through Beaumont, over the Trinity River at Liberty, and straight for Houston. Now Dean got talking about his Houston days in 1947. "Hassel! That mad Hassel! I look for him everywhere I go and I never find him. He used to get us so hung-up in Texas here. We'd drive in with Bull for groceries and Hassel'd disappear. We'd have to go looking for him in every shooting gallery in town." We were entering Houston. "We had to look for him in this spade part of town most of the time. Man, he'd be blasting with every mad cat he could find. One night we lost him and took a hotel room. We were supposed to bring ice back to Jane because her food was rotting. It took us two days to find Hassel. I got hung-up myself—I gunned shopping women in the afternoon, right here, downtown, supermarkets"—we flashed by in the empty night—"and found a real gone dumb girl who was out of her mind and just wandering, trying to steal an orange. She was from Wyoming. Her beautiful body was matched only by her idiot mind. I found her babbling and took her back to the room. Bull was drunk trying to get this young Mexican kid drunk. Carlo was writing poetry on heroin. Hassel didn't show up till midnight at the jeep. We found him sleeping in the back seat. The ice was all melted. Hassel said he took about five sleeping pills. Man, if my memory could only serve me right the way my mind works I could tell you every detail of the things we did. Ah, but we know time. Everything takes care of itself. I could close my eyes and this old car would take care of itself."

In the empty Houston streets of four o'clock in the morning a motorcycle kid suddenly roared through, all bespangled and bedecked with glittering buttons, visor, slick black jacket, a Texas poet of the night, girl gripped on his back like a papoose, hair flying, onward-going, singing, "Houston, Austin, Fort Worth, Dallas—and sometimes Kansas City—and sometimes old Antone, ah-haaaaa!" They pinpointed out of sight. "Wow! Dig that gone gal on his belt! Let's all blow!" Dean tried to catch up with them. "Now wouldn't it be fine if we could all get together and have a real going goofbang together with everybody sweet and fine and agreeable, no hassles, no infant rise of protest or body woes misconceptalized or sumpin? Ah! but we know time." He bent to it and pushed the car.

Beyond Houston his energies, great as they were, gave out and I drove. Rain began to fall just as I took the wheel. Now we were on the great Texas plain and, as Dean said, "You drive and drive and you're still in Texas tomorrow night." The rain lashed down. I drove through a rickety little cowtown with a muddy main street and found myself in a dead end. "Hey, what do I do?" They were both asleep. I turned and crawled back through town. There wasn't a soul in sight and not a single light. Suddenly a horseman in a raincoat appeared in my headlamps. It was the sheriff. He had a ten-gallon hat, drooping in the torrent. "Which way to Austin?" He told me politely and I started off. Outside town I suddenly saw two headlamps flaring directly at me in the lashing rain. Whoops, I thought I was on the wrong side of the road; I eased right and found myself rolling in the mud; I rolled back to the road. Still the headlamps came straight for me. At the last moment I realized the other driver was on the wrong side of the road and didn't know it. I swerved at thirty into the mud; it was flat, no ditch, thank God. The offending car backed up in the downpour. Four sullen fieldworkers, snuck from their chores to brawl in drinking fields, all white shirts and dirty brown arms, sat looking at me dumbly in the night. The driver was as drunk as the lot.

He said, "Which way t'Houston?" I pointed my thumb back. I was thunderstruck in the middle of the thought that they had done this on purpose just to ask directions, as a panhandler advances on you straight up the sidewalk to bar your way. They gazed ruefully at the floor of their car, where empty bottles rolled, and clanked away. I started the car; it was stuck in the mud a foot deep. I sighed in the rainy Texas wilderness.

"Dean," I said, "wake up."

"What?"

"We're stuck in the mud."

"What happened?" I told him. He swore up and down. We put on old shoes and sweaters and barged out of the car into the driving rain. I put my back on the rear fender and lifted and heaved; Dean stuck chains under the swishing wheels. In a minute we were covered with mud. We woke up Marylou to these horrors and made her gun the car while we pushed. The tormented Hudson heaved and heaved. Suddenly it jolted out and went skidding across the road. Marylou pulled it up just in time, and we got in. That was that—the work had taken thirty minutes and we were soaked and miserable.

I fell asleep, all caked with mud; and in the morning when I woke up the mud was solidified and outside there was snow. We were near Fredericksburg, in the high plains. It was one of the worst winters in Texas and Western history, when cattle perished like flies in great blizzards and snow fell on San Francisco and LA. We were all miserable. We wished we were back in New Orleans with Ed Dunkel. Marylou was driving; Dean was sleeping. She drove with one hand on the wheel and the other reaching back to me in the back seat. She cooed promises about San Francisco. I slavered miserably over it. At ten I took the wheel—Dean was out for hours—and drove several hundred dreary miles across the bushy snows and ragged sage hills. Cowboys went by in baseball caps and earmuffs, looking for cows. Comfortable little homes with chimneys smoking appeared along the road at intervals. I wished we could go in for buttermilk and beans in front of the fireplace.

At Sonora I again helped myself to free bread and cheese while the proprietor chatted with a big rancher on the other side of the store. Dean huzzahed when he heard it; he was hungry. We couldn't spend a cent on food. "Yass, yass," said Dean, watching the ranchers loping up and down Sonora main street, "every one of them is a bloody million-aire, thousand head of cattle, workhands, buildings, money in the bank. If I lived around here I'd go be an idjit in the sagebrush, I'd be jackrab-bit, I'd lick up the branches, I'd look for pretty cowgirls—hee-hee-hee-hee! Damn! Bam!" He socked himself. "Yes! Right! Oh me!" We didn't know what he was talking about any more. He took the wheel and flew the rest of the way across the state of Texas, about five hundred miles, clear to El Paso, arriving at dusk and not stopping except once when he took all his clothes off, near Ozona, and ran yipping and leaping naked in the sage. Cars zoomed by and didn't see him. He scurried back to the car and drove on. "Now Sal, now Marylou, I want both of you to do as I'm doing, disemburden yourselves of all that clothes—now what's the sense of clothes? now that's what I'm sayin—and sun your pretty bellies with me. Come on!" We were driving west into the sun; it fell in through the windshield. "Open your belly as we drive into it." Marylou complied; unfuddyduddied, so did I. We sat in the front seat, all three. Marylou took out cold cream and applied it to us for kicks. Every now and then a big truck zoomed by; the driver in high cab caught a glimpse of a golden beauty sitting naked with two naked men: you could see them swerve a moment as they vanished in our rear-view window. Great sage plains, snowless now, rolled on. Soon we were in the orange-rocked Pecos Canyon country. Blue distances opened up in the sky. We got out of the car to examine an old Indian ruin. Dean did so stark naked. Marylou and I put on our overcoats. We wandered among the old stones, hooting and howling. Certain tourists caught sight of Dean naked in the plain but they could not believe their eyes and wobbled on.

Dean and Marylou parked the car near Van Horn and made love while I went to sleep. I woke up just as we were rolling down the tremendous Rio Grande Valley through Clint and Ysleta to El Paso. Marylou jumped to the back seat, I jumped to the front seat, and we rolled along. To our left across the vast Rio Grande spaces were the moorish-red mounts of the Mexican border, the land of the Tarahumare; soft dusk played on the peaks. Straight ahead lay the distant lights of El Paso and Juárez, sown in a tremendous valley so big that you could see several railroads puffing at the same time in every direction, as though it was the Valley of the World. We descended into it.

"Clint, Texas!" said Dean. He had the radio on to the Clint station. Every fifteen minutes they played a record; the rest of the time it was commercials about a high-school correspondence course. "This program is beamed all over the West," cried Dean excitedly. "Man, I used to listen to it day and night in reform school and prison. All of us used to write in. You get a high-school diploma by mail, facsimile thereof, if you pass the test. All the young wranglers in the West, I don't care who, at one time or another write in for this; it's all they hear; you tune the radio in Sterling, Colorado, Lusk, Wyoming, I don't care where, you get Clint, Texas, Clint, Texas. And the music is always cowboy hillbilly and Mexican, absolutely the worst program in the entire history of the country and nobody can do anything about it. They have a tremendous beam; they've got the whole land hogtied." We saw the high antenna beyond the shacks of Clint. "Oh, man, the things I could tell you!" cried Dean, almost weeping. Eyes bent on Frisco and the Coast, we came into El Paso as it got dark, broke. We absolutely had to get some money for gas or we'd never make it.

We tried everything. We buzzed the travel bureau, but no one was going west that night. The travel bureau is where you go for share-the-gas rides, legal in the West. Shifty characters wait with battered suitcases. We went to the Greyhound bus station to try to persuade somebody to give us the money instead of taking a bus for the Coast. We were too bashful to approach anyone. We wandered around sadly. It was cold outside. A college boy was sweating at the sight of luscious Marylou and trying to look unconcerned. Dean and I consulted but decided we weren't pimps. Suddenly a crazy dumb young kid, fresh out of reform school, attached himself to us, and he and Dean rushed out for a beer. "Come on, man, let's go mash somebody on the head and get his money."

"I dig you, man!" yelled Dean. They dashed off. For a moment I was worried; but Dean only wanted to dig the streets of El Paso with the kid and get his kicks. Marylou and I waited in the car. She put her arms around me.

I said, "Dammit, Lou, wait till we get to Frisco."

"I don't care. Dean's going to leave me anyway."

"When are you going back to Denver?"

"I don't know. I don't care what I'm doing. Can I go back east with you?"

"We'll have to get some money in Frisco."

"I know where you can get a job in a lunchcart behind the counter, and I'll be a waitress. I know a hotel where we can stay on credit. We'll stick together. Gee, I'm sad."

"What are you sad about, kid?"

"I'm sad about everything. Oh damn, I wish Dean wasn't so crazy now." Dean came twinkling back, giggling, and jumped in the car.

"What a crazy cat that was, whoo! Did I dig him! I used to know thousands of guys like that, they're all the same, their minds work in uniform clockwork, oh, the infinite ramifications, no time, no time . . ." And he shot up the car, hunched over the wheel, and roared out of El Paso. "We'll just have to pick up hitchhikers. I'm positive we'll find some. Hup! hup! here we go. Look out!" he yelled at a motorist, and swung around him, and dodged a truck and bounced over the city limits. Across the river were the jewel lights of Juárez and the sad dry land and the jewel stars of Chihuahua. Marylou was watching Dean as she had watched him clear across the country and back, out of the corner of her eye—with a sullen, sad air, as though she wanted to cut off his head and hide it in her closet, an envious and rueful love of him so amazingly himself, all raging and sniffy and crazy-wayed, a smile of tender dotage but also sinister envy that frightened me about her, a love she knew would never bear fruit because when she looked at his hang-jawed bony face with its male self-containment and absentmindedness she knew he was too mad. Dean was convinced Marylou was a whore; he confided in me that she was a pathological liar. But when she watched him like this it was love too; and when Dean noticed he always turned with his big false flirtatious smile, with the eyelashes fluttering and the teeth pearly white, while a moment ago he was only dreaming in his eternity. Then Marylou and I both laughed—and Dean gave no sign of discomfiture, just a goofy glad grin that said to us, Ain't we gettin our kicks *anyway?* And that was it.

Outside El Paso, in the darkness, we saw a small huddled figure with thumb stuck out. It was our promised hitchhiker. We pulled up and backed to his side. "How much money you got, kid?" The kid had no money; he was about seventeen, pale, strange, with one undeveloped crippled hand and no suitcase. "Ain't he *sweet?*" said Dean, turning to me with a serious awe. "Come on in, fella, we'll take you out—" The kid saw his advantage. He said he had an aunt in Tulare, California, who owned a grocery store and as soon as we got there he'd have some money for us. Dean rolled on the floor laughing, it was so much like the kid in North Carolina. "Yes! Yes!" he yelled. "We've *all* got aunts; well, let's go, let's see the aunts and the uncles and the grocery stores all the way ALONG that road!!" And we had a new passenger, and a fine little guy he turned out to be, too. He didn't say a word, he listened to us. After a minute of Dean's talk he was probably convinced he had joined a car of madmen. He said he was hitchhiking from Alabama to Oregon, where his home was. We asked him what he was doing in Alabama.

"I went to visit my uncle; he said he'd have a job for me in a lumber mill. The job fell through, so I'm comin back home."

"Goin home," said Dean, "goin home, yes, I know, we'll take you home, far as Frisco anyhow." But we didn't have any money. Then it occurred to me I could borrow five dollars from my old friend Hal

Hingham in Tucson, Arizona. Immediately Dean said it was all settled and we were going to Tucson. And we did.

We passed Las Cruces, New Mexico, in the night and arrived in Arizona at dawn. I woke up from a deep sleep to find everybody sleeping like lambs and the car parked God knows where, because I couldn't see out the steamy windows. I got out of the car. We were in the mountains: there was a heaven of sunrise, cool purple airs, red mountainsides, emerald pastures in valleys, dew, and transmuting clouds of gold; on the ground gopher holes, cactus, mesquite. It was time for me to drive on. I pushed Dean and the kid over and went down the mountain with the clutch in and the motor off to save gas. In this manner I rolled into Benson, Arizona. It occurred to me that I had a pocket watch Rocco had just given me for a birthday present, a four-dollar watch. At the gas station I asked the man if he knew a pawnshop in Benson. It was right next door to the station. I knocked, someone got up out of bed, and in a minute I had a dollar for the watch. It went into the tank. Now we had enough gas for Tucson. But suddenly a big pistol-packing trooper appeared, just as I was ready to pull out, and asked to see my driver's license. "The fella in the back seat has the license," I said. Dean and Marylou were sleeping together under the blanket. The cop told Dean to come out. Suddenly he whipped out his gun and yelled, "Keep your hands up!"

"Offisah," I heard Dean say in the most unctious and ridiculous tones, "offisah, I was only buttoning my flah." Even the cop almost smiled. Dean came out, muddy, ragged, T-shirted, rubbing his belly, cursing, looking everywhere for his license and his car papers. The cop rummaged through our back trunk. All the papers were straight.

"Only checking up," he said with a broad smile. "You can go on now. Benson ain't a bad town actually; you might enjoy it if you had breakfast here."

"Yes yes yes," said Dean, paying absolutely no attention to him, and drove off. We all sighed with relief. The police are suspicious when gangs of youngsters come by in new cars without a cent in their pockets and have to pawn watches. "Oh, they're always interfering," said Dean, "but he was a much better cop than that rat in Virginia. They try to make headline arrests; they think every car going by is some big Chicago gang. They ain't got nothin else to do." We drove on to Tucson.

Tucson is situated in beautiful mesquite riverbed country, over-looked by the snowy Catalina range. The city was one big construction job; the people transient, wild, ambitious, busy, gay; washlines, trailers;

bustling downtown streets with banners; altogether very Californian. Fort Lowell Road, out where Hingham lived, wound along lovely river-bed trees in the flat desert. We saw Hingham himself brooding in the yard. He was a writer; he had come to Arizona to work on his book in peace. He was a tall, gangly, shy satirist who mumbled to you with his head turned away and always said funny things. His wife and baby were with him in the dobe house, a small one that his Indian stepfather had built. His mother lived across the yard in her own house. She was an excited American woman who loved pottery, beads, and books. Hingham had heard of Dean through letters from New York. We came down on him like a cloud, every one of us hungry, even Alfred, the crippled hitchhiker. Hingham was wearing an old sweater and smoking a pipe in the keen desert air. His mother came out and invited us into her kitchen to eat. We cooked noodles in a great pot.

Then we all drove to a crossroads liquor store, where Hingham cashed a check for five dollars and handed me the money.

There was a brief good-by. "It certainly was pleasant," said Hingham, looking away. Beyond some trees, across the sand, a great neon sign of a roadhouse glowed red. Hingham always went there for a beer when he was tired of writing. He was very lonely, he wanted to get back to New York. It was sad to see his tall figure receding in the dark as we drove away, just like the other figures in New York and New Orleans: they stand uncertainly underneath immense skies, and everything about them is drowned. Where go? what do? what for?—sleep. But this foolish gang was bending onward.

9

Outside Tucson we saw another hitchhiker in the dark road. This was an Okie from Bakersfield, California, who put down his story. "*Hot* damn, I left Bakersfield with the travel-bureau car and left my gui-tar in the trunk of another one and they never showed up—gui-tar and cowboy duds; you see, I'm a moo-sician, I was headed for Arizona to play with Johnny Mackaw's Sagebrush Boys. Well, hell, here I am in Arizona, broke, and m'gui-tar's been stoled. You boys drive me back to Bakersfield and I'll get the money from my brother. How much you want?" We wanted just enough gas to make Frisco from Bakersfield, about three dollars. Now we were five in the car. "Evenin, ma'am," he said, tipping his hat to Marylou, and we were off.

In the middle of the night we overtopped the lights of Palm Springs from a mountain road. At dawn, in snowy passes, we labored toward the town of Mojave, which was the entryway to the great Tehachapi Pass. The Okie woke up and told funny stories; sweet little Alfred sat smiling. Okie told us he knew a man who forgave his wife for shooting him and got her out of prison, only to be shot a second time. We were passing the women's prison when he told it. Up ahead we saw Tehachapi Pass starting up. Dean took the wheel and carried us clear to the top of the world. We passed a great shroudy cement factory in the canyon. Then we started down. Dean cut off the gas, threw in the clutch, and negotiated every hairpin turn and passed cars and did everything in the books without the benefit of accelerator. I held on tight. Sometimes the road went up again briefly; he merely passed cars without a sound, on pure momentum. He knew every rhythm and every kick of a first-class pass. When it was time to U-turn left around a low stone wall that overlooked the bottom of the world, he just leaned far over to his left, hands on the wheel, stiff-armed, and carried it that way; and when the turn snaked to the right again, this time with a cliff on our left, he leaned far to the right, making Marylou and me lean with him. In this way we floated and flapped down to the San Joaquin Valley. It lay spread a mile below, virtually the floor of California, green and wondrous from our aerial shelf. We made thirty miles without using gas.

Suddenly we were all excited. Dean wanted to tell me everything he knew about Bakersfield as we reached the city limits. He showed me rooming houses where he stayed, railroad hotels, poolhalls, diners, sidings where he jumped off the engine for grapes, Chinese restaurants where he ate, park benches where he met girls, and certain places where he'd done nothing but sit and wait around. Dean's California—wild, sweaty, important, the land of lonely and exiled and eccentric lovers come to forgather like birds, and the land where everybody somehow looked like broken-down, handsome, decadent movie actors. "Man, I spent hours on that very chair in front of that drugstore!" He remembered all—every pinochle game, every woman, every sad night. And suddenly we were passing the place in the railyards where Terry and I had sat under the moon, drinking wine, on those bum crates, in October 1947, and I tried to tell him. But he was too excited. "This is where Dunkel and I spent a whole morning drinking beer, trying to make a real gone little waitress from Watsonville—no, Tracy, yes, Tracy—and her name was Esmeralda—oh, man, something like that." Marylou was planning what to do the moment she arrived in Frisco. Alfred said his aunt would give him plenty of money up in Tulare. The Okie directed us to his brother in the flats outside town.

We pulled up at noon in front of a little rose-covered shack, and the Okie went in and talked with some women. We waited fifteen minutes. "I'm beginning to think this guy has no more money than I have," said Dean. "We get more hung-up! There's probably nobody in the family that'll give him a cent after that fool escapade." The Okie came out sheepishly and directed us to town.

"*Hot* damn, I wisht I could find my brother." He made inquiries. He probably felt he was our prisoner. Finally we went to a big bread bakery, and the Okie came out with his brother, who was wearing coveralls and was apparently the truck mechanic inside. He talked with his brother a few minutes. We waited in the car. Okie was telling all his relatives his adventures and about the loss of his guitar. But he got the money, and he gave it to us, and we were all set for Frisco. We thanked him and took off.

Next stop was Tulare. Up the valley we roared. I lay in the back seat, exhausted, giving up completely, and sometime in the afternoon, while I dozed, the muddy Hudson zoomed by the tents outside Sabinal where I had lived and loved and worked in the spectral past. Dean was bent rigidly over the wheel, pounding the rods. I was sleeping when we finally arrived in Tulare; I woke up to hear the insane details. "Sal, wake up! Alfred found his aunt's grocery store, but do you know what happened? His aunt shot her husband and went to jail. The store's closed down. We didn't get a cent. Think of it! The things that happen; the Okie told us the same likewise story, the trou-bles on all sides, the complications of events—whee, damn!" Alfred was biting his finger-nails. We were turning off the Oregon road at Madera, and there we made our farewell with little Alfred. We wished him luck and Godspeed to Oregon. He said it was the best ride he ever had.

It seemed like a matter of minutes when we began rolling in the foothills before Oakland and suddenly reached a height and saw stretched out ahead of us the fabulous white city of San Francisco on her eleven mystic hills with the blue Pacific and its advancing wall of potato-patch fog beyond, and smoke and goldenness in the late after-noon of time. "There she blows!" yelled Dean. "Wow! Made it! Just enough gas! Give me water! No more land! We can't go any further 'cause there ain't no more land! Now Marylou, darling, you and Sal go immediately to a hotel and wait for me to contact you in the morning as soon as I have definite arrangements made with Camille and call up Frenchman about my railroad watch and you and Sal buy the first thing hit town a paper for the want ads and workplans." And he drove into the Oakland Bay Bridge and it carried us in. The downtown office buildings were just sparkling on their lights; it made you think of Sam Spade. When we staggered out of the car on O'Farrell Street and sniffed and stretched, it was like getting on shore after a long voyage at sea; the sloppy street reeled under our feet; secret chop sueys from Frisco Chinatown floated in the air. We took all our things out of the car and piled them on the sidewalk.

Suddenly Dean was saying good-by. He was bursting to see Camille and find out what had happened. Marylou and I stood dumbly in the street and watched him drive away. "You see what a bastard he is?" said Marylou. "Dean will leave you out in the cold any time it's in his interest."

"I know," I said, and I looked back east and sighed. We had no money. Dean hadn't mentioned money. "Where are we going to stay?" We wandered around, carrying our bundles of rags in the narrow romantic streets. Everybody looked like a broken-down movie extra, a withered starlet; disenchanted stunt-men, midget auto-racers, poignant California characters with their end-of-the-continent sadness, handsome, decadent, Casanova-ish men, puffy-eyed motel blondes, hustlers, pimps, whores, masseurs, bellhops—a lemon lot, and how's a man going to make a living with a gang like that?

JAZZ OF THE
BEAT GENERATION
1949

EDITOR'S NOTE
Here Kerouac calls himself "Sal," Neal Cassady is called "Dean," and Allen Ginsberg is mentioned as "Carlo Marx."

OUT WE JUMPED in the warm mad night hearing a wild tenorman's bawling horn across the way going "EE-YAH! EE-YAH!" and hands clapping to the beat and folks yelling "Go, go, go!" Far from escorting the girls into the place, Dean was already racing across the street with his huge bandaged thumb in the air yelling "Blow, man, blow!" A bunch of colored men in Saturday night suits were whooping it up in front. It was a sawdust saloon, all wood, with a small bandstand near the john on which the fellows huddled with their hats on blowing over people's heads, a crazy place, not far from Market Street, in the dingy skid-row rear of it, near Harrison and the big bridge causeway; crazy floppy women wandered around sometimes in their bathrobes, bottles clanked in alleys. In back of the joint in a dark corridor beyond the splattered toilets, scores of men and women stood against the wall drinking wine-spodi-odi and spitting at the stars . . . wine, whiskey and beer. The behatted tenorman was blowing at the peak of a wonderfully satisfactory free idea, a rising and falling riff that went from "EE-yah!" to a crazier "EE-de-lee-yah!" and blasted along to the rolling crash of butt-scarred drums hammered by a big brutal-looking curl-sconced Negro with a bullneck who didn't give a damn about anything but punishing his tubs, crash, rattle-ti-boom crash. Uproars of music and the tenorman *had it* and everybody knew he had it. Dean was clutching his head in the crowd and it was a mad crowd. They were all urging that tenorman to hold it and keep it with cries and wild eyes; he was raising himself from a crouch and going down again with his horn, looping it up in a clear cry above the furor. A six-foot skinny Negro woman was rolling her bones at the man's hornbell, and he just jabbed it at her, "Ee! ee! ee!" He had a foghorn tone; his horn was taped; he was a shipyard worker and he didn't care. Everybody was rocking and roaring; Galatea and Alice with beers in their hands were standing on their chairs shaking and jumping. Groups of colored studs stumbled in from the street falling over one another to get there. "Stay with it man!" roared a man with a foghorn voice, and let out a big groan that must have been heard clear to Sacramento, "Ah-haa!"—"Whoo!" said Dean. He was rubbing his chest, his belly, his T-shirt was out, the sweat splashed from his face. Boom, kick, that drummer was kicking his drums down the cellar and rolling the beat upstairs with his murderous sticks, rattlety-boom! A big fat man was jumping on the platform making it sag and creak. "Yoo!" The pianist was only pounding the keys with spread-eagled fingers, chords only, at intervals when the great tenorman was drawing breath for another blast of phrase, Chinese chords, they shuddered the piano in every timber, chink and wire, *boing!* The tenorman jumped down from the platform and just stood buried in the crowd blowing around;

his hat was over his eyes; somebody pushed it back for him. He just hauled back and stamped his foot and blew down a hoarse baughing blast, and drew breath, and raised the horn and blew high wide and screaming in the air. Dean was directly in front of him with his face glued to the bell of the horn, clapping his hands, pouring sweat on the man's keys; and the man noticed and laughed in his horn a long quivering crazy mule's hee-haw and everybody else laughed and they rocked and rocked; and finally the tenorman decided to blow his top and crouched down and held a note in high C for a long time as everything else crashed along skittely-boom and the cries increased and I thought the cops would come swarming from the nearest precinct.

It was just a usual Saturday night goodtime, nothing else; the bebop winos were wailing away, the workingman tenors, the cats who worked and got their horns out of hock and blew and had their women troubles, and came on in their horns with a will, saying things, a lot to say, talkative horns, you could almost hear the words and better than that the harmony, made you hear the way to fill up blank spaces of time with the tune and very consequence of your hands and breath and dead soul; summer, August 1949, and Frisco blowing mad, the dew on the muscat in the interior fields of Joaquin and down in Watsonville the lettuce blowing, the money flowing for Frisco so seasonal and mad, the railroads rolling, extraboards roaring, crates of melons on sidewalks, bananas coming off elevators, tarantulas suffocating in the new crazy air, chipped ice and the cool interior smells of grape tanks, cool bop hepcats standing slumped with horn and no lapels and blowing like Wardell, like Brew Moore softly . . . all of it insane, sad, sweeter than the love of mothers yet harsher than the murder of fathers. The clock on the wall quivered and shook; nobody cared about that thing. Dean was in a trance. The tenorman's eyes were fixed straight on him; he had found a madman who not only understood but cared and wanted to understand more and much more than there was, and they began duelling for this; everything came out of the horn, no more phrases, just cries, cries, "Baugh" and down to "Beep!" and up to "EEEEE!" and down to clinkers and over to sideways echoing horn-sounds and horse-laughs and he tried everything, up, down, sideways, upside down, dog fashion, horizontal, thirty degrees, forty degrees and finally he fell back in somebody's arms and gave up and everybody pushed around and yelled "Yes, yes, he done blowed that one!" Dean wiped himself with his handkerchief.

Up steps Freddy on the bandstand and asks for a slow beat and looks sadly out the open door over people's heads and begins singing "Close Your Eyes." Things quiet down for a minute. Freddy's wearing a tattered suède jacket, a purple shirt with white buttons, cracked shoes and zoot pants without press; he didn't care. He looked like a pimp in Mecca, where there are no pimps; a barren woman's child, which is a dream; he looked like he was beat to his socks; he was down, and bent, and he played us some blues with his vocals. His big brown eyes were concerned with sadness, and the singing of songs slowly and with long thoughtful pauses. But in the second chorus he got excited and embraced the mike and jumped down from the bandstand and bent to it and to sing a note he had to touch his shoe tops and pull it all up to blow, and he blew so much he staggered from the effect, he only recovered himself in time for the next long slow note. "Mu-u-u-u-sic pla-a-a-a-a-a-ay!" He leaned back with his face to the ceiling, mike held at his fly. He shook his shoulders, he gave the hip sneer, he swayed. Then he leaned in almost falling with his pained face against the mike. "Ma-a-a-ke it dream-y for dan-cing"—and he looked at the street outside, Folsom, with his lips curled in scorn—"while we go ro-man-n-n-cing"—he staggered sideways—"Lo-o-o-ove's holi-da-a-a-ay"—he shook his head with disgust and weariness at the whole world—"Will make it seem"—what would it make it seem?—everybody waited, he mourned—"O—kay." The piano hit a chord. "So baby come on and just clo-o-o-o-se your pretty little ey-y-y-es"—his mouth quivered, offered; he looked at us, Dean and me, with an expression that seemed to say "Hey now, what's this thing we're all putting down in this sad brown world"—and then he came to the end of his song and for this there had to be elaborate preparations during which time you could send all the messages to Garcia around the world twelve times and what difference did it make to anybody because here we were dealing with the pit and prune juice of poor beat life itself and the pathos of people in the Godawful streets, so he said and sang it, "Close—your—" and blew it way up to the ceiling with a big voice that came not from training but feeling and that much better, and blew it through to the stars and on up—"Ey-y-y-y-y-es" and in arpeggios of applause staggered off the platform ruefully, broodingly, nonsatisfied, artistic, arrogant. He sat in the corner with a bunch of boys and paid no attention to them. They gave him beers. He looked down and wept. He was the greatest.

Dean and I went over to talk to him. We invited him out to the car. In the car he suddenly yelled "Yes! ain't nothing I like better than good kicks! Where do we go?" Dean jumped up and down in the seat giggling maniacally. "Later! later!" said Freddy. "I'll get my boy to drive us down to Jamson's Nook, I got to sing. Man I *live* to sing. Been singing 'Close Your Eyes' for a month—I don't want to sing nothing else. What are you two boys up to?"

We told him we were going to New York tomorrow. "Lord, I ain't never been there and they tell me it's a real jumping town but I ain't got no cause complaining where I am. I'm married you know." "Oh yes?" said Dean lighting up. "And where is the little darling tonight and I bet she's got a lots of nice friends . . . man . . ." "What do you mean?" said Freddy looking at him half-smiling out of the corner. "I tole you I was married to her, didn't I?"—"Oh yes, Oh yes," blushed Dean. "I was just asking. Maybe she's got a couple of friends downtown, or somethin', you know man, a ball, I'm only lookin for a ball, a gang ball, man."—"Yah, what's the good of balls, life's too sad to be ballin all the time, Jim," said Freddy lowering his eye to the street. "Shee-it," he said, "I ain't got no money and I don't care tonight."

We went back in for more. The girls were so disgusted with Dean and I for jumping around with everybody else that they had left by now, gone to Jamson's Nook on foot; the car we'd come in, and had to push from down Mission, wouldn't run anyway. We saw a horrible sight in the bar; a white hipster fairy of some kind had come in wearing a Hawaiian shirt and was asking the big bull-necked drummer if he could sit in. The musicians looked at him suspiciously. He sat at the tubs and they started the beat of a blues number and he began stroking the snares with soft goofy bop brushes, swaying his neck with that complacent Reich-analyzed ecstasy that doesn't mean anything but too much T and soft foods and goofy kicks in cafeterias and pads at dawn and on the cool order. But he didn't care. The musicians looked at him and said, "Yeah, yeah, that's what the man does, shh-ee-eet." He smiled joyously into space and kept the beat with butterfly brushes, softly, with bop subtleties, a giggling rippling background for big solid foghorn blues. The big Negro bull-neck drummer sat waiting for his turn to come back. "What that man doing?" he said. "Play the music," he said. "What in hell!" he said. "Shh-ee-eet!" and looked away red-eyed. Freddy's boy showed up at this moment; he was a little taut Negro with a great big Cadillac. We all jumped in. He hunched over the wheel and blew the car clear across San Francisco without stopping once, seventy miles per hour; he was fulfilling his mission with a fixed smile, his destiny we'd expected of the rumors and songs of him. Right through traffic and nobody even noticed he was so good. Dean was in ecstasies. "Dig *this* guy, man—dig the way he sits right in that seat with the feel of the car under his both haunches, a little bit forward, to the left, against the gut of the car and he don't make any outward indication and just balls that jack and can talk all night while doing it, only thing is he doesn't bother with life, listen to them, O man the things, the things, he lets Freddy do that, and Freddy's his boy, and tells him about life, listen to them, O man the things . . . the things I could—I wish—let's not stop, man, we've got to keep going now!" And Freddy's boy wound around a corner and bowled us right in front of Jamson's Nook and was parked. "Yes!" yelled Dean. A cab squeaked to a stop in the street; out of it jumped a skinny seventy-year-old withered little Negro preacherman who threw a dollar bill at the cabby and yelled "Blow!" and ran into the club pulling on his coat (just come out of work) and dashed right through the downstairs bar yelling "Go, go, go!" and stumbled upstairs almost falling on his face and blew the door open and fell into the jazz session room with his hands out to support him against anything he might fall on, and he fell right on Lampshade who was reduced to working as a waiter in Jamson's Nook that summer (the great Lampshade whom I'd seen shout the blues with veins helling in his neck and his overcoat on), and the music was there blasting and blasting and the preacherman stood transfixed in the open door screaming "Blowblowblow!" And the man was a little short Negro with an alto horn that Dean said obviously lived with his grandmother, "Just like my boy Jim!", slept all day and blew all night and blew a hundred choruses before he was ready to jump for fair, and that's what he was doing. "It's Carlo Marx!" screamed Dean above the fury. And it was. This little grandmother's boy with the scrapped up alto had beady glittering eyes, small crooked feet, spindly legs in formal black pants, like our friend Carlo, and he hopped and flopped with his horn and threw his feet around and kept his eyes transfixed on the audience (which was just people laughing at a dozen tables, the room thirty by thirty feet and low ceiling) and he never stopped. He was very simple in his ideas. Ideas meant nothing to him. What he liked was the surprise of a new simple variation of chorus. He'd go from "ta-potato-rup, ta-potato-rup" repeating and hopping to it and kissing and smiling into his horn—and then to "ta-potatola-dee-rup, ta-potatola-DEE-rup!" and it was all great moments of laughter and understanding for him and everyone else who heard. His tone was clear as a bell, high, pure, and blew straight in our faces from two feet away. Dean stood in front of him, oblivious to everything else in the world, with his head bowed, his hands socking in together, his whole body jumping on his heels and the sweat, always the sweat pouring and splashing down his tormented neck to literally lie in a pool at his feet. Galatea and Alice were there and it took us five minutes to realize it. Whoo, Frisco nights, the end of the continent and the end of the road and the end of all dull doubt. Lampshade was roaring around with trays of beer: everything he did was in rhythm: he yelled at the waitress with the beat: "Hey now, babybaby, make a way, make a way, it's Lampshade coming your way!" and he hurled by her with the beers in the air and roared through the swinging doors in the kitchen and danced with the cooks and came sweating back. Ronnie Morgan, who'd earlier in the evening performed at the Hey Now Club screaming and kicking over the mike, now sat absolutely motionless at a corner table with an untouched drink in front of him, staring gook-eyed into space, his hands hanging at his sides till they almost touched the floor, his feet outspread like lolling tongues, his body shriveled into absolute weariness and entranced sorrow and what-all was on his mind: a man who knocked himself out every night and let the others put the quietus to him at dawn. Everything swirled around him like a cloud. And that little grandmother's alto, that little Carlo Marx hopped and monkey-danced with his magic horn and blew two hundred choruses of blues, each one more frantic than the other and no signs of failing energy or willingness to call anything a day. The whole room shivered. It has since been closed down, naturally.

Dean and I raced on to the East Coast. At one point we drove a 1947 Cadillac limousine across the state of Nebraska at 110 miles an hour, beating hotshot passenger trains and steel wheel freights in one nervous shuddering snapup of the gas. We told stories and zoomed East. There were hoboes by the tracks, wino bottles, the moon shining on woodfires. There were white-faced cows out in the plains, dim as nuns. There was dawn, Iowa; the Mississippi River at Davenport, and Chicago by nightfall. "Oh man" said Dean to me as we stood in front of a bar on North Clark Street in the hot summer night, "dig these old Chinamen that cut by Chicago. What a weird town—whee! And that woman in that window up there, just looking down with her big breasts hanging from her old nightgown. Just big wide eyes waiting. Wow! Sal we gotta go and never stop going till we get there."—"Where we going man?" —"Obvious question say Charley Chan. But we gotta go, we gotta GO." Then here came a gang of young bop musicians carrying their instruments out of cars. They piled right into a saloon and we followed them. They set themselves up and started blowing. There we were. The leader was a slender drooping curly-haired pursy-mouth tenorman, thin of shoulder, twenty-one, lean, loose, blowing modern and soft, cool in his sports shirt without undershirt, self-indulgent, sneering. Dean and I were like car thieves and juvenile heroes on a mad—with our T-shirts and beards and torn pants—but the bop, the combo! How that cool leader picked up his horn and frowned in it and blew cool and complex and was dainty stamping his foot to catch ideas and ducked to miss others—saying "Wail" very quietly when the other boys took solos. He was the leader, the encourager, the schoolmaker, the Teshmaker, the Bix, the Louis in the great formal school of new underground subterranean American music that would someday be studied all over the universities of Europe and the world. Then there was Pres, a husky handsome blond like a freckled boxer, like Jackie Cooper, meticulously molded in his sharkskin plaid suit with the long drape and the collar falling back and the tie undone for exact sharpness and casualness, sweating and hitching up his horn and writhing into it, and a tone just like Pres Lester Young himself, blowing round and Lester-like as they all leaned and jammed together, the heroes of the hip generation. "You see man Pres has the technical anxieties of a money-making musician, he's the only one who's expensively dressed, obvious big band employee, see him grow worried when he blows a clinker, but the leader, that cool cat, tells him not to worry and just blow truth." They roll into a tune —"Idaho." The Negro alto high-school broad-gash-mouth Yardbird tall kid blows over their heads in a thing of his own, moveless on the horn, fingering, erect, an idealist who reads Homer and Bird, cool, contemplative, grave—raises his horn and blows into it quietly and thoughtfully and elicits birdlike phrases and architectural Miles Davis logics. The children of the great bop innovators. Once there was Louis Armstrong blowing his beautiful bop in the muds of New Orleans; even before him the mad tuba-players and trombone kings who'd paraded on official days and broke up their Sousa marches into ragtime, on Bourbon, Dauphine and South Rampart and Perdido Street too. After which came swing, and Roy Eldridge vigorous and virile blasting the horn for everything it had in waves of power and natural tuneful reason—"I Want a Little Girl," "I Got Rhythm," a thousand choruses of "Wonderful"—leaning to it with glittering eyes and a lovely smile and sending it out broadcast to rock the jazz world. Then had come Charlie Parker, a kid in his mother's woodshed in Kansas City, the dirty snow in late March, smoke from stovepipes, wool hats, pitiful brown mouths breathing vapor, faint noise of music from down the way—

blowing his tied-together alto among the logs, practicing on rainy days, coming out to watch the old swinging Basie and Bennie Moten band that had Hot Lips Page and the rest—lost names in swingin' Kaycee— nostalgia of alcohol, human mouths chewing and talking in smoky noisy jazzrooms, yeah, yah, yeah, yah, last Sunday afternoon and the long red sunset, the lost girl, the spilt wine—Charlie Parker leaving home and unhappiness and coming to the Apple, and meeting mad Monk and madder Gillespie . . . Charlie Parker in his early days when he was out of his mind and walked in a circle while playing his horn. Younger than Lester, also from K.C., that gloomy saintly goof in whom the history of jazz is wrapped: Lester. Here were the children of the modern jazz night blowing their horns and instruments with belief; it was Lester started it all—his fame and his smoothness as lost as Maurice Chevalier in a stage-door poster—his drape, his drooping melancholy disposition in the sidewalk, in the door, his porkpie hat. ("At sessions all over the country from Kansas City to the Apple and back to L.A. they called him Pork Pie because he'd wear that gone hat and blow in it.") What door-standing influence has Dean gained from this cultural master of his generation? What mysteries as well as masteries? What styles, sorrows, collars, the removal of collars, the removal of lapels, the crepe-sole shoes, the beauty goof—that sneer of Lester's, that compassion for the dead which Billy has too, Lady Day—those poor little musicians in Chicago, their love of Lester, early heroisms in a room, records of Lester, early Count, suits hanging in the closet, tanned evenings in the rosy ballroom, the great tenor solo in the shoeshine jukebox, you can hear Lester blow and he is the greatness of America in a single Negro musician—he is just like the river, the river starts in near Butte, Montana, in frozen snow caps (Three Forks) and meanders on down across states and entire territorial areas of dun bleak land with hawthorn crackling in the sleet, picks up rivers at Bismarck, Omaha, and St. Louis just north, another at Kay-ro, another in Arkansas, Tennessee, comes deluging on New Orleans with muddy news from the land and a roar of subterranean excitement that is like the vibration of the entire land sucked of its gut in mad midnight, fevered, hot, the big mudhole rank clawpole old frogular pawed-soul titanic Mississippi from the North, full of wires, cold wood and horn—Lester, so, holding, his horn high in Doctor Pepper chickenshacks, backstreet. Basie Yaycee wearing greasy smeared corduroy bigpants and in torn flap smoking jacket without straw, scuffle-up shoes all slopey Mother Hubbard, soft, pudding, and key ring, early handkerchiefs, hands up, arms up, horn horizontal, shining dull, in wood-brown whiskeyhouse with ammoniac urine from broken gut bottles around fecal pukey bowl and a gal sprawled in it legs spread in brown cotton stockings, bleeding at belted mouth, moaning "yes" as Lester, horn placed, has started blowing, "blow for me mother blow for me," 1938, later, earlier, Miles is still on his daddy's checkered knee, Louis' only got twenty years behind him, and Lester blows all Kansas City to ecstasy and now Americans from coast to coast go mad, and fall by, and everybody's picking up. Stranger flowers now than ever, for as the Negro alto kid mused over everyone's head with dignity, the slender blond kid from Curtis Street, Denver, jeans and studded belt and red shirt, sucked on his mouthpiece while waiting for the others to finish; and when they did he started, and you had to look around to see where the new solo was coming from, for it came from his angelical smiling lips upon the mouthpiece and it was a soft sweet fairy-tale solo he played. A new kind of sound in the night, sweet, plaintive, cold; like cold jazz. Someone from South Main Street, or Market, or Canal, or Streetcar, he's the sweet new alto blowing the tiny heartbreaking salute in the night which is coming, a beauteous and whistling horn; blown easily but fully in a soft flue of air, out comes the piercing thin lament completely softened, the New Sound, the prettiest. And the bass player: wiry redhead with wild eyes jabbing his hips at the fiddle with every driving slap, at hot moments his mouth hung open; behind him, driving, the sad-looking dissipated drummer, completely goofed, chewing gum, wide-eyed, rocking the neck with that Reich kick, dropping bombs with his foot, urging balloons. The piano—a big husky Italian truck-driving kid with meaty hands and a burly and thoughtful joy; anybody start a fight with the band, he will step down; dropping huge chords like a Wolfean horse turding in the steamy Brooklyn winter morn. They played an hour. Nobody was listening. Old North Clark bums lolled at the bar, whores screeched in anger. Secret Chinamen went by. Noises of hootchy-kootchy interfered. They went right on. Out on the sidewalk came an apparition—a sixteen-year-old kid with a goatee and a trombone case. Thin as rickets, mad-faced, he wanted to join this group and blow with them. They knew him from before and didn't want to be bothered with him. He crept into the bar and meekly undid his trombone case and raised the horn to his lips. No opening. Nobody looked at him. They finished, packed up and left for another bar. The boy had his horn out, all assembled and polished of bell and no one cared. He wanted to jump. He was the Chicago Kid. He slapped on his dark glasses, raised the trombone to his lips alone in the bar, and went "Baugh!" Then he rushed out after them. They just wouldn't let him play with them, like the sandlot baseball gang back of the gas tank. "All these guys live with their grandmothers just like my boy Jim and our Carlo Marx alto!" said Dean and we rushed after the whole gang. They went across the street. We went in.

There is no end to the night. At great roar of Chicago dawn we all staggered out and shuddered in the raggedness. It would start all over tomorrow night. We rushed on to New York. "There ain't nothing left after that," said Dean. "Whee!" he said. We seek to find new phrases; we try hard, we writhe and twist and blow; every now and then a clear harmonic cry gives new suggestions of a tune, a thought, that will some-day be the only tune and thought in the world and which will raise men's souls to joy. We find it, we lose, we wrestle for it, we find it again, we laugh, we moan. Go moan for man. It's the pathos of people that gets us down, all the lovers in this dream.

from
THE RAILROAD EARTH
1952

THERE WAS A LITTLE ALLEY in San Francisco back of the Southern Pa-cific station at Third and Townsend in redbrick of drowsy lazy after-noons with everybody at work in offices in the air you feel the impending rush of their commuter frenzy as soon they'll be charging en masse from Market and Sansome buildings on foot and in buses and all well-dressed thru workingman Frisco of Walkup ? ? truck drivers and even the poor grime-bemarked Third Street of lost bums even Ne-groes so hopeless and long left East and meanings of responsibility and *try* that now all they do is stand there spitting in the broken glass some-times fifty in one afternoon against one wall at Third and Howard and here's all these Millbrae and San Carlos neat-necktied producers and commuters of America and Steel civilization rushing by with San Fran-cisco *Chronicles* and green *Call-Bulletins* not even enough time to be disdainful, they've got to catch 130, 132, 134, 136 all the way up to 146 till the time of evening supper in homes of the railroad earth when high in the sky the magic stars ride above the following hotshot freight trains.—It's all in California, it's all a sea, I swim out of it in afternoons of sun hot meditation in my jeans with head on handkerchief on brakeman's lantern or (if not working) on books, I look up at blue sky of perfect lostpurity and feel the warp of wood of old America beneath me and have insane conversations with Negroes in several-story windows above and everything is pouring in, the switching moves of boxcars in that little alley which is so much like the alleys of Lowell and I hear far off in the sense of coming night that engine calling our mountains.

But it was that beautiful cut of clouds I could always see above the little S.P. alley, puffs floating by from Oakland or the Gate of Marin to the north or San Jose south, the clarity of Cal to break your heart. It was the fantastic drowse and drum hum of lum mum afternoon nathin' to do, ole Frisco with end of land sadness—the people—the alley full of trucks and cars of businesses nearabouts and nobody knew or far from cared who I was all my life three thousand five hundred miles from birth-O opened up and at last belonged to me in Great America.

Now it's night in Third Street the keen little neons and also yellow bulblights of impossible-to-believe flops with dark ruined shadows moving back of torn yellow shades like a degenerate China with no money—the cats in Annie's Alley, the flop comes on, moans, rolls, the street is loaded with darkness. Blue sky above with stars hanging high over old hotel roofs and blowers of hotels moaning out dusts of interior, the grime inside the word in mouths falling out tooth by tooth, the reading rooms tick tock bigclock with creak chair and slantboards and old faces looking up over rimless spectacles bought in some West Virginia or Florida or Liverpool England pawnshop long before I was born and across rains they've come to the end of the land sadness end of the world gladness all you San Franciscos will have to fall eventually and burn again. But I'm walking and one night a bum fell into the hole of the construction job where theyre tearing a sewer by day the husky Pacific & Electric youths in torn jeans who work there often I think of going up to some of em like say blond ones with wild hair and torn shirts and say "You oughta apply for the railroad its much easier work you dont stand around the street all day and you get much more pay" but this bum fell in the hole you saw his foot stick out, a British MG also driven by some eccentric once backed into the hole and as I came home from a long Saturday afternoon local to Hollister out of San Jose miles away across verdurous fields of prune and juice joy here's this British MG backed and legs up wheels up into a pit and bums and cops standing around right outside the coffee shop—it was the way they fenced it but he never had the nerve to do it due to the fact that he had no money and nowhere to go and O his father was dead and O his mother was dead and O his sister was dead and O his whereabout was dead was dead.—But and then at that time also I lay in my room on long Saturday afternoons listening to Jumpin' George with my fifth of tokay no tea and just under the sheets laughed to hear the crazy music "Mama, he treats your daughter mean," Mama, Papa, and dont you come in here I'll kill you etc. getting high by myself in room glooms and all wondrous knowing about the Negro the essential American out there always finding his solace his meaning in the fellaheen street and not in abstract morality and even when he has a church you see the pastor out front bowing to the ladies on the make you hear his great vibrant voice on the sunny Sunday afternoon sidewalk full of sexual vibratos saying "Why yes Mam but de gospel do say that man was born of woman's womb—" and no and so by that time I come crawling out of my warmsack and hit the street when I see the railroad ain't gonna call me till 5 AM Sunday morn probably for a local out of Bayshore in fact always for a local out of Bayshore and I go to the wailbar of all the wildbars in the world the one and only Third-and-Howard and there I go in and drink with the madmen and if I get drunk I git.

The whore who come up to me in there the night I was there with Al Buckle and said to me "You wanta play with me tonight Jim, and?" and I didnt think I had enough money and later told this to Charley Low and he laughed and said "How do you know she wanted money always take the chance that she might be out just for love or just out for love you know what I mean man dont be a sucker." She was a goodlooking doll and said "How would you like to oolyakoo with me mon?" and I stood there like a jerk and in fact bought drink got drink drunk that night and in the 299 Club I was hit by the proprietor the band breaking up the fight before I had a chance to decide to hit him back which I didnt do and out on the street I tried to rush back in but they had locked the door and were looking at me thru the forbidden glass in the door with faces like undersea—I should have played with her shurro-uruuruuruuruuruuruuruurkdiei.

Despite the fact I was a brakeman making 600 a month I kept going to the Public restaurant on Howard Street which was three eggs for 26 cents 2 eggs for 21 this with toast (hardly no butter) coffee (hardly no coffee and sugar rationed) oatmeal with dash of milk and sugar the smell of soured old shirts lingering above the cookpot steams as if they were making skidrow lumberjack stews out of San Francisco ancient Chinese mildewed laundries with poker games in the back among the barrels and the rats of the earthquake days, but actually the food some-what on the level of an oldtime 1890 or 1910 section-gang cook of lumber camps far in the North with an oldtime pigtail Chinaman cook-ing it and cussing out those who didnt like it. The prices were incredible but one time I had the beefstew and it was absolutely the worst beefstew I ever et, it was incredible I tell you—and as they often did that to me it was with the most intensest regret that I tried to convey to the geek back of counter what I wanted but he was a tough sonofabitch, ech, ti-ti, I thought the counterman was kind of queer especially he handled gruffly the hopeless drooldrunks, "What now you doing you think you can come in here and cut like that for God's sake act like a man won't you and eat or get out-t-t-t-"—I always did wonder what a guy like that was doing working in a place like that because, but why some sympathy in his horny heart for the busted wrecks, all up and down the street were restaurants like the Public catering exclusively to bums of the black, winos with no money, who found 21 cents left over from wine panhandlings and so stumbled in for their third or fourth touch of food in a week, as sometimes they didnt eat at all and so you'd see them in the corner puking white liquid which was a couple quarts of rancid sauterne rotgut or sweet white sherry and they had nothing on their stomachs, most of them had one leg or were on crutches and had bandages around their feet, from nicotine and alcohol poisoning to-gether, and one time finally on my up Third near Market across the street from Breens, when in early 1952 I lived on Russian Hill and didnt quite dig the complete horror and humor of railroad's Third Street, a bum a thin sickly littlebum like Anton Abraham lay face down on the pavement with crutch aside and some old remnant newspaper sticking out and it seemed to me he was dead. I looked closely to see if he was breathing and he was not, another man with me was looking down and we agreed he was dead, and soon a cop came over and took and agreed and called the wagon, the little wretch weighed about 50 pounds in his bleeding count and was stone mackerel snotnose cold dead as a bleeding doornail—ah I tell you—and who could notice but other half dead deadbums bums bums bums dead dead times X times X times all dead bums forever dead with nothing and all finished and out—there.—And

this was the clientele in the Public Hair restaurant where I ate many's
the morn a 3-egg breakfast with almost dry toast and oatmeal a little
saucer of, and thin sickly dishwater coffee, all to save 14 cents so in my
little book proudly I could make a notation and of the day and prove
that I could live comfortably in America while working seven days a
week and earning 600 a month I could live on less than 17 a week
which with my rent of 4.20 was okay as I had also to spend money to
eat and sleep sometimes on the other end of my Watsonville chaingang
run but preferred most times to sleep free of charge and uncomfortable
in cabooses of the crummy rack—my 26-cent breakfast, my pride.—
And that incredible semiqueer counterman who dished out the food,
threw it at you, slammed it, had a languid frank expression straight in
your eyes like a 1930's lunchcart heroine in Steinbeck and at the steam-
table itself labored coolly a junkey-looking Chinese with an actual
stocking in his hair as if they'd just Shanghai'd him off the foot of
Commercial Street before the Ferry Building was up but forgot it was
1952, dreamed it was 1860 goldrush Frisco—and on rainy days you
felt they had ships in the back room.

I'd take walks up Harrison and the boomcrash of truck traffic towards
the glorious girders of the Oakland Bay Bridge that you could see after
climbing Harrison Hill a little like radar machine of eternity in the sky,
huge, in the blue, by pure clouds crossed, gulls, idiot cars streaking to
destinations on its undinal boom across shmoshwaters flocked up by
winds and news of San Rafael storms and flash boats.—There O I always came and walked and negotiated whole Friscos in one afternoon
from the overlooking hills of the high Fillmore where Orient-bound
vessels you can see on drowsy Sunday mornings of poolhall goof like
after a whole night playing drums in a jam session and a morn in the
hall of cuesticks I went by the rich homes of old ladies supported by
daughters or female secretaries with immense ugly gargoyle Frisco millions fronts of other days and way below is the blue passage of the
Gate, the Alcatraz mad rock, the mouths of Tamalpais, San Pablo Bay,
Sausalito sleepy hemming the rock and bush over yonder, and the sweet
white ships cleanly cutting a path to Sasebo.—Over Harrison and down
to the Embarcadero and around Telegraph Hill and up the back of
Russian Hill and down to the play streets of Chinatown and down
Kearney back across Market to Third and my wild-night neon twinkle
fate there, ah, and then finally at dawn of a Sunday and they did call
me, the immense girders of Oakland Bay still haunting me and all that

eternity too much to swallow and not knowing who I am at all but like a big plump longhaired baby waking up in the dark trying to wonder who I am the door knocks and it's the desk keeper of the flop hotel with silver rims and white hair and clean clothes and sickly potbelly said he was from Rocky Mount and looked like yes, he had been desk clerk of the Nash Buncome Association hotel down there in 50 successive heatwave summers without the sun and only palmos of the lobby with cigar crutches in the albums of the South and him with his dear mother waiting in a buried log cabin of graves with all that mashed past historied underground afoot with the stain of the bear the blood of the tree and cornfields long plowed under and Negroes whose voices long faded from the middle of the wood and the dog barked his last, this man had voyageured to the West Coast too like all the other loose American elements and was pale and sixty and complaining of sickness, might at one time been a handsome squire to women with money but now a forgotten clerk and maybe spent a little time in jail for a few forgeries or harmless cons and might also have been a railroad clerk and might have wept and might have never made it, and that day I'd say he saw the bridgegirders up over the hill of traffic of Harrison like me and woke up mornings with same lost, is now beckoning on my door and breaking in the world on me and he is standing on the frayed carpet of the hall all worn down by black steps of sunken old men for last 40 years since earthquake and the toilet stained, beyond the last toilet bowl and the last stink and stain I guess yes is the end of the world the bloody end of the world, so now knocks on my door and I wake up, saying "How what howp howelk howel of the knavery they've meaking, ek and wont let me slepit? Whey they dool? Whand out wisis thing that comes flarminging around my dooring in the mouth of the night and there everything knows that I have no mother, and no sister, and no father and no bot sosstle, but not crib" I get up and sit up and says "Howowow?" and he says "Telephone?" and I have to put on my jeans heavy with knife, wallet, I look closely at my railroad watch hanging on little door flicker of closet door face to me ticking silent the time, it says 4:30 AM of a Sunday morn, I go down the carpet of the skidrow hall in jeans and with no shirt and yes with shirt tails hanging gray workshirt and pick up phone and ticky sleepy night desk with cage and spittoons and keys hanging and old towels piled clean ones but frayed at edges and bearing names of every hotel of the moving prime, on the phone is the Crew Clerk, "Kerroway?" "Yeah." "Kerroway it's gonna be the Sherman Local at 7 AM this morning." "Sherman Local right."

"Out of Bayshore, you know the way?" "Yeah." "You had that same job last Sunday—Okay Keroway-y-y-y-y." And we mutually hang up and I say to myself okay it's the Bayshore bloody old dirty hagglous old coveted old madman Sherman who hates me so much especially when we were at Redwood Junction kicking boxcars and he always insists I work the rear end tho as one-year man it would be easier for me to follow pot but I work rear and he wants me to be right there with a block of wood when a car or cut of cars kicked stops, so they wont roll down that incline and start catastrophes, O well anyway I'll be learning eventually to like the railroad and Sherman will like me some day, and anyway another day another dollar.

And there's my room, small, gray in the Sunday morning, now all the franticness of the street and night before is done with, bums sleep, maybe one or two sprawled on sidewalk with empty poorboy on a sill —my mind whirls with life.

So there I am in dawn in my dim cell—2½ hours to go till the time I have to stick my railroad watch in my jean watchpocket and cut out allowing myself exactly 8 minutes to the station and the 7:15 train No. 112 I have to catch for the ride five miles to Bayshore through four tunnels, emerging from the sad Rath scene of Frisco gloom gleak in the rainymouth fogmorning to a sudden valley with grim hills rising to the sea, bay on left, the fog rolling in like demented in the draws that have little white cottages disposed real-estatically for come-Christmas blue sad lights—my whole soul and concomitant eyes looking out on this reality of living and working in San Francisco with that pleased semi-loin-located shudder, energy for sex changing to pain at the portals of work and culture and natural foggy fear.—There I am in my little room wondering how I'll really manage to fool myself into feeling that these next 2½ hours will be well filled, fed, with work and pleasure thoughts.—It's so thrilling to feel the coldness of the morning wrap around my thick quilt blankets as I lay there, watch facing and ticking me, legs spread in comfy skidrow soft sheets with soft tears or sew lines in 'em, huddled in my own skin and rich and not spending a cent on— I look at my littlebook—and I stare at the words of the Bible.—On the floor I find last red afternoon Saturday's *Chronicle* sports page with news of football games in Great America the end of which I bleakly see in the gray light entering.—The fact that Frisco is built of wood satisfies me in my peace, I know nobody'll disturb me for 2½ hours and all bums are asleep in their own bed of eternity awake or not, bottle or not—it's the joy I feel that counts for me.—On the floor's my shoes, big lumberboot flopjack workshoes to colomp over rockbed with and not turn the ankle—solidity shoes that when you put them on, yoke-wise, you know you're working now and so for same reason shoes not be worn for any reason like joys of restaurant and shows.—Night-before shoes are on the floor beside the clunkershoes a pair of blue canvas shoes à la 1952 style, in them I'd trod soft as ghost the indented hill sidewalks of Ah Me Frisco all in the glitter night, from the top of Russian Hill I'd looked down at one point on all roofs of North Beach and the Mexican nightclub neons, I'd descended to them on the old steps of Broadway under which they were newly laboring a mountain tunnel—shoes fit for watersides, embarcaderos, hill and plot lawns of park and tiptop vista.—Workshoes covered with dust and some oil of engines—the crumpled jeans nearby, belt, blue railroad hank, knife, comb, keys, switch keys and caboose coach key, the knees white from Pajaro Riverbottom finedusts, the ass black from slick sandboxes in yardgoat after yardgoat—the gray workshorts, the dirty undershirt, sad shorts, tortured socks of my life.—And the Bible on my desk next to the peanut butter, the lettuce, the raisin bread, the crack in the plaster, the stiff-with-old-dust lace drape now no longer laceable but hard as—after all those years of hard dust eternity in that Cameo skid inn with red eyes of rheumy oldmen dying there staring without hope out on the dead wall you can hardlysee thru windowdusts and all you heard lately in the shaft of the rooftop middle way was the cries of a Chinese child whose father and mother were always telling him to shu shand then screaming at him, he was a pest and his tears from China were most persistent and worldwide and represented all our feelings in broken-down Cameo tho this was not admitted by bum one except for an occasional harsh clearing of throat in the halls or moan of nightmarer —by things like this and neglect of a hard-eyed alcoholic oldtime cho-rusgirl maid the curtains had now absorbed all the iron they could take and hung stiff and even the dust in them was iron, if you shook them they'd crack and fall in tatters to the floor and spatter like wings of iron on the bong and the dust would fly into your nose like filings of steel and choke you to death, so I never touched them. My little room at 6 in the comfy dawn (at 4:30) and before me all that time, that fresh-eyed time for a little coffee to boil water on my hot plate, throw some coffee in, stir it, French style, slowly carefully pour it in my white tin cup, throw sugar in (not California beet sugar like I should have been using but New Orleans cane sugar, because beet racks I carried from Oakland out to Watsonville many's the time, a 80-car freight train with nothing but gondolas loaded with sad beets looking like the heads of decapitated women).—Ah me how but it was a hell and now I had the whole thing to myself, and make my raisin toast by sitting it on a little wire I'd especially bent to place over the hotplate, the toast crackled up, there, I spread the margarine on the still red hot toast and it too would crackle and sink in golden, among burnt raisins and this was my toast.—Then two eggs gently slowly fried in soft margarine in my little skidrow frying pan about half as thick as a dime in fact less, a little piece of tiny tin you could bring on a camp trip—the eggs slowly fluffled in there and swelled from butter steams and I threw garlic salt on them, and when they were ready the yellow of them had been slightly filmed with a cooked white at the top from the tin cover I'd put over the frying pan, so now they were ready, and out they came, I spread them out on top of my already prepared potatoes which had been boiled in small pieces and then mixed with the bacon I'd already fried in small pieces, kind of raggely mashed bacon potatoes, with eggs on top steaming, and on the side lettuce, with peanut butter dab nearby on side.—I had heard that peanut butter and lettuce contained all the vitamins you should want, this after I had originally started to eat this combination because of the deliciousness and nostalgia of the taste—my breakfast ready at about 6:45 and as I eat already I'm dressing to go piece by piece and by the time the last dish is washed in the little sink at the boiling hot-water tap and I'm taking my lastquick slug of coffee and quickly rinsing the cup in the hot water spout and rushing to dry it and plop it in its place by the hot plate and the brown carton in which all the groceries sit tightly wrapped in brown paper, I'm already picking up my brake-man's lantern from where it's been hanging on the door handle and my tattered timetable's long been in my backpocket folded and ready to go, everything tight, keys, timetable, lantern, knife, handkerchief, wallet, comb, railroad keys, change and myself. I put the light out on the sad dab mad grub little diving room and hustle out into the fog of the flow, descending the creak hall steps where the old men are not yet sitting with Sunday morn papers because still asleep or some of them I can now as I leave hear beginning to disfawdle to wake in their rooms with their moans and yorks and scrapings and horror sounds, I'm going down the steps to work, glance to check time of watch with clerk cage clock.—A hardy two or three oldtimers sitting already in the dark brown lobby under the tockboom clock, toothless, or grim, or elegantly mustached—what thought in the world swirling in them as they see the young eager brakeman bum hurrying to his thirty dollars of the Sunday—what memories of old homesteads, built without sympathy, horny-handed fate dealt them the loss of wives, childs, moons—libraries collapsed in their time—oldtimers of the telegraph wired wood Frisco in the fog gray top time sitting in their brown sunk sea and will be there when this afternoon my face flushed from the sun, which at eight'll flame out and make sunbaths for us at Redwood, they'll still be here the color of paste in the green underworld and still reading the same editorial over again and wont understand where I've been or what for or what.—I have to get out of there or suffocate, out of Third Street or become a worm, it's alright to live and bed-wine in and play the radio and cook little breakfasts and rest in but O my I've got to go now to work, I hurry down Third to Townsend for my 7:15 train—it's 3 minutes to go, I start in a panic to jog, goddam it I didn't give myself enough time this morning, I hurry down under the Harrison ramp to the Oakland-Bay Bridge, down past Schweibacker-Frey the great dim red neon printshop always spectrally my father the dead executive I see there, I run and hurry past the beat Negro grocery stores where I buy all my peanut butter and raisin bread, past the redbrick railroad alley now mist and wet, across Townsend, the train is leaving!

Fatuous railroad men, the conductor old John J. Coppertwang 35 years pure service on ye olde S.P. is there in the gray Sunday morning with his gold watch out peering at it, he's standing by the engine yelling up pleasantries at old hoghead Jones and young fireman Smith with the baseball cap is at the fireman's seat munching sandwich—"We'll how'd ye like old Johnny O yestiddy, I guess he didnt score so many touchdowns like we thought." "Smith bet six dollars on the pool down in Watsonville and said he's rakin' in thirty four." "I've been in that Watsonville pool—." They've been in the pool of life fleartiming with one another, all the long pokerplaying nights in brownwood railroad places, you can smell the mashed cigar in the wood, the spittoon's been there for more than 750,099 years and the dog's been in and out and these old boys by old shaded brown light have bent and muttered and young boys too with their new brakeman passenger uniform the tie undone the coat thrown back the flashing youth smile of happy fatuous well-fed goodjobbed careered futured pensioned hospitalized taken-care-of railroad men.—35, 40 years of it and then they get to be conductors and in the middle of the night they've been for years called by the Crew Clerk yelling "Cassady? It's the Maximush localized week do you for the right lead" but now as old men all they have is a regular job, a regular train, conductor of the 112 with goldwatch is helling up his pleasantries at all fire dog crazy Satan hoghead Willis why the wildest man this side of France and Frankincense, he was known once to take his engine up that steep grade . . . 7:15, time to pull, as I'm running thru the station hearing the bell jangling and the steam chuff they're pulling out, O I come flying out on the platform and forget momentarily or that is never did know what track it was and whirl in confusion a while wondering what track and cant see no train and this is the time I lose there, 5, 6, 7 seconds when the train tho underway is only slowly unchugging to go and a man a fat executive could easily run up and grab it but when I yell to Assistant Stationmaster "Where's 112?" and he tells me the last track which is the track I never dreamed I run to it fast as I can go and dodge people à la Columbia halfback and cut into track fast as off-tackle where you carry the ball with you to the left and feint with neck and head and push of ball as tho you're gonna throw yourself all out to fly around that left end and everybody psychologically chuffs with you that way and suddenly you contract and you like whiff of smoke are buried in the hole in tackle, cutback play, you're flying into the hole almost before you yourself know it, flying into the track I am and there's the train about 30 yards away even as I look picking up tremendously momentum the kind of momentum I would have been able to catch if I'd a looked a second earlier—but I run, I know I can catch it. Standing on the back platform are the rear brakeman and an old deadheading conductor ole Charley W. Jones, why he had seven wives and six kids and one time out at Lick no I guess it was Coyote he couldnt see on account of the steam and out he come and found his lantern in the igloo regular anglecock of my herald and they gave him fifteen benefits so now there he is in the Sunday har har owlala morning and he and young rear man watch incredulously his student brakeman running like a crazy trackman after their departing train. I feel like yelling "Make your airtest now make your airtest now!" knowing that when a passenger pulls out just about at the first crossing east of the station they pull the air a little bit to test the brakes, on signal from the engine, and this momentarily slows up the train and I could manage it, and could catch it, but they're not making no airtest the bastards, and I hek knowing I'm going to have to run like a sonofabitch. But suddenly I get embarrassed thinking what are all the people of the world gonna say to see a man running so devilishly fast with all his might sprinting thru life like Jesse Owens just to just to catch a goddam train and all of them with their hysteria wondering if I'll get killed when I catch the back platform and Blam, I fall down and go boom and lay supine across the crossing, so the old flagman when the train has flowed by will see that everything lies on the earth in the same stew, all of us angels will die and we dont ever know how or our own diamond, O heaven will enlighten us and open our eyes—open our eyes, open our eyes.—I know I wont get hurt, I trust my shoes, hand grip, feet, solidity of yipe and cripe of gripe and grip and strength and need no mystic strength to measure the musculature in my rib back—but damn it all it's a social embarrassment to be caught sprinting like a maniac after a train especially with two men gaping at me from rear of train and shaking their heads and yelling I cant make it even as I half-heartedly sprint after them with open eyes trying to communicate that I can and not for them to get hysterical or laugh, but I realize it's all too much for me, not the run, not the speed of the train which anyway two seconds after I gave up the complicated chase did indeed slow down at the crossing in the airtest before chugging up again for good and Bayshore. So I was late for work, and old Sherman hated me and was about to hate me more.

The ground I would have eaten in solitude, cronch—the railroad earth, the flat stretches of long Bayshore that I have to negotiate to get to Sherman's bloody caboose on track 17 ready to go with pot pointed to Redwood and the morning's 3-hour work.—I get off the bus at Bayshore Highway and rush down the little street and turn in—boys riding the pot of a switcheroo in the yardgoat day come yelling by at me from the headboards and footboards "Come on down ride with us" otherwise I would have been about 3 minutes even later to my work but now I hop on the little engine that momentarily slows up to pick me up and it's alone not pulling anything but tender, the guys have been up to the other end of the yard to get back on some track of necessity.—That boy will have to learn to flag himself without nobody helping him as many's the time I've seen some of these young goats think they have everything but the plan is late, the word will have to wait, the massive arboreal thief with the crime of the kind, and air and all kinds of ghouls—ZONKed! made tremendous by the flare of the whole crime and encrudalatures of all kinds—San Franciscos and shroudband Bayshores the last and the last furbelow of the eek plot pall prime tit top work oil twicks and wouldn't you?—the railroad earth I would have eaten alone, cronch, on foot head bent to get to Sherman who ticking watch observes with finicky eyes the time to go to give the hiball sign get on going it's Sunday no time to waste the only day of his long seven-day-a-week worklife he gets a chance to rest a little bit at home when "Eee Christ" when "Tell that sonofabitch student this is no party picnic damn this shit and throb tit you tell them something and how do you what the hell expect to underdries out tit all you bright tremendous trouble anyway, we's LATE" and this is the way I come rushing up late. Old Sherman is sitting in the crummy over his switch lists, when he sees me with cold blue eyes he says "You know you're supposed to be here 7:30 dont you so what the hell you doing gettin' in here at 7:50 you're twenty goddam minutes late, what the fuck you think this your birthday?" and he gets up and leans off the rear bleak platform and gives the high sign to the enginemen up front we have a cut of about 12 cars and they say it easy and off we go slowly at first, picking up momentum to the work, "Light that goddam fire" says Sherman he's wearing brand-new workshoes just about bought yestiddy and I notice his clean coveralls that his wife washed and set on his chair just that morning probably and I rush up and throw coal in the potbelly flop and take a fusee and two fussees and light them crack em. Ah fourth of the July when the angels would smile on the horizon and all the racks where the mad are lost are returned to us forever from Lowell of my soul prime and single meditated longsong hope to heaven of prayers and angels and of course the sleep and interested eye of images and but now we detect the missing buffoon there's the poor goodman rear man aint even in the train yet and Sherman looks out sulkily the back door and sees his rear man waving from fifteen yards aways to stop and wait for him and being an old railroad man he certainly isnt going to run or even walk fast, it's well understood, conductor Sherman's got to get up off his switchlist desk chair and pull the air and stop the goddam train for rear man Arkansaw Charley, who sees this done and just come up lopin' in his flop overalls without no care, so he was late too, or at least had gone gossiping in the yard office while waiting for the stupid head brakeman, the tagman's up in front on the presumably pot. "First thing we do is pick up a car in front at Redwood so all's you do get off at the crossing and stand back to flag, not too far." "Dont I work the head end?" "You work the hind end we got not much to do and I wanna get it done fast," snarls the conductor. "Just take it easy and do what we say and watch and flag." So it's peaceful Sunday morning in California and off we go, tack-a-tick, lao-tichi-couch, out of the Bayshore yards, pause momentarily at the main line for the green, ole 71 or ole whatever been by and now we get out and go swamming up the tree browm, browm, the Indians just look up—I see them vanishing like spots—" and sitting in the redbulb room in San Francisco now with sweet Mardou I think, "And this is your father I saw in the gray waste, swallowed by night—from his juices came your lips, your eyes full of suffering and sorrow, and we're not to know his name or name his destiny?"—Her little brown hand is curled in mine, her fingernails are paler than her skin, on her toes too and with her shoes off she has one foot curled in between my thighs for warmth and we talk, we begin our romance on the deeper level of love and histories of respect and shame.—For the greatest key to courage is shame and the blurfaces in the passing train see nothing out on the plain but figures of hoboes rolling out of sight—

"I remember one Sunday, Mike and Rita were over, we had some very strong tea—they said it had volcanic ash in it and it was the strongest they'd ever had."—"Came from L. A.?"—"From Mexico—some guys had driven down in the station wagon and pooled their money, or Tijuana or something, I dunno—Rita was flipping at the time—when we were practically stoned she rose very dramatically and stood there in the middle of the room man saying she felt her nerves burning thru her bones—To see her *flip* right before my eyes—I got nervous and had some kind of idea about Mike, he kept *looking* at me like he wanted to kill me—he has such a funny look anyway—I got out of the house and walked along and didn't know which way to go, my mind kept turning into the several directions that I was thinking of going but my body kept walking straight along Columbus altho I felt the sensation of each of the directions I mentally and emotionally turned into, amazed at all the possible directions you can take with different motives that come in, like it can make you a different *person*—I've often thought of this since childhood, of suppose instead of going up Columbus as I usually did I'd turn into Filbert would something happen that at the time is insignificant enough but would be like enough to influence my whole life in the end?—What's in store for me in the direction I *don't* take?—and all that, so if this had not been such a constant preoccupation that accompanied me in my solitude which I played upon in as many different ways as possible I wouldn't bother now except but seeing the horrible roads this pure *supposing* goes to it took me to *frights,* if I wasn't so damned *persistent*—" and so on deep into the day, a long confusing story only pieces of which and imperfectly I remember, just the mass of the misery in connective form—

Flips in gloomy afternoons in Julien's room and Julien sitting paying

valleys and town vale hollows and main street crossing parking-lot last-night attendant plots and Stanford lots of the world—to our destination in the Pooh which I can see, and, so to while the time I'm up in the cupolo and with my newspaper dig the latest news on the front page and also consider and make notations of the money I spent already for this day Sunday absolutely not jot spend a nothing—California rushes by and with sad eyes we watch it reel the whole bay and the discourse falling off to gradual gils that ease and graduate to Santa Clara Valley then and the fig and behind is the fog immemoriate while the mist closes and we come running out to the bright sun of the Sabbath California—

At Redwood I get off and standing on sad oily ties of the brakie railroad earth with red flag and torpedoes attached and fusees in back-pocket with timetable crushed against and I leave my hot jacket in crummy standing there then with sleeves rolled up and there's the porch of a Negro home, the brothers are sitting in shirtsleeves talking with cigarettes and laughing and little daughter standing amongst the weeds of the garden with her playpail and pigtails and we the railroad men with soft signs and no sound pick up our flower, according to same goodman train order that for the last entire lifetime of attentions ole conductor industrial worker harlotized Sherman has been reading carefully son so's not to make a mistake: "Sunday morning October 15 pick up flower car at Redwood, Dispatcher M.M.S."

from
THE SUBTERRANEANS
1953

EDITOR'S NOTE
In this book Kerouac calls himself "Leo Percepied" and Allen Ginsberg is "Adam Moorad."

IT WAS ON A MORNING when I slept at Adam's that I saw her again, I was going to rise, do some typing and coffee drinking in the kitchen all day since at that time work, work was my dominant thought, not love—not the pain which impels me to write this even while I don't want to, the pain which won't be eased by the writing of this but heightened, but which will be redeemed, and if only it were a dignified pain and could be placed somewhere other than in this black gutter of shame and loss and noisemaking folly in the night and poor sweat on my brow—Adam rising to go to work, I too, washing, mumbling talk, when the phone rang and it was Mardou, who was going to her therapist, but needed a dime for the bus, living around the corner, "Okay come on over but quick I'm going to work or I'll leave the dime with Leo."—"O is he there?"—"Yes."—In my mind man-thoughts of doing it again and actually looking forward to seeing her suddenly, as if I'd felt she was displeased with our first night (no reason to feel that, previous to the balling she'd lain on my chest eating the egg foo young and dug me with glittering glee eyes) (that tonight my enemy devour?) the thought of which makes me drop my greasy hot brow into a tired hand—O love, fled me—or do telepathies cross sympathetically in the night?—Such cacoëthes him befalls—that the cold lover of lust will earn the warm bleed of spirit—so she came in, 8 A.M., Adam went to work and we were alone and immediately she curled up in my lap, at my invite, in the big stuffed chair and we began to talk, she began to tell her story and I turned on (in the gray day) the dim red bulblight and thus began our true love—

She had to tell me everything—no doubt just the other day she'd already told her whole story to Adam and he'd listened tweaking his beard with a dream in his far-off eye to look attentive and loverman in the bleak eternity, nodding—now with me she was starting all over again but as if (as I thought) to a brother of Adam's a greater lover and bigger, more awful listener and worrier.—There we were in all gray San Francisco of the gray West, you could almost smell rain in the air and far across the land, over the mountains beyond Oakland and out beyond Donner and Truckee was the great desert of Nevada, the wastes leading to Utah, to Colorado, to the cold cold come fall plains where I kept imagining that Cherokee-halfbreed hobo father of hers lying bellydown on a flatcar with the wind furling back his rags and black hat, his brown sad face facing all that land and desolation.—At other moments I imagined him instead working as a picker around Indio and on a hot night he's sitting on a chair on the sidewalk among the joking shirtsleeved men, and he spits and they say, "Hey Hawk Taw, tell us that story agin about the time you stole a taxicab and drove it clear to Manitoba,

Canada—d'jever hear him tell that one, Cy?"—I saw the vision of her father, he's standing straight up, proudly, handsome, in the bleak dim red light of America on a corner, nobody knows his name, nobody cares—

Her own little stories about flipping and her minor fugues, cutting across boundaries of the city, and smoking too much marijuana, which held so much terror for her (in the light of my own absorptions concerning her father the founder of her flesh and predecessor terror-ee of her terrors and knower of much greater flips and madness than she in psychoanalytic-induced anxieties could ever even summon up to just imagine), formed just the background for thoughts about the Negroes and Indians and America in general but with all the overtones of "new generation" and other historical concerns in which she was now swirled just like all of us in the Wig and Europe Sadness of us all, the innocent seriousness with which she told her story and I'd listened to so often and myself told—wide eyed hugging in heaven together—hipsters of America in the 1950's sitting in a dim room—the clash of the streets beyond the window's bare soft sill.—Concern for her father, because I'd been out there and sat down on the ground and seen the rail the steel of America covering the ground filled with the bones of old Indians and Original Americans.—In the cold gray fall in Colorado and Wyoming I'd worked on the land and watched Indian hoboes come suddenly out of brush by the track and move slowly, hawk lipped, rill-jawed and wrinkled, into the great shadow of the light bearing burdenbags and junk talking quietly to one another and so distant from the absorptions of the field hands, even the Negroes of Cheyenne and Denver streets, the Japs, the general minority Armenians and Mexicans of the whole West that to look at a three-or-foursome of Indians crossing a field and a railroad track is to the senses like something unbelievable as a dream—you think, "They must be Indians—ain't a soul looking at 'em—they're goin' that way—nobody notices—doesn't matter much which way they go—reservation? What have they got in those brown paper bags?" and only with a great amount of effort you realize "But they were the inhabitors of this land and under these huge skies they were the worriers and keeners and protectors of wives in whole nations gathered around tents—now the rail that runs over their forefathers' bones leads them onward pointing into infinity, wraiths of humanity treading lightly the surface of the ground so deeply suppurated with the stock of their suffering you only have to dig a foot down to find a baby's hand.—The hotshot passenger train with grashing diesel balls by, no attention to her but staring in the gray moth void stirring only occasionally to close the window or change his knee crossings, eyes round staring in a meditation so long and so mysterious and as I say so Christlike really outwardly lamby it was enough to drive anybody crazy I'd say to live there even one day with Julien or Wallenstein (same type) or Mike Murphy (same type), the subterraneans their gloomy longthoughts enduring.—And the meekened girl waiting in a dark corner, as I remembered so well the time I was at Big Sur and Victor arrived on his literally homemade motorcycle with little Dorie Kiehl, there was a party in Patsy's cottage, beer, candlelight, radio, talk, yet for the first hour the newcomers in their funny ragged clothes and he with that beard and she with those somber serious eyes had sat practically out of sight behind the candlelight shadows so no one could see them and since they said nothing whatever but just (if not listened) meditated, gloomed, endured, finally I even forgot they were there—and later that night they slept in a pup tent in the field in the foggy dew of Pacific Coast Starry Night and with the same humble silence mentioned nothing in the morn—Victor so much in my mind always the central exaggerator of subterranean hip generation tendencies to silence, bohemian mystery, drugs, beard, semiholiness and, as I came to find later, insurpassable nastiness (like George Sanders in *The Moon and Sixpence*)—so Mardou a healthy girl in her own right and from the windy open ready for love now hid in a musty corner waiting for Julien to speak.—Occasionally in the general "incest" she'd been slyly silently by some consenting arrangement or secret statesmanship shifted or probably just "Hey Ross you take Mardou home tonight I wanta make it with Rita for a change,"—and staying at Ross's for a week, smoking the volcanic ash, she was flipping—(the tense anxiety of improper sex additionally, the premature ejaculations of these anemic *maquereaux* leaving her suspended in tension and wonder).—"I was just an innocent chick when I met them, independent and like well not happy or anything but feeling that I had something to do, I wanted to go to night school, I had several jobs at my trade, binding in Olstad's and small places down around Harrison, the art teacher the old gal at school was saying I could become a great sculptress and I was living with various roommates and buying clothes and making it"—(sucking in her little lip, and that slick "cuk" in the throat of drawing in breath quickly in sadness and as if with a cold, like in the throats of great drinkers, but she not a drinker but saddener of self) (supreme, dark)—(twining warm arm farther around me) "and he's lying there saying whatsamatter and I can't understand

—." She can't understand suddenly what has happened because she's lost her mind, her usual recognition of self, and feels the eerie buzz of mystery, she really does not know who she is and what for and where she is, she looks out the window and this city San Francisco is the big bleak bare stage of some giant joke being perpetrated on her.—"With my back turned I didn't know what Ross was thinking—even doing." —She had no clothes on, she'd risen out of his satisfied sheets to stand in the wash of gray gloomtime thinking what to do, where to go.—And the longer she stood there finger-in-mouth and the more the man said, "What's the matter ba-by" (finally he stopped asking and just let her stand there) the more she could feel the pressure from inside towards bursting and explosion coming on, finally she took a giant step forward with a gulp of fear—everything was clear: danger in the air—it was writ in the shadows, in the gloomy dust behind the drawing table in the corner, in the garbage bags, the gray drain of day seeping down the wall and into the window—in the hollow eyes of people—she ran out of the room.—"What'd he say?"

"Nothing—he didn't move but was just with his head off the pillow when I glanced back in closing the door—I had no clothes on in the alley, it didn't disturb me, I was so intent on this realization of everything I knew I was an innocent child."—"The naked babe, wow."— (And to myself: "My God, this girl, Adam's right she's crazy, like I'd do that, I'd flip like I did on Benzedrine with Honey in 1945 and thought she wanted to use my body for the gang car and the wrecking and flames but I'd certainly never run out into the streets of San Francisco naked tho I might have maybe if I really felt there was need for action, yah") and I looked at her wondering if she, was she telling the truth.—She was in the alley, wondering who she was, night, a thin drizzle of mist, silence of sleeping Frisco, the B-O boats in the bay, the shroud over the bay of great clawmouth fogs, the aureola of funny eerie light being sent up in the middle by the Arcade Hood Droops of the Pillar-templed Alcatraz—her heart thumping in the stillness, the cool dark peace.—Up on a wood fence, waiting—to see if some idea from outside would be sent telling her what to do next and full of import and omen because it had to be right and just once—"One slip in the wrong direction . . . ," her direction kick, should she jump down on one side of fence or other, endless space reaching out in four directions, bleak-hatted men going to work in glistening streets uncaring of the naked girl hiding in the mist or if they'd been there and seen her would in a circle stand not touching her just waiting for the cop-authorities to come and cart her away and all their uninterested weary eyes flat with blank shame watching every part of her body—the naked babe.—The longer she hangs on the fence the less power she'll have finally to really get down and decide, and upstairs Ross Wallenstein doesn't even move from that junk-high bed, thinking her in the hall huddling, or he's gone to sleep anyhow in his own skin and bone.—The rainy night blooping all over, kissing everywhere men women and cities in one wash of sad poetry, with honey lines of high-shelved Angels trumpet-blowing up above the final Orient-shroud Pacific-huge songs of Paradise, an end to fear below.—She squats on the fence, the thin drizzle making beads on her brown shoulders, stars in her hair, her wild now-Indian eyes now staring into the Black with a little fog emanating from her brown mouth, the misery like ice crystals on the blankets on the ponies of her Indian ancestors, the drizzle on the village long ago and the poorsmoke crawling out of the underground and when a mournful mother pounded acorns and made mush in hopeless millenniums—the song of the Asia hunting gang clanking down the final Alaskan rib of earth to New World Howls (in their eyes and in Mardou's eyes now the eventual Kingdom of Inca Maya and vast Azteca shining of gold snake and temples as noble as Greek, Egypt, the long sleek crack jaws and flattened noses of Mongolian geniuses creating arts in temple rooms and the leap of their jaws to speak, till the Cortez Spaniards, the Pizarro weary old-world sissified pantalooned Dutch bums came smashing canebrake in savannahs to find shining cities of Indian Eyes high, landscaped, boulevarded, ritualled, heralded, beflagged in that selfsame New World Sun the beating heart held up to it)—her heart beating in the Frisco rain, on the fence, facing last facts, ready to go run down the land now and go back and fold in again where she was and where was all—consoling herself with visions of truth—coming down off the fence, on tiptoe moving ahead, finding a hall, shuddering, sneaking—

"I'd made up my mind, I'd erected some structure, it was like, but I can't—." Making a new start, starting from flesh in the rain, "Why should anyone want to harm my little heart, my feet, my little hands, my skin that I'm wrapt in because God wants me warm and Inside, my toes—why did God make all this all so decayable and dieable and harmable and wants to make me realize and scream—why the wild ground and bodies bare and breaks—I quaked when the giver creamed, when my father screamed, my mother dreamed—I started small and ballooned up and now I'm big and a naked child again and only to cry and fear. —Ah—Protect yourself, angel of no harm, you who've never and could never harm and crack another innocent its shell and thin veiled pain—wrap a robe around you, honey lamb—protect yourself from rain and wait, till Daddy comes again, and Mama throws you warm inside her valley of the moon, loom at the loom of patient time, be happy in the mornings."—Making a new start, shivering, out of the alley night naked in the skin and on wood feet to the stained door of some neighbor—knocking—the woman coming to the door in answer to the frightened butter knock knuckles, sees the naked browngirl, frightened—("Here is a woman, a soul in my rain, she looks at me, she is frightened.")—"Knocking on this perfect stranger's door, sure."— "Thinking I was just going down the street to Betty's and back, promised her *meaning* it deeply I'd bring the clothes back and she did let me in and she got a blanket and wrapped it around me, then the clothes, and luckily she was alone—an Italian woman.—And in the alley I'd all come out and *on,* it was now first clothes, then I'd go to Betty's and get two bucks—then buy this brooch I'd seen that afternoon at some place with old seawood in the window, at North Beach, art handicraft ironwork like, a shoppey, it was the first symbol I was going to allow myself."—"Sure."—Out of the naked rain to a robe, to innocence shrouding in, then the decoration of God and religious sweetness.— "Like when I had that fist fight with Jack Steen it was in my mind strongly."—"Fist fight with Jack Steen?"—"This was earlier, all the junkies in Ross's room, tying up and shooting with Pusher, you know Pusher, well I took my clothes off there too—it was . . . all . . . part of the same . . . flip . . ."—"But this *clothes,* this *clothes!*" (to myself).—"I stood in the middle of the room flipping and Pusher was plucking at the guitar, just one string, and I went up to him and said, 'Man don't pluck those dirty notes at ME,' and like he just got up without a word and left."—And Jack Steen was furious at her and thought if he hit her and knocked her out with his fists she'd come to her senses so he slugged at her but she was just as strong as he (anemic pale 110 lb. junkey ascetics of America), blam, they fought it out before the weary others. —She'd pulled wrists with Jack, Julien, beat them practically—"Like Julien finally won at wrists but he really furiously had to put me down to do it and hurt me and was really upset" (gleeful little shniffle thru the little out-teeth)—so there she'd been fighting it out with Jack Steen and really almost licking him but he was furious and neighbors downstairs called cops who came and had to be explained to—"dancing."— "But that day I'd seen this iron thing, a little brooch with a beautiful dull sheen, to be worn around the neck, you know how nice that would look on my breast."—"On your brown breastbone a dull gold beautiful it would be baby, go on with your amazing story."—"So I immediately needed this brooch in spite of the time, 4 A.M. now, and I had that old coat and shoes and an old dress she gave me, I felt like a streetwalker but I felt no one could tell—I ran to Betty's for the two bucks, woke her up—." She demanded the money, she was coming out of death and money was just the means to get the shiny brooch (the silly means invented by inventors of barter and haggle and styles of who owns who, who owns what—). Then she was running down the street with her $2, going to the store long before it opened, going for coffee in the cafeteria, sitting at the table alone, digging the world at last, the gloomy hats, the glistening sidewalks, the signs announcing baked flounder, the reflections of rain in paneglass and in pillar mirror, the beauty of the food counters displaying cold spreads and mountains of crullers and the steam of the coffee urn.—"How warm the world is, all you gotta do is get little symbolic coins—they'll let you in for all the warmth and food you want—you don't have to strip your skin off and chew your bone in alleyways—these places were designed to house and comfort bag-and-bone people come to cry for consolation."—She is sitting there staring at everyone, the usual sexfiends are afraid to stare back because the vibration from her eyes is wild, they sense some living danger in the apocalypse of her tense avid neck and trembling wiry hands.—"This ain't no woman."—"That crazy Indian she'll kill somebody."—Morning coming, Mardou hurrying gleeful and mind-swum, absorbed, to the store, to buy the brooch—standing then in a drugstore at the picture postcard swiveller for a solid two hours examining each one over and over again minutely because she only had ten cents left and could only buy two and those two must be perfect private talismans of the new important meaning, personal omen emblems—her avid lips slack to see the little corner meanings of the cable-car shadows, Chinatown, flower stalls, blue, the clerks wondering: "Two hours she's been in here, no stockings on, dirty knees, looking at cards, some Third Street Wino's wife run away, came to the big whiteman drugstore, never saw a shiny sheen postcard before—." In the night before they would have seen her up Market Street in Foster's with her last (again) dime and a glass of milk, crying into her milk, and men always looking at her, always trying to make her but now doing nothing because frightened, because she was like a child—and because: "Why didn't Julien or Jack Steen or Walt Fitzpatrick give you a place to stay and leave you alone in the corner, or lend you a couple bucks?"—"But they didn't care, they were fright-

ened of me, they *really* didn't want me around, they had like distant
objectivity, watching me, asking *nasty* questions—a couple times Julien
went into his head-against-mine act like you know 'Whatsamatter, Mardou,' and his routines like that and phony sympathy but he really just
was curious to find out why I was flipping—none of them'd ever give
me *money,* man."—"Those guys really treated you bad, do you know
that?"—"Yeah well they never treat anyone—like they never do
anything—you take care of yourself, I'll take care of me."—
"Existentialism."—"But American worse cool existentialism and of
junkies man, I hung around with them, it was for almost a year by then
and I was getting, every time they turned on, a kind of a contact
high."—She'd sit with them, they'd go on the nod, in the dead silence
she'd wait, sensing the slow snakelike waves of vibration struggling
across the room, the eyelids falling, the heads nodding and jerking up
again, someone mumbling some disagreeable complaint, "Ma-a-n, I'm
drug by that son of a bitch MacDoud with all his routines about how
he ain't got enough money for one cap, could he get a half a cap or
pay a half—m-a-a-n, I never seen such nowhereness, no s-h-i-t, why
don't he just go somewhere and *fade,* um." (That junkey "um" that
follows any out-on-the-limb, and anything one says is out-on-the-limb,
statement, *um, he-um,* the self-indulgent baby sob inkept from exploding to the big bawl mawk crackfaced WAAA they feel from the junk
regressing their systems to the crib.)—Mardou would be sitting there,
and finally high on tea or benny she'd begin to feel like she'd been
injected, she'd walk down the street in her flip and actually feel the
electric contact with other human beings (in her sensitivity recognizing
a fact) but some times she was suspicious because it was someone secretly injecting her and following her down the street who was really
responsible for the electric sensation and so independent of any natural
law of the universe.—"But you really didn't believe that—but you did
—when I flipped on benny in 1945 I really believed the girl wanted to
use my body to burn it and put her boy's papers in my pocket so the
cops'd think he was dead—I told her, too."—"Oh what did she do?"
—"She said, 'Ooo daddy,' and hugged me and took care of me, Honey
was a wild bitch, she put pancake makeup on my pale—I'd lost thirty,
ten, fifteen pounds—but what happened?"—"I wandered around with
my brooch."—She went into some kind of gift shop and there was a
man in a wheel chair there. (She wandered into a doorway with cages
and green canaries in the glass, she wanted to touch the beads, watch
goldfish, caress the old fat cat sunning on the floor, stand in the cool

green parakeet jungle of the store high on the green out-of-this-world dart eyes of parrots swivelling witless necks to cake and burrow in the mad feather and to feel that definite communication from them of birdy terror, the electric spasms of their notice, s q u a w k, l a w k, l e e k, and the man was extremely strange.)—"Why?"—"I dunno he was just very strange, he wanted, he talked with me very clearly and insisting —like intensely looking right at me and at great length but smiling about the simplest commonplace subjects but we both knew we meant everything else that we said—you know life—actually it was about the tunnels, the Stockton Street tunnel and the one they just built on Broadway, that's the one we talked of the most, but as we talked this a great electrical current of real understanding passed between us and I could feel the other levels the infinite number of them of every intonation in his speech and mine and the world of meaning in every *word*—I'd never realized before how much is *happening* all the time, and people *know* it—in their eyes they show it, they *refuse* to show it by any other—I stayed a very long time."—"He must have been a weirdy himself."— "You know, balding, and queer like, and middleaged, and with that with-neck-cut-off look or head-on-air," (witless, peaked) "looking all over, I guess it was his mother the old lady with the Paisley shawl— but my god it would take me all day."—"Wow."—"Out on the street this beautiful old woman with white hair had come up to me and saw me, but was asking directions, but liked to talk—." (On the sunny now lyrical Sunday morning after-rain sidewalk, Easter in Frisco and all the purple hats out and the lavender coats parading in the cool gusts and the little girls so tiny with their just whitened shoes and hopeful coats going slowly in the white hill streets, churches of old bells busy and downtown around Market where our tattered holy Negro Joan of Arc wandered hosannahing in her brown borrowed-from-night skin and heart, flutters of betting sheets at corner newsstands, watchers at nude magazines, the flowers on the corner in baskets and the old Italian in his apron with the newspapers kneeling to water, and the Chinese father in tight ecstatic suit wheeling the basket-carriaged baby down Powell with his pink-spot-cheeked wife of glitter brown eyes in her new bonnet rippling to flap in sun, there stands Mardou smiling intensely and strangely and the old eccentric lady not any more conscious of her Negroness than the kind cripple of the store and because of her out and open face now, the clear indications of a troubled pure innocent spirit just risen from a pit in pockmarked earth and by own broken hands self-pulled to safety and salvation, the two women Mardou and the old

lady in the incredibly sad empty streets of Sunday after the excitements
of Saturday night the great glitter up and down Market like wash gold
dusting and the throb of neons at O'Farrell and Mason bars with cocktail glass cherrysticks winking invitation to the open hungering hearts
of Saturday and actually leading only finally to Sunday-morning blue
emptiness just the flutter of a few papers in the gutter and the long
white view to Oakland Sabbath haunted, still—Easter sidewalk of
Frisco as white ships cut in clean blue lines from Sasebo beneath the
Golden Gate's span, the wind that sparkles all the leaves of Marin here
laving the washed glitter of the white kind city, in the lostpurity clouds
high above redbrick track and Embarcadero pier, the haunted broken
hint of song of old Pomos the once only-wanderers of these eleven last
American now white-behoused hills, the face of Mardou's father himself
now as she raises her face to draw breath to speak in the streets of life
materializing huge above America, fading—.) "And like I told her but
talked too and when she left she gave me her flower and pinned it on
me and called me honey."—"Was she white?"—"Yeah, like, she was
very affectionate, very plea-*sant* she seemed to love me—like save me,
bring me out—I walked up a hill, up California past Chinatown, someplace I came to a white garage like with a big garage wall and this guy
in a swivel chair wanted to know what I wanted, I understood all of
my moves as one obligation after another to communicate to whoever
not accidentally but by *arrangement* was placed before me, communicate and exchange this news, the vibration and new meaning that I had,
about everything happening to everyone all the time everywhere and for
them not to worry, nobody as mean as you think or—a colored guy,
in the swivel chair, and we had a long confused talk and he was reluctant, I remember, to look in my eyes and really listen to what I was
saying."—"But what were you saying?"—"But it's all forgotten now—
something as simple and like you'd never expect like those tunnels or
the old lady and I hanging-up on streets and directions—but the guy
wanted to make it with me, I saw him open his zipper but suddenly he
got ashamed, I was turned around and could see it in the glass." (In the
white planes of wall garage morning, the phantom man and the girl
turned slumped watching in the window that not only reflected the
black strange sheepish man secretly staring but the whole office, the
chair, the safe, the dank concrete back interiors of garage and dull sheen
autos, showing up also unwashed specks of dust from last night's rain-
splash and thru the glass the across-the-street immortal balcony of
wooden bay-window tenement where suddenly she saw three Negro

children in strange attire waving but without yelling at a Negro man four stories below in overalls and therefore apparently working on Easter, who waved back as he walked in his own strange direction that bisected suddenly the slow direction being taken by two men, two hatted, coated ordinary men but carrying one a bottle, the other a boy of three, stopping now and then to raise the bottle of Four Star California Sherry and drink as the Frisco A.M. All Morn Sun wind flapped their tragic topcoats to the side, the boy bawling, their shadows on the street like shadows of gulls the color of handmade Italian cigars of deep brown stores at Columbus and Pacific, now the passage of a fishtail Cadillac in second gear headed for hilltop houses bay-viewing and some scented visit of relatives bringing the funny papers, news of old aunts, candy to some unhappy little boy waiting for Sunday to end, for the sun to cease pouring thru the French blinds and paling the potted plants but rather rain and Monday again and the joy of the woodfence alley where only last night poor Mardou'd almost lost.)—"What'd the colored guy do?"—"He zipped up again, he wouldn't look at me, he turned away, it was strange he got ashamed and sat down—it reminded me too when I was a little girl in Oakland and this man would send us to the store and give us dimes then he'd open his bathrobe and show us himself." —"Negro?"—"Yea, in my neighborhood where I lived—I remember I used to never stay there but my girlfriend did and I think she even did something with him one time."—"What'd you do about the guy in the swivel chair?"—"Well, like I wandered out of there and it was a beautiful day, Easter, man."—"Gad, Easter where was I?"—"The soft sun, the flowers and here I was going down the street and thinking 'Why did I allow myself to be bored ever in the past and to compensate for it got high or drunk or rages or all the tricks people have because they want anything but serene understanding of just what there is, which is after all so much, and thinking like angry social deals,—like angry— kicks—like hasseling over social problems and my race problem, it meant so little and I could feel that great confidence and gold of the morning would slip away eventually and had already started—I could have made my whole life like that morning just on the strength of pure understanding and willingness to live and go along, God it was all the most beautiful thing that ever happened to me in its own way—but it was all sinister."—Ended when she got home to her sisters' house in Oakland and they were furious at her anyway but she told them off and did strange things; she noticed for instance the complicated wiring her eldest sister had done to connect the TV and the radio to the kitchen plug in the ramshackle wood upstairs of their cottage near Seventh and Pine the railroad sooty wood and gargoyle porches like tinder in the sham scrapple slums, the yard nothing but a lot with broken rocks and black wood showing where hoboes Tokay'd last night before moving off across the meatpacking yard to the Mainline rail Tracy-bound thru vast endless impossible Brooklyn-Oakland full of telephone poles and crap and on Saturday nights the wild Negro bars full of whores and the Mexicans Ya-Yaaing in their own saloons and the cop car cruising the long sad avenue riddled with drinkers and the glitter of broken bottles (now in the wood house where she was raised in terror Mardou is squatting against the wall looking at the wires in the half dark and she hears herself speak and doesn't understand why she's saying it except that it must be said, come out, because that day earlier when in her wandering she finally got to wild Third Street among the lines of slugging winos and the bloody drunken Indians with bandages rolling out of alleys and the 10¢ movie house with three features and little children of skid row hotels running on the sidewalk and the pawnshops and the Negro chickenshack jukeboxes and she stood in drowsy sun suddenly listening to bop as if for the first time as it poured out, the intention of the musicians and of the horns and instruments suddenly a mystical unity expressing itself in waves like sinister and again electricity but screaming with palpable aliveness the direct *word* from the vibration, the interchanges of statement, the levels of waving intimation, the smile in sound, the same living insinuation in the way her sister'd arranged those wires wriggled entangled and fraught with intention, innocent looking but actually behind the mask of casual life completely by agreement the mawkish mouth almost sneering snakes of electricity purposely placed she'd been seeing all day and hearing in the music and saw now in the wires), "What are you trying to do actually electrocute me?" so the sisters could see something was really wrong, worse than the youngest of the Fox sisters who was alcoholic and made the wild street and got arrested regularly by the vice squad, some nameless horrible yawning *wrong*, "She smokes dope, she hangs out with all those queer guys with beards in the City."—They called the police and Mardou was taken to the hospital—realizing now, "God, I saw how awful what was really happening and about to happen to me and man I pulled out of it fast, and talked sanely with everyone possible and did everything right, they let me out in 48 hours—the other women were with me, we'd look out the windows and the things they said, they made me see the preciousness of really being *out* of those damn bathrobes and *out* of there and out on the street, the sun, we could see ships, out and FREE man to roam around, how great it really is and how we never appreciate it all glum inside our worries and skins, like *fools* really, or blind spoiled detestable children pouting because . . . they can't get . . . all . . . the . . . candy . . . they want, so I talked to the doctors and told them—." "And you had no place to stay, where was your clothes?"—." "Scattered all over—all over the Beach—I had to do something—they let me have this place, some friends of mine, for the summer, I'll have to get out in October."—"In the Lane?"—"Yah."—"Honey let's you and me—would you go to Mexico with me?"—"Yes!"—"If I go to Mexico? that is, if I get the money? altho I do have a hunnerd eighty now and we really actually could go tomorrow and make it—like Indians—I mean cheap and living in the country or in the slums."—"Yes—it would be so nice to get away now."—"But we could or should really wait till I get—I'm supposed to get five hundred see—and—" (and that was when I would have whisked her off into the bosom of my own life)—she saying "I really don't want anything more to do with the Beach or any of that gang, man, that's why—I guess I spoke or agreed too soon, you don't seem so sure now" (laughing to see me ponder).—"But I'm only pondering practical problems."—"Nevertheless if I'd have said 'maybe' I bet—oooo that awright," kissing me—the gray day, the red bulblight, I had never heard such a story from such a soul except from the great men I had known in my youth, great heroes of America I'd been buddies with, with whom I'd adventured and gone to jail and known in raggedy dawns, the boys beat on curbstones seeing symbols in the saturated gutter, the Rimbauds and Verlaines of America on Times Square, kids—no girl had ever moved me with a story of spiritual suffering and so beautifully her soul showing out radiant as an angel wandering in hell and the hell the selfsame streets I'd roamed in watching, watching for someone just like her and never dreaming the darkness and the mystery and eventuality of our meeting in eternity, the hugeness of her face now like the sudden vast Tiger head on a poster on the back of a woodfence in the smoky dumpyards Saturday no-school mornings, direct, beautiful, insane, in the rain.—We hugged, we held close—it was like love now, I was amazed—we made it in the livingroom, gladly, in chairs, on the bed, slept entwined, satisfied—I would show her more sexuality—

from
TRISTESSA
1955

I'M RIDING ALONG with Tristessa in the cab, drunk, with big bottle of Juarez Bourbon whiskey in the till-bag railroad lootbag they'd accused me of holding in railroad 1952—here I am in Mexico City, rainy Saturday night, mysteries, old dream sidestreets with no names reeling in, the little street where I'd walked through crowds of gloomy Hobo Indians wrapped in tragic shawls enough to make you cry and you thought you saw knives flashing beneath the folds—lugubrious dreams as tragic as the one of Old Railroad Night where my father sits big of thighs in smoking car of night, outside's a brakeman with red light and white light, lumbering in the sad vast mist tracks of life—but now I'm up on that Vegetable plateau Mexico, the moon of Citlapol a few nights earlier I'd stumbled to on the sleepy roof on the way to the ancient dripping stone toilet—Tristessa is high, beautiful as ever, goin home gayly to go to bed and enjoy her morphine.

Night before I've in a quiet hassel in the rain sat with her darkly at Midnight counters eating bread and soup and drinking Delaware Punch, and I'd come out of that interview with a vision of Tristessa in my bed in my arms, the strangeness of her love-cheek, Azteca, Indian girl with mysterious lidded Billy Holliday eyes and spoke with great melancholic voice like Luise Rainer sadfaced Viennese actresses that made all Ukraine cry in 1910.

Gorgeous ripples of pear shape her skin to her cheekbones, and long sad eyelids, and Virgin Mary resignation, and peachy coffee complexion and eyes of astonishing mystery with nothing-but-earth-depth expressionless half disdain and half mournful lamentation of pain. "I am seek," she's always saying to me and Bull at the pad—I'm in Mexico City wildhaired and mad riding in a cab down past the Ciné Mexico in rainy traffic jams, I'm swigging from the bottle, Tristessa is trying long harangues to explain that the night before when I put her in the cab the driver'd tried to make her and she hit him with her fist, news which the present driver receives without comment—We're going down to Tristessa's house to sit and get high—Tristessa has warned me that the house will be a mess because her sister is drunk and sick, and El Indio will be there standing majestically with morphine needle downward in the big brown arm, glitter-eyed looking right at you or expecting the prick of the needle to bring the wanted flame itself and going "Hm-za . . . the Aztec needle in my flesh of flame" looking all a whole lot like the big cat in Culiao who presented me the 0 the time I came down to Mexico to see other visions—My whiskey bottle has strange Mexican soft covercap that I keep worrying will slip off and all my bag be drowned in Bourbon 86 proof whiskey.

Through the crazy Saturday night drizzle streets like Hong Kong our cab pushes slowly through the Market ways and we come out on the whore street district and get off behind the fruity fruitstands and tortilla beans and tacos shacks with fixed wood benches—It's the poor district of Rome.

I pay the cab 3.33 by giving cabbie 10 pesos and asking "seis" for change, which I get without comment and wonder if Tristessa thinks I am too splurgy like big John Drunk in Mexico—But no time to think, we are hurrying through the slicky sidewalks of glisten-neon reflections and candle lights of little sidewalk sitters with walnuts on a towel for sale—turn quickly at the stinky alleyway of her tenement cell-house one story high—We go through dripping faucets and pails and boys and duck under wash and come to her iron door, which from adobe withins is unlocked and we step in the kitchen the rain still falling from the leaves and boards that served as the kitchen roof—allowing little drizzles to fizzle in the kitchen over the chicken garbage in the damp corner—Where, miraculously, now, I see the little pink cat taking a little pee on piles of okra and chickenfeed—The inside bedroom is littered completely and ransacked as by madmen with torn newspapers and the chicken's pecking at the rice and the bits of sandwiches on the floor— On the bed lay Tristessa's "sister" sick, wrapped in pink coverlet—it's as tragic as the night Eddy was shot on the rainy Russia Street—

Tristessa is sitting on the edge of the bed adjusting her nylon stockings, she pulls them awkwardly from her shoes with big sad face overlooking her endeavors with pursy lips, I watch the way she twists her feet inward convulsively when she looks at her shoes.

She is such a beautiful girl, I wonder what all my friends would say back in New York and up in San Francisco, and what would happen down in Nola when you see her cutting down Canal Street in the hot sun and she has dark glasses and a lazy walk and keeps trying to tie her kimono to her thin overcoat as though the kimono was supposed to tie to the coat, tugging convulsively at it and goofing in the street saying "Here ees the cab—hey hees hey who—there you go—I breeng you back the moa-ny." Money's moany. She makes money sound like my old French Canadian Aunt in Lawrence "It's not you moany, that I want, it's you loave"—Love is loave. "Eets you lawv." The law is lawv.—Same with Tristessa, she is so high all the time, and sick, shooting ten gramos of morphine per month,—staggering down the city streets yet so beautiful people keep turning and looking at her—Her eyes are radiant and shining and her cheek is wet from the mist and her Indian hair is black and cool and slick hangin in 2 pigtails behind with the roll-sod hairdo behind (the correct Cathedral Indian hairdo)—Her shoes she keeps looking at are brand new not scrawny, but she lets her nylons keep falling and keeps pulling on them and convulsively twisting her feet—You picture what a beautiful girl in New York, wearing a flowery wide skirt a la New Look with Dior flat bosomed pink cashmere sweater, and her lips and eyes do the same and do the rest. Here she is reduced to impoverished Indian Lady gloomclothes—You see the Indian ladies in the inscrutable dark of doorways, looking like holes in the wall not women—their clothes—and you look again and see the brave, the noble *mujer,* the mother, the woman, the Virgin Mary of Mexico.— Tristessa has a huge ikon in a corner of her bedroom.

It faces the room, back to the kitchen wall, in right hand corner as you face the woesome kitchen with its drizzle showering ineffably from the roof tree twigs and hammberboards (bombed out shelter roof)— Her ikon represents the Holy Mother staring out of her blue charaderees, her robes and Damema arrangements, at which El Indio prays devoutly when going out to get some junk. El Indio is a vendor of curios, allegedly.—I never see him on San Juan Letran selling crucifixes, I never see El Indio in the street, no Redondas, no anywhere—The Virgin Mary has a candle, a bunch of glass-fulla-wax economical burners that go for weeks on end, like Tibetan prayer-wheels the inexhaustible aid from our Amida—I smile to see this lovely ikon—

Around it are pictures of the dead—When Tristessa wants to say "dead" she clasps her hands in holy attitude, indicating her Aztecan belief in the holiness of death, by same token the holiness of the essence—So she has photo of dead Dave my old buddy of previous years now dead of high blood pressure at age 55—His vague Greek-Indian face looks out from pale indefinable photograph. I can't see him in all that snow. He's in heaven for sure, hands V-clasped in eternity ecstasy of Nirvana. That's why Tristessa keeps clasping her hands and praying, saying, too, "I love Dave," she had loved her former master—He had been an old man in love with a young girl. At 16 she was an addict. He took her off the street and, himself an addict of the street, redoubled his energies, finally made contact with wealthy junkies and showed her how to live—once a year together they'd taken hikes to Chalmas to the mountain to climb part of it on their knees to come to the shrine of piled crutches left there by pilgrims healed of disease, the thousand *tapete*-straws laid out in the mist where they sleep the night out in blankets and raincoats—returning, devout, hungry, healthy, to light new candles to the Mother and hitting the street again for their morphine—God knows where they got it.

I sit admiring that majestical mother of lovers.

There's no describing the awfulness of that gloom in the holes in the ceiling, the brown halo of the night city lost in a green vegetable height above the Wheels of the Blakean adobe rooftops—Rain is blearing now on the green endlessness of the Valley Plain north of Actopan—pretty girls are dashing over gutters full of pools—Dogs bark at hirshing cars—The drizzle empties eerily into the kitchen's stone Dank, and the door glistens (iron) all shiney and wet—The dog is howling in pain on the bed.—The dog is the little Chihuahua mother 12 inches long, with fine little feet with black toes and toenails, such a "fine" and delicate dog you couldnt touch her without she'd squeal in pain—"Y-eee-p" All you could do was snap your finger gently at her and allow her to nip-nose her cold little wet snout (black as a bull's) against your fingernails and thumb. Sweet little dog—Tristessa says she's in heat and that's why she cries—The rooster screams beneath the bed.

All this time the rooster's been listening under the springs, meditating, turning to look all around in his quiet darkness, the noise of the golden humans above "B e u - v e u - V A A?" he screams, he howls, he interrupts a half a dozen simultaneous conversations raging like torn paper above—The hen chuckles.

The hen is outside, wandering among our feet, pecking gently at the floor—She digs the people. She wants to come up near me and rub illimitably against my pant leg, but I dont give her encouragement, in fact havent noticed her yet and it's like the dream of the vast mad father of the wild barn in howling Nova Scotia with the floodwaters of the sea about to engulf the town and surrounding pine countrysides in the endless north—It was Tristessa, Cruz on the bed, El Indio, the cock, the dove on the mantelpiece top (never a sound except occasional wing flap practice), the cat, the hen, and the bloody howling woman dog blacky Espana Chihuahua pooch bitch.

El Indio's eyedropper is completely full, he jabs in the needle hard and it's dull and it wont penetrate the skin and he jabs in harder and works it in but instead of wincing waits open mouthed with ecstasy and gets the dropful in, down, standing,—"You've got to do me a favor Mr. Gazookus," says Old Bull Gaines interrupting my thought, "come down to Tristessa's with me—I've run short—" but I'm bursting to explode out of sight of Mexico City with walking in the rain splashing through puddles not cursing nor interested but just trying to get home to bed, dead.

It's the raving bloody book of dreams of the cursing world, full of suits, dishonesties and written agreements. And briberies, to children for their sweets, to children for their sweets. "Morphine is for pain," I keep thinking, "and the rest is rest. It is what it is, I am what I am, Adoration to Tathagata, Sugata, Buddha, perfect in Wisdom and Compassion who has accomplished, and is accomplishing, and will accomplish, all these words of mystery."

—Reason I bring the whiskey, to drink, to crash through the black curtain—At same time a comedian in the city in the night—Bepestered by glooms and lull intervenes, bored, drinking, curtsying, crashing, "Where I'm gonna do,"—I pull the chair up to the corner of the foot of the bed so I can sit between the kitty and the Virgin Mary. The kitty, *la gata* in Spanish, the little Tathagata of the night, golden pink colored, 3 weeks old, crazy pink nose, crazy face, eyes of green, mustachio'd golden lion forceps and whiskers—I run my finger over her little skull and she pops up purring and the little purring-machine is started for awhile and she looks around the room glad watching what we're all doing.—"She's having golden thoughts," I'm thinking.—Tristessa likes eggs otherwise she wouldnt allow a male rooster in this female establishment? How should I know how eggs are made. On my right the devotional candles flame before the clay wall.

It's infinitely worse than the sleeping dream I've had of Mexico City where I go dreary along empty white apartments, gray, alone, or where the marble steps of a hotel horrify me—It's the rainy night in Mexico City and I'm in the middle of Mexico Thieves Market district and El Indio is a wellknown thief and even Tristessa was a pickpocket but I dont do more than flick my backhand against the bulge of my folded money sailorwise stowed in the railroad watchpocket of my jeans—And in shirtpocket I have the travelers checks which are unstealable in a sense—That, Ah that side street where the gang of Mexicans stop me and rifle through my dufflebag and take what they want and take me along for a drink—It's gloom as unpredicted on this earth, I realize all the uncountable manifestations the thinking-mind invents to place wall of horror before its pure perfect realization that there is no wall and no horror just Transcendental Empty Kissable Milk Light of Everlasting Eternity's true and perfectly empty nature.—I know everything's alright but I want proof and the Buddhas and the Virgin Marys are there reminding me of the solemn pledge of faith in this harsh and stupid earth where we rage our so-called lives in a sea of worry, meat for Chicagos of Graves—right this minute my very father and my very brother lie side by side in mud in the North and I'm supposed to be smarter than they are—being quick I am dead. I look up at the others glooping, they see I've been lost in thought in my corner chair but are pursuing endless wild worries (all mental 100%) of their own—They're yakking in Spanish, I only understand snatches of that virile conversation—Tristessa keeps saying "chinga" at every other sentence, a swearing Marine,— she says it with scorn and her teeth bite and it makes me worry 'Do you know women as well as you think you do?'—The rooster is unperturbed and lets go a blast.

I take out my whiskey bottle from the bag, the Canady Dry, open both, and pour me a hiball in a cup—making one too for Cruz who has just jumped outa bed to throw up on the kitchen floor and now wants another drink, she's been in the cantina for women all day somewhere back near the whore district of Panama Street and sinister Rayon Street with its dead dog in the gutter and beggars on the sidewalk with no hats looking at you helplessly—Cruz is a little Indian woman with no chin and bright eyes and wears high heel pumps without stockings and battered dresses, what a wild crew of people, in America a cop would have to do a double take seeing them pass all be-wrongled and arguing and staggering on the sidewalk, like apparitions of poverty—Cruz takes a hiball and throws it up too. Nobody notices, El Indio is holding eyedropper in one hand and little piece of paper in the other arguing, tense necked, red, fullblast at a screaming Tristessa whose bright eyes dance to fight it out—The old lady Cruz groans from the riot of it and buries back in her bed, the only bed, under her blanket, her face bandaged and greasy, the little black dog curling against her, and the cat, and she is lamenting something, her drink sickness, and El Indio's constant harassing for more of Tristessa's supply of morphine—I gulp my drink.

Next door the mother's made the little daughter cry, we can hear her praying little woeful squeals enough to make a father's heart break and maybe it might be,—Trucks pass, buses, loud, growling, loaded to the springs with people riding to Tacuyaba and Rastro and Circumvalacion round-routeries of town—the streets of mess puddles that I am going to walk home in at 2 A M splashing without care through streetpools, looking along lone fences at the dismal glimmer of the wet rain shining in the streetlight—The pit and horror of my grit, the Virya tense-neck muscles that a man needs to steel his teeth together to press through lonely roads of rain at night with no hope of a warm bed—My head fells and wearies to think of it. Tristessa says "How is Jack,—?—" She always asks: "Why are you so sad??—'Muy dolorosa'" and as though to mean "You are very full of pain," for pain means *dolor*—"I am sad because all la vida es dolorosa," I keep replying, hoping to teach her Number One of the Four Great Truths,—Besides, what could be truer? With her heavy purple eyes she lids at me the nodding reprisal, "h a - hum," Indian-wise understanding the tone of what I said, and nodding over it, making me suspicious of the bridge of her nose where it looks evil and conniving and I think of her as a Houri Hari Salesman in the hellbottoms Kshitigarbha never dreamed to redeem.—When she looks like an evil Indian Joe of Huckleberry Finn, plotting my demise—El Indio, standing, watching through sad blackened-blue eye flesh, hard and sharp and clear the side of his face, darkly hearing that I say All Life is Sad, nods, agreeing, no comment to make to me or to anyone about it.

Tristessa is bending over the spoon boiling morphine in it with a match boilerfactory. She looks awkward and lean and you see the lean hocks of her rear, in the kimono-like crazydress, as she kneels prayer fashion over the bed boiling her bang over the chair which is cluttered with ashes, hairpins, cottons, Konk material like strange Mexican eyelash lipmakers and teasies and greases—one jiblet of a whole bone of junk, that, had it been knocked down would have added to the mess on the floor only a minor further amount of confusion.—"I raced to find that Tarzan," I'm thinking, remembering boyhood and home as they lament in the Mexican Saturday Night Bedroom, "but the bushes and the rocks weren't real and the beauty of things must be that they end."

I wail on my cup of hiball so much they see I'm going to get drunk so they all permit me and beseech me to take a shot of morphine which I accept without fear because I am drunk—Worse sensation in the world, to take morphine when you're drunk, the result knots in your forehead like a rock and makes great pain there warring in that one field for dominion and none to be had because they've cancelled out each other the alcohol and the alkaloid. But I accept, and as soon as I begin to feel its warning effect and warm effect I look down and perceive that the chicken, the hen, wants to make friends with me—She's walking up close with bobbing neck, looking at my knee cap, looking at my hanging hands, wants to come close but has no authority—So I stick my hand out to its beak to be pecked, to let her know I'm not afraid because I trust her not to hurt me really—which she doesn't—just stares at my hand reasonably and doubtfully and suddenly almost tenderly and I pull away my hand with a sense of the victory. She contentedly chuckles, plucks up a piece of something from the floor, throws it away, a piece of linen thread hangs in her beak, she tosses it away, looks around, walks around the golden kitchen of Time in huge Nirvana glare of Saturday night and all the rivers roaring in the rain, the crash inside my soul when I think of babyhood and you watch the big adults in the room, the wave and gnash of their shadowy hands, as they harangue about time and responsibility, in a Golden Movie inside my own mind without substance not even gelatinous—the hope and horror of the void—great phantoms screeching inside mind with the yawk photograph VLORK of the Rooster as he now ups and emits from his throat intended for open fences of Missouri explodes gunpowder blurts of morningshame, reverend for man—At dawn in impenetrable bleak Oceanities of Undersunk gloom, he blows his rosy morn Collario and still the farmer knows it wont tend that rosy way. Then he chuckles, rooster chuckles, comments on something crazy we might have said, and chuckles—poor sentient noticing being, the beast he knows his time is up in the Chickenshacks of Lenox Avenue—chuckles like we do—yells louder if a man, with special rooster jowls and jinglets—Hen, his wife, she wears her adjustible hat falling from one side of her pretty beak to the other. "Good *morn*ing Mrs. Gazookas," I tell her, having fun by myself watching the chickens as I'd done as a boy in New Hampshire in farmhouses at night waiting for the talk to be done and the wood to be taken in. Worked hard for my father in the Pure Land, was strong and true, went to the city to see Tathagata, leveled the ground for his feet, saw bumps everywhere and leveled the ground, he passed by and saw me and said "First level your own mind, and then the earth will be level, even unto Mount Sumeru" (the ancient name for Everest in Old Magadha) (India).

I wanta make friends with the rooster too, by now I'm sitting in front of the bed in the other chair as El Indio has just gone out with a bunch of suspicious men with mustaches one of whom stared at me curiously and with pleased proud grin as I stood with cup in hand acting drunk before the ladies for his and his friends' edification—Alone in the house with the two women I sit politely before them and we talk earnestly and eagerly about God. "My friends ees seek, I geev them shot," beautiful Tristessa of Dolours is telling me with her long damp expressive fingers dancing little India-Tinkle dances before my haunted eyes."—Ees when, *cuando*, my friend does not pays me back, don I dont care. Because" pointing up with a straight expression into my eyes, finger aloft, "my Lord pay me—and he pay me *more* —M-o-r-e"—she leans quickly emphasizing more, and I wish I could tell her in Spanish the illimitable and inestimable blessing she will get anyway in Nirvana. But I love her, I fall in love with her. She strokes my arm with thin finger. I love it. I'm trying to remember my place and my position in eternity. I have sworn off lust with women,—sworn off lust for lust's sake,—sworn off sexuality and the inhibiting impulse—I want to enter the Holy Stream and be safe on my way to the other shore, but would as lief leave a kiss to Tristessa for her hark of my heart's sake. She knows I admire and love her with all my heart and that I'm holding myself back. "You have you life," she says to Old Bull (of whom in a minute) "and I haff *mind, mine, and Jack has hees life*" indicating me, she is giving me my life back and not claiming it for herself as so many of the women you love do claim.—I love her but I want to leave. She says: "I know it, a man and women iss dead,—" "when they want to be dead"—She nods, confirms within herself some dark Aztecan instinctual belief, wise—a wise woman, who would have graced the herds of Bhikshunis in very Yasodhara's time and made a divine additional nun. With her lidded eyes and clasped hands, a Madonna. It makes me cry to realize Tristessa has never had a child and probably never will because of her morphine sickness (a sickness that goes on as long as the need and feeds off the need and fills in the need simultaneously, so that she moans from pain all day and the pain is real, like abcesses in the shoulder and neuralgia down the side of the head and in 1952 just before Christmas she was supposed to be dying), holy Tristessa will not be cause of further rebirth and will go straight to her God and He will recompense her multibillion-fold in aeons and aeons of dead Karma time. She understands Karma, she says: "What I do, I *reap*" she says in Spanish—"Men and women have *errores*—errors, faults, sins, *faltas*," humanbeings sow their own ground of trouble and stumble over the rocks of their own false erroring imagination, and life is hard. She knows, I know, you know.—"Bot—I weeling to haff jonk—morfina—and be no-seek any more." And she hunches her elbows with peasant face, understanding herself in a way that I cannot and as I gaze at her the candlelight flickers on the high cheekbones of her face and she looks as beautiful as Ava Gardner and even better like a Black Ava Gardner, A Brown Ava with long face and long bones and long lowered lids—Only Tristessa hasnt got that expression of sex-smile, it has the expression of mawkfaced down-mouthed Indian disregard for what you think about its own pluperfect beauty. Not that it's perfect beauty like Ava, it's got faults, errors, but all men and women have them and so all women forgive men and men forgive women and go their own holy ways to death. Tristessa loves death, she goes to the ikon and adjusts flowers and prays,—She bends over a sandwich and prays, looking sideways at the ikon, sitting Burmese fashion in the bed (knee in front of knee) (down) (sitting), she makes a long prayer to Mary to ask blessing or thanks for the food, I wait in respectful silence, take a quick peek at El Indio, who is also devout and even on the point of crying from junk his eyes moist and reverent and sometimes like especially when Tristessa removes her stockings to get in the bed-blankets an undercurrent of reverent love sayings under his breath ("Tristessa, O Yé, comme t'est Belle") (which is certainly what I'm thinking but afraid to look and watch Tristessa remove her nylons for fear I will get a flash sight of her creamy coffee thighs and go mad)— But El Indio is too loaded with the poison solution of morphine to really care and follow up his reverence for Tristessa, he is busy, sometimes busy being sick, has a wife, two children (down the other side of town), has to work, has to cajole stuff off Tristessa when he himself is out (as now)—(reason for his presence in the house)—I see the whole thing popping and parenthesizing in every direction, the story of that house and that kitchen.

• • •

So now El Indio is back and standing at the head of the bed as I sit there, and I turn to look at the rooster ("to tame him")—I put my hand

out exactly as I had done for the hen and allow it to see I'm not scared
if it pecks me, and I will pat it and make it free from fear of me—The
Rooster gazes at my hand without comment, and looks away, and looks
back, and gazes at my hand (the seminal gysmal champion who
dreams a daily egg for Tristessa that she sucks out the end after a little
puncture, fresh)—he looks at my hand tenderly but majestically moreover as the hen can't make that same majestical appraisal, he's
crowned and cocky and can howl, he is the King Fencer biting the duel
with that mosey morn. He chuckles at sight of my hand, meaning Yeh
and turns away—and I look proudly around to see if Tristessa and El
Indio heard my wild *estupiante*—They rave to notice me with avid lips,
"Yes we been talkin about the ten gram-mos we gonna get tomorrar—
Yeh—" and I feel proud to've made the Rooster, now all the little
animals in the room know me and love me and I love them though
may not know them. All except The Crooner on the roof, on the
clothes closet, in the corner away from the edge, against the wall just
under the ceiling, cozy cooing Dove is sitting in nest, ever contemplating the entire scene forever without comment. I look up, my Lord
is flapping his wings and coo doving white and I look at Tristessa
to know why she got a dove and Tristessa lifts up her tender hands
helplessly and looks at me affectionately and sadly, to indicate,
"It is my Pigeon"—"my pretty white Pigeon—what can I do
about it?" "I love it so"—"It is so sweet and white"—"It never make
a noise"—"It got soch prurty eyes you look you see the prurty eyes"
and I look into the eyes of the dove and they are dove's eyes, lidded,
perfect, dark, pools, mysterious, almost Oriental, unbearable to with-
stand the surge of such purity out of eyes—Yet so much like Tristessa's
eyes that I wish I could comment and tell Tristessa "Thou hast the
dove's eyes"—

Or every now and then the Dove rises and flaps her wings for exercise, instead of flying through the bleak air she waits in her golden
corner of the world waiting for perfect purity of death, the Dove in the
grave is a dark thing to rave—the raven in the grave is no white light
illuminating the Worlds pointing up and pointing down throughout up-
pity ten sides of Eternity—Poor Dove, poor eyes,—her breast white
snow, her milk, her rain of pity over me, her even gentle eye-gaze into
mine from rosy heights on a position in a rack and Arcabus in the Ope
Heavens of the Mind World,—rosy golden angel of my days, and I can't
touch her, wouldn't dare get up on a chair and trap her in her corner

and make her leery human teeth-grins trying to impress it to my blood-stained heart—her blood.

El Indio has brought sandwiches back and the little cat is going crazy for some meat and El Indio gets mad and slaps it off the bed and I throw both hands up at him "Non" "Don't do that" and he doesn't even hear me as Tristessa yells at him—the great Man Beast raging in the kitchen meat and slapping his daughter in her chair clear across the room to tumble on the floor her tears start starting as she realizes what he's done—I don't like El Indio for hitting the cat. But he isn't vicious about it, just merely reprimandatory, stern, justified, dealing with the cat, kicking the cat out of his way in the parlor as he walks to his cigars and Television—Old Father Time is El Indio, with the kids, the wife, the evenings at the supper table slapping the kids away and yornching on great meaty dinners in the dim light—"Blurp, blap," he lets go before the kids who look at him with shining and admiring eyes. Now it's Saturday night and he's dealing with Tristessa and wrangling to explain her, suddenly the old Cruz (who is not old, just 40) jumps up crying "Yeh, with our money, Si, con nuestra dinero" and repeating twice and sobbing and El Indio warns her I might understand (as I look up with imperial magnificence of unconcern tinged by regard for the scene) and as if to say "This woman is crying because you take all their money,—what is this? Russia? Mussia? Matamorapussia? as if I didn't care anyway which I couldnt. All I wanted to do was get away. I had completely forgotten about the dove and only remembered it days later.

The wild way Tristessa stands legs spread in the middle of the room to explain something, like a junkey on a corner in Harlem or anyplace, Cairo, Bang Bombayo and the whole Fellah Ollah Lot from Tip of Bermudy to wings of albatross ledge befeathering the Arctic Coastline, only the poison they serve out of Eskimo Gloogloo seals and eagles of Greenland, ain't as bad as that German Civilization morphine she (an Indian) is forced to subdue and die to, in her native earth.

Meanwhile the cat is comfortably ensconced at Cruz's face place where she lies at the foot of the bed, curled, the way she sleeps all night while Tristessa curls at the head and they hook feet like sisters or like mother and daughter and make one little bed do comfortably for two—The little pink kitkat is so certain (despite all his fleas crossing the bridge of his nose or wandering over his eyelids)—that everything is alright—that all is well in the world (at least now)—he wants to be near Cruz's face, where all is well—He (it's a little She) he doesnt notice the bandages and the sorrow and the drunksick horrors she's having, he just knows she's the lady all day her legs are in the kitchen and every now and then she dumps him food, and besides she plays with him on the bed and pretends she's gonna beat him up and holds and scolds him and he yurks in little face into little head and blinks his eyes and flaps back his ears to wait for the beating but she's only playing with him—So now he sits in front of Cruz and even though we may gesture like maniacs as we talk and occasionally a rough hand is waved right by its whiskers almost hitting it or El Indio might roughly decide to throw a newspaper on the bed and land it right on his head, still he sits digging all of us with eyes closed and curled up under Cat Buddha style, meditating among our mad endeavors like the Dove above—I wonder: "Does kittykat know there's a pigeon on the clothes closet." I wish my relatives from Lowell were here to see how people and animals live in Mexico—

But the poor little cat is one mass of fleas, but he doesnt mind, he doesnt keep scratching like American cats but just endures—I pick him up and he's just a skinny little skeleton with great balloons of fur— Everything is so poor in Mexico, people are poor, and yet everything they do is happy and carefree, no matter what is—Tristessa is a junkey and she goes about it skinny and carefree, where an American would be gloomy—But she coughs and complains all day, and by same law, at intervals, the cat explodes into furious scratching that doesnt help—

Meanwhile I keep smoking, my cigarette goes out, and I reach into the ikon for a light from the candle flame, in a glass—I hear Tristessa say something that I interpret to mean "Ack, that stupid fool is using our altar for a light"—To me it's nothing unusual or strange, I just want a light—but perceiving the remark or maintaining belief in the remark without knowing what it was, I ulp and hold back and instead get a light from El Indio, who then shows me later, by quick devout prayer-ito with a piece of newspaper, getting his light indirectly and with a touch and a prayer—Perceiving the ritual I do it too, to get my light a few minutes later—I make a little French prayer: "*Excuse mué ma 'Dame*"—making emphasis on *Dame* because of Damema the Mother of Buddhas.

So I feel less guilty about my smoke and I know all of a sudden all of us will go to heaven straight up from where we are, like golden phantoms of Angels in Gold Strap we go hitch hiking the Deus Ex Machina to heights Apocalyptic, Eucalyptic, Aristophaneac and Divine —I suppose, and I wonder what the cat might think—To Cruz I say "Your cat is having golden thoughts (su gata tienes pensas de or)" but she doesnt understand for a thousand and one billion manifold reasons swimming in the swarm of her milk thoughts Buddha-buried in the stress of her illness enduring—"*What's pensas?*" she yells to the others, she doesnt know that the cat is having golden thoughts—But the cat loves her so, and stays there, little behind to her chin, purring, glad, eyes X-closed and stoopy, kitty kitkat like the Pinky I'd just lost in New York run over on Atlantic Avenue by the swerve dim madtraffics of Brooklyn and Queens, the automatons sitting at wheels automatically killing cats every day about five or six a day on the same road. "But this cat will die the normal Mexican death—by old age or disease— and be a wise old big burn in the alleys around, and you'll see him (dirty as rags) flitting by the garbage heap like a rat, if Cruz ever gets to throw it out—But Cruz won't, and so cat stays at her chin-point like a little sign of her good intentions."

El Indio goes out and gets meat sandwiches and now the cat goes mad yelling and mewing for some and El Indio throws her off the bed—but Cat finally gets a bite of meat and ronches at it like a mad little Tiger and I think "If she was as big as the one in the Zoo, she'd look at me with big green eyes before eating me." I'm having the fairy tale of Saturday night, having a good time actually because of the booze and the good cheer and the careless people—enjoying the little animals—noticing the little Chihuahua pup now meekly waiting for a bite of meat or bread with her tail curled in and woe, if she ever inherits the earth it'll be because of meek—Ears curled back and even whimpering the little Chihuahua smalldog fear-cry—Nevertheless she's been alternately watching us and sleeping all night, and her own reflections on the subject of Nirvana and death and mortals biding time till death, are of a whimpering high frequency terrified tender variety—and the kind that says "Leave me alone, I am so delicate" and you leave her alone in her little fragile shell like the shell of canoes over the ocean deeps—I wish I could communicate to all these creatures and people, in the flush of my moonshine goodtimes, the cloudy mystery of the magic milk to be seen in Mind's Deep Imagery where we learn that everything is nothing—in which case they wouldnt worry any more, except after the instant they think to worry again—All of us trembling in our mortality boots, born to die, BORN TO DIE I could write it on the wall and on Walls all over America—Dove in wings of peace, with her Noah Menagery Moonshine eyes; dog with clitty claws black and shiny, to die is born, trembles in her purple eyes, her little weak bloodvessels down the ribs; yea the ribs of Chihuahua, and Tristessa's ribs too, beautiful ribs, her with her aunts in Chihuahua also born to die, beautiful to be ugly, quick to be dead, glad to be sad, mad to be had—and the El Indio death, born to die, the man, so he plies the needle of Saturday Night every night is Saturday night and goes wild to wait, what else can he do,—The death of Cruz, the drizzles of religion falling on her burial fields, the grim mouth planted the satin of the earth coffin, . . . I moan to recover all that magic, remembering my own *impending* death, "If only I had the magic self of babyhood when I remembered what it was like before I was born, I wouldnt worry about death now knowing both to be the same empty dream"—But what will the Rooster say when it dies, and someone hacks a knife at its fragile chin—And sweet Hen, she who eats out of Tristessa's paw a globule of beer, her beak miffling like human lips to chirn up the milk of the beer—when she dies, sweet hen, Tristessa who loves her will save her lucky bone and wrap it in red thread and keep it in her belongings, nevertheless sweet Mother Hen of our Arc of Noah Night, she the golden purveyor and reaches so far back you can't find the egg that prompted her outward through the first original shell, they'll hack and whack at her tail with hacksaws and make mincemeat out of her that you run through an iron grinder turning handle, and would you wonder why she trembles from fear of punishment too? And the death of the cat, little dead rat in the gutter with twisted yickface—I wish I could communicate to all their combined fears of death the Teaching that I have heard from Ages of Old, that recompenses all that pain with soft reward of perfect silent love abiding up and down and in and out everywhere past, present, and future in the Void unknown where nothing happens and all simply is what it is. But they know that themselves, beast and jackal and love woman, and my Teaching of Old is indeed so old they've heard it long ago before my time.

I become depressed and I gotta go home. Everyone of us, *born to die.*

Bright explanation of the crystal clarity of all the Worlds, I need, to show that we'll all be all right—The measurement of robot machines at this time is rather irrelevant or at any time—The fact that Cruz cooked with a smoky kerosene stove big pottery-fulls of carne meat-general from a whole heifer, bites of veal, pieces of veal tripe and heifer brains and heifer forehead bones . . . this wouldn't ever send Cruz to hell because no one's told her to stop the slaying, and even if someone had, Christ or Buddha or Holy Mohammed, she would still be safe from harm—though by God the heifer ain't—

The little kitty is mewing rapidly for meat—himself a little piece of quivering meat—soul eats soul in the general emptiness.

"Stop complainin!" I yell to the cat as he raves on the floor and finally jumps and joins us on the bed—The hen is rubbing her long feathery side gently imperceptibly against my shoe-tip and I can barely feel it and look in time to recognize, what a gentle touch it is from Mother Maya—She's the Magic henlayer without origin, the limitless chicken with its head cut off—The cat is mewing so violently I begin to worry for the chicken, but no the cat is merely meditating now quietly over a piece of smell on the floor, and I give the poor little fellow a whirr a purr on the thin sticky shoulders with my fingertip—Time to go, I've petted the cat, said goodbye to God the Dove, and wanta leave the heinous kitchen in the middle of a vicious golden dream—It's all taking place in one vast mind, us in the kitchen. I don't believe a word of it or a substantial atom-empty hunk of flesh of it, I see right through it, right through our fleshy forms (hens and all) at the bright amethyst future whiteness of reality—I am worried but I aint glad—"Foo," I say, and rooster looks at me, "what z he mean by *foo!*" and Rooster goes "Cork a Loodle Doo" a real Sunday morning (which it is now, 2 A M) Squawk and I see the brown corners of the dream house and remember my mother's dark kitchen long ago on cold streets in the other part of the same dream as this cold present kitchen with its drip-pots and horrors of Indian Mexico City—Cruz is feebly trying to say goodnight to me as I prepare to go, I've petted her several times a pat on the shoulder thinking that's what she wanted at the right moments and reassured her I loved her and was on her side "but I had no side of my own," I lie to myself—I've wondered what Tristessa thought of my patting her—for awhile I almost thought she was her mother, one wild moment I divined this: "Tristessa and El Indio are brother and sister, and this is their Mother, and they're driving her crazy yakking in the night about poison and morphine'—Then I realize: "Cruz is a junkey too, uses three gramos a month, she'll be on the same time and antenna of their dream trouble, moaning and groaning they'll all three go through the rest of their lives sick. Addiction and affliction. Like diseases of the mad, insane inside encephilitises of the brain where you knock out your health purposely to hold a feeling of feeble chemical gladness that has no basis in anything but the thinking-mind—Gnosis, they will certainly change me the day they try to lay morphine on me. And on ye."

Though the shot has done me some good and I haven't touched the bottle since, a kind of weary gladness has come over me tinged with wild strength—the morphine has gentlized my concerns but I'd rather not have it for the weakness it brings to my ribs,—I shall have them bashed in—"I don't want no more morphine after this," I vow, and I yearn to get away from all the morphine talk which, after sporadic listens, has finally wearied me.

I get up to go, El Indio will go with me, walk me to the corner, though at first he argues with them as though he wanted to stay or wanted something further—We go out quickly, Tristessa closes the door in back of us, I don't even give her a close look, just a glance as she closes indicating I'll see her later—El Indio and I walk vigorously down the slimey rainy aisles, turn right, and cut out to the market street, I've already commented on his black hat, and now here I am on the street with the famous Black Bastard—I've already laughed and said "You're just like Dave" (Tristessa's ex husband) "you even wear the black hat" as I'd seen Dave one time, on Redondas—in the moil and wild of a warm Friday night with buses parading slowly by and mobs on the sidewalk; Dave hands the package to his boy, the seller calls the cop, cop comes running, boy hands it back to Dave, Dave says "Okay take it and run" and tosses it back and boy hits ledge of a flying bus and hangs in to the crowd with his loins his body hanging over the street and his arms rigidly holding the bus door pole, the cops can't catch, Dave meanwhile has vamoosed into a saloon, removed his legendary black hat, and sat at the counter with other men looking straight ahead—cops no find—I had admired Dave for his guts, now admire El Indio for *his*—As we come out of the Tristessa tenement he lets loose a whistle and a shout at a bunch of men on the corner, we walk right along and they spread and we come up to the corner and walk right on talking. I've not paid attention to what he's done, all I wanta do is go straight home—It's started to drizzle—

"Ya voy dormiendo, I go sleep now" says El Indio putting his palms together at side of his mouth—I say "Okay" then he makes a further elaborate statement I think repeating in words what done before by sign.

I fail to acknowledge complete understanding of his new statement, he disappointedly says "Yo un untiende" (you dont understand) but I do understand that he wants to go home and go to bed—"Okay" I say—We shake—We then go through an elaborate smiling routine on the streets of man, in fact on broken cobbles of Redondas—

To reassure him I give him a parting smile and start off but he keeps alertly watching every flicker of my smiler and eyelash, I can't turn away with an arbitrary leer, I want to smile him on his way, he replies by smiles of his own equally elaborate and psychologically corroborative, we swing informations back and forth with crazy smiles of farewell, so much so, El Indio stumbles in the extreme strain of this, over a rock, and throws still a further parting smile of reassurance capping my own, till no end in sight, but we stumble in our opposite directions as though reluctant—which reluctance lasts a brief second, the fresh air of the night hits your newborn solitude and both you and your Indio go off in a new man and the smile, part of the old, is removed, no longer necessita—He to his home, I to mine, why smile about it all night long except in company—The dreariness of the world politely—

from
THE DHARMA BUMS
1955

EDITOR'S NOTE
*In this book Kerouac calls himself "Ray Smith" and Gary Snyder is
"Japhy Ryder."*

1

HOPPING A FREIGHT out of Los Angeles at high noon one day in late September 1955 I got on a gondola and lay down with my duffel bag under my head and my knees crossed and contemplated the clouds as we rolled north to Santa Barbara. It was a local and I intended to sleep on the beach at Santa Barbara that night and catch either another local to San Luis Obispo the next morning or the firstclass freight all the way to San Francisco at seven p.m. Somewhere near Camarillo where Charlie Parker'd been mad and relaxed back to normal health, a thin old little bum climbed into my gondola as we headed into a siding to give a train right of way and looked surprised to see me there. He established himself at the other end of the gondola and lay down, facing me, with his head on his own miserably small pack and said nothing. By and by they blew the highball whistle after the eastbound freight had smashed through on the main line and we pulled out as the air got colder and fog began to blow from the sea over the warm valleys of the coast. Both the little bum and I, after unsuccessful attempts to huddle on the cold steel in wraparounds, got up and paced back and forth and jumped and flapped arms at each our end of the gon. Pretty soon we headed into another siding at a small railroad town and I figured I needed a poorboy of Tokay wine to complete the cold dusk run to Santa Barbara. "Will you watch my pack while I run over there and get a bottle of wine?"

"Sure thing."

I jumped over the side and ran across Highway 101 to the store, and bought, besides wine, a little bread and candy. I ran back to my freight train which had another fifteen minutes to wait in the now warm sunny scene. But it was late afternoon and bound to get cold soon. The little bum was sitting crosslegged at his end before a pitiful repast of one can of sardines. I took pity on him and went over and said, "How about a little wine to warm you up? Maybe you'd like some bread and cheese with your sardines."

"Sure thing." He spoke from far away inside a little meek voicebox afraid or unwilling to assert himself. I'd bought the cheese three days ago in Mexico City before the long cheap bus trip across Zacatecas and Durango and Chihuahua two thousand long miles to the border at El Paso. He ate the cheese and bread and drank the wine with gusto and gratitude. I was pleased. I reminded myself of the line in the Diamond Sutra that says, "Practice charity without holding in mind any conceptions about charity, for charity after all is just a word." I was very devout in those days and was practicing my religious devotions almost to perfection. Since then I've become a little hypocritical about my lip-service and a little tired and cynical. Because now I am grown so old and neutral. . . . But then I really believed in the reality of charity and kindness and humility and zeal and neutral tranquillity and wisdom and ecstasy, and I believed that I was an oldtime bhikku in modern clothes wandering the world (usually the immense triangular arc of New York to Mexico City to San Francisco) in order to turn the wheel of the True Meaning, or Dharma, and gain merit for myself as a future Buddha (Awakener) and as a future Hero in Paradise. I had not met Japhy Ryder yet, I was about to the next week, or heard anything about "Dharma Bums" although at this time I was a perfect Dharma Bum myself and considered myself a religious wanderer. The little bum in the gondola solidified all my beliefs by warming up to the wine and talking and finally whipping out a tiny slip of paper which contained a prayer by Saint Teresa announcing that after her death she will return to the earth by showering it with roses from heaven, forever, for all living creatures.

"Where did you get this?" I asked.

"Oh, I cut it out of a reading-room magazine in Los Angeles couple of years ago. I always carry it with me."

"And you squat in boxcars and read it?"

"Most every day." He talked not much more than this, didn't amplify on the subject of Saint Teresa, and was very modest about his religion and told me little about his personal life. He is the kind of thin quiet little bum nobody pays much attention to even in Skid Row, let alone Main Street. If a cop hustled him off, he hustled, and disappeared, and if yard dicks were around in bigcity yards when a freight was pulling out, chances are they never got a sight of the little man hiding in the weeds and hopping on in the shadows. When I told him I was planning to hop the Zipper firstclass freight train the next night he said, "Ah you mean the Midnight Ghost."

"Is that what you call the Zipper?"

"You musta been a railroad man on that railroad."

"I was, I was a brakeman on the S.P."

"Well, we bums call it the Midnight Ghost cause you get on it at L.A. and nobody sees you till you get to San Francisco in the morning the thing flies so fast."

"Eighty miles an hour on the straightaways, pap."

"That's right but it gits mighty cold at night when you're flyin up that coast north of Gavioty and up around Surf."

"Surf that's right, then the mountains down south of Margarita."

"Margarity, that's right, but I've rid that Midnight Ghost more times'n I can count I guess."

"How many years been since you've been home?"

"More years than I care to count I guess. Ohio was where I was from."

But the train got started, the wind grew cold and foggy again, and we spent the following hour and a half doing everything in our power and will power not to freeze and chatter-teeth too much. I'd huddle and meditate on the warmth, the actual warmth of God, to obviate the cold; then I'd jump up and flap my arms and legs and sing. But the little bum had more patience than I had and just lay there most of the time chewing his cud in forlorn bitterlipped thought. My teeth were chattering, my lips blue. By dark we saw with relief the familiar mountains of Santa Barbara taking shape and soon we'd be stopped and warm in the warm starlit night by the tracks.

I bade farewell to the little bum of Saint Teresa at the crossing, where we jumped off, and went to sleep the night in the sand in my blankets, far down the beach at the foot of a cliff where cops wouldn't see me and drive me away. I cooked hotdogs on freshly cut and sharpened sticks over the coals of a big wood fire, and heated a can of beans and a can of cheese macaroni in the redhot hollows, and drank my newly bought wine, and exulted in one of the most pleasant nights of my life. I waded in the water and dunked a little and stood looking up at the splendorous night sky, Avalokitesvara's ten-wondered universe of dark and diamonds. "Well, Ray," sez I, glad, "only a few miles to go. You've done it again." Happy. Just in my swim shorts, barefooted, wild-haired, in the red fire dark, singing, swigging wine, spitting, jumping, running—that's the way to live. All alone and free in the soft sands of the beach by the sigh of the sea out there, with the Ma-Wink fallopian virgin warm stars reflecting on the outer channel fluid belly waters. And if your cans are redhot and you can't hold them in your hands, just use good old railroad gloves, that's all. I let the food cool a little to enjoy more wine and my thoughts. I sat crosslegged in the sand and contemplated my life. Well, there, and what difference did it make? "What's going to happen to me up ahead?" Then the wine got to work on my taste buds and before long I had to pitch into those hotdogs, biting them right off the end of the stick spit, and chomp chomp, and dig down into the two tasty cans with the old pack spoon, spooning up rich bites of hot beans and pork, or of macaroni with sizzling hot sauce, and maybe a little sand thrown in. "And how many grains of sand are there on this beach?" I think. "Why, as many grains of sand as there are stars in that sky!" (chomp chomp) and if so "How many human beings have there been, in fact how many living creatures have there been, since before the *less* part of beginningless time? Why, oy, I reckon you would have to calculate the number of grains of sand on this beach and on every star in the sky, in every one of the ten thousand great chilicosms,

which would be a number of sand grains uncomputable by IBM and
Burroughs too, why boy I don't rightly know" (swig of wine) "I don't
rightly know but it must be a couple umpteen trillion sextillion infideled
and busted up unnumberable number of roses that sweet Saint Teresa
and that fine little old man are now this minute showering on your head,
with lilies."

Then, meal done, wiping my lips with my red bandana, I washed
up the dishes in the salt sea, kicked a few clods of sand, wandered
around, wiped them, put them away, stuck the old spoon back in the
salty pack, and lay down curled in my blanket for a night's good and
just rest. Waking up in the middle of the night, "Wa? Where am I, what
is the basketbally game of eternity the girls are playing here by me in
the old house of my life, the house isn't on fire is it?" but it's only the
banding rush of waves piling up higher closer high tide to my blanket
bed. "I be as hard and old as a conch shell," and I go to sleep and
dream that while sleeping I use up three slices of bread breathing. . . .
Ah poor mind of man, and lonely man alone on the beach, and God
watching with intent smile I'd say. . . . And I dreamed of home long
ago in New England, my little kitkats trying to go a thousand miles
following me on the road across America, and my mother with a pack
on her back, and my father running after the ephemeral uncatchable
train, and I dreamed and woke up to a gray dawn, saw it, sniffed (because I had seen all the horizon shift as if a sceneshifter had hurried to
put it back in place and make me believe in its reality), and went back
to sleep, turning over. "It's all the same thing," I heard my voice say in
the void that's highly embraceable during sleep.

•   •   •

from
GOOD BLONDE
1955

. . . "DAMN," SAID I, "I'll just hitchhike on that highway" (101) seeing
the fast flash of many cars. The old Greek was still wandering on the
water's edge when I looked back, right on that mystical margin men-

tioned by Whitman where sea kisses sand in the endless sigh kiss of time. Like the three bos in Lordsburg New Mexico his direction in the void seemed so much sadder than my own, they were going east to hopeless sleeps in burlap in Alabama fields and the eventual Texas chaingang, he was going up and down the beach alone kicking sand . . . but I knew that in reality my own direction, going up to San Francisco to see the gang and whatever awaited me there, was no higher and no lower than his own humble and unsayable state. The little store had a tree in front, shade, I laid my pack down and went in and came out with a ten-cent ice cream on a stick and sat awhile eating, resting, then combed my hair with water out of an outside faucet and went to the highway all ready to thumb. I walked a few blocks up to the light and got on the far side and stood there, pack at my feet, for a good half hour during which time I got madder and madder and finally I was swearing to myself "I will never hitchhike again, it's getting worse and worse every goddamn year." Meanwhile I kept a sharp eye on the rails a block toward the sea watching for convenient freight trains. At the moment when I was the maddest, and was standing there, thumb out, completely infuriated and so much so that (I remember) my eyes were slitted, my teeth clenched, a brand new cinnamon colored Lincoln driven by a beautiful young blonde in a bathingsuit flashed by and suddenly swerved to the right and put to a stop in the side of the road for me. I couldn't believe it. I figured she wanted road information. I picked up my pack and ran. I opened the door and looked in to smile and thank her.

She said "Get in. Can you drive?" She was a gorgeous young blonde girl of about 22 in a pure white bathingsuit, barefooted with a little ankle bracelet around her right ankle. Her bathingsuit was shoulderless and low cut. She sat there in the luxurious cinnamon sea in that white suit like a model. In fact she was a model. Green eyes, from Texas, on her way back to the City.

"Sure I can drive but I don't have a license."

"You drive all right?"

"I drive as good as anybody."

"Well I'm dog tired, I've been driving all the way from Texas without sleep, I went to see my family there" (by now she had the heap jet gone up the road and went up to 60 and kept it there hard and clean on the line, driving like a good man driver). "Boy," she said, "I sure wish I had some Benzedrine or sumptin to keep me awake. I'll have to give you the wheel pretty soon."

"Well how far you going?"

"Far as you are I think . . . San Francisco."

"Wow, great." (To myself: who will ever believe I got a ride like this from a beautiful chick like that practically naked in a bathingsuit, wow, what does she expect me to do next?) "And Benzedrine you say?" I said "I've got some here in my bag, I just got back from Mexico, I got plenty."

"Crazy!" she yelled. "Pull it out. I want some."

"Baby you'll drive all the way when you get high on that stuff, Mexican you know."

"Mexican Shmexican just give it to me."

"OK." Grinning I began dumping all my dirty old unwashed rags and gear and claptraps of cookpot junk and pieces of food in wrapper on the floor of her car searching feverishly for the little tubes of Benny suddenly I couldn't find anymore. I began to panic. I looked in all the flaps and sidepockets. "Goddamnit where is it!" I kept worrying the smell of my old unwashed clothes would be repugnant to her, I wanted to find the stuff as soon as possible and repack everything away.

"Never mind man, take your time," she said looking straight ahead at the road, and in a pause in my search I let my eye wander to her ankle bracelet, as damaging a sight as Cleopatra on her poop of beaten gold, and the sweet little snowy bare foot on the gas pedal, enough to drive a man mad. I kept wondering why she'd really picked me up.

I asked her "How come you picked up a guy like me? I never seen a girl alone pick up a guy."

"Well I tell you I need someone to help me drive to the City and I figured you could drive, you looked like it anyway . . ."

"O where are those Bennies!"

"Take your time."

"Here they are!"

"Crazy! I'll pull into that station up ahead and we'll go in and have a Coke and swallow em down." She pulled into the station which also had an inside luncheonette. She jumped out of the car barefooted in her low-cut bathingsuit as the attendant stared and ordered a full tank as I went in and bought two bottles of Coke to go out, cold. When I came back she was in the car with her change, ready to go. What a wild chick. I looked at the attendant to see what he was thinking. He was looking at me enviously. I kept having the urge to tell him the true story.

"Here," and I handed her the tubes, and she took out two. "Hey, that's too many, your top'll fly out . . . better take one and a half, or one. I take one myself."

"I don't want no one and a half, I want two."

"You've had it before?"

"Of course man and everything else."

"Pot too?"

"Sure pot . . . I know all the musicians in L.A. and the City, when I come into the Ramador Shelly Manne sees me coming and stops whatever they're playing and they play my theme song which is a little bop arrangement."

"How does it go?"

"Ha! and it goes: boop boop be doodleya dap."

"Wow, you can sing."

"I walk in, man, and they play that, and everybody knows I'm back." She took her two Bennies and swigged down, and buzzed the car up to a steady 70 as we hit the country north of Santa Barbara, the traffic thinning and the road getting longer and straighter. "Long drive to San Francisco, four hundred miles just about. I hope these Bennies are good, I'd like to go all the way."

"Well if you're tired I can drive," I said but hoped I wouldn't have to drive, the car was so brand new and beautiful. It was a '55 Lincoln and here it was October 1955. Beautiful, lowslung, sleek. Zip, rich. I leaned back with my Benny in my palm and threw it down with the Coke and felt good. Up ahead suddenly I realized the whole city of San Francisco would be all bright lights and glittering wide open waiting for me this very night, and no strain, no hurt, no pain, no freight train, no sweating on the hitchhike road but up there zip zoom inside about eight hours. She passed cars smoothly and went on. She turned on the radio and began looking for jazz, found rock 'n' roll and left that on, loud. The way she looked straight ahead and drove with no expression and sending no mincing gestures my way or even telepathies of mincingness, you'd never believe she was a lovely little chick in a bathingsuit. I was amazed. And in the bottom of that scheming mind I kept wondering and wondering (dirtily) if she hadn't picked me up because she was secretly a sex-fiend and was waiting for me to say "Let's park the car somewhere and make it" but something so inviolately grave about her prevented me from saying this, more than that my own sudden bashfulness (as the holy Benny began taking effect) prevented me from making such an importunate and really insulting proposition seeing I'd just met the young lady. But the thought stuck and stuck with me. I was afraid to turn and look at her and only occasionally dropped my eyes to that ankle bracelet and the little white lily foot on the gas pedal. And we talked and talked. Finally the Benny began hitting us strong after Los Alamos and we were talking a blue streak, she did most of the talking. She'd been a model, she wanted to be an actress, so forth, the usual beautiful-California-blonde designs but finally I said "As for me I don't want anything . . . I think life is suffering, a suffering dream, and all I wanta do is rest and be kind somewhere, preferably in the woods, under a tree, live in a shack."

"Ain't you ever gonna get married?"

"Been married twice and I've had it."

"Well you oughta take a third crack at it, maybe this time you'd hit a homerun."

"That ain't the point, in the first place I wouldn't wanta have children, they only born to die."

"You better not tell that to my mom and dad, they had eight kids in Texas, I was the second, they've had a damn good long life and the kids are great, you know what my youngest brother did when I walked in the house last week and hadn't seen him for a year: he was all grown up tall and put on a rock-'n'-roll record for me and wanted me to do the lindy with him. O what laughs we had in the old homestead last week. I'm glad I went."

"I'll bet when you were a little girl you had a ball there in Texas huh? hunting, wandering around."

"Everything man, sometimes I think my new life now modeling and acting in cities isn't half as good as that was."

"And there you were on long Texas nights Grandma readin the Bible, right?"

"Yeah and all the good food we made, nowadays I have dates in good restaurants and man—"

"Dates . . . you ain't married hey?"

"Not yet, pretty soon."

"Well what does a beautiful girl like you think about?" This made her turn and look at me with bland frank green eyes.

"What do you mean?"

"I don't know . . . I'd say, for a man, like me, what I say is best for him . . . but for a beautiful girl like you I guess what you're doing is best." I wasn't going to say get thee to a nunnery, she was too gone, too pretty too, besides she wouldn't have done it by a long shot, she just didn't care. In no time at all we were way up north of Los Alamos and coming into a little bumper to bumper traffic outside Santa Maria where she pulled up at a gas station and said:

"Say do you happen to have a little change?"

"About a dollar and a half."

"Hmmmm . . . I want to call longdistance to South City and tell my man I'll be in at eight or so."

"Call him collect if he's your man."

"Now you're talkin like a man" she said and went trottin barefoot to the phone booth in the driveway and got in and made a call with a dime. I got out of the car to stretch out, high and dizzy and pale and sweating and excited from the Benzedrine, I could see she was the same way in the phone booth, chewing vigorously on a wad of gum. She got her call and talked while I picked up an orange from the ground and wound up and did the pitcher-on-the-mound bit to stretch my muscles. I felt good. A cool wind was blowing across Santa Maria, with a smell of the sea in it somehow. The palm trees waved in a cooler wind than the one in Barbara and L.A. Tonight it would be the cool fogs of Frisco again! After all these years! She came out and we got in.

"Who's the guy."

"He's my man, Joey King, he runs a bar in South City . . . on Main Street."

"Say I used to be a yardclerk in the yards there and I'd go to some of those bars on Main Street for a beer . . . with a little cocktail glass neon in front, with a stick in it?"

"All the bars have that around here," she laughed and gunned on up the road fast. Pretty soon, yakking happily about jazz and even singing a lot of jazz, we got to San Luis Obispo, went through town, and started up the pass to Santa Margarita.

"There you see it," I said, "see where the railroad track winds around to go up the pass, I was a brakeman on that for years, on drizzly nights I'd be squattin under lumber boards ridin up that pass and when I'd go through the tunnels I'd hold my bandanna over my nose not to suffocate."

"Why were you riding on the outside of the engine."

"Because I was the guy assigned to puttin pops up and down, air valves, for mountain brakes, all that crap . . . I don't think it would interest you."

"Sure, my brother's a brakeman in Texas. He's about your age."

"I'm thirty-three."

"Well he's a little younger but his eyes are greener than yours, yours are blue."

"Yours are green."

"No, mine are hazel."

"Well that's what green-eyed girls always say."

"What do hazel-eyed girls always say?"

"They say, hey now." We were (as you see) talking like two kids and completely unself-conscious and by this time I'd quite forgotten the lurking thought of us sexing together in some bushes by the side of the road, though I kept smelling her, the Benny sweat, which is abundant, and perfumy in the way it works, it filled the car with a sweet perfume, mingled with my own sweat, in our noses if not in our minds there was a thought of sweating love . . . at least in my mind. Sometimes I felt the urge to just lay my head in her lap as she drove but then I got mad and thought "Ah hell it's all a dream including beauty, leave the Angel Alone you dirty old foney Duluoz" which I did. To this day I never know what she wanted, I mean, what she really secretly thought of me, of picking me up, and she got so high on the Benny she drove all the way anyway, or perhaps she woulda drove all the way anyway, I don't know. She balled up over the pass in the gathering late afternoon golden shadows of California and came out on the flats of the Margarita plateau, where we stopped for gas, where in the rather cool mountain wind she got out and ran to the ladies room and the gas attendant said to me:

"Where'd you pick her up?" thinking the car was mine.

"She picked *me* up, pops."

"Well I oughta be glad if I was you."

"I ain't unglad."

"Sure is a nice little bundle."

"She's been wearing that bathingsuit clear from Texas."

"Geez." She came out and we went up the Salinas valley as it got dark slowly with old orange sunsets behind the rim where I'd seen bears as a brakeman, at night, standing by the track as we'd in the Diesel ball by with a hundred-car freight behind us, and one time a cougar. Wild country. And the floor of the dry Salinas riverbottom is all clean white sand and bushes, ideal for bhikkuing (outdoor camping where nobody bothers you) because you can hide good and hide your campfire and the only people to bother you are cattle, and snakes I guess, and beautiful dry climate with stars, even now at dusk, I could see flashing in the pale plank of heaven, like bhaghavat nails. I told Pretty about it:

"Someday I'm gonna bring my pack and a month's essential groceries right down to that riverbottom and build a little shelter with twigs and stuff and a tarpaulin or a poncho and lay up and do nothing for a month."

"What you wanta do that for? There's no fun in that."

"Sure there is."

"Well I can't figure all this out but . . . it's all right I guess." At times I didn't like her, at one point I definitely didn't like her because there was something so cold and yawny distant about her, I felt that in her secret bedroom she probably yawned a lot and didn't know what to do with herself and to compensate for that had a lot of boyfriends who bought her expensive presents (just because she was beautiful, which compensated not for her inside unbeautiful feeling), and going to restaurants and bars and jazz clubs and yooking it up because there was nothing else inside. And I thought: "Truly, I'm better off *without* a doll like this . . . out there in that riverbottom, pure and free, what immensities I'd have, in real riches . . . alone, in old clothes, cooking my own food, finding my own peace . . . instead of sniffin around her ankles day in day out wonderin whether in some mean mood she's going to throw me out anyway and then I would have to clap her one or something and all of it a crock for sure—" I didn't dare tell her all this, besides the point being she wouldn't have been interested in the least. It got dark, we flew on, soon we saw the sealike flats of Salinas valley stretching on both sides of us, with occasional brown farmlamps, the stars overhead, a vast storm cloud gathering in the night sky in the east and the radio announcer predicting rain for the night, then finally far up ahead the jeweled cluster of Salinas the city and airport lights. Outside Salinas on the four lane, about five miles, suddenly she said "The car's run out of gas, Oho" and she began wobbling the car from side to side in a graceful dance.

"What you doin that for?"

"That's to splash what's left of the gas into the carburetor . . . I can do this for a few miles, let's pray we see a station or we don't get to South City by eight." She swayed and wobbled along, grinning faintly over her wheel, and in the cuddly dark and little emergency of the night, I began to love her again and thought "Ah well and what a strong sweet angel to spend the rest of your life with, though, damn." Pretty soon the wobbles were wider and the speed slower and she finally pulled over by the side of the road and parked and said "That's that, we're out of gas."

"I'll go out and hail a car."

"While you're doing that I'll go in the backseat and put something over my bathingsuit, it's getting cold," which it was. I unsuccessfully tried to hail down cars for five minutes or so, they were all zipping at a steady 70, and I said:

"Say when you're ready come on out, when they see *you* they'll stop." She came out and we joked a bit in the dark dancing and showing our legs at the cars and finally a big truck stopped and I ran after it to talk to him. It was a big burly guy eager to help, he'd seen the blonde. He got out a chain and tied her car on and off we went at about 15 miles per hour to the gas station three miles down. He had air-brakes and she was worried about ramming him and hoped he wouldn't go too fast. He went perfect. In the gas station driveway he got out to admire her some more.

"Boy, that's a little bit of sumptin" he said to me as she went to the toilet.

"She picked me up in Santa Barbara, she's been driving all the way from Texas alone."

"Well, well, you're a lucky hitchhiker." He undid the chain. She came out and stood around chatting with the big truck-driver and the attendant. Now she was clad in tightfitting black slacks and a neat keen throwover of some kind, and sandals, in which she padded like a little tightfit Indian. I felt humble and foolish with the two men staring at her and me waiting by the car for my poor world ride. She came back and off we went, getting through Salinas and out on the dark road and now finally we found some real fine jazz from San Francisco, the Pat Henry show or some other show, and we didn't speak much anymore but just sang with the music and kept our eyes glued on the headlamp swatch and the inwinding kiss-in of the white line in the road where it again became a two-laner. Soon we were going through Watsonville, a little behind schedule.

"Here's where I did most of my work as a brakeman . . . insteada sleeping in the railroad dormitory I'd go out to the sandbottom of that river, the Pajaro, and cook woodfires and eat hotdogs like last night and sleep in the sand . . ."

"You're always in some riverbottom or other." The music on the radio got louder and louder as we began to approach San Jose and the City. The storm to the east hadn't formed yet. It was exciting to be coming into the City now. On Bayshore we really felt it, all the cars flashing by both ways in the lanes, the lights, the roadside restaurants, the antennas, nothing had looked like that all day, the big city, "The Apple," I said, "the Apple of California but have you ever been to *the* Apple, New York!" to which she replied: "Yeah man."

"But nothing wrong with this little old town, it's got everything . . . isn't it . . . don't you feel a funny feeling in your belly coming into the City."

"Yeah man I always do." We agreed on that and talked about it, and soon we were coming into South San Francisco where I suddenly realized she was going to let me out in a few minutes and I hadn't anticipated parting from her ever, somehow. She pulled up right smack in front of the little station where I'd worked as a yardclerk and there were the same old tracks, I knew every number and name of them, and the same old overpass, and the spurs leading off to the slaughterhouses Armour and Swift east, the same sad lamps and sad dim red switchlights in the darkness. The car stopped, our bodies were still vibrating as we sat in the stillness, the radio booming.

"Well I'll get out and let you get home," I said, "and I needn't tell you how great it was and how glad I am you gave me this great ride."

"Oh man, nothing, it was fun."

"Why don't you give me your phone, I'll call you and we'll go down and hear Brue Moore, I hear he's in town."

"O he's my favorite tenor, I've seen him . . . OK, I'll give you my address, I haven't got a phone in yet."

"OK." She wrote out the address in my little breastpocket notebook and I could see she was anxious to get on home to her man so I said "OK, here I go," and got my bag and went out and stuck my hand in to shake and off she went, up Main Street, probably to her pad to take a shower and dress up and go down to her man's bar. And I put my bag on my back and walked down the same old homey familiar rail and felt glad . . . probably gladder than she did, but who knows?

• • •

from
THE DHARMA BUMS
1955–1956

EDITOR'S NOTE
In this book Kerouac calls himself "Ray Smith," Allen Ginsberg is "Alvah Goldbook," Gary Snyder is "Japhy Ryder," Neal Cassady is "Cody Pomeray," Philip Whalen is "Warren Coughlin," Michael McClure is "Ike O'Shay," Kenneth Rexroth is "Rheinhold Cacoethes," Philip Lamantia is "Francis DaPavia," and John Montgomery is "Henry Morley."

2

THE LITTLE SAINT TERESA BUM was the first genuine Dharma Bum I'd met, and the second was the number one Dharma Bum of them all and in fact it was he, Japhy Ryder, who coined the phrase. Japhy Ryder was a kid from eastern Oregon brought up in a log cabin deep in the woods with his father and mother and sister, from the beginning a woods boy, an axman, farmer, interested in animals and Indian lore so that when he finally got to college by hook or crook he was already well equipped for his early studies in anthropology and later in Indian myth and in the actual texts of Indian mythology. Finally he learned Chinese and Japanese and became an Oriental scholar and discovered the greatest Dharma Bums of them all, the Zen Lunatics of China and Japan. At the same time, being a Northwest boy with idealistic tendencies, he got interested in oldfashioned I.W.W. anarchism and learned to play the guitar and sing old worker songs to go with his Indian songs and general folksong interests. I first saw him walking down the street in San Francisco the following week (after hitchhiking the rest of the way from Santa Barbara in one long zipping ride given me, as though anybody'll believe this, by a beautiful darling young blonde in a snow-white strapless bathing suit and barefooted with a gold bracelet on her ankle, driving a next-year's cinnamon-red Lincoln Mercury, who wanted benzedrine so she could drive all the way to the City and when I said I had some in my duffel bag yelled "Crazy!")—I saw Japhy loping along in that curious long stride of the mountainclimber, with a small knapsack on his back filled with books and toothbrushes and whatnot which was his small "goin-to-the-city" knapsack as apart from his big full rucksack complete with sleeping bag, poncho, and cookpots. He wore a little goatee, strangely Oriental-looking with his somewhat slanted green eyes, but he didn't look like a Bohemian at all, and was far from being a Bohemian (a hanger-onner around the arts). He was wiry, suntanned, vigorous, open, all howdies and glad talk and even yelling hello to bums on the street and when asked a question answered right off the bat from the top or bottom of his mind I don't know which and always in a sprightly sparkling way.

"Where did you meet Ray Smith?" they asked him when we walked into The Place, the favorite bar of the hepcats around the Beach.

"Oh I always meet my Bodhisattvas in the street!" he yelled, and ordered beers.

It was a great night, a historic night in more ways than one. He and some other poets (he also wrote poetry and translated Chinese and Japanese poetry into English) were scheduled to give a poetry reading at the Gallery Six in town. They were all meeting in the bar and getting high. But as they stood and sat around I saw that he was the only one who didn't look like a poet, though poet he was indeed. The other poets were either hornrimmed intellectual hepcats with wild black hair like Alvah Goldbook, or delicate pale handsome poets like Ike O'Shay (in a suit), or out-of-this-world genteel-looking Renaissance Italians like Francis DaPavia (who looks like a young priest), or bow-tied wild-haired old anarchist fuds like Rheinhold Cacoethes, or big fat bespectacled quiet booboos like Warren Coughlin. And all the other hopeful poets were standing around, in various costumes, worn-at-the-sleeves corduroy jackets, scuffly shoes, books sticking out of their pockets. But Japhy was in rough workingman's clothes he'd bought secondhand in Goodwill stores to serve him on mountain climbs and hikes and for sitting in the open at night, for campfires, for hitchhiking up and down the Coast. In fact in his little knapsack he also had a funny green alpine cap that he wore when he got to the foot of a mountain, usually with a yodel, before starting to tromp up a few thousand feet. He wore mountainclimbing boots, expensive ones, his pride and joy, Italian make, in which he clomped around over the sawdust floor of the bar like an oldtime lumberjack. Japhy wasn't big, just about five foot seven, but strong and wiry and fast and muscular. His face was a mask of woeful bone, but his eyes twinkled like the eyes of old giggling sages of China, over that little goatee, to offset the rough look of his handsome face. His teeth were a little brown, from early backwoods neglect, but you never noticed that and he opened his mouth wide to guffaw at jokes. Sometimes he'd quiet down and just stare sadly at the floor, like a man whittling. He was merry at times. He showed great sympathetic interest in me and in the story about the little Saint Teresa bum and the stories I told him about my own experiences hopping freights or hitchhiking or hiking in woods. He claimed at once that I was a great "Bodhisattva," meaning "great wise being" or "great wise angel," and that I was ornamenting this world with my sincerity. We had the same favorite Buddhist saint, too: Avalokitesvara, or, in Japanese, Kwannon the Eleven-Headed. He knew all the details of Tibetan, Chinese, Mahayana, Hinayana, Japanese and even Burmese Buddhism but I warned him at once I didn't give a goddamn about the mythology and all the names and national flavors of Buddhism, but was just interested in the first of Sakyamuni's four noble truths, *All life is suffering*. And to an extent interested in the third, *The suppression of suffering can be achieved*, which I didn't quite believe was possible then. (I hadn't yet digested the Lankavatara Scripture which eventually shows you that there's nothing in the world but the mind itself, and therefore all's possible including the suppression of suffering.) Japhy's buddy was the aforementioned booboo big old goodhearted Warren Coughlin a hundred and eighty pounds of poet meat, who was advertised by Japhy (privately in my ear) as being more than meets the eye.

"Who is he?"

"He's my big best friend from up in Oregon, we've known each other a long time. At first you think he's slow and stupid but actually he's a shining diamond. You'll see. Don't let him cut you to ribbons. He'll make the top of your head fly away, boy, with a choice chance word."

"Why?"

"He's a great mysterious Bodhisattva I think maybe a reincarnation of Asagna the great Mahayana scholar of the old centuries."

"And who am I?"

"I dunno, maybe you're Goat."

"Goat?"

"Maybe you're Mudface."

"Who's Mudface?"

"Mudface is the mud in your goatface. What would you say if someone was asked the question 'Does a dog have the Buddha nature?' and said 'Woof!' "

"I'd say that was a lot of silly Zen Buddhism." This took Japhy back a bit. "Lissen Japhy," I said, "I'm not a Zen Buddhist, I'm a serious Buddhist, I'm an oldfashioned dreamy Hinayana coward of later Mahayanism," and so forth into the night, my contention being that Zen Buddhism didn't concentrate on kindness so much as on confusing the intellect to make it perceive the illusion of all sources of things. "It's *mean*," I complained. "All those Zen Masters throwing young kids in the mud because they can't answer their silly word questions."

"That's because they want them to realize mud is better than words, boy." But I can't recreate the exact (will try) brilliance of all Japhy's answers and come-backs and come-ons with which he had me on pins and needles all the time and did eventually stick something in my crystal head that made me change my plans in life.

Anyway I followed the whole gang of howling poets to the reading at Gallery Six that night, which was, among other important things, the night of the birth of the San Francisco Poetry Renaissance. Everyone was there. It was a mad night. And I was the one who got things jumping by going around collecting dimes and quarters from the rather stiff audience standing around in the gallery and coming back with three huge gallon jugs of California Burgundy and getting them all piffed so that by eleven o'clock when Alvah Goldbook was reading his, wailing his poem "Wail" drunk with arms outspread everybody was yelling "Go! Go! Go!" (like a jam session) and old Rheinhold Cacoethes the father of the Frisco poetry scene was wiping his tears in gladness. Japhy himself read his fine poems about Coyote the God of the North American Plateau Indians (I think), at least the God of the Northwest Indians, Kwakiutl and what-all. "Fuck you! sang Coyote, and ran away!" read Japhy to the distinguished audience, making them all howl with joy, it was so pure, fuck being a dirty word that comes out clean. And he had his tender lyrical lines, like the ones about bears eating berries, showing his love of animals, and great mystery lines about oxen on the Mongolian road showing his knowledge of Oriental literature even on to Hsuan Tsung the great Chinese monk who walked from China to Tibet, Lanchow to Kashgar and Mongolia carrying a stick of incense in his hand. Then Japhy showed his sudden barroom humor with lines about Coyote bringing goodies. And his anarchistic ideas about how Americans don't know how to live, with lines about commuters being trapped in living rooms that come from poor trees felled by chainsaws (showing here, also, his background as a logger up north). His voice was deep and resonant and somehow brave, like the voice of oldtime American heroes and orators. Something earnest and strong and humanly hopeful I liked about him, while the other poets were either too dainty in their aestheticism, or too hysterically cynical to hope for anything, or too abstract and indoorsy, or too political, or like Coughlin too incomprehensible to understand (big Coughlin saying things about "unclarified processes" though where Coughlin did say that revelation was a personal thing I noticed the strong Buddhist and idealistic feeling of Japhy, which he'd shared with goodhearted Coughlin in their buddy days at college, as I had shared mine with Alvah in the Eastern scene and with others less apocalyptical and straighter but in no sense more sympathetic and tearful).

Meanwhile scores of people stood around in the darkened gallery straining to hear every word of the amazing poetry reading as I wandered from group to group, facing them and facing away from the stage, urging them to glug a slug from the jug, or wandered back and sat on the right side of the stage giving out little wows and yesses of approval and even whole sentences of comment with nobody's invitation but in the general gaiety nobody's disapproval either. It was a great night. Delicate Francis DaPavia read, from delicate onionskin yellow pages, or pink, which he kept flipping carefully with long white fingers, the poems of his dead chum Altman who'd eaten too much peyote in Chihuahua (or died of polio, one) but read none of his own poems—a charming elegy in itself to the memory of the dead young poet, enough to draw tears from the Cervantes of Chapter Seven, and read them in a delicate Englishy voice that had me crying with inside laughter though I later got to know Francis and liked him.

Among the people standing in the audience was Rosie Buchanan, a girl with a short haircut, red-haired, bony, handsome, a real gone chick and friend of everybody of any consequence on the Beach, who'd been a painter's model and a writer herself and was bubbling over with excitement at that time because she was in love with my old buddy Cody. "Great, hey Rosie?" I yelled, and she took a big slug from my jug and shined eyes at me. Cody just stood behind her with both arms around her waist. Between poets, Rheinhold Cacoethes, in his bow tie and shabby old coat, would get up and make a little funny speech in his snide funny voice and introduce the next reader; but as I say come eleven-thirty when all the poems were read and everybody was milling around wondering what had happened and what would come next in American poetry, he was wiping his eyes with his handkerchief. And we all got together with him, the poets, and drove in several cars to Chinatown for a big fabulous dinner off the Chinese menu, with chopsticks, yelling conversation in the middle of the night in one of those free-swinging great Chinese restaurants of San Francisco. This happened to be Japhy's favorite Chinese restaurant, Nam Yuen, and he showed me how to order and how to eat with chopsticks and told anecdotes about the Zen Lunatics of the Orient and had me going so glad (and we had a bottle of wine on the table) that finally I went over to an old cook in the doorway of the kitchen and asked him "Why did Bodhidharma come from the West?" (Bodhidharma was the Indian who brought Buddhism eastward to China.)

"I don't care," said the old cook, with lidded eyes, and I told Japhy and he said, "Perfect answer, absolutely perfect. Now you know what I mean by Zen."

I had a lot more to learn, too. Especially about how to handle girls—Japhy's incomparable Zen Lunatic way, which I got a chance to see firsthand the following week.

3

In Berkeley I was living with Alvah Goldbook in his little rose-covered cottage in the backyard of a bigger house on Milvia Street. The old rotten porch slanted forward to the ground, among vines, with a nice old rocking chair that I sat in every morning to read my Diamond Sutra. The yard was full of tomato plants about to ripen, and mint, mint, everything smelling of mint, and one fine old tree that I loved to sit under and meditate on those cool perfect starry California October nights unmatched anywhere in the world. We had a perfect little kitchen with a gas stove, but no icebox, but no matter. We also had a perfect little bathroom with a tub and hot water, and one main room, covered with pillows and floor mats of straw and mattresses to sleep on, and books, books, hundreds of books everything from Catullus to Pound to Blyth to albums of Bach and Beethoven (and even one swinging Ella Fitzgerald album with Clark Terry very interesting on trumpet) and a good three-speed Webcor phonograph that played loud enough to blast the roof off: and the roof nothing but plywood, the walls too, through which one night in one of our Zen Lunatic drunks I put my fist in glee and Coughlin saw me and put his head through about three inches.

About a mile from there, way down Milvia and then upslope toward the campus of the University of California, behind another big old house on a quiet street (Hillegass), Japhy lived in his own shack which was infinitely smaller than ours, about twelve by twelve, with nothing in it but typical Japhy appurtenances that showed his belief in the simple monastic life—no chairs at all, not even one sentimental rocking chair, but just straw mats. In the corner was his famous rucksack with cleaned-up pots and pans all fitting into one another in a compact unit and all tied and put away inside a knotted-up blue bandana. Then his Japanese wooden pata shoes, which he never used, and a pair of black inside-pata socks to pad around softly in over his pretty straw mats, just room for your four toes on one side and your big toe on the other. He had a slew of orange crates all filled with beautiful scholarly books, some of them in Oriental languages, all the great sutras, comments on sutras, the complete works of D. T. Suzuki and a fine quadruple-volume edition of Japanese haikus. He also had an immense collection of valuable general poetry. In fact if a thief should have broken in there the only things of real value were the books. Japhy's clothes were all old hand-me-downs bought secondhand with a bemused and happy expression in Goodwill and Salvation Army stores: wool socks darned, colored undershirts, jeans, workshirts, moccasin shoes, and a few turtleneck sweaters that he wore one on top the other in the cold mountain nights of the High Sierras in California and the High Cascades of Washington and Oregon on the long incredible jaunts that sometimes lasted weeks and weeks with just a few pounds of dried food in his pack. A few orange crates made his table, on which, one late sunny afternoon as I arrived, was steaming a peaceful cup of tea at his side as he bent his serious head to the Chinese signs of the poet Han Shan. Coughlin had given me the address and I came there, seeing first Japhy's bicycle on the lawn in front of the big house out front (where his landlady lived) then the few odd boulders and rocks and funny little trees he'd brought back from mountain jaunts to set out in his own "Japanese tea garden" or "tea-house garden," as there was a convenient pine tree soughing over his little domicile.

A peacefuller scene I never saw than when, in that rather nippy late red afternoon, I simply opened his little door and looked in and saw him at the end of the little shack, sitting crosslegged on a Paisley pillow on a straw mat, with his spectacles on, making him look old and scholarly and wise, with book on lap and the little tin teapot and porcelain cup steaming at his side. He looked up very peacefully, saw who it was, said, "Ray, come in," and bent his eyes again to the script.

"What you doing?"

"Translating Han Shan's great poem called 'Cold Mountain' writ-

ten a thousand years ago some of it scribbled on the sides of cliffs
hundreds of miles away from any other living beings."

"Wow."

"When you come into this house though you've got to take your
shoes off, see those straw mats, you can ruin 'em with shoes." So I took
my softsoled blue cloth shoes off and laid them dutifully by the door
and he threw me a pillow and I sat crosslegged along the little wooden
board wall and he offered me a cup of hot tea. "Did you ever read the
Book of Tea?" said he.

"No, what's that?"

"It's a scholarly treatise on how to make tea utilizing all the knowledge of two thousand years about tea-brewing. Some of the descriptions
of the effect of the first sip of tea, and the second, and the third, are
really wild and ecstatic."

"Those guys got high on nothing, hey?"

"Sip your tea and you'll see; this is good green tea." It was good
and I immediately felt calm and warm. "Want me to read you parts of
this Han Shan poem? Want me to tell you about Han Shan?"

"Yeah."

"Han Shan you see was a Chinese scholar who got sick of the big
city and the world and took off to hide in the mountains."

"Say, that sounds like you."

"In those days you could really do that. He stayed in caves not far
from a Buddhist monastery in the T'ang Hsing district of T'ien Tai and
his only human friend was the funny Zen Lunatic Shih-te who had a
job sweeping out the monastery with a straw broom. Shih-te was a poet
too but he never wrote much down. Every now and then Han Shan
would come down from Cold Mountain in his bark clothing and come
into the warm kitchen and wait for food, but none of the monks would
ever feed him because he didn't want to join the order and answer the
meditation bell three times a day. You see why in some of his utterances,
like—listen and I'll look here and read from the Chinese," and I bent
over his shoulder and watched him read from big wild crowtracks of
Chinese signs: "Climbing up Cold Mountain path, Cold Mountain path
goes on and on, long gorge choked with scree and boulders, wide creek
and mist-blurred grass, moss is slippery though there's been no rain,
pine sings but there's no wind, who can leap the world's ties and sit
with me among white clouds?"

"Wow."

"Course that's my own translation into English, you see there are five signs for each line and I have to put in Western prepositions and articles and such."

"Why don't you just translate it as it is, five signs, five words? What's those first five signs?"

"Sign for climbing, sign for up, sign for cold, sign for mountain, sign for path."

"Well then, translate it 'Climbing up Cold Mountain path.' "

"Yeah, but what do you do with the sign for long, sign for gorge, sign for choke, sign for avalanche, sign for boulders?"

"Where's that?"

"That's the third line, would have to read 'Long gorge choke avalanche boulders.' "

"Well that's even better!"

"Well yeah, I thought of that, but I have to have this pass the approval of Chinese scholars here at the university and have it clear in English."

"Boy what a great thing this is," I said looking around at the little shack, "and you sitting here so very quietly at this very quiet hour studying all alone with your glasses. . . ."

"Ray what you got to do is go climb a mountain with me soon. How would you like to climb Matterhorn?"

"Great! Where's that?"

"Up in the High Sierras. We can go there with Henry Morley in his car and bring our packs and take off from the lake. I could carry all the food and stuff we need in my rucksack and you could borrow Alvah's small knapsack and carry extra socks and shoes and stuff."

"What's these signs mean?"

"These signs mean that Han Shan came down from the mountain after many years roaming around up there, to see his folks in town, says, 'Till recently I stayed at Cold Mountain, et cetera, yesterday I called on friends and family, more than half had gone to the Yellow Springs,' that means death, the Yellow Springs, 'now morning I face my lone shadow, I can't study with both eyes full of tears.' "

"That's like you too, Japhy, studying with eyes full of tears."

"My eyes aren't full of tears!"

"Aren't they going to be after a long long time?"

"They certainly will, Ray . . . and look here, 'In the mountains it's cold, it's always been cold not just this year,' see, he's real high, maybe twelve thousand or thirteen thousand feet or more, way up there, and says, 'Jagged scarps always snowed in, woods in the dark ravines spitting mist, grass is still sprouting at the end of June, leaves begin to fall in early August, and here am I high as a junkey—' "

"As a junkey!"

"That's my own translation, he actually says here am I as high as the sensualist in the city below, but I made it modern and high translation."

"Great." I wondered why Han Shan was Japhy's hero.

"Because," said he, "he was a poet, a mountain man, a Buddhist dedicated to the principle of meditation on the essence of all things, a vegetarian too by the way though I haven't got on that kick from figuring maybe in this modern world to be a vegetarian is to split hairs a little since all sentient beings eat what they can. And he was a man of solitude who could take off by himself and live purely and true to himself."

"That sounds like you too."

"And like you too, Ray, I haven't forgotten what you told me about how you made it in the woods meditating in North Carolina and all." Japhy was very sad, subdued, I'd never seen him so quiet, melancholy, thoughtful his voice was as tender as a mother's, he seemed to be talking from far away to a poor yearning creature (me) who needed to hear his message he wasn't putting anything on he was in a bit of a trance.

"Have you been meditating today?"

"Yeah I meditate first thing in the morning before breakfast and I always meditate a long time in the afternoon unless I'm interrupted."

"Who interrupts you?"

"Oh, people. Coughlin sometimes, and Alvah came yesterday, and Rol Sturlason, and I got this girl comes over to play yabyum."

"Yabyum? What's that?"

"Don't you know about yabyum, Smith? I'll tell you later." He seemed to be too sad to talk about yabyum, which I found out about a couple of nights later. We talked a while longer about Han Shan and poems on cliffs and as I was going away his friend Rol Sturlason, a tall blond goodlooking kid, came in to discuss his coming trip to Japan with him. This Rol Sturlason was interested in the famous Ryoanji rock garden of Shokokuji monastery in Kyoto, which is nothing but old boulders placed in such a way, supposedly mystically aesthetic, as to cause thousands of tourists and monks every year to journey there to stare at the boulders in the sand and thereby gain peace of mind. I have never met such weird yet serious and earnest people. I never saw Rol Sturlason again, he went to Japan soon after, but I can't forget what he said about the boulders, to my question, "Well who placed them in that certain way that's so great?"

"Nobody knows, some monk, or monks, long ago. But there is a definite mysterious form in the arrangement of the rocks. It's only through form that we can realize emptiness." He showed me the picture of the boulders in well-raked sand, looking like islands in the sea, looking as though they had eyes (declivities) and surrounded by a neatly screened and architectural monastery patio. Then he showed me a diagram of the stone arrangement with the projection in silhouette and showed me the geometrical logics and all, and mentioned the phrases "lonely individuality" and the rocks as "bumps pushing into space," all meaning some kind of koan business I wasn't as much interested in as in him and especially in good kind Japhy who brewed more tea on his noisy gasoline primus and gave us added cups with almost a silent Oriental bow. It was quite different from the night of the poetry reading.

* * *

11

At about noon we started out, leaving our big packs at the camp where nobody was likely to be till next year anyway, and went up the scree valley with just some food and first-aid kits. The valley was longer than it looked. In no time at all it was two o'clock in the afternoon and the sun was getting that later more golden look and a wind was rising and I began to think "By gosh how we ever gonna climb that mountain, tonight?"

I put it up to Japhy who said: "You're right, we'll have to hurry."

"Why don't we just forget it and go on home?"

"Aw come on Tiger, we'll make a run up that hill and then we'll go home." The valley was long and long and long. And at the top end it got very steep and I began to be a little afraid of falling down, the rocks were small and it got slippery and my ankles were in pain from yesterday's muscle strain anyway. But Morley kept walking and talking and I noticed his tremendous endurance. Japhy took his pants off so he could look just like an Indian, I mean stark naked, except for a jockstrap, and hiked almost a quarter-mile ahead of us, sometimes waiting a while, to give us time to catch up, then went on, moving fast, wanting to climb the mountain today. Morley came second, about fifty yards ahead of me all the way. I was in no hurry. Then as it got later afternoon

I went faster and decided to pass Morley and join Japhy. Now we were at about eleven thousand feet and it was cold and there was a lot of snow and to the east we could see immense snowcapped ranges and whooee levels of valleyland below them, we were already practically on top of California. At one point I had to scramble, like the others, on a narrow ledge, around a butte of rock, and it really scared me: the fall was a hundred feet, enough to break your neck, with another little ledge letting you bounce a minute preparatory to a nice goodbye one-thousand-foot drop. The wind was whipping now. Yet that whole afternoon, even more than the other, was filled with old premonitions or memories, as though I'd been there before, scrambling on these rocks, for other purposes more ancient, more serious, more simple. We finally got to the foot of Matterhorn where there was a most beautiful small lake unknown to the eyes of most men in this world, seen by only a handful of mountainclimbers, a small lake at eleven thousand some odd feet with snow on the edges of it and beautiful flowers and a beautiful meadow, an alpine meadow, flat and dreamy, upon which I immediately threw myself and took my shoes off. Japhy'd been there a half-hour when I made it, and it was cold now and his clothes were on again. Morley came up behind us smiling. We sat there looking up at the imminent steep scree slope of the final crag of Matterhorn.

"That don't look much, we can do it!" I said glad now.

"No, Ray, that's more than it looks. Do you realize that's a thousand feet more?"

"That much?"

"Unless we make a run up there, double-time, we'll never make it down again to our camp before nightfall and never make it down to the car at the lodge before tomorrow morning at, well at midnight."

"Phew."

"I'm tired," said Morley. "I don't think I'll try it."

"Well that's right," I said. "The whole purpose of mountainclimbing to me isn't just to show off you can get to the top, it's getting out to this wild country."

"Well I'm gonna go," said Japhy.

"Well if you're gonna go I'm goin with you."

"Morley?"

"I don't think I can make it. I'll wait here." And that wind was strong, too strong, I felt that as soon as we'd be a few hundred feet up the slope it might hamper our climbing.

Japhy took a small pack of peanuts and raisins and said "This'll be our gasoline, boy. You ready Ray to make a double-time run?"

"Ready. What would I say to the boys in The Place if I came all this way only to give up at the last minute?"

"It's late so let's hurry." Japhy started up walking very rapidly and then even running sometimes where the climb had to be to the right or left along ridges of scree. Scree is long landslides of rocks and sand, very difficult to scramble through, always little avalanches going on. At every few steps we took it seemed we were going higher and higher on a terrifying elevator, I gulped when I turned around to look back and see all of the state of California it would seem stretching out in three directions under huge blue skies with frightening planetary space clouds and immense vistas of distant valleys and even plateaus and for all I knew whole Nevadas out there. It was terrifying to look down and see Morley a dreaming spot by the little lake waiting for us. "Oh why didn't I stay with old Henry?" I thought. I now began to be afraid to go any higher from sheer fear of being too high. I began to be afraid of being blown away by the wind. All the nightmares I'd ever had about falling off mountains and precipitous buildings ran through my head in perfect clarity. Also with every twenty steps we took upward we both became completely exhausted.

"That's because of the high altitude now Ray," said Japhy sitting beside me panting. "So have raisins and peanuts and you'll see what kick it gives you." And each time it gave us such a tremendous kick we both jumped up without a word and climbed another twenty, thirty steps. Then sat down again, panting, sweating in the cold wind, high on top of the world our noses sniffling like the noses of little boys playing late Saturday afternoon their final little games in winter. Now the wind began to howl like the wind in movies about the Shroud of Tibet. The steepness began to be too much for me; I was afraid now to look back any more; I peeked: I couldn't even make out Morley by the tiny lake.

"Hurry it up," yelled Japhy from a hundred feet ahead. "It's getting awfully late." I looked up to the peak. It was right there, I'd be there in five minutes. "Only a half-hour to go!" yelled Japhy. I didn't believe it. In five minutes of scrambling angrily upward I fell down and looked up and it was still just as far away. What I didn't like about that peak-top was that the clouds of all the world were blowing right through it like fog.

"Wouldn't see anything up there anyway," I muttered. "Oh why did I ever let myself into this?" Japhy was way ahead of me now, he'd left the peanuts and raisins with me, it was with a kind of lonely solemnity now he had decided to rush to the top if it killed him. He didn't sit down any more. Soon he was a whole football field, a hundred yards ahead of me, getting smaller. I looked back and like Lot's wife that did it. "*This is too high!*" I yelled to Japhy in a panic. He didn't hear me. I raced a few more feet up and fell exhausted on my belly, slipping back just a little. "*This is too high!*" I yelled. I was really scared. Supposing I'd start to slip back for good, these screes might start sliding any time anyway. That damn mountain goat Japhy, I could see him jumping through the foggy air up ahead from rock to rock, up, up, just the flash of his boot bottoms. "How can I keep up with a maniac like that?" But with nutty desperation I followed him. Finally I came to a kind of ledge where I could sit at a level angle instead of having to cling not to slip, and I nudged my whole body inside the ledge just to hold me there tight, so the wind would not dislodge me, and I looked down and around and I had had it. "*I'm stayin here!*" I yelled to Japhy.

"Come on Smith, only another five minutes. I only got a hundred feet to go!"

"*I'm staying right here! It's too high!*"

He said nothing and went on. I saw him collapse and pant and get up and make his run again.

I nudged myself closer into the ledge and closed my eyes and thought "Oh what a life this is, why do we have to be born in the first place, and only so we can have our poor gentle flesh laid out to such impossible horrors as huge mountains and rock and empty space," and with horror I remembered the famous Zen saying, "When you get to the top of a mountain, keep climbing." The saying made my hair stand on end; it had been such cute poetry sitting on Alvah's straw mats. Now it was enough to make my heart pound and my heart bleed for being born at all. "In fact when Japhy gets to the top of that crag he *will* keep climbing, the way the wind's blowing. Well this old philosopher is staying right here," and I closed my eyes. "Besides," I thought, "rest and be kind, you don't have to prove anything." Suddenly I heard a beautiful broken yodel of a strange musical and mystical intensity in the wind, and looked up, and it was Japhy standing on top of Matterhorn peak letting out his triumphant mountain-conquering Buddha Mountain Smashing song of joy. It was beautiful. It was funny, too, up here on the not-so-funny top of California and in all that rushing fog. But I had to hand it to him, the guts, the endurance, the sweat, and now the crazy human singing: whipped cream on top of ice cream. I didn't have enough strength to answer his yodel. He ran around up there and went out of sight to investigate the little flat top of some kind (he said) that ran a few feet west and then dropped sheer back down maybe as far as I care to the sawdust floors of Virginia City. It was insane. I could hear him yelling at me but I just nudged farther in my protective nook, trembling. I looked down at the small lake where Morley was lying on his back with a blade of grass in his mouth and said out loud "Now there's the karma of these three men here: Japhy Ryder gets to his triumphant mountaintop and makes it, I almost make it and have to give up and huddle in a bloody cave, but the smartest of them all is that poet's poet lyin down there with his knees crossed to the sky chewing on a flower dreaming by a gurgling *plage,* goddammit they'll never get me up here again."

12

I really was amazed by the wisdom of Morley now: "Him with all his goddamn pictures of snowcapped Swiss Alps" I thought.

Then suddenly everything was just like jazz: it happened in one insane second or so: I looked up and saw Japhy *running down the mountain* in huge twenty-foot leaps, running, leaping, landing with a great drive of his booted heels, bouncing five feet or so, running, then taking another long crazy yelling yodelaying sail down the sides of the world and in that flash I realized *it's impossible to fall off mountains you fool* and with a yodel of my own I suddenly got up and began running down the mountain after him doing exactly the same huge leaps, the same fantastic runs and jumps, and in the space of about five minutes I'd guess Japhy Ryder and I (in my sneakers, driving the heels of my sneakers right into sand, rock, boulders, I didn't care any more I was so anxious to get down out of there) came leaping and yelling like mountain goats or I'd say like Chinese lunatics of a thousand years ago, enough to raise the hair on the head of the meditating Morley by the lake, who said he looked up and saw us flying down and couldn't believe it. In fact with one of my greatest leaps and loudest screams of joy I came flying right down to the edge of the lake and dug my sneakered heels into the mud and just fell sitting there, glad. Japhy was already taking his shoes off and pouring sand and pebbles out. It was great. I took off my sneakers and poured out a couple of buckets of lava dust and said "Ah Japhy you taught me the final lesson of them all, you can't fall off a mountain."

"And that's what they mean by the saying, When you get to the top of a mountain keep climbing, Smith."

"Dammit that yodel of triumph of yours was the most beautiful thing I ever heard in my life. I wish I'd a had a tape recorder to take it down."

"Those things aren't made to be heard by the people below," says Japhy dead serious.

"By God you're right, all those sedentary bums sitting around on pillows hearing the cry of the triumphant mountain smasher, they don't deserve it. But when I looked up and saw you running down that mountain I suddenly understood everything."

"Ah a little satori for Smith today," says Morley.

"What were you doing down here?"

"Sleeping, mostly."

"Well dammit I didn't get to the top. Now I'm ashamed of myself because now that I know how to come *down* a mountain I know how to go *up* and that I can't fall off, but now it's too late."

"We'll come back next summer Ray and climb it. Do you realize that this is the first time you've been mountainclimbin and you left old veteran Morley here way behind you?"

"Sure," said Morley. "Do you think, Japhy, they would assign Smith the title of Tiger for what he done today?"

"Oh sure," says Japhy, and I really felt proud. I was a Tiger.

"Well dammit I'll be a lion next time we get up here."

"Let's go men, now we've got a long long way to go back down this scree to our camp and down that valley of boulders and then down that lake trail, wow, I doubt if we can make it before pitch dark."

"It'll be mostly okay." Morley pointed to the sliver of moon in the pinkening deepening blue sky. "That oughta light us a way."

"Let's go." We all got up and started back. Now when I went around that ledge that had scared me it was just fun and a lark, I just skipped and jumped and danced along and I had really learned that you can't fall off a mountain. Whether you *can* fall off a mountain or not I don't know, but I had learned that you can't. That was the way it struck me.

It was a joy, though, to get down into the valley and lose sight of all that open sky space underneath everything and finally, as it got graying five o'clock, about a hundred yards from the other boys and walking alone, to just pick my way singing and thinking along the little black cruds of a deer trail through the rocks, no call to think or look ahead or worry, just follow the little balls of deer crud with your eyes cast down and enjoy life. At one point I looked and saw crazy Japhy who'd climbed for fun to the top of a snow slope and skied right down to the bottom, about a hundred yards, on his boots and the final few yards on his back, yippeeing and glad. Not only that but he'd taken off his pants again and wrapped them around his neck. This pants bit of his was simply he said for comfort, which is true, besides nobody around to see him anyway, though I figured that when he went mountainclimbing with girls it didn't make any difference to him. I could hear Morley talking to him in the great lonely valley: even across the rocks you could tell it was his voice. Finally I followed my deer trail so assiduously I was by myself going along ridges and down across creekbottoms completely out of sight of them, though I could hear them, but I trusted the instinct of my sweet little millennial deer and true enough, just as it was getting dark their ancient trail took me right to the edges of the familiar shallow creek (where they stopped to drink for the last five thousand years) and there was the glow of Japhy's bonfire making the side of the big rock orange and gay. The moon was bright high in the sky. "Well that moon's gonna save our ass, we got eight miles to go downtrail boys."

We ate a little and drank a lot of tea and arranged all our stuff. I had never had a happier moment in my life than those lonely moments coming down that little deer trace and when we hiked off with our packs I turned to take a final look up that way, it was dark now, hoping to see a few dear little deer, nothing in sight, and I thanked everything up that way. It had been like when you're a little boy and have spent a whole day rambling alone in the woods and fields and on the dusk homeward walk you did it all with your eyes to the ground, scuffling, thinking, whistling, like little Indian boys must feel when they follow their striding fathers from Russian River to Shasta two hundred years ago, like little Arab boys following their fathers, their fathers' trails; that singsong little joyful solitude, nose sniffling, like a little girl pulling her little brother home on the sled and they're both singing little ditties of their imagination and making faces at the ground and just being themselves before they have to go in the kitchen and put on a straight face again for the world of seriousness. "Yet what could be more serious than to follow a deer trace to get to your water?" I thought. We got to the cliff and started down the five-mile valley of boulders, in clear moonlight now, it was quite easy to dance down from boulder to boulder, the boulders were snow white, with patches of deep black shadow. Everything was cleanly whitely beautiful in the moonlight. Sometimes you could see the silver flash of the creek. Far down were the pines of the meadow park and the pool of the pond.

At this point my feet were unable to go on. I called Japhy and apologized. I couldn't take any more jumps. There were blisters not only on the bottoms but on the sides of my feet, from there having been no protection all yesterday and today. So Japhy swapped and let me wear his boots.

With these big lightweight protective boots on I knew I could go on fine. It was a great new feeling to be able to jump from rock to rock without having to feel the pain through the thin sneakers. On the other hand, for Japhy, it was also a relief to be suddenly lightfooted and he enjoyed it. We made double-time down the valley. But every step was getting us bent, now, we were all really tired. With the heavy packs it was difficult to control those thigh muscles that you need to go *down* a mountain, which is sometimes harder than going up. And there were all those boulders to surmount, for sometimes we'd be walking in sand awhile and our path would be blocked by boulders and we had to climb them and jump from one to the other then suddenly no more boulders and we had to jump down to the sand. Then we'd be trapped in impassable thickets and had to go around them or try to crash through and sometimes I'd get stuck in a thicket with my rucksack, standing there cursing in the impossible moonlight. None of us were talking. I was angry too because Japhy and Morley were afraid to stop and rest, they said it was dangerous at this point to stop.

"What's the difference the moon's shining, we can even sleep."

"No, we've got to get down to that car tonight."

"Well let's stop a minute here. My legs can't take it."

"Okay, only a minute."

But they never rested long enough to suit me and it seemed to me they were getting hysterical. I even began to curse them and at one point I even gave Japhy hell: "What's the sense of killing yourself like this, you call this fun? Phooey." (Your ideas are a crock, I added to myself.) A little weariness'll change a lot of things. Eternities of moonlight rock and thickets and boulders and ducks and that horrifying valley with the two rim walls and finally it seemed we were almost out of there, but nope, not quite yet, and my legs screaming to stop, and me cursing and smashing at twigs and throwing myself on the ground to rest a minute.

"Come on Ray, everything comes to an end." In fact I realized I had no guts anyway, which I've long known. But I have joy. When we got to the alpine meadow I stretched out on my belly and drank water and enjoyed myself peacefully in silence while they talked and worried about getting down the rest of the trail in time.

"Ah don't worry, it's a beautiful night, you've driven yourself too hard. Drink some water and lie down here for about five even ten minutes, everything takes care of itself." Now I was being the philosopher. In fact Japhy agreed with me and we rested peacefully. That good long rest assured my bones I could make it down to the lake okay. It was beautiful going down the trail. The moonlight poured through thick foliage and made dapples on the backs of Morley and Japhy as they walked in front of me. With our packs we got into a good rhythmic walk and enjoying going "Hup hup" as we came to switchbacks and swiveled around, always down, down, the pleasant downgoing swinging rhythm trail. And that roaring creek was a beauty by moonlight, those flashes of flying moon water, that snow white foam, those black-as-pitch trees, regular elfin paradises of shadow and moon. The air began to get warmer and nicer and in fact I thought I could begin to smell people again. We could smell the nice raunchy tide-smell of the lake water, and flowers, and softer dust of down below. Everything up there had smelled of ice and snow and heartless spine rock. Here there was the smell of sun-heated wood, sunny dust resting in the moonlight, lake mud, flowers, straw, all those good things of the earth. The trail was fun coming down and yet at one point I was as tired as ever, more than in that endless valley of boulders, but you could see the lake lodge down below now, a sweet little lamp of light and so it didn't matter. Morley and Japhy were talking a blue streak and all we had to do was roll on down to the car. In fact suddenly, as in a happy dream, with the suddenness of waking up from an endless nightmare and it's all over, we were striding across the road and there were houses and there were automobiles parked under trees and Morley's car was sitting right there.

"From what I can tell by feeling this air," said Morley, leaning on the car as we slung our packs to the ground, "it mustn't have froze at all last night, I went back and drained the crankcase for nothing."

"Well maybe it did freeze." Morley went over and got motor oil at the lodge store and they told him it hadn't been freezing at all, but one of the warmest nights of the year.

"All that mad trouble for nothing," I said. But we didn't care. We were famished. I said "Let's go to Bridgeport and go in one of those

lunchcarts there boy and eat hamburg and potatoes and hot coffee."
We drove down the lakeside dirt road in the moonlight, stopped at the
inn where Morley returned the blankets, and drove on into the little
town and parked on the highway. Poor Japhy, it was here finally I found
out his Achilles heel. This little tough guy who wasn't afraid of anything
and could ramble around mountains for weeks alone and run down
mountains, was afraid of going into a restaurant because the people in
it were too well dressed. Morley and I laughed and said "What's the
difference? We'll just go in and eat." But Japhy thought the place I chose
looked too bourgeois and insisted on going to a more workingman-
looking restaurant across the highway. We went in there and it was a
desultory place with lazy waitresses letting us sit there five minutes without even bringing a menu. I got mad and said "Let's go to that other
place. What you afraid of, Japhy, what's the difference? You may know
all about mountains but I know about where to eat." In fact we got a
little miffed at each other and I felt bad. But he came to the other place,
which was the better restaurant of the two, with a bar on one side,
many hunters drinking in the dim cocktail-lounge light, and the restaurant itself a long counter and a lot of tables with whole gay families
eating from a very considerable selection. The menu was huge and good:
mountain trout and everything. Japhy, I found, was also afraid of spending ten cents more for a good dinner. I went to the bar and bought a
glass of port and brought it to our stool seats at the counter (Japhy:
"You sure you can do that?") and I kidded Japhy awhile. He felt better
now. "That's what's the trouble with you Japhy, you're just an old
anarchist scared of society. What difference does it make? Comparisons
are odious."

"Well Smith it just looked to me like this place was full of old rich
farts and the prices would be too high, I admit it, I'm scared of all this
American wealth, I'm just an old bhikku and I got nothin to do with
all this high standard of living, goddammit, I've been a poor guy all my
life and I can't get used to some things."

"Well your weaknesses are admirable. I'll buy 'em." And we had a
raving great dinner of baked potatoes and porkchops and salad and hot
buns and blueberry pie and the works. We were so honestly hungry it
wasn't funny and it was honest. After dinner we went into a liquor store
where I bought a bottle of muscatel and the old proprietor and his old
fat buddy looked at us and said "Where you boys been?"

"Climbin Matterhorn out there," I said proudly. They only stared
at us, gaping. But I felt great and bought a cigar and lit up and said

"Twelve thousand feet and we come down outa there with such an appetite and feelin so good that now this wine is gonna hit us just right." The old men gaped. We were all sunburned and dirty and wildlooking, too. They didn't say anything. They thought we were crazy.

We got in the car and drove back to San Francisco drinking and laughing and telling long stories and Morley really drove beautifully that night and wheeled us silently through the graying dawn streets of Berkeley as Japhy and I slept dead to the world in the seats. At some point or other I woke up like a little child and was told I was home and staggered out of the car and went across the grass into the cottage and opened my blankets and curled up and slept till late the next afternoon a completely dreamless beautiful sleep. When I woke up the next day the veins in my feet were all cleared. I had worked the blood clots right out of existence. I felt very happy.

• • •

Now, as though Japhy's finger were pointing me the way, I started north to my mountain.

It was the morning of June 18, 1956. I came down and said goodbye to Christine and thanked her for everything and walked down the road. She waved from the grassy yard. "It's going to be lonely around here with everybody gone and no big huge parties on weekends." She really enjoyed everything that had gone on. There she was standing in the yard barefooted, with little barefooted Prajna, as I walked off along the horse meadow.

I had an easy trip north, as though Japhy's best wishes for me to get to my mountain that could be kept forever, were with me. On 101 I immediately got a ride from a teacher of social studies, from Boston originally, who used to sing on Cape Cod and had fainted just yesterday at his buddy's wedding because he'd been fasting. When he left me off at Cloverdale I bought my supplies for the road: a salami, Cheddar cheese wedge, Ry-Krisp and also some dates for dessert, all put away neatly in my foodwrappers. I still had peanuts and raisins left over from our last hike together. Japhy had said, "I won't be needing those peanuts and raisins on that freighter." I recalled with a twinge of sadness how Japhy was always so dead serious about food, and I wished the whole world was dead serious about food instead of silly rockets and machines and explosives using everybody's food money to blow their heads off anyway.

I hiked about a mile after eating my lunch in back of a garage, up to a bridge on the Russian River, where, in gray gloom, I was stuck for as much as three hours. But suddenly I got an unexpected short ride from a farmer with a tic that made his face twitch, with his wife and boy, to a small town, Preston, where a truckdriver offered me a ride all the way to Eureka ("Eureka!" I yelled) and then he got talking to me and said "Goldang it I get lonesome driving this rig, I want someone to talk to all night, I'll take you all the way to Crescent City if you want." This was a little off my route but farther north than Eureka so I said okay. The guy's name was Ray Breton, he drove me two hundred and eighty miles all night in the rain, talking ceaselessly about his whole life, his brothers, his wives, sons, his father and at Humboldt Redwood Forest in a restaurant called Forest of Arden I had a fabulous dinner of fried shrimp with huge strawberry pie and vanilla ice cream for dessert and a whole pot of coffee and he paid for the whole works. I got him off talking about his troubles to talk about the Last Things and he said, "Yeah, those who're good stay in Heaven, they've been in Heaven from the beginning," which was very wise.

We drove through the rainy night and arrived at Crescent City at dawn in a gray fog, a small town by the sea, and parked the truck in the sand by the beach and slept an hour. Then he left me after buying me a breakfast of pancakes and eggs, probably sick and tired of paying for all my meals, and I started walking out of Crescent City and over on an eastward road, Highway 199, to get back to big-shot 99 that would shoot me to Portland and Seattle faster than the more picturesque but slower coast road.

Suddenly I felt so free I began to walk on the wrong side of the road and sticking out my thumb from that side, hiking like a Chinese Saint to Nowhere for no reason, going to my mountain to rejoice. Poor little angel world! I suddenly didn't care any more, I'd walk all the way. But just because I was dancing along on the wrong side of the road and didn't care, anybody began to pick me up immediately, a goldminer with a small caterpillar up front being hauled by his son, and we had a long talk about the woods, the Siskiyou Mountains (through which we were driving, toward Grants Pass Oregon), and how to make good baked fish, he said, just by lighting a fire in the clean yellow sand by a creek and then burying the fish in the hot sand after you've scraped away the fire and just leaving it there a few hours then taking it out and cleaning it of sand. He was very interested in my rucksack and my plans.

He left me off at a mountain village very similar to Bridgeport

California where Japhy and I had sat in the sun. I walked out a mile and took a nap in the woods, right in the heart of the Siskiyou Range. I woke up from my nap feeling very strange in the Chinese unknown fog. I walked on the same way, wrong side, got a ride at Kerby from a blond used-car dealer to Grants Pass, and there, after a fat cowboy in a gravel truck with a malicious grin on his face deliberately tried to run over my rucksack in the road, I got a ride from a sad logger boy in a tin hat going very fast across a great swooping up and down dream valley thruway to Canyonville, where, as in a dream, a crazy store-truck full of gloves for sale stopped and the driver, Ernest Petersen, chatting amiably all the way and insisting that I sit on the seat that faced him (so that I was being zoomed down the road backward) took me to Eugene Oregon. He talked about everything under the sun, bought me two beers, and even stopped at several gas stations and hung out displays of gloves. He said, "My father was a great man, his saying was 'There are more horses' asses than horses in this world.' " He was a mad sports fan and timed outdoor track meets with a stopwatch and rushed around fearlessly and independently in his own truck defying local attempts to get him in the unions.

At red nightfall he bade me farewell near a sweet pond outside Eugene. There I intended to spend the night. I spread my bag out under a pine in a dense thicket across the road from cute suburban cottages that couldn't see me and wouldn't see me because they were all looking at television anyway, and ate my supper and slept twelve hours in the bag, waking up only once in the middle of the night to put on mosquito repellent.

At morning I could see the mighty beginnings of the Cascade Range, the northernmost end of which would be my mountain on the skirt of Canada, four hundred more miles north. The morning brook was smoky because of the lumber mill across the highway. I washed up in the brook and took off after one short prayer over the beads Japhy had given me in Matterhorn camp: "Adoration to emptiness of the divine Buddha bead."

I immediately got a ride on the open highway from two tough young hombres to outside Junction City where I had coffee and walked two miles to a roadside restaurant that looked better and had pancakes and then walking along the highway rocks, cars zipping by, wondering how I'd ever get to Portland let alone Seattle, I got a ride from a little funny lighthaired housepainter with spattered shoes and four pint cans of cold beer who also stopped at a roadside tavern for more beer and finally we were in Portland crossing vast eternity bridges as draws went up behind us to allow crane barges through in the big smoky river city scene surrounded by pine ridges. In downtown Portland I took the twenty-five-cent bus to Vancouver Washington, ate a Coney Island hamburger there, then out on the road, 99, where a sweet young mustached one-kidney Bodhisattva Okie picked me up and said "I'm s'proud I picked you up, someone to talk to," and everywhere we stopped for coffee he played the pinball machines with dead seriousness and also he picked up all hitchhikers on the road, first a big drawling Okie from Alabama then a crazy sailor from Montana who was full of crazed intelligent talk and we balled right up to Olympia Washington at eighty m.p.h. then up Olympic Peninsula on curvy woodsroads to the Naval Base at Bremerton Washington where a fifty-cent ferry ride was all that separated me from Seattle!

We said goodbye and the Okie bum and I went on the ferry, I paid his fare in gratitude for my terrific good luck on the road, and even gave him handfuls of peanuts and raisins which he devoured hungrily so I also gave him salami and cheese.

Then, while he sat in the main room, I went topdeck as the ferry pulled out in a cold drizzle to dig and enjoy Puget Sound. It was one hour sailing to the Port of Seattle and I found a half-pint of vodka stuck in the deck rail concealed under a *Time* magazine and just casually drank it and opened my rucksack and took out my warm sweater to go under my rain jacket and paced up and down all alone on the cold fog-swept deck feeling wild and lyrical. And suddenly I saw that the Northwest was a great deal more than the little vision I had of it of Japhy in my mind. It was miles and miles of unbelievable mountains grooking on all horizons in the wild broken clouds, Mount Olympus and Mount Baker, a giant orange sash in the gloom over the Pacific-ward skies that led I knew toward the Hokkaido Siberian desolations of the world. I huddled against the bridgehouse hearing the Mark Twain talk of the skipper and the wheelman inside. In the deepened dusk fog ahead the big red neons saying: PORT OF SEATTLE. And suddenly everything Japhy had ever told me about Seattle began to seep into me like cold rain, I could feel it and see it now, and not just think it. It was exactly like he'd said: wet, immense, timbered, mountainous, cold, exhilarating, challenging. The ferry nosed in at the pier on Alaskan Way and immediately I saw the totem poles in old stores and the ancient 1880-style switch goat with sleepy firemen chug chugging up and down the waterfront spur like a scene from my own dreams, the old Casey Jones locomotive of America, the only one I ever saw that old outside of Western movies, but actually working and hauling boxcars in the smoky gloom of the magic city.

I immediately went to a good clean skid row hotel, the Hotel Stevens, got a room for the night for a dollar seventy-five and had a hot tub bath and a good long sleep and in the morning I shaved and walked out First Avenue and accidentally found all kinds of Goodwill stores with wonderful sweaters and red underwear for sale and I had a big breakfast with five-cent coffee in the crowded market morning with blue sky and clouds scudding overhead and waters of Puget Sound sparkling and dancing under old piers. It was real true Northwest. At noon I checked out of the hotel, with my new wool socks and bandanas and things all packed in gladly, and walked out to 99 a few miles out of town and got many short rides.

Now I was beginning to see the Cascades on the northeast horizon, unbelievable jags and twisted rock and snow-covered immensities, enough to make you gulp. The road ran right through the dreamy fertile valleys of the Stilaquamish and the Skagit, rich butterfat valleys with farms and cows browsing under that tremendous background of snow-pure heaps. The further north I hitched the bigger the mountains got till I finally began to feel afraid. I got a ride from a fellow who looked like a bespectacled careful lawyer in a conservative car, but turned out he was the famous Bat Lindstrom the hardtop racing champion and his conservative automobile had in it a souped-up motor that could make it go a hundred and seventy miles an hour. But he just demonstrated it by gunning it at a red light to let me hear the deep hum of power. Then I got a ride from a lumberman who said he knew the forest rangers where I was going and said "The Skagit Valley is second only to the Nile for fertility." He left me off at Highway 1-G, which was the little highway to 17-A that wound into the heart of the mountains and in fact would come to a dead-end as a dirt road at Diablo Dam. Now I was really in the mountain country. The fellows who picked me up were loggers, uranium prospectors, farmers, they drove me through the final big town of Skagit Valley, Sedro Woolley, a farming market town, and then out as the road got narrower and more curved among cliffs and the Skagit River, which we'd crossed on 99 as a dreaming belly river with meadows on both sides, was now a pure torrent of melted snow pouring narrow and fast between muddy snag shores. Cliffs began to

appear on both sides. The snow-covered mountains themselves had disappeared, receded from my view, I couldn't see them any more but now
I was beginning to feel them more.

32

In an old tavern I saw an old decrepit man who could hardly move
around to get me a beer behind the bar, I thought "I'd rather die in a
glacial cave than in an eternity afternoon room of dust like this." A
Min 'n' Bill couple left me off at a grocery store in Sauk and there I got
my final ride from a mad drunk fastswerving dark long-sideburned
guitar-playing Skagit Valley wrangler who came to a dusty flying stop
at the Marblemount Ranger Station and had me home.

The assistant ranger was standing there watching. "Are you
Smith?"

"Yeah."

"That a friend of yours?"

"No, just a ride he gave me."

"Who does he think he is speeding on government property."

I gulped, I wasn't a free bhikku any more. Not until I'd get to my
hideaway mountain that next week. I had to spend a whole week at
Fire School with whole bunches of young kids, all of us in tin hats which
we wore either straight on our heads or as I did at a rakish tilt, and we
dug fire lines in the wet woods or felled trees or put out experimental
small fires and I met the oldtimer ranger and onetime logger Burnie
Byers, the "lumberjack" that Japhy was always imitating with his big
deep funny voice.

Burnie and I sat in his truck in the woods and discussed Japhy. "It's
a damn shame Japhy ain't come back this year. He was the best lookout
we ever had and by God he was the best trailworker *I* ever seen. Just
eager and anxious to go climbin around and so durn cheerful, I ain't
never seen a better kid. And he wasn't afraid of nobody, he'd just come
right out with it. That's what I like, cause when the time comes when
a man can't say whatever he pleases I guess that'll be when I'm gonna
go up in the backcountry and finish my life out in a lean-to. One thing
about Japhy, though, wherever he'll be all the resta his life, I don't care
how old he gets, he'll always have a good time." Burnie was about sixty-
five and really spoke very paternally about Japhy. Some of the other
kids also remembered Japhy and wondered why he wasn't back. That
night, because it was Burnie's fortieth anniversary in the Forest Service,

the other rangers voted him a gift, which was a brand new big leather belt. Old Burnie was always having trouble with belts and was wearing a kind of cord at the time. So he put on his new belt and said something funny about how he'd better not eat too much and everybody applauded and cheered. I figured Burnie and Japhy were probably the two best men that had ever worked in this country.

After Fire School I spent some time hiking up the mountains in back of the Ranger Station or just sitting by the rushing Skagit with my pipe in my mouth and a bottle of wine between my crossed legs, afternoons and also moonlit nights, while the other kids went beering at local carnivals. The Skagit River at Marblemount was a rushing clear snowmelt of pure green; above, Pacific Northwest pines were shrouded in clouds; and further beyond were peak tops with clouds going right through them and then fitfully the sun would shine through. It was the work of the quiet mountains, this torrent of purity at my feet. The sun shined on the roils, fighting snags held on. Birds scouted over the water looking for secret smiling fish that only occasionally suddenly leaped flying out of the water and arched their backs and fell in again into water that rushed on and obliterated their loophole, and everything was swept along. Logs and snags came floating down at twenty-five miles an hour. I figured if I should try to swim across the narrow river I'd be a half-mile downstream before I kicked to the other shore. It was a river wonderland, the emptiness of the golden eternity, odors of moss and bark and twigs and mud, all ululating mysterious visionstuff before my eyes, tranquil and everlasting nevertheless, the hillhairing trees, the dancing sunlight. As I looked up the clouds assumed, as I assumed, faces of hermits. The pine boughs looked satisfied washing in the waters. The top trees shrouded in gray fog looked content. The jiggling sunshine leaves of Northwest breeze seemed bred to rejoice. The upper snows on the horizon, the trackless, seemed cradled and warm. Everything was everlastingly loose and responsive, it was all everywhere beyond the truth, beyond emptyspace blue. "The mountains are mighty patient, Buddha-man," I said out loud and took a drink. It was coldish, but when the sun peeped out the tree stump I was sitting on turned into a red oven. When I went back in the moonlight to my same old tree stump the world was like a dream, like a phantom, like a bubble, like a shadow, like a vanishing dew, like a lightning's flash.

Time came finally for me to be packed up into my mountain. I bought forty-five dollars' worth of groceries on credit in the little Marblemount grocery store and we packed that in the truck, Happy the muleskinner and I, and drove on up the river to Diablo Dam. As we proceeded the Skagit got narrower and more like a torrent, finally it was crashing over rocks and being fed by side-falls of water from heavy timbered shores, it was getting wilder and craggier all the time. The Skagit River was dammed back at Newhalem, then again at Diablo Dam, where a giant Pittsburgh-type lift took you up on a platform to the level of Diablo Lake. There'd been a gold rush in the 1890s in this country, the prospectors had built a trail through the solid rock cliffs of the gorge between Newhalem and what was now Ross Lake, the final dam, and dotted the drainages of Ruby Creek, Granite Creek, and Canyon Creek with claims that never paid off. Now most of this trail was under water anyway. In 1919 a fire had raged in the Upper Skagit and all the country around Desolation, my mountain, had burned and burned for two months and filled the skies of northern Washington and British Columbia with smoke that blotted out the sun. The government had tried to fight it, sent a thousand men in with pack string supply lines that then took three weeks from Marblemount fire camp, but only the fall rains had stopped that blaze and the charred snags, I was told, were still standing on Desolation Peak and in some valleys. That was the reason for the name: Desolation.

"Boy," said funny old Happy the muleskinner, who still wore his old floppy cowboy hat from Wyoming days and rolled his own butts and kept making jokes, "don't be like the kid we had a few years ago up on Desolation, we took him up there and he was the greenest kid I ever saw, I packed him into his lookout and he tried to fry an egg for supper and broke it and missed the friggin fryingpan and missed the stove and it landed on his boot, he didn't know whether to run shit or go blind and when I left I told him not to flog his damn dummy too much and the sucker says to me 'Yes sir, yes sir.' "

"Well I don't care, all I want is to be alone up there this summer."

"You're sayin that now but you'll change your tune soon enough. They all talk brave. But then you get to talkin to yourself. That ain't so bad but don't start *answerin* yourself, son." Old Happy drove the pack mules on the gorge trail while I rode the boat from Diablo Dam, to the foot of Ross Dam where you could see immense dazzling openings of vistas that showed the Mount Baker National Forest mountains in wide panorama around Ross Lake that extended shiningly all the way back to Canada. At Ross Dam the Forest Service floats were lashed a little way off from the steep timbered shore. It was hard sleeping on those bunks at night, they swayed with the float and the log and the wave combined to make a booming slapping noise that kept you awake.

The moon was full the night I slept there, it was dancing on the waters. One of the lookouts said "The moon is right on the mountain, when I see that I always imagine I see a coyote silhouettin."

Finally came the gray rainy day of my departure to Desolation Peak. The assistant ranger was with us, the three of us were going up and it wasn't going to be a pleasant day's horseback riding in all that downpour. "Boy, you shoulda put a couple quarts of brandy in your grocery list, you're gonna need it up there in the cold," said Happy looking at me with his big red nose. We were standing by the corral, Happy was giving the animals bags of feed and tying it around their necks and they were chomping away unmindful of the rain. We came plowing to the log gate and bumped through and went around under the immense shrouds of Sourdough and Ruby mountains. The waves were crashing up and spraying back at us. We went inside to the pilot's cabin and he had a pot of coffee ready. Firs on steep banks you could barely see on the lake shore were like ranged ghosts in the mist. It was the real Northwest grim and bitter misery.

"Where's Desolation?" I asked.

"You ain't about to see it today till you're practically on top of it," said Happy, "and then you won't like it much. It's snowin and hailin up there right now. Boy, ain't you sure you didn't sneak a little bottle of brandy in your pack somewheres?" We'd already downed a quart of blackberry wine he'd bought in Marblemount.

"Happy when I get down from this mountain in September I'll buy you a whole quart of scotch." I was going to be paid good money for finding the mountain I wanted.

"That's a promise and don't you forget it." Japhy had told me a lot about Happy the Packer, he was called. Happy was a good man; he and old Burnie Byers were the best oldtimers on the scene. They knew the mountains and they knew pack animals and they weren't ambitious to become forestry supervisors either.

Happy remembered Japhy too, wistfully. "That boy used to know an awful lot of funny songs and stuff. He shore loved to go out loggin out trails. He had himself a Chinee girlfriend one time down in Seattle, I seen her in his hotel room, that Japhy I'm tellin you he shore was a grunge-jumper with the women." I could hear Japhy's voice singing gay songs with his guitar as the wind howled around our barge and the gray waves plashed up against the windows of the pilot house.

"And this is Japhy's lake, and these are Japhy's mountains," I thought, and wished Japhy were there to see me doing everything he wanted me to do.

from
DESOLATION ANGELS
1956–1957

EDITOR'S NOTE
In this book Kerouac calls himself "Jack Duluoz," Allen Ginsberg is "Irwin Garden," William Burroughs is "Bull Hubbard," Neal Cassady is "Cody Pomeray," Gary Snyder is "Jarry Wagner," Philip Whalen is "Ben Fagan," Peter Orlovsky is "Simon Darlovsky," and Gregory Corso is "Raphael Urso."

PART ONE
DESOLATION IN SOLITUDE

1

THOSE AFTERNOONS, those lazy afternoons, when I used to sit, or lie down, on Desolation Peak, sometimes on the alpine grass, hundreds of miles of snowcovered rock all around, looming Mount Hozomeen on my north, vast snowy Jack to the south, the encharmed picture of the lake below to the west and the snowy hump of Mt. Baker beyond, and to the east the rilled and ridged monstrosities humping to the Cascade Ridge, and after that first time suddenly realizing "It's me that's changed and done all this and come and gone and complained and hurt and joyed and yelled, not the Void" and so that every time I thought of the void I'd be looking at Mt. Hozomeen (because chair and bed and meadowgrass faced north) until I realized "Hozomeen is the Void—at least Hozomeen means the void to my eyes"— Stark naked rock, pinnacles and thousand feet high protruding from hunch-muscles another thousand feet high protruding from immense timbered shoulders, and the green pointy-fir snake of my own (Starvation) ridge wriggling to it, to its awful vaulty blue smokebody rock, and the "clouds of hope" lazing in Canada beyond with their tittlefaces and parallel lumps and sneers and grins and lamby blanks and puffs of snout and mews of crack saying "Hoi! hoil earth!"—the very top tittermost peak abominables of Hozomeen made of black rock and only when storms blow I dont see them and all they do is return tooth for tooth to storm an imperturbable surl for cloudburst mist—Hozomeen that does not crack like cabin rigging in the winds, that when seen from upsidedown (when I'd do my headstand in the yard) is just a hanging bubble in the illimitable ocean of space—

Hozomeen, Hozomeen, most beautiful mountain I ever seen, like a tiger sometimes with stripes, sunwashed rills and shadow crags wriggling lines in the Bright Daylight, vertical furrows and bumps and Boo! crevasses, boom, sheer magnificent Prudential mountain, nobody's even heard of it, and it's only 8,000 feet high, but what a horror when I first saw that void the first night of my staying on Desolation Peak waking up from deep fogs of 20 hours to a starlit night suddenly loomed by Hozomeen with his two sharp points, right in my window black—the Void, every time I'd think of the Void I'd see Hozomeen and understand—Over 70 days I had to stare it.

2

Yes, for I'd thought, in June, hitch hiking up there to the Skagit Valley in northwest Washington for my fire lookout job "When I get to the top of Desolation Peak and everybody leaves on mules and I'm alone I will come face to face with God or Tathagata and find out once and for all what is the meaning of all this existence and suffering and going to and fro in vain" but instead I'd come face to face with myself, no liquor, no drugs, no chance of faking it but face to face with ole Hateful Duluoz Me and many's the time I thought I die, suspire of boredom, or jump off the mountain, but the days, nay the hours dragged and I had no guts for such a leap, I had to *wait* and get to see the face of reality —and it finally comes that afternoon of August 8 as I'm pacing in the high alpine yard on the little wellworn path I'd beaten, in dust and rain, on many a night, with my oil lamp banked low inside the cabin with the four-way windows and peaked pagoda roof and lightning rod point, it finally comes to me, after even tears, and gnashing, and the killing of a mouse and attempted murder of another, something I'd never done in my life (killing animals even rodents), it comes in these words: "The void is not disturbed by any kind of ups and downs, my God look at Hozomeen, is he worried or tearful? Does he bend before storms or snarl when the sun shines or sigh in the late day drowse? Does he smile? Was he not born out of madbrained turmoils and upheavals of raining fire and now's Hozomeen and nothing else? Why should I choose to be bitter or sweet, he does neither?—Why cant I be like Hozomeen and O Platitude O hoary old platitude of the bourgeois mind "take life as it comes"—Twas that alcoholic biographer, W. E. Woodward, said, "There's nothing to life but just the living of it"— But O God I'm bored! But is Hozomeen bored? And I'm sick of words and explanations. Is Hozomeen?

> Aurora Borealis
> over Hozomeen—
> The void is stiller

—Even Hozomeen'll crack and fall apart, nothing lasts, it is only a faring-in-that-which-everything-is, a passing-through, that's what's going on, why ask questions or tear hair or weep, the burble blear purple Lear on his moor of woes he is only a gnashy old flap with winged whiskers beminded by a fool—to be *and* not to be, that's what we are— Does the Void take any part in life and death? does it have funerals? or birth cakes? why not I be like the Void, inexhaustibly fertile, beyond serenity, beyond even gladness, just Old Jack (and not even that) and conduct my life from this moment on (though winds blow through my windpipe), this ungraspable image in a crystal ball is not the Void, the Void is the crystal ball itself and all my woes the Lankavatara Scripture hairnet of fools, "Look sirs, a marvelous sad hairnet" — Hold together, Jack, pass through everything, and everything is one dream, one appearance, one flash, one sad eye, one crystal lucid mystery, one word— Hold still, man, regain your love of life and go down from this mountain and simply *be*—*be*—be the infinite fertilities of the one mind of infinity, make no comments, complaints, criticisms, appraisals, avowals, sayings, shooting stars of thought, just *flow, flow,* be you all, be you what it is, it is only what it always is— Hope is a word like a snow-drift— This is the Great Knowing, this is the Awakening, this is Voidness— So shut up, live, travel, adventure, bless and dont be sorry— Prunes, prune, eat your prunes— And you have been forever, and will be forever, and all the worrisome smashings of your foot on innocent cupboard doors it was only the Void pretending to be a man pretending not to know the Void—

I come back into the house a new man.

All I have to do is wait 30 long days to get down from the rock and see sweet life again—knowing it's neither sweet nor bitter but just what it is, and so it is—

So long afternoons I sit in my easy (canvas) chair facing Void Hozomeen, the silence hushes in my little shack, my stove is still, my dishes glitter, my firewood (old sticks that are the form of water and welp, that I light small Indian fires with in my stove, to make quick meals) my firewood lies piled and snaky in the corner, my canned goods wait to be opened, my old cracked shoes weep, my pans lean, my dish rags hang, my various things sit silent around the room, my eyes ache, the wind wallows and belts at the window and upped shutters, the light in late afternoon shades and bluedarks Hozomeen (revealing his streak of middle red) and there's nothing for me to do but wait—and breathe (and breathing is difficult in the thin high air, with West Coast sinus wheezings) —wait, breathe, eat, sleep, cook, wash, pace, watch, never any forest fires—and daydream, "What will I do when I get to Frisco? Why first thing I'll get a room in Chinatown"—but even nearer and sweeter I daydream what I'll do Leaving Day, some hallowed day in early September, "I'll walk down the trail, two hours, meet Phil in the boat, ride to the Ross Float, sleep there a night, chat in the kitchen, start early in the morning on the Diablo Boat, go right from that little pier (say hello to Walt), hitch right to Marblemount, collect my pay, pay my debts, buy a bottle of wine and drink it by the Skagit in the afternoon, and leave next morning for Seattle"—and on, down to Frisco, then L.A., then Nogales, then Guadalajara, then Mexico City— And still the Void is still and'll never move—

But I will be the Void, moving without having moved.

3

Aw, and I remember sweet days of home that I didnt appreciate when I had them—afternoons then, when I was 15, 16, it meant Ritz Brothers crackers and peanut butter and milk, at the old round kitchen table, and my chess problems or self-invented baseball games, as the orange sun of Lowell October'd slant thru the porch and kitchen curtains and

make a lazy dusty shaft and in it my cat'd be licking his forepaw laplap
with tiger tongue and cue tooth, all undergone and dust betided, Lord
—so now in my dirty torn clothes I'm a bum in the High Cascades and
all I've got for a kitchen is this crazy battered stove with cracked stovepipe rust—stuffed, yea, at the ceiling, with old burlap, to keep the rats
of night out—days long ago when I could have simply walked up and
kissed either my mother or my father and say "I like you because someday I'll be an old bum in desolation and I'll be alone and sad"— O
Hozomeen, the rocks of it gleam in the downgo sun, the inaccessible for-
tress parapets stand like Shakespeare in the world and for miles around
not a thing knows the name of Shakespeare, Hozomeen or me—

Late afternoon long ago home, and even recently in North Carolina
when, to recall childhood, I did eat Ritz and peanut butter and milk at
four, and played the baseball game at my desk, and it was schoolboys
in scuffed shoes coming home just like me hungry (and I'd make them
special Jack Bananasplits, only a measly six months ago)— But here on
Desolation the wind whirls, desolate of song, shaking rafters of the
earth, progenitating night— Giant bat shadows of cloud hover on the
mountain.

Soon dark, soon my day's dishes done, meal eaten, waiting for September, waiting for the descent to the world again.

4

Meanwhile the sunsets are mad orange fools raging in the gloom, whilst
far in the south in the direction of my intended loving arms of señoritas,
snowpink piles wait at the foot of the world, in general silver ray
cities—the lake is a hard pan, gray, blue, waiting at the mist bottoms
for when I ride her in Phil's boat—Jack Mountain as always receives
his meed of little cloud at highbrow base, his thousand football fields
of snow all raveled and pink, that one unimaginable abominable snow-
man still squatted petrified on the ridge— Golden Horn far off is yet
golden in a gray southeast— Sourdough's monster hump overlooks the
lake— Surly clouds blacken to make fire rims at that forge where the
night's being hammered, crazed mountains march to the sunset like
drunken cavaliers in Messina when Ursula was fair, I would swear that
Hozomeen would move if we could induce him but he spends the night
with me and soon when stars rain down the snowfields he'll be in the
pink of pride all black and yaw-y to the north where (just above him
every night) North Star flashes pastel orange, pastel green, iron orange,

iron blue, azurite indicative constellative auguries of her makeup up
there that you could weigh on the scales of the golden world—

The wind, the wind—

And there's my poor endeavoring human desk at which I sit so often
during the day, facing south, the papers and pencils and the coffee cup
with sprigs of alpine fir and a weird orchid of the heights wiltable in
one day— My Beechnut gum, my tobacco pouch, dusts, pitiful pulp
magazines I have to read, view south to all those snowy majesties—
The waiting is long.

> On Starvation Ridge
> little sticks
> Are trying to grow.

5

Only the night before my decision to live loving, I had been degraded,
insulted, and made mournful by this dream:

"And get a good tenderloin steak!" says Ma handing Deni Bleu the
money, she's sending us to the store to get a good supper, also she's
suddenly decided to put all her confidence in Deni these later years now
that I've become such a vague ephemeral undeciding being who curses
the gods in his bed sleep and wanders around bareheaded and stupid
in the gray darkness— It's in the kitchen, it's all agreed, I dont say
anything, we go off— In the front bedroom by the stairs Pa is dying,
is in his death bed and practically dead already, it's in spite of *that* that
Ma wants a good steak, wants to plank her last human hope on Deni,
on some kind of decisive solidarity— Pa is thin, pale, his bed sheets
white, it seems to me he's dead already— We go down in the gloom
and negotiate our way somehow to the butcher store in Brooklyn in the
downtown main streets around Flatbush— Bob Donnelly is there and
the rest of the gang, bareheaded and bummy in the street— A gleam
has now come in Deni's eyes as he sees his chance to turn tail and
become a con man with all Ma's money in his hand, in the store he
orders the meat but I see him pulling shortchange tricks and stuffing
money in his pocket and making some kind of arrangement to renege
on *her* agreement, her *last* agreement— She had pinned her hopes on
him, I was of no more avail— Somehow we wander from there and
dont go back to Ma's house and wind up in the River Army which is
dispatched, after watching a speedboat race, to swim downstream in

the cold swirling dangerous waters— The speedboat, if it had been a "long" one could have dived right under the flotilla'd crowd and come up the other side and completed its time but because of faulty short design the racer (Mr. Darling) complains that that was the reason his boat just ducked under the crowd and got stuck there and couldnt go on—big official floats took note.

Me in the lead gang, the Army starts swimming downstream, we are going to the bridges and cities below. The water is cold and the current extremely bad but I swim and struggle on. "How'd I get here?" I think. "What about Ma's steak? What did Deni Bleu do with her money? Where is he now? O I have no time to think!" Suddenly from a lawn by the St. Louis de France church on the shore I hear kids shouting a message at me, "Hey your mother's in the insane asylum! Your mother's gone to the insane asylum! Your father's dead!" and I realize what's happened and still, swimming and in the Army, I'm stuck struggling in the cold water, and all I can do is grieve, grieve, in the hoar necessitous horror of the morning, bitterly I hate myself, bitterly it's too late yet while I feel better I still feel ephemeral and unreal and unable to straighten my thoughts or even really grieve, in fact I feel too stupid to be really bitter, in short I dont know what I'm doing and I'm being told what to do by the Army and Deni Bleu has played a wood on me too, at last, to get his sweet revenge but mostly it's just that he's decided to become an out-and-out crook and this was his chance—

. . . And even though the saffron freezing message may come from the sunny ice caps of this world, O haunted fools we are, I add an appendage to a long loving letter I'd been writing to my mother for weeks:

> Dont despair, Ma, I'll take care of you whenever you need me—just yell. . . . I'm right there, swimming the river of hardships but I know how to swim— Dont ever think for one minute that you are left alone.

> She is 3,000 miles away living in bondage to ill kin.
> Desolation, desolation, how shall I ever repay thee?

6

I could go mad in this— O carryall menaya but the weel may track the rattle-burr, poniac the avoid devoidity runabout, minavoid the crail—

Song of my all the vouring me the part de rail-ing carry all the pone—
part you too may green and fly—welkin moon wrung salt upon the
tides of come-on night, swing on the meadow shoulder, roll the boulder
of Buddha over the pink partitioned west Pacific fog mow— O tiny tiny
tiny human hope, O molded cracking thee mirror thee shook pa t n a
watalaka—and more to go—

   Ping.

7

Every night at 8 the lookouts on all the different mountaintops in the
Mount Baker National Forest have a bull session over their radios—I
have my own Packmaster set and turn it on, and listen.

   It's a big event in the loneliness—

   "He asked if you was goin to sleep, Chuck."

   "You know what he does Chuck when he goes out on patrol?—he
finds a nice shady spot and just goes to sleep."

   "Did you say Louise?"

   "—I doant knaow—"

   "—Well I only got three weeks to wait—"

   "—right on 99—"

   "Say Ted?"

   "Yeah?"

   "How do you keep your oven hot for makin those, ah, muffins?"

   "Oh just keep the fire hot—"

   "They only got one road that ah zigzags all over creation—"

   "Yeh well I hope so—I'll be there waitin anyway."

   Bzzzzz bzgg radio—long silence of pensive young lookouts—

   "Well is your buddy gonna come up here and pick you up?"

   "Hey Dick— Hey Studebaker—"

   "Just keep pourin wood in it, that's all, it stays hot—"

   "Are you still gonna pay him the same thing as you did ah pay him
comin out?"

   "—Yeah but ah three four trips in three hours?"

   My life is a vast and insane legend reaching everywhere without
beginning or ending, like the Void—like Samsara— A thousand memories come like tics all day perturbing my vital mind with almost muscular spasms of clarity and recall— Singing in a false limey accent to
Loch Lomond as I heat my evening coffee in cold rose dusk, I immediately think of that time in 1942 in Nova Scotia when our seedy ship

put in from Greenland for a night's shore leave, Fall, pines, cold dusk and then dawn sun, over the radio from wartime America the faint voice of Dinah Shore singing, and how we got drunk, how we slipped and fell, how the joy welled up in my heart and exploded fuming into the night that I was back to my beloved America almost—the cold dog dawn—

Almost simultaneously, just because I'm changing my pants, or that is putting on an extra pair for the howling night, I think of the marvelous sex fantasy of earlier in the day when I'm reading a cowboy story about the outlaw kidnapping the girl and having her all alone on the train (except for one old woman) who (the old woman now in my daydream sleeps on the bench while ole hard hombre me outlaw pushes the blonde into the men's compartment, at gun point, and she wont respond but scratch (natch) she loves an honest killer and I'm old Erdaway Molière the murderous sneering Texan who slit bulls in El Paso and held up the stage to shoot holes in people only) —I get her on the seat and kneel and start to work, French postcard style, till I've got her eyes closed and mouth open until she cant stand it and loves this lovin outlaw so she by her own wild willin volition jumps to kneel and works, then when I'm ready turns while the old lady sleeps and the train rattles on— "Most delightful my dear" I'm saying to myself in Desolation Peak and as if to Bull Hubbard, using his way of speech, and as if to amuse him, as if he's here, and I hear Bull saying "Dont act effeminate Jack" as he seriously told me in 1953 when I had started joking with him in *his* effeminate manner routine "On *you* it dont look good Jack" and here I am wishing I could be in London with Bull tonight—

And the new moon, brown, sinks early yonder by Baker River dark.

My life is a vast inconsequential epic with a thousand and a million characters—here they all come, as swiftly we roll east, as swiftly the earth rolls east.

8

For smoking all I have is Air Force paper to roll my tobacco in, an eager sergeant had lectured us on the importance of the Ground Observer Corps and handed out fat books of blank paper to record whole armadas apparently of enemy bombers in some paranoiac Conelrad of his brain— He was from New York and talked fast and was Jewish and made me homesick—"Aircraft Flash Message Record," with lines and numbers, I take my little aluminum scissors and cut a square and roll a butt and when airplanes pass I mind my own business although he (the Sgt) did say "If you see a flying saucer report the flying saucer"— It says on the blank: "Number of aircraft, one, two, three, four, many, unknown," reminds me of the dream I had of me and W. H. Auden standing at a bar on the Mississippi River joking elegantly about "women's urine"—"Type of aircraft," it goes on, "single—, bi—, multi—, jet, unknown"— Naturally I love that unknown, got nothin else to do up there on Desolation—"Altitude of aircraft" (and dig this) "Very low, low, high, very high, unknown"—then "SPECIAL REMARKS: EXAMPLES: Hostile aircraft, blimp" (bloop), "helicopter balloon, aircraft in combat or distress, etc." (or whale)— O distressed rose unknown sorrow plane, come!

My cigarette paper is so sad.

"When will Andy and Fred get here!" I yell, when they come up that trail on mules and horses I'll have real cigarette paper and my dear mail from my millions of characters—

For the trouble with Desolation, is, no characters, alone, isolated, but is Hozomeen isolate?

9

My eyes in my hand, welded to wheel to welded to whang.

10

To while away the time I play my solitaire card baseball game Lionel and I invented in 1942 when he visited Lowell and the pipes froze for Christmas—the game is between the Pittsburgh Plymouths (my oldest team, and now barely on top of the 2nd division) and the New York Chevvies rising from the cellar ignominiously since they were world champions last year—I shuffle my deck, write out the lineups, and lay out the teams— For hundreds of miles around, black night, the lamps of Desolation are lit, to a childish sport, but the Void is a child too— and here's how the game goes:—what happens:—how it's won, and by whom:—

The opposing pitchers are, for the Chevvies, Joe McCann, old vet of 20 years in my leagues since first at 13 age I'd belt iron rollerbearings with a nail in the appleblossoms of the Sarah backyard, Ah sad—Joe McCann, with a record of 1-2, (this is the 14th game of the season for both clubs), and an earned run average of 4.86, the Chevvies naturally heavily favored and especially as McCann is a star pitcher and Gavin a secondrater in my official effectiveness rulings—and the Chevvies are hot anyway, comin up, and took the opener of this series 11–5 . . .

The Chevvies jump right out ahead in their half of the first inning as Frank Kelly the manager belts a long single into center bringing home Stan Orsowski from second where he'd gone on a single and walk to Duffy—yag, yag, you can hear those Chevvies (in my mind) talking it up and whistling and clapping the game on— The poor greenclad Plymouths come on for their half of the opening inning, it's just like real life, real baseball, I cant tell the difference between this and that howling wind and hundreds of miles of Arctic Rock without—

But Tommy Turner with his great speed converts a triple into an inside-the-park homerun and anyway Sim Kelly has no arm out there and it's Tommy's sixth homerun, he is the "magnificent one" all right —and his 15th run batted in and he's only been playin six games because he was injured, a regular Mickey Mantle—

Followed immediately back to back by a line drive homerun over the rightfield fence from the black bat of old Pie Tibbs and the Plyms out ahead 2–1 . . . wow . . .

(the fans go wild in the mountain, I hear the rumble of celestial racing cars in the glacial crevasses)

—Then Lew Badgurst singles to right and Joe McCann is really getting belted (and him with his fancy earned run average) (pah, goes to show)—

In fact McCann is almost batted out of the box as he further gives up a walk to Tod Gavin but Ole Reliable Henry Pray ends up the inning grounding out to Frank Kelly at third—it will be a slugfest.

Then suddenly the two pitchers become locked in an unexpected brilliant pitching duel, racking up goose egg after goose egg, neither one of them giving up a hit except one single (Ned Gavin the pitcher got it) in the second inning, right on brilliantly up to the uttermost eighth when Zagg Parker of the Chevs finally breaks the ice with a single to right which (he too for great super runner speed) unopposed stretches into a double (the throw is made but he makes it, sliding) —and a new tone comes in the game you'd think but no!—Ned Gavin makes Clyde Castleman fly out to center then calmly strikes out Stan the Man Orsowski and stalks off the mound chewing his tobacco unperturbed, the very void— Still, a 2–1 ballgame favor of his team—

McCann yields a single to big bad Lew Badgurst (with big arms southpawing that bat) in *his* half of the eighth, and there's a base stolen on him by pinch runner Allen Wayne, but no danger as he gets Tod Gavin on a grounder—

Going into the final inning, still the same score, the same situation.

All Ned Gavin has to do is hold the Chevvies for 3 long outs. The fans gulp and tense. He has to face Byrd Duffy (batting .346 up to this game), Frank Kelly, and pinch hitter Tex Davidson—

He hitches up his belt, sighs, and faces the chubby Duffy—and winds up— Low, one ball.

Outside, ball two.

Long fly to center field but right in the hands of Tommy Turner. *Only two to go.*

"Come on Neddy!" yells manager Cy Locke from the 3rd base box, Cy Locke who was the greatest shortstop of all time in his time in my appleblossom time when Pa was young and laughed in the summernight kitchen with beer and Shammy and pinochle—

Frank Kelly up, dangerous, menacing, the manager, hungry for money and pennants, a whiplash, a firebrand—

Neddy winds up: delivers: inside.

Ball one.

Delivers.

Kelly belts it to right, off the flagpole, Tod Gavin chases, it's a standup double, the tying run is on second, the crowd is wild. Whistles, whistles, whistles—

Speedboy Selman Piva is sent out to run for Kelly.

Tex Davidson is a big veteran chaw-chawin old outfielder of the old wars, he drinks at night, he doesnt care— He strikes out with a big wheeling whackaround of the empty bat.

Ned Gavin has thrun him 3 curves. Frank Kelly curses in the dugout, Piva, the tying run, is still on second. *One more to go!*

The batter: Sam Dane, Chevvy catcher, old veteran chawi-drink-buddy in fact of Tex Davidson's, only difference is Sam bats lefty— same height, lean, old, dont care—

Ned pitches a call strike across the letters—

And there it comes:—a booming homerun over the centerfield barrier, Piva comes home, Sam comes loping around chewing his tobacco, still doesnt care, at the plate he is mobbed by the Kellies and the crazies—

Bottom of the 9th, all Joe McCann has to do is hold the Plymouth—Pray gets on an error, Gucwa singles, they hold at second and first, and up steps little Neddy Gavin and doubles home the tying run and sends the winning run to third, pitcher eat pitcher—Leo Sawyer pops up, it looks like McCann'll hold out, but Tommy Turner simply slaps a sacrifice grounder and in comes the winning run, Jake Gucwa who'd singled so unobtrusively, and the Plymouths rush out and carry Ned Gavin to the showers atop their shoulders.

Tell me Lionel and I didnt invent a good game!

11

Great day in the morning, he's committed another murder, in fact the same one, only this time the victim sits happily in my father's chair just about on Sarah Avenue location and I'm just sitting at my desk writing on, unconcerned, when I hear of the new murder I go on writing (presumably about it, he he)—All the ladies have gone to the lawns but what horror when they come back just to sense murder in that room, what will Ma say, but he has cut up the body and washed it down the toilet— Dark brewing face bends over us in the gloomdream.

I wake up in the morning at seven and my mop is still drying on the rock, like a woman's head of hair, like Hecuba forlorn, and the lake is a misty mirror a mile below out of which soon the ladies of the lake shall rise in wrath and all night long I hardly slept (I hear faint thunder in my eardrums) because the mice, the rat, and the two fawns befawdledawdled all over my place, the fawns unreal, too skinny, too strange to be deer, but new kinds of mystery mountain mammals— They cleaned out utterly the plate of cold boiled potatoes I laid out for them— My sleepingbag is flat for another day—I sing at the stove: "How coffee, you sure look good when you brewin"—

"How how lady, you sure look good when you lovin"

(the ladies of the North Pole Snow I heard sing in Greenland)

12

My toilet is a little peaked wood outhouse on the edge of a beautiful Zen precipice with boulders and rock slate and old gnarled enlightened trees, remnants of trees, stumps, torn, tortured, hung, ready to fall, unconscious, Ta Ta Ta—the door I keep jammed open with a rock, faces vast triangular mountain walls across Lightning Gorge to the east, at 8:30 A.M. the haze is sweet and pure—and dreamy—Lightning Creek mores and mores her roar—Three Fools join in, and Shull and Cinammon feed him, and beyond, Trouble Creek, and beyond, other forests, other primitive areas, other gnarled rock, straight east to Montana—On foggy days the view from my toilet seat is like a Chinese Zen drawing in ink on silk of gray voids, I half expect to see two giggling old dharma bums, or one in rags, by the goat-horned stump, one with a broom, the other with a pen quill, writing poems about the Giggling Lings in the Fog—saying, "Hanshan, what is the meaning of the void?"

"Shihte, did you mop your kitchen floor this morning?"

"Hanshan, what is the meaning of the void?"

"Shihte, did you mop—Shihte, did you mop?"

"He he he he."

"Why do you laugh, Shihte?"

"Because my floor is mopped."

"Then what is the meaning of the void?"

Shihte picks up his broom and sweeps empty space, like I once saw Irwin Garden do—they wander off, giggling, in the fog, and all's left are the few near rocks and gnarls I can see and above, the Void goes into the Great Truth Cloud of upper fogs, not even one black sash, it is a giant vertical drawing, showing 2 little masters and then space endlessly above them— "Hanshan, where is your mop?"

"Drying on a rock."

A thousand years ago Hanshan wrote poems on cliffs like these, on foggy days like these, and Shihte swept out the monastery kitchen with a broom and they giggled together, and King's Men came from far and wide to find them and they only ran, hiding, into crevasses and caves — Suddenly I see Hanshan now appearing before my Window pointing to the east, I look that way, it's only Three Fools Creek in the morning haze, I look back, Hanshan has vanished, I look back at what he showed me, it's only Three Fools Creek in the morning haze.

What else?

13

Then come the long daydreams of what I'll do when I get out of there, that mountaintop trap. Just to drift and roam down that road, on 99, fast, mebbe a filet mignon on hot coals in a riverbottom some night, with good wine, and on in the morning—to Sacramento, Berkeley, go up to Ben Fagan's cottage and say first off this Haiku:

> Hitch hiked a thousand
> miles and brought
> You wine

—mebbe sleep in his grass yard that night, at least one night in a Chinatown hotel, one long walk around Frisco, one big Chinese two big Chinese dinners, see Cody, see Mal, look for Bob Donnelly and the others—few things here and there, a present for Ma—why plan? I'll just drift down the road looking at unexpected events and I wont stop till Mexico City

14

I have a book up there, confessions of ex communists who quit when they recognized its totalitarian beastliness, *The God That Failed* the title (including one dull O awfully dull account of André Gide's that old postmortem bore) —all I have, for reading—and become depressed by the thought of a world (O what a world is this, that friendships cancel enmity of the heart, people fighting for something to fight, everywhere) a world of GPU's and spies and dictators and purges and midnight murders and marijuana revolutions with guns and gangs in the desert —suddenly, just by tuning in on America via the lookout radio listening to the other boys in the bull session, I hear football scores, talk of so-and-so "Bo Pelligrini!—what a bruiser!! I dont talk to anybody from Maryland"—and the jokes and the laconic stay, I realize, "America is as free as that wild wind, out there, still free, free as when there was no name to that border to call it Canada and on Friday nights when Canadian Fishermen come in old cars on the old road beyond the lake tarn" (that I can see, the little lights of Friday night, thinking then immediately of their hats and gear and flies and lines) "on Friday nights it was the nameless Indian came, the Skagit, and a few log forts were up there, and down here a ways, and winds blew on free feet and free antlers, and still do, on free radio waves, on free wild young-talk of America on the radio, college boys, fearless free boys, a million miles from Siberia this is and Amerikay is a good old country yet—"

For the whole blighted darkness-woe of thinking about Russias and plots to assassinate whole peoples' souls, is lifted just by hearing "My God, the score is 26–0 already—they couldn't gain anything thru the line"—"Just like the All Stars"—"Hey Ed when you comin down off your lookout?"—"He's goin steady, he'll be wantin to go home straight"—"We might take a look at Glacier National Park"—"We're goin home thru the Badlands of North Dakota"—"You mean the Black Hills"—"I dont talk to anybody from Syracuse"—"Anybody know a good bedtime story?"—"Hey it's eight thirty, we better knock off— How 33 ten-seven till tomorrow morning. Good night"—"Ho! How 32 ten-seven till tomorrow morning— Sleep tight"—"Did you say you had Honkgonk on your portable radio?"—"Sure, listen, hingya hingya hingya"—"That does it, good night"—

And I know that America is too vast with people too vast to ever be degraded to the low level of a slave nation, and I can go hitch hiking down that road and on into the remaining years of my life knowing that outside of a couple fights in bars started by drunks I'll have not a hair on my head (and I need a haircut) harmed by Totalitarian cruelty—

Indian scalp say this, and prophesy:

"From these walls, laughter will run over the world, infecting with courage the bent laborious peon of antiquity."

15

And I buy Buddha, who said, that what he said was neither true nor untrue, and there's the only true thing or good thing I ever heard and it rings a cloudy bell, a mighty supramundane gong— He said, "Your trip was long, illimitable, you came to this raindrop called your life, and call it *yours*—we have purposed that you vow to be awakened— whether in a million lifetimes you disregard this Kingly Heeding, it's still a raindrop in the sea and who's disturbed and what is time—? This Bright Ocean of Infinitude sails many fish afar, that come and go like the sparkle on your lake, mind, but dive into the rectangular white blaze of this thought now: You have been assigned to wake up, this is the golden eternity, which knowledge will do you no earthly good for earth's not pith, a crystal myth—face the A-H truth, awakener, be you not knuckled under the wile of cold or heat, comfort or unrepose, be you mindful, moth, of eternity—be you loving, lad, lord, of infinite variety—be you one of us, Great Knowers Without Knowing, Great Lovers Beyond Love, whole hosts and unnumberable angels with form or desire, supernatural corridors of heat—we heat to hold you woke— open your arms embrace the world, it and we rush in, we'll lay a silver meeting brand of golden hands on your milky embowered brow, power, to make you freeze in love forever— Believe! and ye shall live forever

— Believe, that ye have lived forever—overrule the fortresses and pen-ances of dark isolate suffering life on earth, there's more to life than earth, there's Light Everywhere, look—"

In these strange words I hear every night, in many other words, varieties and threads of discourse pouring in from that ever-mindful rich—

Take my word for it, something will come of it, and it will wear the face of sweet nothingness, flappy leaf—

The bullnecks of strong raft drivers the color of purple gold and kirtles of silk will carry us uncarried uncrossing crossable no-cross voids to the ulum light, where Ragamita the lidded golden eye opes to hold the gaze— Mice skitter in the mountain night with little feet of ice and diamonds, but's not my time yet (mortal hero) to know what I know I know, so, come in

> Words . . .
> The stars are words . . .
> Who succeeded? Who failed?

16

Ah yair, and when
I gets to Third and
Townsend,
    I'll ketch me
the Midnight Ghost—
We'll roll right down
    to San Jose
As quick as you can boast—
—Ah ha, Midnight,
    midnight ghost,
Ole Zipper rollin
    down the line—
Ah ha, Midnight,
    midnight ghost,
Rollin
            down
                the
                    line
We'll come a blazing

To Watson-ville,
And whang on through
    the line—
Salinas Valley
    in the night,
On down to Apaline—
Whoo Whoo
  Whoo ee
Midnight Ghost
Clear t'Obispo Bump
—Take on a helper
and make that mountain,
and come on down the town,
—We'll rail on through
to Surf and Tangair
and on down by the sea—
The moon she shines
   the midnight ocean
goin down the line—
Gavioty, Gavioty,
O Gavi-oty,
Singin and drinkin wine—
Camarilla, Camarilla,
Where Charley Parker
    went mad
We'll roll on to L.A.
—O Midnight
    midnight,
  midnight ghost,
rollin down the line.
Sainte Teresa
Sainte Teresa, dont you worry,
We'll make it on time,
  down that midnight
    line

And that's how I figure I'll make San Francisco to L.A. in 12 hours, ridin the Midnight Ghost, under a lashed truck, the Firstclass Zipper freight train, zooam, zom, right down, sleepingbag and wine—a day-dream in the form of a song.

17

Getting tired of looking at all the angles of my lookout, as for instance, looking at my sleepingbag in the morning from the point of view of opening it again at night, or at my stove with high supper heat of mid-afternoon from the point of view of midnight when the mouse'll be scratching in it cold, I turn my thoughts to Frisco and I see it like a movie what'll be there when I get there, I see myself in my new (to-be-bought-in-Seattle-I-plan) black large-sized leather jacket that hangs and ties over my waist low (mebbe hangs over my hands) and my new gray Chino pants and new wool sports shirt (orange and yellow and blue!) and my new haircut, there I go bleakfaced Decembering the steps of my Skid Row Chinatown hotel, or else I'm at Simon Darlovsky's pad at 5 Turner Terrace in the crazy Negro housing project at Third & 22nd where you see the giant gastanks of eternity and a whole vista of the smoky industrial Frisco including the bay and the railroad mainline and factories—I see myself, rucksack on one shoulder, coming in the ever-unlocked backdoor to Lazarus' bedroom (Larazus is Simon's strange 15½ year old mystic brother who never says anything but "D'ja have any dreams?") (last night in your sleep?) (he means), I come, in, it's October, they're at school, I go out and buy ice cream, beer, canned peaches, steaks and milk and stock the icebox and when they come home at late afternoon and in the courtyard the little kids have started screaming for Fall Dusk Joy, I've been at that kitchen table all day drinking wine and reading the papers, Simon with his bony hawk nose and crazy glittering green eyes and glasses looks at me and says through his ever-sinus nostrils "*Jack! You!* When'd you get here, hnf!" as he sniffs (horribly the torment of his sniff, I hear it now, cant tell how he breathes)—"Just today—look, the icebox is full of food— Mind if I stay here a few days?"—"Plenty room"—Lazarus is behind him, wearing his new suit and all combed to make the junior highschool lovelies, he just nods and smiles and then we're having a big feast and Lazarus finally says "Where dja sleep last night?" and I say "In a yard in Berkeley" so he says "Djav any dreams?"— So tell him a long dream. And at midnight when Simon and I have gone out walking all the way up Third Street drinking wine and talking about girls and talking to the spade whores across from the Cameo Hotel and going to North Beach to look for Cody and the gang, Lazarus all alone in the kitchen fries himself three steaks for a midnight snack, he's a big goodlooking crazy kid, one of many Darlovsky brothers, in the madhouse most of them, for some reason, and Simon hitch hiked all the way to New York to rescue Laz and brought him back to live with him, on relief, two Russian brothers, in the city, in the void, Irwin's protégés, Simon a Kafka writer—Lazarus a mystic who stares at pictures of monsters on weird magazines, for hours, and wanders around the city zombie like, and when he was 15 claimed he would weigh 300 pounds before the year was out and also had set himself a deadline to make a million dollars by New Year's Eve—to this crazy pad Cody ofttimes goes in his shabby blue brakeman's uniform and sits at the kitchen table then leaps out and jumps in his car yelling "Short on time!" and races off to North Beach to look for the gang or to work to catch his train, and girls everywhere in the streets and in our bars and the whole Frisco scene one insane movie—I see myself arriving on the scene, across that screen, looking around, all done with desolation— White masts of ships at the foot of streets.

I see myself wandering among the wholesale markets—down past the deserted MCS union hall where I'd tried so hard to get a ship, for years— There I go, chewing on a Mister Goodbar—

I wander by Gumpy's department store and look in the artframe shop where Psyche, who always wears jeans and turtleneck sweater with a little white collar falling over, works, whose pants I would like to remove and just leave the turtleneck sweater and the little collar and the rest is all for me and all too sweet for me—I stand in the street staring in at her—I sneak by our bar several times (The Place) and peek in—

18

I wake up and I'm on Desolation Peak and the firs are motionless in the blue morning— Two butterflies comport, with worlds of mountains as their backdrop— My clock ticks the slow day— While I slept and traveled in dreams all night, the mountains didnt move at all and I doubt they dreamed—

I go out to fetch a pail of snow to put in my old tin washtub that reminds me of my grandfather's in Nashua and I find that my shovel has disappeared from the snowbank on the precipice, I look down and figure it will be a long climb down and up but I cant see it— Then I do see it, right in the mud at the foot of the snow, on a ledge, I go down very carefully, slipping in the mud, for fun yank out a big boulder from the mud and kick it down, it goes booming and crashes on a rock and splits in two and thunders 1500 feet down to where I see the final rock of it rolling in long snowfields and coming to rest against boulders with a knock that I only hear 2 seconds later— Silence, the beautiful gorge shows no sign of animal life, just firs and alpine heather and rocks, the snow beside me blinds whitely in the sun, I loose down at the cerulean neutral lake a look of woe, little pink or almost brown clouds hover in its mirror, I look up and there's mighty Hozomeen redbrown pinnacles high in the sky—I get the shovel and come up carefully in the mud, slipping—fill the pail with clean snow, cover the stash of carrots and cabbage in a new deep snowhole, and go back, dumping the lump in the tin tub and splashing water over the sides onto my dusty floor— Then I get an old pail and like the old Japanese woman go down among beautiful heather meadows and gather sticks for my stove. It's Saturday afternoon all over the world.

19

"If I were in Frisco now," I think in my chair in the late after-solitudes, "I'd buy a great big quart of Christian Brothers Port or some other excellent special brand and go up to my Chinatown room and empty half its contents in an empty pint, stick that in my pocket, and take off, around the little streets of Chinatown watching the children, the little Chinese children so happy with their little hands in their parents' wrapt, I'd look in grocery stores and see the noncommittal Zen butchers cutting the necks of chickens, I'd gaze water mouthed at the beautiful glazed cured roasted ducks in the window, I'd wander around, stand on the corner of Italian Broadway too, to get the feel of life, blue skies and white clouds above, I'd go back and into the Chinese movie with my pint and sit there drinking it (from now, 5 P.M.) three hours digging the weird scenes and unheard-of dialogs and developments and maybe some of the Chinese would see me drink-a-pint and they'd think "Ah, a drunken white man in the Chinese movie"—at 8 I'd come out to a blue dusk with sparkling lights of San Francisco on all the magic hills around, now I'd refill my pint in the hotel room and really take off for a long hike around the city, to work up an appetite for my midnight feast in a booth in Sun Heung Hung's marvelous old restaurant—I'd strike over the hill, over Telegraph, and right down to the rail spur where I know a place in a narrow alley where I can sit and drink and wallgaze a vast black cliff that has magic vibratory properties that send back messages of swarming holy light in the night, I know I tried it—then, drinking,

sipping, re-capping the bottle, I walk the lonely way along the Embarcadero through Fisherman's Wharf restaurant areas where the seals
break my heart with their coughing cries of love, I go, past shrimp
counters, out, past the masts of the last docked ships, and then up Van
Ness and over and down into the Tenderloin—the winking marquees
and bars with cocktail cherrysticks, the sallow characters the old alcoholic blondes stumbling to the liquor store in slacks—then I go (wine
almost gone and me high and glad) down main arterial Market Street
and the honkytonk of sailors, movies, and sodafountains, across the
alley and into Skid Row (finishing my wine there, among scabrous old
doorways chalked and be-pissed and glass-crashed by a hundred thousand grieving souls in Goodwill rags) (the same old boys who roam the
freights and cling to little bits of paper on which you always find some
kind of prayer or philosophy)— Wine finished, I go singing and hand-
clapping quietly to the beat of my feet all the way up Kearney back to
Chinatown, almost midnight now, and I sit in the Chinatown park on
a dark bench and take the air, drinking in the sight of the foody delicious neons of my restaurant blinking in the little street, occasionally
crazy drunks go by in the dark looking for half finished bottles on the
ground, or, butts, and across Kearney there you see the blue cops goin
in and out of the big gray jailhouse— Then I go in my restaurant, order
from the Chinese menu, and instantly they bring me smoked fish, curried
chicken, fabulous duck cakes, unbelievably delicious and delicate silver
platters (on stems) containing steaming marvels, that you raise the cover
off and look and sniff—with tea pot, cup, ah I eat—and eat—till
midnight—maybe then over tea write a letter to beloved Ma, telling
her—then, done, I either go to bed or to our bar, The Place, to find the
gang and get drunk . . .

20

On a soft August evening I scramble down the slope of the mountain
and find a steep place to sit crosslegged near firs and blasted old tree
stumps, facing the moon, the yellow halfmoon that's sinking into the
mountains to the southwest— In the western sky, warm rose— About
8:30— The wind over the mile-down lake is balmy and reminiscent of
all the ideas you've ever had about enchanted lakes—I pray and ask
Awakener Avalokitesvara to lay his diamond hand on my brow and
give me the immortal understanding— He is the Hearer and Answerer
of Prayer, I know that this business is self hallucination and crazy busi-

ness but after all it is only the awakeners (the Buddhas) who have said they do not exist— In about twenty seconds comes this understanding to my mind and heart: "When a baby is born he falls asleep and dreams the dream of life, when he dies and is buried in his grave he wakes up again to the Eternal Ecstasy"—"And when all is said and done, it doesnt matter"—

Yea, Avalokitesvara did lay his diamond hand . . .

And then the question of why, why, it's only the Power, the one mental nature exuding its infinite potentialities— What a strange feeling reading that in Vienna in February of 1922 (month before I was born) such and such was going on in the streets, how could there have been a Vienna, nay even the conception of a Vienna before I was born?!— It's because the one mental nature goes on, has nothing to do with individual arrivers and departers that bear it and fare in it and that are fared in by it— So that 2500 years ago was Gotama Buddha, who thought up the greatest thought in Mankind, a drop in the bucket those years in that Mental Nature which is the Universal Mind—I see in my mountainside contentment that the Power delights and joys in both ignorance and enlightenment, else there wouldnt be ignorant existence alongside enlightened inexistence, why should the Power limit itself to one or the other—whether as the form of pain, or as impalpable ethers of formlessness and painlessness, what matters it?—And I see the yellow moon a-sinkin as the earth rolls away. I twist my neck around to see upsidedown and the mountains of the earth are just those same old hanging bubbles hanging into an unlimited sea of space— Ah, if there was another sight besides *eye* sight what atomic otherlevels wouldnt we see?—but here we see moons, mountains, lakes, trees and sentient beings only, with our eyesight— The Power delights in all of it— It is reminding itself that it is the Power, that's why, for it, The Power, is really only ecstasy, and its manifestations dream, it is the Golden Eternity, ever peaceful, this bleary dream of existence is just a blear in its —I run out of words— The warm rose in the west becomes a hushed pastel park of gray, the soft evening sighs, little animals rustle in the heather and holes, I shift my cramped feet, the moon yellows and mellows and finally begins to hit the topmost crag and as always you see silhouetted in its magic charm some snag or stump that looks like the legendary Coyotl, God of the Indians, about to howl to the Power—

O what peace and content I feel, coming back to my shack knowing that the world is a babe's dream and the ecstasy of the golden eternity is all we're going back to, to the essence of the Power—and the Primordial Rapture, *we all know it*—I lie on my back in the dark, hands joined, glad, as the northern lights shine like a Hollywood premiere and at that too I look upsidedown and see that it's just big pieces of ice on earth reflecting the other-side sun in some far daylight, in fact, too, the curve of the earth silhouetted is also seen arching over and around— Northern lights, bright enough to light my room, like ice moons.

What content to know that when all is said and done it doesnt matter— Woes? the piteousnesses I feel when I think of my mother?— but it all has to be roused and remembered, it isnt there by itself, and that's because the mental nature is by nature free of the dream and free of everything— It's like those pipe-smoking Deist philosophers who say "O mark the marvelous creation of God, the moon, the stars etc., would you trade it for anything?" not realizing they wouldnt be saying this at all if it wasnt for some primordial memory of when, of what, of how nothing was— "It's only recent," I realize, looking at the world, some recent cycle of creation by The Power to joy in its reminder to its selfless self that it is The Power—and all of it in its essence swarming tender mystery, that you can see by closing your eyes and letting the eternal silence in your ears—that blessedness and bliss surely to be believed, my dears—

The awakeners, if they choose, are born as babes— This is my first awakening— There are no awakeners and no awakening.

In my shack I lie, remembering the violets in our backyard on Phebe Avenue when I was eleven, on June nights, the blear dream of it, ephemeral, haunted, long gone, going further out, till it shall be all gone out.

21

I wake up in the middle of the night and remember Maggie Cassidy and how I might have married her and been old Finnegan to her Irish Lass Plurabelle, how I might have got a cottage, a little ramshackle Irish rose cottage among the reeds and old trees on the banks of the Concord and woulda worked as a grim bejacketed gloved and bebaseballhatted brakeman in the cold New England night, for her and her Irish ivory thighs, her and her marshmallow lips, her and her brogue and "God's Green Earth" and her two daughters— How I would of laid her across the bed at night all mine and laborious sought her rose, her mine of a thing, that emerald dark and hero thing I want—remember her silk thighs in tight jeans, the way she folded back one thigh under her hands and sighed as we watched Television together—in her mother's parlor that last haunted 1954 trip I took to October Lowell— Ah, the rose vines, the river mud, the run of her, the eyes— A woman for old Duluoz? Unbelievable by my stove in desolation midnight that it should be true—Maggie Adventure—

The claws of black trees by moonlit rosy dusk mayhap and by chance hold me much love too, and I can always leave them and roam along—but when I'm old by my final stove, and the bird fritters on his branch of dust in O Lowell, what'll I think, willow?—when winds creep inside my sack and give me bareback blues and I go bent about my meritorious duties in the sod-cover earth, what lovesongs then for old bedawdler bog bent foggy Jack O—?—no new poets will bring laurels like honey to my milk, sneers— Sneers of love woman were better I guess—I'd fall down ladders, brabac, and wash me river underwear— gossip me washlines—air me Mondays—fantasm me Africas of housewives— Lear me daughters—panhandle me marble heart—but it might have been better than what it may be, lonesome unkissed Duluoz lips surling in a tomb

22

Early Sunday mornings I always remember home in Ma's house in Long Island, recent years, when she's reading the Sunday papers and I get up, shower, drink a cup of wine, read the scores and then eat the charming little breakfast she'll lay out for me, just all I have to do is ask her, her special way of crisping bacon and the way she sunnysides the eggs— The TV not turned because there's nothing much of note on Sunday mornings—I grieve to think that her hair is turning gray and she's 62 and will be 70 when I'm in my owlish 40's—soon it will be my "old mother"—in the bunk I try to think of how I'll take care of her—

Then as day lengthens and Sunday drags and the mountains wear the pious dullish aspect Sabbathini I always begin to think instead of earlier days in Lowell when the redbrick mills were so haunted by the riverside about 4 in the afternoon, the kids coming home from the Sunday movies, but O the sad redbrick and everywhere in America you see it, in the reddening sun, and clouds beyond, and people in their best clothes in all that— We all stand on the sad earth throwing long shadows, breath cut with flesh.

Even the skitter of the mouse in my shack attic on Sundays has a Sunday halidom about it, as though churchgoing, churchment, preachments— We'll have a whack at it around.

Mostly Sundays I'm bored. And all my memories are bored. The sun is too golden bright. I shudder to think what people are doing in North Carolina. In Mexico City they wander around eating vast planks of fried porkskin, among parks, even their Sunday is a Blight— It must be the Sabbath was invented to soften joy.

For normal peasants Sunday is a smile, but us black poets, agh—I guess Sunday is God's lookingglass.

Compare the churchyards of Friday night, with the pulpits of Sunday morn—

In Bavaria, men with bare knees walk around with hands behind their backs— Flies drowse behind a lace curtain, in Calais, and out the window see the sailboats— On Sunday Céline yawns and Genêt dies— In Moscow there's no pomp— Only in Benares on Sundays peddlers scream and snakecharmers open baskets with a lute— On Desolation Peak in the High Cascades, on Sundays, agh—

I think in particular of that redbrick wall of the Sheffield Milk Company by the mainline of the Long Island Railroad in Richmond Hill, the mud tracks of workers' cars left in the lot during the week, one or two forlorn Sundayworker cars parked there now, the clouds passing in the pools of brown puddlewater, the sticks and cans and rags of debris, the commute local passing by with pale blank faces of Sunday Travelers—presaging the ghostly day when industrial America shall be abandoned and left to rust in one long Sunday Afternoon of oblivion.

23

With his ugly many bud legs the green alpine caterpillar comports in his heather world, a head like a pale dewdrop, his fat body reaching up straight to climb, hanging upsidedown like a South American ant eater to fiddle and fish and sway around in search, then cromming up like a boy making a limb he aligns himself hidden under heather limbs and plucks and monsters at the innocent green—the part of the green, he is, that was given moving juice—he twists and peers and intrudes his head everywhere—he is in a jungle of dappled shady old lastyear's gray heather pins—sometimes motionless like the picture of a boa constrictor he yaws to heaven a songless gaze, sleeps snakeheaded, then turns in like a busted-out tube when I blow on him, swift to duck, quick to retire, meek to obey the level injunction of lie still that's meant by the sky whatever may chance from it— He is very sad now as I blow again, puts head in shoulder mourning, I'll let him free to roam unobserved, playing possum as he wists—there he goes, disappearing, making little jiggles in the jungle, eye level to his world I perceive that he too is overtopped by a few fruits and then infinity, he too's upsidedown and clinging to his sphere—we are all mad.

I sit there wondering if my own travels down the Coast to Frisco and Mexico wont be just as sad and mad—but by bejesus j Christ it'll be bettern hangin around *this* rock—

24

Some of the days on the mount, tho hot, are permeated with a pure cool beauty that presages October and my freedom in the Indian Plateau of Mexico which will be even purer and cooler— O old dreams I've had of the mountains on the plateau of Mexico when the skies are filled with clouds like the beards of patriarchs and indeed I'm the Patriarch himself standing in a flowing robe on the green hill of gold— In the Cascades summer may heat in August but you get the Fall hint, especially on the eastern slope of my hill in the afternoons, away from the burn of the sun, where the air is sharp and mountainlike and the trees have well withered to a beginning of the end— Then I think of the World Series, the coming of football across America (the cries of a keen Middle-western voice on the scratchy radio)—I think of shelves of wine in stores along the mainline of the California Railroad, I think of the pebbles in the ground of the West under vast Fall-booming skies, I think of the long horizons and plains and the ultimate desert with his cactus and dry mesquites stretching to red tablelands far away where my traveler's old hope always wends and wends and only void-returns from nowhere, the long dream of the Western hitch hiker and hobo, the harvest tramps who sleep in their cottonpickin bags and rest content under the flashy star— At night, Fall hints in the Cascade Summer where you see Venus red on her hill and think "Who will be my lady?"—It will all, the haze shimmer and the beezing bugs, be wiped off the slate of summer and hurled to the east by that eager sea west wind and that's when hairflying me'll be stomping down the trail for the last time, rucksack and all, singing to the snows and jackpines, en route for further adventures, further yearnings for adventures—and all behind me (and you) the ocean of tears which has been this life on earth, so old, that when I look at my panoramic photographs of the Desolation area and see the old mules and wiry roans of 1935 (in the picture) hackled at a no-more corral fence, I marvel that the mountains lookt the same in 1935 (Old Jack Mountain to an exact degree with the same snow arrangement) as they do in 1956 so that the oldness of the earth strikes me recalling primordially that it was the same, they (the mountains) looked the same too in 584 B.C.—and all that but a sea spray drop— We live to long, so long I will, and jounce down that mountain highest perfect knowing or no highest perfect knowing full of glorious ignorant looking to sparkle elsewhere—

Later in the afternoon the west wind picks up, comes from smileless wests, invisible, and sends clean messages thru my cracks and screens — More, more, let the firs wither more, I want to see the white marvels south—

• • •

70

Everything is so keen when you come down from solitude, I notice all Seattle with every step I take—I'm going down the sunny main drag now with pack on back and room rent paid and lotsa pretty girls eating ice cream cones and shopping in the 5 & 10— On one corner I see an eccentric paperseller with a wagonbike loaded with ancient issues of magazines and bits of string and thread, an oldtime Seattle character— "The *Reader's Digest* should write about him," I think, and go to the bus station and buy my ticket to Frisco.

The station is loaded with people, I stash my rucksack in the baggage room and wander around unencumbered looking everywhere, I sit in the station and roll a cigarette and smoke, I go down the street for hot chocolate at a soda fountain.

A pretty blonde woman is running the fountain, I come in there and order a thick milkshake first, move down to the end of the counter and drink it there— Soon the counter begins to fill up and I see she's overworked— She cant keep up with all the orders—I even order hot chocolate myself finally and she does a little "Hmf O my"— Two teenage hepcats come in and order hamburgers with catsup, she cant find the catsup, has to go in the backroom and look while even then fresh further people sit at the counter hungry, I look around to see if anybody'll help her, the drug clerk is a completely unconcerned type with glasses who in fact comes over and sits and orders something himself, free, a *steak sandwich*—

"I cant find the catsup!" she almost weeps—

He turns over a page of the newspaper, "Is that a fact"—

I study him—the cold neat white-collar nihilistic clerk who doesnt care about anything but does believe that women should wait on him! —She I study, a typical West Coast type, probable ex-showgirl, maybe even (sob) ex-burlesque dancer who didnt make it because she wasnt naughty enough, like O'Grady last night— But she lives in Frisco too, she always lives in the Tenderloin, she is completely respectable, very attractive, works very hard, very good hearted, but somehow something's wrong and life deals her a complete martyr deck I dont know why—something like my mother— Why some man doesnt come and latch on her I dont know— The blonde is 38, fulsome, beautiful Venus body, a beautiful and perfect cameo face, with big sad Italianized eyelids, and high cheekbones creamy soft and full, but nobody notices her, nobody wants her, her man hasnt come yet, her man will never come and she'll age with all that beauty in that selfsame rockingchair by the potted-flower window (O West Coast!)—and she'll complain, she'll say her story: "All my life I've tried to do the best I could"— But the two teenagers insist they want catsup and finally, when she has to admit she's out they get surly and start to eat— One, an ugly kid, takes his straw and to pop it out of its paper wrapper stabs viciously at the counter, as tho stabbing someone to death, a real hard fast death-stab that frightens me— His buddy is very beautiful but for some reason he likes this ugly murderer and they pal around together and probably stab old men at night— Meanwhile she's all fuddled in a dozen different orders, hot dogs, hamburgers, (myself I want a hamburger now), coffee, milk, lime-ades for children, and cold clerk sits reading his paper and chewing his steak sandwich— He notices nothing— Her hair is falling over one eye, she's almost *weeping*— Nobody cares because nobody notices— And tonight she'll go to her little clean room with the kitchenette and feed the cat and go to bed with a sigh, as pretty a woman as you'll ever see— No Lochinvar at the door— An angel of a woman— And yet a bum like me, with no one to love her tonight— That's the way it goes, there's your world— Stab! Kill!—Dont care!— There's your Actual Void Face—exactly what this empty universe holds in store for us, the Blank— Blank Blank Blank!

When I leave I'm surprised that, instead of treating me contemptuously for watching her sweat a whole hour, she actually sympathetically counts up my change, with a little harried look from tender blue eyes—I picture myself in her room that night listening first to her list of legitimate complaints.

But my bus is going—

71

The bus pulls out of Seattle and goes barreling south to Portland on swish-swish 99—I'm comfortable in the back seat with cigarettes and paper and near me is a young Indonesian-looking student of some intelligence who says he's from the Philippines and finally (learning I speak Spanish) confesses that white women are shit—

"Las mujeres blancas son la mierda"

I shudder to hear it, whole hordes of invading Mongolians shall overrun the Western world saying that and they're only talking about the poor little blonde woman in the drugstore who's doing her best— By God, if I were Sultan! I wouldnt allow it! I'd arrange for something better! But it's only a dream! Why fret?

The world wouldnt exist if it didnt have the power to liberate itself.

Suck! suck! suck at the teat of Heaven!

Dog is God spelled backwards.

72

And I had raged purely among rocks and snow, rocks to sit on and snow to drink, rocks to start avalankies with and snow to throw snowballs at my house—raged among gnats and dying male ants, raged at a mouse and killed it, raged at the hundred mile cyclorama of snow-capped mountains under the blue sky of day and the starry splendor of night— Raged and been a fool, when I shoulda loved and repented—

Now I'm *back* in that goddam movie of the world and *now* what do I do with it?

> Sit in fool and be fool,
> thats all—

The shades come, night falls, the bus roars downroad— People sleep, people read, people smoke— The busdriver's neck is stiff and alert— Soon we see the lights of Portland all bleak bluff and waters and soon

the city alleys and drivearounds flash by—And after that the body of
Oregon, the Valley of the Willamette—

At dawn I restless wake to see Mount Shasta and old Black Butte,
mountains dont amaze me anymore—I dont even look out the window—It's too late, who cares?

Then the long hot sun of the Sacramento Valley in her Sunday
afternoon, and bleak little stop-towns where I chew up popcorn and
squat and wait— Bah!— Soon Vallejo, sights of the bay, the beginnings
of something new on the cloud-splendrous horizon—San Francisco on
her Bay!

Desolation anyway—

73

It's the bridge that counts, the coming-into-San Francisco on that
Oakland-Bay Bridge, over waters which are faintly ruffled by ocean-
going Orient ships and ferries, over waters that are like taking you to
some other shore, it had always been like that when I lived in
Berkeley—after a night of drinking, or two, in the city, bing, the old
F-train'd take me barreling across the waters back to that other shore
of peace and contentment— We'd (Irwin and I) discuss the Void as we
crossed— It's seeing the rooftops of Frisco that makes you excited and
believe, the big downtown hulk of buildings, Standard Oil's flying red
horse, Montgomery Street highbuildings, Hotel St. Francis, the hills,
magic Telegraph with her Coit-top, magic Russian, magic Nob, and
magic Mission beyond with the cross of all sorrows I'd seen long ago
in a purple sunset with Cody on a little railroad bridge—San Francisco,
North Beach, Chinatown, Market Street, the bars, the Bay-Oom, the
Bell Hotel, the wine, the alleys, the poorboys, Third Street, poets, paint-
ers, Buddhists, bums, junkies, girls, millionaires, MG's, the whole fabulous movie of San Francisco seen from the bus or train on the Bridge
coming in, the tug at your heart like New York—

And they're all there, my friends, somewhere in those little toy-
streets, and when they see me the angel'll smile— That's not so bad—
Desolation aint so bad—

74

Wow, an entirely different scene, San Francisco always is, it always gives
you the courage of your convictions— "This city will see to it that you

make it as you wish, with limitations which are obvious, in stone and memory"— Or such—thus—that feeling, of, "Wow O Alley, I'm gonna get me a poorpoy of Tokay and drink it on the way"— The only city I know of where you can drink the open in the street as you walk and nobody cares—everybody avoids you like poison sailor O Joe McCoy just off the Lurline—"one of the bottlewashers there?"—"No, just a old seedy S.I.U. deckhand, and's been to Hongkong and Singapore and back more time's almost's he's et that wine in backalleys of Harrison"—

Harrison is the street the bus comes in on, ramping, and we go twaddling seven blocks north to Seventh Street, where he turns into the city traffic of Sunday—and there's all your Joes on the street.

Things happening everywhere. Here comes Longtail Charley Joe from Los Angeles, suitcase, blond hair, sports shirt, big thick wrist watch, with him's Minnie O'Pearl the gay girl who sings in the band at Rooey's—"Whooey?"

There're the Negro baggagehandlers of the Greyhound Company, described by Irwin as Mohammedan Angels I believe—sending precious cargo to Loontown and Moontown and Moonlight in Colorado the bar where they'll be tonight whanging with the chicks among U-turning cars and Otay Spence on the box—down among the Negro housing projects, where we'd gone at morning, with whisky and wine and oolyakoo'd with the sisters from Arkansas who'd seen their father hanged— What notion could they get of this country, this Mississippi— There they are, neat and welldressed, perfect neckties and collars, the cleanest dressers in America, presenting their Negro faces at the employer-judge, who judges harshly on the basis of their otay perfect neckties—some with glasses, rings, polite pipe-smokers, college boys, sociologists, the whole we-all-know-the-great-scene-in-otay that I know so well in San Fran— sound—I come dancing through this city with big pack on my back and so I have to hustle not to bump into anybody but nevertheless make time down that Market Street parade— A little deserted and desolate, Sunday— Tho Third Street be crowded, and great big Pariahs bark a-doors and discuss Wombs of Divinity, it's all houndsapack—I crap along and farty up Kearney, towards Chinatown, watching all stores and all faces to see which way the Angel points this fine and perfect day—

"By God I'm gonna give myself a haircut in my room," I say, "and make it look like sumptin"—"Because first thing I'm gonna do is hit that otay sweet saxophone Cellar." Where I'll immediately go for the

Sunday afternoon jam session. O they'll all be there, the girls with dark glasses and blonde hair, the brunettes in pretty coats by the side of their little boy (The Man)—raising beers to their lips, sucking in cigarette smoke, beating to the beat of the beat of Brue Moore the perfect tenor saxophone— Old Brue he'll be high on Brew, and me too—"I'll tap him on the toenail," I think— "We'll hear what the singers gotto say today"— Because all summer I've provided myself my own jazz, singing in the yard or in the house at night, whenever I had to hear some music, see which way the Angel pours the bucket, what stairs down she goes, and otay jazz afternoons in the Maurie O'Tay nightclub okay—music — Because all these serious faces'll only drive you mad, the only truth is music—the only meaning is without meaning— Music blends with the heartbeat universe and we forget the brain beat.

75

I'm in San Francisco and I'm gonna take it all in. Incredible the things I saw.

I get out of the way for two Filipino gentlemen crossing California. I pass through to the Bell Hotel, by the Chinese playground, and go in get my room.

The attendant is immediately succinctly anxious to please me, and there are women in the hall gossiping Malay, I shudder to think the sounds will come in through the courtyard window, all Chinese and melodious, I hear even choruses of French talk, from the owners. A medley of a hotel of rooms in dark carpeted halls, and old creaky night steps and blinking wallclock and 80-year-old bent sage behind the grille, with open doors, and cats— The attendant brings me back my change as I wait with waited door. I take out my little tiny aluminium scissors that cant cut buttons off a sweater, but cut my hair anyway— Then I examine the effect with mirrors— Okay, then I go and shave anyway. I get hot water and I shave and I square away and on the wall is a nude calendar of a Chinese girl. Lot I can do with a calendar. ("Well," said the bum in the burlesque to the other bum, two Limies, "I'm avin er naow.")

In hot little flames.

76

I go out and hit the street crossing at Columbus and Kearney, by Barbary Coast, and a bum in a long bum overcoat sings out to me "When we cross streets in New York we cross em!—None a this waitin shit for me!" and both of us barrel across and walk among cars and shoot back and forth about New York— Then I get to the Cellar and jump down, steep wooden steps, in a broad cellar hall, right to the right is the room with the bar and the bandstand otay where now as I come Jack Minger is blowing on trumpet and behind him's Bill the mad blond pianist scholar of music, on the drums that sad kid with the sweating handsome face who has such a desperate beat and strong wrists, and on bass I cant see him bobbing in the dark with beard— Some crazy Wigmo or other—but it's not the session, it's the regular group, too early, I'll come back later, I've heard every one of Jack Minger's ideas alone with the group, but first (as I'd just dropped into the bookstore to look around) (and a girl called Sonya had prettily come up to me, 17, and said "O do you know Raphael? He needs some money, he's waiting at my place") (Raphael being my old New York crony) (and more about Sonya later), I run in there and am about to turn around and swing out, when I see a cat looks like Raphael, wearing dark glasses, at the foot of the bandstand talking to a chick, so I run over (walking fast) (to avoid goofing the beat as the musicians play on) (some little tune like "All Too Soon") I look right down to see if it's Raphael, almost turning over, looking at him upsidedown, as he notices nothing talking to his girl, and I see it aint Raphael and cut out— So the trumpetplayer who's playing his solo wonders what he sees, knowing me from before as always crazy, running in now to look upsidedown at someone then running out—I go running up to Chinatown to eat and come back to the session. Shrimp! Chicken! Spare ribs! I go down to Sun Heung Hung's and sit there at their new bar drinking cold beers from an incredibly clean bartender who keeps mopping the bar and polishing glasses and even mops under my beer several times and I tell him "This is a nice clean bar" and he says "Brand new"—

Meanwhile I watch for a booth to sit in—none—so I go upstairs and sit in a big curtained booth for families but they throw me outa there ("You cannot sit there, that's for families, big parties") (then they dont come and serve me as I wait) so I slonk back my chair and stomp downstairs fast on quiet feet and get a booth and tell the waiter "Dont let nobody sit with me, I like to eat alone" (in restaurants, naturally)—

Shrimp in a brown sauce, curried chicken, and sweet and sour spare ribs, in a Chinese menu dinner, I eat it with another beer, it's a terrific meal I can hardly finish—but I finish it clean, pay and cut out— To the now late afternoon park where the children are playing in sandboxes and swings, and old men are staring on benches—I come over and sit down.

The little Chinese children are waging big dramas with sand— Meanwhile a father gathers up his three different little ones and heads them home— Cops are going into the jailhouse across the street. Sunday in San Francisco.

A bearded point-bearded patriarch nods at me then sits near an old crony and they start talking loudly in Russian. I know olski-dolski when I hear it, nyet?

Then I amble along in the gathering cool and do walk through Chinatown duskstreets like I said I would on Desolation, the wink of pretty neons, the faces in the stores, the festooned bulbs across Grant Street, the Pagodas.

I go to my hotel room and rest awhile on the bed, smoking, listening to the sounds coming in the window from the Bell Hotel court, the noises of dishes and traffic and Chinese— It is all one big wailing world, all over, even in my own room there is sound, the intense roaring silence sound that swishes in my ear and swashes the diamond persepine—I let go and feel my astral body leave, and lay there completely in a trance, seeing through everything. It's all white.

77

It's a North Beach tradition, Rob Donnelly had done it in a Broadway hotel and floated away and saw whole worlds and came back and woke up in his room on the bed, all dressed to go out—

Like as not, too, Old Rob, wearing Mal Damlette's sharp cap on the side of his head, would be in the Cellar even right now—

By now the Cellar is waiting for the musicians, not a sound, nobody I know in there, I hang on the sidewalk and here comes Chuck Berman one way, and Bill Slivovitz the other, a poet, and we talk at a fender of a car—Chuck Berman looks tired, his eyes are all puffed, but he's wearing soft smart shoes and looking so cool in the twilight—Bill Slivovitz doesnt care, he's wearing a shabby sports coat and scuffed out shoes and carrying poems in his pocket—Chuck Berman is high, says he's high, lingers a minute looking around; then cuts— He'll be back— Bill

Slivovitz the last time I saw him'd said "Where you goin?" and I'd yelled "Ah what's the difference?" so now I apologize and explain I was hungover— We repair to The Place for a beer.

The Place is a brown lovely bar made of wood, with sawdust, barrel beer in glass mugs, an old piano for anybody to bang on, and an upstairs balcony with little wood tables—who care? the cat sleeps on the bench. The bartenders are usually friends of mine except today, now—I let Bill get the beers and we talk at a little round table about Samuel Beckett and prose and poetry. Bill thinks Beckett is the end, he talks about it all over, his glasses glint in my eyesight, he has a long serious face, I cant believe he's serious about death but he must be—"I'm dead," he says, "I wrote some poems about death"—

"Well where are they?"

"They're not finished, man."

"Let's go to the Cellar and hear the jazz," so we cut around the corner and just as we walk in the streetdoor I hear them baying down there, a full group of tenors and altos and trumpets riding in for the first chorus— Boom, we walk in just in time for the break, bang, a tenor is taking the solo, the tune is simply "Georgia Brown"—the tenor rides it big and heavy with a big tone— They've come from Fillmore in cars, with their girls or without, the cool colored cats of Sunday San Fran in incredibly beautiful neat sports attire, to knock your eyes out, shoes, lapels, ties, no-ties, studs— They've brought their horns in taxis and in their own cars, pouring down into the Cellar to really give it some class and jazz now, the Negro people who will be the salvation of America—I can see it because the last time I was in the Cellar it was full of surly whites waiting around a desultory jam session to start a fight and finally they did, with my boy Rainey who was knocked out when he wasnt looking by a big mean brutal 250-pound seaman who was famous for getting drunk with Dylan Thomas and Jimmy the Greek in New York— Now everything is too cool for a fight, now it's jazz, the place is roaring, all beautiful girls in there, one mad brunette at the bar drunk with her boys— One strange chick I remember from some-where, wearing a simple skirt with pockets, her hands in there, short haircut, slouched, talking to everybody— Up and down the stairs they come— The bartenders are the regular band of Jack, and the heavenly drummer who looks up in the sky with blue eyes, with a beard, is wailing beer-caps of bottles and jamming on the cash register and every-thing is going to the beat— It's the beat generation, its *béat,* it's the beat to keep, it's the beat of the heart, it's being beat and down in the world

and like oldtime lowdown and like in ancient civilizations the slave
boatmen rowing galleys to a beat and servants spinning pottery to a
beat— The faces! There's no face to compare with Jack Minger's who's
up on the bandstand now with a colored trumpeter who outblows him
wild and Dizzy but Jack's face overlooking all the heads and smoke—
He has a face that looks like everybody you've ever known and seen on
the street in your generation, a sweet face— Hard to describe—sad eyes,
cruel lips, expectant gleam, swaying to the beat, tall, majestical—waiting in front of the drugstore— A face like Huck's in New York (Huck
whom you'll see on Times Square, somnolent and alert, sad-sweet, dark,
beat, just out of jail, martyred, tortured by sidewalks, starved for sex
and companionship, open to anything, ready to introduce new worlds
with a shrug)— The colored big tenor with the big tone would like to
be blowing Sonny Stitts clear out of Kansas City roadhouses, clear,
heavy, somewhat dull and unmusical ideas which nevertheless never
leave the music, always there, far out, the harmony too complicated for
the motley bums (of music-understanding) in there—but the musicians
hear— The drummer is a sensational 12-year-old Negro boy who's not
allowed to drink but can play, tremendous, a little lithe childlike Miles
Davis kid, like early Fats Navarro fans you used to see in Espan Harlem,
hep, small—he thunders at the drums with a beat which is described to
me by a near-standing Negro connoisseur with beret as a "fabulous
beat"— On piano is Blondey Bill, good enough to drive any group—
Jack Minger blows out and over his head with these angels from Fillmore, I dig him— It's terrific—

I just stand in the outside hall against the wall, no beer necessary,
with collections of in-and-out listeners, with Sliv, and now here returns
Chuck Berman (who is a colored kid from West Indies who barged into
my party six months earlier high with Cody and the gang and I had a
Chet Baker record on and we hoofed at each other in the room, tremendous, the perfect grace of his dancing, casual, like Joe Louis casually
hoofing)— He comes now in dancing like that, glad— Everybody looks
everywhere, it's a jazz-joint and beat generation madtrick, you see someone, "Hi," then you look away elsewhere, for something someone else,
it's all insane, then you look back, you look away, around, everything
is coming in from everywhere in the sound of the jazz— "Hi"—
"Hey"—

Bang, the little drummer takes a solo, reaching his young hands all
over traps and kettles and cymbals and foot-peddle BOOM in a fantastic crash of sound—12 years old—what will happen?

Me'n Sliv stand bouncing to the beat and finally the girl in the skirt comes talk to us, it's Gia Valencia, the daughter of the mad Spanish anthropologist sage who'd lived with the Pomo and Pit River Indians of California, famous old man, whom I'd read and revered only three years ago while working the railroad outa San Luis Obispo— "Bug, give me back my shadow!" he yelled on a recorded tape before he died, showing how the Indians made it at brooks in old California pre-history before San Fran and Clark Gable and Al Jolson and Rose Wise Lazuli and the jazz of the mixed generations— Out there's all that sun and shade as same as old doodlebug time, but the Indians are gone, and old Valencia is gone, and all's left is his charming erudite daughter with her hands in her pockets digging the jazz— She's also talking to all the goodlooking men, black and white, she likes em all— They like her— To me she suddenly says "Arent you going to call Irwin Garden?"

"Sure I just got into town!"

"You're Jack Duluoz arent you!"

"And yeah, you're—"

"Gia"

"Ah a Latin name"

"Oh you frightening man," she says seriously, suddenly meaning my impenetrable of myself way of talking to a woman, my glare, my eyebrows, my big lined angry yet crazy eye-gleaming bony face— She really means it—I feel it— Often frighten myself in the mirror— But for some tender chicken to look into my mirror of all-the-woes-you-know . . . it's worse!

She talks to Sliv, he doesnt frighten her, he's sympathetic and sad and serious and she stands there I watch her, the little thin body just faintly feminine and the low pitch of her voice, the charm, the veritable elegant oldworld way she comes on, completely out of place in the Cellar— Should be at Katherine Porter's cocktail—should be exchanging duet-os of art talk in Venice and Fiorenza with Truman Capote, Gore Vidal and Compton-Burnett—should be in Hawthorne's novels— I really like her, I feel her charm, I go over and talk some more—

Alternately bang bang the jazz crashes in to my consciousness and I forget everything and just close my eyes and listen to the ideas—I feel like yelling "Play A Fool Am I!" which would be a great tune— But now they're on some other jam—whatever they feel like, the downbeat, the piano chord, off—

"How can I call Irwin?" I ask her— Then I remember I've got Raphael's phone number (from sweet Sonya in the bookshop) and I slip into the booth with my dime and dial, typical jazz joint stuff, like the time I'd slipped into the booth at Birdland in New York and in the comparative silence suddenly heard Stan Getz, who was in the toilet nearby, blowing his saxophone quietly to the music of Lennie Tristano's group out front, when I realized he could do anything— (Warne Marsh me no Warne Marsh! his music said)—I call Raphael who answers "Yes?"

"*Raphael?* This is Jack—Jack Duluoz!"

"Jack! Where are you?"

"The Cellar—come on down!"

"I cant, I have no money!"

"Cant you walk?"

"*Walk?*"

"I'll call and get Irwin and we'll come over get you in a cab— Call you back half hour!"

I try to call Irwin, it wont do, he's nowhere— Everybody in the Cellar is goofing, now the bartenders are beginning to whip at beers themselves and get flushed and high and drunk— The drunken brunette falls off her stool, her cat carries her to the ladies' room— Fresh gangs roam in— It's mad— And finally to cap everything (O Desolation Me Silent Me) here comes Richard de Chili the insane Richard de Chili who wanders around Frisco at night in long fast strides, all alone, examining the examples of architecture, strange hodgepodge notions and bay windows and garden walls, giggling, alone in the night, doesnt drink, hoards funny soapy candy bars and bits of string in his pockets and half out combs and half toothbrushes and when he comes to sleep at any of our pads he'll burn toothbrushes at the stove jet, or stay in the bathroom hours running water, and brush his hair with assorted brushes, completely homeless, always sleeping on someone's couch and yet once a month he goes to the bank (the night watchman vault) and there's his monthly income waiting for him (the daytime bank's embarrassed), just enough money to live on, left to him by some mysterious unknown elegant family he never talks about— No teeth in the front of his mouth whatever— Crazy clothes, like a scarf around his neck and jeans and a silly jacket he found somewhere with paint on it, and offers you a peppermint candy and it tastes like soap—Richard de Chili, the Mysterious, who was for a long time out of sight (six months earlier) and finally as we're driving down the street we see him striding into a supermarket "There's Richard!" and all jump out to follow him and there he is in the store lifting candybars and cans of peanuts on the sly and not only that he's seen by the Okie storeman and we have to pay his way out and he comes with us with his incomprehensible low-spoken remarks, like, "The moon is a piece of tea," looking up at it in the rumble seat — Whom finally I welcomed to my 6-month-earlier shack in Mill Valley to stay a few days and he takes all the sleepingbags and slings them (except mine, hidden in the grass) over the window, where they tear, so the last time I see my Mill Valley shack as I start hitch hiking for Desolation Peak there's Richard de Chili sleeping in a great roomful of duck feathers, an incredible sight—a typical sight—with his underarm paper bags full of strange esoteric books (one of the most intelligent persons I know in the world) and his soaps and candles and giblets of junk, O my, the catalogue is out of my memory— Who finally took me on a long walk around Frisco one drizzly night to go peek through the street window of an apartment occupied by two homosexual *midgets* (who werent there)—Richard comes in and stands by me and as usual and in the roar I cant hear what he's saying and it doesnt matter anyway— He too goofing nervously, looking around everywhere, everybody reaching for that next kick and there's no next-kick . . .

"What are we gonna do?" I say—

Nobody knows—Sliv, Gia, Richard, the others, they all just stand shuffling around in the Cellar of Time waiting, waiting, like so many Samuel Beckett heroes in the Abyss— Me, I've *got* to do something, go somewhere, establish a rapport, get the talk and the action going, I fidget and shuffle with them—

The beautiful brunette is even worse— Clad so beautifully in a tightfitting black silk dress exhibiting all her perfect dusky charms she comes out of the toilet and falls down again— Crazy characters are milling around— Insane conversations I cant remember anymore, it's too mad!

"I'll give up, I'll go sleep, tomorrow I'll find the gang."

A man and a woman ask us to move over please so they can study the map of San Francisco on the hall wall— "Tourists from Boston, hey?" says Richard, with his witless grin—

I get on the phone again and cant find Irwin so I'll go home to my room in the Bell Hotel and sleep— Like sleep on the mountain, the generations *are* too mad—

Yet Sliv and Richard dont want me to leave, everytime I edge off they follow me, shuffling, we're all shuffling and waiting for nothing, it gets on my nerves— It takes all my willpower and sad regret to say so long to them and cut out into the night—

"Cody'll be at my place at eleven tomorrow," shouts Chuck Berman so I'll make that scene—

At the corner of Broadway and Columbus, in the famous little open eatery, I call Raphael to tell him to meet me in the morning at Chuck's— "Okay—but listen! While I was waiting for you I wrote a poem! A terrific poem! It's all about you! I address it to you! Can I read it to you over the phone?"

"Go ahead"

"*Spit* on Bosatsu!" he yells. "*Spit* on Bosatsu!"

"Oo," I say, "that's beautiful"

"The poem is called 'To Jack Duluoz, Buddha-fish'— Here's the way it goes—" And reads me this long insane poem over the phone as I stand there against the counter of hamburgs, as he yells and reads (and I take in every word, every meaning of this Lower Eastside New York Italian genius reborn from the Renaissance) I think "O God, how sad! —I have poet friends who yell me their poems in cities—it's just as I predicted on the mount, it's celebrating in cities upsidedown—

"Sweet, Raphael, great, you're a greater poet than ever—you're really going now—great—dont stop—remember to write without stopping, without thinking, just go, I wanta hear what's in the bottom of your mind."

"And that's what I'm doing, see?—do you dig it? do you under*stand?*" The way he says "under*stand,*" like, "stahnd," like Frank Sinatra, like something New York, like something new in the world, a real down-from-the-bottom city Poet at last, like Christopher Smart and Blake, like Tom O Bedlam, the song of the streets and of the alley cats, the great great Raphael Urso who'd made me so mad in 1953 when he made it with my girl—but whose fault was that? mine as much as theirs—it's all recorded in *The Subterraneans*—

"Great great Raphael I'll see you tomorra— Let's sleep and be silent— Let's dig silence, silence is the end, I've had it all summer, I'll teach you."

"Great, great, I dig that you dig silence," comes his sad enthusiastic voice over the pitiful telephone machine, "it makes me sad to think you dig silence, but I will dig silence, believe it, I *will*"—

I go to my room to sleep.

And lo! There's the old night clerk, an old Frenchman, I dont know his name, when Mal my buddy used to live in the Bell (and we'd drink big toasts of port wine to Omar Khayyam and pretty girls with short haircuts in his bulb-hanging room) this old man used to be angry all

the time and screaming at us incoherently, annoyed— Now, two years
later, he's completely changed and with it his back has bent all the way,
he's 75 and walks completely bent over muttering down the hall to
unlock your transient room, he's completely sweetened, death is soothing his eyelids, he's seen the light, he's no longer mad and annoyed—
He smiles sweetly even when I come on him (1 A.M.) standing bent on
a chair trying to fix the clerk cage clock— Comes down painfully and
leads me to my room—

"*Vous êtes francais, monsieur?*" I say. "*Je suis francais moimême.*"

In his new sweetness is also new Buddha-blankness, he doesnt even
answer, he just unlocks my door and smiles sadly, way down bent, and
says "Good night, sir—everything all right, sir"— I'm amazed—
Crotchety for 73 years and now he'll bide right out of time with a few
dewdrop sweet years and they'll bury him all bent in his tomb (I dont
know how) and I would bring him flowers— *Will* bring him flowers a
million years from now—

In my room invisible eternal golden flowers drop on my head as I
sleep, they drop everywhere, they are Ste. Terese's roses showering and
pouring everywhere on the heads of the world— Even the shufflers and
madcaps, even the snarling winos in alleys, even the bleating mice still
in my attic a thousand miles and six thousand feet up in Desolation,
even on the least her roses shower, perpetually— We all know that in
our sleep.

78

I sleep a good solid ten hours and wake up roses-refreshed— But I'm
late for my meet with Cody and Raphael and Chuck Berman—I jump
up and put on my little checkered cotton shortsleeved sportshirt, my
canvas jacket over that, and my chino pants, and hurry out into the
bright ruffling Monday Morning harbor wind— What a city of whites
and blues!—What air!— Great churchbells bonging, the hint of tinkling
flutes from Chinatown markets, the incredible Old Italy scene on Broadway where old dark-garmented Wops gather with twisted black little
cigarillos and chot the black coffee— It's their dark shadows on the
white sidewalk in the clean bell-ringing air, with white ships seen
coming in the Golden Gate down below the etched Rimbaud milky
rooftops—

It's the wind, the cleanness, great stores like Buon Gusto's with all
the hanging salamis and provelones and assortments of wine, and veg-

etable bins—and the marvelous oldworld pastry shops—then the view of the tangled wood tenement child-screaming daydrowsy Telegraph Hill—

I swing along on my new heavenly softsoled canvas blueshoes ("Oog, like the shoes queers wear!" comments Raphael next day) and lo! there's bearded Irwin Garden coming down the opposite side of the street— Wow!—I yell and whistle and wave, he sees me and throws out his arms with rounded eyes and comes running across the traffic with that peculiar gazotsky run of his, flapping feet—but his face is immense and serious surrounded by a great solemn Abrahamic beard and his eyes are steady in a candlesteady gleam in their ogling sockets, and his sensuous fulsome red mouth shows out thru the beard like the poopoo lips of old prophets about to say something— Long ago I'd dug him as a Jewish prophet wailing at the final wall, now it was official, a big article had just been written about him in the New York *Times* mentioning that— The author of "Howling," a big wild free verse poem about all of us beginning with the lines:—

"*I have seen the best minds of my generation destroy'd by madness*"—etc.

But I never know what he means by mad, like, he had a vision in a Harlem pad in 1948 one night of a "giant machine descending from the sky," a big ark-dove of his imagination, and keeps saying "But do you realize the state of mind I was in—have you ever really had a real vision?"

"Sure, whattayou mean?"

I never understand what he's driving at and sometimes I suspect he's Jesus of Nazareth reborn, sometimes I get mad and think he's only Dostoevsky's poor devil in poorclothes, giggling in the room— An early idealistic hero of my days, who'd come on the scene of my life at 17— I remember the strangeness of the firmness of his voice-tone even then — He talks low, distinct, excited—but he looks a little pooped with all his San Francisco excitement which for that matter will wear me out in 24 hours— "Guess who's in town?"

"I know, Raphael—I'm going there to meet him and Cody now."

"Cody?—where?"

"Chuck Berman's pad—everybody's there—I'm late—let's hurry"

We talk a million forgettable little things as we race, almost run up the sidewalk—Desolation Jack is now ankling along with a bearded compatriot—my roses wait—"Simon and I are going to Europe!" he announces. "Why dont you come with us! My mother left me a thousand dollars. I've got another thousand saved! We'll all go visit the Old World Strange!"

"Okay with me"—"I've got a few bucks too— Might as well— About time, hey ole buddy?"

For Irwin and I had discussed and dreamed Europe, and of course read everything, even unto the "weeping on the old stones of Europe" of Dostoevsky and the gutters-saturated-with-symbols of early Rimbaud excitements when we wrote poems and ate potato soup together (1944) on the Columbia Campus, even unto Genêt and the Apache heroes— even unto Irwin's own sad dreams of spectral visits to a Europe all drenched with old rain and woe, and standing on the Eiffel Tower feeling silly and effete— Arm over each other's shoulder we hurry up the hill to Chuck Berman's streetdoor, knock and walk in— There's Richard de Chili on the couch, as foretold, turning around to give us a weak grin— A couple other cats with Chuck in the kitchen, one a crazy Indian with black hair who wants change for a poorboy, a French-Canadian like me, I'd talked to him the night before in the Cellar and he'd called out "So long brother!"— Now it's "Good morning brother!" and we're all milling around, no Raphael there yet, Irwin suggests we go down to the hep coffee place and meet everybody there—

"They all go there anyway"

But nobody's there so we head for the bookstore and bang! up Grant here comes Raphael with his John Garfield long-stride and swinging arms, talking and yelling as he comes, bursting all over with poems, we're all yelling at the same time— We mill around bumping into one another, across streets, down streets, looking for a place to drink coffee—

We go in the coffee joint (on Broadway) and sit in a booth and out come all the poems and books and bang! here comes a redheaded girl and behind her Cody—

"Jackson me boyyyy" says Cody as usual imitating old W. C. Fields railroad conductors—

"Cody! Aye! Sit down! Wow! Everything's happening!"

For it comes, it always comes in great vibrating seasons.

. . .

PART THREE
PASSING THROUGH TANGIERS

50

What a crazy picture, maybe the picture of the typical American, sitting on a boat mulling over fingernails wondering where to really go, what to do next—I suddenly realized I had nowhere to turn at all.

But it was on this trip that the great change took place in my life which I called a "complete turningabout" on that earlier page, turning from a youthful brave sense of adventure to a complete nausea concerning experience in the world at large, a *revulsion* in all the six senses. And as I say the first sign of that revulsion had appeared during the dreamy solitary comfort of the two months on Desolation mountain, before Mexico, since which time I'd been melanged again with all my friends and old adventures, as you saw, and not so 'sweetly,' but now I was alone again. And the same feeling came to me: Avoid the World, it's just a lot of dust and drag and means nothing in the end. But what to do instead? And here I was relentlessly being carried to further "adventures" across the sea. But it was really in Tangiers after an overdose of opium the turningabout really clicked down and locked. In a minute—but meanwhile another experience, at sea, put the fear of the world in me, like an omen warning. This was a huge tempest that whacked at our C-4 from the North, from the Januaries and Pleniaries of Iceland and Baffin Bay. During wartime I'd actually sailed in those Northern seas of the Arctic but it was only in summertime: now, a thousand miles south of these in the void of January Seas, gloom, the cappers came glurring in gray spray as high as a house and plowed rivers all over our bow and down the washes. Furyiating howling Blakean glooms, thunders of thumping, washing waving sick manship diddling like a long cork for nothing in the mad waste. Some old Breton knowledge of the sea still in my blood now shuddered. When I saw those walls of water advancing one by one for miles in gray carnage I cried in my soul WHY DIDNT I STAY HOME!? But it was too late. When the third night came the ship was heaving from side to side so badly even the Yugoslavs went to bed and jammed themselves down between pillows and blankets. The kitchen was insane all night with crashing and toppling pots even tho they'd been secured. It scares a seaman to hear the Kitchen scream in fear. For eating at first the steward had placed dishes on a wet tablecloth, and of course no soup in soupbowls but in deep cups, but now it was too late for even that. The men chewed at biscuits as they staggered to their knees in their wet sou'westers. Out on deck where I went a minute the heel of the ship was enough to kick you over the gunwale straight *at* walls of water, sperash. Deck lashed trucks groaned and broke their cables and smashed around. It was a Biblical Tempest like an old dream. In the night I prayed with fear to God Who was now taking all of us, the souls on board, at this dread particular time, for reasons of His own, at last. In my semi delirium I thought I saw a snow white ladder being held down to us from the sky. I saw Stella Maris over the Sea like a statue of Liberty in all shining white. I thought of all the sailors that ever drowned and O the choking thought of it, from Phoenicians of 3000 years ago to poor little teenage sailors of America only last war (some of whom I'd sailed in safety with)— The carpets of sinking water all deep blue *green* in the middle of the ocean, with their damnable patterns of foam, the sickening choking *too-much* of it even tho you're only looking at the surface—beneath all that the upwell of cold miles of fathoms—swaying, rolling, smashing, the tonnages of Peligroso Roar beating, heaving, swirling—not a face in sight! Here comes more! Duck! The whole ship (only as long as a Village) ducks into it shuddering, the crazy screws furiously turn in nothingness, shaking the ship, slap, the bow's now up, thrown up, the screws are dreaming deep below, the ship hasnt gained ten feet—it's like that— It's like frost in your face, like the cold mouths of ancient fathers, like wood cracking in the sea. Not even a fish in sight. It's the thunderous jubilation of Neptune and his bloody wind god canceling men. "All I had to do was stay home, give it all up, get a little home for me and Ma, meditate, live quiet, read in the sun, drink wine in the moon in old clothes, pet my kitties, sleep good dreams—now look at this *petrain* I got me in, Oh dammit!" ("Petrain" is a 16th Century French word meaning "mess.") But God chose to let us live as at dawn the captain turned the ship the other way and gradually left the storm behind, then headed back east towards Africa and the stars.

51

I feel I didnt explain that right, but it's too late, the moving finger crossed the storm and that's the storm.

I thereafter spent ten quiet days as that old freighter chugged and chugged across the calmest seas without seeming to get anywhere and

I read a book on world history, wrote notes, and paced the deck at night. (How insouciantly they write about the sinking of the Spanish fleet in the storm off Ireland, ugh!) (Or even one little Galilean fisherman, drowned forever.) But even in so peaceful and simple an act as reading world history in a comfortable cabin on comfortable seas I felt that awful revulsion for everything—the insane things done in human history even before us, enough to make Apollo cry or Atlas drop his load, my God the massacres, purges, tithes stolen, thieves hanged, crooks imperatored, dubs praetorian'd, benches busted on people's heads, wolves attacked nomad campfires, Genghiz Khans ruining— testes smashed in battle, women raped in smoke, children belted, animals slaughtered, knives raised, bones thrown— Clacking big slurry meatjuiced lips the dub Kings crapping on everybody thru silk— The beggars crapping thru burlap— The mistakes everywhere the mistakes! The smell of old settlements and their cookpots and dungheaps—The Cardinals like "Silk stockings full of mud," the American congressmen who "shine and stink like rotten mackerel in the moonlight"— The scalpings from Dakota to Tamurlane— And the human eyes at Guillotine and burning stake at dawn, the glooms, bridges, mists, nets, raw hands and old dead vests of poor mankind in all these thousands of years of "history" (they call it) and all of it an awful mistake. Why did God do it? or is there really a Devil who led the Fall? Souls in Heaven said "We want to try mortal existence, O God, Lucifer said it's great!"—Bang, down we fall, to this, to concentration camps, gas ovens, barbed wire, atom bombs, television murders, Bolivian starvation, thieves in silk, thieves in neckties, thieves in office, paper shufflers, bureaucrats, insult, rage, dismay, horror, terrified nightmares, secret death of hangovers, cancer, ulcers, strangulation, pus, old age, old age homes, canes, puffed flesh, dropped teeth, stink, tears, and goodbye. Somebody else write it, I dont know how.

How to live with glee and peace therefore? By roaming around with your baggage from state to state each one worse deeper into the darkness of the fearful heart? And the heart only a thumping tube all delicately murderable with snips of artery and vein, with chambers that shut, finally someone eats it with the knife and fork of malice, laughing. (Laughing for awhile anyway.)

Ah but as Julien would say "There's nothing you can do about it, revel in it boy— Bottoms up in every way, Fernando." I think of Fernando his puffed alcoholic eyes like mine looking out on bleak palmettos at dawn, shivering in his scarf: beyond the last Frisian Hill a big scythe is cutting down the daisies of his hope tho he's urged to celebrate this each New Years Eve in Rio or in Bombay. In Hollywood they swiftly slide the old director in his crypt. Aldous Huxley half blind watches his house burn down, seventy years old and far from the happy walnut chair of Oxford. Nothing, nothing, nothing O but *nothing* could interest me any more for one god damned minute in anything in the *world*. But where else to go?

On the overdose of opium this was intensified to the point where I actually got up and packed to go back to America and find a *home*.

52

At first the sea fear slept, I actually enjoyed the approach to Africa and of course I had a ball the first week in Africa.

It was sunny afternoon February 1957 when we first saw the pale motleys of yellow sand and green meadow which marked the vague little coast line of Africa far away. It grew bigger as the afternoon drowsed on till a white spot that had troubled me for hours turned out to be a gas tank in the hills. Then like seeing sudden slow files of Mohammedan women in white I saw the white roofs of the little port of Tangiers sitting right there in the elbow of the land, on the water. This dream of white robed Africa on the blue afternoon Sea, wow, who dreamed it? Rimbaud! Magellan! Delacroix! Napoleon! White sheets waving on the rooftop!

And suddenly a small Moroccan fishing boat with a motor but a high balconied poop in carved Lebanese wood, with cats in jalabas and pantaloons chattering on deck, came plopping by turning south down the Coast for the evening's fishing beneath the star (now) of Stella Maris, Mary of the Sea who protects all fishermen by investing with grace of hope in the dangers of the sea her own Archangelic prayer of Safety. And some Mahomet Star of the Sea of their own to guide them. The wind ruffled on their clothes, their hair, "their real hair of real Africa" I said to myself amazed. (Why travel if not like a child?)

Now Tangiers grew, you saw sandy barrens of Spain on the left, the hump leading to Gibraltar around the Horn of Hesperid, the very amazing spot the entryway to the Mediterranean Atlantis of old flooded by the Ice Caps so celebrate in the Book of Noah. Here's where Mister Hercules held the world up groaning as "rough rocks groaning vegetate" (Blake). Here the patch-eyed international gem smugglers sneaked up with blue .45's to steal the Tangier harem. Here the crazy Scipios

came to trounce the blue eyed Carthage. Somewhere in that sand beyond the Atlas Range I saw my blue eyed Gary Cooper winning the
"Beau Geste." And a night in Tangiers with Hubbard!

The ship anchored in the sweet little harbor and spun slowly around
giving me all kinds of views of city and headland from my porthole as
I packed to leave the ship. On the headland around Tangiers Bay was
a beacon turning in the blue dusk like St. Mary assuring me port is
made and all's all safe. The city turns on magical little lights, the hill of
the Casbah hums, I wanta be out there in those narrow Medina alleys
looking for hasheesh. The first Arab I see is too ridiculous to believe: a
little bum boat puts out to our Jacob's Ladder, the motor men ragged
teenage Arabs in sweaters like the sweaters of Mexico, but in the mid
boat stands a fat Arab in a grimy red fez, in a blue business suit, hands
behind him, looking for to sell cigarettes or buy something or anything
at all. Our handsome Yugo captain shouts them away from the bridge.
At about seven we dock and I go ashore. Big Arabic Letterings are
stamped on my fresh innocent passport by clerks in dusty fezzes and
baggy pants. In fact it's exactly like Mexico, the Fellaheen world, that
is, the world that's not making History in the present: *making* History,
manufacturing it, shooting it up in H bombs and Rockets, reaching for
the grand conceptual finale of Highest Achievement (in our times the
Faustian "West" of America, Britain and Germany high and low).

I get a cab to Hubbard's address on a narrow hilly street in the
European quarter beneath the Medina twinkle hill.

Poor Bull has been on a health kick and is already asleep at 9:30
when I knock on his garden door. I'm amazed to see him strong and
healthy, no longer skinny from drugs, all tanned and muscular and vigorous. He's six foot one, blue eyes, glasses, sandy hair, 44, a scion of a
great American industrial family but they've only a-scioned him a $200
a month trust fund and are soon to cut that down to $120, finally two
years later rejecting him completely from their interior decorated livingrooms in retirement Florida because of the mad book he's written and
published in Paris (*Nude Supper*) —a book enough to make any mother
turn pale (more anon). Bull grabs his hat and says "Come on, let's go
dig the Medina" (after we turn on) and vigorously striding like an insane
German Philologist in Exile he leads me thru the garden and out the
gate to the little magic street. "Tomorrow morning first thing after I've
had my simple breakfast of tea and bread, we'll go rowing in the Bay."

This is a command. This is the first time I've seen "Old Bull" (actually a friend of the "Old Bull" in Mexico) since the days in New

Orleans when he was living with his wife and kids near the Levee (in Algiers Louisiana)— He doesnt seem any older except he doesnt seem to comb his hair as carefully any more, which I realize the next day is only because he's distraught and completely bemused in the midst of his writing, like a mad haired genius in a room. He's wearing American Chino pants and pocketed shirts, a fisherman's hat, and carries a huge clicking switchblade a foot long. "Yessir, without this switchblade I'd be dead now. Bunch of Ay-rabs surrounded me in an alley one night. I just let this old thing click out and said 'Come on ya buncha bastards' and they cut out."

"How do you *like* the Arabs?"

"Just push em aside like little pricks" and suddenly he walked right thru a bunch of Arabs on the sidewalk, making them split on both sides, muttering and swinging his arms with a vigorous unnatural pumping motion like an insane exaggerated Texas oil millionaire pushing his way thru the Swarms of Hong Kong.

"Come on Bull, you cant do that every day."

"*What?*" he barked, almost squeaking. "Just brush em aside, son, dont take no shit from them little pricks." But by next day I realized *everybody* was a little prick:—me, Irwin, himself, the Arabs, the women, the merchants, the President of the U.S.A. and Ali Baba himself: Ali Baba or whatever his name was, a child leading a flock of sheep in the field and carrying a baby lamb in his arms with a sweet expression like the expression of St. Joseph when he himself was a child:—"Little prick!" I realized it was just an expression, a sadness on Bull's part that he would never regain the innocence of the Shepherd or in fact of the little prick.

Suddenly as we climbed the hill of white street steps I remembered an old sleeping dream where I climbed such steps and came to a Holy City of Love. "Do you mean to tell me that my life is going to change after all that?" I say to myself, (high), but suddenly to the right there was a big Kaplow! (hammer into steel) ca blam! and I looked into the black inky maw of a Tangiers garage and the white dream died right there, for good, right in the greasy arm of a big Arab mechanic crashing furiously at the fenders and hems of Fords in the oil rag gloom under one Mexican lightbulb. I kept on climbing the holy steps with weariness, to the next horrible disappointment. Bull kept yelling back "Come on, step on it, young man like you cant even keep up with old man like me?"

"You *walk* too fast!"

"Lard assed hipsters, aint no good for nothin!" says Bull.

We walk almost running down a steep hill of grass and boulders, with a path, to a magical little street with African tenements and again I'm hit in the eye by an old magic dream: "I was born here: This is the street where I was born." I even look up at the exact tenement window to see if my crib's still there. (Man, that hasheesh in Bull's room—and it's amazing how American potsmokers have gone around the world by now with the most exaggerated phantasmagoria of gooey details, hallucinations actually, by which their machine-ridden brains though are actually given a little juice of the ancient life of man, so God bless pot.) ("If you were born on this street you musta drowned a long time ago," I add, thinking.)

Bull goes arm swinging and swaggering like a Nazi into the first queer bar, brushing Arabs aside and looking back at me with: "Hey what?" I cant see how he can have managed this except I learn later he's spent a whole year in the little town sitting in his room on huge overdoses of morfina and other drugs staring at the tip of his shoe too scared to take one shuddering bath in eight months. So the local Arabs remember him as a shuddering skinny ghost who's apparently recovered, and let him rant. Everybody seems to know him. Boys yell "Hi" "Boorows!" "Hey!"

In the dim queer bar which is also the lunching spot of most of the queer Europeans and Americans of Tangiers with limited means, Hubbard introduces me to the big fat Dutch middleaged owner who threatens to return to Amsterdam if he dont find a good "poy" very soon, as I mentioned in an article elsewhere. He also complains about the declining peseta but I can surely see him moaning in his private bed at night for love or something in the sorry *internationale* of his night. Dozens of weird expatriates, coughing and lost on the cobbles of Moghreb—some of them sitting at the outdoor cafe tables with the glum look of foreigners reading zigzag newspapers over unwanted Vermouth. Ex-smugglers with skipper hats straggling by. No joyful Moroccan tambourine anywhere. Dust in the street. The same old fish heads everywhere.

Hubbard also introduces me to his lover, a boy of 20 with a sweet sad smile just the type poor Bull has always loved, from Chicago to Here. We have a few drinks and go back to his room.

"Tomorrow the Frenchwoman who runs this pension will probably rent you that excellent room on the roof with bath and patio, my dear. I prefer being down here in the garden so I can play with the cats and

I'm growing some roses." The cats, two, belong to the Chinese house-keeper who does the cleaning for the shady lady from Paris, who owns the apartment building on some old Roulette bet or some old rearview of the Bourse, or something—but later I find all the real work is done by the big Nubian Negress who lives in the cellar (I mean, if you wanted big romantic novels about Tangiers.)

53

But no time for that! Bull insists we go rowing. We pass whole cafes of sour Arab men on the waterfront, they're all drinking green mint tea in glasses and chain smoking pipes of kief (marijuana)— They watch us pass with those strange redrimmed eyes, as tho they were half Moorish and half Carthaginian (half Berber)— "God those guys must hate us, for some reason."

"No," says Bull, "they're just waiting for someone to run amok. D'jever see an amok trot? An amok occurs here periodically. He is a man who suddenly picks up a machete and starts trotting thru the market with a regular monotonous trot slashing people as he passes. He usually kills or maims about a dozen before these characters of the cafes get wind of it and get up and rush after him and tear him to bits. In between that they smoke their endless pipes of pot."

"What they think of you trottin down to the waterfront every morning to rent a boat?"

"Somewhere among them is the guy that gets the profits—" Some boys are tending rowboats at the quai. Bull gives them money and we get in and Bull rows off vigorously, standing facing forward, like a Venetian oarsman. "When I was in Venice I noticed that this is the only real way to row a boat, standing up, boom and bam, like this," rowing with forward motion. "Outside of that Venice is the dreariest town this side of Beeville Texas. Dont ever go to Beeville boy, or Venice either." (Beeville a sheriff'd caught him making love to his wife June in the car, parked on the highway, for which he spent two days in jail with a sinister deputy in steel rimmed spectacles.) "Venice—my God, on a clear night you can hear the shrieks of the fairies on St. Marks Plaza a mile away. You can see successful young novelists being rowed away into the night. In the middle of the Canal they suddenly assault the poor Italian Gondoleer. They have palazzos with people straight out of Princeton amortifyin' chauffeurs." The funny thing is that when Bull was in Venice he was invited to an elegant party in a Palace, and when

he appeared at the door, with his old Harvard friend Irwin Swenson
the hostess held out her hand to be kissed—Irwin Swenson said: "You
see in these circles you must kiss the hand of the hostess, customarily"
— But as everybody stared at the pause in the door Bull yelled out "Aw
gee, I'd rather kiss her *cont!*" And that was the end of that.

There he is rowing energetically as I sit on the poop digging Tangiers Bay. Suddenly a boatload of Arab boys rows up and they yell in
Spanish to Bull: "*Tu nuevo amigo Americano? Quieren muchachos?*"

"No, *quieren mucha*-CHAS'"

"*Por que?*"

"*Es macho por muchachas mucho!*"

"Ah," they all wave their hands and row away, looking for money
from visiting queers, they'd asked Hubbard if I was queer. Bull rowed
on but suddenly he was tired and had me row. We were nearing the
end of the harbor wall. The water got choppy. "Ah shit, I'm tired."

"Well for God's sake make a little effort to get us back a ways."
Bull was already tired and wanted to go back to his room to make
majoun and write his book.

54

Majoun is a candy you make with honey, spices and raw marijuana
(kief)— Kief is actually mostly stems with fewer leaves of the plant
chemically known as Muscarine— Bull rolled it all up into edible balls
and we ate it, chewing for hours, picking it out of our teeth with tooth-
picks, drinking it down with hot plain tea— In two hours our eyes'
irises would get huge and black and off we'd go walking to the fields
outside town— A tremendous high giving vent to many colored sensations like, "Notice the delicate white shade of those flowers under the
tree." We stood under the tree overlooking the Bay of Tangiers. "I get
many visions at this spot," says Bull, serious now, telling me about his
book.

In fact I hung around his room several hours a day altho I now
had a great room on the roof, but he wanted me to hang around about
noon till two, then cocktails and dinner and most of the evening together (a very formal man) so I happened to be sitting on his bed reading
when often, while typing out his story, he'd suddenly double up in
laughter at what he done and sometimes roll on the floor. A strange
compressed laugh came out of his stomach as he typed. But so wont no
Truman Capote think he's only a typewriter, sometimes he'd whip out

his pen and start scribbling on typewriter pages which he threw over his shoulder when he was through with them, like Doctor Mabuse, till the floor was littered with the strange Etruscan script of his handwriting. Meanwhile as I say his hair was all askew, but as that was the gist of my worries about him he twice or thrice looked up from his writing and said to me with frank blue eyes "You know you're the only person in the world who can sit in the room while I'm writing and I dont even know you're *there?*" A great compliment, too. The way I did it was to concentrate on my own thoughts and just dream away, mustn't disturb Bull. "All of a sudden I look up from this horrible pun and there you are reading a label on a bottle of Cognac."

I'll leave the book for the reader to see, *Nude Supper,* all about shirts turning blue at hangings, castration, and lime— Great horrific scenes with imaginary doctors of the future tending machine catatonics with negative drugs so they can wipe the world out of people but when that's accomplished the Mad Doctor is alone with a self operated self tape recording he can change or edit at will, but no one left, not even Chico the Albino Masturbator in a Tree, to notice— Whole legions of shitters patched up like bandaged scorpions, something like that, you'll have to read it yourself, but so horrible that when I undertook to start typing it neatly doublespace for his publishers the following week I had horrible nightmares in my roof room—like of pulling out endless bolognas from my mouth, from my very entrails, feet of it, pulling and pulling out all the horror of what Bull saw, and wrote.

You may talk to me about Sinclair Lewis the great American writer, or Wolfe, or Hemingway, or Faulkner, but none of them were as honest, unless you name . . . but it aint Thoreau either.

"Why are all these young boys in white shirts being hanged in limestone caves?"

"Dont ask me—I get these messages from other planets—I'm apparently some kind of agent from another planet but I havent got my orders clearly decoded yet."

"But why all the vile rheum—like r-h-e-u-m."

"I'm shitting out my educated Middlewest background for once and for all. It's a matter of catharsis where I say the most horrible thing I can think of— Realize that, the most *horrible* dirty slimy awful niggardliest posture possible— By the time I finish this book I'll be as pure as an angel, my dear. These great existential anarchists and terrorists socalled never even their own drippy fly *mentioneth,* dear— They should poke sticks thru their shit and analyze *that* for social progress."

"But where'll all this shit get us?"

"Simply get us rid of shit, *really Jack*." He whips out (it's 4 P.M.) the afternoon's apéritif cognac bottle. We both sigh to see it. Bull has suffered so much.

• • •

56

And I had really liked Tangiers, the fine Arabs who never even looked at me in the street but minded their eyes to themselves (unlike Mexico which is *all* eyes), the great roof room with tile patio looking down on the little dreamy Spanish Moroccan tenements with an empty lot hill that had a shackled goat grazing— The view over those roofs to the Magic Bay with its sweep to the Headland Ultimo, on clear days the distant shadow mump of Gibraltar far away— The sunny mornings I'd sit on the patio enjoying my books, my kief and the Catholic churchbells— Even the kids' basketball games I could see by leaning far over and around and—or down straight I'd look to Bull's garden, see his cats, himself mulling a minute in the sun— And on heavenly starlit nights just to lean on the roof rail (concrete) and look to sea till sometimes often I saw glittering boats putting in from Casablanca I felt the trip had been worthwhile. But now on the opium overdose I felt snarling dreary thoughts about all Africa, all Europe, the world—all I wanted somehow now was Wheaties by a pine breeze kitchen window in America, that is, I guess a vision of my childhood in America— Many Americans suddenly sick in foreign lands must get the same childlike yen, like Wolfe suddenly remembering the lonely milkman's bottle clink at dawn in North Carolina as he lies there tormented in an Oxford room, or Hemingway suddenly seeing the autumn leaves of Ann Arbor in a Berlin brothel. Scott Fitz tears coming into his eyes in Spain to think of his father's old shoes in the farmhouse door. Johnny Smith the Tourist wakes up drunk in a cracked Istanbul room crying for ice cream sodas of Sunday Afternoon in Richmond Hill Center.

So by the time Irwin and Simon finally arrived for their big triumphant reunion with us in Africa, it was too late. I was spending more and more time on my roof and now actually reading Van Wyck Brooks' books (all about the lives of Whitman, Bret Harte, even Charles Nimrod of South Carolina) to get the feel of home, forgetting entirely how bleak and grim it had been only a short while ago like in Roanoke Rapids the lost tears— But it *has* been ever since then that I've lost my yen for any further outside searching. Like Archbishop of Canterbury says "A constant detachment, a will to go apart and wait upon God in quiet and silence," which more or less describes his own feeling (he being Dr. Ramsey the scholar) about retirement in this gadfly world. At the time I sincerely believed that the only decent activity in the world was to pray for everyone, in solitude. I had many mystic joys on my roof, even while Bull or Irwin were waiting for me downstairs, like the morning I felt the whole living world ripple joyfully and all the dead things rejoice. Sometimes when I saw the priests watching me from seminary windows, where they too leaned looking to sea, I thought they knew about me already (happy paranoia). I thought they rang the bells with special fervor. The best moment of the day was to slip in bed with bedlamp over book, and read facing the open patio windows, the stars and the sea. I could also hear it sighing out there.

• • •

58

My money came and it was time to go but there's poor Irwin at midnight calling up to me from the garden "Come on down Jack-Kee, there's a big bunch of hipsters and chicks from Paris in Bull's room." And just like in New York or Frisco or anywhere there they are all hunching around in marijuana smoke, talking, the cool girls with long thin legs in slacks, the men with goatees, all an enormous drag after all and at the time (1957) not even started yet officially with the name of "Beat Generation." To think that I had so much to do with it, too, in fact at that very moment the manuscript of *Road* was being linotyped for imminent publication and I was already sick of the whole subject. Nothing can be more dreary than "coolness" (not Irwin's cool, or Bull's or Simon's, which is natural quietness) but postured, actually secretly *rigid* coolness that covers up the fact that the character is unable to convey anything of force or interest, a kind of sociological coolness soon to become a fad up into the mass of middleclass youth for awhile. There's even a kind of insultingness, probably unintentional, like when I said to the Paris girl just fresh she said from visiting a Persian Shah for Tiger hunt "Did you actually shoot the tiger yourself?" she gave me a cold look as tho I'd just tried to kiss her at the window of a Drama School. Or tried to trip the Huntress. Or *something*. But all I could do was sit on the edge of the bed in despair like Lazarus listening to their awful "likes" and "like you know" and "wow crazy" and "a wig, man" "a real gas"— All this was about to sprout out all over America even down to High School level and be attributed in part to my doing! But Irwin paid no attention to all that and just wanted to know what they were thinking anyway.

Lying on the bed stretched out as tho gone forever was Joe Portman son of a famous travel writer who said to me "I hear you're going to Europe. How about traveling with me on the Packet? We'll get tickets this week."

"Okay."

Meanwhile the Parisian jazz musician was explaining that Charley Parker wasnt disciplined enough, that jazz needed European classical patterns to give it depth, which sent me upstairs whistling "Scrapple," "Au Privave" and "I Get a Kick."

• • •

63

So I raced out of New York and down South to get my mother, loaded with another publisher's installment ($100)— Just stopping long enough to spend two days with Alyce who was now soft and pretty in a Spring-time dress and glad to see me— A few beers, a few lovings, a few whispered words in ear, and off I was to my "new life" promising I'd see her soon.

My mother and I packed all the pitiful junks of life and called the movers giving them the only Californian address I knew, Ben Fagan's cottage in Berkeley—I figured we'd go there by bus, all three thousand awful miles of it, rent an apartment in Berkeley and have plenty of time to re-route the movers to our new home which I promised myself would be my final glad sanctuary (hoping for pine trees).

Our "junk" consisted of old clothes I never would wear again, cartons of old manuscripts of mine some from 1939 with the paper already yellowed, pitiful heat lamps and *overshoes* of all things (overshoes of old New England), bottles of shaving lotion and holy water, even light-bulbs saved from years ago, old smoking pipes of mine, a basketball, a baseball glove, my God even a bat, old curtains that had never been put up for lack of a home, rolled-up useless rag rugs, books weighing a ton (even old editions of Rabelais with no covers) and all kinds of inconceivable pots and pans and sad shifts that people somehow need to keep to go on— Because I still remember the America when men traveled with nothing but a paperbag for luggage, always tied with string—I still remember the America of people waiting in line for coffee and donuts— The America of 1932 when people foraged in riverside dumps looking for junk to sell— When my father sold neckties or dug ditches for the W.P.A.— When old men with burlap bags at night fwished thru garbage cans or collected rare horse dung in the streets— When yams were something to joy about. But here it was 1957 prosperous America and people laughing at all our junk in the center of which nevertheless my mother'd hidden her essential sewing basket, her essential crucifix, and her essential family photo album— Not to mention her essential salt shaker, pepper shaker, sugar shaker (all full) and her essential bar of soap already half used, all wrapped in the essential sheets and blankets of beds not yet seen.

64

Here now I'm telling about the most important person in this whole story and the best. I've noticed how most of my fellow writers all seem to "hate" their mothers and make big Freudian or sociological philosophies around that, in fact using it as the straight theme of their fantasies, or at least saying as much—I often wonder if they've ever slept till four in the afternoon and woke up to see their mother darning their socks in a sad window light, or come back from revolutionary horrors of weekends to see her mending the rips in a bloody shirt with quiet eternal bowed head over needle— And not with martyred pose of resentment, either, but actually seriously bemused over *mending,* the mending of torture and folly and all loss, mending the very days of your life with almost glad purposeful gravity— And when it's cold she puts on that shawl, and mends on, and on the stove potatoes are burbling forever— Making some neurotics go mad to see such sanity in a room— Making *me* mad sometimes because I'd been so foolish tearing shirts and losing shoes and losing and tearing hope to tatters in that silly thing called *wild*— "You've got to have an escape valve!" Julien'd often yelled at me, "let out that steam or go mad!" tearing my shirt, only to have Memère two days later sitting in her chair mending that very shirt just because it was a shirt and it was mine, her son's— Not to make me feel guilty but to fix the shirt— Though it always made me feel guilty to hear her say: "It was such a nice shirt, I paid $3.25 for it in Woolworth's, why do you let those nuts tear at your shirt like that. *Ça pas d'bon sens.*" And if the shirt was beyond repair she'd always wash it and put it away "for patching" or to make a rag rug with. In one of her rag rugs I recognized three decades of tortured life not only by myself but herself, my father, my sister. She'd have sewn up the grave and used it if possible. As for food, nothing went wasted: an odd potato half eaten ends up delightfully tidbit fried by a piece of later meat, or a quarter of an onion finds its way into a jar of home-pickled onions or old corners of roastbeef into a delicious homey burbling fricassee. Even a torn old handkerchief is washed and mended and better to blow your nose in than ten thousand crinkly new Brooks Brothers Handker-chiefs with idle monogram. Any stray toy I bought for her "doodad" shelf (little Mexican burros in plastic, or piggy banks or vaselets) re-mained on that shelf for years and years, duly dusted and arranged according to her taste esthetically. A minor cigarette hole in old jeans is suddenly patched with pieces of 1940 jean. Her sewing basket con-tains a wooden darner (like a small bowling duckpin) older than I am. Her needles some of them come from Nashua 1910. As the years go by her family write her increasingly loving letters realizing what they lost when they took her orphan money and spent it. At the TV which I bought her with my pitiful 1950 money she stares believingly, only a battered old 1949 Motorola set. She watches the commercials where the women primp or the men boast and doesnt even know I'm in the room. It's all a show for her eyes. I have nightmares of her and I finding pastrami slabs in old junkyards of New Jersey on a Saturday morning, or of the top drawer of her dresser open in the road of America showing silk bloomers, rosaries, tin cans full of buttons, rolls of ribbon, needle hassocks, powder pouffes, old berets and boxes of cotton saved from old medicine bottles. Who could put down a woman like that? When-ever I need something she has it somewhere:—an aspirin, an ice bag, a bandage, a can of cheap spaghetti in the cupboard (cheap but good). Even a candle when the big civilized power blows out.

For the bathtub, the toilet and the sink she has big cans of deterring powder and disinfectants. She has a dry mop and twice a week is reach-ing under my bed for gobs of dust which are rapped out the window sill, "*Tiens!* Your room is clean!" Wrapped somewhere in the moving carton is a big basket of clothespins to hang out the wash wherever she goes—I see her with basket of wet wash going out with clothespin in mouth, and when we have no yard, *right in the kitchen!* Duck under the wash and get your beer in the icebox. Like the mother of Hui Neng,

I'd bet, enough to enlighten anybody with the actual true "Zen" of how to live in any time and just right.

Tao say, in more words than one, that a woman who takes care of her home has equalized Heaven and Earth.

Then on Saturday nights she's ironing on the battered ironing board bought by her a lifetime ago, the cloth all brown with burns, the creaky wooden legs, but all the wash comes out ironed and white and to be folded away in perfect paper-lined cupboards for use.

At night when she sleeps I bow my head in shame. And I know that in the morning when I wake up (maybe noon) she'll already have walked to the store on her strong "peasant" legs and brought back all the food towering in bags with the lettuce at the top, my cigarettes at the top, the hotdogs and hamburgs and tomatos and grocery slips to "show me," the pitiful nylon stockings on the bottom apologetically admitted to my sight— Ah me, and all the girls I'd known in America who dabbled at blue cheese and let it harden on the sill! Who'd spent hours before the mirror with blue eye shade! Who'd wanted taxis for their milk! Who'd groaned on Sunday without roasts! Who'd left me because I complained!

The trend nowadays is to say that mothers stand in the way of your sex life, as tho my sex life in the apartments of girls in New York or San Francisco had anything to with my quiet Sunday nights reading or writing in the privacy of my clean homey bed room, when breezes riffle the curtain and cars shirsh by— When the cat meows at the icebox and already there's a can of Nine Lives for my baby, bought by Ma on Saturday morning (writing her lists)— As tho sex was the be-all of my love for the woman.

65

My mother provided me with the means for peace and good sense— She didnt tear at her slip and rant I didnt love her and knock over dressers of makeup— She didnt harpy at me or croon at me for thinking my own thoughts— She only yawned at eleven and went to bed with her rosary, like living in a monastery with the Reverend Mother O'Shay—I might lie there in my clean sheets and think of running out to find a raunchy wild whore with stockings in her hair but it had nothing to do with my mother—I was free to do so— Because any man who's loved a friend and therefore made the vow to leave him and his wife alone, can do the same for his friend his father— To each his own, and she belonged to my father.

But wretched leering thieves of life say no: say, "if a man lives with his mother he's *frustrated*": and even Genêt the divine knower of Flowers said a man who loves his mother is the worst scoundrel of them all: or psychiatrists with hairy wrists like Ruth Heaper's psychiatrists trembling for the snowy thighs of young patients: or sick married men with no peace in their eyes ranting at the bachelor's hole: or deadly chemists with no thought of hope: all say to me: "Duluoz you liar! Go out and live with a woman and fight and suffer with her! Go swarming in your bliss hair! Go ratcheting after fury! Find the furies! Be historical!" and all the time I'm sitting there enjoying and *in*-joying the sweet silly peace of my mother, a lady the likes of which you wont find any more unless you travel to Sinkiang, Tibet or Lampore.

66

But here we are in Florida with two tickets to California waiting standing for the bus to New Orleans where we'll change for El Paso and L.A.— It's hot in May in Florida—I long to get out and go west beyond the East Texas Plain to that High Plateau and on over the Divide to dry Arizonies and beyond— Poor Ma is standing there absolutely dependent on me, foolish as I've been as you see. I wonder what my father is saying in Heaven? "That crazy Ti Jean is carting her three thousand miles in wretched buses just for a dream about a holy pine tree." But a kid is talking to us waiting in line at our side, when I say that I wonder if we'll ever get there or the bus will ever come he says:—

"Dont worry, you'll get there." I wonder how he knows we'll get there. "You'll not only get there, you'll come back and go elsewhere. Ha ha ha!"

Yet there's hardly anything in the world or at least in America more miserable than a transcontinental bus trip with limited means— More than three days and three nights wearing the same clothes, bouncing around in town after town, even at three o'clock in the morning when you've finally fallen asleep there you are being bounced over the railroad tracks of Oshkosh and all the lights are turned on bright to reveal your raggedness and weariness in the seat— To do that, as I'd done so often, as a strong young man, bad enough, but to have to do that when you're a 62-year-old lady . . . I really wondered quite often what my father was thinking in Heaven and prayed for him to give my mother strength to make it without too much horror— Yet was she more cheerful than I was— And she devised a terrific trick to keep us in fairly good shape, aspirins with Coke three times a day to calm the nerves.

From mid-Florida we rolled in the late afternoon over orange grove hills towards the panhandle Tallahassees and Mobile Alabamas of morning, no prospect of New Orleans till noon and already fair exhausted. Such an enormous country you realize when you cross it on buses, the dreadful stretches between equally dreadful cities all of them looking the same when seen from the bus of woes, the inescapable bus of never-get-there stopping everywhere (the joke about Greyhound stopping at every post) and worst of all the string of fresh enthusiastic drivers at every two or three hundred miles warning everyone to relax and be happy.

Sometimes during the night I'd look at my poor sleeping mother cruelly *crucified* there in the American night because of no-money, no-hope-of-money, no family, no nothing, just myself the stupid son of plans all of them compacted of eventual darkness. God how right Hemingway was when he said there was no remedy for life—and to think that negative little paper-shuffling prissies should write condescending obituaries about a man who told the truth, nay who drew breath in pain to tell a tale like that! . . . No remedy but in my mind I raise a fist to High Heaven promising that I shall bull whip the first bastard who makes fun of human hopelessness anyway—I know it's ridiculous to pray to my father that hunk of dung in a grave yet I pray to him anyway, what else shall I do? sneer? shuffle paper on a desk and burp with rationality? Ah thank God for all the Rationalists the worms and vermin got. Thank God for all the hate mongering political pamphleteers with no left or right to yell about in the Grave of Space. I say that we shall all be reborn with The Only One, that we will not be ourselves any more but simply the Companion of The Only One, and that's what makes me go on, and my mother too. She has her rosary in the bus, dont deny her that, that's *her* way of stating the fact. If there cant be love among men let there be love at least between men and God. Human courage is an opiate but opiates are human too. If God is an opiate so am I. Therefore *eat me. Eat* the night, the long desolate America between Sanford and Shlamford and Blamford and Crapford, eat the hematodes that hang parasitically from dreary southern trees, eat the blood in the ground, the dead Indians, the dead pioneers, the dead Fords and Pontiacs, the dead Mississippis, the dead arms of forlorn hopelessness washing underneath— Who are men, that they can insult men?

Who are these people who wear pants and dresses and sneer? What am I talking about? I'm talking about human helplessness and unbelievable loneliness in the darkness of birth and death and asking "What is there to laugh about in that?" "How can you be *clever* in a meatgrinder?" "Who makes fun of misery?" There's my mother a hunk of flesh that didnt ask to be born, sleeping restlessly, dreaming hopefully, beside her son who also didnt ask to be born, thinking desperately, praying hopelessly, in a bouncing earthly vehicle going from nowhere to nowhere, all in the night, worst of all for that matter all in noonday glare of bestial Gulf Coast roads— Where is the rock that will sustain us? Why are we here? What kind of crazy college would feature a seminar where people talk about hopelessness, forever?

And when Ma wakes up in the middle of the night and groans, my heart breaks— The bus goes belumping over back lots of Shittown to go pick up one package in a dawn station. Groans everywhere, all the way to the back seats where black sufferers suffer no less because their skin is black. Yes, "Freedom Riders" indeed, just because you've got "white" skin and ride in the front dont make you suffer less—

And there's just no hope anywhere because we're all disunited and ashamed: if Joe says life is sad Jim will say that Joe is silly because it doesnt matter. Or if Joe says we need help Jim will say that Joe's a sniveler. Or if Joe says Jim is mean Jim'll bust down crying in the night. Or something. It's just awful. The only thing to do is be like my mother: patient, believing, careful, bleak, self-protective, glad for little favors, suspicious of great favors, beware of Greeks bearing Fish, make it your own way, hurt no one, mind your own business, and make your compact with God. For God is our Guardian Angel and this is a fact that's only proven when proof exists no more.

Eternity, and the Here-and-Now, are the same thing.

Send that message back to Mao, or Schlesinger at Harvard, or Herbert Hoover too.

67

As I say, the bus arrives in New Orleans at noon and we have to disembark with all our tangled luggage and wait four hours for the El Paso express so me and Ma decide to investigate New Orleans and stretch our legs. In my mind I imagine a big glorious lunch in a Latin Quarter Abalone restaurant among grilleworked balconies and palms but as soon as we find such a restaurant near Bourbon Street the prices on the menu are so high we have to walk out sheepishly as gay businessmen and councilmen and tax collectors dine on. At 3 P.M. they'll be back at their office desks shuffling quintuplicates of onionskinned news concerning negative formalities and shoving them thru further paper machines that will multiply them ten times to be sent out to be done in triplicate to end up in wastebaskets when their salaries are in. For all the strong food and drink they get give back triplicates of paper, signed, tho I cant understand it how it's done when I see sweating arms digging ditches in the streets in the Gulf shattering sun—

Just for the hell of it Ma and I just decide to walk into a New Orleans saloon that has an oyster bar. And there by God she has the time of her life drinking wine, eating oysters on the half shell with *piquante,* and yelling crazy conversations with the old Italian oyster man. "Are you married, eh?" (She's always asking old men if they're married, it's amazing how women are looking for husbands right up to the end.) No, he's not married, and would she like some clams now, maybe steamed? and they exchanged names and addresses but later never write. Meanwhile Ma is all excited to be in famous New Orleans at last and when we walk around she buys pickaninny dolls and praline candies all excited in stores and packs them in our luggage to send back by mail as presents to my sister in Florida. A relentless hope. Just like my father she just wont let anything discourage her. I walk sheepishly by her side. And she's been doing this for 62 years: at the age of 14 there she was, at dawn, walking to the shoe factory to work till six that evening, till Saturday evening, 72-hour workweek, all gleeful in anticipation of that pitiful Saturday night and Sunday when there'd be popcorn and swings and singing. How can you beat people like that? When Feudal tithe-barons made their grab, did they feel sheepish before the glee of their peasants? (surrounded as they were by all those dull knights all yearning to be buggered by masterful sadists from another burgh).

So we get back on the El Paso bus after an hour standing in line in blue bus fumes, loaded with presents and luggage, talking to everybody, and off we roar up the river and then across the Louisiana plains, sitting in front again, feeling gay and rested now and also because I've bought a little pint of booze to nip us along.

"I dont care what anybody say," says Ma pouring a nip into her ladylike portable shot container, "a little drink never hurt nobody!" and I agree ducking down beneath the driver's rear vision seat and gulping up a snort. Off we go to Lafayette. Where to our amazement we hear the local people talking French exactly as we do in Quebecois, the

Cajuns are only *Acadians* but there's no time, the bus is leaving for Texas now.

68

In reddish dusk we're rolling across the Texas plains talking and drinking but soon the pint runs out and poor Ma's sleeping again, just a hopeless baby in the world, and all that distance yet to go, and when we get there *what?* Corrigan, and Crockett, and Palestine, the dull bus stops, the sighs, the endlessness of it, only half way across the continent, another night of sleeplessness ahead and another one later, and still another one— Oh me—

Exactly 24 hours and then six more after arriving in New Orleans we are finally bashing down the Rio Grande Valley into the wink of El Paso night, all nine hundred *miserere* miles of Texas behind us, both of us completely doped and numb with tiredness, I realize there's nothing to do but get off the bus and get a hotel suite and get a good night's sleep before goin on to California more than another thousand bumpy miles—

And at the same time I will show my mother Mexico across the little bridge to Juarez.

69

Everybody knows what it feels like after two days of vibration on wheels to suddenly lie in still beds on still ground and sleep— Right next to the bus station I got a suite and went out to buy chicken-in-the-basket while Ma washed up— As I look back on it now I realize she was having a big adventurous trip visiting New Orleans and staying in hotel suites ($4.50) and now going to Mexico for the first time tomorrow— We drank another half pint and ate the chicken and slept like logs.

In the morning, with eight hours till bus time, we sallied forth strong with all our luggage repacked and stored in 25¢ bus station lockers—I even made her walk the one mile to the Mexico bridge for exercise— At the bridge we paid three cents each and went over.

Immediately we were in Mexico, that is, among Indians in an Indian earth—among the smells of mud, chickens, including that Chihuahua dust, lime peels, horses, straw, Indian weariness— The strong smell of cantinas, beer, dank— The smell of the market—and the sight of beautiful old Spanish churches rising in the sun with all their woeful majestical Maria Guadalupes and Crosses and cracks in the wall— "O Ti Jean! I want to go in that church and light a candle to Papa!"

"Okay." And when we go in we see an old man kneeling in the aisle with his arms outstretched in penitence, a *penitente,* hours like that he kneels, old serape over his shoulder, old shoes, hat on the church floor, raggedy old white beard. "O Ti Jean, what's he done that he's so sad for? I cant believe that old man has ever done anything really bad!"

"He's a *penitente,*" I tell her in French. "He's a sinner and he doesnt want God to forget him."

"*Pauvre bonhomme!*" and I see a woman turn and look at Ma thinking she said "*Pobrecito*" which is exactly what she said anyway. But the most pitiful sight suddenly in the old Juarez church is a shawled woman all dressed in black, barefooted, with a baby in her arms advancing slowly on her knees up the aisle to the altar. "What has happened *there?*" cries my mother amazed. "That poor lil mother has done no wrong! Is it her husband who's in prison? She's carrying that leetle baby!" I'm glad now I took Ma on this trip for her to see the real church of America if nothing else. "Is *she* a penitente *too?* Dat little baby is a penitente? She's got him all wrapped up in a leetle ball in her shawl!"

"I dont know why."

"Where's the priest that he dont bless her? There's nobody here but that poor leetle mother and that poor old man! This is the Church of Mary?"

"This is the church of Maria de Guadalupe. A peasant found a shawl in Guadalupe Mexico with Her Face imprinted on it like the cloth the women had at the cross of Jesus."

"It happened in Mexico?"

"*Si.*"

"And they pray to Marie? But that poor young mother is only half way to the altar— She comes slow slow slow on her knees all quiet. Aw but these are good people the *Indians* you say?"

"*Oui*—Indians just like the American Indians but here the Spaniards did not destroy them" (in French). "*Içi les espanols sont marié avec les Indiens.*"

"*Pauvre monde!* They believe in God just like us! I didnt know that, Ti Jean! I never saw anything like this!" We creeped up to the altar and lighted candles and put dimes in the church box to pay for the wax. Ma made a prayer to God and did the sign of the cross. The Chihuahua desert blew dust into the church. The little mother was still advancing on her knees with the infant quietly asleep in her arms. Memère's eyes blurred with tears. Now she understood Mexico and why I had come there so often even tho I'd get sick of dysentery or lose weight or get pale. "*C'est du monde qu'il on du coeur,*" she whispered, "these are people who have *heart!*"

"*Oui.*"

She put a dollar in the church machine hoping it would do some good somehow. She never forgot that afternoon: in fact even today, five years later, she still adds a prayer for the little mother with the child crawling to the altar on her knees: "There was something was wrong in her life. Her husband, or maybe her *baby* was sick— We'll never know— But I shall always pray for that leetle woman. Ti Jean when you took me there you showed me something I'd never believed I'd ever *ever* see—"

Years later, when I met the Reverend Mother in the Bethlehem Benedictine Monastery talking to her thru wooden nunnery bars, and told her this, she cried . . .

And meanwhile the old man *Penitente* still kneeled there arms outspread, all your Zapatas and Castros come and go but the Old Penitence is still there and will always be there, like Coyotl Old Man in the Navajo Mountains and Mescalero Foothills up north:—

Chief Crazy Horse looks north	*	Geronimo weeps—
with tearful eyes—	*	no pony
The first snow flurries.	*	With a blanket.

70

It was also very funny to be in Mexico with my mother for when we came out of the church of Santa Maria we sat in the park to rest and enjoy the sun, and next to us sat an old Indian in his shawl, with his wife, saying nothing, looking straight ahead on their big visit to Juarez from the hills of the desert out beyond— Come by bus or burro— And Ma offered them a cigarette. At first the old Indian was afraid but finally he took a cigarette, but she offered him one for his wife, in French, in Quebecois Iroquois French, "*Vas il, ai paw 'onte, un pour ta famme*" so he took it, puzzled— The old lady never looked at Memère— They knew we were American tourists but never tourists like these— The old man slowly lighted his cigarette and looked straight ahead— Ma said to me: "They're afraid to talk?"

"They dont know what to do. They never meet anybody. They

come from the desert. They dont even speak Spanish just Indian. Say Tarahumare."

"How's anybody can say dat?"

"Say Chihuahua."

Ma says "Chihuahua" and the old man grins at her and the old lady smiles. "Goodbye" says Memère as we leave. We go wandering across the sweet little park full of children and people and ice cream and balloons and come to a strange man with birds in a cage, who catches our eye and yells for our attention (I had taken my mother around to the back streets of Juarez.) "What does he want?"

"Fortune! His birds will tell your fortune! We give him one peso and his little birds grab a slip of paper and your fortune's written on it!"

"Okay! *Seenyor!*" The little bird beaks up a clip of paper from a pile of papers and hands it to the man. The man with his little mustache and gleeful eyes opens it. It reads as follows:—

"You will have goods fortuna with one who is your son who love you. Say the bird."

He gives the little paper to us laughing. It's amazing.

71

"Now," says Memère as we walk arm in arm thru the streets of Old Juarez, "how could that little silly bird know I have a son or *any*thing about me— Phew there's a lot of dust around here!" as that million million grained desert blows dust along the doors. "Can you explain me that? What is one peso, *eight cents?* And the little bird knew all dat? Hah?" Like Thomas Wolfe's Esther, "Hah?", only a longer lasting love. "Dat guy with the mustache doesnt know us. His little bird knew everything." She had the bird's slip of paper securely in her purse.

"A little bird that knew Gerard."

"And the little bird picked out the paper with his crazy face! Ah but the people are poor here, eh?"

"Yeh—but the government is taking care of that a lot. Used to be there were families sleeping on the sidewalk wrapped in newspapers and bullfight posters. And girls sold themselves for twenty cents. They have a good government since Aleman, Cardenas, Cortines—"

"The poor little bird of Mexica! And the little mother! I can always say I've seen Mexica." She pronounced it "Mexica."

So I bought a pint of Juarez Bourbon in a store and back we went to the American bus station in El Paso, got on a big doubledecker Grey-hound that said "Los Angeles" on it, and roared off in a red desert dusk drinking from the pint in our front seats yakking with American sailors who knew nothing about Santa Maria de Guadalupe or the Little Bird but were good old boys nevertheless.

And as the bus rammed down that empty road among desert buttes and lava humps like the landscape of the moon, miles and miles of desolation towards that last faint Chihuahuan Mountain to the South or New Mexico dry rock range to the North, Memère drink-in-hand said: "I'm afraid of those mountains—they're trying to say something to us—they might fall right over us any minute!" And she leaned over to tell the sailors that, who laughed, and she offered them a drink and even kissed their polite cheeks, and they enjoyed it, such a crazy mother—Nobody in America was ever going to understand again what she'd try to tell them about what she saw in Mexico or in the Universe Entire. "Those mountains aint out there for nothing! They're there to tell us something! They're just sweet boys," and she fell asleep, and that was it, and the bus droned on to Arizona.

72

But we're in America now and at dawn it's the city called Los Angeles tho nobody can see what it can possibly have to do with angels as we stash our gear in lockers to wait for the 10 A.M. San Francisco bus and go out in gray streets to find a place for coffee and toast— It's 5 A.M. even too early for anything and all we get to see are the night's remnants of horrified hoodlums and bloody drunks staggering around—I'd wanted to show her the bright happy L.A. of Art Linkletter Television shows or glimpses of Hollywood but all we saw was horror of Grue-some's end, the battered junkies and whores and suitcases tied with string, the empty traffic lights, no birds here, no Maria here—but dirt and death yes. Tho a few miles beyond those embittered awful paves were the soft shiny shores of a Kim Novak Pacific she'd never see, where *hors d'oeuvres* are thrown away to the dogs of sea— Where Producers mingle with their wives in a movie they never made—But all poor Me-mère ever saw of L.A. was dawn batteredness, hoodlums, some of them Indians of America, dead sidewalks, crops of cop cars, doom, early morning whistles like the early morning whistles of Marseilles, haggard ugly awful California City I-cant-go-on-what-am-I-doing-here *mierda*— Oh, who ever hath lived and suffered in America knows what I mean!

Whoever rode coal cars out of Cleveland or stared at mailboxes in Washington D. C. knows! Whoever bled again in Seattle or bled again in Montana! Or peeled in Minneapolis! Or died in Denver! Or cried in Chicago or said "Sorry I'm burning" in Newark! Or sold shoes in Winchendon! Or flared out in Philadelphia? Or pruned in Toonerville? But I tell you there's nothing more awful than empty dawn streets of an American city unless it's being thrown to the Crocodiles in the Nile for nothing as cat-priests smile. Slaves in every toilet, thieves in every hole, pimps in every dive, Governors signing redlight warrants— Gangs of ducktailed blackjacketed hoods on every corner some of them Pachucos, I pray in fact to my Papa "Forgive me for dragging Memère thru all this in search of a cup of coffee"— The same streets I've known before but not with *her*— But every evil dog in evildom understands it when he sees a man with his mother, so bless you all.

73

After a whole day riding thru the green fields and orchards of beautiful San Joaquin Valley, even my mother impressed tho she mentions the dry furze on those distant hills (and has already complained and rightly so about the caney wastes of Tucson and Mojave deserts)—as we sit there stoned to death with tiredness, of course, but almost there, only five hundred miles of valley up to north and the City—a long complicated way of telling you that we arrive at Fresno at dusk, walk around a little, get back on now with a fantastically vigorous Indian driver (some Mexican kid from Madera) off we go bashing to Oakland as the driver bears down on everything in that two way Valley lane (99) making whole populations of oncoming cars quake and revert into line— He'll just ram em right down.

So we arrive in Oakland at night, Saturday, (me finishing the last sip of my California rotgut port mixed with bus station ice) bang, we first thing see a battered drunkard all covered with blood staggering thru the bus station for emergency aid— My mother cant even see anymore, she's been sleeping all the way from Fresno, but she does see that sight and sighs wondering what next, New York? maybe Hell's Kitchen or Lower East Side East? I promise myself I'm going to show her something, a good little home and some quiet and trees, just like my father must've promised when he moved her from New England to New York—I get all the bags and hail a Berkeley bus.

Pretty soon we're out of Oakland downtown streets of empty movie marquees and dull fountains and we're rolling thru little long streets full of old 1910 white cottages and palms. But mostly other trees, your California northern trees, walnut and oak and cypress, and finally we come to near the University of California where I lead her down a leafy little street with all our gear towards the dull dimlamp of old Bhikku Ben Fagan studying in his backyard cabin. He's going to show us where to get a hotel room and help us find an apartment tomorrow either the upstairs or downstairs of a cottage. He's my only connection in Berkeley. By God as we come walking across his tall grass there we see him in a rose covered window with his head bent over the Lankavatara Scripture, and he's *smiling!* I cant understand what he's smiling about, *maya?* Buddha laughing on Mount Lanka or something? But here comes woesome old me and my maw down the yard with battered suitcases arriving almost like phantoms dripping from the sea. He's *smiling!*

For a moment, in fact, I hold my mother back and shush so I can watch him (the Mexicans call me an "adventurer") and by God he's just alone in the night smiling over old Bodhisattva truths of India. You cant go wrong with him. He's smiling *happily,* in fact, it's really a crime to disturb him—but it's got to be done, besides he'll be pleased and maybe even shocked into Seeing Maya but I have to clomp on his porch and say "Ben, it's Jack, I'm with my mother." Poor Memère is standing behind me with her poor eyes half closed from inhuman weariness, and despair too, wondering *now what* as big old Ben comes clomping to the little rose covered door with pipe in mouth and says "Well, well, well, whaddaya know?" Ben is too smart and really too nice to say anything like "Well hello there, when did you get in?" I'd already written ahead to him but had rather expected to arrive somehow in the daytime and find a room before dropping in on him, maybe alone while Memère could read a *Life* Magazine or eat sandwiches in her hotel room. But here it was 2 A.M., I was utterly stupefied, I'd seen no hotels or rooms to rent from the bus—I wanted to lean my shoulder on Ben somehow. He had to work in the morning too. But that smile, in the flowery silence, everybody in Berkeley asleep, and over such a text as the Lankavatara Scripture which says things like *Behold the hairnet, it is real, say the fools,* or like *Life is like the reflection of the moon on the water, which one is the true moon?* meaning: Is reality the unreal part of unreality? or vice versa, when you open the door does anyone enter or is it you?

74

And smiling over that in the western night, stars waterfalling over his roof like drunkards stumbling downstairs with lanterns in their asses, the whole cool dew night I loved so much of northern California (that rainforest freshness), that smell of fresh green mint growing among tangled rubbery weeds and flowers.

The little cottage had quite a history, too, as I've shown earlier, had been the haven of Dharma Bums in the past where we'd had big tea discussions on Zen or sex orgies and yabyum with girls, where we'd played phonograph music and drank loudly in the night like Gay Mexicans in that quiet collegiate neighbourhood, no one complaining somehow— The same old battered rocking chair was still on the little Walt Whitman rosey porch of vines and flowerpots and warped wood — In the back were still the little God-leak pots of Irwin Garden, his tomato plants, maybe some of our lost dimes or quarters or snapshots —Ben (a California poet from Oregon) had inherited this sweet little spot after everybody'd dispersed east some as far east as Japan (like old Dharma Bum Jarry Wagner)— So he sat there smiling over the Lankavatara Scripture in the quiet California night a strange and sweet sight to see after all those three thousand miles from Florida, for me— He was still smiling as he invited us to sit down.

"What now?" sighs poor Memère. "Jacky drag me all the way from my daughter's house in Florida with no plans, no money."

"There's lots of nice apartments around here for fifty dollars a month," I say, "and besides Ben can show us where to get a room tonight." Smoking and smiling and carrying most of our bags good old Ben leads us to a hotel five blocks away on University and Shattuck where we hire two rooms and go to sleep. That is, while Memère sleeps I walk back to the cottage with Ben to rehash old times. For us it was a strange quiet time between the era of our Zen Lunatic days of 1955 when we read our new poems to big audiences in San Francisco (tho I never read, just conducted sort of with a jug of wine) and the upcoming era of the paper and critics writing about it and calling it the "San Francisco Beat Generation Poetry Renaissance"— So Ben sat crosslegged sighing and said: "Oh nothing much happening around here. Think I'll go back to Oregon pretty soon." Ben is a big pink fellow with glasses and great calm blue eyes like the eyes of a Moon Professor or really of a Nun. (Or of Pat O'Brien, but he almost killed me when I asked him if he was an Irishman the first time I met him.) Nothing ever surprises him not even my strange arrival in the night with my mother; the moon'll shine on the water anyway and chickens'll lay more eggs and nobody'll know the origin of the limitless chicken without the egg. "What were you *smiling* about when I saw you in the window?" He goes into the tiny kitchen and brews a pot of tea. "I hate to disturb your hermitage."

"I was probably smiling because a butterfly got caught in the pages. When I extricated it, the black cat and the white cat both chased it."

"And a flower chased the cats?"

"No, Jack Duluoz arrived with a long face worrying about something, at 2 A.M. not even carrying a candle."

"You'll like my mother, she's a *real* Bodhisattva."

"I like her already. I like the way she puts up with you, you and your crazy three-thousand-mile ideas."

"She'll take care of everything . . ."

Funny thing about Ben, the first night me and Irwin had met him he cried all night face down on the floor, nothing we could do to console him. Finally he ended up never crying ever since. He had just come down from a summer on a mountain (Sourdough Mountain) just like me later, and had a whole book of new poems he hated, and cried: "Poetry is a lotta bunk. Who wants to bother with all that mental discrimination in a world already dead, already gone to the other shore? There's just nothin to do." But now he felt better, with that *smile*, saying: "It doesnt matter any more, I dreamed I was a Tathagata twelve feet long with gold toes and I didnt even care any more." There he sits crosslegged, leaning slightly to the left, flying softly thru the night with a Mount Malaya smile. He appears as blue mist in the huts of poets five thousand miles away. He's a strange mystic living alone smiling over books, my mother says next morning in the hotel "What kind of fella is that Benny? No wife, no family, nothing to do? Does he have a job?"

"He has a part time job inspecting eggs in the university laboratory up the hill. He earns just enough for his beans and wine. He's a *Buddhist!*"

"You and your Buddhists! Why dont you stick to your own religion?" But we go forth at nine in the morning and immediately miraculously find a fine apartment, groundfloor with a flowery yard, and pay a month's rent in advance and move our suitcases in. At 1943 Berkeley Way right near all the stores and from my bedroom window I can actually see the Golden Gate Bridge over the waters beyond the rooftops ten miles away. There's even a fireplace. When Ben gets home from work I go get him at his cottage and we go buy a whole frying chicken, a quart of whiskey, cheese and bread and accessories, and that night by firelight as we all get drunk in the new apartment I fry the chicken in the rucksack cookpots right on the logs and we have a great feast. Ben has already bought me a present, a tamper to tamp down the tobacco in my pipe, and we sit smoking by the fire with Memère.

But too much whiskey and we all get woozy and pass out. There are already two beds in the apartment and in the middle of the night I wake up to hear Memère's groan from the whiskey and somehow I realize our new home is already cursed thereby.

* * *

And then to top it all off one day Cody is rushing across our porch and into the house dying to borrow ten dollars from me for an urgent pot connection. I've practically *come* to California to be near old buddy Cody but his wife has refused to help this time, probably because I have Memère with me, probably because she's afraid he'll go mad with me again like he did on the road years ago— To him it makes no difference, he hasnt changed, he just wants to borrow ten dollars. He says he'll be back. Meanwhile he also borrows Ben's tendollar *Tibetan Book of the Dead* and rushes off, all muscular as usual in T-shirt and frayed jeans, crazy Cody. "Any girls around here?" he cries anxiously as he drives off.

But a week later I take Memère into San Francisco to let her ride the cable cars and eat in Chinatown and buy toys in Chinatown and I have her wait for me in the big Catholic church on Columbus while I rush to the Place, Cody's hangout, to see if I can recoup that $10 from him. By God there he is sipping a beer, playing chess with "The Beard." He looks surprised but he knows I want my ten bucks. He cashes a twenty at the bar and pays me and then even comes with me to meet Memère in the church. As we walk in he kneels and does the sign of the Cross, as I do, and Memère turns to see us do that. She realizes Cody and I are fatal lovely friends who are not bad boys at all.

So three days later as I'm kneeling on the floor unpacking a crate of advance copies of my novel *Road* which is all about Cody and me and Joanna and big Slim Buckle, and Memère's at the store so I'm alone in the house, I look up as a golden light appears in the porch door silently: and there stands Cody, Joanna (golden blonde beauty), big tall Slim Buckle, and behind them the midget 4:2 inch Jimmy Low (known not as a "midget" at all but simply Jimmy, or as Deni Bleu calls him,

"A Little Man.") We all stare at one another in the golden light. Not a sound. I'm also caught red handed (as we all grin) with a copy of *Road* in my hands *even before I've looked at it for the first time!* I automatically hand one to Cody who is after all the hero of the poor crazy sad book. It's one of the several occasions in my life when a meeting with Cody seems to be suffused with a silent golden light, as I'll show another later, altho I dont even know what it means, unless it means that Cody is actually some kind of angel or archangel come down to this world and I recognize it. A fine thing to say in this day and age! And especially with the wild life he was now leading that was going to end in tragedy in six months, as I'll tell in a minute— A fine thing to be talking about angels in this day when common thieves smash the holy rosaries of their victims in the street . . . When the highest ideals on earth are based on the month and the day of some cruel bloody revolution, nay when the highest ideals are simply new *reasons* for murdering and despoiling people— And Angels? Since we've never seen an angel what angel do you mean? But it was Christ said "Since you've never seen my Father then how can you know my Father?"

81

Ah yes, maybe I'm wrong and all the Christian, Islamic, Neo Platonist, Buddhist, Hindu, and Zen Mystics of the world were wrong about the transcendental mystery of existence but I dont think so— Like the thirty birds who reached God and saw themselves reflected in His Mirror. The thirty Dirty Birds, those 970 of us birds who never made it across the Valley of Divine Illumination did really make it anyway in Perfection — So now let me explain about poor Cody, even tho I've already told most of his story. He is a *believer* in life and he *wants* to go to Heaven but because he loves life so he embraces it so much he thinks he sins and will never see Heaven— He was a Catholic altar boy as I say even when he was bumming dimes for his hopeless father hiding in alleys. You could have ten thousand cold eyed Materialistic officials claim they love life too but can never embrace it so near sin and also never see Heaven— They will condemn the hot-blooded lifelover with their cold papers on a desk because they have no blood and therefore have no sin? No! They sin by lifelessness! They are the ogres of Law entering the Holy Realm of Sin! Ah, I've got to explain myself without essays and poems—Cody had a wife whom he really loved, and three kids he really loved, and a good job on the railroad. But when the sun went down his blood got hot:—hot for old lovers like Joanna, for old pleasure like marijuana and talk, for jazz, for the gayety that any respectable American wants in a life growing more arid by the year in Law Ridden America. But he did not hide his desire and cry *Dry!* He went all out. He filled his car with friends and booze and pot and batted around looking for ecstasy like some fieldworker on a Saturday night in Georgia when the moon cools the still and guitars are twangin down the hill. He came from sturdy Missouri stock that walked on strong feet. We've all seen him kneel *sweating* praying to God! When we went to San Francisco that day whole cordons of police were surrounding the streets of North Beach looking for crazy people like him. Somehow by some miracle we walked with pockets full of bottles and pot right thru them, laughing with girls, with little Jimmy, to parties, to bars, to jazz cellars. I couldnt understand what the cops were doing! Why werent they looking for murderers and robbers? When I once suggested this to a policeman who stopped us because I was flagging my buddy's car back with a railroad lamp so there'd be no accidents anywhere the policeman said "You've got quite an imagination, havent you?" (meaning I might be a murderer or robber myself.) I'm no such thing and neither is Cody, you have to be DRY to be those things! You have to HATE life to kill it and rob it!

82

But enough about California for now—I later had adventures in Big Sur down there that were really horrible and only as horrible as you get when you get older and your last moment impels you to test *all,* to go *mad,* just to see what the Void'll do— Suffice it to say that when Cody said goodbye to all of us that day he for the first time in our lives failed to look me a goodbye in the eye but looked away shifty-like—I couldn't understand it and still dont—I knew something was bound to be wrong and it turned out very wrong, he was arrested a few months later for possession of pot and spent two years sweeping out the cotton room in San Quentin tho I happen to know the real reason for this horrible ordeal in the real world is not because of having two cigarettes in his pocket (two bearded bluejeaned beatniks in a car saying "What's the hurry kid?" and Cody says "Drive me down to the station real quick I'll be late for my train") (his driving license taken away for speeding) ("and I'll give ya some pot for your trouble") and they turn out to be disguised cops— The real reason aside from he didnt look in my eyes, was, I once saw him belt his daughter across the room in a chastising crying scene and that's why his Karma devolved that way— Tit for Tat, and Jot for Tittle— Tho in two years Cody was about to become a greater man than ever as maybe he realizes all this— But, and, according to the laws of tit-for-tat what do I deserve myself?

from
BIG SUR
1960

EDITOR'S NOTE
In this book Kerouac calls himself "Jack Duluoz," Allen Ginsberg is "Irwin Garden," Neal Cassady is "Cody Pomeray," Carolyn Cassady is "Evelyn," Gary Snyder is "Jarry Wagner," Philip Whalen is "Ben Fagan," Michael McClure is "Pat McLear," Lenore Kandel is "Romana Swartz," Lew Welch is "David Wain," Lawrence Ferlinghetti is "Lorenzo Monsanto, and Robert La Vigne is "Robert Browning."

THE CHURCH IS BLOWING a sad windblown "Kathleen" on the bells in the skid row slums as I wake up all woebegone and goopy, groaning from another drinking bout and groaning most of all because I'd ruined my "secret return" to San Francisco by getting silly drunk while hiding in the alleys with bums and then marching forth into North Beach to see everybody altho Lorenz Monsanto and I'd exchanged huge letters outlining how I would sneak in quietly, call him on the phone using a code name like Adam Yulch or Lalagy Pulvertaft (also writers) and then he would secretly drive me to his cabin in the Big Sur woods where I would be alone and undisturbed for six weeks just chopping wood, drawing water, writing, sleeping, hiking, etc. etc.—But instead I've bounced drunk into his City Lights bookshop at the height of Saturday night business, everyone recognized me (even tho I was wearing my disguise-like fisherman's hat and fishermen coat and pants waterproof) and 't'all ends up a roaring drunk in all the famous bars the bloody "King of the Beatniks" is back in town buying drinks for everyone— Two days of that, including Sunday the day Lorenzo is supposed to pick me up at my "secret" skid row hotel (the Mars on 4th and Howard) but when he calls for me there's no answer, he has the clerk open the door and what does he see but me out on the floor among bottles, Ben Fagan stretched out partly beneath the bed, and Robert Browning the beatnik painter out on the bed, snoring—So says to himself "I'll pick him up next weekend, I guess he wants to drink for a week in the city (like he always does, I guess)" so off he drives to his Big Sur cabin without me thinking he's doing the right thing but my God when I wake up, and Ben and Browning are gone, they've somehow dumped me on the bed, and I hear "I'll Take You Home Again Kathleen" being bell-roped so sad in the fog winds out there that blow across the rooftops of eerie old hangover Frisco, wow, I've hit the end of the trail and cant even drag my body any more even to a refuge in the woods let alone stay upright in the city a minute—It's the first trip I've taken away from home (my mother's house) since the publication of "Road" the book that "made me famous" and in fact so much so I've been driven mad for three years by endless telegrams, phonecalls, requests, mail, visitors, reporters, snoopers (a big voice saying in my basement window as I prepare to write a story:— ARE YOU BUSY?) or the time the reporter ran upstairs to my bedroom as I sat there in my pajamas trying to write down a dream—Teenagers jumping the six-foot fence I'd had built around my yard for privacy—Parties with bottles yelling at my study window "Come on out and get drunk, all work and no play makes Jack a dull boy!"—A woman coming to my door and saying "I'm not going to ask you if you're Jack Duluoz because I know he wears a beard, can you tell me where I can find him, I want a real beatnik at my annual Shindig party"—Drunken visitors puking in my study, stealing books and even pencils—Uninvited acquaintances staying for days because of the clean beds and good food my mother provided—Me drunk practically all the time to put on a jovial cap to keep up with all this but finally realizing I was surrounded and outnumbered and had to get away to solitude again or die—So Lorenzo Monsanto wrote and said "Come to my cabin, no one'll know," etc. so I had sneaked into San Francisco as I say, coming 3000 miles from my home in Long Island (Northport) in a pleasant roomette on the California Zephyr train watching America roll by outside my private picture window, really happy for the first time in three years, staying in the roomette all three days and three nights with my instant coffee and sandwiches—Up the Hudson Valley and over across New York State to Chicago and then the Plains, the mountains, the desert, the final mountains of California, all so easy and dreamlike compared to my old harsh hitch hikings before I made enough money to take transcontinental trains (all over America high-school and college kids thinking "Jack Duluoz is 26 years old and on the road all the time hitch hiking" while there I am almost 40 years old, bored and jaded in a roomette bunk crashin across that Salt Flat)—But in any case a wonderful start towards my retreat so generously offered by sweet old Monsanto and instead of going thru smooth and easy I wake up drunk, sick, disgusted, frightened, in fact terrified by that sad song across the roofs mingling with the lachrymose cries of a Salvation Army meeting on the corner below "*Satan* is the cause of your alco-holism, *Satan* is the cause of your immorality, Satan is *everywhere* workin to destroy you unless you repent *now*" and worse than that the sound of old drunks throwing up in rooms next to mine, the creak of hall steps, the moans everywhere—Including the moan that had awak-ened me, my own moan in the lumpy bed, a moan caused by a big roaring Whoo Whoo in my head that had shot me out of my pillow like a ghost.

2

And I look around the dismal cell, there's my hopeful rucksack all neatly packed with everything necessary to live in the woods, even unto the minutest first aid kit and diet details and even a neat little sewing kit cleverly reinforced by my good mother (like extra safety pins, buttons, special sewing needles, little aluminum scissors)—The hopeful medal of St. Christopher even which she'd sewn on the flap—The survival kit all in there down to the last little survival sweater and handkerchief and tennis sneakers (for hiking)—But the rucksack sits hopefully in a strewn mess of bottles all empty, empty poorboys of white port, butts, junk, horror. . . ."One fast move or I'm gone," I realize, gone the way of the last three years of drunken hopelessness which is a physical and spiritual and metaphysical hopelessness you cant learn in school no matter how many books on existentialism or pessimism you read, or how many jugs of vision-producing Ayahuasca you drink, or Mescaline take, or Peyote goop up with—That feeling when you wake up with the delirium tre-mens with the *fear* of eerie death dripping from your ears like those special heavy cobwebs spiders weave in the hot countries, the feeling of being a bentback mudman monster groaning underground in hot steam-ing mud pulling a long hot burden nowhere, the feeling of standing ankledeep in hot boiled pork blood, ugh, of being up to your waist in

a giant pan of greasy brown dishwater not a trace of suds left in it—
The face of yourself you see in the mirror with its expression of unbearable anguish so hagged and awful with sorrow you cant even cry
for a thing so ugly, so lost, no connection whatever with early perfection
and therefore nothing to connect with tears or anything: it's like William
Seward Burroughs' "Stranger" suddenly appearing in your place in the
mirror—Enough! "One fast move or I'm gone" so I jump up, do my
headstand first to pump blood back into the hairy brain, take a shower
in the hall, new T-shirt and socks and underwear, pack vigorously, hoist
the rucksack and run out throwing the key on the desk and hit the cold
street and walk fast to the nearest little grocery store to buy two days
of food, stick it in the rucksack, hike thru lost alleys of Russian sorrow
where bums sit head on knees in foggy doorways in the goopy eerie city
night I've got to escape or die, and into the bus station—In a half hour
into a bus seat, the bus says "Monterey" and off we go down the clean
neon hiway and I sleep all the way, waking up amazed and well again
smelling sea air the bus driver shaking me "End of the line, Monterey."—And by God it *is* Monterey, I stand sleepy in the 2 A.M. seeing
vague little fishing masts across the street from the bus driveway. Now
all I've got to do to complete my escape is get 14 miles down the coast
to the Raton Canyon bridge and hike in.

3

"One fast move or I'm gone" so I blow $8 on a cab to drive me down
that coast, it's a foggy night tho sometimes you can see stars in the sky
to the right where the sea is, tho you cant see the sea you can only hear
about it from the cabdriver—"What kinda country is it around here?
I've never seen it."

"Well, you cant see it tonight—Raton Canyon you say, you better
be careful walkin around there in the dark."

"Why?"

"Well, just use your lamp like you say—"

And sure enough when he lets me off at the Raton Canyon bridge
and counts the money I sense something wrong somehow, there's an
awful roar of surf but it isnt coming from the right place, like you'd
expect it to come from "over there" but it's coming from "under
there"—I can see the bridge but I can see nothing below it—The bridge
continues the coast highway from one bluff to another, it's a nice white
bridge with white rails and there's a white line runnin down the middle

familiar and highwaylike but something's wrong—Besides the headlights of the cab just shoot out over a few bushes into empty space in
the direction where the canyon's supposed to be, it feels like being up
in the air somewhere tho I can see the dirt road at our feet and the dirt
overhang on the side—"What in the hell is this?"—I've got the directions all memorized from a little map Monsanto's mailed me but in my
imagination dreaming about this big retreat back home there'd been
something larkish, bucolic, all homely woods and gladness instead of
all this aerial roaring mystery in the dark—When the cab leaves I therefore turn on my railroad lantern for a timid peek but its beam gets lost
just like the car lights in a void and in fact the battery is fairly weak
and I can hardly see the bluff at my left—As for the bridge I cant see
it anymore except for graduating series of luminous shoulder buttons
going off further into the low sea roar—The sea roar is bad enough
except it keeps bashing and barking at me like a dog in the fog down
there, sometimes it booms the earth but my God where is the earth and
how can the sea be underground!—"The only thing to do," I gulp, "is
to put this lantern shinin right in front of your feet, *kid*do, and follow
that lantern and make sure it's shinin on the road rut and hope and
pray it's shinin on ground that's gonna be there when it's shining," in
other words I actually fear that even my lamp will carry me astray if I
dare to raise it for a minute from the ruts in the dirt road—The only
satisfaction I can glean from this roaring high horror of darkness is that
the lamp wobbles huge dark shadows of its little rim stays on the overhanging bluff at the left of the road, because to the right (where the
bushes are wiggling in the wind from the sea) there aint no shadows
because there aint no light can take hold—So I start my trudge, pack
aback, just head down following my lamp spot, head down but eyes
suspiciously peering a little up, like a man in the presence of a dangerous
idiot he doesnt want to annoy—The dirt road starts up a little, curves
to the right, starts down a little, then suddenly up again, and up—By
now the sea roar is further back and at one point I even stop and look
back to see nothing—"I'm gonna put out my light and see what I can
see" I say rooted to my feet where they're rooted to that road—Fat
lotta good, when I put out the light I see nothing but the dim sand at
my feet.

   Trudging up and getting further away from the sea roar I get to
feel more confident but suddenly I come to a frightening thing in the
road, I stop and hold out my hand, edge forward, it's only a cattle
crossing (iron bars imbedded across the road) but at the same time a

big blast of wind comes from the left where the bluff should be and I
spot that way and see nothing. "What the hell's going on!" "Follow the
road," says the other voice trying to be calm so I do but the next instant
I hear a rattling to my right, throw my light there, see nothing but
bushes wiggling dry and mean and just the proper high canyonwall kind
of bushes fit for rattlesnakes too—(which it was, a rattlesnake doesnt
like to be awakened in the middle of the night by a trudging humpbacked monster with a lamp.)

But now the road's going down again, the reassuring bluff reappears on my left, and pretty soon according to my memory of Lorry's
map there she is, the creek, I can hear her lappling and gabbing down
there at the bottom of the dark where at least I'll be on level ground
and done with booming airs somewhere above—But the closer I get to
the creek as the road dips steeply, suddenly, almost making me trot
forward, the louder it roars, I begin to think I'll fall right into it before
I can notice it—It's screaming like a raging flooded river right below
me—Besides it's even *darker* down there than anywhere! There are
glades down there, ferns of horror and slippery logs, mosses, dangerous
plashings, humid mists rise coldly like the breath of death, big dangerous
trees are beginning to bend over my head and brush my pack—There's
a noise I know can only grow louder as I sink down and for fear how
loud it can grow I stop and listen, it rises up crashing mysteriously at
me from a raging battle among dark things, wood or rock or something
cracked, all smashed, all wet black sunken earth danger—I'm *afraid* to
go down there—I am *affrayed* in the old Edmund Spenser sense of being
frayed by a whip, and a wet one at that—A slimy green dragon racket
in the bush—An angry war that doesnt want me pokin around—It's
been there a million years and it doesnt want me clashing darkness with
it—It comes snarling from a thousand crevasses and monster redwood
roots all over the map of creation—It is a dark clangoror in the rain
forest and doesnt want no skid row bum to carry to the sea which is
bad enough and waitin back there—I can almost feel the sea pulling at
that racket in the trees but there's my spotlamp so all I gotta do is follow
the lovely sand road which dips and dips in rising carnage and suddenly
a flattening, a sight of bridge logs, there's the bridge rail, there's the
creek just four feet below, cross the bridge you woken bum and see
what's on the other shore.

Take one quick peek at the water as you cross, just water over
rocks, a small creek at that.

And now before me is a dreamy meadowland with a good old corral gate and a barbed wire fence the road running right on left but this where I get off at last. Then I crawl thru the barbed wire and find myself trudging a sweet little sand road winding right thru fragrant dry heathers as tho I'd just popped thru from hell into familiar old Heaven on Earth, yair and Thank God (tho a minute later my heart's in my mouth again because I see black things in the white sand ahead but it's only piles of good old mule dung in Heaven).

4

And in the morning (after sleeping by the creek in the white sand) I do see what was so scary about my canyon road walk—The road's up there on the wall a thousand feet with a sheer drop sometimes, especially at the cattle crossing, way up highest, where a break in the bluff shows fog pouring through from another bend of the sea beyond, scary enough in itself anyway as tho one hole wasnt enough to open into the sea— And worst of all is the bridge! I go ambling seaward along the path by the creek and see this awful thin white line of bridge a thousand un-bridgeable sighs of height above the little woods I'm walking in, you just cant believe it, and to make things heart-thumpingly horrible you come to a little bend in what is now just a trail and there's the booming surf coming at you whitecapped crashing down on sand as tho it was higher than where you stand, like a sudden tidal wave world enough to make you step back or run back to the hills—And not only that, the blue sea behind the crashing high waves is full of huge black rocks rising like old ogresome castles dripping wet slime, a billion years of woe right there, the moogrus big clunk of it right there with its slaverous lips of foam at the base—So that you emerge from pleasant little wood paths with a stem of grass in your teeth and drop it to see doom—And you look up at that unbelievably high bridge and feel death and for a good reason: because underneath the bridge, in the sand right beside the sea cliff, *hump*, your heart sinks to see it: the automobile that crashed thru the bridge rail a decade ago and fell 1000 feet straight down and landed upsidedown, is still there now, an upsidedown chassis of rust in a strewn skitter of sea-eaten tires, old spokes, old car seats sprung with straw, one sad fuel pump and no more people—

Big elbows of Rock rising everywhere, sea caves within them, seas plollocking all around inside them crashing out foams, the boom and pound on the sand, the sand dipping quick (no Malibu Beach here)— Yet you turn and see the pleasant woods winding upcreek like a picture in Vermont—But you look up into the sky, bend way back, my God you're standing directly under that aerial bridge with its thin white line running from rock to rock and witless cars racing across it like dreams! From rock to rock! All the way down the raging coast! So that when later I heard people say "Oh Big Sur must be beautiful!" I gulp to wonder why it has the reputation of being beautiful above and beyond its *fearfulness,* its Blakean groaning roughrock Creation throes, those vistas when you drive the coast highway on a sunny day opening up the eye for miles of horrible washing sawing.

5

It was even frightening at the other peaceful end of Raton Canyon, the east end, where Alf the pet mule of local settlers slept at night such sleepfull sleeps under a few weird trees and then got up in the morning to graze in the grass then negotiated the whole distance slowly to the sea shore where you saw him standing by the waves like an ancient sacred myth character motionless in the sand—Alf the Sacred Burro I later called him—The thing that was frightening was the mountain that rose up at the east end, a strange Burmese like mountain with levels and moody terraces and a strange ricepaddy hat on top that I kept staring at with a sinking heart even at first when I was healthy and feeling good (and I would be going mad in this canyon in six weeks on the fullmoon night of September 3rd)—The mountain reminded me of my recent recurrent nightmares in New York about the "Mountain of Mien Mo" with the swarms of moony flying horses lyrically sweeping capes over their shoulders as they circled the peak a "thousand miles high" (in the dream it said) and on top of the mountain in one haunted nightmare I'd seen the giant empty stone benches so silent in the topworld moonlight as tho once inhabited by Gods or giants of some kind but long ago vacated so that they were all dusty and cobwebby now and the evil lurked somewhere inside the pyramid nearby where there was a monster with a big thumping heart but also, even more sinister, just ordinary seedy but muddy janitors cooking over small woodfires—Narrow dusty holes through which I'd tried to crawl with a bunch of tomato plants tied around my neck—Dreams—Drinking nightmares—A recurrent series of them all swirling around that mountain, seen the very first time as a beautiful but somehow horribly green verdant mist enshrouded jungle peak rising out of green tropical country in "Mexico" so called but beyond which were pyramids, dry rivers, other countries full of infantry

enemy and yet the biggest danger being just hoodlums out throwing
rocks on Sundays—So that the sight of that simple sad mountain, together with the bridge and that car that had flipped over twice or so
and landed flump in the sand with no more sign of human elbows or
shred neckties (like a terrifying poem about America you could write),
agh, HOO HOO of Owls living in old evil hollow trees in that misty
tangled further part of the canyon where I was always afraid to go
anyhow—That unclimbably tangled steep cliff at the base of Mien Mo
rising to gawky dead trees among bushes so dense and up to heathers
God knows how deep with hidden caves no one not even I spose the
Indians of the 10th Century had ever explored—And those big gooky
rainforest ferns among lightningstruck conifers right beside sudden
black vine cliff faces rising right at your side as you walk the peaceful
path—And as I say that ocean coming at you higher than you are like
the harbors of old woodcuts always higher than the towns (as Rimbaud
pointed out shuddering)—So many evil combinations even unto the bat
who would come at me later while I slept on the outdoor cot on the
porch of Lorenzo's cabin, come circle my head coming real low sometimes filling me with the traditional fear it'll get tangled in my hair, and
such silent wings, how would you like to wake up in the middle of the
night and see silent wings beating over you and you ask yourself "Do
I really believe in Vampires?"—In fact, flying silently around my lamplit
cabin at 3 o'clock in the morning as I'm reading (of all things) (shudder)
Doctor Jekyll and Mister Hyde—Small wonder maybe that I myself
turned from serene Jekyll to hysterical Hyde in the short space of six
weeks, losing absolute control of the peace mechanisms of my mind for
the first time in my life.

But Ah, at first there were fine days and nights, right after Monsanto drove me to Monterey and back with two boxes of a full grub
list and left me there alone for three weeks of solitude, as we'd agreed
—So fearless and happy I even spotted his powerful flashlight up at the
bridge the first night, right thru the fog the eerie finger reaching the pale
bottom of that high monstrosity, and even spotted it out over the farm-
less sea as I sat by caves in the crashing dark in my fisherman's outfit
writing down what the sea was saying—Worst of all spotting it up at
those tangled mad cliffsides where owls hooted ooraloo—Becoming acquainted and swallowing fears and settling down to life in the little
cabin with its warm glow of woodstove and kerosene lamp and let the
ghosts fly their asses off—The Bhikku's home in his woods, he only
wants peace, peace he will get—Tho why after three weeks of perfect

happy peace and adjustment in these strange woods my soul so went down the drain when I came back with Dave Wain and Romana and my girl Billie and her kid, I'll never know—Worth the telling only if I dig deep into everything.

Because it was so beautiful at first, even the circumstance of my sleepingbag suddenly erupting feathers in the middle of the night as I turned over to sleep on, so I curse and have to get up and sew it by lamplight or in the morning it might be empty of feathers—And as I bend poor mother head over my needle and thread in the cabin, by the fresh fire and in the light of the kerosene lamp, here come those damned silent black wings flapping and throwing shadows all over my little home, the bloody bat's come in my house—Trying to sew a poor patch on my old crumbly sleepingbag (mostly ruined by my having to sweat out a fever inside of it in a hotel room in Mexico City in 1957 right after the gigantic earthquake there), the nylon all rotten almost from all that old sweat, but still soft, tho so soft I have to cut out a piece of old shirt flap and patch over the rip—I remember looking up from my middle of the night chore and saying bleakly "They, yes, have bats in Mien Mo valley"—But the fire crackles, the patch gets sewn, the creek gurgles and thumps outside—A creek having so many voices it's amazing, from the kettledrum basin deep bumpbumps to the little gurgly feminine crickles over shallow rocks, sudden choruses of other singers and voices from the log dam, dibble dabble all night long and all day long the voices of the creek amusing me so much at first but in the later horror of that madness night becoming the babble and rave of evil angels in my head—So not minding the bat or the rip finally, ending up cant sleep because too awake now and it's 3 A.M. so the fire I stoke and I settle down and read the entire *Doctor Jekyll and Mister Hyde* novel in the wonderful little handsized leather book left there by smart Monsanto who also must've read it with wide eyes on a night like that—Ending the last elegant sentences at dawn, time to get up and fetch water from gurgly creek and start breakfast of pancakes and syrup—And saying to myself "So why fret when something goes wrong like your sleepingbag breaking in the night, use self reliance"—"Screw the bats" I add.

Marvelous opening moment in fact of the first afternoon I'm left alone in the cabin and I make my first meal, wash my first dishes, nap, and wake up to hear the rapturous ring of silence or Heaven even within and throughout the gurgle of the creek—When you say AM ALONE and the cabin is suddenly home only because you made one meal and washed your firstmeal dishes—Then nightfall, the religious vestal lighting of the beautiful kerosene lamp after careful washing of the mantle in the creek and careful drying with toilet paper, which spoils it by specking it so you again wash it in the creek and this time just let the mantle drip dry in the sun, the late afternoon sun that disappears so quickly behind those giant high steep canyon walls—Nightfall, the kerosene lamp casts a glow in the cabin, I go out and pick some ferns like the ferns of the Lankavatara Scripture, those hairnet ferns, "Look sirs, a beautiful hairnet!"—Late afternoon fog pours in over the canyon walls, sweep, cover the sun, it gets cold, even the flies on the porch are as so sad as the fog on the peaks—As daylight retreats the flies retreat like polite Emily Dickinson flies and when it's dark they're all asleep in trees or someplace—At high noon they're in the cabin with you but edging further towards the open doorsill as the afternoon lengthens, how strangely gracious—There's the hum of the bee drone two blocks away the racket of it you'd think it was right over the roof, when the bee drone swirls nearer and nearer (gulp again) you retreat into the cabin and wait, maybe they got a message to come and see you all two thousand of em—But getting used to the bee drone finally which seems to happen like a big party once a week—And so everything eventually marvelous.

Even the first frightening night on the beach in the fog with my notebook and pencil, sitting there crosslegged in the sand facing all the Pacific fury flashing on rocks that rise like gloomy sea shroud towers out of the cove, the bingbang cove with its seas booming inside caves and slapping out, the cities of seaweed floating up and down you can even see their dark leer in the phosphorescent seabeach nightlight—That first night I sit there and all I know, as I look up, is the kitchen light is on, on the cliff, to the right, where somebody's just built a cabin overlooking all the horrible Sur, somebody up there's having a mild and tender supper that's all I know—The lights from the cabin kitchen up there go out like a little weak lighthouse beacon and ends suspended a thousand feet over the crashing shore—Who would build a cabin up there but some bored but hoary old adventurous architect maybe got sick of running for congress and one of these days a big Orson Welles tragedy with screaming ghosts a woman in a white nightgown'll go flying down that sheer cliff—But actually in my mind what I really see is the kitchen lights of that mild and tender maybe even romantic supper up there, in all that howling fog, and here I am way below in the Vulcan's Forge itself looking up with sad eyes—Blanking my little Camel cigarette on a billion year old rock that rises behind my head to a height unbelievable—The little kitchen light on the cliff is only on the end of it, behind it the shoulders of the great sea hound cliff go rising up and back and sweeping inland higher and higher till I gasp to think "Looks like a reclining dog, big friggin shoulders on that sonofabitch"—Riseth and sweepeth and scareth men to death but what is death anyway in all this water and rock.

I fix up my sleepingbag on the porch of the cabin but at 2 A.M. the fog starts dripping all wet so I have to go indoors with wet sleepingbag and make new arrangements but who cant sleep like a log in a solitary cabin in the woods, you wake up in the late morning so refreshed and realizing the universe namelessly: the universe is an Angel —But easy enough to say when you've had your escape from the gooky city turn into a success—And it's finally only in the woods you get that nostalgia for "cities" at last, you dream of long gray journeys to cities where soft evenings'll unfold like Paris but never seeing how sickening it will be because of the primordial innocence of health and stillness in the wilds—So I tell myself "Be Wise."

• • •

7

Because on the fourth day I began to get bored and noted it in my diary with amazement, "Already bored?"—Even tho the handsome words of Emerson would shake me out of that where he says (in one of those little redleather books, in the essay on "Self Reliance" a man "is relieved and gay when he has put his heart into his work and done his best") (applicable both to building simple silly little millraces and writing big stupid stories like this)—Words from that trumpet of the morning in America, Emerson, he who announced Whitman and also said "Infancy conforms to nobody"—The infancy of the simplicity of just being happy in the woods, conforming to nobody's idea about what to do, what should be done—"Life is not an apology"—And when a vain and malicious philanthropic abolitionist accused him of being blind to the issues of slavery he said "Thy love afar is spite at home" (maybe the philanthropist had Negro help anyway)—So once I again I'm Ti Jean the Child, playing, sewing patches, cooking suppers, washing dishes (always kept the kettle boiling on the fire and anytime dishes need to be washed I just pour hot hot water into pan with Tide soap and soak them good and then wipe them clean after scouring with little 5-&-10 wire

scourer)—Long nights simply thinking about the usefulness of that little
wire scourer, those little yellow copper things you buy in supermarkets
for 10 cents, all to me infinitely more interesting than the stupid and
senseless "Steppenwolf" novel in the shack which I read with a shrug,
this old fart reflecting the "conformity" of today and all the while he
thought he was a big Nietzsche, old imitator of Dostoevsky 50 years
too late (he feels tormented in a "personal hell" he calls it because he
doesnt like what other people like!)—Better at noon to watch the orange and black Princeton colors on the wings of a butterfly—Best to go
hear the sound of the sea at night on the shore.

   Maybe I shouldna gone out and scared or bored or belabored myself so much, tho, on that beach at night which would scare any ordinary mortal—Every night around eight after supper I'd put on my big
fisherman coat and take the notebook, pencil and lamp and start down
the trail (sometimes passing ghostly Alf on the way) and go under that
frightful high bridge and see through the dark fog ahead the white
mouths of ocean coming high at me—But knowing the terrain I'd walk
right on, jump the beach creek, and go to my corner by the cliff not far
from one of the caves and sit there like an idiot in the dark writing
down the sound of the waves in the notebook page (secretarial notebook) which I could see white in the darkness and therefore without
benefit of lamp scrawl on—I was afraid to light my lamp for fear I'd
scare the people way up there on the cliff eating their nightly tender
supper—(later found out there was nobody up there eating tender suppers, they were overtime carpenters finishing the place in bright lights)
—And I'd get scared of the rising tide with its 15 foot waves yet sit
there hoping in faith that Hawaii warnt sending no tidal wave I might
miss seeing in the dark coming from miles away high as Groomus—
One night I got scared anyway so sat on top of 10 foot cliff at the foot
of the big cliff and the waves are going "Rare, he rammed the gate
rare"—"Raw roo roar"—"Crowsh"—the way waves sound especially
at night—The sea not speaking in sentences so much as in short lines:
"Which one? . . . the one ploshed?. . . . the same, ah Boom" . . . Writing
down these fantastic inanities actually but yet I felt I had to do it because
James Joyce wasnt about to do it now he was dead (and figuring "Next
year I'll write the different sound of the Atlantic crashing say on the
night shores of Cornwall, or the soft sound of the Indian Ocean crashing
at the mouth of the Ganges maybe")—And I just sit there listening to
the waves talk all up and down the sand in different tones of voice "Ka
bloom, kerplosh, ah ropey otter barnacled be, crowsh, are rope the an-

gels in all the sea?" and such—Looking up occasionally to see rare cars crossing the high bridge and wondering what they'd see on this drear foggy night if they knew a madman was down there a thousand feet below in all that windy fury sitting in the dark writing in the dark— Some sort of sea beatnik, tho anybody wants to call me a beatnik for THIS better try it if they dare—The huge black rocks seem to move— The bleak awful roaring isolateness, no ordinary man could do it I'm telling you—*I am a Breton!* I cry and the blackness speaks back "*Les poissons de la mer parlent Breton*" (the fishes of the sea speak Breton) —Nevertheless I go there every night even tho I dont feel like it, it's my duty (and probably drove me mad), and write these sea sounds, and all the whole insane poem "Sea."

Always so wonderful in fact to get away from that and back to the more human woods and come to the cabin where the fire's still red and you can see the Bodhisattva's lamp, the glass of ferns on the table, the box of Jasmine tea nearby, all so gentle and human after that rocky deluge out there—So I make an excellent pan of muffins and tell myself "Blessed is the man can make his own bread"—Like that, the whole three weeks, happiness—And I'm rolling my own cigarettes, too—And as I say sometimes I meditate how wonderful the fantastic use I've gotten out of cheap little articles like the scourer, but in this instance I think of the marvelous belongings in my rucksack like my 25 cent plastic shaker with which I've just made the muffin batter but also I've used it in the past to drink hot tea, wine, coffee, whisky and even stored clean handkerchiefs in it when I traveled—The top part of the shaker, my holy cup, and had it for five years now—And other belongings so valuable compared to the worthlessness of expensive things I'd bought and never used—Like my black soft sleeping sweater also five years which I was now wearing in the damp Sur summer night and day, over a flannel shirt in the cold, and just the sweater for the night's sleep in the bag—Endless use and virtue of it!—And because the expensive things were of ill use, like the fancy pants I'd bought for recent recording dates in New York and other television appearances and never even wore again, useless things like a $40 raincoat I never wore because it didnt even have slits in the side pockets (you pay for the label and the so called "tailoring")—Also an expensive tweed jacket bought for TV and never worn again—Two silly sports shirts bought for Hollywood never worn again and were 9 bucks each!—And it's almost tearful to realize and remember the old green T-shirt I'd found, mind you, eight years ago, mind you, on the DUMP in Watsonville California mind you, and got fantastic use and comfort from it—Like working to fix that new stream in the creek to flow through the convenient deep new waterhole near the wood platform on the bank, and losing myself in this like a kid playing, it's the little things that count (clichés are truisms and all truisms are true)—On my deathbed I could be remembering that creek day and forgetting the day MGM bought my book, I could be remembering the old lost green dump T-shirt and forgetting the sapphired robes—Mebbe the best way to get into Heaven.

I go back to the beach in the daytime to write my "Sea," I stand there barefoot by the sea stopping to scratch one ankle with one toe, I hear the rhythm of those waves, and they're saying suddenly "Is Virgin you trying to fathom me"—I go back to make a pot of tea.

> Summer afternoon—
> Impatiently chewing
> The Jasmine leaf

At high noon the sun always coming out at last, strong, beating down on my nice high porch where I sit with books and coffee and the noon I thought about the ancient Indians who must have inhabited this canyon for thousands of years, how even as far back at the 10th Century this valley must have looked the same, just different trees: these ancient Indians simply the ancestors of the Indians of only recently say 1860— How they've all died and quietly buried their grievances and excitements—How the creek may have been an inch deeper since logging operations of the last 60 years have removed some of the watershed in the hills back there—How the women pounded the local acorns, acorns or shmacorns, I finally found the natural nuts of the valley and they were sweet tasting—And men hunted deer—In fact God knows what they did because I wasnt here—But the same valley, a thousand years of dust more or less over their footsteps of 960 A.D.—And as far as I can see the world is too old for us to talk about it with our new words—We will pass just as quietly through life (passing through, passing through) as the 10th century people of this valley only with a little more noise and a few bridges and dams and bombs that wont even last a million years—The world being just what it is, moving and passing through, actually alright in the long view and nothing to complain about—Even the rocks of the valley had earlier rock ancestors, a billion billion years ago, have left no howl of complaint—Neither the bee, or the first sea urchins, or the clam, or the severed paw—All sad So-Is sight of the world, right there in front of my nose as I look,—And looking at that valley in fact I also realize I have to make lunch and it wont be any different than the lunch of those olden men and besides it'll taste good—Everything is the same, the fog says "We are fog and we fly by dissolving like ephemera," and the leaves say "We are leaves and we jiggle in the wind, that's all, we come and go, grow and fall" —Even the paper bags in my garbage pit say "We are man-transformed paper bags made out of wood pulp, we are kinda proud of being paper bags as long as that will be possible, but we'll be mush again with our sisters the leaves come rainy season"—The tree stumps say "We are tree stumps torn out of the ground by men, sometimes by wind, we have big tendrils full of earth that drink out of the earth"—Men say "We are men, we pull out tree stumps, we make paper bags, we think wise thoughts, we make lunch, we look around, we make a great effort to realize everything is the same"—While the sand says "We are sand, we already know," and the sea says "We are always come and go, fall and plosh"—The empty blue sky of space says "All this comes back to me, then goes again, and comes back again, then goes again, and I dont care, it still belongs to me"—The blue sky adds "Dont call me eternity, call me God if you like, all of you talkers are in paradise: the leaf is paradise, the tree stump is paradise, the paper bag is paradise, the man is paradise, the sand is paradise, the sea is paradise, the man is paradise, the fog is paradise"—Can you imagine a man with marvelous insights like these can go mad within a month? (because you must admit all those talking paper bags and sands were telling the truth)—But I remember seeing a mess of leaves suddenly go skittering in the wind and into the creek, then floating rapidly down the creek towards the sea, making me feel a nameless horror even then of "Oh my God, we're all being swept away to sea no matter what we know or say or do"—And a bird who was on a crooked branch is suddenly gone without my even hearing him.

• • •

10

With my mind even and upright and abiding nowhere, as Hui Neng would say, I go dancing off like a fool from my sweet retreat, rucksack on back, after only three weeks and really after only 3 or 4 days of boredom, and go hankering back for the city—"You go out in joy and in sadness you return," says Thomas à Kempis talking about all the fools who go forth for pleasure like high school boys on Saturday night hurrying clacking down the sidewalk to the car adjusting their ties and rubbing their hands with anticipatory zeal, only to end up Sunday morning groaning in bleary beds that Mother has to make anyway—It's a beautiful day as I come out of that ghostly canyon road and step out on the coast highway, just this side of Raton Canyon bridge, and there they are, thousands and thousands of tourists driving by slowly on the high curves all oo ing and aa ing at all that vast blue panorama of seas washing and raiding at the coast of California—I figure I'll get a ride into Monterey real easy and take the bus there and be in Frisco by nightfall for a big ball of wino yelling with the gang, I feel in fact Dave Wain oughta be back by now, or Cody will be ready for a ball, and there'll be girls, and such and such, forgetting entirely that only three weeks previous I'd been sent fleeing from that gooky city by the horrors—But hadnt the sea told me to flee back to my own reality?

But it is beautiful especially to see up ahead north a vast expanse of curving seacoast with inland mountains dreaming under slow clouds, like a scene of ancient Spain, or properly really like a scene of the real essentially Spanish California, the old Monterey pirate coast right there, you can see what the Spaniards must've thought when they came around the bend in their magnificent sloopies and saw all that dreaming fatland beyond the seashore whitecap doormat—Like the land of gold—The old Monterey and Big Sur and Santa Cruz magic—So I confidently adjust my pack straps and start trudging down the road looking back over my shoulder to thumb.

This is the first time I've hitch hiked in years and I soon begin to see that things have changed in America, you cant get a ride any more (but of course especially on a strictly tourist road like this coast highway with no trucks or business)—Sleek long stationwagon after wagon comes sleering by smoothly, all colors of the rainbow and pastel at that, pink, blue, white, the husband is in the driver's seat with a long ridiculous vacationist hat with a long baseball visor making him look witless and idiot—Beside him sits wifey, the boss of America, wearing dark glasses and sneering, even if he wanted to pick me up or anybody up she wouldn't let him—But in the two deep backseats are children, children, millions of children, all ages, they're fighting and screaming over ice cream, they're spilling vanilla all over the Tartan seatcovers—There's no room anymore anyway for a hitch hiker, tho conceivably the poor bastard might be allowed to ride like a meek gunman or silent murderer in the very back platform of the wagon, but here no, alas! here is ten thousand racks of drycleaned and perfectly pressed suits and dresses of all sizes for the family to look like millionaires every time they stop at a roadside dive for bacon and eggs—Every time the old man's trousers start to get creased a little in the front he's made to take down a fresh pair of slacks from the back rack and go on, like that, bleakly, tho he might have secretly wished just a good oldtime fishing trip alone or with his buddies for this year's vacation—But the P.T.A. has prevailed over every one of his desires by now, 1960's, it's no time for him to yearn for Big Two Hearted River and the old sloppy pants and the string of fish in the tent, or the woodfire with Bourbon at night—It's time for motels, roadside driveins, bringing napkins to the gang in the car, having the car washed before the return trip—And if he thinks he wants to explore any of the silent secret roads of America it's no go, the lady in the sneering dark glasses has now become the navigator and sits there sneering over her previously printed blue-lined roadmap distributed by happy executives in neckties to the vacationists of America who would also wear neckties (after having come along so far) but the vacation fashion is sports shirts, long visored hats, dark glasses, pressed slacks and baby's first shoes dipped in gold oil dangling from the dashboard —So here I am standing in that road with that big woeful rucksack but also probably with that expression of horror on my face after all those nights sitting in the seashore under giant black cliffs, they see in me the very apotheosical opposite of their every vacation dream and of course drive on—That afternoon I say about 5 thousand cars or probably 3 thousand passed me not one of them ever dreamed of stopping—Which didnt bother me anyway because at first seeing that gorgeous long coast up to Monterey I thought "Well I'll just hike right in, it's only 14 miles, I oughta do that easy"—And on the way there's all kindsa interesting things to see anyway like the seals barking on rocks below, or quiet old farms made of logs on the hills across the highway, or sudden up-stretches that go along dreamy seaside meadows where cows grace and graze in full sight of endless blue Pacific—But because I'm wearing de-sert boots with their fairly thin soles, and the sun is beating hot on the tar road, the heat finally gets through the soles and I begin to deliver heat blisters in my sockiboos—I'm limping along wondering what's the matter with me when I realize I've got blisters—I sit by the side of the road and look—I take out my first aid kit from the pack and apply unguents and put on cornpads and carry on—But the combination of the heavy pack and the heat of the road increases the pain of the blisters until finally I realize I've got to hitch hike a ride or never make it to Monterey at all.

But the tourists bless their hearts after all, they couldnt know, only think I'm having a big happy hike with my rucksack and they drive on, even tho I stick out my thumb—I'm in despair because I'm really stranded now, and by the time I've walked seven miles I still have seven to go but I cant go on another step—I'm also thirsty and there are absolutely no filling stations or anything along the way—My feet are ruined and burned, it develops now into a day of complete torture, from nine o'clock in the morning till four in the afternoon I negotiate those nine or so miles when I finally have to stop and sit down and wipe the blood off my feet—And then when I fix the feet and put the shoes on again, to hike on, I can only do it mincingly with little twinkletoe steps like Babe Ruth, twisting footsteps every way I can think of not to press too hard on any particular blister—So that the tourists (lessening now as the sun starts to go down) can now plainly see that there's a man on the highway limping under a huge pack and asking for a ride, but still they're afraid he may be the Hollywood hitch hiker with the hidden gun and besides he's got a rucksack on his back as tho he'd just escaped from the war in Cuba—Or's got dismembered bodies in the bag anyway—But as I say I dont blame them.

The only car that passes that might have given me a ride is going in the wrong direction, down to Sur, and it's a rattly old car of some kind with a big bearded "South Coast Is the Lonely Coast" folksinger in it waving at me but finally a little truck pulls up and waits for me 50 yards ahead and I limprun that distance on daggers in my feet—It's a guy with a dog—He'll drive me to the next gas station, then he turns off—But when he learns about my feet he takes me clear to the bus station in Monterey—Just as a gesture of kindness—No particular reason, and I've made no particular plea about my feet, just mentioned it.

I offer to buy him a beer but he's going on home for supper so I go into the bus station and clean up and change and pack things away, stow the bag in the locker, buy the bus ticket, and go limping quietly in the blue fog streets of Monterey evening feeling light as feather and happy as a millionaire—The last time I ever hitch hiked—And NO RIDES a sign.

• • •

30

I do understand the strange day Ben Fagan finally came to visit me alone, bringing wine, smoking his pipe, and saying "Jack you need some sleep, that chair you say you've been sitting in for days have you noticed the bottom is falling out of it?"—I get on the floor and by God look and it's true, the springs are coming out—"How long have you been sitting in that chair?"—"Every day waiting for Billie to come home and talking to Perry and the others all day . . . My God let's go out and sit in the park," I add—In the blur of days McLear has also been over on a forgotten day when, on nothing but his chance mention that maybe I could get his book published in Paris I jump up and dial longdistance for Paris and call Claude Gallimard and only get his butler apparently in some Parisian suburb and I hear the insane giggle on the other end of the line—"Is this the home, *c'est le chez eux de Monsieur Gallimard?*"— Giggle—"*Où est Monsieur Gallimard?*"—Giggle—A very strange phone call—McLear waiting there expectantly to get his "Dark Brown" published—So in a fury of madness I then call London to talk to my old buddy Lionel just for no reason at all and I finally reach him at home he's saying on the wire "You're calling me from San Francisco? but why?"—Which I cant answer any more than the giggling butler (and to add to my madness, of course, why should a longdistance call to Paris to a publisher end up with a giggle and a longdistance call to an old friend in London end up with the friend getting mad?)—So Fagan now sees I'm going overboard crazy and I need sleep—"We'll get a bottle!" I yell—But end up, he's sitting in the grass of the park smoking his pipe, from noon to 6 P.M., and I'm passed out exhausted sleeping in the grass, bottle unopened, only to wake up once in a while wondering where I am and by God I'm in Heaven with Ben Fagan watching over men and me.

And I say to Ben when I wake up in the gathering 6 P.M. dusk "Ah Ben I'm sorry I ruined our day by sleeping like this" but he says: "You needed the sleep, I told ya"—"And you mean to tell me you been sitting all afternoon like that?"—"Watching unexpected events," says he, "like there seems to be sound of a Bacchanal in those bushes over there" and I look and hear children yelling and screaming in hidden bushes in the park—"What they doing?"—"I dont know: also a lot of strange people

went by"—"How long have I been sleeping?"—"Ages"—"I'm sorry"
—"Why should be sorry, I love you anyway"—"Was I snoring?"—
"You've been snoring all day and I've been sitting here all day"—"What
a beautiful day!"—"Yes it's been a beautiful day"—"How strange!"—
"Yes, strange . . . but not so strange either, you're just tired"—"What
do you think of Billie?"—He chuckles over his pipe: "What do you
expect me to say? that the frog bit your leg?"—"Why do you have a
diamond in your forehead?"—"I dont have a diamond in my forehead
damn you and stop making arbitrary conceptions!" he roars—"But
what am I doing?"—"Stop thinking about yourself, will ya, just float
with the world"—"Did the world float by the park?"—"All day, you
should have seen it, I've smoked a whole package of Edgewood, it's
been a very strange day"—"Are you sad I didnt talk to you?"—"Not
at all, in fact I'm glad: we better be starting back," he adds, "Billie be
coming home from work soon now"—"Ah Ben, Ah Sunflower"—"Ah
shit" he says—"It's strange"—"Who said it wasnt"—"I dont understand it"—"Dont worry about it"—"Hmm holy room, sad room, life
is a sad room"—"All sentient beings realize that," he says sternly—
Benjamin my real Zen Master even more than all our Georges and Ar-
thurs actually—"Ben I think I'm going crazy"—"You said that to me
in 1955"—"Yeh but my brain's gettin soft from drinkin and drinkin
and drinkin"—"What you need is a cup of tea I'd say if I didnt know
that you're too crazy to know how really crazy you are"—"But why?
what's going on?"—"Did you come three thousand miles to find
out?"—"Three thousand miles from where, after all? from whiney old
me"—"That's alright, everything is possible, even Nietzsche knew
that"—"Aint nothin wrong with old Nietzsche"—" 'Xcept he went
mad too"—"Do you think I'm going mad?"—"Ho ho ho" (hearty
laugh)—"What's that mean, laughing at me?"—"Nobody's laughing at
you, dont get excited"—"What'll we do now?"—"Let's go visit the
museum over there"—There's a museum of some sort across the grass
of the park so I get up wobbly and walk with old Ben across the sad
grass, at one point I put my arm over his shoulder and lean on him—
"Are you a ghoul?" I ask—"Sure, why not?"—"I like ghouls that let
me sleep?"—"Duluoz it's good for you to drink in a way 'cause you're
awful stingy with yourself when You're sober"—"You sound like
Julien"—"I never met Julien but I understand Billie looks like him, you
kept saying that before you went to sleep"—"What happened while I
was asleep?"—"Oh, people went by and came back and forth and the
sun sank and finally sank down and's gone now almost as you can see,

what you want, just name it you got it"—"Well I want sweet salvation"—"What's sposed to be sweet about salvation? maybe it's sour"—"It's sour in my mouth"—"Maybe your mouth is too big, or too small, salvation is for little kitties but only for awhile"—"Did you see any little kitties today?"—"Shore, hundreds of em came to visit you while you were sleeping"—"Really?"—"Sure, didnt you know you were saved?"—"Now come on!"—"One of them was real big and roared like a lion but he had a big wet snout and kissed you and you said *Ah*"—"What's this museum up here?"—"Let's go in and find out"—That's the way Ben is, he doesnt know what's going on either but at least he waits to find out maybe—But the museum is closed—We stand there on the steps looking at the closed door—"Hey," I say, "the temple is closed."

So suddenly in red sundown me and Ben Fagan arm in arm are walking slowly sadly back down the broad steps like two monks going down the esplanade of Kyoto (as I imagine Kyoto somehow) and we're both smiling happily suddenly—I feel good because I've had my sleep but mainly I feel good because somehow old Ben (my age) has blessed me by sitting over my sleep all day and now with these few silly words—Arm in arm we slowly descend the steps without a word—It's been the only peaceful day I've had in California, in fact, except alone in the woods, which I tell him and says "Well, who said you werent alone now?" making me realize the ghostliness of existence tho I feel his big bulging body with my hands and say: "You sure some pathetic ghost with all that ephemeral heavy crock a flesh"—"I didnt say nottin" he laughs—"Whatever I say Ben, dont mind it, I'm just a fool"—"You said in 1957 in the grass drunk on whiskey you were the greatest thinker in the world"—"That was before I fell asleep and woke up: now I realize I'm no good at all and that makes me feel free"—"You're not even free being no good, you better stop thinking, that's all"—"I'm glad you visited me today, I think I might have died"—"It's all your fault" —"What are we gonna do with our lives?"—"Oh," he says, "I dunno, just watch em I guess"—"Do you hate me? . . . well, do you like me? . . . well, how are things?"—"The hicks are alright"—"Anybody hex ya lately . . . ?"—"Yeh, with cardboard games?"—"Cardboard games?" I ask—"Well you know, they build cardboard houses and put people in them and the people are cardboard and the magician makes the dead body twitch and they bring water to the moon, and the moon has a strange ear, and all that, so I'm alright, Goof."

"Okay."

So there I am as it starts to get dark standing with one hand on the window curtain looking down on the street as Ben Fagan walks away to get the bus on the corner, his big baggy corduroy pants and simple blue Goodwill workshirt, going home to the bubble bath and a famous poem, not really worried or at least not worried about what I'm worried about tho he too carries that anguishing guilt I guess and hopeless remorse that the potboiler of time hasnt made his early primordial dawns over the pines of Oregon come true—I'm clutching at the drapes of the window like the Phantom of the Opera behind the masque, waiting for Billie to come home and remembering how I used to stand by the windows like this in my childhood and look out on dusky streets and think how awful I was in this development everybody said was supposed to be "my life" and "their lives."—Not so much that I'm a drunkard that I feel guilty about but that others who occupy this plane of "life on earth" with me dont feel guilty at all—Crooked judges shaving and smiling in the morning on the way to their heinous indifferences, respectable generals ordering soldiers by telephone to go die or drop dead, pickpockets nodding in cells saying "I never hurt anybody," "that's one thing you can say for me, yes sir," women who regard themselves saviors of men simply stealing their substance because they think their swan-rich necks deserve it anyway (though for every swan-rich neck you lose there's another ten waiting, each one ready to lay for a lemon), in fact awful hugefaced monsters of men just because their shirts are clean deigning to control the lives of working men by running for Governor saying "Your tax money in my hands will be aptly used," "You should realize how valuable I am and how much you need me, without me what would you be, not led at all?"—Forward to the big designed mankind cartoon of a man standing facing the rising sun with strong shoulders with a plough at his feet, the necktied governor is going to make hay while the sun rises—?—I feel guilty for being a member of the human race—Drunkard yes and one of the worst fools on earth— In fact not even a genuine drunkard just a fool—But I stand there with hand on curtain looking down for Billie, who's late, Ah me, I remember that frightening thing Milarepa said which is other than those reassuring words of his I remembered in the cabin of sweet loneness on Big Sur: "When the various experiences come to light in meditation, do not be proud and anxious to tell other people, else to Goddesses and Mothers you will bring annoyance" and here I am a perfectly obvious fool American writer doing just that not only for a living (which I was always able to glean anyway from railroad and ship and lifting boards and sacks with humble hand) but because if I dont write what actually I see happening in this unhappy globe which is rounded by the contours of my deathskull I think I'll have been sent on earth by poor God for nothing—Tho being a Phantom of the Opera why should that worry me?—In my youth leaning my brow hopelessly on the typewriter bar, wondering why God ever was anyway?—Or biting my lip in brown glooms in the parlor chair in which my father's died and we've all died a million deaths—Only Fagan can understand and now he's got his bus—And when Billie comes home with Elliott I smile and sit down in the chair and it utterly collapses under me, blang, I'm sprawled on the floor with surprise, the chair has gone.

"How'd that happen?" wonders Billie and at the same time we both look at the fishbowl and both the goldfishes are upsidedown floating dead on the surface of the water.

I've been sitting in that chair by that fishbowl for a week drinking and smoking and talking and now the goldfish are dead.

"What killed them?"—"I dont know"—"Did I kill them because I gave them some Kelloggs corn flakes?"—"Mebbe, you're not supposed to give them anything but their fish food"—"But I thought they were hungry so I gave them a few flicks of corn flakes?—"Well I dont know what killed them"—"But why dont anybody know? what happened? why do they do this? otters and mouses and every damn thing dyin on all sides Billie, I cant stand it, it's all my goddam fault every time!"—"Who said it was your fault dear?"—"Dear? you call me dear? why do you call me dear?"—"Ah, let me love you" (kissing me), "just because you dont deserve it"—(Chastised): "Why dont I deserve it"—"Because you say so . . ."—"But what about the fish"—"I dont know, really"—"Is it because I've been sitting in that crumbling chair all week blowing smoke on their water? and all the others smoking and all the talk?"—But the little kid Elliott comes crawling up his mommy's lap and starts asking questions: "Billie," he calls her, "Billie, Billie, Billie," feeling her face, I'm almost going mad from the sadness of it all—"What did you do all day?"—"I was with Ben Fagan and slept in the park . . . Billie what are we gonna do?"—"Anytime you say like you said, we'll get married and fly to Mexico with Perry and Elliott"—"I'm afraid of Perry and I'm afraid of Elliott"—"He's only a little boy"—"Billie I dont wanta get married, I'm afraid . . ."—"Afraid?"—"I wanta go home and die with my cat." I could be a handsome thin young president in a suit sitting in an oldfashioned rocking chair, no instead I'm just the Phantom of the Opera standing by a drape among dead fish and broken chairs —Can it be that no one cares who made me or why?—"Jack what's the matter, what are you talking about?" but suddenly as she's making supper and poor little Elliott is waiting there with spoon upended in fist I realize it's just a little family home scene and I'm just a nut in the wrong place—And in fact Billie starts saying "Jack we should be married and have quiet suppers like this with Elliott, something would sanctify you forever I'm positive."

"What have I done wrong?"—"What you've done wrong is withhold your love from a woman like me and from previous women and future women like me—can you imagine all the fun we'd have being married, putting Elliott to bed, going out to hear jazz or even taking planes to Paris suddenly and all the things I have to teach you and you teach me—instead all you've been doing is wasting life really sitting around sad wondering where to go and all the time it's right there for you to take"—"Supposin I dont want it"—"That's part of the picture where you say you dont want it, of course you want . . ."—"But I dont, I'm a creepy strange guy you dont even know"—("Cweepy? what's cweepy? Billie? what's cweepy?" is asking poor little Elliott)—And meanwhile Perry comes in for a minute and I pointblank say to him "I dont understand you Perry, I love you, dig you, you're wild, but what's all this business where you wanta kidnap little girls?" but suddenly as I'm asking that I see tears in his eyes and I realize he's in love with Billie and has always been, wow—I even say it, "You're in love with Billie aint ya? I'm sorry, I'm cuttin out"—"What are you talkin about man?"—It's a big argument then about how he and Billie are just friends so I start singing *Just Friends* like Sinatra "Two friends but not like before" but goodhearted Perry seeing me sing runs downstairs to get another bottle for me—But nevertheless the fish are dead and the chair is broken.

● ● ●

33

It sounds all so sad but it was actually such a gay night as Dave and Romana came over and there's all the business of packing boxes and clothes down to the car, nipping out of bottles, getting ready in fact to sing all the way to Big Sur "Home On the Range" and "I'm Just a

Lonesome Old Turd" by Dave Wain—Me sitting up front next to Dave and Romana for some reason maybe because I wanted to identify with my old broken front rockingchair and lean there flapping and singing but with Romana between us the seat is pinned down and no longer flaps—Meanwhile Billie is on the back mattress with sleeping child and off we go booming down Bay Shore to that other shore whatever it will bring, the way people always feel whenever they essay some trip long or short especially in the night—The eyes of hope looking over the glare of the hood into the maw with its white line feeding in straight as an arrow, the lighting of fresh cigarettes, the buckling to lean forward to the next adventure something that's been going on in America ever since the covered wagons clocked the deserts in three months flat—Billie doesnt mind that I dont sit in back with her because she knows I wanta sing and have a good time—Romana and I hit up fantastic medleys of popular and folk songs of all kinds and Dave contributes his New York Chicago blue light nightclub romantic baritone specialties—My wavering Sinatra is barely heard in fact—Beat on your knees and yell and sing Dixie and Banjo On My Knee, get raucous and moan out Red River Valley, "Where's my harmonica, I been meanin to buy me a eight dollar harmonica for eight years now."

It always starts out good like that, the bad moments—Nothing is gained or lost also by the fact that I insist we stop at Cody's en route so I can pick up some clothes I left there but secretly I want Evelyn to finally come face to face with Billie—It surprises me more however to see the look of absolute fright on Cody's face as we pour into his livingroom at midnight and I announce that Billie's in the jeep sleeping—Evelyn is not perturbed at all and in fact says to me privately in the kitchen "I guess it was bound to happen sometime she'd come here and see it but I guess it was destined to be you who'd bring her"—"What's Cody so worried about?"—"You're spoiling all his chance to be real secretive"—"He hasnt come and seen us for a whole week, that's in a way what happened, he just left me stranded there: I've been feeling awful, too"—"Well if you want you can ask her to come in"—"Well we're leaving in a minute anyway, you wanta see her at least?"—"I dont care"—Cody is sitting in the livingroom absolutely rigid, stiff, formal, with a big Irish stone in his eye: I know he's really mad at me this time tho I dont really know why—I go out and there's Billie alone in the car over sleeping Elliott biting her fingernail—"You wanta come in and meet Evelyn?"—"I shouldnt, she wont like that, is Cody there?"— "Yah"—So Willamine climbs out (I remember just then Evelyn telling me seriously that Cody always calls his women by their full first names, Rosemarie, Joanna, Evelyn, Willamine, he never gives them silly nick-names nor uses them).

The meeting is not eventful, of course, both girls keep their silence and hardly look at each other so it's all me and Dave Wain carrying on with the usual boloney and I see that Cody is really very sick and tired of me bringing gangs arbitrarily to his place, running off with his mis-tress, getting drunk and thrown out of family plays, hundred dollars or no hundred dollars he probably feels I'm just a fool now anyway and hopelessly lost forever but I dont realize that myself because I'm feeling good—I want us to resume down that road singing bawdier and darker songs till we're negotiating narrow mountain roads at the pitch of the greatest songs.

I try to ask Cody about Perry and all the other strange characters who visit Billie in the City but he just looks at me out of the corner eye and says "Ah, yah,hm,"—I dont know and I never will know what he's up to anyway in the long run: I realize I'm just a silly stranger goofing with other strangers for no reason far away from anything that ever mattered to me whatever that was—Always an ephemeral "visitor" to the Coast never really involved with anyone's lives there because I'm always ready to fly back across the country but not to any life of my own on the other end either, just a traveling stranger like Old Bull Balloon, an exemplar of the loneliness of Doren Coit actually waiting for the only real trip, to Venus, to the mountain of Mien Mo—Tho when I look out of Cody's livingroom window just then I do see my star still shining for me as it's done all these 38 years over crib, out ship windows, jail windows, over sleepingbags only now it's dummier and dimmer and getting blurreder damnit as tho even my own star be now fading away from concern for me as I from concern for it—In fact we're all strangers with strange eyes sitting in a midnight livingroom for nothing—And small talk at that, like Billie saying "I always wanted a nice fireplace" and I'm yelling "Dont worry we got one at the cabin hey Dave? and all the wood's chopped!" and Evelyn:—"What does Mon-santo think of you using his cabin all summer, weren't you supposed to go there alone in secret?"—"It's too late now!" I sing swigging from the bottle without which I'd only drop with shame face flat on the floor or on the gravel driveway—And Dave and Romana look a little uneasy finally so we all get up to go, zoom, and that's the last time I see Cody or Evelyn anyway.

And as I say our songs grow mightier as the road grows darker and wilder, finally here we are on the canyon road the headlights just reaching out there around bleak sand shoulders—Down to the creek where I unlock the corral gate—Across the meadow and back to the haunted cabin—Where on the strength of that night's booze and getaway gladness Billie and I actually have a good time lighting fires and making coffee and *gong* to be together in the one sleepingbag easy as pie after we've bundled up little Elliott and Dave and Romana have retired in his double nylon bag by the creek in the moonlight.

No, it's the next day and night that concerns me.

34

The whole day begins simply enough with me getting up feeling fair and going down to the creek to slurp up water in my palms and wash up, seeing the languid waving of one large brown thigh over the mass of Dave's nylons indicative of an early morning love scene, in fact Romana telling us later at breakfast "When I woke up this morning and saw all those trees and water and clouds I told Dave 'It's a beautiful universe we created' "—A real Adam and Eve waking up, in fact this being one of Dave's gladdest days because he'd really wanted to get away from the City again anyway and this time with a pretty doll, and's brought his surf casting gear planning a big day—And we've brought a lot of good food—The only trouble is there's no more wine so Dave and Romana go off in Willie to get some more anyway at a store 13 miles south down the highway—Billie and I are alone talking by the fire—I begin to feel extremely low as soon as last night's alcohol wears off.

Everything is trembly again, the trembling hand, I cant for a fact even light the fire and Billie has to do it—"I cant light a fire any more!" I yell—"Well I can" she says in a rare instance when she lets me have it for being such a nut—Little Elliott is constantly pulling at her asking this and that, "What is that stick for, to put in the fire? why? how does it burn? why does it burn? where are we? when are we leaving" and the pattern develops where she begins to talk to him instead of me anyway because I'm just sitting there staring at the floor sighing—Later when he takes his nap we go down the path to the beach, about noon, both of us sad and silent—"What's the matter I wonder" I say out loud—She:—"Everything was alright last night when we slept in the bag together now you wont even hold my hand . . . goddamit I'm going to kill myself!"—Because I've begun to realize in my soberness that this thing has come too far, that I dont love Billie, that I'm leading her on, that I made a mistake dragging everyone here, that I simply wanta go home now, I'm just plumb sick and tired just like Cody I guess of the whole nervewracking scene bad enough as it is always pivoting back to this poor haunted canyon which again gives me the willies as we walk under the bridge and come to those heartless breakers busting in on sand higher than earth and looking like the heartlessness of wisdom— Besides I suddenly notice as if for the first time the awful way the leaves of the canyon that have managed to be blown to the surf are all hesi- tantly advancing in gusts of wind then finally plunging into the surf, to be dispersed and belted and melted and taken off to sea—I turn around and notice how the wind is just harrying them off trees and into the sea, just hurrying them as it were to death—In my condition they look human trembling to that brink—Hastening, hastening—In that awful huge roar blast of autumn Sur wind.

Boom, clap, the waves are still talking but now I'm sick and tired of whatever they ever said or ever will say—Billie wants me to stroll with her down towards the caves but I dont want to get up from the sand where I'm sitting back to boulder—She goes alone—I suddenly remember James Joyce and stare at the waves realizing "All summer you were sitting here writing the so called sound of the waves not re- alizing how deadly serious our life and doom is, you fool, you happy kid with a pencil, dont you realize you've been using words as a happy game—all those marvelous skeptical things you wrote about graves and sea death it's ALL TRUE YOU FOOL! Joyce is dead! The sea took him! it will take YOU!" and I look down the beach and there's Billie wading in the treacherous undertow, she's already groaned several times earlier (seeing my indifference and also of course the hopelessness at Cody's and the hopelessness of her wrecked apartment and wretched life) "Someday I'm going to commit suicide," I suddenly wonder if she's going to horrify the heavens and me too with a sudden suicide walk into those awful undertows—I see her sad blonde hair flying, the sad thin figure, alone by the sea, the leaf-hastening sea, she suddenly reminds me of something—I remember her musical sighs of death and I see the words clearly imprinted in my mind over her figure in the sand:— ST.CAROLYN BY THE SEA—"You were my last chance" she's said but dont all women say that?—But can it be by "last chance" she doesnt mean mere marriage but some profoundly sad realization of something in me she really needs to go on living, at least that impression coming across anyway on the force of all the gloom we've shared—Can it be I'm withholding from her something sacred just like she says, or am I just a fool who'll never learn to have a decent eternally minded deep-down relation with a woman and keep throwing that away for a song at a bottle?—In which case my own life is over anyway and there are the Joycean waves with their blank mouths saying "Yes that's so," and there are the leaves hurrying one by one down the sand and dumping in—In fact the creek is freighting hundreds more of them a minute right direct from the back hills—That big wind blasts and roars, it's all yellow sunny and blue fury everywhere—I see the rocks wobble as it seems God is really getting mad for such a world and's about to destroy it: big cliffs wobbling in my dumb eyes: God says "It's gone too far, you're all destroying everything one way or the other wobble boom the end is NOW."

"The Second Coming, tick tock," I think shuddering—St.Carolyn by the Sea is going in further—I could run and go see her but she's so far away—I realize that if that nut is going to try this I'll have to make an awful run and swim to get her—I get up and edge over but just then she turns around and starts back . . . "And if I call her 'that nut' in my secret thoughts wonder what she calls me?"—O hell, I'm sick of life— If I had any guts I'd drown myself in that tiresome water but that wouldnt be getting it over at all, I can just see the big transformations and plans jellying down there to curse us up in some other wretched suffering form eternities of it—I guess that's what the kid feels—She looks so sad down there wandering Ophelialike in bare feet among thunders.

On top of that now here come the tourists, people from other cabins in the canyon, it's the sunny season and they're out two three times a week, what a dirty look I get from the elderly lady who's apparently heard about the "author" who was secretly invited to Mr. Monsanto's cabin but instead brought gangs and bottles and today worst of all trollopes—(Because in fact earlier that morning Dave and Romana have already made love on the sand in broad daylight visible not only to others down the beach but from that high new cabin on the shoulder of the cliff) (tho hidden from sight from the bridge by cliffwall)—So it's all well known news now there's a ball going on in Mr. Monsanto's cabin and him not even here—This elderly lady being accompanied by children of all kinds—So that when Billie returns from the far end of the beach and starts back with me down the path (and I'm silly with a big footlong wizard pipe in my mouth trying to light it in the wind to cover up) the lady gives her the once over real close but Billie only smiles lightly like a little girl and chirps hello.

I feel like the most disgraceful and nay disreputable wretch on earth, in fact my hair is blowing in beastly streaks across my stupid and moronic face, the hangover has now worked paranoia into me down to the last pitiable detail.

Back at the cabin I cant chop wood for fear I'll cut a foot off, I cant sleep, I cant sit, I cant pace, I keep going to the creek to drink water till finally I'm going down there a thousand times making Dave Wain wonder as he's come back with more wine—We sit there slugging out of our separate bottles, in my paranoia I begin to wonder why I get to drink just the one bottle and he the other—But he's gay "I am now going out surf castin and catch us a grabbag of fish for a marvelous supper; Romana you get the salad ready and anything else you can think of; we'll leave you alone now" he adds to gloomy me and Billie thinking he's in our way, "and say, why dont we go to Nepenthe and *private* our grief tonight and enjoy the moonlight on the terrace with Manhattans, or go see Henry Miller?"—"No!" I almost yell, "I mean I'm so exhausted I dont wanta do anything or see anybody"—(already feeling awful guilt about Henry Miller anyway, we've made an appointment with him about a week ago and instead of showing up at his friend's house in Santa Cruz at seven we're all drunk at ten calling long distance and poor Henry just said "Well I'm sorry I dont get to meet you Jack but I'm an old man and at ten o'clock it's time for me to go to bed, you'd never make it here till after midnight now") (his voice on the phone just like on his records, nasal, Brooklyn, goodguy voice, and him disappointed in a way because he's gone to the trouble of writing the preface to one of my books) (tho I suddenly now think in my remorseful paranoias "Ah the hell with it he was only gettin in the act like all these guys write prefaces so you dont even get to read the author first") (as an example of how really psychotically suspicious and loco I was getting).

Alone with Billie's even worse—"I cant see anything to do now," she says by the fire like an ancient Salem housewife ("Or Salem witch?" I'm leering)—"I could have Elliott taken care of in a private home or an orphanage and just go to a nunnery myself, there's a lot of them around—or I could kill myself and Elliott both"—"Dont talk like that"—"There's no other way to talk when there's no more directions to take"—"You've got me all wrong I wouldnt be any good for you"

—"I know that now, you want to be a hermit you say but you dont do it much I noticed, you're just tired of life and wanta sleep, in a way that's how I feel too only I've got Elliott to worry about . . . I could take both our lives and solve that"—"You, creepy talk"—"You told me the first night you loved me, that I was most interesting, that you hadnt met anyone you liked so much then you just went on drinking, I really can see now what they say about you is true: and all the others like you: O I realize you're a writer and suffer through too much but you're really ratty sometimes . . . but even that I know you cant help and I know you're not really ratty but awfully broken up like you explained to me, the reasons . . . but you're always groaning about how sick you are, you really dont think about others enough and I KNOW you cant help it, it's a curious disease a lot of us have anyway only better hidden sometimes . . . but what you said the first night and even just now about me being St.Carolyn in the Sea, why dont you follow through with what your heart knows is Good and best and true, you give up so easy to discouragement . . . then I guess too you dont really want me and just wanta go home and resume your own life maybe with Louise your girlfriend"—"No I couldn't with her either, I'm just bound up inside like constipation, I cant move emotionally like you'd say emotionally as tho that was some big grand magic mystery everybody saying 'O how wonderful life is, how miraculous, God made this and God made that,' how do you know he doesnt hate what He did: He might even be drunk and not noticing what he went and done tho of course that's not true"—"Maybe God is dead"—"No, God cant be dead because He's the unborn"—"But you have all those philosophies and sutras you were talking about"—"But dont you see they've all become empty words, I realize I've been playing like a happy child with words words words in a big serious tragedy, look around"—"You could make some effort, damn it!"

But what's even ineffably worse is that the more she advises me and discussed the trouble the worse and worse it gets, it's as tho she didnt know what she was doing, like an unconscious witch, the more she tries to help the more I tremble almost too realizing she's doing it on purpose and knows she's witching me but it's all gotta be formally understood as "help" dingblast it—She must be some kind of chemical counterpart to me, I just cant stand her for a minute, I'm racked with guilt because all the evidence there seems to say she's a wonderful person sympathizing in her quiet sad musical voice with an obvious rogue nevertheless none of these rational guilts stick—All I feel is the invisible stab from her—She's hurting me!—At some points in our conversation I'm a veritable ham actor jumping up to twitch my head, that's the effect she has—"What's the matter?" she asks softly—Which makes me almost scream and I've never screamed in my life—It's the first time in my life I'm not confident I can hold myself together no matter what happens and be inly calm enough to even smile with condescension at the screaming hysterias of women in madwards—I'm in the same madward all of a sudden—And what's happened? what's caused it—"Are you driving me mad on purpose?" I finally blurt—But naturally she protests I'm talking out of my head, there's no such evident intention anywhere, we're just on a happy weekend in the country with friends, "Then there's something wrong with ME!" I yell—"That's obvious but why dont you try to calm down and for instance like make love to me, I've been begging you all day and all you do is groan and turn away as tho I was an ugly old bat"—She comes and offers herself to me softly and gently but I just stare at my quivering wrists—It's really very awful—It's hard to explain—Besides then the little boy is constantly coming at Billie when she kneels at my lap or sits on it or tries to soothe my hair and comfort me, he keeps saying in the same pitiful voice "Dont do it Billie dont do it Billie dont do it Billie" till finally she has to give up that sweet patience of hers where she answers his every little pathetic question and yell "Shut up! Elliott will you shut up! DO I have to beat you again!" and I groan "No!" but Elliott yells louder "Dont do it Billie dont do it Billie dont do it Billie!" so she sweeps him off and starts whacking him screamingly on the porch and I am about to throw in the towel and gasp up my last, it's horrible.

Besides when she beats Elliott she herself cries and then will be yelling madwoman things like "I'll kill both of us if you dont stop, you leave me no alternative! O my child!" suddenly picking him up and embracing him rocking tears, and gnashing of hair and all under those old peaceful bluejay trees where in fact the jays are still waiting for their food and watching all this—Even so Alf the Sacred Burro is in the yard waiting for somebody to give him an apple—I look up at the sun going down golden throughout the insane shivering canyon, that blasted rogue wind comes topping down trees a mile away with an advancing roar that when it hits the broken cries of mother and son in grief are blown away with all those crazy scattering leaves—The creek screeches—A door bangs horribly, a shutter follows suit, the house shakes—I'm beating my knees in the din and cant even hear that.

"What's I got to do with you committing suicide anyway?" I'm yelling—"Alright, it has nothing to do with you"—"So okay you have no husband but at least you've got little Elliott, he'll grow up and be okay, you can always meanwhile go on with your job, get married, move away, do something, maybe it's Cody but more than that I'd say it's all those mad characters making you insane and wanta kill yourself like that—Perry—"—"Dont talk about Perry, he's wonderful and sweet and I love him and he's much kinder to me than you'll ever be: at least he gives of himself"—"But what's all this giving of ourselves, what's there to give that'll help anybody"—"You'll never know you're so wrapped up in yourself"—We're now starting to insult each other which would be a healthy sign except she keeps breaking down and crying on my shoulder more or less again insisting I'm her last chance (which isnt true)—"Let's go to a monastery together," she adds madly—"Evelyn, I mean Billie you might go to a nunnery at that, by God get thee to a nunnery, you look like you'd make a nun, maybe that's what you need all that talk about Cody about religion maybe all this worldly horror is just holding you back from what you call your true realizing, you could become a big reverend mother someday with not a worry on your mind tho I met a reverend mother once who cried . . . ah it's all so sad"—"What did she cry about?"—"I dont know, after talking to me, I remember I said some silly thing like 'the universe is a woman because it's round' but I think she cried because she was remembering her early days when she had a romance with some soldier who died, at least that's what they say, she was the greatest woman I ever saw, big blue eyes, big smart woman . . . you could do that, get out of this awful mess and leave it all behind"—"But I love love too much for that"—"And not because you're sensual either you poor kid"—In fact we quiet down a little and do actually make love in spite of Elliott pulling at her "Billie dont do it dont do it Billie dont do it" till right in the middle I'm yelling "Dont do what? what's he mean?—can it be he's right and Billie you shouldnt do it? can it be we're sinning after all's said and done? O this is insane!—but he's the most insane of them all," in fact the child is up on bed with us tugging at her shoulder just like a grownup jealous lover tryin to pull a woman off another man (she being on top indication of exactly how helpless and busted down I've become and here it is only 4 in the afternoon)—A little drama going on in the cabin maybe a little different than what cabins are intended for or the local neighbors are imagining.

35

But there's an awful paranoiac element sometimes in orgasm that suddenly releases not sweet genteel sympathy but some token venom that splits up in the body—I feel a great ghastly hatred of myself and everything, the empty feeling far from being the usual relief is now as tho I've been robbed of my spinal power right down the middle on purpose by a great witching force—I feel evil forces gathering down all around me, from her, the kid, the very walls of the cabin, the trees, even the sudden thought of Dave Wain and Romana is evil, they're all coming now—I leave poor Billie face in hand and rush off to drink water in the creek but every time I do something like that I have to run back to be sorry and say so, but the moment I see her again "She's doing something else" I leer and I dont feel sorry at all—She's mumbling face in hands and the little boy's crying at her side—"My God she should get to a nunnery!" I think rushing back to the creek—Suddenly the water in the creek tastes different as tho somebody's thrown gasoline or kerosene in it upstream—"Maybe those neighbors wanta get back at me that's what!"—I taste the water carefully and I'm positive that's what happened.

Like an idiot I'm sitting by the creek staring when Dave Wain comes striding down with one fish on the line and his big cheerful western twang as tho nothing unusual's happened "Well boy I spent a whole two hours and look what I got! one measly but beautiful pathetic as you'll see holy little rainbow sea trout that I'm now going to clean—Now the way to clean fish is as follows," and he kneels innocently by the creek to show me how—I have nothing else to do but watch and smile—He says: "Be prepared to be taken on tour of Farollone Island within next two years, boy, with wild canaries actually lighting on your boat hundreds of miles out at sea—See I'm tryna to save money for a fishboat of my own, I think fishing is bettern anything and I intend to entirely reorganize my life for this tho I see the stern image of Fagan shrieking with a Roshi stick, but you ought to see how fast you can bait up hundreds of herring and clean salmon in one and a half minutes, it's a fact, and you walk around in hickory shirts and wool knit caps —Man I know all about it and I'm writing a final definitive article on how clean hard work is the saviour of us all—When you're out there it's a very primal light, fishing is—You're a hunter—Birds find fish for you—Weather drives you—Foolish mind-hangs dissolve before utter fatigue and everything comes in"—As I squat there I imagine maybe Billie is telling Romana what happened in the cabin and Dave'll know in a while tho he seems to know a lot that's going on—He's hinted several times, like now, "You look like you're having the worse time of your life, that kid Elliott is enough to drive anybody crazy and Billie is sure a nervous little wench—Now here's the way you scale, with this here knife"—And I marvel that I cant be so useful and humanly simple and good enough to make small talk to make others feel better, like Dave, there he is long and hollow of cheeks from long drinking himself the past few weeks, but he's not complaining or moaning in the corner like me, at least he does something about it, he puts himself to the test— He gives me that feeling again that I'm the only person in the world who is devoid of humanbeingness, damn it, that's true, that's the way I feel anyway—"Ah Dave someday you and me'll go fishing in your abandoned mining camp on the Rogue River, huh, we'll be feeling better by then somehow gaddamit"—"Well we've got to cut down on the sauce a whole lot, Jack," saying "Jack" sadly a lot like Jarry Wagner used to do on our Dharmabumming mountain climbs where we'd confide dolors, "yes, and we drink too many SWEET drinks in a way, you know all that sugar and no food is bound to upset your metabolism and fill your blood with sugar to the point where you aint got the strength of a hen; you especially you've been drinking nothin but sweet port and sweet Manhattans now for weeks—I promise you the holy flesh of this little fish will heal you," (chuckle).

I suddenly look at the fish and feel horrible all over again, that old death scheme is back only now I'm gonna put my big healthy Anglo-saxon teeth into it and wrench away at the mournful flesh of a little living being that only an hour ago was swimming happily in the sea, in fact even Dave thinking this and saying: "Ah yes that little muzzling mouth was blindly sucking away in the glad waters of life and now look at it, here's where the fittin head's chopped off, you dont have to look, us big drunken sinners are now going to use it for our sacrificial supper so in fact when we cook it I'm going to say an Indian prayer for it hoping it's the same prayer the local Indians used—Jack in a way we might even start havin fun here and make a great week out of it!"— "Week?"—"I thought we was coming here for a week"—"Oh I said that didnt I . . . I feel awful about everything . . . I dont think I can make it . . . I'm going crazy with Billie and Elliott and me too . . . maybe I'll have to, maybe we'll have to leave or something, I think I'll die here"—And Dave is disappointed naturally and here I've already routed him up out of his own affairs to drive down here anyway, another matter to make me feel like a rat.

36

But Dave's making the best of clomping up and down the cabin preparing the bag of cornmeal and starting the corn oil in the frying pan, Romana too she's making an exquisite big salad with lots of mayonnaise and in fact poor Billie is mutely helping her setting the table and the little boy is crooning by the stove it's almost like a happy domestic scene suddenly—Only I watch it from the porch with horrified eyes—Also because their shadows in the lamplight gone casting on the walls look huge and monsterlike and witch-like and warlock-like, I'm alone in the woods with happy ghosts—The wind is howling as the sun goes down so I go in, but I go out at once again madly to my creek, always thinking the creek itself will give me water that will clear away everything and reassure me forever (also remembering in my distress Edgar Cayce's advice "Drink a lot of water") but "There's kerosene in the water!" I yell in the wind, nobody hearing—I feel like kicking the creek and screaming—I turn around and there's the cabin with its warm interiors, the silent people inside all noticeably glum because they cant understand anyway what's with the nut wandering in and out from cabin to creek, silent, wan faced, stupefacted, trembling and sweating like midsummer was on the roof and instead it's even cold now—I sit in the chair with my back to the door and watch Dave as he lectures on bravely.

"What we're having is a sacrificial banquet with all kinds of goodies you see laid in a regal spread around one little delicious fish so that we all have to pray to the fish and take tiny little bites, we only have about four bites apiece and there's all kinds of parts of the fish where the bites are more significant—But beyond that the way to properly fry a fresh-caught fish is to be sure the oil is burning and furiously so when you lay the fish in it, not burning but real hot oil, well yeh even burning, hand me the spat, you then gently lay the fish into the oil and create a tremendous crackling racket" (which he does as Romana cheers) (and I glance at Billie and she's thinking of something else like a nun in the corner) but Dave keeps on making jokes till he actually has us all smiling—While the fish is cooking, tho, Romana as she's been doing all day is constantly handing me a bite to eat, some *hors d'oeuvres* or piece of tomato or other, apparently trying to help me feel better—"You've got to EAT" she and Dave keep saying but I dont want to eat and yet they're always holding out bites to my mouth until finally now I begin to frown thinking "What's all these bites they keep throwing at me, poison?—and what's wrong with my eyes, they're all dilated black like I've had drugs, all I've had is wine, did Dave put drugs in my wine or something? thinking it will help or something? or are they members of a secret society that dopes people secretly the idea being to enlighten them or something?" even as Romana is handing me a bite and I take it from her big brown hands and chew—She's wearing purple panties and purple bras, nothing else, just for fun, Dave's slappin her on the can joyfully as he cooks the supper, it's some big erotic natural thing to do for Romana, she believes in showing her beautiful big body anyway—In fact at one point when Billie's up leaning over a chair Dave goes behind Billie and playfully touches *her* and winks at me, but I'm not of all this like a moron and we could all be having fun such as soldiers dream the day away imagining, dammit—But the venoms in the blood are asexual as well as asocial and a-everything—"Billie's so nice and thin, like I'm used to Romana maybe I should switch around here for variety," says Dave at the sizzling frying pan—I look over my shoulder and see at first with a leap of joy but then with ominous fear an enormous full moon at full fat standing there between Mien Mo mountain and the north canyon wall, like saying to me as I look over my trembling shoulder "Hoo doo you."

But I say "Dave, look, as if all this wasnt enough" and I point out the moon to him, there's dead silence in the trees and also among us inside, there she is, vast lugubrious fullmoon that frights madmen and makes waters wave, she's got one or two treetops silhouetted and's got that whole side of the canyon lit up in silver—Dave just looks at the moon with his tired madness eyes (overexcited eyes, my mother'd said) and says nothing—I go out to the creek and drink water and come back and wonder about the moon and suddenly the four shadows in the cabin are all dead silent as tho they had conspired with the moon.

"Time to eat, Jack," says Dave coming out on the porch suddenly —No one's saying anything—I go in and sheepishly sit at the table like the useless pioneer who doesnt do anything to help the men or please the women, the idiot in the wagon train who nevertheless has to be fed—Dave stands there saying "Oh full moon, here is our little fish which we are now going to partake of to feed us so that we shall be stronger; thank you Fish people, thank you Fish god; thank you moon for making our light tonight; this is the night of the fullmoon fish which we now consecrate with the first delicate bite"—He takes his fork and opens the little fish carefully, it's beautifully breaded and fried and centered in a dazzle of salads and vegetables and cornmeal johnnycakes, he opens a funny gill, goes under, removes a strange bite and projects it to my mouth saying "Take the first bite Jack, just a little bite, and be sure to chew very slowly"—I do so, oily delicious bite but nothing delicious any more in my tongue—Then the others take their little holy bites, little Elliott's eyes shining with delight at this wonderful game that however has started to frighten me—For obvious reasons by now.

As we eat Dave announces that he and I are sick from too much drinking and by God we're going to reform and see to it that we shape up, then he launches into stories as usual, ending in a talkative ordinary supper that I think will sorta straighten me out at first but after supper I feel even worse, "That fish has all the death of otters and mouses and snakes right in it or something" I'm thinking—Billie is quietly washing the dishes without complaint, Dave is gladly smoking after-dinner cigarettes on the porch, but here I am again mooning by the creek hiding from all of them each five minutes tho I cant understand what makes me do it—I HAVE to get out of there—But I have no right to STAY AWAY—So I keep coming back but it's all an insane revolving automatic directionless circle of anxiety, back and forth, around and around, till they're really by now so perturbed by my increasing silent departures and creepy returns they're all sitting without a word by the stove but now their heads are together and they're whispering—From the woods I see those three shadowy heads whispering me by the stove—What's Dave saying?—And why do they look like they're plotting something further?—Can it be it was all arranged by Dave Wain via Cody that I would meet Billie and be driven mad and now they've got me alone in the woods and are going to give me final poisons tonight that will utterly remove all my control so that in the morning I'll have to go to a hospital forever and never write another line?—Dave Wain is jealous because I wrote 10 novels?—Billie has been assigned by Cody to get me to marry her so he'll get all my money? Romana is a member of the expert poisoning society (I've heard her mention tree spirits already, earlier in the car, and she's sung some strange songs the night before)—The three of them, Dave Wain in fact the chief conspirator because I know he does have amphetomine on his person and the needles in a little box, just one injection of a tomato, or of a portion of fish, or drops into a bottle of wine, and my eyes become mad wide and black like they are now, my nerves OO ouch, this is what I'm thinking—Still they sit there by the fire in dead silence, when I tromp into the cabin in fact they all start up again talking: sure sign—I walk out again, "I'm going down the road a ways"—"Okay"—But the moment I'm alone on the path a million waving moony arms are thrashing around me and every hole in the cliffs and burnt out trees I'd calmly passed a hundred times all summer in dead of fog, now has something moving in it quickly—I hurry back—Even on the porch I'm scared to see the familiar bushes near the outhouse or down by the broken treetrunk—And now a babble in the creek has somehow entered my head and with all the rhythm of the sea waves going "Kettle blomp you're up, you rop and dop, ligger lagger ligger" I grab my heat but it keeps babbling.

Masks explode before my eyes when I close them, when I look at the moon it waves, moves, when I look at my hands and feet they creep—Everything is moving, the porch is moving like ooze and mud, the chair trembles under me—"Sure you dont wanta go to Nepenthe for a Manhattan Jack?"—"No" ("Yeh and you'd dump poison in it" I think darkly but seriously hurt I could ever allow myself to think that about poor Dave)—And I realize the unbearable anguish of insanity: how uninformed people can be thinking insane people are "happy," O God, in fact it was Irwin Garden once warned me not to think the madhouses are full of "happy nuts," "There's a tightening around the head that hurts, there's a terror of the mind that hurts even more, they're so unhappy and especially because they cant explain it to anybody or reach out and be helped through all the hysterical paranoia they are really suffering more than anyone in the world and I think in the universe in fact," and Irwin knew this from observing his mother Naomi who finally had to have a lobotomy—Which sets me thinking how nice to cut away therefore all that agony in my forehead and STOP IT! STOP THAT BABBLING!—Because now the babbling's not only in the creek, as I say it's left the creek and come in my head, it would be alright for coherent babbling meaning something but it's all brilliantly enlightened babble that does more than mean something: it's telling me to die because everything is over—Everything is swarming all over me.

Dave and Romana retire again by the creek for a night's sweet sleep under the moon while Billie and I sit there gloomy by the fire—Her voice is crying: "It might make you feel better to just come in my arms"—"I've got to try something, Billie after all I've told you I cant make you see what's happening to me, you dont understand"—"Come into our sleepingbag again like last night, just sleep"—We get in naked but now I'm not drunk I'm aware of the real tight squeeze in there and besides in my fever I'm perspiring so much it's unbearable, her own skin is soaking wet from mine, yet our arms are outside in the cold—"This won't do!"—"What'll you do?"—"Let's try the cot inside" but maniacally I arrange the cot all screwy with a board on top of it forgetting to put sleepingbag pads underneath like I'd done all summer, I simply forget all that, Billie, poor Billie lies down with me on this absurd board thinking I'm trying to drive my madness away by self torturing ordeals—It's ridiculous, we lie there stiff as boards on a board—I roll off and saying "We'll try something else"—I try laying out the sleepingbag on the floor of the porch but the moment she's in my arms a mosquito comes at me, or I burst out sweating, or I see a flash of lightning, or I hear a big roaring Hymn in my head, or imagine a thousand people are coming down the creek talking, or the roar of the wind is bringing flying treetrunks that will crush us—"Wait a minute," I yell and get up to pace awhile and run down to drink water by the creek where Dave and Romana are peacefully entangled—I start cursing Dave "Bastard's got the only decent spot there is to sleep in anyway, right there in that sand by the creek, if he wasnt here I could sleep there and the creek would cover the noise in my head and I could sleep there, with Billie even, all night, bastard's got my spot," and I kick back to the porch—Poor Billie's arms are outstretched to me: "Please Jack, come on, love me, love me"—"I CANT"—"But why cant you, if even we'll never see each other again let us our last night be beautiful and something to remember forever."

"Like a big ideal memory for both of us, cant you give me just that?"—"I would if I could" I'm muttering around like a fussy old nut inside the cabin looking for a match—I cant even light my cigarette, something sinister blows it out, when it's lit it mortifies my hot mouth anyway like a mouthful of death—I grab up another batch of bags and blankets and start piling myself up on the other side of the porch saying to Billie who's sighing now realizing it's hopeless "First I'll try to take a nap by myself here then when I wake up I'll feel better and come over to you"—So I try that, turning over rigidly my eyes wide open staring full fright into the dark like the time in the movie Humphrey Bogart who's just killed his partner trying to sleep by the fire and you see his eyes staring into the fire rigid and insane—That's just the way I'm staring—If I try to close my eyes some elastic pulls them open again—If I try to turn over the whole universe turns over with me but it's no better on the other side of the universe—I realize I may never come out of this and my mother is waiting for me at home praying for me because she must know what's happening tonight, I cry out to her to pray and help me—I remember my cat for the first time in three hours and let out a yell that scares Billie—"All right Jack?"—"Give me a little time"—But now she's started to sleep, poor girl is exhausted, I realize she's going to abandon me to my fate anyway and I cant help thinking she and Dave and Romana are all secretly awake waiting for me to die—"For what reason?" I'm thinking "this secret poisoning society, I know, it's because I'm a Catholic, it's a big anti-Catholic scheme, it's Communists destroying everybody, systematic individuals are poisoned till finally they'll have everybody, this madness changes you completely and in the morning you no longer have the same mind—the drug is invented by Airapatianz, it's the brainwash drug, I always thought that Romana was a Communist being a Rumanian, and as for Billie that gang of hers is strange, and Cody dont care, and Dave's all evil just like I always figured maybe" but soon my thoughts arent even as "rational" as that any more but become hours of raving—There are forces whispering in my ear in rapid long speeches advising and warning, suddenly other voices are shouting, the trouble is all the voices are longwinded and talking very fast like Cody at his fastest and like the creek so that I have to keep up with the meaning tho I wanta bat it out of my ears —I keep waving at my ears—I'm afraid to close my eyes for all the turmoiled universes I see tilting and expanding suddenly exploding suddenly clawing in to my center, faces, yelling mouths, long haired yellers, sudden evil confidences, sudden rat-tat-tats of cerebral committees arguing about "Jack" and talking about him as if he wasnt there—Aimless moments when I'm waiting for more voices and suddenly the wind explodes huge groans in the million treetop leaves that sound like the moon gone mad—And the moon rising higher, brighter, shining down in my eyes now like a streetlamp—The huddled shadowy sleeping figures over there so coy—So human and safe, I'm crying "I'm not human any more and I'll never be safe any more, Oh what I wouldnt give to be home on Sunday afternoon yawning because I'm bored, Oh for that again, it'll never come back again—Ma was right, it was all bound to drive me mad, now it's done—What'll I say to her?—She'll be terrified and go mad herself—*Oh ti Tykey, aide mué*—me who's just eaten fish have no right to ask for brother Tyke again—"—An argot of sudden screamed reports rattles through my head in a language I never heard but understand immediately—For a moment I see blue Heaven and the Virgin's white veil but suddenly a great evil blur like an ink spot spreads over it, "The devil!—the devil's come after me tonight! tonight is the night! that's what!"—But angels are laughing and having a big barn dance in the rocks of the sea, nobody cares any more—Suddenly as clear as anything I ever saw in my life, I see the Cross.

37

I see the cross, it's silent, it stays a long time, my heart goes out to it, my whole body fades away to it, I hold out my arms to be taken away to it, by God I am being taken away my body starts dying and swooning out to the Cross standing in a luminous area of the darkness, I start to scream because I know I'm dying but I dont want to scare Billie or anybody with my death scream so I swallow the scream and just let myself go into death and the Cross: as soon as that happens I slowly sink back to life—Therefore the devils are back, commissioners are sending out orders in my ear to think anew, babbling secrets are hissed, suddenly I see the Cross again, this time smaller and far away but just as clear and I say through all the noise of the voices "I'm with you, Jesus, for always, thank you"—I lie there in cold sweat wondering what's come over me for years my Buddhist studies and pipesmoking assured meditations on emptiness and all of a sudden the Cross is manifested to me—My eyes fill with tears—"We'll all be saved—I wont even tell Dave Wain about it, I wont go wake him up down there and scare him, he'll know soon enough—now I can sleep."

I turn over but it's only begun—It's only one o'clock in the morning and the night wears on to the wheeling moon worse and worse till dawn by which time I've seen the Cross again and again but there's a battle somewhere and the devils keep coming back—I know if I could only sleep for an hour the whole complex of noisy brains would settle down, some control would come back somewhere inside there, some blessing would soothe the whole issue—But the bat comes silently flapping around me again, I see him clearly in the moonlight now his little head of darkness and wings that zigzag maddeningly so you cant even get a look at them—Suddenly I hear a hum, a definite flying saucer is hovering right over those trees where the hum must be, there are orders in there, "They're coming to get me O my God!"—I jump up and glare at the tree, I'm going to defend myself—The bat flaps in front of my face—"The bat is their representative in the canyon, his radar message they got, why dont they leave? doesnt Dave hear that awful hum?"—Billie is dead asleep but little Elliott suddenly thumps his foot, once—I realize he's not even asleep and knows everything that's going on—I lie down again and peek at him across the porch floor: I suddenly realizing he's staring at the moon and there he goes again, thumping his foot: he's sending messages—He's a warlock disguised as a little boy, he's also destroying Billie!—I get up to look at him feeling guilty too realizing this is all nonsense probably but he is not properly covered, his little bare arms are outside the blankets in the cold night, he hasnt even got a nightshirt, I curse at Billie—I cover him up and he whimpers—I go back and lie down with mad eyes looking deep inside me, suddenly a bliss comes over me as the sleep mechanism takes sinking hold—And there I am dreaming me and two kids are hired to work in the mountains on the same "ridge" as Desolation Peak (i.e. Mien Mo Mountain again) and start with a cliffside river crew who tell us two workers have apparently sunk in the cliffside snow and we must lean over sheer drops and see if we can "dump them out" or haul them in—All we do is lie there on crumbly snow a thousand foot fall to the river crumbling the snow off in slabs so big you wouldnt know if men were trapped in em or not—Not only that the bosses have special shoes on sliders that are holding them to the safe shore (like ski clamps) so I begin to realize they're only fooling us poor kids and we could have fallen too (I almost do)—(did)—(almost)—As observer of the story I see it's just an annual ritualistic joke to fool the new kids on the job who are then dispatched to the other side of the river to slump off *more* snow from sheer banks in hopes of finding the lost workmen—So we start there on a big trip, downriver first, but en route all the peasants tell us stories of the God Monster Machine on the other shore who makes sounds like certain birds and owls and has a million infernal contraptions enough to make you sick with all the slipshod windmill rickety details, as "Observer of the story" again I see it's just a trick to make us scared when we get there at night and hear actual natural sounds of birds, owls, etc. thinking as green rookies in the country it's that "Monster"—Meanwhile we sign on to go to the main mountain but I promise myself if I dont like the work there I'll come back get my old job on Desolation—Already our employers have shown a murderous sense of humor—I arrive at Mien Mo Mountain which is like Raton Canyon again but has a large tho dry rot river running in the wide hole and down there on many rocks are huge brooding vultures—Old bums row out to them and pull them clumsily off the rocks and start feeding them like pets, bites of red meat or red mite, tho at first I thought the eccentric old town bums wanted them to eat or to sell (still maybe so) because before I study this I look and see hundreds of slowly fornicating vulture couples on the town dump—These are now humanly formed vultures with human shaped arms, legs, heads, torsos, but they have rainbow colored feathers, and the men are all quietly sitting *behind* Vulture Women slowly somehow fornicating at them in all the same slow obscene movement —Both man and woman sit facing the same direction and somehow there's contact because you can see all their feathery rainbow behinds slowly dully monotonously fornicating on the dumpslopes—As I pass I even see the expression on the face of a youngish blond vulture man eternally displeased because his Vulture Mistress is an old Yakker who's been arguing with him all the time—His face is completely human but inhumanly pasty like uncooked pale pie dough with dull seamed buggy horror that he's doomed to all this enough to make me shudder in sympathy, I even see her awful expression of middleaged pie dough tormentism—They're so human!—But suddenly me and the two kid workers are taken to the Vulture People respectable quarter of town to our apartment where a Vulture Woman and her daughter show us our rooms—Their faces are leprous thick with softy yeast but painted with makeup to make them like thick Christmas dolls and dull and fuzzy but human expressions, like with thick lips of rubber muzz, fat expressions all crumbly like cracker meal, yellow pizza puke faces, disgusting us tho we say nothing—The apartment has dirty beatnik beds and mattresses everywhere but I walk thru the back looking for a sink—It's *huge*—An endless walk thru long greasy pantries and vast washrooms a block long with single filthy little sink all dark and slimey like underground Lowell High School crumbling basements—Finally I come to the Kitchen where we "new workers" are s'posed to cook little meals all summer—It's vast stone fireplaces and stone stoves all rancid and greasy from a month-old Vulture People Banquet Orgy with still dozens of uncooked chickens lying around on the floor, among garbage and bottles—Rancid stale grease everywhere, nobody's ever cleaned it up or knew how and the place as big as a garage—I push my way out of there pushing a huge greasystink foodstained tray of some sort hurrying away from the big stinky emptiness and horror—The fat golden chickens lie rotten up-sidedown on littered stone slabs—I hurry out never having seen such a dirty sight in my life. Meanwhile I learn the two boys are studying a hamper full of Vulture Food for us and one of them wisely says "Blisters in our sugar," meaning the Vultures put their blisters in our sugar so we'll "die" but instead of being really dead we'll be taken to the Underground Slimes to walk neck deep in steaming mucks pulling huge groaning wheels (among small forked snakes) so the devil with the long ears can mine his Purple Magenta Square Stone that is the secret of all this Kingdom—You end up down there groaning and pulling thru dead bodies of other people even your own family floating in the ooze—If you succeed you can become a pasty Vulture Person obscenely fornicating slowly on the dump above, I think, either that or the devil just invents the Vulture People with what's left over out of the underground Hell—"Beans anyone?" I hear myself saying as *thump!* I'm awake again! Elliott has thumped his foot just at that moment on the porch! —I look over there!—He's doing it on purpose, he knows everything that's going on!—What on earth have I brought these people for and why just this particular night of that moon that moon that moon?

I'm up again and pacing up and down and drinking water at the creek, Dave and Romana's lump figures in the moonlight dont move, like hypocrites, "Bastard has my only sleeping spot"—I clutch my head, I'm so alone in all this—I go fearfully casting about for control back inside the cabin by the lighted lamp, a smoke, trying to squeeze the last red drop out of the rancid port bottle, no go—Now that Billie's asleep and so still and peaceful I wonder if I can sleep just by lying beside her and holding her—I do just this, crawling in with all my clothes which I've put on because I'm afraid of going mad naked or of not being able to suddenly run away from everything, in my shoes, she moans a little in her sleep and resumes sleeping as I hold her with those rigid staring eyes—Her blonde flesh in the moonlight, the poor blonde hair so carefully washed and combed, the ladylike little body also a burden to carry around like my own but so frail, thinnish, I just stare at her shoulders with tears—I'd wake her up and confess everything but I'll only scare her—I've done irreparable harm ("Garradarable narm!" yells the creek)—All my self sayings suddenly blurting babbles so the meaning cant even stay a minute I mean a moment to satisfy my rational endeavors to hold control, every thought I have is smashed to a million pieces by millionpieced mental explosions that I remember I thought were so wonderful when I'd first seen them on Peotl and Mescaline, I'd said then (when still innocently playing with words) "Ah, the manifestation of multiplicity, you can actually see it, it aint just words" but now it's "Ah the keselamaroyot you rot"—Till when dawn finally comes my mind is just a series of explosions that get louder and more "multiply" broken in pieces some of them big orchestral and then rainbow explosions of sound and sight mixed.

At dawn also I've almost dimmed into sleep three times but I swear (and this is something I remember that makes me realize I dont understand what happened at Big Sur even now) the little boy somehow thumped his foot just at the moment of drowse, to instantly wake me up, wide awake, back to my horror which when all is said and done is the horror of all the worlds the showing of it to me being damn well what I deserve anyway with my previous blithe yakkings about the sufferings of others in books.

Books, shmooks, this sickness has got me wishing if I can ever get out of this I'll gladly become a millworker and shut my big mouth.

38

Dawn is most horrible of all with the owls suddenly calling back and forth in the misty moon haunt—And even worse than dawn is morning, the bright sun only GLARING in on my pain, making it all brighter, hotter, more maddening, more nervewracking—I even go roaming up and down the valley in the bright Sunday morning sunshine with bag under arm looking hopelessly for some spot to sleep in—As soon as I find a spot of grass by the path I realize I cant lie down there because the tourists might walk by and see me—As soon as I find a glade near the creek I realize it's too sinister there, like Hemingway's darker part of the swamp where "the fishing would be more tragic" somehow—All the haunts and glades having certain special evil forces concentrated there and driving me away—So haunted I go wandering up and down the canyon crying with that bag under my arm: "What on earth's happened to me? and how can earth be like that?"

Am I not a human being and have done my best as well as anybody else? never really trying to hurt anybody or half-hearted cursing Heaven?—The words I'd studied all my life have suddenly gotten to me in all their serious and definite deathliness, never more I be a "happy poet" "Singing" "about death" and allied romantic matters, "Go thou crumb of dust you with your silt of a billion years, here's a billion pieces of silt for you, shake that out of your shaker"—And all the green nature of the canyon now waving in the morning sun looking like a cruel idiot convocation.

Coming back to the sleepers and staring at them wild eyed like my brother'd once stared at me in the dark over my crib, staring at them not only enviously but lonely inhuman isolation from their simple sleeping minds—"But they all look dead!" I'm carking in my canyon, "Sleep is death, everything is death!"

The horrible climax coming when the others finally get up and pook about making a troubled breakfast, and I've told Dave I cant possibly stay here another minute, he must drive us all back to town, "Okay but I sure wish we could stay a week like Romana wants to do,"—"Well you drive me and come back"—"Well I dunno if Monsanto would like that we've already dirtied up the place aplenty, in fact we've got to dig a garbage pit and get rid of the junk"—Billie offers to dig the garbage pit but does so by digging a neat tiny coffinshaped grave instead of just a garbage hole—Even Dave Wain blinks to see it—It's exactly the size fit for putting a little dead Elliott in it, Dave is thinking the same thing I am I can tell by a glance he gives me—We've all read Freud sufficiently to understand something there—Besides little Elliott's been crying all morning and has had two beatings both of them ending up crying and Billie saying she cant stand it any more she's going to kill herself—

And Romana too notices it, the perfect 4 foot by 3 foot neatly sided grave like you're ready to sink a little box in it—Horrifying me so much I take the shovel and go down to dump junk into it and mess up the neat pattern somehow but little Elliott starts screaming and grabs the shovel and refuses I go near the hole—So Billie herself goes and starts filling the garbage in but then looks at me significantly (I'm sure sometimes she really did aspire to make me crazy) "Do you want to finish the job yourself?"—"What do you mean?"—"Cover the earth on, do the honors?"—"What do you mean do the honors!"—"Well I said I'd dig the garbage pit and I've done that, aint you supposed to do the rest?"—Dave Wain is watching fascinated, there's something screwy he sees there too, something cold and frightening—"Well okay" I say, "I'll dump the earth over it and tamp it down" but I go down to do this Elliott is screaming "NO no no no no!" ("My God, the fishes' bones are in that grave" I realize too)—"What's the matter he wont let me go near that hole! why did you make it look like a grave?" I finally yell—But Billie is only smiling quietly and steadily at me, over the grave, shovel in hand, the kid weeping tugging the shovel, rushing up to block my way, trying to shove me back with his little hands—I cant understand any of it—He's screaming as I grab the shovel as tho I'm about to bury Billie in there or something or himself maybe—"What's the matter with this kid is he a cretin?" I yell.

With the same quiet steady smile Billie says "Oh you're so fucking neurotic!"

I simply get mad and dump earth over the garbage and tromp it all down and say "The hell with all this madness!"

I get mad and stomp up on the porch and throw myself in the

canvas chair and close my eyes—Dave Wain says he's going down the road to investigate the canyon a bit and when he comes back the girls will have finished packing and we'll all leave—Dave goes off, the girls clean up and sweep, the little kid is sleeping and suddenly hopelessly and completely finished I sit there in the hot sun and close my eyes: and there's the golden swarming peace of Heaven in my eyelids—It comes with a sure hand a soft blessing as big as it is beneficent, i.e., endless—I've fallen asleep.

I've fallen asleep in a strange way, with my hands clasped behind my head thinking I'm just going to sit there and think, but I'm sleeping like that, and when I wake up just one short minute later I realize the two girls are both sitting behind me in absolute silence—When I'd sat down they were sweeping, but now they were squatting behind my back, facing each other, not a word—I turn and see them there—Blessed relief has come to me from just that minute—Everything has washed away—I'm perfectly normal again—Dave Wain is down the road looking at fields and flowers—I'm sitting smiling in the sun, the birds sing again, all's well again.

I still cant understand it.

Most of all I cant understand the miraculousness of the silence of the girls and the sleeping boy and the silence of Dave Wain in the fields—Just a golden wash of goodness has spread over all and over all my body and mind—All the dark torture is a memory—I know now I can get out of there, we'll drive back to the City, I'll take Billie home, I'll say goodbye to her properly, she wont commit no suicide or do anything wrong, she'll forget me, her life'll go on, Romana's life will go on, old Dave will manage somehow, I'll forgive them and explain everything (as I'm doing now)—And Cody, and George Baso, and ravened McLear and perfect starry Fagan, they'll all pass through one way or the other—I'll stay with Monsanto at his home a few days and he'll smile and show me how to be happy awhile, we'll drink dry wine instead of sweet and have quiet evenings in his home—Arthur Ma will come to quietly draw pictures at my side—Monsanto will say "That's all there is to it, take it easy, everything's okay, dont take things too serious, it's bad enough as it is without you going the deep end over imaginary conceptions just like you always said yourself"—I'll get my ticket and say goodbye on a flower day and leave all San Francisco behind and go back home across autumn America and it'll all be like it was in the beginning—Simple golden eternity blessing all—Nothing ever happened—Not even this—St.Carolyn by the Sea will go on being golden one way or the other—The little boy will grow up and be a great man—There'll be farewells and smiles—My mother'll be waiting for me glad—The corner of the yard where Tyke is buried will be a new and fragrant shrine making my home more homelike somehow—On soft Spring nights I'll stand in the yard under the stars—Something good will come out of all things yet—And it will be golden and eternal just like that—There's no need to say another word.

POETRY

EDITOR'S INTRODUCTION

THIS SELECTION OF KEROUAC'S POETRY begins with his introduction to *San Francisco Blues,* his first book of poetry, followed by the first five poems from the book, which give a sense of what he was trying to do in the blues poetry form. He wrote them, as he says in one of the poems, "in a rocking chair/In the Cameo Hotel/San Francisco Skid row/Nineteen Fifty Four."

As his fellow poet Amiri Baraka understood, Kerouac was deeply influenced by "black improvisational music." He loved to listen to the "scatting" or vocalization of jazz lines by performers like King Pleasure, and he made amateur recordings of himself singing and scatting with his friends Neal Cassady and John Clellon Holmes. When he came to write down his improvisations as poetry, the form that he first chose was his free response to the instrumental blues chorus he heard in jazz. This is a freely improvised variation on a harmonic phrase that recurs in a continuous if varied pattern over the duration of twelve bars of music.

Kerouac was attracted to the blues form for many reasons, perhaps because he felt that its structure allowed him the most free and spontaneous approach to the merging of text and sound. Like the black musicians who'd created the form, Kerouac intended the poems he wrote to be heard, preferably with a jazz background. The three recordings he made reading his poetry for Verve and Hanover in 1958 and 1959 are the best indication of how he wanted it to sound.

Kerouac finished other books of blues—like *Mexico City Blues, Macdougal Street Blues,* and *Orizaba Blues*—and he also wrote many individual poems; "Daydreams for Ginsberg," "Rose Pome," and "Woman" follow the selections from *San Francisco Blues.*

Kerouac's most complete statement about his view of himself as a poet was published in the *Chicago Review* in the spring of 1958, titled "The Origins of Joy in Poetry." In this short essay he pointed out his affinities to his poet friends in the San Francisco Renaissance group, saying they all shared his dedication to spontaneity and confession:

The new American poetry as typified by the SF Renaissance (which means Ginsberg, me, Rexroth, Ferlinghetti, McClure,

Corso, Gary Snyder, Phil Lamantia, Philip Whalen, I guess) is a kind of new-old Zen Lunacy poetry, writing whatever comes into your head as it comes, poetry returned to its origin, in the bardic child, truly ORAL as Ferling said, instead of gray faced Academic quibbling. Poetry & prose had for long-time fallen into the false hands of the false. These new pure poets confess forth for the sheer joy of confession. They are CHILDREN. They are also childlike graybeard Homers singing in the street. They SING, they SWING. It is diametrically opposed to the Eliot shot, who so dismally advises his dreary negative rules like the objective correlative, etc. which is just a lot of constipation and ultimately emasculation of the pure masculine urge to freely sing. In spite of the dry rules he set down his poetry itself is sublime. I could say lots more but aint got time or sense. But SF is the poetry of a new Holy Lunacy like that of ancient times (Li Po, Han Shan, Tom O Bedlam, Kit Smart, Blake) yet it also has that mental discipline typified by the haiku (Basho, Buson), that is, the discipline of pointing out things directly, purely, concretely, no abstractions or explanations, wham wham the true blue song of man.

More surprising than the implicit sexism ("the pure masculine urge to freely sing") in this statement is Kerouac's praise of T. S. Eliot's poetry as "sublime." Eliot's work is so different from Kerouac's that we would expect the younger writer to express admiration instead for the "American grain" of William Carlos Williams's poetry, which his friend Ginsberg revered. Kerouac was full of contradictions. He was responsive to Eliot's use of the French poetic tradition and honored it himself in the poem "Rimbaud."

The next selections "Hymn," "Poem," "A Pun for Al Gelpi," "Two Poems Dedicated to Thomas Merton," and "How to Meditate" reflect Kerouac's study of Buddhism. "Hitch Hiker" and "Pome on Doctor Sax" are humorous poems in which he attempted what he called "the easy lightness of Beatnik poetry." Kerouac had his "own way," or style, and in 1959 he tried to define it for his editor Donald Allen:

Add alluvials to the end of your line when all is exhausted but something has to be said for some specified irrational reason, since reason can never win out, because poetry is NOT a science. The rhythm of how you decide to "rush" yr statement determines the rhythm of the poem, whether it is a poem in verse-separated lines, or an endless one-line poem called prose . . . (with its paragraphs). So let there be no equivocation about statement, and if you think this is not hard to do, try it. You'll find that your lies are heavier than your intentions. And your confessions lighter than Heaven.

Otherwise, who wants to read?

I myself have difficulty covering up my bullshit lies.

Next come selections from Kerouac's *Book of Haikus*. Kerouac enjoyed writing in this traditional form throughout his life, often enclosing haikus in letters to friends or jotting them down on the endpapers of books in his library. In 1959 he noted the difference he saw between Japanese haiku and his own work:

The American Haiku is not exactly the Japanese haiku. The Japanese Haiku is strictly disciplined to seventeen syllables but since the language structure is different I don't think American Haikus (short three-line poems intended to be completely packed with Void of Whole) should worry about syllables because American speech is something again . . . bursting to pop.

This section ends with the experimental poem "Sea," in which Kerouac attempted to transcribe the sound of the waves of the Pacific Ocean crashing on the beach at Bixby Canyon in 1960. On his trip to France five years later, in search of the origin of what he called his "real name," Jean-Louis Lebris de Kérouac, he hoped to write another poem based on the sound of the Atlantic Ocean off the coast of Brittany, but he was unable to complete the project.

San Francisco Blues

from
SAN FRANCISCO BLUES—
IN 79 CHORUSES

SAN FRANCISCO BLUES was my first book of poems, written back in 1954 & hinting the approach of the final blues poetry form I developed for the *Mexico City Blues.*

In my system, the form of blues choruses is limited by the small page of the breastpocket notebook in which they are written, like the form of a set number of bars in a jazz blues chorus, and so sometimes the word-meaning can carry from one chorus into another, or not, just like the phrase-meaning can carry harmonically from one chorus to the other, or not, in jazz, so that, in these blues as in jazz, the form is determined by time, and by the musician's spontaneous phrasing & harmonizing with the beat of the time as it waves & waves on by in measured choruses.

It's all gotta be non stop ad libbing within each chorus, or the gig is shot.

—Jack Kerouac

(1)

I see the backs
Of old men
Rolling slowly into
Black stores
Line-faced, moustached
Black men
With Army weathered brown hats
Stomp on by with bags
Of burlap and rue
Talking to secret companions
With long hair
In the sidewalk on Third Street
San Francisco
With the rain of exhaust

Plicking in the mist
You see in black store doors
Heading trucks plopping
    Vastly city

(2)

Third Street, Market
TO LEASE
Has a washed down tile entrance
Once white
Now caked with gum
Of a hundred thousand feet
Of passers who didn't go straight on
Bending to flap the time
Pap page on back
With smoke emanating from their noses
But slowly like old
Lantern-jawed junkmen
Hurrying with the lump
Wondrous potato bag
Through the avenues of sunshine
    Came
Bending to spit
And shuffled a while there

(3)

The rooftop of the beatup
Tenement
On 3rd & Harrison
Has Belfast painted
Black on yellow
On the side
The old Frisco wood is
Shown with weatherbeaten
Rainboards, & a
Washed out blue bottle
Once painted for wild
Commercial reasons by

An excited seltzerite
As firemen came last
Afternoon & raised the
Ladder to a fruitless
Fire that was not there,
So, is Belfast singing
          in this time
When brand's forgotten
Taste washed in
Rain the gullies broadened
And everybody gone
And acrobats of the
          Tenement
          Who dug bel fast
          Divers all
          And the divers all dove

(4)

Ah
          Little girls make
          Shadows on the
          Sidewalk shorter
          Than the shadow
          Of death
In this town—

(5)

Fat girls
In red coats
With flat, white out shoes
Harried Mexican laborers
Become respectable San Francisco
Carry newspapers of culture burden
And packages of need
Walk sadly, reluctant to work
And dawn
Stalking with not cat
In the feel of their stride

Touching to hide the sidewalk
Black, shiny last night
Parlor shoes
Hitting the slippery
With hard slicky heels
To slide and fall—
B-b-whack
Crack!

DAYDREAMS FOR GINSBERG

I lie on my back at midnight
hearing the marvelous strange chime
of the clocks, and know it's midnight and in that instant the whole
world swims into sight for me
in the form of beautiful swarming m u t t a worlds—
everything is happening, shining
Buhudda-lands, *bhuti*
blazing in faith, I know I'm
forever right & all's I got to
do (as I hear the ordinary
extant voices of ladies talking
in some kitchen at midnight
oilcloth cups of cocoa
cardore to mump the
rinnegain in his
darlin drain—) i will write
it, all the talk of the world
everywhere in this morning, leaving open parentheses sections
for my own accompanying inner
thoughts—with roars of me
all brain—all world
roaring—vibrating—I put
it down, swiftly, 1,000 words

(of pages) compressed into one second
of time—I'll be long
robed & long gold haired in
the famous Greek afternoon
of some Greek City
Fame Immortal & they'll
have to find me where they find
the t h n u p f t of my
shroud bags flying
flag yagging Lucien
Midnight back in their
mouths—Gore Vidal'll
be amazed, annoyed—
   my words'll be writ in gold
& preserved in libraries like
Finnegans Wake & Visions of Neal

ROSE POME

I'd rather be thin than famous,
I dont wanta be fat,
And a woman throws me outa bed
Callin me Gordo, & everytime
      I bend
      to pickup
      my suspenders
      from the davenport
      floor I explode
      loud huge grunt-o
      and disgust
      every one
      in the familio

   I'd rather be thin than famous
   But I'm fat

Paste that in yr. Broadway Show

WOMAN

A woman is beautiful
  but
    you have to swing
    and swing and swing
    and swing like
    a handkerchief in the
                wind

RIMBAUD

  Arthur!
   On t'appela pas Jean!
Born in 1854 cursing in Charle-
ville thus paving the way for
the abominable murderousnesses
of Ardennes—
No wonder your father left!
So you entered school at 8
—Proficient little Latinist you!
In October of 1869
Rimbaud is writing poetry
in Greek French—
Takes a runaway train

to Paris without a ticket,
the miraculous Mexican Brakeman
throws him off the fast
train, to Heaven, which
he no longer travels because
Heaven is everywhere—
Nevertheless the old fags
intervene—
Rimbaud nonplussed Rimbaud
trains in the green National
Guard, proud, marching
in the dust with his heroes—

[handwritten annotation:] Heaven, to which he no longer must travel because Heaven is everywhere

hoping to be buggered,
dreaming of the ultimate Girl.
—Cities are bombarded as
he stares & stares & chews
his degenerate lip & stares
with gray eyes at
      Walled France—

André Gill was forerunner
to André Gide—
Long walks reading poems
in the Genet Haystacks—
The Voyant is born,
the deranged seer makes his
      first Manifesto,
gives vowels colors
      & consonants carking care,
comes under the influence
of old French Fairies
who accuse him of constipation
of the brain & diarrhea
of the mouth—
Verlaine summons him to Paris
with less aplomb than he
did banish girls to
      Abyssinia—

"Merde!" screams Rimbaud
at Verlaine salons—
Gossip in Paris—Verlaine Wife
is jealous of a boy
with no seats to his trousers
—Love sends money from Brussels
—Mother Rimbaud hates
the importunity of Madame
Veraline—Degenerate Arthur
      is suspected of being a poet
      by now—
Screaming in the barn
      Rimbaud writes Season in Hell,

"The Ultimate Girl"

alliteration

his mother trembles—
Verlaine sends money & bullets
      into Rimbaud—
            Rimbaud goes to the police
            & presents his innocence
            like the pale innocence
            of his divine, feminine Jesus
—Poor Verlaine, 2 years
in the can, but could have
got a knife in the heart

—Illuminations! Stuttgart!
Study of Languages!
On foot Rimbaud walks
& looks thru the Alpine
passes into Italy, looking
            for clover bells, rabbits,
            Genie Kingdoms & ahead
            of him nothing but the old
                  Canaletto death of sun
                  on old Venetian buildings
—Rimbaud studies language
—hears of the Alleghanies,
of Brooklyn, of last
      American Plages—
His angel sister dies—
            Vienne! He looks at pastries
            & pets old dogs! I hope!
This mad cat joins
            the Dutch Army
            & sails for Java
commanding the fleet
      at midnight
      on the bow, alone,
      no one hears his Command
but every fishy shining
            in the sea—August is no
time to stay in Java—
            Aiming at Egypt, he's again
hungup in Italy so he goes

back home to deep armchair
but immediately he goes
again, to Cyprus, to
    run a gang of quarry
workers,—what did he
    look like now, this Later
    Rimbaud?—Rock dust
& black backs & hacks
    of coughers, the dream rises
in the Frenchman's Africa
mind,—Invalids from
  the tropics are always
    loved—The Red Sea
    in June, the coast clanks
    of Arabia—Havar,
    Havar, the magic trading
    post—Aden, Aden,
      South of Bedouin—
      Ogaden, Ogaden, never
      known—Meanwhile
      Verlaine sits in Paris
  over cognacs wondering
what Arthur looks like
  now, & how bleak their
eyebrows because they believed
in earlier eyebrow beauty—
Who cares? What kinda
Frenchmen are these?
Rimbaud, hit me over the
head with that rock!

Serious Rimbaud composes
elegant & learned articles
for National Geographic
Societies, & after wars
commands Harari Girl
(Ha *Ha!*) back
to Abyssinia, & she
was young, had black
    eyes, thick lips, hair

curled, & breasts like
polished brown with
copper teats & ringlets
on her arms & joined
    her hands upon her
    central loin & had
    shoulders as broad as
    Arthur's, & little ears
—A girl of some
    caste, in Bronzeville—

Rimbaud also knew
thinbonehipped Polynesians
with long tumbling hair
    & tiny tits & big feet

    Finally he starts
trading illegal guns
    in Tajoura
    riding in caravans, mad,
with a belt of gold
    around his waist—
Screwed by King Menelek!
The Shah of Shoa!
    The noises of these names
    in that noisy French
    mind!

    Cairo for the summer,
bitter lemon wind
& kisses in the dusty park
    where girls sit folded
    at dusk thinking
    nothing—

    Havar! Havar!
    By litter to Zeyla
    he's carried moaning his
    birthday—the boat
    returns to chalk castle

Marseilles sadder than
time, than dream,
sadder than water
—Carcinoma, Rimbaud
is eaten by the disease
of overlife—They cut
off his beautiful leg—

He dies in the arms
of Ste. Isabelle
his sister
& before rising to Heaven
sends his francs
to Djami, Djami
the Havari boy
his body servant
8 years in the African
Frenchman's Hell,
& it all adds up
to nothing, like

Dostoevsky, Beethoven
or Da Vinci—
So, poets, rest awhile
& shut up:
Nothing ever came
of nothing.

HYMN

And when you showed me Brooklyn Bridge
in the morning,
Ah God,
And the people slipping on ice in the street,
twice,
twice,
two different people
came over, goin to work,

so earnest and tryful,
clutching their pitiful
morning Daily News
slip on the ice & fall
both inside 5 minutes
and I cried I cried
That's when you taught me tears, Ah
   God in the morning,
       Ah Thee
And me leaning on the lamppost wiping
eyes,

       eyes,
           nobody's known I'd cried
           or woulda cared anyway
           but O I saw my father
           and my grandfather's mother
           and the long lines of chairs
           and tear-sitters and dead,
           Ah me, I knew God You
           had better plans than that
So whatever plan you have for me
Splitter of majesty
Make it short
   brief
Make it snappy
   bring me home to the Eternal Mother
   today
At your service anyway,
   (and until)

POEM

I demand that the human race
ceases multiplying its kind
           and bow out
           I advise it

And as punishment & reward
for making this plea I know
      I'll be reborn
      the last human   *what a concept*
Everybody else dead and I'm
an old woman roaming the earth
        groaning in caves
        sleeping on mats

And sometimes I'll cackle, sometimes
pray, sometimes cry, eat & cook
      at my little stove
      in the corner
"Always knew it anyway,"
      I'll say
And one morning won't get up from my mat   *wow.*

A PUN FOR AL GELPI

Jesus got mad one day
  at an apricot tree.
He said, "Peter, you
  of the Holy See,
Go see if the tree is ripe."
  "The tree is not yet ripe,"
  reported back Peter the Rock.
"Then let it wither!"
Jesus wanted an apricot.
In the morning, the tree
  had withered,
Like the ear in the agony
  of the garden,
Struck down by the sword.
  Unready.
  What means this parable?
Everybody
  better see.

You're really sipping
When your glass
  is always empty.

TWO POEMS DEDICATED
TO THOMAS MERTON

I

It's not that
everybody's trying
  to get into the act,
as Jimmy Durante
says—it's that
  EVERYBODY *IS*
    IN THE ACT
      (from the point
        of view of
        Universality)

      Rhymes
        With
          Durante

II

Not oft
    the snow
        so soft
          the holy bow

HOW TO MEDITATE

        —lights out—
fall, hands a-clasped, into instantaneous
ecstasy like a shot of heroin or morphine,

the gland inside of my brain discharging
the good glad fluid (Holy Fluid) as
I hap-down and hold all my body parts
down to a deadstop trance—Healing
all my sicknesses—erasing all—not
even the shred of a "I-hope-you" or a
Loony Balloon left in it, but the mind
blank, serene, thoughtless. When a thought
comes a-springing from afar with its held-
forth figure of image, you spoof it out,
you spuff it off, you fake it, and
it fades, and thought never comes—and
with joy you realize for the first time
"Thinking's just like not thinking—
So I don't have to think
   any
   more"

HITCH HIKER

"Tryna get to sunny Californy"—
   Boom. It's the awful raincoat
making me look like a selfdefeated self-
murdering imaginary gangster, an idiot in
a rueful coat, how can they understand
my damp packs—my mud packs—
      "Look John, a hitchhiker"
      "He looks like he's got a gun underneath
that I.R.A. coat"
      "Look Fred, that man by the road"
      "Some sexfiend got in print in 1938
in Sex Magazine"—
      "You found his blue corpse in a
greenshade edition, with axe blots"

POME ON DOCTOR SAX

In his declining years Doctor Sax was an old bum living in Skid
  Row hotel rooms in the blighted area of SF around 3rd
    Street—He was a madhaired old genius now with hair
      growing out of his nose and, like the hair growing out of
        the nose of Aristidamis Kaldis the painter, and had
          eyebrows growing out an inch long, like the eyebrows
            of Daisetz Suzuki the Zen Master of whom
              it has been said, of *which*, eyebrows like that
                take a lifetime to grow so long &
                  therefore resemble the bush of the
                    Dharma which once rooted
                      is too tough to be
                        pulled out by hand
                          or horse—

Let that be a lesson to all you young
  girls plucking your eyebrows & you
    (also) young choir singers jacking off
      behind the marechal's hilt
        in St Paul's
          Cathedral
            (& yelling home to Mother
              "Mater Mine, b' ome
                for Easter")

Dr Sax the master knower of
  Easter was now reduced to penury
    & looking at Stained glass windows
    in old churches—His only 2
    last friends in this life, this impossibly
    hard life no matter under what
  conditions it appears, were Bela
  Lugosi & Boris Karloff, who visited
him annually in his room on 3rd Street
  & cut thru the fogs of evening with
    their heads bent as the bells of St Simon
    tolled a heartbroken "Kathleen" across
    the rooftops of old hotels where similar old

men like Doctor Sax sat bent headed
on beds of woe with prayerbeads between
    their feet, Oh moaning, homes for
        lost pigeons or time's immemorial
        white dove
            of the roses
                of the unborn
                    astonished bliss—

    And there they'd sit in the little
room, Sax on the edge of the bed with a
    bottle of rotgut Tokay in his hand, Bela
    in the old rocking chair, Boris standing by
        the sink, & sigh------------
            & then Sax wd always say

    "Please play the monster for me" & of course
the old actors, who loved him dearly & came to
see him for human tender sentimentality not
    monstrous reasons protested but he always
    got drunk & cried so that Boris first had
        to get up & extend his arms do
        Frankenstein go UK! then Bela
        wd stand & arm cape & leer &
        approach Sax, who squealed

from BOOK OF HAIKUS:
SOME WESTERN HAIKUS

EXPLANATORY NOTE BY AUTHOR: The "Haiku" was invented and developed over hundreds of years in Japan to be a complete poem in seventeen syllables and to pack in a whole vision of life in three short lines. A "Western Haiku" need not concern itself with the seventeen syllables since Western languages cannot adapt themselves to the fluid syllabic Japanese. I propose that the "Western Haiku" simply say a lot in three short lines in any Western language.

Above all a Haiku must be very simple and free of all poetic trickery

and make a little picture and yet be as airy and graceful as a Vivaldi
Pastorella. Here is a great Japanese Haiku that is simpler and prettier
than any Haiku I could ever write in any language:

> A day of quiet gladness,
> Mount Fuji is veiled
> In misty rain.
>   (Basho) (1644–1694)

Here is another:

> Nesetsukeshi ko no
> Sentaku ya natsu
> No tsuki

> She has put the child to sleep,
> And now washes the clothes;
> The summer moon.
>   (Issa) (1763–1827)

And another, by Buson (1715–1783):

> The nightingale is singing,
> Its small mouth
> Open.

                    • • •

Arms folded
 to the moon,
Among the cows.

> Birds singing
> in the dark
> —Rainy dawn.

Elephants munching
 on grass—loving
Heads side by side.

> Missing a kick
> at the icebox door
> It closed anyway.

Perfect moonlit night
 marred
By family squabbles.

Catfish fighting for his life,
 and winning,
Splashing us all.

Evening coming—
 the office girl
Unloosing her scarf.

The low yellow
 moon above the
Quiet lamplit house

Shall I say no?
 —fly rubbing
its back legs

Unencouraging sign
 —the fish store
Is closed.

Nodding against
 the wall, the flowers
Sneeze

Straining at the padlock,
 the garage doors
At noon

The taste
 of rain
—Why kneel?

The moon,
 the falling star
—Look elsewhere

The rain has filled
 the birdbath
Again, almost

And the quiet cat
 sitting by the post
Perceives the moon

Useless, useless,
 the heavy rain
Driving into the sea.

Juju beads on the
 Zen Manual:
My knees are cold.

Those birds sitting
 out there on the fence—
They're all going to die.

The bottoms of my shoes
 are wet
from walking in the rain

In my medicine cabinet,
 the winter fly
has died of old age.

November—how nasal
 the drunken
Conductor's call

The moon had
 a cat's mustache
For a second

A big fat flake
 of snow
Falling all alone

The summer chair
 rocking by itself
In the blizzard

                                                    This July evening,
                                                     a large frog
                                                    On my door sill.

SEA

 Cherson!
  Cherson!
   You aint just whistlin
    Dixie, Sea—
   Cherson! Cherson!
    We calcimine fathers
     here below!
   Kitchen lights on—
    Sea Engines from Russia
     seabirding here below—
 When rocks outsea froth
    I'll know Hawaii
     cracked up & scramble
     up my doublelegged cliff
   to the silt of
    a million years—

Shoo—Shaw—Shirsh—
Go on die salt light
 You billion yeared
  rock knocker

Gavroom
Seabird ——————⟶
Gabroobird
Sad as wife & hill
Loved as mother & fog
Oh! Oh! Oh!

Sea! Osh!
Where's yr little Neppytune
    tonight?

These gentle tree pulp pages
which've nothing to do
with yr crash roar,
    liar sea, ah,
were made for rock
tumble seabird digdown
    footstep hollow weed
  move bedarvaling
  crash? Ah again?
Wine is salt here?
  Tidal wave kitchen?
Engines of Russia
    in yr soft talk—

Les poissons de la mer
    parle Breton—
Mon nom es Lebris
    de Keroack—
  Parle, Poissons, Loti,
    parle—
Parlning Ocean sanding
  crash the billion rocks—

  Ker plotsch—
    Shore—shoe—
god—brash—

The headland looks like
a longnosed Collie sleeping
with his light on his
    nose, as the ocean,
  obeying its accommodations
  of mind, crashes in
    rhythm which could
  & will intrude, in thy
    rhythm of sand

thought—
—Big frigging shoulders
on *that* sonofabitch

Parle, O, parle, mer, parle,
 Sea speak to me, speak
  to me, your silver you light
  Where hole opened up in Alaska
   Gray—shh—wind in
    The canyon wind in the rain
    Wind in the rolling rash
   Moving and t wedel
    Sea
     sea
      Diving sea
O bird—la vengeance
 De la roche
   Cossez
    Ah

Rare, he rammed the gate
rare over by Cherson, Cherson,
we calcify fathers here below
—a watery cross, with weeds
entwined—This grins restoredly,
 low sleep—Wave—Oh, no,
shush—Shirk—Boom plop
Neptune now his arms extends
 while one millions of souls
  sit lit in caves of darkness
 —What old bark? The dog
mountain? Down by the Sea
 Engines? God rush—Shore—
Shaw—Shoo—Oh soft sigh
 we wait hair twined like
 larks—Pissit—Rest not
—Plottit, bisp tesh, cashes,
 re tav, plo, aravow,
shirsh,—Who's whispering over
  there—the silly earthen creek!

The fog thunders—We put
   silver light on face—We
      took the heroes in—A billion
         years aint nothing—

O the cities here below!
The men with a thousand
arms! the stanchions of
their upward gaze! the
coral of their poetry! the
   sea dragons tenderized, meat
   for fleshy fish—
      Navark, navark, the fishes
   of the Sea speak Breton—
   wash as soft as people's
dreams—We got peoples
   in & out the shore, they call
   it shore, sea call it
      pish rip plosh—The
      5 billion years since
      earth we saw substantial
      chan—Chinese are
         the waves—the woods
         are dreaming

No human words bespeak
   the token sorrow older
   than old this wave
   becrashing smarts the
      sand with plosh
      of twirléd sandy
thought—Ah change
   the world? Ah set
   the fee? Are rope the
      angels in all the sea?
      Ah ropey otter
   barnacle'd be—
      Ah cave, Ah crosh!
      A feathery sea

Too much short—Where
  Miss Nop tonight?
Wroten Kerarc'h
  in the labidalian
  aristotelian park
with slime a middle
—And Ranti forner
  who pulled pearls by
  rope to throne
    the King by
      the roll in the
      forest of everseas?
Not everseas, *be* seas
  ——Creep
    Crash

ON SPONTANEOUS
PROSE

EDITOR'S INTRODUCTION

KEROUAC WAS INTERESTED in writing, rather than in writing about writing, and he made few efforts to explain or theorize about his work. "Belief & Technique for Modern Prose," thirty terse, sometimes enigmatic phrases and commands, was an attempt to describe what he was doing, but "The Essentials of Spontaneous Prose" was a more extensive effort. He wrote it at the request of Allen Ginsberg and William Burroughs in the fall of 1953, after he had shown them the manuscript of *The Subterraneans*. His friends were so impressed by the fact that he'd written the entire book in three nights sitting at a table in the kitchen of his mother's apartment in Queens that they asked him to describe how he'd done it.

Later in an introduction to a Norwegian edition of the book, Kerouac referred to the compositional process again, stating his belief that his method of writing produced

the prose of the future, from both the conscious top and the unconscious bottom of the mind, limited only by the limitations of time flying by as your mind flies by with it. Not a word of this book was changed after I had finished writing it in three sessions from dusk to dawn at the typewriter like a long letter to a friend. This I believe to be the only possible literature of the future.
UNINTERRUPTED AND UNREVISED FULL CONFESSIONS ABOUT WHAT ACTUALLY HAPPENED IN REAL LIFE.

Describing what he considered the nine essentials of spontaneous prose—set-up, procedure, method, scoping, lag in procedure, timing, center of interest, structure of work, and mental state—Kerouac compared himself explicitly to a jazz musician.

With Ginsberg and Burroughs, the poet Robert Creeley was on Kerouac's wavelength. In an essay titled "Thinking of Jack," Creeley wrote that what Kerouac's method of spontaneous prose both wanted to do and did was to "take in" all that the senses apprehended, to move with the complexity of the moment's demand, to be "with it," as jazz was, not "about it" as authoritarian writing and criticism then argued. . . . No precedent "form" or preconception could ever be there in the same way. Jazz was the parallel. Our evident lives were the proof. . . . We thought to be honest, like they say, to be true to our own origins and persons, to break through the literary habits and social determinants we felt our generation particularly to face. We took such risks as we could find as a badge of honor. Security of any sort was a dirty word.

Writing spontaneous prose was a risky business for Kerouac in more ways than Creeley described. In an essay that appeared in *Escapade* magazine in 1967, "Jack Kerouac Takes a Fresh Look at Jack Kerouac," Kerouac reviewed his career in the decade since publication of *On the Road*. There he mentioned that his method of spontaneous prose had led him "to the edges of language where the babble of the subconscious begins" and confessed that he "began to rely too much on babble" in his attempt to "race away from cantish cliches," ending up "ravingly enslaved to sounds. . . . There's a delicate balancing point between bombast and babble."

Finally, in the article "Are Writers Made or Born?" written for *Writers' Digest* in 1962, Kerouac analyzed the difference between literary talent and genius. His piece was introduced in the magazine by a condescending paragraph: "Chanting the offbeat of the Beat Generation, writers like Jack Kerouac read poems, yen for Zen, strut the streets of the lower East Side and 'dig' the offbeat cats and damsels in the Bohemian lofts that have become the center of a new 'village.' Like any sick people, they want to be left alone; but what about cultures where the highest value is withdrawal? Who would be sick in such a culture? The 'beatniks' feign no answers. Rebels against reality, and protestors against the provincial, they decry naming what they stand for."

BELIEF & TECHNIQUE
FOR MODERN PROSE

List of Essentials

1. Scribbled secret notebooks, and wild typewritten pages, for yr own joy
2. Submissive to everything, open, listening
3. Try never get drunk outside yr own house
4. Be in love with yr life
5. Something that you feel will find its own form
6. Be crazy dumbsaint of the mind
7. Blow as deep as you want to blow
8. Write what you want bottomless from bottom of the mind
9. The unspeakable visions of the individual
10. No time for poetry but exactly what is
11. Visionary tics shivering in the chest
12. In tranced fixation dreaming upon object before you
13. Remove literary, grammatical and syntactical inhibition
14. Like Proust be an old teahead of time
15. Telling the true story of the world in interior monolog
16. The jewel center of interest is the eye within the eye
17. Write in recollection and amazement for yourself
18. Work from pithy middle eye out, swimming in language sea
19. Accept loss forever
20. Believe in the holy contour of life
21. Struggle to sketch the flow that already exists intact in mind
22. Dont think of words when you stop but to see picture better
23. Keep track of every day the date emblazoned in yr morning
24. No fear or shame in the dignity of yr experience, language & knowledge
25. Write for the world to read and see yr exact pictures of it
26. Bookmovie is the movie in words, the visual American form
27. In praise of Character in the Bleak inhuman Loneliness
28. Composing wild, undisciplined, pure, coming in from under, crazier the better

29. You're a Genius all the time
30. Writer-Director of Earthly movies Sponsored & Angeled in Heaven

ESSENTIALS OF
SPONTANEOUS PROSE

SET-UP.   The object is set before the mind, either in reality, as in sketching (before a landscape or teacup or old face) or is set in the memory wherein it becomes the sketching from memory of a definite image-object.

PROCEDURE.   Time being of the essence in the purity of speech, sketching language is undisturbed flow from the mind of personal secret idea-words, *blowing* (as per jazz musician) on subject of image.

METHOD.   No periods separating sentence-structures already arbitrarily riddled by false colons and timid usually needless commas—but the vigorous space dash separating rhetorical breathing (as jazz musician drawing breath between outblown phrases)—"measured pauses which are the essentials of our speech"—"divisions of the *sounds* we hear"— "time and how to note it down." (William Carlos Williams)

SCOPING.   Not "selectivity" of expression but following free deviation (association) of mind into limitless blow-on-subject seas of thought, swimming in sea of English with no discipline other than rhythms of rhetorical exhalation and expostulated statement, like a fist coming down on a table with each complete utterance, bang! (the space dash) —Blow as deep as you want—write as deeply, fish as far down as you want, satisfy yourself first, then reader cannot fail to receive telepathic shock and meaning-excitement by same laws operating in his own human mind.

LAG IN PROCEDURE.   No pause to think of proper word but the infantile pileup of scatalogical buildup words till satisfaction is gained, which will turn out to be a great appending rhythm to a thought and be in accordance with Great Law of timing.

TIMING.   Nothing is muddy that *runs in time* and to laws of *time*—Shakespearian stress of dramatic need to speak now in own unalterable way or forever hold tongue—*no revisions* (except obvious rational mistakes, such as names or *calculated* insertions in act of not writing but *inserting*).

CENTER OF INTEREST.   Begin not from preconceived idea of what to say about image but from jewel center of interest in subject of image at *moment* of writing, and write outwards swimming in sea of language to peripheral release and exhaustion—Do not afterthink except for poetic or P.S. reasons. Never afterthink to "improve" or defray impressions, as, the best writing is always the most painful personal wrung-out tossed from cradle warm protective mind—tap from yourself the song of yourself, *blow!*—*now!*—*your* way is your only way—"good"—or "bad"—always honest, ("ludicrous"), spontaneous, "confessional" interesting, because not "crafted." Craft *is* craft.

STRUCTURE OF WORK.   Modern bizarre structures (science fiction, etc.) arise from language being dead, "different" themes give illusion of "new" life. Follow roughly outlines in out-fanning movement over subject, as river rock, so mindflow over jewel-center need (run your mind over it, *once*) arriving at pivot, where what was dim formed "beginning" becomes sharp-necessitating "ending" and language shortens in race to wire of time-race of work, following laws of Deep Form, to conclusion, last words, last trickle—Night is The End.

MENTAL STATE.   If possible write "without consciousness" in semi-trance (as Yeats' later "trance writing") allowing subconscious to admit in own uninhibited interesting necessary and so "modern" language what conscious art would censor, and write excitedly, swiftly, with writing-or-typing-cramps, in accordance (as from center to periphery) with laws of orgasm, Reich's "beclouding of consciousness." *Come* from within, out—to relaxed and said.

THE FIRST WORD:
JACK KEROUAC TAKES
A FRESH LOOK AT JACK KEROUAC

MY POSITION in the current American literary scene is simply that I got
sick and tired of the conventional English sentence which seemed to me
so ironbound in its rules, so inadmissable with reference to the actual
format of my mind as I had learned to probe it in the modern spirit of
Freud and Jung, that I couldn't express myself through that form any
more. How many sentences do you see in current novels that say, "The
snow was on the ground, and it was difficult for the car to climb the
hill"? By the childish device of taking what was originally two short
sentences, and sticking in a comma with an "and," these great contemporary prose "craftsmen" think they have labored out a sentence. As
far as I can see it is two short sets of picturization belonging to a much
longer sentence the total picturization of which would finally say something we never heard before if the writer dared to utter it out.

Shame seems to be the key to repression in writing as well as in
psychological malady. If you don't stick to what you first thought, and
to the words the thought brought, what's the sense of bothering with it
anyway, what's the sense of foisting your little lies on others, or, that
is, hiding your little truths from others? What I find to be really "stu-
pefying in its unreadability" is this laborious and dreary lying called
craft and revision by writers, and certainly recognized by the sharpest
psychologists as sheer blockage of the mental spontaneous process
known 2,500 years ago as "The Seven Streams of Swiftness."

In the *Surangama Sutra,* Gotama Buddha says, "If you are now
desirous of more perfectly understanding Supreme Enlightenment, you
must learn to answer questions spontaneously with no recourse to discriminative thinking. For the Tathagatas (the Passers-Through) in the
ten quarters of the universes, because of the straight-forwardness of
their minds and the spontaneity of their mentations, have ever remained,
from beginningless time to endless time, of one pure Suchness with the
enlightening nature of pure Mind Essence."

Which is pretty strange old news. You can also find pretty much
the same thing in Mark 13:11. "Take no thought beforehand what ye
shall speak, neither do ye premeditate: but whatsoever shall be given

you in that hour, that speak ye: for it is not ye that speak, but the Holy Ghost." Mozart and Blake often felt they weren't pushing their own pens, 'twas the "Muse" singing and pushing.

But I would also like to compare spontaneous composition of prose and verse to the incomparable, heartbreaking discipline of the fire ordeal. You had to get through the fire "to prove your innocence" or just die in it "guilty"—there was certainly no chance to stop and think it over, to chew on the end of your pencil and erase something. O maybe you could pause a second or two for another direction but the trick was to act now (or speak now, as in writing) or forever hold your tongue.

In another sense spontaneous, or ad lib, artistic writing imitates as best it can the flow of the mind as it moves in its space-time continuum, in this sense it may really be called Space Age Prose someday because when astronauts are flowing through space and time they too have no chance to stop and reconsider and go back. It may be they won't be reading anything else but spontaneous writing when they do get out there, the science of the language to fit their science of movement.

But I'd gone so far to the edges of language where the babble of the subconscious begins, because words "come from the Holy Ghost" first in the form of a babble which suddenly by its sound indicates the word truly intended (in describing the stormy sea in *Desolation Angels* I heard the sound "Peligroso" for "Peligroso Roar" without knowing what it meant, wrote it down involuntarily, later found out it means "dangerous" in Spanish)—I began to rely too much on babble in my nervous race away from cantish cliches, chased the proton too close with my microscope, ended up ravingly enslaved to sounds, became unclear and dull as in my ultimate lit'ry experiment "Old Angel Midnight" (*Evergreen Review* and *Lui* in Paris in French). There's a delicate balancing point between bombast and babble.

And now my hand doesn't move as fast as it used to, and so many critics have laughed at me for those 16 originally-styled volumes of mine published in 16 languages in 42 countries, never for one moment calling me "sensitive" or artistically dignified but an unlettered literary hoodlum with diarrhea of the mouth, I'm having to retreat closer back to the bombast (empty abstraction) of this world and make my meaning plainer, i.e., dimmer, but the Space Age of the future won't bother with my "later" works if any, or with any of these millions of other things written today that sound alike.

To break through the barrier of language with WORDS, you have to be in orbit around your mind, and I may go up again if I regain my strength. It may sound vain but I've been wrestling with this angelic problem with at least as much discipline as Jacob.

The little kid in the Lowell House at Harvard, whose professor I was for an hour, looked me right in the eye and asked, "Why do you have no discipline?" I said, "Is that the way to talk to your professor? Try it if you can. If you can you'll pull the rug out from everybody."

ARE WRITERS MADE OR BORN?

WRITERS ARE MADE, for anybody who isn't illiterate can write; but geniuses of the writing art like Melville, Whitman or Thoreau are born. Let's examine the word "genius." It doesn't mean screwiness or eccentricity or excessive "talent." It is derived from the Latin word *gignere* (to beget) and a genius is simply a person who *originates* something never known before. Nobody but Melville could have written *Moby Dick*, not even Whitman or Shakespeare. Nobody but Whitman could have conceived, originated and written *Leaves of Grass*; Whitman was born to write a *Leaves of Grass* and Melville was born to write a *Moby Dick*. "It ain't whatcha do," Sy Oliver and James Young said, "it's the way atcha do it." Five thousand writing-class students who study "required reading" can put their hand to the legend of Faustus but only one Marlowe was born to do it the way he did.

I always get a laugh to hear Broadway wiseguys talk about "talent" and "genius." Some perfect virtuoso who can interpret Brahms on the violin is called a "genius," but the genius, the originating force, really belongs to Brahms; the violin virtuoso is simply a talented interpreter —in other words, a "Talent." Or you'll hear people say that so-and-so is a "major writer" because of his "large talent." There can be no major writer without original genius. Artists of genius, like Jackson Pollock, have painted things that have never been seen before. Anybody who's seen his immense Samapattis of color has no right to criticize his "crazy method" of splashing and throwing and dancing around.

Take the case of James Joyce: people said he "wasted" his "talent" on the stream of consciousness style, when in fact he was simply *born* to originate it. How would you like to spend your old age reading books about contemporary life written in the pre-Joycean style of, say, Ruskin, or William Dean Howells, or Taine? Some geniuses come with heavy feet and march solemnly forward like Dreiser, yet no one ever wrote about that America of his as well as he. Geniuses can be scintillating and geniuses can be somber, but it's that inescapable sorrowful depth that shines through—*originality*.

Joyce was insulted all his life by practically all of Ireland and the world for being a genius. Some Celtic Twilight idiots even conceded he had *some* talent. What else could they say, since they were all going to start imitating him? But five thousand university-trained writers could put their hand to a day in June in Dublin in 1904, or one night's dreams, and never do with it what Joyce did with it: he was simply born to do it. On the other hand, if the five thousand "trained" writers, plus Joyce, all put their hands to a *Reader's Digest*-type article about "Vacation Hints" or "Homemaker's Tips," even then I think Joyce would stand out because of his inborn originality of language insight. Bear well in mind what Sinclair Lewis told Thomas Wolfe: "If Thomas Hardy had been given a contract to write stories for *The Saturday Evening Post*, do you think he would have written like Zane Grey or like Thomas Hardy? I can tell you the answer to that one. He would have written like Thomas Hardy. He couldn't have written like anyone else but Thomas Hardy. He would have kept on writing like Thomas Hardy, whether he wrote for *The Saturday Evening Post* or *Captain Billy's Whiz-Bang*."

When the question is therefore asked, "Are writers made or born?" one should first ask, "Do you mean writers with talent or writers with originality?" Because anybody can write, but not everybody invents new forms of writing. Gertrude Stein invented a new form of writing and her imitators are just "talents." Hemingway later invented his own form also. The criterion for judging talent or genius is ephemeral, speaking rationally in this world of graphs, but one gets the feeling definitely when a writer of genius amazes him by strokes of force never seen before and yet hauntingly familiar (Wilson's famous "shock of recognition"). I got that feeling from *Swann's Way*, as well as from *Sons and Lovers*. I do not get it from Colette, but I do get it from Dickinson. I get it from Céline, but I do not get it from Camus. I get it from Hemingway, but not from Raymond Chandler, except when he's dead serious. I get it from the Balzac of *Cousin Bette*, but not from Pierre Loti. And so on.

The main thing to remember is that talent imitates genius because there's nothing else to imitate. Since talent can't originate it has to imitate, or interpret. The poetry on page 2 of the *New York Times*, with all its "silent wings of urgency in a dark and seldom wood" and other lapidary trillings, is but a poor imitation of previous poets of genius, like Yeats, Dickinson, Apollinaire, Donne, Suckling. . . .

Genius gives birth, talent delivers. What Rembrandt or Van Gogh saw in the night can never be seen again. No frog can jump in a pond like Basho's frog. *Born* writers of the future are amazed already at what they're seeing now, what we'll all see in time for the first time, and then see imitated many times by *made* writers.

So in the case of a born writer, genius involves the original formation of a new style. Though the language of Kyd is Elizabethan as far as period goes, the language of Shakespeare can truly be called only *Shakespearean*. Oftentimes an originator of new language forms is called "pretentious" by jealous talents. But it ain't whatcha write, it's the way atcha write it.

THE MODERN
SPONTANEOUS
METHOD

EDITOR'S INTRODUCTION

THE PIECES IN THIS SECTION chart the range of Kerouac's journey through his exploration of his experimental prose style. "In the Ring" appeared in *The Atlantic* in 1968. It is a classic Kerouac exposition of associations stemming from what he called his "jewel center of interest," an image from his childhood "of a young teen-age boxer hurrying down the street with a small blue bag in which all his fundamental things were packed. . . ."

"On the Road to Florida," published posthumously in the *Evergreen Review*, is Kerouac's free-wheeling account of a trip to Florida with the Swiss-American photographer Robert Frank. The essay was originally commissioned by Grove Press as the introduction to a collection of Frank's brilliant photographs of the American people and landscape, *The Americans* (1960). Kerouac's spontaneous prose method began with what he called a "definite image-object." He had a particular affinity for Frank's work as a photographer, seeing America through Frank's eyes as they drove down back roads and rural highways, identifying with his outsider's view of the country.

When Kerouac began thinking of selections that he would like to see in an anthology of his work, he told his agent, Sterling Lord, that he wanted to be sure it contained at least two specific pieces from *Visions of Cody*, his first experimental book, begun in the fall of 1951, six months after he'd finished *On the Road*. There he used spontaneous prose to give not "just a horizontal account of travels on the road" with Neal Cassady (renamed "Cody Pomeray" in *Visions of Cody*), but instead "a vertical, metaphysical study of Cody's character and its relationship to the general 'America.' This feeling may soon be obsolete as America enters its High Civilization period and no one will get sentimental or poetic any more about trains and dew on fences at dawn in Missouri."

The two selections from *Visions of Cody* that were among Kerouac's favorites were "The Three Stooges" and "Joan Rawshanks in the Fog." At one point Kerouac envisioned his friend Neal Cassady "in his whirlwinds," walking down a San Francisco street accompanied by the

Three Stooges, the slapstick movie comedians whom he and Neal loved to watch. "Joan Rawshanks in the Fog" is one of Kerouac's spontaneous prose masterpieces. He wrote it in 1952, while staying with Neal and Carolyn Cassady in San Francisco. He took a walk one foggy night near their apartment and watched a film crew at work with Joan Crawford, who was shooting a scene from a movie. The two pieces are joined in the reader by a short selection in which Kerouac experimented with allowing his "French-Canadian side" to monitor his thoughts about Cassady.

Another of Kerouac's writing experiments continued for years, a project begun in 1952 that he considered his private dream-record, what the publisher Lawrence Ferlinghetti called "the poetic raw material of the Kerouac saga, the substrata of his novels and a commentary upon them." These are the selections from *Book of Dreams*, published by City Lights in 1961. Kerouac kept several sheets of paper and a pencil attached to a clipboard on a string tied to the headboard of his bed, so he could write down his dreams immediately after awakening. He typed up the selections for Ferlinghetti, and his friend Philip Whalen put them in order for publication. Kerouac referred to his nightmare about the "Flying Horses of Mien Mo" in his book *Big Sur*.

This section concludes with several selections from *Old Angel Midnight*, in which Kerouac, influenced by James Joyce's experiments in *Finnegan's Wake* (1939), pushed spontaneous prose to its ultimate expression. Kerouac told John Clellon Holmes that his work in progress was "an endless automatic writing piece which raves on and on with no direction and no story." He experimented with free association in this poem, attempting to write down "the sounds of the entire world . . . now swimming thru the window." The San Francisco poet Michael McClure recognized that in *Old Angel Midnight*, Kerouac had achieved one of his most remarkable works:

> Never before has inconsequentiality been raised to such a peak that it becomes a breakthrough. . . . Inconsequentiality becomes a skewing of the established values of the senses and imagination into strange and yet familiar, but elusive, tantalizing and remarkable, constructs of image and sound. . . . The politics of *Old Angel Midnight* is that it is a reply by Jack to heavily armored, socially approved literature, as it was then taught and admired in colleges. . . . *Old Angel Midnight* is contemporary

with exploratory jazz and with the painting which sought to make spiritual autobiography utilizing the gestures of the artist and his materials. . . . *Old Angel Midnight* is struggling to be occupied by consciousness and nothingness, and not by social commands.

IN THE RING

MY JEWEL CENTER OF INTEREST when I think of sports as is, or as we say in the academic circles, *per se*, which means "as is" in Latin, is that sight I had one time of a young teen-age boxer hurrying down the street with a small blue bag in which all his fundamental things were packed: jockstrap I guess (I know), trunks, liniment, toothbrush, money, vitamin pills mayhap, T-shirts, sweat shirt, mouthpiece for all I know, under the grimly drab lamps of New England on a winter night on his way to, say, Lewiston Maine for a semifinal lightweight bout for 10 bucks a throw for all I know, or for (O worse!) Worcester Massachusetts or Portland Maine, or Laconia N.H., to the Greyhound or Trailways bus a-hurrying and where his father is I'll never have known, or his mother in what gray tenement, or his sister or brothers in what war and lounge—With a nose not yet broken, and luminous eyes, and meaningful glance at the sidewalk 'pon which he pounds to his destination the likes of which, whatever it ever became, shall never be visited on any angel that was fallen from heaven—I mean it, what's the sense of knocking your brains out for a few bucks?—I saw this guy outside the little training gym my father ran in Centerville, Lowell Mass., about 1930, when he first introduced me to sports by taking me in there to watch the boys hammer away at punching bags and big sandbags, and if you ever see an amateur heavyweight whacking away full-fisted at a sandbag and making the whole gym creak, you'll learn never to start a fight with any big boy you ever do meet in any bar from Portland Maine to Portland Oregon—And the young pug's name on the street was probably Bobby Sweet.

I was 8 at the time and soon after that my big fat cigarsmoking Pa (a printer by trade) had turned the place into a wrestling club, organization, gymnasium, and promotion, call it what you will, but the same guys who were boxers the year before were now wrestlers; especially old Roland Bouthelier, who was my father's unofficial chauffeur 'cause my father couldn't drive his 1929 Ford himself his legs being too short, or him having to try to talk too much while driving, and Roland being also a young friend of the family's (about 22) and a worker in his printing plant to boot—Now Roland was a wrestler and my sister Nin

(10) and I always beseeched him to show us his muscles when he came in the house for occasional supper and certainly for holiday suppers and he always obliged and Nin hung from one biceps and I hung from the other, whee . . . What a build! Like Mister America. One time he swallowed his tongue and almost choked at Salisbury Beach. He had a touch of epilepsy. During his youth there, my father was his friend and employer and protector. No capitalism involved, as tho a two-bit wrestling promoter and a one-bit printer could be a capitalist in a city of 100,000 people and him as honest as the day pretended to be long.

So I remember the time in about 1931 when I heard Roland being given sincere instructions in a dressing room smelling of big men sweat and liniment and all the damp smells that come from the showers and the open windows, "Go out there etc.," and out comes me and my Pa and we sit right at ringside, he lights up his usual 7-20-4 or Dexter cigar, the first match is on, his own promoted match, it's Roland Bouthelier against wild Mad Turk McGoo of the Lower Highlands and they come out and face each other; they lean over and clap big arms and hands over each other's necks and start mauling around and pretty soon one of them makes a big move and knocks the other guy down on the soft hollowly bouncing canvas, "Ugh, OO," he's got a headlock around Roland's head with his big disgusting legs full of hair, I can see Roland's face (my hero) turn red, he struggles there, but the guy squeezes harder and harder. This was before wrestling matches had begun to be fixed? you say? Well Roland had just got his instructions to lose the match in the first minute and then in the next minute if possible, to make time for the semifinal and the main match. But I saw his face turn red with French-Canadian rage and he suddenly threw his legs out and shot himself out of the leg hold and landed on his behind and leaped up in one acrobatic move on his feet, turned, and took the Turk by the shoulders and shoved him against the ropes, and when the Turk bounced back he had him direct in the stomach with a Gus Sonnenberg head charge and knocked the guy so hard back against the ropes the ropes gave and the guy tilted over and landed at some used cigars under the apron of the ring, where he lay gazing up with bleary nonunderstanding eyes. So naturally the referee gives the count, slow as he can, but that guy is slow coming back in; as soon as he crawls thru the ropes Roland's got him by the neck and throws him over his shoulder, the poor guy lands slam on his back, Roland's on top of him and pins his two shoulders down, but the guy wriggles out and Roland falls on his behind, clips him with his two sneakered feet, knocks him over on his stomach, jumps on his back, gives him the Full Nelson (which means both arms under the other guy's armpits and twined around to join at the neck), makes him hurt and weep and cry and curse and wince awhile, then, with one imperious angry shove, knocks him over again to his back (one big biceped arm) and pins his two shoulders down and he's gone and thrown the match, so to speak, which he was supposed to lose, out of angry real wrestling fury.

I'm even in the showers afterward listening to my Pa and the men give Roland hell for making them lose all that money, Roland says simply, "OK but he spit in my face in the leg lock when he had me down there, I wont take that from nobody."

A week later Roland is driving me and Pa, my ma and my sister to Montreal Canada for a big Fourth of July weekend where Roland is going to be introduced to the most beautiful little French dolls in town, my elder cousin girls. He turns and looks at me in the back seat as we're passing Lake Champlain, yells in French, "Are you still there, Ti Pousse?" (Lil Thumb?)

About this time too my Pa takes me and my ma to see every big wrestling match which happened at the time (dont ask me why, except Lowell must have been a big wrestling town) between the two world champs, Gus Sonnenberg of Topsfield (or thereabouts Massachusetts, originally from Germany) and the great Henri DeGlane, world's champion from France—In those days wrestling was still for keeps, dont you see—In the first fall Gus Sonnenberg rushes off the ropes with a bounce and does his famous head-into-belly rush that knocks DeGlane right over the ropes upside down bouncing and into my mother's lap . . . He is abashed, says, "I'm sorry, Madame," she says, "I dont mind as long as it's a good French man." Then on the next play he pins Sonnenberg down with his famous leg stranglehold and wins the first fall. Later on, in the incredible cigarsmoke which always made me wonder how those guys could even breathe let alone wrestle (in the Crescent Rink in Lowell) somebody applies a wrenching awful hellish leg-spreading hold that makes some people rush home in fear and somebody wins, I forget who.

It was only shortly after that that wrestling matches began to be fixed.

Meanwhile in this Crescent there were boxing matches and what I liked, besides the action, and since I didnt gamble, being 10 and not caring about money bets then as even now, I saw some marvelous aes-

thetical nuances connected with indoor fight sports: heard: smelled the
cigarsmoke, the hollow cries, the poem of it all . . . (which I wont go
into just now).

Because now there's no time for poetry anyway. The only way to
organize what you're going to say about anything is to organize it on
a grand and emotional scale based on the way you've felt about life all
along. Only recently, now at age 45, I saw I swear the selfsame young
pug with the sad blue bag a-hurrying to the bus station in Massachusetts
to make his way to Maine for another dreary prelim bout, with no hope
now but maybe 50 bucks, and maybe a broken nose, but why should
a young man do things like that and wind up in the bottom pages of
smalltown newspapers where they always have the UPI or AP reports
of fights: "Manila, Philippines, Jose Ortega, 123, of San Juan Puerto
Rico, outpointed Sam Vreska, 121, Kearney, Nebraska, in ten rounds.
. . . Hungry Kelly, 168, Omaha, Nebraska, kayoed Ross Raymond, 169,
Ottawa, Canada, in round 2." You read those things and you wonder
what makes them so eagerly helpless in the corner when their seconds
are sponging their reddened nose. Well never expect me to go into the
ring! I'm too yellow! Could it say in the lexicon of publishing stories
that Grass Williams outpointed or kayoed Gray Glass in the fifth? in
Beelzabur Town? I say, God bless young fighters, and now I'll take a
rest and wait for my trainer's bottle, and my trainer's name is Johnny
Walker.

ON THE ROAD
TO FLORIDA

JUST TOOK A TRIP BY CAR to Florida with Photographer Robert Frank,
Swiss born, to get my mother and cats and typewriter and big suitcase
full of original manuscripts, and we took this trip on a kind of provi-
sional assignment from *Life* magazine who gave us a couple hundred
bucks which paid for the gas and oil and chow both ways. But I was
amazed to see how a photographic artist does the bit, of catching those
things about the American Road writers write about. It's pretty amazing
to see a guy, while steering at the wheel, suddenly raise his little 300-

dollar German camera with one hand and snap something that's on the move in front of him, and through an unwashed windshield at that. Later on, when developed, the unwashed streaks dont harm the light, composition or detail of the picture at all, seem to enhance it. We started off in N.Y. at noon of a pretty Spring day and didnt take any pictures till we had negotiated the dull but useful stretch of the New Jersey Turnpike and come on down to Highway 40 in Delaware where we stopped for a snack in a roadside diner. I didnt see anything in particular to photograph, or "write about," but suddenly Robert was taking his first snap. From the counter where we sat, he had turned and taken a picture of a big car-trailer with piled cars, two tiers, pulling in the gravel driveyard, but through the window and right over a scene of leftovers and dishes where a family had just vacated a booth and got in their car and driven off, and the waitress not had time yet to clear the dishes. The combination of that, plus the movement outside, and further parked cars, and reflections everywhere in chrome, glass and steel of cars, cars, road, road, I suddenly realized I was taking a trip with a genuine artist and that he was expressing himself in an art-form that was not unlike my own and yet fraught with a thousand difficulties quite unlike those of my own. Contrary to the general belief about photography, you don't need bright sunlights: the best, moodiest pictures are taken in the dim light of almost-dusk, or of rainy days, like it was now in Delaware, late afternoon with rain impending in the sky and lights coming on on the road. Outside the diner, seeing nothing as usual, I walked on, but Robert suddenly stopped and took a picture of a solitary pole with a cluster of silver bulbs way up on top, and behind it a lorn American Landscape so unspeakably indescribable, to make a Marcel Proust shudder . . . how beautiful to be able to detail a scene like that, on a gray day, and show even the mud, abandoned tin cans and old building blocks laid at the foot of it, and in the distance the road, the old going road with its trucks, cars, poles, roadside houses, trees, signs, crossings . . . A truck pulls into the gravel flat, Robert plants himself in front of it and catches the driver in his windshield wild-eyed and grinning mad like an Indian. He catches that glint in his eye . . . He takes a picture of a fantastic truck door announcing all the licenses from Arkansas to Washington, Florida to Illinois, with its confusion of double mirrors arranged so the driver can see to the rear around the body of the trailer . . . little details writers usually forget about. In darkening day, rain coming on the road, lights already on at 3 PM, mist descending on Highway 40, we see the insect swoop of modern sulphur lamps, the distant haze of forgotten trees, the piled cars being tolled into the Baltimore Harbor Tunnel, all of which Robert snaps casually while driving, one eye to the camera, snap. Thence down into Maryland, lights flashing now in a 4 PM rain, the lonely look of a crossroad stoplight, the zing of telephone wires into the glooming distance where another truck heads obstinately toward some kind of human goal, of zest, or rest. And GULF, the big sign, in the gulf of time . . . a not unusual yet somehow always startling sight in all the pure hotdog roadstand and motel whiteness in a nameless district of U.S.A. where red traffic lights always seem to give a sense of rain and green traffic lights a sense of distance, snow, sand . . .

Then the colored girl laughing as she collects the dollar toll at the Potomac River Bridge at dusk, the toll being registered in lights on the board. Then over the bridge, the flash and mystery of oncoming car lights (something a writer using words can never quite get), the sense of old wooden jetties however unphotographable far below rotting in the mud and bushes, the old Potomac into Virginia, the scene of old Civil War battles, the crossing into the country known as The Wilderness, all a sadness of steel a mile long now as the waters roll on anyway, mindless of America's mad invention, photographs, words. The glister of rain on the bridge paving, the reds of brakelights, the gray reflections from open holes in the sky with the sun long gone behind rain to the westward hills of Maryland. You're in the South now.

A dreary thing to drive through Richmond Virginia in a drenching midnight downpour.

But in the morning, after a little sleep, America wakes up for you again in the bright morning sun, fresh grass and the hitchhiker flat on his back sleeping in the sun, with his carton suitcase and coat before him, as a car goes by on the road—he knows he'll get there anyway, if at all, why not sleep. His America. And beyond his sleep, the old trees and the long A.C.L. freight balling on by on the main line, and patches of sand in the grass. I sit in the car amazed to see the photographic artist prowling like a cat, or an angry bear, in the grass and roads, shooting whatever he wants to see. How I wished I'd have had a camera of my own, a mad mental camera that could register pictorial shots, of the photographic artist himself prowling about for his ultimate shot—an epic in itself.

We drove down into Rocky Mount North Carolina where, at a livestock auction right outside town, hundreds of out-of-work Southerners of the present recession milled about in the Russia-looking mud staring at things like the merchant's clutter of wares in the back trunk of his fintail new-car . . . there he sits, before his tools, drills, toothpaste, pipe tobacco, rings, screwdrivers, fountain pens, gloomy and jut jawed and sad, in the gray Southern day, as livestock moo and moan within and everywhere the cold sense of drizzle and hopelessness. "I should imagine," said Robert Frank to me that morning over coffee, "though I've never been to Russia, that America is really more like Russia, in feeling and look, than any other country in the world . . . the big distances, the faces, the look of families traveling . . ." We drove on, down near South Carolina got out of the car to catch a crazy picture of a torndown roadside eatery that still announced "Dinner is ready, this is It, welcome" and you could see through the building to the fields the other side and around it bulldozers wrecking and working.

In a little town in South Carolina, as we floated by in the car, as I steered for him slowly down Main Street, he leaned from the driver's window and caught three young girls coming home from school. In the sun. Their complaint: "O Jeez."

Further down, the little girl in the front seat with pin curls, her mother doubleparked in front of some Five and Ten.

A car parked near a diner near a junkyard further down, and in the back seat, strung to a necessary leash, a frightened little cat . . . the pathos of the road and of Modern America: "What am I doing in all this junk?"

We went off our route a little to visit Myrtle Beach, South Carolina, and got a girl being very pensive leaning on the pinball machine watching her boy's score.

A little down the road to McClellanville South Carolina, scene of beautiful old houses and incredible peace, and the old "Coastal Barber Shop" run by 80 year old Mr. Bryan who proudly declared "I was the first white barber in McClellanville." We asked him where in town we could get a cup of coffee. "Aint no place, but you go down to the sto and get you a jar of powder coffee and bring it back, I got a nice pot on the stove here and got three cups . . ." Mr. Bryan lived on the highway a few miles away, where, "All's I like to do is sit on my porch and watch the cars run." Wanted to make a trade for Robert Frank's 1952 Stationwagon. "Got a nice Thirty Six Ford and another car." "How old is the other car?" "It aint quite as young . . . but you boys need two cars, dont ya? You goin to get married, aint ya?" Insists on giving us haircuts. With comb in the hair in the old barber tradition, he gives the photographer a weird haircut and chuckles and reminisces. Barber shop hasnt changed since Photographer Frank was by here about five years ago to photograph the shop from the street door, even the bottles on the shelf are all the same and apparently havent been moved.

A little ways down a country road, to the colored houses of McClellanville, a Negro funeral, Strawhat Charley with razor scar looking out the window of his black shiny car, "Yay" . . . And the graves, simple mounds covered with clam shells, sometimes one symbolic Coca Cola bottle. Things you cant capture in words, the moody poem of death . . .

A little more sleep, and Savannah in the morning. Prowling around we see a brand new garbage truck of the City of Savannah with fantastic propped-up dolls' heads that blink their eyes as the truck lumbers through back alleys and women in their bathrobes come out and supervise . . . the dolls, the American flag, the horseshoe in the windshield, the emblems, mirrors, endless pennons and admirable spears, and the boss driver himself, colored, all decked out in boots and cap and a "garbage" knife in his belt. He says "Wait here till we come around the corner and you catch a pitcher of the truck in the SUN" and Robert Frank obliges . . . prowling around the back alleys of Savannah in the morning with his all-seeing camera . . . the Dos Passos of American photographers.

We investigate bus stations, catch an old boy from the South with floppy Snopes hat waiting at Gate One of the station fingering a roadmap and saying "I dont know where this line go." (*The new Southern Aristocracy!* yell my friends seeing this picture.)

Night, and Florida, the lonely road night of snow white roadsigns at a wilderness crossing showing four endless unreadable nowhere directions, and the oncoming ghost cars. And the roadside gift shoppes of Florida by night, clay pelicans stuck in grass being a simple enough deal but not when photographed at night against the oncoming atom-ball headlights of a northbound car.

A trailer camp . . . a swimming pool . . . Spanish moss waving from old trees . . . and while prowling around to photograph a white pony tethered by the pool we spot four frogs on a stick floating in the cerulean pool . . . look closely and judge for yourself whether the frogs are meditating. A Melody Home trailer, the canaries in the window cage, and a little way down the road, the inevitable roadside Florida zoo and the old alligator slumbering like a thousand years and too lazy to shake his horny snout and shake off the peanut shells on his nose and eyes . . . mooning in his gravy. Other, grimmer trailer camps, like the one in Yukon Florida, the outboard motorboat on wheels, ready to go, the butane tank, the new lounge chair in the sun, the baby's canvas seat swing, the languorous pretty wife stepping out, cigarette in mouth . . . beyond her all wavy grass and swamps . . .

Now we're in Florida, we see the lady in the flowery print dress in a downtown Orlando Fla. drugstore looking over the flowery postcards on the rack, for now she's finally made it to Florida it's time to send postcards back to Newark.

Sunday, the road to Daytona Beach, the fraternity boys in the Ford with bare feet up on the dashboard, they love that car so much they even lie on top of it at the beach.

Americans, you cant separate them from their cars even at the most beautiful natural beach in the world, there they are taking lovely sunbaths practically under the oil pans of their perpetually new cars . . . The Wild Ones on their motorcycles, with T-shirt, boots, dark glasses, and ivy league slacks, the mad painting job on the motorcycle, and beyond, the confusion of cars by the waves. Another "wild one," not so wild, conversing politely from his motorcycle to a young family sprawled in the sand beside their car . . . in the background others leaning on car fenders. Critics of Mr. Frank's photography have asked "Why do you take so many pictures of cars?"

He answers, shrugging, "It's all I see everywhere . . . look for yourself."

Look for yourself, the soft day Atlantic waves washing in to the pearly flat hard sand, but everywhere you look, cars, fishtail Cadillacs, one young woman and a baby in the breeze to ten cars, or whole families under swung-across blankets from car to car camping in front of dreary motels.

The great ultimate shot of Mrs. Jones from Dubuque Iowa, come fifteen hundred miles just to turn her back to the very ocean and sit behind the open trunk of her husband's car (a car dealer), bored among blankets and spare tires.

A lesson for any writer . . . to follow a photographer and look at what he shoots . . . I mean a great photographer, an artist . . . and how he does it. The result: Whatever it is, it's America. It's the American Road and it awakens the eye every time.

from
VISIONS OF CODY

THE THREE STOOGES

BUT THE LATEST AND PERHAPS REALLY, next to Mexico and the jazz tea high I'll tell in a minute, best, vision, also on high, but under entirely different circumstances, was the vision I had of Cody as he showed me one drowsy afternoon in January, on the sidewalks of workaday San Francisco, just like workaday afternoon on Moody Street in Lowell when boyhood buddy funnguy G.J. and I played zombie piggybacks in mill employment offices and workmen's saloons (the Silver Star it was), what and how the Three Stooges are like when they go staggering and knocking each other down the street, Moe, Curly (who's actually the bald domed one, big husky) and meaningless goof (though somewhat mysterious as though he was a saint in disguise, a masquerading super-duper witch doctor with good intentions actually)—can't think of his name; Cody knows his name, the bushy feathery haired one. Cody was supposed to be looking after his work at the railroad, we had just blasted in the car as we drove down the hill into wild mid-Market traffics and out Third past the Little Harlem where two and a half years ago we jumped with the wild tenor cats and Freddy and the rest (I dig the Little Harlem in rainy midnights comin home from work in the black slouch hat, from the corner, the pale pretty pink neons, the mod-ernistic front, the puddles so rosy glowing at the foot of the entrance, the long arrowing deserted Folsom Street which, as I hadn't remembered in my back East reveries runs straight into the far lights of the Mission or Richmond or whatever district, all glitters in the indigo distance of the night, to make you think of trucks and long hauls to Paso Robles, bleak Obispo or Monterrey, or Fresno in the mist of highways, the last highways, the California up and down coast highways, the ones with an end which is water orients and the empurpled Golgothan panoplies of Pacific Bowl and Abyss), past the dingy bars with their incredible names (colored bars) like Moonlight in Colorado (that one's actually in Fillmore) or Blue Midnight or Pink Glass and inside it's all wretched raw brown whiskey and mauve boilermakers, past Mission Street earlier too (before Folsom) with its corner conglomerate of bums or sometimes lines of dragged winos so torpid that when pretty women pass they don't even look (even though they're waiting in line to give blood for four dollars at Cutters so they can rush off and buy wine and pissberry brandy for the Embarcadero Night) or if they do look it's accidental, they seem to be too guilty to look at ordinary women, only Steamboat Annies of pierfront *bouges* with knots in their sticks for calf muscles and hagless toothmarks in their purply gums, Jey-sas Crise!; bums of Mission and Howard, that live in miserable flop hotels like the Skylark in Denver that Cody and his father Old Cody Pomeray the Barber lived in and from which they took their Sunday afternoon walks together hand in hand and amiable after the previous Saturday night's hassles over his overdrinking wine in the ceremonial saved-up evening movie so he'd snore at usher closeup time and lights on in the showhouse would reveal to shuffling audiences of whole Mexican and Arky families the sight of one of their fellow Americans a bit under the weather in a seat, this being the capper to a whole day of Saturday joys for little Cody such as reading the *Count of Monte Cristo* while his father barbered in the busy weekend morning, cleanup at the Skylark, and a regular good meal in a fairly good restaurant in late afternoon, and maybe a moment's lingering with the majority of noncelebrating Saturday night bums wrangled around in seated positions in the sitting room the longer winter nights of which Cody endured aiming spitballs at plaster targets and celestial ceiling cracks as old big clock tocketytocked the Jinuaries away and like in a movie the calendars flapped and still the land and the man survived, stood fixed and immovable in a blurflap of white pages representing time, usually the man was Cody's dad, the land Colorado, the occasion and occupation Hope, good boy hope for a change; but now it's May and they're going to a show and saying good evening to the bums who sit in state over this like old French sewing sisters in a Provincial town; May and Larimer Street is humbuzzing with that same excitement, that same countrified wrangly sad toot and tinkle of old Main line shopping streets in Charleston, West Virginia with all its spotted farmer cars ranged and the Kanawha flowing, and the Southern railroad town with moils of activity at sun tortured five-and-tens across from the tracks, awnings, nations of Negroes lounging by beater stores in near the tobacco warehouses flashing aluminum lights in the southern day-fire; and Los Angeles when the parade goes up and down both sides and the cracked old crazy John Gaunt from a rackety house in a telegraph grove outside the Bakersfield flats with his entire brood of nine packed and pushed up to the torn flapass black tarpaulin roof of his fantastic ancient 1929 touring Imperial Buick with the wooden spokes two of them cracked and a siderack for spares like a snail's shell goof on the runningboard, old John Gaunt and Ma Gaunt with her overalls and sorrow (has to wait while Pa gets his fill at the shooting gallery at South Main, two blocks from System Auto Parks); it's May and little Cody and old man go cutting together into the adventures of a hard won evening and one which of course like all life is doomed to tragic, unnamable, to-make-you-speechless and sadfaced forever death; just as I used to hurry with my father in May dusks of Saturday, towards unspeakable seashores, with lights before them, and swooping spaces fit for gulls and clouds scuds, towards ramps of yellow sulphur lamp light, overdrives, sudden dank side alleys when there came among the greases and irons and blackdust of ramps in cobbled avenues like the avenues of factories in Germany, those secret chop sueys from Boston China-town to make my mouth water and my thoughts hasten to the wink of Chinese lanterns hung in red doorways at the base of golden tinsel porch steps leading up to the Mandarin secrets of within (so when Cody dreamed of being Cristo thrown in the sea in a bag, I was kidnapped and Shanghaied and orphaned to a strange but friendly old Chinaman who was my only contact with hopes of returning to my former life, orphaned in the interesting old void, hey?); May night on Larimer, when the sun is red on green store fronts and Army-Navy suits by the door, and makes a ray and a frazzle by an empty bottle, foot of a hydrant; illuminates the reveries of an aged lady in a window above the windows of empty store rooms, she looks on Wynkoop, Wazee and the rails— we passed Third Street and all its *that,* and came, driving slowly, notic-ing everything, talking everything, to the railyards where we worked and got out of the car to cross the warm airy plazas of the day and there particularly with a fine soot-scent of coal and tide and oil and big works (a fly across haze oil shimmers) (the tar soft undershoe), noticing how great the day and how in the experience of our lives together we were always finding ourselves on a golden sleepy good afternoon just like fishing or really like the afternoons that must have been experienced by the noble sons of great Homeric warriors after (like Telemachus and the noble son of his host, Nestor's friend) wild night charioteerings across the ghosts and white horses of Phallic Classical Fate in the gray plain to the Sea, rewardful afternoons for tired winners, caresses of cups and figs in the loll of Heroes, just like that, Cody and Me, only Amer-ican and Cody saying "Now goddammit Jack you've gotta admit that we're high and that was real good shit" and more instant and interest-

ing, and always happening, and *everything always all right.* We sauntered thus—had come in the green clunker for some reason, wore our
usual greasy bum clothes that put real bums to shame but nobody with
the power to reprimand and arrest us in his house—began somehow
talking about the Three Stooges—were headed to see Mrs. So-and-So
in the office and on business and around us conductors, executives,
commuters, consumers rushed or sometimes just maybe ambling Russian spies carrying bombs in briefcases and sometimes ragbags I bet—
just foolishness—and the station there, the creamy stucco suggestive of
palms, like the Union Station in L.A. with its palms and mission arches
and marbles, is so unlike a railroad station to an Easterner like myself
used to old redbrick and sootirons and exciting gloom fit for snows and
voyages across pine forests to the sea, or like that great NYCEP whatever station I ran to over the ice that morning en route in Pittsburgh,
so unlike a railroad station that I couldn't imagine anything good and
adventurous coming from it (we, in our youth, had spent goof hours
around railroad stations, in fact the last time I was in Lowell we staggered and laughed past the depot to the nearest bar and jumped and
whooped over four-foot snowbanks to boot, bareheaded and coatless).
Nothing, only bright California gloom and propriety (and I suppose
because Cody works for them here), nothing but whiteness and everything busy, official, let's say Californian, no spitting, no grabbing your
balls, you're at the carven arches of a great white temple of commercial
travel in America, if you're going to blank your cigar do it on the sly
up your asshole or in the sand behind the vine if they had a sand vine
or sandpot palm, but really—when it came into Cody's head to imitate
the stagger of the Stooges, and he did it wild, crazy, yelling in the sidewalk right there by the arches and by hurrying executives, I had a vision
of him which at first (manifold it is!) was swamped by the idea that this
was one hell of a wild unexpected twist in my suppositions about how
he might now in his later years feel, twenty-five, about his employers
and their temple and conventions, I saw his (again) rosy flushing face
exuding heat and joy, his eyes popping in the hard exercise of staggering, his whole frame of clothes capped by those terrible pants with six,
seven holes in them and streaked with baby food, come, ice cream,
gasoline, ashes—I saw his whole life, I saw all the movies we'd ever
been in, I saw for some reason he and his father on Larimer Street not
caring in May—their Sunday afternoon walks hand in hand in back of
great baking soda factories and along deadhead tracks and ramps, at
the foot of that mighty red brick chimney à la Chirico or Chico Velas-

quez throwing a huge long shadow across their path in the gravel and the flat—

Supposing the Three Stooges were real? and so I saw them spring into being at the side of Cody in the street right there front of the Station, Curly, Moe and Larry, that's his bloody name, *Larry;* Moe the leader, mopish, mowbry, mope-mouthed, mealy, mad, hanking, making the others quake; whacking Curly on the iron pate, backhanding Larry (who wonders); picking up a sledgehammer, honk, and ramming it down nozzle first on the flatpan of Curly's skull, boing, and all big dumb convict Curly does is muckle and yukkle and squeal, pressing his lips, shaking his old butt like jelly, knotting his Jell-o fists, eyeing Moe, who looks back and at him with that lowered and surly "Well what are you gonna do about it?" under thunderstorm eyebrows like the eyebrows of Beethoven, completely ironbound in his surls, Larry in his angelic or rather he really looks like he conned the other two to let him join the group, so they had to pay him all these years a regular share of the salary to them who work so hard with the props—Larry, goofhaired, mopple-lipped, lisped, muxed and completely flunk—trips over a pail of whitewash and falls face first on a seven-inch nail that remains imbedded in his eyebone; the eyebone's connected to the shadowbone, shadowbone's connected to the luck bone, luck bone's connected to the, foul bone, foul bone's connected to the, high bone, high bone's connected to the, air bone, air bone's connected to the, sky bone, sky bone's connected to the, angel bone, angel bone's connected to the, God bone, *God bone's connected to the bone bone;* Moe yanks it out of his eye, impales him with an eight-foot steel rod; it gets worse and worse, it started on an innocent thumbing, which led to backhand, then the pastries, then the nose yanks, blap, bloop, going, going, gong; and now as in a sticky dream set in syrup universe they do muckle and moan and pull and mop about like I told you in an underground hell of their own invention, they are involved and alive, they go haggling down the street at each other's hair, socking, remonstrating, falling, getting up, flailing, as the red sun sails—So supposing the Three Stooges were real and like Cody and me were going to work, only they forget about that, and tragically mistaken and interallied, begin pasting and cuffing each other at the employment office desk as clerks stare; supposing in real gray day and not the gray day of movies and all those afternoons we spent looking at them, in hooky or officially on Sundays among the thousand crackling children of peanuts and candy in the dark show when the Three Stooges (as in that golden dream B-movie of mine round the corner from the Strand) are providing scenes for wild vibrating hysterias as great as the hysterias of hipsters at Jazz at the Philharmonics, supposing in real gray day you saw them coming down Seventh Street looking for jobs—as ushers, insurance salesmen—that way. Then I saw the Three Stooges materialize on the sidewalk, their hair blowing in the wind of things, and Cody was with them, laughing and staggering in savage mimicry of them and himself staggering and gooped but they didn't notice . . . I followed in back. . . . There was an afternoon when I had found myself hungup in a strange city, maybe after hitch-hiking and escaping something, half tears in my eyes, nineteen, or twenty, worrying about my folks and killing time with B-movie or any movie and suddenly the Three Stooges appeared (just the name) goofing on the screen and in the streets that are the same streets as outside the theater only they are photographed in Hollywood by serious crews like Joan Rawshanks in the fog, and the Three Stooges were bopping one another . . . until, as Cody says, they've been at it for so many years in a thousand climactic efforts superclimbing and worked out every refinement of bopping one another so much that now, in the end, if it isn't already over, in the baroque period of the Three Stooges they are finally bopping mechanically and sometimes so hard it's impossible to bear (wince), but by now they've learned not only how to master the style of the blows but the symbol and acceptance of them also, as though inured in their souls and of course long ago in their bodies, to buffetings and crashings in the rixy gloom of Thirties movies and B short subjects (the kind made me yawn at 10 A.M. in my hooky movie of high school days, intent I was on saving my energy for serious-jawed features which in my time was the cleft jaw of Cary Grant), the Stooges don't feel the blows any more, Moe is iron, Curley's dead, Larry's gone, off the rocker, beyond the hell and gone (so ably hidden by his uncombable mop, in which, as G.J. used to say, he hid a Derringer pistol), so there they are, bonk, boing, and there's Cody following after them stumbling and saying "Hey, lookout, houk" on Larimer or Main Street or Times Square in the mist as they parade erratically like crazy kids past the shoeboxes of simpletons and candy corn arcades—and seriously Cody talking about them, telling me, at the creamy Station, under palms or suggestions thereof, his huge rosy face bent over the time and the thing like a sun, in the great day—So then I knew that long ago when the mist was raw Cody saw the Three Stooges, maybe he just stood outside a pawnshop, or hardware store, or in that perennial poolhall door but maybe more likely on the pavings of the city under tragic rainy telephone poles, and thought of the Three Stooges, suddenly realizing—that life is strange and the Three Stooges exist—that in 10,000 years—that . . . all the goofs he felt in him were justified in the outside world and he had nothing to reproach himself for, bonk, boing, crash, skittely boom, pow, slam, bang, boom, wham, blam, crack, frap, kerplunk, clatter, clap, blap, fap, slapmap, splat, crunch, crowsh, bong, splat, splat, *BONG!*

WELL, CODY IS ALWAYS INTERESTED IN HIMSELF . . .

Well, Cody is always interested in himself: from behind his iron bars he's always talking and conning somebody all day. Like the lyrics of popular songs you can't believe a word of it. I hear him from far away; his voice urgent, anxious, high-pitched, explanatory, full of rapine; he's on the bed convincing her, who's turned her head away in disgust, for now, that she need worry about nothing, he didn't drown the kittens at all, they fell down the drain by themselves, or it wasn't because he wanted to see Jimmy he was late but because (she having made no issue about lateness) in passing the bakery it reminded him she had mentioned that very morning she was sick and tired of store bread and so he went right to the store and bought some, twenty-two cents . . . something like that. For years I've listened to him con women; supreme; first Joanna the lost lovely blond of his early and first passions under those bleak electric neons by hotel windows in the wind-whip of Wyoming born, first her; then Evelyn; finally that horrible Diane who has every-body frightened with her lawsuits and quiddities. That first con in Har-lem, make the breakfast, was followed by . . . Damn Cody, I'm tired of him and I'm going; my benefactor whispers his wife to me in the dark.

His sad face permeates the mere mention of Sioux City; if he says it himself, and wasn't ever there, I know it's an American city. A true, real American is a mystery to us, to U.S., somewhere and somehow he became like Cody and stands here among us. In my romance I have traveled far to find a cousin to the Greek. And in my romance I have traveled far to see an American, one that reminded me of the Civil War soldier in the old photo who stands by a pile of lumber in a drizzle, waiting for arrest, backgrounded by pine brush bottoms all wet and dismal in an Alabama afternoon in the wilderness of hoar. Beside him is a superior officer, Rebel Colonel or Captain, Confederate Wildcat, teeth bared, coat over arm, defiant to the very wind. "Ho! don't forget those two prisoners by the lumber," shouts the Yankee captain perceiving the prisoners but not the camera, and old Johnny Youngpants who looks like Cody just stands there beside his rosehog Confederacy wildboar and waits for tomorrows of capture with that implacable sad and slightly gaunted look of the Sioux Cities of the mind, the one I mean, his father had it, and has it in that photo, that teary, dreary look of old torment and of old mists, that hangjaw ancientness and goodhearted tragicness of the old entire; a piss-ass poor agrarian whore "Why do I stop in my grains?" couldn't look worse in a cornfield with her legs spread, or honester. (Splat, or as B. O. Plenty says, Ptoo.) But sadness, sadism, all, let's hear what my French-Canadian side has to say about him. Now we're conning nature.

"Si tu veux parlez apropos d'Cody pourquoi tu'l fa—tu m'a arretez avant j'ai eu une chance de continuez, ben arrete donc. Écoute, j'va t'dire—lit bien. Il faut t'u te prend soin—attend?—donne moi une chance—tu pense j'ai pas d'art moi français?—ca? —idiot—crapule—tas'd marde—enfant shiene—batard—cochon—buffon—bouche de marde, granguele, face laite, shienculotte, morceau d'marde, susseu, gros fou, envi d'chien en culotte, ca c'est pire—en face!—fam toi!—crashe!—varge!—frappe!—mange!—foure!—foure moi'l Gabin!—envalle Céline, mange l'e rond ton Genêt, Rabelais? El terra essuyer l'coup au derriere. Mais assez, c'est pas interessant. C'est pas interessant l'maudit Francais. Écoute, Cody ye plein

"If you want to talk about Cody why do you do it—you stopped me before I had a chance to continue, stop won't you! Listen, I'm going to tell you—read well: you have to take care of yourself, hear it?—give me a chance—you think I've no art me French?—eh?—idiot—crapule—piece of shit—sonofabitch—bastard—pig —clown—shitmouth—long mouth—ugly face, shitpants, piece of shit, sucktongue, big fool, wantashitpants, that's worse —right in the face!—shut up!—spit!—hit it! (varge!)—hit! (frappe)—eat it!—fuck!—scram me Gabin!—swallow Céline, eat him raw your Genêt, Rabelais? He woulda wiped your neck on his ass. But enough, it's not interesting. It's not interesting goddamn French. Listen, Cody is full

d'marde; les lé allez; il est ton
ami, les le songée; yé pas ton
frere, yé pas ton pere, yé pas ton
ti Saint Michel, yé un gas, ye
marriez, il travaille, v'as t'couchez
l'autre bord du monde, v'a pen-
sant dans la grand nuit Euro-
peene. Je t'l' explique, ma
manière, pas la tienne, enfant,
chien—ecoutes:—va trouvez ton
âme, vas sentir le vent, vas loin—
La vie est d' hommage. Ferme le
livre, vas—n' écrit plus sur l'mur,
sa lune, au chien, dans la mer au
fond neigant, un petit poème. Va
trouvez Dieu dans les nuits. Les
nuées aussi. Quantesse s'a peut
arrêtez s'grand tour au cerveux
de Cody; il ya des hommes, des
affaires en dehors a faire, des
grosses tombeaux d'activité dans
les désert d'l'Afrique du coeur, les
anges noires, les femmes couchée
avec leur beaux bras ourvert pour
toi dans leur jennesse, d'la ten-
dresse enfermez dans l'meme lit,
les gros nuees de nouveaux conti-
nents, le pied fatiguee dans de
climes mystères, descend pas le
côté de l'autre bord de ta vie (30)
pour rien.
A Cody, un corp.

of shit; let him go; he is your
friend, let him dream; he's not
your brother, he's not your father, he's not your Saint Michael,
he's a guy, he's married, he
works, go sleeping on the other
side of the world, go thinking in
the great European night. I'm explaining him to you, my way, not
yours, child, dog—listen:—go
find your soul, go smell the wind
—go far—Life is a pity. Close
the book, go on—write no more
on the wall, on the moon, at the
dog's, in the sea in the snowing
bottom, a little poem. Go find
God in the nights. The clouds
too. When can it stop this big
tour at the skull of Cody; there
are men, things outside to do,
great huge tombs of activity in
the desert of Africa of the heart,
the black angels, the women in
bed with the beautiful arms open
for you in their youth, some tenderness shrouded in the same
bed, the big clouds of new conti-
nents, the foot tired in climes so
mysterious, don't go down the
hill of the other side of your life
(30) for nothing.
To Cody, a body.

JOAN RAWSHANKS
IN THE FOG

Joan Rawshanks stands all alone in the fog. Her name is Joan Rawshanks and she knows it, just as anybody knows his name, and she knows who she is, same way, Joan Rawshanks stands alone in the fog and a thousand eyes are fixed on her in all kinds of ways; above Joan Rawshanks rises the white San Francisco apartment house in which the terrified old ladies who spend their summers in lake resort hotels are now wringing their hands in the illuminated (by the floodlights outside) gloom of their livingrooms, some of them having Venetian blinds in them but none drawn; Joan Rawshanks leans her head in her hands, she's wearing a mink coat by the wet bushes, she leans against the dewy wire fence separating the slopeyard of the magnificent San Francisco DeLuxe Arms from the neat white Friscoan street-driveway sloping abruptly at seventy-five degrees; in back where the angry technicians muster and make gestures in the blowing fog that rushes past kleig lights and ordinary lights in infinitesimal cold showers, to make everything seem miserable and storm-hounded, as though we were all on a mountain top saving the brave skiers in the howl of the elements, but also just like the lights and the way the night mist blows by them at the scene of great airplane disasters or train wrecks or even just construction jobs that have reached such a crucial point that there's overtime in muddy midnight Alaskan conditions; Joan Rawshanks, wearing a mink coat, is trying to adjust herself to the act of crying but has a thousand eyes of local Russian Hill spectators who've been hearing about the Hollywood crew filming for the last hour, ever since dinner's end, and are arriving on the scene here despite the fog (move over from my microphone wire, there) in driblets; pretty girls with fresh dew fog faces and bandanas and moonlit (though no moon) lips; also old people who customarily at this hour make grumpy shows of walking the dog in dismal and empty slope streets of the rich and magnificently quiet; the fog of San Francisco in the night, as a buoy in the bay goes b-o, as a buoy in the bag goes b-o, bab-o, as a buoy in the bag goes bab-o; the young director eagerly through the rain like an Allen Minko (crazy type in floppy stylish bought-at-Brooks-Brothers-deliberately clothes who talks his way entirely into his careers and stands there, gesticulating, ducking to see, measuring with his eyes, hand over brow to estimate just right, darting up, shadowing himself, looking furtively over his shoulder, long director's coat flying, hang-jawed sullen face, long Semitic ears, curly handsome hair, face with the Hollywood Tan which is the most successful and beautiful tan in the world, that rich tan, intent in the foggy night on his great-genius studies of light on light, for he has technicians standing around with punctured boards that they adjust and meander in their hands to cast certain glows and shadows on the essences at hand, hark, though methinks the ghost now comes along the splintered pale, entry made for him, intent on his great-tennis studies of the night) eagerly through the rain he watches Joan through his fist telescopes and then rushes down to her.

"Now baby, remember what I said about the so-and-so" and she says "With the flip on the end of it?"

"Yes, that and what I've been trying to explain to Schultz for ten minutes, the meaneander there when you come in at the end byazacking along the trull, I told him and he won't listen, we called Red, it's absolutely—got the rest straight though?"

"Yes and tell Rogeroo to make room for me at the other end; o those horrible bores in there"—Joan adding the last to mean the people who live on the bottom floor of the apartment house and who invited them in, while waiting for exact arrangements to get underway, offering Joan Rawshanks tea and warmth in her hard stint of the night; the same fog-stint she must have gone through when she was a poor dear hustler but now and everything is happening all over at the exact moment. In the back is Leon Errol—suddenly you think, "No this is not Leon Errol" (he's dead) and yet he walks exactly like Leon Errol, on rubber legs, is on a movie lot, has a big floppy gabardine coat in which he must have got drunk at the racetrack in that same afternoon; the two local cops on the beat, according apparently to Hollywood custom, consented to have their pictures taken by a member of the camera crew, who if not delighted was appealed upon to take their pictures; this being Leon Errol; and the police stand passively, side by side, two blue coats, one fortyish, one a boy cop, a thirty-year-old-married-with-two-children-might-have-been-brakeman who instead in the brutality of his instincts migrated to the police force, though with a mild and malleable nature and without military ostentation; these two men, father and son in their nightly duty and relationship in the cold torpors of Russian Hill *haute* through which their tragic figures cut, swinging clubs, in the rare occasions when residents of the neighborhood happen to cast a bored glance from their evening window (there being nothing to see or do in enemy, the crowd was cooped up in an Alamo, I heard one woman say "I'll be damned if I don't go home *between* scenes!" though no one, not even the Inspector at the rope line hastily thrown up, had mentioned or heard of between-scenes or anything like that, if someone in the crowd hadn't used some democratic social intelligence the crowd would have stood rooted on forbidden ground freezing all night before some kindly and courtly state trooper decided to tell them they didn't have to stand there at all, perfectly proper to walk right up to the kleig lights and even in fact bump into them. Personal, or private, property still prevailed in the presence of several portly gentlemen from upstairs, excuse me; gentlemen, bankers, businessmen, who lived in the creamy Russian Hill apartment and others on the same little driveway semi-privated street (a street, incidentally, with a vista that draws unofficial tourists like myself on sunny red Sunday gloomdusks that show you the Golden Gate opening purple to the wild gray banners of the orient sea way out, and the quiet of the wild hills across the Bridge, Marin County, bushy, dark, filled with cragous canyons of strange traffic, oversurmounted as a scene by Mt. Tamalpais, a real vista and one which now of course in the foggy night no one and none of the Hollywood cameras could see) businessmen who lived in this charming district congregating as interested neighbors in an unofficial spectacle (impulsive, organic spectacle) taking place in their backyards, on their private but not hotly debated property, their hospitable property that's it; so that when a cop, a trooper Nazi type with sharp jaw, boots, protruberant gun, etc. steel eyes, told everybody with equal icy calm to move back, women included, but went up to our cluster of neighbors they apparently looked back at him with ample-bellied slow surprise and one of them decided to say that he had talked with Mr. So-and-So the producer or Assistant Camera Technician and they knew certainly well the entire proceedings by which the apartment management itself had rented out its grounds and impedimenta for a Hollywood location shot, so that if the trooper should try to make them move back, he would do so under duress of the knowledge that they were interested clients of the management of the property upon which that hired taxfree trooper stood, only fat businessmen having the gall nowadays to stay by the letter of the law give or take; so that, damn it all, when I tried to winny my way into the center of the camera crew (I was dressed exactly like they were, at least in the dark, I had a leather jacket with a fur collar, wino chino pants, etc. in other words like a soldier in the arctic, a worker in the fog, etc.) why when the trooper came up to me he wasn't quite sure where I

these streets, morning, noon and night); so the cops stand there having their picture took but suddenly and everybody watching (crowds in the cold fog, hand in pockets, like little kids at the back end of semi-pro football games on scuffled wild neighborhood fields of Saturday afternoon cold and red and hard in the month of November in the North;) everybody in the crowd realizes that the Leon Errol fotografter is actually only just fiddling with his lightbulbs and put-up arrangements of tripods and subsidiary lights (with a cat standing next to him again wielding those strange riddled cardboards they use for estimating the inch-ounch of light they want, though how can anybody in a movie audience get to detect that when the picture finally flashes on the screen;) so the cops are temporarily and suddenly under the glare of floodlights and there they are, they don't know what to do, perhaps they should look coply, very well they do, folding arms, looking away. But actually at first they waited with comradely joy while the fotog took his first bending licks at the dark rig, with accommodating nineteenth-century buddy joy they in fact almost locked arms, and waited, as if with mustachions and beer-jowl, were posing for the Beanbag Afternoon Set of the German Band Union that invites the Police Force to participate in the old days; the dark suspicion crept now around the crowd perhaps (it certainly did on me, I was alone, watching, Cody was at home not letting anything happen but himself, lamenting in his dark heart's house with lovemasks and tangled flesh shrouds, as usual) that the Hollywood cameramen were such cynics and played such stupendous private jokes in their travels around, that they were putting the cops to a phony hangup; evidently however Leon Errol did snap their pictures, because when it was all over, while the cops nervously took his name and gave their own (to have the pics mailed) he, with the gesture of the narcotic cameraman, sucked the film out of his box and plopped it, hot with reality, instant, into his pocket; just like a teahead might lick the ash-end of a roach for the exact feel of his smoking hots, like a linotypist must feel late in the night before the groaning hot machine that somewhere in its balls and bowels it has some metallic heat that would be good to lick, would kick you like a can of beer; evidently, Leon Errol, sucking, had made the picture alright and would actually—but now, the cops for just a moment had been in the glare of floodlights, watched by others, by a thousand eyes, by my eyes, the eyes of commen and maybe murderers in the crowd, the poor cops stood there dumbly for the first time in not only their careers but lives that they had been subjected to scrutiny by thousands of eyes under the glare of floodlights (this being of course the Hollywood cameramen stunt trick, they'd get their kicks making cops pose like that all over the country, at least till the cops joined the unions); but now, the leading man was standing at the fringed end of the crowd and he was a strange one, I told Mrs. Brown standing next to me, "I think he looks sorta handsome and all that, you could say that he's handsome—but my God when he turns this way and looks this way I can't stand the great hollow sorrow and strange emptiness and alcoholic lostness and vagueity of his eyes . . . and what is he looking for? look how eagerly he bends and grins and fawns; wouldn't it be terrible to be married to a man like that, you'd never, you'd have to make faces all the livelong day," but Mrs. Brown said, "Yes but on the other hand look at that sharp, almost shroudy clothes he wears, it makes him look like a part in a nineteenth-century castle picture, he's the hero, the son of the Count, the favored of the Peasants, a carriage awaits him by rainsplashed rose arbor down the road, they're going to capture a lovely gowned lady in a black mask tonight; he looks exactly like that, I know what you means about his awful falseness and iridescence of almost homosexual charm but consider that he is a gentleman, a nice fellow, not harming anybody, sorta sissy, probably loves someone very dearly, maybe he has seven kids how do you know? maybe he lives in a rose covered cottage in Catalina and paints rococo Gaugins of his wife covered with suntan lotion with the kids around the big candy ball; so what's it to you that he fawns and flickers all over" (Two misplaced verbs there.) Joan Ashplant stands in the fog, the director is explaining what he wants done; they sound like they're arguing about prices in a delicatessen, or with a ski attendant in Berne; over at the misty stone steps the lights are strongest bent; under a canvas that flaps out from the back of a truck that has red boards in the back to make it a proper circus wagon but nevertheless (it's a kleig truck, with tools) a real cluttered up truck, coils of wire, you'd almost expect to find a clown's mask among the soldiers, it's so damned . . . under the tent top sit the great generals of the vast activity which is the filming of Joan Clawthighs running up the white driveway (asphalt) (hic) and up the white stone steps and to the door, pausing, at the foot of the steps (not steps where she goes, but gradation of concrete, a driveway, garage ramp, deluxe style, creamy in fact) pausing there to cast a frightened glance into the general night; which she did but when she had to, the glance had to be in the direction of the crowd; at first Joan apparently wanted to weep in this scene, the young director dissuaded her; this explains the early head on hands business, she was

fixing up to cry, in fact the scene was run off and shot and Joan, weeping, ran up the ramp to the door; nope, the director made her do this over again, substituting for the tears a frightened run from something down into the general driveway of the night so that he had all of us in the fogswept audience fearful already of some new menace to come from his fantasy; in fact people now began to crane down the ramp to, I mean down the driveway to see; I expected a Cadillac with crooks; (doesn't it seem as though the script would have been materially altered on the point of this decision about whether to cry or be frightened? . . . it must have been some wild decision and inspiration in the clear ear of this post-Kwakiutl American culture, the clear air of early times) (of course I stood amazed) all the crowd was amazed, little teenage girls took care to notice that the director, absentmindedly explaining to Joan in the wind, swept and held her scarf when she took a drag off a cigarette, the teenage girls thought this to be extra-special polite to her as Movie Queen but actually I noticed to make his point clear and to do so drawing her head down by the scarf noose around her neck and really make her listen his pithy best instruction; I thought it was just a little on this side of cruel, I feel a twinge of sorriness for Joan, either because all this time she'd been suffering real horrors nevertheless as movie queen that I had no idea about, or, in the general materialism of Hollywood she is being maltreated as a star "on the way out"; which she certainly is not at this moment (probably is), though of course all the teenage girls were quick to say, in loud voices for everyone to hear, that her makeup was very heavy, she'd practically have to stagger under it, and leaving it up to us to determine how saggy and baggy her face; well, naturally, I didn't expect Joan Crawfish in the fog to be anything but Joan Crawfish in the fog;—(there were subsidiary love affairs that is, apart from the movie one, going on in the audience itself): but I was determined not to let the audience distract me. It was so arranged finally, so decided upon: the area of grass where I'd originally stood to witness my first kicks of this debacle spectacle was finally and suddenly used (I say suddenly because it apparently was not really necessary judging from the scene being shot) and the whole crowd had to move over into a limited area (as though that's what the directors wanted not for kicks but in serious fascistic interest in the movement of crowds) which was also cut off from the street by floodlights on restricted ground, truly "cameras" area, action, cameras, so nobody could go home in these fascistic intervals; there was no backway out, the audience, the crowd had been finally surrounded and looped in and forted in by this invading belonged and said "Are you with the company?" and had I said "Yes," and I was just then walking or on the movement of deciding to walk up to the midst of the cameras and wires nonchalantly, I went and said "No," automatically, and, automatically, he sent me back to the crowd, where I spent the rest of my time craning, which is an occupation in itself, proper old men move away from you slyly, enjoying the suspicion that you're a pickpocket. Joan Rawshanks stood in the fog. . . .

I said to her "Blow, baby, blow!" when I saw that thousands' eyes were fixed on her and in the huge embarrassment of that, really, on a human-like level, or humane, all these people are going to see you muster up a falsehood for money, you'll have to whimper tears you yourself probably never had any intention of using; on some gray morning in your past what was your real tear, Joan, your real sorrows, in the terrible day, way back in the Thirties when women writhed with a sexual torment and as now they writhe with a sexual frustration, they used to, now they don't, they learned to be a generation not liking it; everybody can see her plain as day fabricating tears on her arm, but she really does; there's no applause but there is later when she finally gets the apartment house door open after three or four instructed yanks . . . now there's only the great silence of the great moment of Hollywood, the actual TAKE (how many producers got high on Take do you think?) just as in a bullfight, when the moment comes for the matador to stick his sword into the bull and kill it, and the matador makes use firmly of this allotted moment, you, the American who never saw a bullfight realize this is what you came to see, the actual kill, and it surprises you that the actual kill is a distant, vague, almost dull flat happening like when Lou Gherig actually did connect for a home run and the sharp flap of the bat on ball seems disappointing even though Gherig hits another home run next time up, this one loud and clout in its sound, the actual moment, the central kill, the riddled middle idea, the thing, the Take, the actual juice suction of the camera catching a vastly planned action, the moment when we all know that the camera is germinating, a thing is being born whether we planned it right or not; there were three takes of every area of the action; Joan rushing up the drive, then Joan fiddling with her keys at the door, and later a third take that I never got to see, three shots of each, each shot carefully forewarned; and the exact actual moment of the Take is when silence falls over just like a bullfight. Joan Rawshanks, with her long pinched tragic face with its remaining hints of wild Twenties dissolution, a flapper girl then, then the writhey girl of the Thirties, under a ramp, in striped blouse, Anna

Lucasta, the girl camping under the lamp like today you can on a real waterfront see a butch queer in seamanlongshoreman peacap bowcoat toga, with simpering fat lips, standing exactly like Joan used to do in old pictures that followed the Claudette Colbert of *I Cover the Waterfront* (busy little girl): Joan Rawshanks, actually in the fog, but as we can see with our own everyday eyes in the fog all lit by kleig lights, and in a furcoat story now, and not really frightened or anything but the central horror we all feel for her when she turns her grimace of horror on the crowd preparatory to running up the ramp, we've seen that face, ugh, she turns it away herself and rushes on with the scene, for a moment we've all had a pang of disgust, the director however seems pleased; he sucks on his red lollipop.

I begin to wonder or that is realize about his red lollipop; at first I thought it was a whistle; and then a gadget; and then an eccentricity; and then a gag; and then a plain lollipop that happens to be on location; the Director with the Lollipop, he gets his ideas better by suddenly lifting it to his lips, in the glare of kleigs, at a moment when the crowd expects him to do something else, so that they're all arrested and bemused and made to comment about the lollipop. Meanwhile I looked anxiously everywhere not only for a better place to see from, but up at the apartment house where the old ladies wrung their hands in hysteria. Apparently (for they could have drawn their blinds or rigged something up) they wanted actually to see what was going on in the street, what the actual hysteria of the scene being filmed, in which subconsciously I sensed their belief; so that in the midst of some awful sprawl by kleiglight grayscreen gangster extras getting all wet and bloody in the street with ketchup as the camera actions, the old ladies would come plummeting down from their five-story window in a double wild believing religious hysterical screaming suicide which would be accidentally filmed by the expensive grinding huge cameras and make a picture so stark that for another century Hollywood tycoons would feature this film as the capper to an evening of dominoes and deals, for relaxation of the nerves; two wild women flying in the night suddenly into the area of the lamps, but so suddenly as to look to the eye like rags, then instrumentations of the eyeball, then tricks of the camera, then flickers of electricity, then finally humanizations in twisted hideous form under the bright glares of the wild fear of old women in America, plunk on the ground, and Joan Rawshanks in the fog, not smiling, or fabricating tears, standing, legs aspraddle in a moment of dubious remembrance of what a moment ago she'd thought to decide to remember about just where, halfway up the ramp, to start walking very fast so that her momentum and carrythrough would really get her up that ramp so that in the last steps she wouldn't be a middleaged struggling lady on a cement slope but a young despairing woman of the foggy night walking with lean absentminded pumping legs (being more concerned with affairs of the soul, love, night, tears, rings, fog, sorrowtomorrow) straight up that thing, no hassle. Reason, I saw those ladies, in the kitchen the old damsel had stood up a lamp, took off the sides of it somehow, so that she had a pathetic private kleig light of her own now shining down on the eyes of the crowd (didn't want people looking into her room) (her kitchen or anything) but in the general glare unnoticed, though on an ordinary night it would have upset and gassed and turned on the whole area; but nevertheless she had her lights out in the livingroom and stood there, with a sister or a neighbor, looking down on the scene wringing her hands and I could see declaiming, as though she wanted somehow to be in the movies, be photographed somehow as she declaimed in the general vicinity of a Take, very hysterical, strange, I thought she was crazy and was one of those old sisters who end up hermits if it wasn't for hotel apartments like these that provide them with a minimum of service, saving them from the fate of the Collier brothers, really, and all over America dotty old rich ladies live like this in hotel apartments; well imagine their horror this evening with all those lights suddenly literally turned right on their windows and into their livingrooms and how they wail and cling to each other and think, naturally, the end of the world is bound to come soon if it hasn't and isn't in the process of right now. There was a fat guy with a red baseball cap; he ran up and down the driveway in some capacity allied with that of the police guards, keeping it clear of incoming cars, of people, or something; every time they shot Joan Rawshanks fiddling with her keys and yanking at that door, traffic had to be stopped on Hyde Street because of the arrangement apparently of the cameras. So I began noticing another crowd sort of thickening on Hyde Street itself, and restricted to one side there, for no reason really, of course, every now and then the fabled-cable-so-photographable coming by with a ringdingding and people, passengers, who are just riding home and have nothing to do with artistic San Francisco societies that fight to keep the colorful cable car (and so in fact the Hollywood men, I expected them to look with interest at the passing cable car in the night but they didn't from which I concluded that the sharpsters of Hollywood apparently, like New Yorkers, think all the rest of California is square so anything they do or have is of absolutely no serious interest, in fact feeling a twinge of civic pride and wondering, why, on the sly, one of them didn't just snap a photo of the cable car) (Budd Schulberg, that's who the director looked like.)—passengers who are riding by are surprised to pass a movie lot but really californially don't give a shit or shinola. In the back, tragic tent flaps move in the shroudy wind that comes smack from the great hidden dark bay where also poor broken tragic King Alcatraz like a muzzle of the cannon sits in the center of the bay, all bright lights in its pavilion in the night, its arcade and bat shrouds, the sleephouse of two thousand dead criminals, who with great devouring eyes must look at San Francisco all day from behind bars and plot huge crimes and paranoias and love-triumphs such as the world has never known, ahem—the tents flap, the technicians bend to stricken tasks by flashlight, there's mud at the wheels of their trucks, somehow wagons surround them, they're the backbone of Hollywood for the movies have nothing now but great technique to show, a great technique is ready for a great incoming age, and these workmen of the progress of machine to aid and relieve the world, these ambiguous wonderers at the limits of set and imposed but useful and will-get-you-there (ho ho) task huddled in the night doing their work behind the fuffoonery and charaderees of Hollywood so mad, Hollywood, the Death of Hollywood is upon us, and the wild semi-producers and booted lieutenants of said same, the group huddled beneath the wet flapshroud, the generals of Antietam, how they huddle there in dark *misère,* looking for every possible angle, they think important, actually utterly unimportant; for the director will leap out in the drizzle to test a strand of bushes that forms the edge of a shot of Joan Rawshanks down the driveway (it's not Joan who stands there waiting all this time as the geniuses speculate and gape, it's the extra, young, prettier, gamer, just a girl, tired on her feet, working for a living, etcetera, but ambitious, she'll get there, all she's gotta do is bang the right people is what I say, that'll get you there fastern anything why did I ever tell you what C. S. Jones the hoghead on the, you know that old engineer with the grimy wrinkles that spits and leans beneath the watertower at dusk in New Mexico and from his wrinkly sacks of eyes surveys, appraises land tracts reaching to the mist of the mountains under a cloudheap that on the horizon sits like the, like God on a couch; why, shore, (spitting), I could tell you stories about that there Hollywood—only assuming;) the director will go to all that foolish trouble to move and test a twig and if he wants to cut it he can, as if that would add reality, but he ends up not cutting it, just testing it, this consumes the attention of a thousand eyes and the tickings of moments that cost a company that puts up props by an actual apartment the same amount of money it would cost them to build an actual apartment house itself likely, what with all those union technicians milled and snarling in the background and all them kleig lights and bought cops and mad producers and geniuses with lollipops spending their precious time in a rainy Frisco night—Joan Rawshanks in the fog. . . .

I had no difficulty picking her out, I knew her well; "Good evening lady" uttered a little teenage girl when the director first ran up to talk to Joan, the little girl throwing in her own line of dialog about how'd she feel meeting Joan Rawshanks like that say on a cable car, as oft you see, here in Frisco, dignified ladies in furs riding the cold and draughty inconveniences of the city; Joan Rawshanks in the fog, I didn't rub my eyes, I didn't blink across the fog and darkness of the night where stood the very bridge from which in a dream a friend of mine once fell, like a floppydoll, while I, the last to arrive at the carnival in the canyon, was given first-prize on the last prize, a stale sandwich, as sadly the elephant tents were folded and a dust proceeded to emanate from the plain. . . . Yes, because when I thought of Hollywood camera crews I always pictured them in the California night, by moonlight, on some sand road back of Pasadena or something, or maybe in some treey canyon at the foot of the Mojave Desert, or some dreaming copse like the one in Nathanael West where the cowboy who kills the chicken is pausing suddenly at eventide to answer the chirp of a bird luting in the dewy bushes over by the lemon dusk just showing at the foot and mouth of the grove down there in the canyon where they went for a Technicolor picnic it seems with their red shirts glowing phosphorescent in the campfire—I thought of movie crews in a location like that; best of all I thought of them in the San Joaquin Valley of California, on a warm night, on a sand road running through some rolling browngrass fields that at this point happen not to be in cultivation, just ragged indecipherable-by-moonlight fields, and a few fences, and overhanging inky trees with the ghosts of old outlaws hanging from the cottonwood limb, and maybe a wagon standing in back of crazy-ranch corral where maybe actually an old Italian fruiterer lives with fat-wife and dogs but in the moonlight it looks like the corral of a cursed homesteader; and on the soft dust of the starwhite dirtroad in the moonlight softly roll the big pneumatic tires of the camera truck, about forty miles an hour, scooping up a low cloud for the stars; and on the back of it the camera, pointing backwards, handled by gumchewing California Nightmen on the Local A.O.U.; and on the road itself Hopalong Cassidy, in his white hat and on his famed pony, loping along intently with beck and bent, holding one rein up daintily, stiffly, like a fist, instead of hanging to the pommel; grave, bemused in the night, thinking thoughts; an escapee; followed by a band of rustlers posing as a posse, they catch up by the moment; the camera truck is leading and rolling them down the slope of a long hill; soon we will see views of a roadside cut, a sudden little crick bridge made of a log or two; then the great moony grove suddenly appearing and disappearing; all pure California night scenery and landscape; the great hairy trees of its night; then through a sudden splash of dark that completely and miraculously amazingly obscures Hoppy in a momentary invisibility; then the posse comes pell-mell from the other hand; what will happen, how will Hoppy escape? what his secret thoughts and stratagems! but he doesn't seem to be worried at all, in fact then you realize he's going to hide in those dark bushes of space and let the posse ride by on momentum, then he'll simply cut back silently on his horse which is good at these tricks, (Cody "And etcetera that's exactly right and more"); I thought of the camera crew doing this in the soft Southern California night, and of their dinners by campfire later, and talk. I had never imagined them going through these great Alexandrian strategies just for the sake of photographing Joan Rawshanks fumbling with her keys at a goggyfoddy door while all traffic halts in real world life only half a block away and everything waits on a whistle blown by a hysterical fool in a uniform who suddenly decided the importance of what's going on by some convulsive phenomena in the lower regions of his twitching hips, all manifesting itself in a sudden freezing grimace of idiotic wonder just exactly like the look of the favorite ninny in every B-movie you and I and Cody ever saw (the same expression as the cop posing, the older cop, probably himself it was) to suddenly realize that he is completely witless and therefore achieving the only thought of his life, the single adult realization of anykind, before twitching and reverting back to his puppy roles, puppythorities of a kind, going down the stairs of his own home without realizing that he is doing so in the great dark shadow of time and himself falling . . . with what fascination another oldtimer in the crowd watched that older's face under the floodlights of Leon Errol the rubberlegged tragic mistaken comedian of an accident, how else could I or the oldtimer get to know—when he saw that he was under floodlights, when it, the simple symbol (Wherewereyouonthenightofjunefourteen) finally dawned on him long after it had dawned on the whole crowd who also got their fill looking before he realized, but when it did assert itself on his very tiny brain he looked, he let his lower lip slip up over his upper teeth in a simper of complete idiocy and looked to his companion, with a nose wrinkled complete giveup of what to figure or what to do next; recalling, not instantly but after awhile, that he is a policeman, and at that moment striking the copy coply pose in the flare of lights to return his attention to the drama of the filming of Joan Rawshanks in the fog, whom I saw even then looking fitfully into the sky as the camera took. Joan Rawshanks in the fog . . . it isn't that Hollywood has won us with its dreams, it has only enhanced our own wild dreams, we the populace so strange and unknown, so uncalculable, mad, eee . . . Joan Rawshanks in the fog . . . the little girls in the crowd were pretty, wore bandanas, so did Joan; the little girls were witty, pretty and nice; we had a gay time; out of the corner of my evil eyes I caught sight of little dumplings of every order, cherry lipped, nipptious, virvacious, flauntin their eyes at the boys, and I, an innocent ghost, gaping, a shadow; Joan Rawshanks in the fog, could it be the terrible dolors we all felt when we saw her suddenly alone in the silence, standing by the litup fence making ready to emote to millions, to erupt, vomit and obhurt to others; we are so decadent with our moues. No discussion was on among the shroudy shadows in the litup raining shadowy background of Franklin Delano Roosevelt, the Technician magicians, the mysteries, no discussion as to whether the emotional, political and social issues out front had anything to do with the state of a coil, or the kilowatt of a fowder, when of course she is eminently layable, but as to her flaunts and sundances, well, they'd have to take it up with the advisory committee on sex down at the union hall, the guys down there—at one point a millionaire dweller in the rich apartment below which all this was taking place took his stand along the circus electric jutter truck and far from, as me, looking nirpatiously over his shoulder for sign of anyone seein him, rather brushes lightly with his hand against the material of the truckfence he's about to lean on, not that it's not his own truck but it might be dirty; far from me, as I stood, behind the crowd, couldn't see nothin—meanwhile the great drama ever unfolded in the area of the blazing lights that were so bright and white when I first saw them coming up Hyde Street thinking I'd terminate my walk on top of Russian Hill and get me a prospect then return home, so bright I thought they were being used by a new kind of civil defense organization crew that makes tests to see how bright lights have to be for bomber planes to catch them on foggy frisco nights; in this brightness, so bright that it embarrasses, I myself and all the crowd were finally delivered up judged and damned to them, because we couldn't leave except through that restricted zone and because of that they put the light on the alley of exit, for Hollywood of course is eager to see the populace itself, ahem, I mean, Hollywood wants to see more than anyone of us, than we do, than anything, we all had to cross that catwalk of lights and felt ourselves melt into identity as we crossed from the fingerprint rack to the blue desk, so much so that I took quick refuge beside two conmen who had commented on the old ladies upstairs as they really—they were burglars or eager to meet rich old dames say in a capacity as servant and then rob them, I took cover in their shadow so persistently as we walked the catwalk that one of them observed the tenacity of my presence somehow and looked annoyedly, so I had to dart forward, for a moment be caught, flying, etched in whiteheat wild Hollywoodian blazos, to take cover behind a librarian girl who'd had enough of her first glimpse of Hollywood filming since she'd arrived from Little Rock on her first sojourn in California. Earlier in the performance a beautiful crazy girl in glasses and ordinary coat and low heels came rushing up the driveway before the first Take as though she was lost and stopped to talk, or to be talked to really, by the pretty stand-in girl, who only and quite in a natural way began to explain something to her, but then we in the whole crowd saw the girl goof and titter and get that camera feeling and we all laughed her off as an eccentric movie crasher not a serious ordinary girl lost going home in the maze of a movie location scene; well she was a luscious little girl and came around with the rest of the crowd, finally, where it stood, on a grassy slope, watching; stood in the back, smiling, isolated, bashful still . . . with a kind of crazy dream in her eyes. But I was determined to see the spectacle of Hollywood. There she was . . . Joan Rawshanks in the fog; she had taken up the stand-in's place; they were ready for the last great Take. The whistle shrilled, that of the cop who by now had, in the background to all the moil and counter-confusion, worked like a ferret to finally achieve a pinnacle of success and power which had increased to the point now where he was actually blowing his whistle after every Take, in order to signal not only Hyde Street traffic it could move on but the remnants of the trapped crowd who wanted to sneak out the illuminated scandalous escape alley and go home, and had to face that ordeal to do it, running a gauntlet more cruel than any Cecil B. De Mille ever dreamed. So traffic, whitefaced and panicked, stayed suspended on the street; subinterior lieutenants of the uniformed corps rushed out; one big particular lug who was of course a perfect Hollywood version of the cop, they must have hired him for looks and not for training, he'd go running frantically with his hand on his gunhock across or that is along the great Italian balconean rail that juts out from the front of Elite Arms and in full sight, in bright lights, against white marble, dressed all in crazy blackshirt black, he'd go running after some imaginary traffic disturbance that had somehow took root in the porch, otherwise he had no right immediately prior to each take to suddenly dart off shouting some fake name or ambiguous imitation of someone shouting for somebody, hand on gun as if they were filming him, the which I assure you if you've at all trusted my previous observations, they were not; understand; and so, ah, but, running to the end of the thing, darting a look over the precipice, the whole thing and the whole scene, the top of Russian Hill, overlooking great etceteras of the city and the Bay Bridge down there—the crowd gently surged forward to see Joan enact the scene of the frightened woman with the fiddling keys and the door that would only open to three tugs. Through the rain I try to discern signs of whether the camera is turning or not; then I could be ready for the big moment; I endeavor to hear someone shout a signal like "Camera!" There are strident disturbances in the crowd itself; feeling cold, surrounded, foolishified, foolified, trapped, they now make cracks, the kids wrestle in the dark, little dogs break away from the leashes so that pretty lovergirls previously turning smiling faces to suitors in the interesting dark are now scurrying among legs of pedestrians very ungirllike and so forth to refetch their little doggies, and an eccentric but goodlooking middleaged woman who never goes out alone but has decided to come down in a hasty coat to see a real Hollywood filming is now hysterically looking around with a smile of gratitude and goodcheer and light, can't name it, she was watching so intently from the park curb that she didn't notice when she started to teeter off it, so when she landed on her feet not realizing the instinct perfection she was caught surprised and stumbled forward and teetered and almost fell, but didn't; to atone for this smiled at everyone in the immediate vicinity close enough to have caught her in the act, as I did; but no one acknowledged in the least, we all turned away, she ended up smiling in a void, understand, smiling too in the opposite direction from the cameras, the cameras are focused on the rainy asphalt all white, her vacant and inexcusable and imoondable smile is fixed on nothing but the rainy cape of night, the whole part of the wind and the night that sits out here juttin over the bay and a raw wet mountain or two that comes from Seattle and even the cold regions further North. Joan Rawshanks hugged herself, she was getting ready for another Take; she had her head bowed; I felt tired standing. She moves forward . . . ah, the signal must have come; the cameras are actually turning; just like when the great punter punts, the ball soars high and magnificent and spiral but the sound of the kick was unsatisfying; now the cruel cameras grind and gravel and turn and pick up Joan, and there she goes, hustling like mad up that ramp, fumbling for her keys in her purse, now she's got them; it's exactly the same thing they've already done twice, this is almost as perfect as a vaudeville act; she goes to the door, fumbles, gets the keyhole, plunges into the keyhole, with rapture, like she was coming, she has that awful ugh desperation we all saw at this moment, the door won't yield to her first tug, gad, the door is closed, obstreperous, you can feel it in the crowd, their hostility for that door is already aroused and the picture isn't even cut yet or the film dry; they're going to hate that door en masse opening night; it's just a door, though; I see Joan tugging at it, she tosses her frightened face to the sky, the overhead, actually, creamy concrete garage ramp light on the ramp steps; two tugs, three, the door finally opens, the crowd cheers scattered and forlorn in the rainy dismalities; and Joan has made her third Take— The camera men suddenly begin mutilating and dissecting parts of their equipment and camera, something is being slapped to the ground like a doggie, a cigarette lights, the director's assistant (tall sort of grave fellow like a railroad baggage handler foreman with his hat on the back of his head only this one here wears a hunting hat casually and when an intelligent little boy in glasses impulsively wandered on-set to ask intelligent questions or be let to sit he was kind and fatherly and not police-like in succeeding in getting him, the puffy cheek wide-eyed educated curious boy, back, pudgylegged and all, into the crowd, to watch, where he oughta watch from, like us); the Take was over. Joan vanished in a flare of cloaks, a Carriage was pulling up; just back of the rose vine wall there . . . but, no, then, actually, Joan was in the tent with the Generals; it appears they'll take another Take and then everybody knock off for the night, see what Frisco's got to offer; one technician saying to another "I don't know as I wanta do that *tonight*," in other words everybody on the job starting to relax and talk about afterwork matters, so that the crowd began to file away in great numbers that ate at its presence, in fact I went with this slice and batch, across those guilt provoking judgment day lights of greatlamps . . . the director's assistant is going around clearing up things it seems. The prettiest girl in the crowd, darkeyed Susan, is in love with

James, the tall young beautiful handsomeboy of the neighborhood who will probably win a prize soon, go to Hollywood and become a basketball star simultaneously and also be sought, because of his demure purple eyes, which he can't help, (and long-eyelashed languor) by queers of every kind; but Barbara, whose mother and elder sister are out witnessing with her, is also on the make for James but at the same time on the outs with Susan; so both she and Susan have been occupied all this time (while cops gain power, while producers gain time, while movie stars win thousands of dollars etc. and while old ladies wring their hands in despair, while the fog rolls and ships are sailing out into the darkness of the sea this very instant) occupied all this time in a catfight for James' attention; James, however, being well attended by his squire, junior brother, and dog, and not unconscious of his power; so that after Barbara makes an elaborate fuss saying goodnight to her mother and elder past-prime sister, so that past-prime sister will whimper and coo for James, who loves it and withers, and writhes, past-prime says "Well if you insist on staying out, Barbara, you can tell us all the details in the morning . . ." so that James has to duck a little to miss the object, after that play-act going on simultaneous with the show down there, Barbara officially installs herself to talk to James but he is in love with Susan and keeps casting to her, and when that slice of the crowd I spoke of leaves, Susan is in it, simply going home, leaving James forlorn, defeating Barbara, but Barbara thinks she's won! (defeat and victory all around); all this, too, after Susan and James leapt madly and gaily over the hedges together earlier, in the second try of the first Take, say. So long have I been here that the original interest I had found in observing the director, who was not much older than myself, got lost and with it the director got lost, I couldn't see him anymore, he faded away into something rich and distant, like sitting by swimmingpools on drizzly nights in Beverly Hills in a topcoat, with a drink, to brood. As for poor Joan Rawshanks in the fog, she too was gone . . . I guess they'd raise a glass of champagne to her lips tonight in some warmly lit room atop the roof of a hilltop hotel roofgarden swank arrangement somewhere in town. At dawn when Joan Rawshanks sees the first hints of great light over Oakland, and there swoops the bird of the desert, the fog will be gone.

from
BOOK OF DREAMS

EDITOR'S NOTE
In this book Neal Cassady is called "Cody Pomeray," Carolyn Cassady is "Evelyn," Allen Ginsberg is "Irwin Garden," and William S. Burroughs is "Bull Hubbard."

OH! THE HORRIBLE VOYAGES I've had to take across the country and back with gloomy railroads and stations you never dreamed of—one of em a horrible pest of bats and crap holes and incomprehensible parks and rains, I can't see the end of it on all horizons, this is the book of dreams.

Jesus life is dreary, how can a man live let alone work—sleeps and dreams himself to the other side—and that's where your Wolf is ten times worse than preetypop knows—and how, look, I stopped—*how can a man lie and say shit when he has gold in his mouth.* Cincinnati, Philarkadelphia, Frohio, stations in the Flue—rain town, graw flub, Beelzabur and Hemptown I've been to all of them and read Finnegain's Works what will it do me good if I dont stop and righten the round wrong in my poor bedighted b— what word is it?—skull . . .

Talk, talk, talk—

I went and saw Cody and Evelyn, it all began in Mexico, on Bull's ratty old couch I purely dreamed that I was riding a white horse down a side street in that North town like in Maine but really off Highway Maine with the rainy night porches in the up and down America, you've all seen it you ignorant pricks that cant understand what you're reading, *there,* with sidestreets, trees, night, mist, lamps, cowboys, barns, hoops, girls, leaves, something so familiar and never been seen it tears your heart out—I'm dashing down this street, cloppity clip, just left Cody and Evelyn at a San Francisco spectral restaurant or cafeteria table at Market and Third where we talked eagerly plans for a trip *East* it was (as if!) (as if there could be East or West in that waving old compass of the sack, base set on the pillow, foolish people and crazy people dream, the world wont be saved at this rate, these are the scravenings of a—lost—sheep)—the Evelyn of these dreams is an amenable—Cody is—(cold and jealous)—something—dont know—dont care—Just that after I talk to them—Good God it's taken me all this time to say, I'm riding down the hill—it becomes the Bunker Hill Street of Lowell—I'm headed for the black river on a white horse—it broke my heart when I woke up, to realize that I was going to make that trip *East* (pathetic!) —by myself—alone in eternity—to which now I go, on white horse, not knowing what's going to happen, predestined or not, if predestined why bother, if not why try, not if try why, but try if why not, or not why—At the present time I have nothing to say and refuse to go on without further knowledge.

• • •

Last night my father was back in Lowell—O Lord, O haunted life— and he wasnt interested in anything much—He keeps coming back in this dream, to Lowell, has no shop, no job even—a few ghostly friends are rumored to be helping him, looking for connections, he has many especially among the quiet misanthropic old men—but he's feeble and he aint supposed to live long anyway so it doesnt matter—He has de- parted from the living so much his once-excitement, tears, argufying, it's all gone, just paleness, he doesnt care any more—has a lost and distant air—We saw him in a cafeteria, across street from Paige's but not Waldorf's—he hardly talks to me—it's mostly my mother talking to me about him—"Ah well, ah bien, he vivra pas longtemps ce foi *icit!*"—"he wont live long *this* time!"—she hasnt changed—tho she too mourns to see his change—but God Oh God this haunted life I keep hoping against hope against hope he's going to live anyway even tho I not only know he's sick but that it's a dream and he did die in real life—ANYWAY—I worry myself . . . (When writing *Town and the City* I wanted to say "Peter worried himself white"—for the haunted sadness that I feel in these dreams is white—) Maybe Pop is very quietly sitting in a chair while we talk—he happened to come home from downtown to sit awhile but not because it's home so much as he has no other place to go at the moment—in fact he hangs out in the poolhall all day— reads the paper a little—he himself doesnt want to live much longer— that's the point—He's so different than he was in real life—in haunted life I think I see now his true soul—which is like mine—life means nothing to him—or, I'm my father myself and this is me (especially the Frisco dreams)—but it *is* Pa, the big fat man, but frail and pale, but so mysterious and un-Kerouac—but is that me? Haunted life, haunted life—and all this takes place within inches of the ironclouds dream of 1946 that saved my soul (the bridge across the Y, 10 blocks up from "cafeteria"—) Oh Dammit God—

*   *   *

They're hanging the political traitor in my closet up in my room at Phebe Avenue, crowd watching from near the window and I (with friend) from near the corner—It's an old man like the actor Ray Collins, he isnt too scared, not at all in fact—The executioner puts the rope around his neck and for an instant we see a look of distaste (for the rope) (itself) (not Death) on the face of the condemned old man—I stand horrified to see it's all "really going to happen!"—the hangman ties the knot and then with no ado puts up laboriously the body of the big man, I had intended not to "watch" but I do "see" and the rope tightens, the politician grimaces to choke, his body rises, silent—no complaint—no comment from the audience—I "dream" his twisted side down dead-neck, not moved at all but curious—going downstairs then with Lionel to the parlor where I turn on the television though it's 5 A M and Ma's in the kitchen cheerily making her go-to-work lunch and chatting with also up Nin—I say to Lionel "But he really wasnt all Anti Fascist!" and it's my father I'm talking about, my father was hanged—My mother looks at me as if she didnt recognize me immediately or what I was doing down there—The red livingroom rattle furniture of Lilly Street flat in 1929 is responsible for the horror, the hanging, the guilt, the old Victrola's just a new TV now, is all—the coffin that's never been removed from the parlor of the Kerouacs—*le mort dans salle des Kerouac*—

*   *   *

Night of miraculous dreams March 16 Sunday night—There had been a national catastrophe, it was announced over the radio at gray rainy dawn, it was riot of so great proportions it was some kind of revolu-tion—over "police brutality"—bandages were strewn in the street—people had revolted against the police—survivors were stretched out in annexes—announcers were grimly announcing everything in quiet voices on the dawn radio—I knew something would happen when I went to bed the night before—this would change the course of history, America and the world—no school no work—Like days when I was a boy, rain, I'd stay home with Ma and see before me sweet hours of playing with my marble horse races and papers and as in Gloomy Book-movie in *Sax* she'd occasionally look in on my games, bring cake, milk, fresh pies, show socks she was darning and *assure* me it would rain much too hard for this afternoon too and so like the national riot ca-tastrophe now she cant go to work (if so I'll walk her to the bus, there may be bricks flying—but it's a good idea not to—but she insists, "I dont wanta lose my job, it's the only security I have")—

Then there was Lowell, the Gershom street house, Iddyboy looking young and thin now that he's in his 30's came rushing in in a white shirt, with Rudy Loval—I had been all around the world and away from Lowell, I was back, with Ma, in the 34 Gershom street house "Hee thee Boy!" cried Iddyboy joyfully so glad to see me—sweet sun and flowers outdoors of a Sunday morning everybody Pawtucketville going to church—Rudy Loval as ever eager, warm—this is the happiest dream of my life—

• • •

The most incredible beat dream in the world, it's near St. Rita's church, on that street from Moody, but as my mother and sister Nin and I are traveling up Mammoth Road on some kind of train a woman rushes up shouting "I want to see Dinah Shore!"—She, Dinah, lives right up the street, right at the location of that grammar school—in a house— she has a "canary yellow" jeepster or convertible, which I point out to the lady saying, "That'll be her house there, Olivia DeHaviland has a canary yellow car"—(confusing the names)—My mother and sister ac-company the woman: but I stay behind in a kind of suddenly trans-placed Sarah Avenue house, it's Sunday, I'm the 30 year old beat brother and loafer of the family—"Dinah Shore" is standing in front of her house, and, seeing that I had directed the woman autograph hound to her she says, bleakly looking at me in an "official" or "Hollywood courteous" way—"Wont you come in with us?" (for a bleary visit)—

"Oh no—I'm busy—" but, they can see that I'm yielding and in my head I've started calculating advantages I can get from knowing "Olivia de Haviland"—So I give in, but in such a beat obvious way, and we go on in—

"I'm a novelist," I announce forthwith, "you should read my book," I say to the hostess—"Your husband is a writer too—a very great writer, Marcus Goodrich." Then the persistent fiction I have that Dinah Shore is really Olivia De Haviland has to break down here and

I say "Oh well, of course, yes, you're Dinah Shore, I keep thinking you're Olivia de Haviland"—but this is so gauche—and I havent shaved and stand there in her parlor, she is bleakly attentive, I'm like a thinner younger Major Hoople who really had a small taste of early success but then lost it and came home to live off his mother and sister but goes on "writing" and acting like an "author"—on the little street—But now, my sister sees that I am botching everything so she steps in and in an even more beat awful gauche way begins to try to impress Dinah with a kind of halting Canuck-English speech (attempts at "social smartness") (and really painful to hear) goes into some speech about how this and that, and so on, to show how really chic she's been at one time, we've been, our really more elegant real back-grounds than what shows (and in spite of this pitiful brother, and she's spoken up really to cover me up and also cut me, as she has her own ideas about how to impress people like Dinah Shore) to which Dinah listens even more bleakly—and my mother standing by like the original lady who wanted an autograph—it ends on this bleak beat note . . . with me all anxious and chewing my nails—the comic opera of our real days—

I'm also a neighborhood self-styled roué ready to make all the housewives but they dont really want any part of me, except a few of the older ones who want to have something on my mother—

• • •

In a dismal studio room in New York my whole family Ma Pa & Nin and I have taken up quarters and "all got jobs" and here it's night, one dim light burning, we're conversing but it's a weird conversation, it seems I dont realize what I'm doing and involuntarily or carelessly (be-cause not fearing wrath of women relatives and forgotten the father's because he so long gone in death) I'm rolling a stick of tea and talking right at them some wild excited inanities (born of T) they dont even listen to, rather they're discussing me solemnish and my father gets up and says "He's not worried about marijuana? Eh?" and he comes over to my side—I see him coming and I go blind, darkness takes the place of the entire scene, nevertheless now I feel his touch on my arm, he may have an axe, he may have anything and I cant see—I fall fainting dead in the darkness, with a groan that wakes me up and prevents me from being found dead (if there is such a thing as death) in my bed in the morning—for my blood stop't beating when that Shroudy Traveller fi-nally got his hand on me—He's getting closer & closer—I know how to be beyond him now—by not being concerned not believing in either life or death, if this can be possible in a humble Pratyeka at this time

. . .

Digging in this woman's cellar to plant, or transplant, my marijuana—under clutters of papers (just a minute before was going thru my own things, in a huge new room)—clutters of rubber bands, etc., and digging into dirt to make plant bed but realized how deep her hole was beneath her junk, thought to myself, "The old lady's—the older you get the deeper your cellar gets, more like a grave—the more your cellar looks like a grave—" There was a definite hole to the left—a definite saying—

I was foraging for my stories and paper—earlier I was in a room, working for a man as secretary, he was a masquerader, a fraud—and an evil pulp magazine crook genius leader of some evil—My mother visited me as if I was in jail—I turned over in my bed, my cot, interested in these things—

. . .

That recurrent dream where I'm always in California in Frisco, and have to travel all the way back and have no money—I see a woman suspended in midair giving her son a strange rich pie thru a window of a wooden Frisco building, which he accepts graciously over the rushing traffics of the street, and I think first of Evelyn (Pomeray) in Los Gatos and the sad trains there-to, then I think of Ma in the East (N.Y.?) and how I gotta go home for Christmas—There've been events all night, a bloody season, Irwin Gardens everywhere, Codies, et ceteras, I've had my up-to-here—it's time to go—wearing that seedy old topcoat and my muffcap over my ears there I go driving down the spectral boulevard in an old car (it's actually Cody's '40 Packard) and I think of hitch hiking all in the snow and decide, "Wyoming? No! I'll just drive all the way, at same time get this car home" (it's been given me)—What will I do for gas money? from hitch hikers—I'll work! "But if I work I wont make it for Christmas!"—the whole spectral hump o the continent's ahead a me, ephemeral as snow, awful as Edom,—my Arcady of Ribs, my Troy of Bones I'll crack and Waterloo on such a hopeless run and as if not remarmant & cartchaptoed enuf and once again and *again again!*—but here I am already, driving wrong way on the Oneway boulevard and seeing I cant turnoff I make a neat proud U-turn and go back where I started from still debatin how to make that 3,000 miles east,

in that miserable coat and muff hat, driving slow like an old man, sunk
low at the seat—"La Marde"—and all on account of a pie.

What an arbitrary conception this Coming Home For Christmas is
—I've done it twice now, and each time it bugged out on me—the first
time my mother fell asleep, the second time she had to go to a funeral
—big gay cities have huge sad cemeteries right outside, need em—

Rattling tenements and spectral girls (I call em tenements, I mean
the wooden houses of San Fran)—(like the one Rosemarie jumped off-
of)—this drear dreaming of necessitous sad traveling and I wake up in
a vast comfortable double bed in Rocky Mount in a house in the country with nothing to do but write *Visions of Gerard*, wash the dishes
and feed the cat!—and pop the *Book of Dreams*—Cant remember the
haunting taunting earlier details of this dream, the girls, cops, floors,
sex, suicides, pies, pastiches, parturiences, wallpapers, transcendencies
—the stations, gray—Garden, who never laughs, mines information—
June Ogilvie Blabbery Adams McCracken my girl—June John Boabus
Protapolapalopos the the Greek All-Mix Lover—Pain Twang—

*   *   *

I'm married to Josephine and with all her friends around in the kitchen
she makes fun of me and my "writing", I'm there with all my manuscripts, gooping—a cuckold paramoured to a dike—I make up feeble
stories and try to write them or act them out with disinterested friends
—Later Ed Buckle or Buddy Van Buder comes to try kitchen window,
sees me, says the publishers want another novel to look at (a falsehood,
what he really wants is a jolt of heroin again and I know it)—a bleak
laterlife with no balls, no joy, no Ma, no Kerouacism, nothing but the
possibilities of the present ripened to full horror—without any of the
charm now apparent—I'm like old Uncle Mike in the cubab tears of
afternoon or that incredible teary old Canuck lush in the Papineau Tavern in Montreal who cried when we carried him over (called him over)
and I was amazed to learn this lonely broken heartsensitive wretch was
one of the richest men in the neighborhood—people avoided his big
Weeping countenance and frank blue breton eyes—he was the one said
I should drink Caribou Blood—Le Sang du Caribou—something Breton
& Lost—

*   *   *

With my crayons I drew a marvelously beautiful scene of some buildings
in late afternoon, maybe churches or stores but using pink and deep

inkblue lavishly and very heavy with the hand I have put up a color of awe and mystery of the late sun on old stone that is so beautiful, something never before seen by human eyes, a work of art worthy of a DaVinci, a Rembrandt even—I'm amazed just a little to see I'm a great artist—Unfortunately I drew the picture on the TV screen "during a color broadcast" and now as I'm just about to show it to my mother the colorcast ends and ordinary pale luminous gray faces show and my whole masterpiece is completely wiped away—"Damn bastards changed!" I yell—It was a scene like Venice in the late Fall afternoon, blues & pink & stone salmon & awe gulp dark sorrow that made you think of Jesus & Magdalene

· · ·

And Mexico City, a spectral one with wished for piers sitting at the base of gloomy gray Liverpool-like Ferrocarril—I and a horde of young generation in suits with prom flower girls attend a melee, a gathering, at a building, a tower—so crowded, I, among bachelors, have to wait outside—rousing applause, speeches, music inside—Strange how in my dreams it doesnt seem that everything's already happened in a more interesting way, but awe, sweet awe remains—for my rage is eating my heart away, What am I doing in this sinister North Carolina as a clerk getting up at 6:00—a clerk among sinister oldfaced clerks in an old gloomy railroad office—no dream could be as frightening and more like hell.—I finally manage to get in the party—no, the idiot dog woke me up at just the point where I might have made a story of the deal—and lately anyway I wake at dawn with the horrors. In New York they're stealing my ideas, getting published, being feted, fucking other men's wives, getting laurel wreaths from old poets—and I wake on this bed of horror to a nightmare only life could have devised. To Hell with it.

· · ·

My poor sad mother Angie is trying to get off a crummy, I see her up the track, she's carrying burdens, she's "followed me on the railroad," it's hard for her with her old legs to jump off the high caboose step, but she does—How short, squat, sad she looks—how long suffering, that now in these last tired years she "follows me on the railroad"— Finally, after a series of "moves," in the night, she's standing by a switch, we're finished for the night—she looks so tired, old and gray-haired and finally weary now, heavier, much slower, no longer bubbling —my heart breaks when she says "Ride ton *point,* Jean—and dont walk on your poor legs—ride—and come back home." I'm going to "ride my point" to the other end, that'll be the end of my day's work, we'll rest now—worked so hard—my heart is broken, God, by this sad lonely mother you made me come from and by the poor way she used the railroad word "point" with a French Canadian accent and sadly as if talking to her baby—having to use this harsh Okie word under the stress of earth's harsh inhospitable circumstances—Ah Lord, save her —save me—she is my Angel and my Truth—Why does it tear my heart out that she pronounced it "pwaint"—that French Canadian way of using English to express its humility—meanings—no non-French Canadian knows this—

• • •

I'm in Mexico peering into windows while neighbors stare, finally I ask one woman "A donde es Senor Gaines?" but I really mean Hubbard and shows me a window with Hubbard inside standing in the middle of his room surrounded by a dozen beatnik and hoodlum and other visitors—I knock on window, he rushes out politely to let me in but I have my hunting cap over my eyes not even looking at him and go in —In the middle of the floor Bull (no room for himself to sit) expounds on guns and finally fishes out a small automatic from a silk wrapping & hands it to a young darkhaired hoodlum—Later, in his shorts like the John L. Sullivan boxing-pose photo in BIG TABLE magazine, Bull is advised by the Sergeant to report up the sandbank to his officers the "Allies"—Other guys in shorts are listening—I marvel that Bull is so sardonic with the sergeant & about the whole Army in general—"Give my regards to the Allies," says I, "if you gets there" (imitating Charles Laughton for Bull's benefit & also knowing he wont even go) & Bull laughs but I lamely add "*When* you gets there," as always nervous when trying to be funny for Bull, & like in the door with the hunting cap he politely refrains from comments on my awkwardness—I marvel at the respect he gets from the men and officers of the world

• • •

I had a white bandage on my head from a wound, the police are after me around the dark stairs of wood near the Victory Theater in Lowell, I sneak away—come to the boulevard where a parade of children chanting my name hide me from the searching police as I duck along their endless ranks, keeping low—The parade of children is endless—Chant-

ing and singing we go marching into Mongolia with me with my white
bandaged head in front

(dreamed the day after the publication of ON THE ROAD)

. . .

I'm looking for a place to sit and write quietly at the baseball park and
go around a fountain and batting cage wire to a bench on the side where
there's an old typewriter & desks under a tree and here I turn into
"Malcolm Cowley" and start typing—but so old the Machine, to register letters ya gotta hit it one finger at a time *hard,* which I do,—&
there's a sad young kid there, of 18, definite personality, curly brown
hair, thoughtful, as an interested old Man of Letters I begin to interview
him sympathetically and find he's a young tender poet so saddened he
doesnt write much, or some such,—walked 2½ miles before I wrote
this, so part forgot—So he stares into space in my dream and I worry
about him—Who's subjective? Who's objective?

. . .

At a big "Swenson" party in his huge complicated hard-to-find-your-
way-around apartments, there's been a weekend, drinking—We've gone
down the street of some mixed-up California town (Los Altos!) and saw
a colored girl across the street, wellknown, to whom one of our party
called, "Come on over Joo Jee!"—and she derisively said no, with a
remark, waving, going on alone, the colored guy in our party emphatically saying to me "You should know Joo Jee, you really should know
her—she's something—" and later the big banquet for everybody—
hysterical eaters—I start in the kitchen with tidbits on the table, toast
butter and crisp in a dish on a side board, various crumbs en route in
the livingroom, ending up in the parlor where people are standing or
sitting around in various attitudes of wellfedness, not saying much,
picking their teeth, drinking black coffee, or port, or Scotch—I see a
lovely pecan pie in the middle of the diningroom table and take a knife
to cut a piece, which brings it to the attention of everyone else so that
when I wake up we've all slowly silently stepped up a tempo at the pie,
cutting, lifting pieces, dropping them, hands mixing and clashing and
sweating as at gold, hands trembling in growing hunger as the more
Swenson morsels are laid out and the better, the hungrier more desperate the dark voracious guests fighting now to freeload at the curious
pecan pie "I discovered"—but the whole dream filled with the gray

indisoluble hopelessness like a stone—an emptybelly 3-beer nightmare, alcoholically lost, grim—

. . .

The Flying Horses of Mien Mo—I'm riding a bus thru Mexico with Cody sleeping at my side, at the dawn the bus stops in the countryside and I look out at the quiet warm fields & think: "Is this really Mexico? why am I here?"—The fields look too calm & grassy & bugless to be Mexico—Later I'm sitting on the other side of the bus, Cody is gone, I look up in the sky & see that old ten thousand foot or hundred mile high mountain cliff with its enormous hazy blue palaces and temples where they have giant granite benches & tables for Giant Gods bigger than the ones who hugged skyscrapers on Wall Street—And in the air, Ah the silence of that horror, I see flying winged horses with capes furling over their shoulders, the slow majestic pawing of their front hooves as they clam thru the air flight—Griffins they are!—So I realize we're in "Coyocan" & this is the famous legendary place—I start telling 4 Mexicans in the seat in front of me the story of the Mountain of Coyocan & its Secret Horses but they laugh not only to hear a stranger talk about it but the ridiculousness of anybody even mentioning or noticing it—There's some secret they wont tell me concerning ignoration of the Frightful Castle—They even get wise with Gringo Me and I feel sand pouring down my shirt front, the big Mexican is sitting there with sand in his hand, smiling—I leap up & grab one, he is very tiny & skinny & I hold his hand against his belly so he wont pull a knife on me but he has none—They're really laughing at me for my big ideas about the Mountain—

We arrive at Coyocan town over which the hazy blue Mountain rises and now I notice that the Flying Horses are constantly swirling over this town & around the cliff, swooping, flying, sometimes sweeping low, yet nobody looks up & bothers with them—I cant bring myself to believe that they are actually flying horses & I look & look but that's what they have to be, even when I see them in moon profile: horses pawing thru air, slow, slow, eerie griffin horror men-horses—I realize they've been there all the time swirling around the Eternal Mountain Temple & I think: "The bastards have something to do with that Temple, that's where they come from, I always knew that Mountain was all horror!"—I go inside the Coyocan Maritime Union Hall to sign for a Chinese sea job, it's in the middle of Mexico, I dont know why I've come all the way from New York to the landlocked center of Mexico for a sea voyage but there it is: a Seaman's hiring hall full of confusion & pale officials who dont understand why I came also—One of them makes a great intelligent effort to have letters in duplicate written to New York to begin straightening out the reason why I came—So if it's a job I'll get, it wont be for a week at least, or *more*—The town is evil & completely sinister because everybody is ugly sneering (the natives, I mean,) and they refuse to recognize the existence of that Terrible Swirl of Flying horses—"Mien Mo," I think, remembering the name of the Mountain in Burma they call the world, with Dzapoudiba the southern island (India), on account of Himalayan secret horrors—The beating heart of the Giant Beast is up there, the Griffins are just incidental insects—but those Flying Horses are happy! how beautifully they claw slow fore-hooves thru the blue void!—

Meanwhile 2 young American seamen and I study them flying up there miles high & watch them swoop lower, when they come low they change into blue and white birds to fool everybody—Even I say: "Yep, they're not flying horses, they only seem to be, they're Birds!" but even as I say that I see a distinct horse motioning lyrically thru the moon with a cape furling from his infernal shoulders—

A broken nosed ex boxer approaches me hinting that for 50¢ a job can be arranged on a ship—He is so sinister & intense I'm afraid to even give him 50¢—Up comes a blonde with her fiance announcing her forthcoming marriage but she interrupts her speech every now and then to wail on my joint in front of everybody in the streets of COYOCAN!

And the Flying Horses of Mien Mo are galloping with silent ease in the happy empty air way up there—Tinkle Tinkle go the streets of Coyocan as the sun falls, but up there is all silence & the Giant Gods are up—How can I describe it?

• • •

"Cool it" I say to a gang of crazy boys I been playin on the rollercoasters with, as one starts shouting loudly about the marijuana exploits I taught them—"Ah hell, cool it yaself" is the answer from my disciples—We're in our shorts and T-shirts, I feel tired of trying to keep up with the consequences of the Beat Generation and all lugubrious in the dream— Wake up in Lowell Skidrow—

'T'is only in the quiet of the Sainte Jeanne d'Arc church on the great gray day of Nov. 21 1954 that I saw: "The *Beati*fic Generation"

• • •

Happy dream of Canada, the illuminated Northern land—I'm there at first on Ste. Catherine or some other Boulevard with a bunch of brother French-Canadians and among old relatives and at one point Nat King Cole is there talking with my mother (is not dark, but light, friendly, I call him "Nat")—We all go to the Harsh Northern School and are sitting (like the gray wood room of Mechanical Drawing class in Bartlett J H shack) and the teacher is a freckled redhaired Scotchman and acts a little contemptuous of the Frenchies, has his favorite teacher's boy in the front row and he too is a sarcastic freckled redhaired British Canadian—I've been close and talkative and like Saintly Ti Jean with everyone so now contemplatively I lean forward and study the situation, watch the teacher and his asskissing sarcastic prototype, and softly, in French, nodding, for I see it all and only because an outsider American Genius Canuck can see, "Ca-na-da"—(I say) Ca-na-daw—and my brother darkhaired anxious angry Canucks vehemently agree with me —"It's always them!" they cry and I see that sarcastic non-French smirk on the redheads' faces, smashable faces, something hateful I must have seen on Ste. Catherine St. in 1953 March, that arrogant Britishified look—or from ancestors' memories of old French-Indian canoe wars— Had I gone back to Canada I wouldnt have taken shit one from any non Frenchman of Canada . . . took everything from Brother Noel and mourned—but God the fist mashed face of my redhaired English Canadian enemy—

This was such a happy dream, I woke up at 5 AM from the comradeship and glow of it—no anger (as now, afternoon) at all—I should have written it at dawn—it was Ti Jean the happy Saint back among his loyal brothers at last—That's why

from
OLD ANGEL MIDNIGHT

1

FRIDAY AFTERNOON IN THE UNIVERSE, in all directions in & out you got your men women dogs children horses pones tics perts parts pans pools palls pails parturiences and petty Thieveries that turn into heav-

enly Buddha—I know boy what's I talkin about case I made the world
& when I made it I no lie & had Old Angel Midnight for my name
and concocted up a world so *nothing* you had forever thereafter make
believe it's real—but that's alright because now everything'll be alright
& we'll soothe the forever boys & girls & before we're thru we'll find
a name for this Goddam Golden Eternity & tell a story too—and but
d y aver read a story as vast as this that begins Friday Afternoon with
workinmen on scaffolds painting white paint & ants merlying in lil
black dens & microbes warring in yr kidney & mesaroolies microbing
in the innards of mercery & microbe microbes dreaming of the ultimate
microbe-hood which then ultimates outward to the endless vast empty
atom which is this imaginary universe, ending nowhere & ne'er e'en
born as Bankei well poled when he ferried his mother over the rocks to
Twat You Tee and people visit his hut to enquire "What other planet
features this?" & he answers "What other planet?" tho the sounds of
the entire world are now swimming thru this window from Mrs Mc-
Cartiola's twandow & Ole Poke's home dronk again & acourse you
hear the cats wailing in the wail-bar wildbar wartfence moonlight midnight Angel Dolophine immensity Visions of the Tathagata's Seat of
Purity & Womb so that here is all this infinite immaterial meadowlike
golden ash swimswarming in our enlighten brains & the silence Shh
shefallying in our endless ear & still we refuse naked & blank to hear
What the Who? the Who? Too What You? will say the diamond boat
& Persepine, Recipine, Mill town, Heroine, & Fack matches the silver
ages everlasting swarmswallying in a simple broom—and at night ya
raise the square white light from your ghost beneath a rootdrinkin tree
& Coyote wont hear ya but you'll ward off the inexistency devils just
to pass the time away & meanwhile it's timeless to the ends of the last
lightyear it might as well be gettin-late Friday afternoon where we start
so's old Sound can come home when worksa done & drink his beer &
tweak his children's eyes—

2

and what talents it takes to bail boats out you'd never flank till flail
pipe throwed howdy who was it out the bar of the seven seas and all
the Italians of 7th Street in Sausaleety slit sleet with paring knives that
were used in the ream kitchens to cut the innards of gizzards out on a
board, wa, twa, wow, why, shit, Ow, man, I'm tellin you—Wait—We
bait the rat and forget to mark the place and soon Cita comes and eat

it and puke out grit—fa yen pas d case, chanson d idiot, imbecile, vas malade—la sonora de madrigal—but as soon as someone wants to start then the world takes on these new propensities:

1. Bardoush (the way the craydon bi fa shta ma j en vack)
2. Flaki—arrete—interrupted chain saw sting eucalyptus words inside the outside void that good God we cant believe is anything so arsaphallawy any the pranajara of madore with his bloody arse kegs, shit—go to three.

3

Finally just about the time they put wood to the poets of France & fires broke out recapitulating the capitulation of the continent of Mu located just south of Patch, Part, with his hair askew and wearing goldring ears & Vaseline Hair Oil in his arse ass hole flaunted all the old queers and lecherous cardinals who wrote (write) pious manuals & announced that henceforth he was to be the sole provender provider this side of Kissthat.

Insteada which hey marabuda you son of a betch you cucksucker you hey hang dat board down here I'll go cot you on the Yewneon ya bum ya—lick, lock, lick, lock, mix it for pa-tit a a lamana lacasta reda va da Poo moo koo—la—swinging Friday afternoon in eternity here comes Kee pardawac with long golden robe flowing through the Greek Islands with a Bardic (forgot) with a lard (?) with a marde manual onder his Portugee Tot Sherry Rotgut, singing "Kee ya".

Tried to warn all of you, essence of stuff wont do—God why did you make the world?

Answer:—Because I gwt pokla renamash ta va in ming the atss are you forever with it?

I like the bliss of mind.

Awright I'll call up all the fuckin Gods, right now! Parya! Arrive! Ya damn hogfuckin lick lip twillerin fishmonger! Kiss my purple royal ass baboon! Poota! Whore! You and yr retinues of chariots & fucks! Devadatta! Angel of Mercy! Prick! Lover! Mush! Run on ya dog eared kiss willying nilly Dexter Michigan ass-warlerin ratpole! The rat in my cellar's an old canuck who wasnt fooled by rebirth but b God gotta admit I was born for the same reason I bring this glass to my lip—?

Rut! Old God whore, the key to ecstasy is forevermore blind! Potanyaka! God of Mercy! Boron O Mon Boron! All of ye! Rush! Ghosts & evil spirits, if you appear I'm saved. How can you fool an old man with a stove & wine drippin down his chin? The flowers are my little sisters and I love them with a dear heart. Ashcans turn to snow and milk when I look. I know sinister alleys. I had a vision of Han Shan a darkened by sun bum in odd rags standing short in the gloom scarey to see. Poetry, all these vicious writers and bores & Scriptural Apocraphylizers fucking their own dear mothers because they want ears to sell—

And the axe haiku.

All the little fine angels amercyin and this weary prose hand handling dumb pencils like in school long ago the first redsun special. Henry Millers everywhere Fridaying the world—Rexroths. Rexroths not a bad egg. Creeley. Creeley. Real magination realizing rock roll rip snortipatin oyster stew of Onatona Scotiat Shores where six birds week the nest and part wasted his twill till I.

Mush. Wish. Wish I could sing ya songs of a perty nova spotia patonapeein pack wallower wop snot polly—but caint—cause I'll get sick & die anyway & you too, born to die, little flowers. Fiorella. Look around. The burlap's buried in the wood on an angle, axe haiku. La religion c'est de la marde! Pa! d la marde! J m en dor—

God's asleep dreaming, we've got to wake him up! Then all of a sudden when we're asleep dreaming, he comes and wakes us up—how gentle! How are you Mrs Jones? Fine Mrs Smith! Tit within Tat—Eye within Tooth—Bone within Light, like—Drop some little beads of sweetness in that stew (O Phoney Poetry!)—the heart of the onion— That stew's too good for me to eat, you!—

People, shmeople

4

Boy, says Old Angel, this amazing nonsensical rave of yours wherein I spose you'd think you'd in some lighter time find hand be-almin ya for the likes of what ya devote yaself to, pah—bum with a tail only means one thing,—They know that in sauerkraut bars, god the chew chew & wall lips—And not only that but all them in describable paradises— aye—ah—Old Angel m boy—Jack, the born with a tail bit is a deal that you never dream'd to redeem—verify—try to see as straight—you wont believe even in God but the devil worries you—you & Mrs Tourian—great gaz-zuz & I'd as lief be scoured with a leaf rust as hear this poetizin horseshit everywhere I want to hear the sounds thru the window you promised me when the Midnight bell on 7th St did toll bing bong & Burroughs and Ginsberg were asleep & you lay on the couch in that timeless moment in the little red bulblight bus & saw drapes of eternity parting for your hand to begin & so's you could affect—and *ee*ffect—the total turningabout & deep revival of world robeflowing literature till it shd be something a man'd put his eyes on & continually read for the sake of reading & for the sake of the Tongue & not just these insipid stories writ in insipid aridities & paranoias bloomin & why yet the image—let's hear the Sound of the Universe, son, & no more part twaddle—And dont expect nothing from me, my middle name is Opprobrium, Old Angel Midnight Opprobrium, boy, O.A.M.O.—

Pirilee pirilee, tzwe tzwi tzwa,—tack tick—birds & firewood. The dream is already ended and we're already awake in the golden eternity.

ON BOP AND THE
BEAT GENERATION

EDITOR'S INTRODUCTION

In April 1959, Kerouac began writing articles for *Escapade* magazine as a regular columnist. Before publication of *On the Road*, his work had appeared in little magazines like *The Chicago Review*, *Ark II/Moby I*, the *Berkeley Bussei*, the *Paris Review*, and the *Black Mountain Review*; but when *On the Road* became a bestseller his agent, Sterling Lord, started selling his articles and stories to mainstream magazines like *Esquire*, *Playboy*, *Pageant*, and *Holiday*, adding substantially to Kerouac's income. The *Escapade* editors contracted for Kerouac to write for them on a regular basis, and "The Beginning of Bop" was his first appearance in the magazine.

To stimulate discussion about his article, the editors advertised a contest with a hundred-dollar prize for the best letters, pro and con, about—as they put it—"the article and the controversial Mr. Kerouac." The best pro letter argued that the writing in Kerouac's article might be unconventional, but it communicated "a vivid word picture" of the FEEL of jazz. The winning con letter found Kerouac's article "a drag, man." "Jack is a no-blow," the letter added, for mistakenly writing that Lionel Hampton played the saxophone (instead of vibes and drums), and it concluded that "Kerouac's poor ear and his lack of feeling and respect for the language defy conception." *Escapade* also ran excerpts from other letters about the article, ending with the opinion of a reader who understood that "Kerouac does not ask us to follow his philosophy. For if we did, then we would all once again be playing the worn out game of follow-the-leader. Rather, in his very thinking, he challenges us to be ourselves. . . . Kerouac has given us an insight into society's lost art, the art of encouraging and creating the thoughts of the individual."

By the time of the *Escapade* contest, Kerouac was highly visible as the key spokesman for the Beat Generation, and the public debate about him and his writing was at its height. In 1948, more than a decade before, Kerouac had coined the term "Beat Generation" in a conversation with John Clellon Holmes. Kerouac took the term only half seriously, and he never sat down to define what he meant by it until requested to do so by Patricia MacManus, the publicist at Viking Press, shortly before the publication of *On the Road* in the summer of 1957. Kerouac wrote "About the Beat Generation" in Mexico City, and when he told Ginsberg about it in a letter, he said that he wanted to show that Beat was a religious movement prophesized in Oswald Spengler's *Decline of the West*. Burroughs had given him a copy of this book in 1944, with the instruction to "edify your mind, me boy, with the grand actuality of fact."

The essay was retitled and published as "Aftermath: The Philosophy of the Beat Generation" in *Esquire* in March 1958, nearly intact but with a major omission. In his original version, reprinted here, Kerouac had described the different visions "all inspired and fervent and free of Bourgeois-Bohemian Materialism" of the people who were what he called "the early hipsters" in the original group of Beats: Herbert Huncke, Allen Ginsberg, William Burroughs, Neal Cassady, Gregory Corso, Gary Snyder, Philip Whalen, Philip Lamantia, and Alene L., the only woman in the crowd, whose love affair with Kerouac became his subject in *The Subterraneans*.

"Lamb, No Lion" appeared in *Pageant* magazine a month before the *Esquire* article. In this essay Kerouac went directly to the question of "hoodlumism" in the Beat Generation, responding to charges that his portrayal of "Dean Moriarty" (the character based on Neal Cassady) in *On the Road* was "just a lot of frantic nowhere hysteria." As someone once observed, Kerouac tried to reply to hostile questions about his intent as a writer with "weirdly courteous patience."

"Beatific: The Origins of the Beat Generation," published in *Playboy* in June 1959, is Kerouac's most extensive discussion of the term. It was originally written as a talk that he delivered at a seminar at Hunter College on the topic "Beat and Its Beginnings." *Playboy* published his article with a respectful introduction, and Kerouac's piece was later anthologized in Thomas Parkinson's textbook *A Casebook on the Beat* (1961).

The newspaper article "After Me, the Deluge"—or as the piece was also titled, "Man, Am I the Granddaddy-O of the Hippies" and "Kerouac: The Last Word from the Father of the Beats"—appeared in the *Miami Tropic* (October 12, 1969), the *Washington Post* (October 22, 1969), and the *Los Angeles Times* (October 26, 1969) just before and soon after Kerouac's death on October 21, 1969. He published little in periodicals during the last years of his life, with the notable exception of his long interview on the "Art of Fiction" with Ted Berrigan and Aram Saroyan in the *Paris Review* summer 1968 issue.

Escalation of the war in Vietnam and the rise of the "Hippie-Yippie" movement caused Kerouac to feel himself caught in the middle between radicals and conservatives. At the conclusion of his last article, he defined what he saw as his position as a creative artist, paradoxically hinting at his lifelong conservatism by saying "So I'll be 'generous with the liberality of poets, which is conservative to the bone.' "

THE BEGINNING
OF BOP
1959

BOP BEGAN WITH JAZZ but one afternoon somewhere on a sidewalk maybe 1939, 1940, Dizzy Gillespie or Charley Parker or Thelonious Monk was walking down past a men's clothing store on 42nd Street or South Main in L.A. and from the loudspeaker they suddenly heard a wild impossible mistake in jazz that could only have been heard inside their own imaginary head, and that is a new art. Bop. The name derives from an accident, America was named after an Italian explorer and not after an Indian king. Lionel Hampton had made a record called "Hey Baba Ree Bop" and everybody yelled it and it was when Lionel would jump in the audience and whale his saxophone at everybody with sweat, claps, jumping fools in the aisles, the drummer booming and belaboring on his stage as the whole theater rocked. Sung by Helen Humes it was a popular record and sold many copies in 1945, 1946. First everyone looked around then it happened—bop happened—the bird flew in— minds went in—on the streets thousands of new-type hepcats in red shirts and some goatees and strange queerlooking cowboys from the West with boots and belts, and the girls began to disappear from the street—you no longer saw as in the Thirties the wrangler walking with his doll in the honkytonk, now he was alone, rebop, bop, came into being because the broads were leaving the guys and going off to be middleclass models. Dizzy or Charley or Thelonious was walking down the street, heard a noise, a sound, half Lester Young, half raw-rainy-fog that has that chest-shivering excitement of shack, track, empty lot, the sudden vast Tiger head on the woodfence rainy no-school Saturday morning dumpyards, "Hey!" and rushed off dancing.

On the piano that night Thelonious introduced a wooden off-key note to everybody's warmup notes, Minton's Playhouse, evening starts, jam hours later, 10 p.m., colored bar and hotel next door, one or two white visitors some from Columbia some from Nowhere—some from ships—some from Army Navy Air Force Marines—some from Europe —The strange note makes the trumpeter of the band lift an eyebrow.

Dizzy is surprised for the first time that day. He puts the trumpet to lips and blows a wet blur—

"Hee ha ha!" laughs Charley Parker bending down to slap his ankle. He puts his alto to his mouth and says "Didn't I tell you?"—with jazz of notes—Talking eloquent like great poets of foreign languages singing in foreign countries with lyres, by seas, and no one understands because the language isn't alive in the land yet—Bop is the language from America's inevitable Africa, *going* is sounded like *gong*, Africa is the name of the flue and kick beat, off to one side—the sudden squeak uninhibited that screams muffled at any moment from Dizzy Gillespie's trumpet—do anything you want—drawing the tune aside along another improvisation bridge with a reach-out tear of claws, why be subtle and false?

The band of 10 p.m. Minton's swings into action. Bird Parker who is only 18 year old has a crew cut of Africa looks impossible has perfect eyes and composures of a king when suddenly you stop and look at him in the subway and you can't believe that bop is here to stay—that it is real, Negroes in America are just like us, we must look at them understanding the exact racial counterpart of what the man is—and figure it with histories and lost kings of immemorial tribes in jungle and Fellaheen town and otherwise and the sad mutts sleeping on old porches in Big Easonburg woods where just 90 years ago old Roost came running calling "Maw" through the fence he'd just deserted the Confederate Army and was running home for pone—and flies on watermelon porches. And educated judges in hornrimmed glasses reading the Amsterdam News.

The band realized the goof of life that had made them be not only misplaced in a white nation but mis-noticed for what they really were and the goof they felt stirring and springing in their bellies, suddenly Dizzy spats his lips tight-drum together and drives a high screeching fantastic clear note that has everybody in the joint look up—Bird, lips hanging dully to hear, is turning slowly in a circle waiting for Diz to swim through the wave of the tune in a toneless complicated wave of his own grim like factories and atonal at any minute and the logic of the mad, the sock in his belly is sweet, the rock, zonga, monga, bang —In white creamed afternoons of blue Bird had leaned back dreamily in eternity as Dizzy outlined to him the importance of becoming Mohammedans in order to give a solid basis of *race* to their ceremony. "Make that rug swing, mother,—When you say Race bow your head and close your eyes." Give them a religion no Uncle Tom Baptist—

make them wearers of skull caps of respectable minarets in actual New York—picking hashi dates from their teeth—Give them new names with zonga sounds—make it weird—

Thelonious was so weird he wandered the twilight streets of Harlem in winter with no hat on his hair, sweating, blowing fog—In his head he heard it all ringing. Often he heard whole choruses by Lester. There was a strange English kid hanging around Minton's who stumbled along the sidewalk hearing Lester in his head too—hours of hundreds of developing choruses in regular beat all day so in the subway no dissonance could crash against unalterable choruses in implacable bars—erected in mind's foundation jazz.

The tune they were playing was *All the Things You Are* . . . they slowed it down and dragged behind it at half tempo dinosaur proportions—changed the placing of the note in the middle of the harmony to an outer more precarious position where also its sense of not belonging was enhanced by the general atonality produced with everyone exteriorizing the tune's harmony, the clonk of the millenial piano like anvils in Petrograd—"Blow!" said Diz, and Charley Parker came in for his solo with a squeaky innocent cry. Monk punched anguished nub fingers crawling at the keyboard to tear up foundations and guts of jazz from the big masterbox, to make Charley Parker hear his cry and sigh —to jar the orchestra into vibrations—to elicit gloom from the doom of the black piano. He stared down wild eyed at his keys like a matador at the bull's head. Groan. Drunken figures shaded in the weaving background, tottering—the boys didn't care. On cold corners they stood three backs to one another, facing all the winds, bent—lips don't care —miserable cold and broke—waiting like witchdoctors—saying, "Everything belongs to me because I am poor." Like 12th Century monks high in winter belfries of the Gothic Organ they wildeyed were listening to their own wild sound which was heralding in a new age of music that would eventually require symphonies, schools, centuries of technique, declines and falls of master-ripe styles—the Dixieland of Louis Armstrong sixteen in New Orleans and of big Pops Forest niggerlips jim in the white shirt whaling at a big scarred bass in raunchy nongry New Orleans on South Rampart street famous for parades and old Perdido Street—all that was mud in the river Mississippi, pasts of 1910 gold rings, derby hats of workers, horses steaming turds near breweries and saloons,—Soon enough it would leap and fill the gay Twenties like champagne in a glass, pop!—And crawl up to the Thirties with tired Rudy Vallees lamenting what Louis had laughed in a Twenties Transoceanic Jazz, sick and tired early Ethel Mermans, and old beat bed-springs creaking in that stormy weather blues when people lay in bed all day and moaned and had it good—The world of the United States was tired of being poor and low and gloomy in a line. Swing erupted as the Depression began to crack, it was the year marijuana was made illegal, 1937. Young teenagers took to the first restraint, the second, the third, some still wandered on hobo trains (lost boys of the Thirties numbered in the hundreds of thousands, Salvation Armies put up full houses every night and some were ten years old)—teenagers, alienated from their parents who have suddenly returned to work and for good to get rid of that dam old mud of the river—and tear the rose vine off the porch—and paint the porch white—and cut the trees down—castrate the hedges—burn the leaves—build a wire fence—get up an antenna—listen—the alienated teenager in the 20th Century finally ripe gone wild modern to be rich and prosperous no more just around the corner—became the hepcat, the jitterbug, and smoked the new law weed. World War II gave everybody two pats of butter in the morning on a service tray, including your sister. Up from tired degrading swing wondering what happened between 1937 and 1945 and because the Army'd worked it canned it played it to the boys in North Africa and raged it in Picadilly bars and the Andrews Sisters put the corn on the can—swing with its heroes died—and Charley Parker, Dizzy Gillespie and Thelonious Monk who were hustled through the chow lines—came back remembering old goofs—and tried it again—and Zop! Dizzy screamed, Charley squealed, Monk crashed, the drummer kicked, dropped a bomb—the bass questionmark plunked—and off they whaled on Salt Peanuts jumping like mad monkeys in the grey new air. "Hey Porkpie, Porkpie, Hey Porkpie!"

"Skidilibee-la-bee you, -oo, -e bop she bam, ske too ria—Parasakiliaoolza—menooriastibatiolyait -oon ya koo." They came into their own, they jumped, they had jazz and took it in their hands and saw its history vicissitudes and developments and turned it to their weighty use and heavily carried it clanking like posts across the enormity of a new world philosophy and a new strange and crazy grace came over them, fell from the air free, they saw pity in the hole of heaven, hell in their hearts, Billy Holiday had rocks in her heart, Lester droopy porkpied hung his horn and blew bop lazy ideas inside jazz had everybody dreaming (Miles Davis leaning against the piano fingering his trumpet with a cigarette hand working making raw iron sound like wood speaking in long sentences like Marcel Proust)—"Hey Jim," and the stud comes swinging down the street and says he's real *bent* and he's *down* and he has a *twisted* face, he works, he wails, he bops, he bangs, this man who was sent, stoned and stabbed is now *down, bent* and *stretched-out*—he is home at last, his music is here to stay, his history has washed over us, his imperialistic kingdoms are coming.

ABOUT THE
BEAT GENERATION
1957

THE BEAT GENERATION, that was a vision that we had, John Clellon Holmes and I, and Allen Ginsberg in an even wilder way, in the late Forties, of a generation of crazy, illuminated hipsters suddenly rising and roaming America, serious, curious, bumming and hitchhiking everywhere, ragged, beatific, beautiful in an ugly graceful new way—a vision gleaned from the way we had heard the word "beat" spoken on streetcorners on Times Square and in the Village, in other cities in the downtown city night of postwar America—beat, meaning down and out but full of intense conviction—We'd even heard old 1910 Daddy Hipsters of the streets speak the word that way, with a melancholy sneer—It never meant juvenile delinquents, it meant characters of a special spirituality who didn't gang up but were solitary Bartlebies staring out the dead wall window of our civilization—the subterraneans heroes who'd finally turned from the "freedom" machine of the West and were taking drugs, digging bop, having flashes of insight, experiencing the "derangement of the senses," talking strange, being poor and glad, prophesying a new style for American culture, a new style (we thought) completely free from European influences (unlike the Lost Generation), a new incantation—The same thing was almost going on in the postwar France of Satre and Genet and what's more we knew about it—But as to the actual existence of a Beat Generation, chances are it was really just an idea in our minds—We'd stay up 24 hours drinking cup after cup of black coffee, playing record after record of Wardell Gray, Lester Young, Dexter Gordon, Willie Jackson, Lennie Tristano and all the rest, talking madly about that holy new feeling out there in

the streets—We'd write stories about some strange beatific Negro hepcat saint with goatee hitchhiking across Iowa with taped up horn bringing the secret message of blowing to other coasts, other cities, like a
veritable Walter the Penniless leading an invisible First Crusade—We
had our mystic heroes and wrote, nay sung novels about them, erected
long poems celebrating the new "angels" of the American underground—In actuality there was only a handful of real hip swinging cats
and what there was vanished mighty swiftly during the Korean War
when (and after) a sinister new kind of efficiency appeared in America,
maybe it was the result of the universalization of Television and nothing
else (the Polite Total Police Control of Dragnet's "peace" officers) but
the beat characters after 1950 vanished into jails and madhouses, or
were shamed into silent conformity, the generation itself was shortlived
and small in number.

But there'd be no sense in writing this article if it weren't equally
true that by some miracle of metamorphosis, suddenly, the Korean postwar youth emerged cool and beat, had picked up the gestures and the
style, soon it was everywhere, the new look, the "twisted" slouchy look,
finally it began to appear even in movies (James Dean) and on television,
bop arrangements that were once the secret ecstasy music of beat con-
templatives began to appear in every pit in every square orchestral book
(cf. the works of Neil Hefti and not meaning Basie's book), the bop
visions became common property of the commercial popular cultural
world, the use of expressions like "crazy," "hungup," "hassle," "make
it," "like" ("like make it over sometime, like"), "go," became familiar
and common usage, the ingestion of drugs became official (tranquillizers
and the rest), and even the clothes style of the beat hipsters carried over
to the new Rock'n'Roll youth via Montgomery Clift (leather jacket),
Marlon Brando (T-shirt), and Elvis Presley (long sideburns), and the
Beat Generation, though dead, was suddenly resurrected and justified.

It really happened, and the sad thing is, that while I am asked to
explain the Beat Generation, there is no actual original Beat Generation
left.

Yet today from Montreal to Mexico City, from London to Casablanca kids in blue jeans are now playing Rock'n'Roll records on
jukeboxes.

As to an analysis of what it means . . . who knows? Even in this
late stage of civilization when money is the only thing that really matters, to everybody, I think perhaps it is the Second Religiousness that
Oswald Spengler prophesied for the West (in America the final home of

Faust), because there are elements of hidden religious significance in the way, for instance, that a guy like Stan Getz, the highest jazz genius of his "beat" generation, was put in jail for trying to hold up a drug store, suddenly had visions of God and repented (something gracefully Villon-esque in that story)—Or take the case of the posthumous canonization of James Dean by millions of kids—Strange talk we'd heard among the early hipsters, of "the end of the world" at the "second coming," of "stoned-out visions" and even visitations, all believing, all inspired and fervent and free of Bourgeois-Bohemian Materialism, such as P.L.'s[1] being knocked off his chair by the Angel and his vision of the books of the Fathers of the Church and of Christ crashing through Time, G.C.'s[2] visions of the devil and celestial Heralds, A.G.'s[3] visions in Harlem and elsewhere of the tearful Divine Love, W.S.B.'s[4] reception of the word that he is the One Prophet, G.S.'s[5] Buddhist visions of the vow of sal-vation, peotl visions of all the myths being true, P.W.'s[6] visions of ma-lific flashes and forms and the roof flying off the house, J.K.'s[7] numerous visions of Heaven, the "Golden Eternity," bright light in the night woods, H.H.'s[8] geekish visions of Armaggedon (experienced in Sing Sing), N.C.'s[9] visions of reincarnation under God's will [. . .] A.L.'s[10] vision of everything as mysterious electricity, and one unnamed Times Square kid's vision of the Second Coming being televised (all taking place, a definite fact, in the midst of everyday contemporary life in the minds of typical members of my generation whom I know), reappear-ances of the early Gothic Springtime feeling of Western mankind before it went on its "Civilization" Rationale and developed relativity, jets and superbombs and supercolossal bureaucratic totalitarian benevolent Big Brother structures—so, as Spengler says, when comes the sunset of our culture (due now, according to his morphological graphs) and the dust of civilized striving settles, lo, the clear late-day glow reveals the original

1. Philip Lamantia.
2. Gregory Corso.
3. Allen Ginsberg.
4. William S. Burroughs.
5. Gary Snyder.
6. Philip Whalen.
7. Jack Kerouac.
8. Herbert Huncke.
9. Neal Cassady.
10. Alene L., the African-American woman with whom Kerouac had an affair in New York City in 1953; she is called "Mardou" in *The Subterraneans*.

concerns again, reveals a beatific indifference to things that are Caesar's, for instance, a tiredness of that, and a yearning for, a regret for, the transcendent value, or "God," again, "Heaven," the spiritual regret for Endless Love which our theory of electromagnetic gravitation, our conquest of space will prove, and instead of only techniques of efficiency, all will be left, as with a population that has gone through a violent earthquake, will be the Last Things . . . again (for the fact that everybody dies makes the world kind).

We all know about the Religious Revival, Billy Graham and all, under which the Beat Generation, even the existentialists with all their intellectual overlays and pretenses of indifference, represent an even deeper religiousness, the desire to be gone, out of this world (which is not our kingdom), "high," ecstatic, saved, as if the visions of the cloistral saints of Chartres and Clairvaux were back with us again bursting like weeds through the sidewalks of stiffened Civilization wearying through its late motions.

Or maybe the Beat Generation, which is the offspring of the Lost Generation, is just another step towards that last, pale generation which will not know the answers either.

In any case, indications are that its effect has taken root in American culture.

Maybe.

Or, what difference does it make?

LAMB, NO LION
1958

THE BEAT GENERATION is no hoodlumism. As the man who suddenly thought of that word "beat" to describe our generation, I would like to have my little say about it before everyone else in the writing field begins to call it "roughneck," "violent," "heedless," "rootless." How can *people* be rootless? Heedless of what? Wants? Roughneck because you don't come on elegant?

Beat doesn't mean tired, or bushed, so much as it means *beato,* the Italian for beatific: to be in a state of beatitude, like St. Francis, trying to love all life, trying to be utterly sincere with everyone, practicing endurance, kindness, cultivating joy of heart. How can this be done in our mad modern world of multiplicities and millions? By practicing a little solitude, going off by yourself once in a while to store up that most precious of golds: the vibrations of sincerity.

Being bugged is not being beat. You may be withdrawn, but you don't have to be mean about it. Beatness is not a form of tired old criticism. It is a form of spontaneous affirmation. What kinda culture you gonna have with everybody's gray faces saying "I don't think that's quite correct"?

Let's start at the beginning. After publishing my book about the beat generation I was asked to explain beatness on TV, on radio, by people everywhere. They were all under the impression that being beat was just a lot of frantic nowhere hysteria. What are you searching for? they asked me. I answered that I was waiting for God to show his face. (Later I got a letter from a 16-year-old girl saying that was exactly what she'd been waiting for too.) They asked: How could this have anything to do with mad hepcats? I answered that even mad happy hepcats with all their kicks and chicks and hep talk were creatures of God laid out here in this infinite universe without knowing what for. And besides I have never heard more talk about God, the Last Things, the soul, the where-we-going than among the kids of my generation: and not the intellectual kids alone, *all* of them. In the faces of my questioners was the hopeless question: But Why? Billy Graham has a half million spiritual babies. This generation has many more "beat kiddies," and the relationship is close.

The Lost Generation of the 20s believed in nothing so they went their rather cynical way putting everything down. That generation forms the corpus of our authority today, and is looking with disfavor upon us, under beetling brows, at us who want to swing—in life, in art, in everything, in the confession of everything to everyone. The Lost Generation put it down; the Beat Generation is picking it all up again. The Beat Generation *believes* that there will be some justification for all the horror of life. The first of the Four Noble Truths is: All Life Is Suffering. Yet I hear them talk about how it's worth it, if you only *believed*, if you let that holy flow gush endlessly out of that secret source of living bliss.

"Man, I dig everything!" So many cats said that to me on the sidewalks of the 1940s when beatness rose like an ethereal flower out of the squalor and madness of the times. "But why?" I'd say. "You haven't got a cent, no place to sleep." Answer: "Man, you gotta stay high, that's all." Then I'd see these same characters next day all bushed and beat brooding on a bench in the park, refusing to talk to anybody, *storing* up for more belief.

And there they all were, at night, the bop musicians were on the stand blowing, the beat was great, you'd see hundreds of heads nodding in the smoky dimness, nodding to the music, "Yes, yes, yes" is what their nodding heads said, so musingly, so prettily, so *mystically*. Musicians waiting for their turn to take a solo also listened nodding, Yes. I saw a whole generation nodding yes. (I also saw the junkies nod No over their bed-edges.)

I don't think the Beat Generation is going to be a moronic band of dope addicts and hoodlums. My favorite beat buddies were all *kind,* good kids, eager, sincere ("Now lend me five minutes of your time and listen to *every word* I'm going to say!") . . . such tender concern! Such a pathetic human hope that all will be communicated and received, and all made well by this mysterious union of minds. The dope thing will die out. That was a fad, like bathtub gin. In the Beat Generation instead of an old Lost Generation champagne bottle intertwined in one silk stocking, you found an old benny tube in the closet, or an ancient roach in a dresser, all covered with dust. The dope thing was confined to a handful of medical metabolic junkies before it was given such publicity by the authorities. Then it got out of hand.

As to sex, why not? One woman interviewer asked me if I thought sexual passion was messy, I said "No, it's the gateway to paradise."

Only bitter people put down life. The Beat Generation is going to be a sweetie (as the great Pinky Lee would say, Lee who loves children, and all generations are children).

I only hope there won't be a war to hurt all these beautiful people, and I don't think there will be. There appears to be a Beat Generation all over the world, even behind the Iron Curtain. I think Russia wants a share of what America has—food and clothing and pleasantries for most everyone.

I prophesy that the Beat Generation which is supposed to be nutty nihilism in the guise of new hipness, is going to be the most sensitive generation in the history of America and therefore it can't help but do good. Whatever wrong comes will come out of evil interference. If there is any quality that I have noticed more strongly than anything else in this generation, it is the spirit of non-interference with the lives of others. I had a dream that I didn't want the lion to eat the lamb and the lion suddenly becoming the frantic Shadow going mwee hee hee ha ha in the alleys of New York imagination. To Popeye the sailor and the Sea Hag and the meaty gunwales of boats, to Cap'n Easy and Wash Tubbs screaming with ecstasy over canned peaches on a cannibal isle, to Wimpy looking X-eyed for a juicy hamburger such as they make no more. To Jiggs ducking before a household of furniture flying through the air, to Jiggs and the boys at the bar and the corned beef and cabbage of old woodfence noons—to King Kong his eyes looking into the hotel window with tender huge love for Fay Wray—nay, to Bruce Cabot in mate's cap leaning over the rail of a fogbound ship saying "Come aboard." It goes back to when grapefruits were thrown at crooners and harvestworkers at bar-rails slapped burlesque queens on the rump. To when fathers took their sons to the Twi League game. To the days of Babe Callahan on the waterfront, Dick Barthelmess camping under a London streetlamp. To dear old Basil Rathbone looking for the Hound of the Baskervilles (a dog big as the Grey Wolf who will destroy Odin)—to dear old bleary Doctor Watson with a brandy in his hand. To Joan Crawford her raw shanks in the fog, in striped blouse smoking a cigarette at sticky lips in the door of the waterfront dive. To train whistles of steam engines out above the moony pines. To Maw and Paw in the Model A clanking on to get a job in California selling used cars making a whole lotta money. To the glee of America, the honesty of America, the honesty of oldtime grafters in straw hats as well as the honesty of oldtime waiters in line at the Brooklyn Bridge in *Winterset*, the funny spitelessness of old bigfisted America like Big Boy Williams saying "Hoo? Hee? Huh?" in a movie about Mack Trucks and sliding-door lunchcarts. To Clark Gable, his certain smile, his confident leer. Like my grandfather this America was invested with wild selfbelieving individuality and this had begun to disappear around the end of World War II with so many great guys dead (I can think of half a dozen from my own boyhood groups) when suddenly it began to emerge again, the hipsters began to appear gliding around saying "Crazy, man."

When I first saw the hipsters creeping around Times Square in 1944 I didn't like them either. One of them, Huncke of Chicago, came up to me and said "Man, I'm beat." I knew right away what he meant somehow. At that time I still didn't like bop which was then being introduced by Bird Parker and Dizzy Gillespie and Bags Jackson (on vibes), the last of the great swing musicians was Don Byas who went to Spain right after, but then I began . . . but earlier I'd dug all my jazz in the old Clinton Playhouse (Lester Young, Ben Webster, Joey Guy, Charlie

came up and lapped my face like a big puppy dog and then I picked up the lamb and it kissed me. This is the dream of the Beat Generation.

BEATIFIC:
THE ORIGINS OF
THE BEAT GENERATION
1959

THIS ARTICLE necessarily'll have to be about myself. I'm going all out.

That nutty picture of me on the cover of *On the Road* results from the fact that I had just gotten down from a high mountain where I'd been for two months completely alone and usually I was in the habit of combing my hair of course because you have to get rides on the highway and all that and you usually want girls to look at you as though you were a man and not a wild beast but my poet friend Gregory Corso opened his shirt and took out a silver crucifix that was hanging from a chain and said "Wear this and wear it outside your shirt and don't comb your hair!" so I spent several days around San Francisco going around with him and others like that, to parties, arties, parts, jam sessions, bars, poetry readings, churches, walking talking poetry in the streets, walking talking God in the streets (and at one point a strange gang of hoodlums got mad and said "What right does he got to wear that?" and my own gang of musicians and poets told them to cool it) and finally on the third day *Mademoiselle* magazine wanted to take pictures of us all so I posed just like that, wild hair, crucifix, and all, with Gregory Corso, Allen Ginsberg and Phil Whalen, and the only publication which later did not erase the crucifix from my breast (from that plaid sleeveless cotton shirt-front) was *The New York Times*, therefore *The New York Times* is as beat as I am, and I'm glad I've got a friend. I mean it sincerely, God bless *The New York Times* for not erasing the crucifix from my picture as though it was something distasteful. As a matter of fact, who's *really* beat around here, I mean if you wanta talk of Beat as "beat down" the people who erased the crucifix are really the "beat down" ones and not *The New York Times*, myself, and Gregory Corso the poet. I am not ashamed to wear the crucifix of my Lord. It is because I am Beat, that is, I believe in beatitude and that God so loved the world that he gave his only begotten son to it. I am sure no priest would've condemned me for wearing the crucifix outside my shirt everywhere and *no matter where* I went, even to have my picture taken by *Mademoiselle*. So you people don't believe in God. So you're all big smart know-it-all Marxists and Freudians, hey? Why don't you come back in a million years and tell me all about it, angels?

Recently Ben Hecht said to me on TV "Why are you afraid to speak out your mind, what's wrong with this country, what is everybody afraid of?" Was he talking to me? And all he wanted me to do was speak out my mind *against* people, he sneeringly brought up Dulles, Eisenhower, the Pope, all kinds of people like that habitually he would sneer at with Drew Pearson, *against* the world he wanted, this is his idea of freedom, he calls it freedom. Who knows, my God, but that the universe is not one vast sea of compassion actually, the veritable holy honey, beneath all this show of personality and cruelty. In fact who knows but that it isn't the solitude of the oneness of the essence of everything, the solitude of the actual oneness of the unbornness of the unborn essence of everything, nay the true pure foreverhood, that big blank potential that can ray forth anything it wants from its pure store, that blazing bliss, *Mattivajrakaruna* the Transcendental Diamond Compassion! No, I want to speak *for* things, for the crucifix I speak out, for the Star of Israel I speak out, for the divinest man who ever lived who was a German (Bach) I speak out, for sweet Mohammed I speak out, for Buddha I speak out, for Lao-tse and Chuang-tse I speak out, for D.T. Suzuki I speak out . . . why should I attack what I love out of life. This is Beat. Live your lives out? Naw, *love* your lives out. When they come and stone you at least you won't have a glass house, just your glassy flesh.

That wild eager picture of me on the cover of *On the Road* where I look so Beat goes back much further than 1948 when John Clellon Holmes (author of *Go* and *The Horn*) and I were sitting around trying to think up the meaning of the Lost Generation and the subsequent Existentialism and I said "You know, this is really a beat generation" and he leapt up and said "That's it, that's right!" It goes back to the 1880s when my grandfather Jean-Baptiste Kerouac used to go out on the porch in big thunderstorms and swing his kerosene lamp at the lightning and yell "Go ahead, go, if you're more powerful than I am strike me and put the light out!" while the mother and the children

cowered in the kitchen. And the light never went out. Maybe since I'm supposed to be the spokesman of the Beat Generation (I *am* the originator of the term, and around it the term and the generation have taken shape) it should be pointed out that all this "Beat" guts therefore goes back to my ancestors who were Bretons who were the most independent group of nobles in all old Europe and kept fighting Latin France to the last wall (although a big blond bosun on a merchant ship snorted when I told him my ancestors were Bretons in Cornwall, Brittany, "Why, we Wikings used to swoop down and steal your nets!") Breton, Wiking, Irishman, Indian, madboy, it doesn't make any difference, there is no doubt about the Beat Generation, at least the core of it, being a swinging group of new American men intent on joy . . . Irresponsibility? Who wouldn't help a dying man on an empty road? No and the Beat Generation goes back to the wild parties my father used to have at home in the 1920s and 1930s in New England that were so fantastically loud nobody could sleep for blocks around and when the cops came they always had a drink. It goes back to the wild and raving childhood of playing the Shadow under windswept trees of New England's gleeful autumn, and the howl of the Moon Man on the sandbank until we caught him in a tree (he was an "older" guy of 15), the maniacal laugh of certain neighborhood madboys, the furious humor of whole gangs playing basketball till long after dark in the park, it goes back to those crazy days before World War II when teenagers drank beer on Friday nights at Lake ballrooms and worked off their hangovers playing baseball on Saturday afternoon followed by a dive in the brook—and our fathers wore straw hats like W.C. Fields. It goes back to the completely senseless babble of the Three Stooges, the ravings of the Marx Brothers (the tenderness of Angel Harpo at harp, too).

It goes back to the inky ditties of old cartoons (Krazy Kat with the irrational brick)—to Laurel and Hardy in the Foreign Legion—to Count Dracula and his *smile* to Count Dracula shivering and hissing back before the Cross—to the Golem horrifying the persecutors of the Ghetto—to the quiet sage in a movie about India, unconcerned about the plot—to the giggling old Tao Chinaman trotting down the sidewalk of old Clark Gable Shanghai—to the holy old Arab warning the bloods that Ramadan is near. To the Werewolf of London a distinguished doctor in his velour smoking jacket smoking his pipe over a lamplit tome on botany and suddenly hairs grown on his hands, his face, he hisses, and he slips out into the night with a cape and a slanty hat over the caps of people in breadlines—to Lamont Cranston so cool and

Christian, others) and when I first heard Bird and Diz in the Three Deuces I knew they were serious musicians playing a goofy new sound and didn't care what I thought, or what my friend Seymour thought. In fact I was leaning against the bar with a beer when Dizzy came over for a glass of water from the bartender, put himself right against me and reached both arms around both sides of my head to get the glass and danced away, as though knowing I'd be singing about him someday, or that one of his arrangements would be named after me someday by some goofy circumstance. Charlie Parker was spoken of in Harlem as the greatest new musician since Chu Berry and Louis Armstrong.

Anyway, the hipsters, whose music was bop, they looked like criminals but they kept talking about the same things I liked, long outlines of personal experience and vision, nightlong confessions full of hope that had become illicit and repressed by War, stirrings, rumblings of a new soul (that same old human soul). And so Huncke appeared to us and said "I'm beat" with radiant light shining out of his despairing eyes . . . a word perhaps brought from some midwest carnival or junk cafeteria. It was a new language, actually spade (Negro) jargon but you soon learned it, like "hung-up" couldn't be a more economical term to mean so many things. Some of these hipsters were raving mad and talked continually. It was jazzy. Symphony Sid's all-night modern jazz and bop show was always on. By 1948 it began to take shape. That was a wild vibrating year when a group of us would walk down the street and yell hello and even stop and talk to anybody that gave us a friendly look. The hipsters had eyes. That was the year I saw Montgomery Clift, unshaven, wearing a sloppy jacket, slouching down Madison Avenue with a companion. It was the year I saw Charley Bird Parker strolling down Eighth Avenue in a black turtleneck sweater with Babs Gonzales and a beautiful girl.

By 1948 the hipsters, or beatsters, were divided into cool and hot. Much of the misunderstanding about hipsters and the Beat Generation in general today derives from the fact that there are two distinct styles of hipsterism: the cool today is your bearded laconic sage, or schlerm, before a hardly touched beer in a beatnik dive, whose speech is low and unfriendly, whose girls say nothing and wear black: the "hot" today is the crazy talkative shining eyed (often innocent and openhearted) nut who runs from bar to bar, pad to pad looking for everybody, shouting, restless, lushy, trying to "make it" with the subterranean beatniks who ignore him. Most Beat Generation artists belong to the hot school, naturally since that hard gemlike flame needs a little heat. In many cases the mixture is 50-50. It was a hot hipster like myself who finally cooled it in Buddhist meditation, though when I go in a jazz joint I still feel like yelling "Blow baby blow!" to the musicians though nowadays I'd get 86d for this. In 1948 the "hot hipsters" were racing around in cars like in *On the Road* looking for wild bawling jazz like Willis Jackson or Lucky Thompson (the early) or Chubby Jackson's big band while the "cool hipsters" cooled it in dead silence before formal and excellent musical groups like Lennie Tristano or Miles Davis. It's still just about the same, except that it has begun to grow into a national generation and the name "Beat" has stuck (though all hipsters hate the word).

The word "beat" originally meant poor, down and out, deadbeat, on the bum, sad, sleeping in subways. Now that the word is belonging officially it is being made to stretch to include people who do not sleep in subways but have a certain new gesture, or attitude, which I can only describe as a new *more.* "Beat Generation" has simply become the slogan or label for a revolution in manners in America. Marlon Brando was not really first to portray it on the screen. Dane Clark with his pinched Dostoievskyan face and Brooklyn accent, and of course Garfield, were first. The private eyes were Beat, if you will recall. Bogart. Lorre was Beat. In *M*, Peter Lorre started a whole revival, I mean the slouchy street walk.

I wrote *On the Road* in three weeks in the beautiful month of April 1951 while living in the Chelsea district of lower West Side Manhattan, on a 100-foot roll and put the Beat Generation in words in there, saying at the point where I am taking part in a wild kind of collegiate party with a bunch of kids in an abandoned miner's shack "These kids are great but where are Dean Moriarty and Carlo Marx? Oh well I guess they wouldn't belong in this gang, they're too *dark,* too strange, too subterranean and I am slowly beginning to join a new kind of *beat* generation." The manuscript of *Road* was turned down on the grounds that it would displease the sales manager of my publisher at that time, though the editor, a very intelligent man, said "Jack this is just like Dostoyevsky, but what can I do at this time?" It was too early. So for the next six years I was a bum, a brakeman, a seaman, a panhandler, a pseudo-Indian in Mexico, anything and everything, and went on writing because my hero was Goethe and I believed in art and hoped some day to write the third part of *Faust,* which I have done in *Doctor Sax.* Then in 1952 an article was published in *The New York Times* Sunday magazine saying, the headline, " 'This is a Beat Generation' " (in quotes like that) and in the article it said that I had come up with the term first "when the face was harder to recognize," the face of the generation. After that there was some talk of the Beat Generation but in 1955 I published an excerpt from *Road* (melling it with parts of *Visions of Neal*) under the pseudonym "Jean-Louis," it was entitled *Jazz of the Beat Generation* and was copyright as being an excerpt from a novel-in-progress entitled *Beat Generation* (which I later changed to *On the Road* at the insistence of my new editor) and so then the term moved a little faster. The term and the cats. Everywhere began to appear strange hepcats and even college kids went around hep and cool and using the terms I'd heard on Times Square in the early Forties, it was growing somehow. But when the publishers finally took a dare and published *On the Road* in 1957 it burst open, it mushroomed, everybody began yelling about a Beat Generation. I was being interviewed everywhere I went for "what I meant" by such a thing. People began to call themselves beatniks, beats, jazzniks, bopniks, bugniks and finally I was called the "avatar" of all this.

Yet it was as a Catholic, it was not at the insistence of any of these "niks" and certainly not with their approval either, that I went one afternoon to the church of my childhood (one of them), Ste. Jeanne d'Arc in Lowell, Mass., and suddenly with tears in my eyes and had a vision of what I must have really meant with "Beat" anyhow when I heard the holy silence in the church (I was the only one in there, it was five p.m., dogs were barking outside, children yelling, the fall leaves, the candles were flickering alone just for me), the vision of the word Beat as being to mean beatific . . . There's the priest preaching on Sunday morning, all of a sudden through a side door of the church comes a group of Beat Generation characters in strapped raincoats like the I.R.A. coming in silently to "dig" the religion . . . I knew it then.

But this was 1954, so then what horror I felt in 1957 and later 1958 naturally to suddenly see "Beat" being taken up by everybody, press and TV and Hollywood borscht circuit to include the "juvenile delinquency" shot and the horrors of a mad teeming billyclub New York and L.A. and they began to call *that* Beat, *that* beatific . . . bunch of fools marching against the San Francisco Giants protesting baseball, as if (now) in my name and I, my childhood ambition to be a big league baseball star hitter like Ted Williams so that when Bobby Thomson hit that homerun in 1951 I trembled with joy and couldn't get over it for days and wrote poems about how it is possible for the human spirit to win after all! Or, when a murder, a routine murder took place in North Beach, they labeled it a Beat Generation slaying although in my childhood I'd been famous as an eccentric in my block for stopping the younger kids from throwing rocks at the squirrels, for stopping them from frying snakes in cans or trying to blow up frogs with straws. Because my brother had died at the age of nine, his name was Gerard Kerouac, and he'd told me "Ti Jean never hurt any living being, all living beings whether it's just a little cat or squirrel or whatever, all, are going to heaven straight into God's snowy arms so never hurt anything and if you see anybody hurt anything stop them as best you can" and when he died a file of gloomy nuns in black from St. Louis de France parish had filed (1926) to his deathbed to hear his last words about Heaven. And my father too, Leo, had never lifted a hand to punish me, or to punish the little pets in our house, and this teaching was delivered to me by the men in my house and I have never had anything to do with violence, hatred, cruelty, and all that horrible nonsense which, nevertheless, because God is gracious beyond all human imagining, he will forgive in the long end . . . that million years I'm asking about you, America.

And so now they have beatnik routines on TV, starting with satires about girls in black and fellows in jeans with snap-knives and sweat-shirts and swastikas tattooed under their armpits, it will come to respectable m.c.s of spectaculars coming out nattily attired in Brooks Brothers jean-type tailoring and sweater-type pull-ons, in other words, it's a simple change in fashion and manners, just a history crust—like from the Age of Reason, from old Voltaire in a chair to romantic Chatterton in the moonlight—from Teddy Roosevelt to Scott Fitzgerald . . . So there's nothing to get excited about. Beat comes out, actually, of old American whoopee and it will only change a few dresses and pants and make chairs useless in the livingroom and pretty soon we'll have Beat Secretaries of State and there will be instituted new tinsels, in fact new reasons for malice and new reasons for virtue and new reasons for forgiveness . . .

But yet, but yet, woe, woe unto those who think that the Beat Generation means crime, delinquency, immorality, amorality . . . woe unto those who attack it on the grounds that they simply don't understand history and the yearnings of human souls . . . woe unto those who don't realize that America must, will, is, changing now, for the better I say. Woe unto those who believe in the atom bomb, who believe in hating mothers and fathers, who deny the most important of the Ten Commandments, woe unto those (though) who don't believe in the unbelievable sweetness of sex love, woe unto those who are the standard bearers of death, woe unto those who believe in conflict and horror and violence and fill our books and screens and livingrooms with all that crap, woe in fact unto those who make evil movies about the Beat Generation where innocent housewives are raped by beatniks! Woe unto those who are the real dreary sinners that even God finds room to forgive . . . woe unto those who spit on the Beat Generation, the wind'll blow it back.

AFTER ME,
THE DELUGE
1969

WHAT AM I THINKING ABOUT? I'm trying to figure out where I am between the established politicians and the radicals, between cops and hoods, tax collectors and vandals.

I'm not a Tax-Free, not a Hippie-Yippie—I must be a Bippie-in-the-Middle.

No, I'd better go around and tell everybody, or let others convince me, that I'm the great white father and intellectual forebear who spawned a deluge of alienated radicals, war protestors, dropouts, hippies and even "beats," and thereby I can make some money maybe and a "new Now-image" for myself (and God forbid I dare call myself the intellectual forebear of modern spontaneous prose), but I've got to figure out first how I could possibly spawn Jerry Rubin, Mitchell Goodman, Abbie Hoffman, Allen Ginsberg and other warm human beings from the ghettos who say they suffered no less than the Puerto Ricans in their barrios and the blacks in their Big and Little Harlems, and all because I wrote a matter-of-fact account of a true adventure on the road (hardly an agitational propaganda account) featuring an ex-cowhand and an ex-footballer driving across the continent north, northwest, midwest and southland looking for lost fathers, odd jobs, good times, and girls and winding up on the railroad. Yup, I'd better convince myself that these thinkers were not on an entirely different road.

But now, where will I turn? Oh, I know, I'll go to the "top echelons" of American Society, all sleeked up, and try to forget the ships' crews of World War II who grew beards and long haircuts till a mission was finished, or the "disheveled aspect" of G.I. Joe in the foxholes, yair, the "slovenly appearance" of men and women in 1930's breadlines, and understand that appearance *does* make the man, just like clothes, and go rushing to a Politico fund-raising dinner. House Appropriations Chairmen, assistants, Health Directors, Commission Chairmen, assistants, Assistants to the Director of Regional Planning, Neighborhood Center Directors, Executive Presidents of Banks, Chairmen of Interior Subcommittees, Officials of the Department of Rehabilitative Services, Planners of the Preliminary Regional Plan, ethical Members of Rules Committees, House Insurance Committees, Utilities Commission entrepreneurs, Expressway Authority Directors, county news hacks, spokesmen, pleaders, applauders, aides and wives in organdy, $2500 worth of food and $5000 worth of booze and the caterer's cut thrown in, for one "lunch," tax-exempt, televised for a 15-second spot on the evening news to show how well they can put on the dog. At your expense. Here every handshake, every smile, every gibberous applause is shiny hypocrisy, is political lust and concupiscence, a ninny's bray of melody backed by a ghastly neurological drone of money-grub accompanied by the anvil chorus of garbage can covers being banged over half-eaten filet mignons which don't even get to the dogs, let alone hungry children of the absent "constituency."

I'll try to forget that the Hippie Flower Children out in the park with their peanut butter sandwiches and their live-and-let-live philosophy nevertheless are not too proud of being robbed of their simplified attempt at primitive dignity, but the banquet guests are proud, proud.

The banquet guests, the Politicos and their grinnish entourage in glistering suits and dresses, paper-shufflers all, plutocrats *salient* with hind paws and forepaws together, last night's *nouveau riche*, would be even prouder if they could get the "non-productive parasite Hippies" to get to work digging new roads and cooking and washing dishes at these fund-raising galas so the dirty punks could at least make cash contributions, or, at best, pay taxes to enable the paper-shufflers to order more paper and copying machines with which they now *rampant* could form a further "planning" committee (of three-year duration, on pollution, sex, think of anything dirty) while sitting back and admiring the view of their back lawn where all the trees that only God can make have been cut down along with the birds' nests.

No, I think I'll go back to the alienated radicals who are quite understandably alienated, nay disgusted by this scene, but I'll have to try to overlook the fact that the "alienated" radicals and activist Yippies and SDS'ers who pretended holily inside the Hippie Flower Movement of a few years ago till their colors withdrew into the basal portions of the chromatophores like the dwarf lizard's have no better plan to offer the grief-stricken American citizenry but fund-raising dinners of their own, and if not for the same reasons, I'd better forget I'd be willing to bet for worse reasons.

Because so what if these brand new alienated radical chillun of Kropotkin and Bakunin don't believe in Western-style capitalism, private property, simple privacy even of individuals or families, for instance, or in Jesus or any cluster of reasons for honesty; or in education of course, that is, the bigotry of classic historical scholarship which enables one to know one, the better to see what other ambitious vandals and liars did before; or don't believe in government wrenched away by any others but themselves? Ah, so what if they don't even believe in the written word which is the only way to keep the record straight?

Really, so *what's new* if they would like to see to it that under Timothy Leary's guiding proselytization no one in America could address a simple envelope or keep a household budget or a checkbook balanced or for that matter legible? In fact wouldn't it be better if nobody at all could count change any more and of course forget how to read any kind of book, newspaper or document, the P.O.B.'s (The Print-Oriented-Bastards!), and stick to the psychedelic multi-media nude "Commune" dance at retardate happenings inside of giant plastic balloons, the better to cart the *branle-cul* fools off to camps when used? (Documented as insane, of course).

In fact, who cares, shucks, Toronto, that if Marshall McLuhan had wanted to be the biggest barbarianizing influence in the globe he couldn't have come up with a better idea (even if you can't go to the toilet nowadays without having an affidavit on it) than that linear reasonableness of the printed word is out, and the jiggling behinds in back of placards are in? (Electronic All-Now mosaic dots on said behinds somewhat suspect).

Of course the alienated radicals, the would-be fund-raisers of the Peking-oriented Castro-jacketed New Left who hate be-necktied plutocrats so much because clothes don't make the man, themselves won't take LSD or STP acid (which stupefy the mind and hand for weeks on end) but will keep perfect records of their own, even incorporate tax-exempt Libertarian Foundations for vocal poets who are really agitational propagandists, why, the alienated radicals, they'll be exuding transactions maybe with the help of a relative who's a lawyer. Their anarchism extends just so far, after all. The relative wants to be a commissar too, hey. No sense starting trouble unless you get a "top job" straightening it out. Commissar of Chaos, say.

Addresses anyone? Red China's international propaganda and subversive apparatus is the Teh Wu (do-thus) section of Peking's overall Hai-Wai-Tiao-Cha-Pu espionage organization.

Russia: The Kremlin's KGB (State Security Committee) at 19 Stanislavskaya St. opposite the East German Embassy in Moscow.

Vietcong: propaganda headquarters near the late Ho Chi Minh's French mansion in center of Hanoi. This leaves everybody "poor peasants" except the bastard Party cadres who figured it all out, even if they have to compromise a little with the "bourgeois" now, although I wish I could tell them that the only bourgeois I ever knew was Paul Bourgeois, a rough-and-tumble French-Canadian Indian high-steel worker on bridges who would tell them to go jump in the Lake of St. Louis de Ha Ha.

O New World!—Yay, if joy were proponent of coin, what grand economy. It's much like: what do you think a parasite is thinking when he's sucking on the belly of a whale or the back of a shark? "Where did this big stupid brute get all that blood, not being a parasite like me? How come he's so strong and free, not knowing how to live like I do?" So with human parasites feeding on their juicy national, personal, political, or racial host.

So who cares anyhow that if it hadn't been for Western-style capitalism so-called (nothing to do with the black market capitalism in jeeps and rice in Asia), or Laissez-Faire, free economic byplay, movement north south east and west, haggling, pricing, and the political balance of power carved into the U.S. Constitution and active thus far in the history of our government, and my perfectly recorded and legitimatized U.S. Coast Guard papers, just as one instance of arch (non-anarchic) credibility in our proveable system, I wouldn't have been able or allowed to hitchhike half broke through 47 states of this union and see the scene with my own eyes, unmolested? Who cares, Walt Whitman?

But now, I'll have to switch and become a "war protestor" and stick to my guns and try to insult the Military-Industrial Complex for safeguarding our offensive weapons inside of an electronic armory instead of leaving them out in the rain. I'll try to forget old armory raids. Maybe Jerome Weisner of M.I.T. already does. At least I can always yell "ABM system too expensive!" but who'm I going to blame, Military

Industrial Complex? or Industrial Military Complex? or Industrial Civilian Military Labor Academic Complex? or . . . or maybe, yippee! no national right at all to be granted to the United States to defend itself against its own perimeter of enemies in its own bigger scale, that's best. Advised by the pacifists who faced Genghis Khan. By international pacifist demonstrators who now face further demonstrations by Chairman Mao's IBM warheads.

Or I can always try to see aggression by the U.S. in Vietnam as different from other armies' "defensive ripostes" and "counterfoils" and the good old brisk reply to "blind hatred": a "lesson" not an attack.

I'll try to see the difference between bombing of "civilians" in one town and bombing of "women and children" in another and "reprisals" instead of raids, and, elsewhere on our map, rocket "warnings" on the very ricepot rooftops of Saigon and Hue by the Viet Cong and brutal U.S. Imperialist bombings of Ho Chi Minh trail and rails round Hanoi. Then I'll get a Ph.D. in the distinguishing of this ideological difference, become expert, disinterested, warm, the diploma being mailed to me by General David Dellinger in Hanoi as a sign I should be grateful and I've done my duty and the word is out I need never be ashamed of myself again, because I'm one of the "kids" who's been out there just like them "doughboys in the trenches Over There," like "our boys in the war effort," yes, "one of the kids down there in the Park" in Chicago 1968 as seen from a quiet thirdfloor suite by Martini-mitted Protest Leaders who look pretty shipshape and pretty presentable as generals go (although I still think I look silly with that billyclub sticking out of my ear which is also smeared with a bag of you-know-what).

Warm human beings everywhere. In Flanders Field they're piled ten high.

The Mekong, it's just a long, soft river.

I'll do this, I'll do that—

You can't fight City Hall, it keeps changing its name—

Ah Phooey on 'em—you pays your taxes and you passes to your grave, why study their "matters"? Let them present their problematical matters before the zoning board, or present complaint six on matters before the kidnapped Dean (problem planning committees for planning problem solutions) 'cause "I've got," as Neal Cassady said, "my own lil old bangtail mind."

I think I'll drop out—Great American tradition—Dan'l Boone, U.S. Grant, Mark Twain—I think I'll go to sleep and suddenly in my deepest inadequacy nightmares wake up haunted and see everyone in the world as unconsolable orphans yelling and screaming on every side to make arrangements for making a living yet all bespattered and gloomed-up in the nightsoil of poor body and soul all present and accounted for as some kind of sneakish, craft gift, and all so *lonered.*

Martin Heidegger says, "Why are there existing essential things, instead of nothing?" Founder of Existentialism, never mind your Sartre, and also said: "And there is no philosophy without this doozie as a starter." Ever look closely at *anybody* and see that particularized patience all their own, eyes hid, waiting with lips sewn down for time to pass, for something to lift them up, for their yesterday's daily perseverance to succeed, for the long night of life to take them in its arms and say, "Ah, Cherubim, this silly stupid business . . . What *is* it, existence."

A lifelong struggle to avoid disaster. Idiot PTA's and gurus call it Cre-a-tive? Politics, gambling, hard work, drinking, patriotism, protest, pooh-poohings, all therapeutic shifts against the black void. To make you forget it really isn't there, nor you anywhere.

It's like saying, if there are no elephants in the room, then you can safely say the room is empty of elephants. Ah, your immemorial golden ashes shall seem to be scattered anywhere in Paradise.

All caught in the middle.

Ah! I know what I'll do, I'll be like Andy Capp the British comic strip character and go to the rub-a-dub-dub for a bout-a-doubt (Cockney lingo for "pub" and "stout"). After all, doubt parades a lout. And I'll yell "WHAT I NEED IS LESS PEOPLE TELLIN' ME WHAT I NEED!" (Copyright 1969 by Smythe).

So I'll be "generous with the liberality of poets, which is conservative to the bone." (Copyright 1969 by Donald Phelps).

"No cede malis" (cede not to malfortune) (don't give in to bad times). (Copyright 130 A.D. by Juvenal).

Some deluge.

ON BUDDHISM

EDITOR'S INTRODUCTION

DESPITE HIS CATHOLIC BACKGROUND, Kerouac read widely in Buddhist literature with a sense of self-recognition. He was profoundly in agreement with the First Noble Truth of the Buddha's teaching, that all life is suffering. He found the practice of Buddhism more difficult to accept than the teaching—not only the regular meditation practice or "sitting," which he found unbearably painful because of his tendency toward thrombophlebitis, but also the Buddhist dictim to live in the here and now, moment after moment. Sharing a house with his mother, an ardent Catholic who kept a religious medal fastened to her apron with a safety pin, Kerouac had to fend off her steady resistance to his practice of Buddhism at home.

Early in 1954 Kerouac began reading Buddhist literature and practicing meditation on his own without a formal teacher. He began writing about Buddhism a short time later, first copying texts out of books from the public library for his own personal use and for Allen Ginsberg, whom he encouraged to study Buddhism. In this early period of Kerouac's involvement with Buddhism, he tried to live what he called a "Modified Ascetic Life," outlining a strenuous regime for himself of disciplined activities for the next fifteen years: "No chasing after women anymore. No more drunkenness or alcohol, no more 'sipping.' No more rich or/and expensive foods—elementary diet of salt pork, beans, bread, greens, peanuts, figs, coffee & later grow everything and pick acorns, pinyon nuts, cacti fruit myself. . . . Finally no more writing or I art-ego of any kind, finally no I-self, or Name. . . ." He found these ideals impossible to realize.

For the next two years Kerouac was intensely absorbed in his studies, compiling his reading notes into what he called "an endlessly continuing notebook . . . reports on dhyanas and samadhis and all kinds of Buddhist poems and notes and outcries"; he titled this notebook *Buddha Tells Us* or *Some of the Dharma*. In 1955 he told his literary agent, Sterling Lord, that he planned to translate Tibetan manuscripts from the French, and he completed his own version of a biography of Shakyamuni Buddha, the founder of Buddhism, titled *Wake Up*. Finally, encouraged by Gary Snyder in the spring of 1956, he attempted an entirely original Buddhist work of his own, *The Scripture of the Golden Eternity*.

In 1959—the year after Kerouac published *The Dharma Bums*, a book dramatizing his adventures on the West Coast with Ginsberg, Snyder, and other poets he called "Zen Lunatics"—his writing was criticized by Alan Watts, an authority on Buddhism, who said that his work was "always a shade too self-conscious, too subjective, and too strident to have the flavor of Zen." Many of Kerouac's books after 1954 contain references to Buddhist terms and doctrines, particularly *Mexico City Blues, Visions of Gerard,* and *The Dharma Bums*. Although he developed his practice of spontaneous prose before he discovered his interest in Buddhism, Zen doctrine emphasizing spontaneity and the natural flow of the mind was particularly congenial to him.

Near the end of Kerouac's life he tried to clarify the effects of his Buddhist studies on his writing for Ted Berrigan and Aram Saroyan, who interviewed him for the *Paris Review*. Kerouac said that

> what's really influenced my work is the Mahayana Buddhism, the original Buddhism of Gotama Sakyamuni, the Buddha himself of the India of old. . . . Zen is what's left of his Buddhism, or Bodhi, after its passing into China and then into Japan. The part of Zen that's influenced my writing is the Zen contained in the haiku. . . . But my serious Buddhism, that of ancient India, has influenced that part in my writing that you might call religious, or fervent, or pious, almost as much as Catholicism has. Original Buddhism referred to continual conscious compassion, brotherhood, the dana paramita meaning the perfection of charity.

As the critic Beongcheon Yu understood, Kerouac found an essential affinity between Buddhism and Catholicism in their similar views of life as pain and suffering and in their teachings of charity and compassion. Yet Kerouac was also ambivalent about his involvement in Buddhism. In *Big Sur* (1962) he saw an image of the Cross, not Avalokitesvara, the Buddhist diety of mercy, during his emotional breakdown at Bixby Canyon; in *Satori in Paris* (1966), he wrote "But I'm not a Buddhist, I'm a Catholic—revisiting the ancestral land that fought for Catholicism against impossible odds yet won in the end."

Perhaps the best introduction to Kerouac's involvement with Buddhism is his essay beginning "Because none of us want to think that the universe is a blank dream," which was published as his "Last Word" column in *Escapade* magazine in October 1959. Kerouac had written two other columns for the magazine that year (one on sports and the other an early version of his essay that begins "My position in the current American literary scene") before turning to Buddhism as a subject. In the article he referred to his first encounter with the Four Noble Truths as propounded by Buddha, which he read in a library after sitting "in my lonely November room" in 1953, a month after writing *The Subterraneans,* still trying to get over the breakup of the love affair described in that book.

The selection of dreams from Kerouac's *Book of Dreams* suggests his ambivalence toward Buddhism. He recorded the dreams in that book during the years 1952–1960, during which time his nighttime fantasies included about two dozen "Oriental" and Buddhist references.

The excerpts from *The Scripture of the Golden Eternity* comprise a sample of Kerouac's most inspired writing about Buddhism. As the historian Rick Fields recognized, the sixty-six verse paragraphs of the text are a remarkable achievement, "one of the most successful attempts yet to catch emptiness, nonattainment and egolessness in the net of American poetic language." Written during the contented weeks that Kerouac shared a Mill Valley cabin with Gary Snyder, *The Scripture* expresses Kerouac's mind at rest, at once both playful and enlightened, effortlessly weaving Catholic images and Buddhist concepts into the seamless cloth of his own spiritual experience. As he wrote in section 22, "A Hummingbird/can come into a house and a hawk will not; so rest/and be assured. While looking for the light, you/may suddenly be devoured by the darkness/and find the true light."

THE LAST WORD
October 1959

BECAUSE NONE OF US want to think that the universe is a blank dream
on account of our minds so we want *belief* and plenty names, we want
lists of laws and a little bit of harrumph shouldersback separation from
the faceless UGH of True Heaven, I see men now standing erect in
bleaky fields waving earnest hands to explain, yet ghosts, pure naught
ghosts—And even the great Chinese who've known so much for so long,
will paint delicately on silk the Truth Cloud upper skies that lead off
over rose-hump unbelievable mountains and crunchy trees, indefinable
waterfalls of white, then the earthbound scraggle tree twisted to a rock,
then, because Human Chinese, the little tiny figures of men on horseback lost in all that, usually leaving 8/10ths of the upper silk to scan
th'unscannable Void—So I was wiser when I was younger after a bad
love affair and sat in my lonely November room thinking: "It's all a big
crrrock, I wanta die," and thinking: "The dead man's lips are pressed
tasting death, as bitter as dry musk, but he might as well be tasting
saccharine for all he knows," yet these thoughts didn't stand up to the
Four Noble Truths as propounded by Buddha and which I memorized
under a streetlamp in the cold wind of night:

(1) All Life is Sorrowful
(2) The Cause of Suffering is Ignorant Desire
(3) The Suppression of Suffering Can Be Achieved
(4) The Way is the Noble Eightfold Path (which you might as well say
     is just as explicit in Bach's Goldberg variations.)

Not knowing it could just as well be:

(1) All Life is Joy
(2) The Cause of Joy is Enlightened Desire
(3) The Expansion of Joy Can Be Achieved
(4) The Way is the Noble Eightfold Path

since what's the difference, in supreme reality, we are neither subject to suffering nor joy—Why not?—Because who says?

But it was Asvaghosha's incomparable phrase that hooked me on the true morphine of Buddha: "REPOSE BEYOND FATE"—because since life is nothing but a short vague dream encompassed round by flesh and tears, and the ways of men are the ways of death (if not now, eventually, you'll see), the ways of beautiful women such as those pictured in this magazine are eventually the ways of old age, and since nothing we do seems to go right in the end, goes sour, but no more sour than what Nature intends in need of sour fertilizer for continuers and continuees, "repose beyond fate" meant "rest beyond what happens to you," "give it up, sit, forget it, stop thinking," YOUR OWN PRIVATE MIND IS GREATER THAN ALL—So that my first meditation was a tremendous sensation of "When did I do this last?" (it seemed so natural so right) "Why didn't I do it before?"—And all things vanished, what was left was the United Stuff out of which all things appeared to be made of without being made into anything really, all things I then saw as unsubstantial trickery of the mind, furthermore it was already long gone out of sight, the liquid waterball earth a speck in sizeless spaces but O then—

But it *is* a bleary blank, how foreign to our sweet hopeful (some of us) natures are the blind worms that'll eat our beloved vitals, beloved hands, holy noses, remembered jaws, the flesh on us which burns before eyes in 70 years burns slow burn, just as impersonal as if a hydrogen bomb should blow up the whole earth in a second to scarring fireball as prophesied aplenty—That's why when I recently bent my lips to my beloved's neck it seemed ephemeral to think "Is it *her* neck? her real me-neck, my-neck?" because it isn't anybody's neck at all because nothing's there but imaginary concatenation of mind—So O the ecstasy of that first meditation when I closed my eyes and saw golden swarms of nothing, the true thing, the thus-ness of Creation—All of us pieces of the United Stuff rising up awhile in shroudy form, to wave a minute (70 years among the myriad mindless multibillions), *bling,* mindless neck lovely human beings and all the animals and insects and otherplanet creatures thinking they have a true SELF somewhere somehow in this sea of gold naught—Dust takes a flyer, then folds under, as flighty as a baby twister in the Pecos Plains of Texas you see across the sand swirling to no eyes, by nightfall where did it go?—Clap hands, lovely Buddha!

In my ancient books I read about Bodhisattva who said: "All living beings who discipline themselves in listening to Silence shall hear Heaven," (the blessedness that penetrates through appearances), "shall attain to the unattainable, shall enter the doorless, shall cross the river on the ferry and reach the other shore" and (no river, no ferry, no other shore) come New Year's Eve my mother and I toast martinis to each other and as she says "Happy New Year, dear boy, and I hope you'll be happy" and on the T.V. the horns and tootles are blowing (and in fleecy beds little boys wake up to hear the midnight bong below) I see that I *have* reached the other shore because it no longer matters to me about "happiness" in this or any other world, "crossing the shore" has simply been the recognition that there's nothing to yearn after, nothing to think, my Essence of Mind, the universal One Sea of mysterious mentality, so that I raise a private toast to my mother and all beings (silently) wishing them the Sweet Dharma Truth instead of a Happy "New Year" the sweet Dharma Truth, the unrecognizable recognition, that which blots out (as snow blots out) the blottable pitiful shapeliness of ogroid earth—

"The best lack all conviction," said Yeats, because as the ancient Chinese say: "He who knows does not speak."

from
BOOK OF DREAMS
1952-1960

FOR THE FIRST TIME—dreamed I climbed a gradual cliff from slope to slope and got up on top and sat down but suddenly in looking down I saw it was not a gradual cliff at all but sheer—in the dream no thought of getting down on other side—in the dream as always in Highplaces Dreams I'm concerned with *getting down the way I came,* or rectifying my own mistakes—and even though I know it's a dream, within the dream I insist I must get down off the high cliff I climbed—the same old fear grips me in mortal throes—"But if it's a dream then the cliff is not real," I tell myself "so just wake up & the cliff will vanish"—I hardly believe it's possible, and trembling, open my eyes & the dream is gone, the cliff is gone, the terror is gone—This is the Sign from Bud-

dha's Compassion at last—In other words, for the first time I dreamed
that I was on a high place & was afraid to get down but I knew it was
a dream & something told me to wake up & the high place would
disappear, & I opened my eyes & it was all gone

SAVED!

Buddha rectified by mistake for me—AWAKEN FROM THE
DREAM

For a moment too I thought of jumping down to get down—O
pitiful reality! (but that would mean mortal pain, the falling, mortal
horror, or, death)—

Also, in many other Highplace Dreams I knew it was a dream too,
but insisted within the dream *on getting down*—dream-activity in the
dreamworld—dream-activity in the dreamworld—dream-action down
the dream-cliff—

The cliff seemed to be, and now the cliff doesnt seem to be—

Dream-analysis in only cause-and-condition explanation (such, as,
cliff from symbol during waking day, like, murderer with knife because
window left unlocked)—dream-analysis is only a measurement of the
maya-like and has no value—dream-dispersion has the only value—
Freudianism is a big stupid mistaken dealing with causes & conditions
instead of the mysterious, essential, permanent reality of Mind
Essence—(My only problem is how to practice the Eightfold Path day
in, day out, as long as I don't live in solitude—) It's more than just the
high cliff of the other-night's-reading-Dante,—it's the high cliff of mortal anxiety—

• • •

At dawn (after yesterday's initiation of One Meal A day-No Drink-No
Friends "Western" device for Buddhism) a namelessly beautiful joy in
my dreambrain concerning the Single Taste of all things, a transcendental sensation of Singleness in the Universe, a Solitary Ecstasy—Interrupted by the daily morning vulgar throat-clearing of the Fat Pole next
door and yet I blessed him in my happiness and all anger had disappeared—Later my mind went ignorantly deeply asleep & consumed itself with visions of rough seas, seamen struggling with a lifeboat over
the side of a freighter & suddenly all disappearing to drown and you
dont see anything on the sea till a minute after the floating rowboat
hulk 300 yards down the starboard stern, the men gone except for inky
seablobs—Earlier I'd been in the old Sun Building in Lowell and asleep
upstairs & some man, thinking me drunk, carries me downstairs to

Kearney Square & I fake outness, a tender scene, he's got me like a baby—then I walk on up to a lunch cart near the Y and up Merrimac Street and report my story to someone in the dark rainy day—evil weirdness of Kearney Square, the whole thing is nothing but a discriminated cerebral hassel and this I may say for the entire book of dreams of images to disturb its unbroken serenity & preoccupations with imagelessness though *how* this is so I cant tell yet in words that are in themselves discriminative hassels of arbitrary conception—As I say, words, images & dreams are fingers of false imagination pointing at the reality of Holy Emptiness—but my words are still many & my images stretch to the holy void like a road that has an end—It's the ROAD OF THE HOLY VOID this writing, this life, this image of regrets———

· · ·

At a California camp the Americans, on orders from the Russians who keep flying overhead in big planes threatening to drop the H-Bomb, have imprisoned a large group of people in a wire-enclosed trap and are preparing them to be the first victims of the H-Bomb Detonation right on the button. Meanwhile the doomed boys play basketball and even have gang fights. At H-Hour the people will be made to lie down in bomb shelters right under the bomb; some will be given certain shots, some not; offensive liquid mixtures to drink so the cause of your death can be traced like chalk through your guts—Everybody's saying "We'll all die of Mastoids anyway"—"from the concussion on the ears of the upper explosion"—My mother and I are there, trapped, so is Julien, Joe, many others—Ma and I foolishly came to California just in time to be trapped—At H-Hour fools with earphones will hysterically count off the seconds while people wait for death—it is sad—At the end, near the end, Julien and I are sitting together on a step—We have received no shots, we are among the lot who are going to be allowed to die straight without shots and for straight research of our blue remains— It seems to me now that I have been taking care of Julien, who is like a helpless little brother, in many a life, many a rebirth—I am the Bodhisattva entrusted with his care—He barely begins to realize this, I can see, by his new silence and introspective respect—I am writing a poem to commemorate the Scene—it ends with these lines:–

The Silent Hush
Of the Pure Land Thrush.

————meaning Avalokitesvara's Transcendental Sound of Nirvana which is within and beyond the Bomb. It is a great Idealistic Poem and I finish it with a flourish of the pencil, beside the silent non committal Julien whose thoughts are bent on death—It is gray dusk, warm, withered flowers lay around—

> The Ground Divine
> Of Mortal Mind

I think on waking up—

. . .

I'm going down the stone steps of the great Buddhist World Cave saying to watchers on the parapet "It's inward suicide"—and going down the Holy Hall ways with followers, to the big Reclining Face & the swarming dark full of light irradiating from the Center—there's nowhere to go but inward—The Cave of the World, the Cave of Reality beyond conceptions of sun, air, etc., contains the Well of Shining Reality

. . .

from
THE SCRIPTURE OF
THE GOLDEN ETERNITY
1956

1

Did I create that sky? Yes, for, if it was anything other than a conception in my mind I wouldnt have said "Sky"—That is why I am the golden eternity. There are not two of us here, reader and writer, but one, one golden eternity, One-Which-It-Is, That-Which-Everything-Is.

2

The awakened Buddha to show the way, the chosen Messiah to die in the degradation of sentience, is the golden eternity. One that is what is, the golden eternity, or God, or, Tathagata—the *name*. The Named One. The human God. Sentient Godhood. Animate Divine. The Deified One. The Verified One. The Free One. The Liberator. The Still One. The Settled One. The Established One. Golden Eternity. All is Well. The Empty One. The Ready One. The Quitter. The Sitter. The Justified One. The Happy One.

3

That sky, if it was anything other than an illusion of my mortal mind I wouldnt have said "that sky." Thus I made that sky, I am the golden eternity. I am Mortal Golden Eternity.

4

I was awakened to show the way, chosen to die in the degradation of life, because I am Mortal Golden Eternity.

5

I am the golden eternity in mortal animate form.

6

Strictly speaking, there is no me, because all is emptiness. I am empty, I am non-existent. All is bliss.

7

This truth law has no more reality than the world.

8

You are the golden eternity because there is no me and no you, only one golden eternity.

9

The Realizer. Entertain no imaginations whatever, for the thing is a
no-thing. Knowing this then is Human Godhood.

10

This world is the movie of what everything is, it is one movie, made
of the same stuff throughout, belonging to nobody, which is what
everything is.

11

If we were not all the golden eternity we wouldnt be here. Because we
are here we cant help being pure. To tell man to be pure on account
of the punishing angel that punishes the bad and the rewarding angel
that rewards the good would be like telling the water "Be Wet"—
Never the less, all things depend on supreme reality, which is already
established as the record of Karma-earned fate.

12

God is not outside us but is just us, the living and the dead, the
never-lived and never-died. That we should learn it only now, is
supreme reality, it was written a long time ago in the archives of
universal mind, it is already done, there's no more to do.

13

This is the knowledge that sees the golden eternity in all things, which
is us, you, me, and which is no longer us, you, me.

14

What name shall we give it which hath no name, the common eternal
matter of the mind? If we were to call it essence, some might think it
meant perfume, or gold, or honey. It is not even mind. It is not even
discussable, groupable into words; it is not even endless, in fact it is
not even mysterious or inscrutably inexplicable; it is what is; it is that;

it is this. We could easily call the golden eternity "This." But "what's in a name?" asked Shakespeare. The golden eternity by another name would be as sweet. A Tathagata, A God, a Buddha by another name, an Allah, a Sri Krishna, a Coyote, a Brahma, a Mazda, a Messiah, an Amida, an Aremedeia, a Maitreya, a Palalakonuh, 1 2 3 4 5 6 7 8 would be as sweet. The golden eternity is X, the golden eternity is A, the golden eternity is $\triangle$, the golden eternity is $\bigcirc$, the golden eternity is $\square$, the golden eternity is t-h-e g-o-l-d-e-n e-t-e-r-n-i-t-y. In the beginning was the word; before the beginning, in the beginningless infinite neverendingness, was the essence. Both the word "God" and the essence of the word, are emptiness. The form of emptiness which is emptiness having taken the form of form, is what you see and hear and feel right now, and what you taste and smell and think as you read this. Wait awhile, close your eyes, let your breathing stop three seconds or so, listen to the inside silence in the womb of the world, let your hands and nerve-ends drop, re-recognize the bliss you forgot, the emptiness and essence and ecstasy of ever having been and ever to be the golden eternity. This is the lesson you forgot.

15

The lesson was taught long ago in the other world systems that have naturally changed into the empty and awake, and are here now smiling in our smile and scowling in our scowl. It is only like the golden eternity pretending to be smiling and scowling to itself; like a ripple on the smooth ocean of knowing. The fate of humanity is to vanish into the golden eternity, return pouring into its hands which are not hands. The navel shall receive, invert, and take back what'd issued forth; the ring of flesh shall close; the personalities of long dead heroes are blank dirt.

16

The point is we're waiting, not how comfortable we are while waiting. Paleolithic man waited by caves for the realization of why he was there, and hunted; modern men wait in beautified homes and try to forget death and birth. We're waiting for the realization that this is the golden eternity.

17

It came on time.

18

There is a blessedness surely to be believed, and that is that everything abides in eternal ecstasy, now and forever.

• • •

53

Everything's alright, form is emptiness and emptiness is form, and we're here forever, in one form or another, which is empty. Everything's alright, we're not here, there, or anywhere. Everything's alright, cats sleep.

54

The everlasting and tranquil essence, look around and see the smiling essence everywhere. How wily was the world made, Maya, not-even-made.

55

There's the world in the daylight. If it was completely dark you wouldnt see it but it would still be there. If you close your eyes you really see what it's like: mysterious particle-swarming emptiness. On the moon big mosquitos of straw know this in the kindness of their hearts. Truly speaking, unrecognizably sweet it all is. Dont worry about nothing.

56

Imaginary judgments about things, in this Nothing-Ever-Happened wonderful Void, you dont even have to reject them, let alone accept them. "That looks like a tree, let's call it a tree," said Coyote to Earthmaker at the beginning, and they walked around the rootdrinker patting their bellies.

57

Perfectly selfless, the beauty of it, the butterfly doesnt take it as a personal achievement, he just disappears through the trees. You too, kind and humble and not-even-here, it wasnt in a greedy mood that you saw the light that belongs to everybody.

58

Look at your little finger, the emptiness of it is no different than the emptiness of infinity.

59

Cats yawn because they realize that there's nothing to do.

60

Up in heaven you wont remember all these tricks of yours. You wont even sigh "Why?" Whether as atomic dust or as great cities, what's the difference in all this stuff. A tree is still only a rootdrinker. The puma's twisted face continues to look at the blue sky with sightless eyes, Ah sweet divine and indescribable verdurous paradise planted in mid-air! Caitanya, it's only consciousness. Not with thoughts of your mind, but in the believing sweetness of your heart, you snap the link and open the golden door and disappear into the bright room, the everlasting ecstasy, eternal Now. Soldier, follow me!—there never was a war. Arjuna, dont fight!—why fight over nothing? Bless and sit down.

61

I remember that I'm supposed to be a man and consciousness and I focus my eyes and the print reappears and the words of the poor book are saying, "The world, as God has made it" and there are no words in my pitying heart to express the knowless loveliness of the trance there was before I read those words, I had no such idea there was a world.

62

This world has no marks, signs or evidence of existence, nor the
noises in it, like accident of wind or voices or heehawing animals, yet
listen closely the eternal hush of silence goes on and on throughout all
this, and has been going on, and will go on and on. This is because
the world is nothing but a dream and is just thought of and the
everlasting eternity pays no attention to it. At night under the moon,
or in a quiet room, hush now, the secret music of the Unborn goes on
and on, beyond conception, awake beyond existence. Properly
speaking, awake is not really awake because the golden eternity never
went to sleep: you can tell by the constant sound of Silence which
cuts through this world like a magic diamond through the trick of
your not realizing that your mind caused the world.

63

The God of the American Plateau Indian was Coyote. He says:
"Earth! those beings living on your surface, none of them
disappearing, will all be transformed. When I have spoken to them,
when they have spoken to me, from that moment on, their words and
their bodies which they usually use to move about with, will all
change. I will not have heard them."

64

I was smelling flowers in the yard, and when I stood up I took a deep
breath and the blood all rushed to my brain and I woke up dead on
my back in the grass. I had apparently fainted, or died, for about
sixty seconds. My neighbor saw me but he thought I had just
suddenly thrown myself on the grass to enjoy the sun. During that
timeless moment of unconsciousness I saw the golden eternity. I saw
heaven. In it nothing had ever happened, the events of a million years
ago were just as phantom and ungraspable as the events of now or of
a million years from now, or the events of the next ten minutes. It
was perfect, the golden solitude, the golden emptiness, Something-Or-
Other, something surely humble. There was a rapturous ring of
silence abiding perfectly. There was no question of being alive or not
being alive, of likes and dislikes, of near or far, no question of giving
or gratitude, no question of mercy or judgment, or of suffering or its

opposite or anything. It was the womb itself, aloneness, alaya vijnana the universal store, the Great Free Treasure, the Great Victory, infinite completion, the joyful mysterious essence of Arrangement. It seemed like one smiling smile, one adorable adoration, one gracious and adorable charity, everlasting safety, refreshing afternoon, roses, infinite brilliant immaterial golden ash, the Golden Age. The "golden" came from the sun in my eyelids, and the "eternity" from my sudden instant realization as I woke up that I had just been where it all came from and where it was all returning, the everlasting So, and so never coming or going; therefore I call it the golden eternity but you can call it anything you want. As I regained consciousness I felt so sorry I had a body and a mind suddenly realizing I didnt even have a body and a mind and nothing had ever happened and everything is alright forever and forever and forever, O thank you thank you thank you.

65

This is the first teaching from the golden eternity.

66

The second teaching from the golden eternity is that there never was a first teaching from the golden eternity. So be sure.

SELECTED
LETTERS

EDITOR'S INTRODUCTION

ONE OF THE EARLIEST SURVIVING LETTERS by Kerouac was written to his sister Caroline when he was nineteen, a short time before he returned to Columbia College to begin his sophomore year in the fall of 1941. Kerouac typed most of his letters, and he kept drafts and carbons of many of the hundreds of letters he wrote to family, friends, and literary associates over the next twenty-eight years. He was an indefatigible correspondent, neatly filing his own letters and those sent to him in case he wanted to use them later on in his books. For example, details in this early letter to his sister were recycled in 1967, when he wrote *Vanity of Duluoz* about this period of his life.

Letters played an important part when Kerouac broke through to finding his own voice as a writer with *On the Road* in April of 1951. The previous December he had been impressed by a letter many thousands of words long sent to him by Neal Cassady, telling about Cassady's sexual exploits in Denver. When Kerouac sat down to write *On the Road,* he imagined he was telling the story of his adventures with Neal Cassady to his newly married second wife, Joan Haverty. While she was away from their Manhattan apartment in the daytime, working as a waitress in Stouffer's Restaurant and, as she remembered, busying herself at home scrubbing and painting the shabby apartment at night, Kerouac worked steadily on his book, as if he were writing her a series of long letters. He was even able to weave into his narrative sections of Cassady's letters, which he'd been saving since 1947. Later Kerouac said he also wrote *The Subterraneans* "like a long letter to a friend."

The letters in this section of the reader begin on August 25, 1942, after twenty-year-old Kerouac had signed up in Boston as a merchant seaman, taking out ordinary seaman's papers. He wrote the letter to a Barnard College student named Norma Blickfelt, whom he'd dated in New York City that spring. This was Kerouac's second letter to the girl, but apparently he never mailed either letter, keeping the first one written in July, he told her, "as a monument to my emotional 'teens."

This letter from August 25, 1942, was written on board the Merchant Marine ship S.S. *Dorchester,* after Kerouac had signed on as a scullion. Transporting a construction crew to Greenland, the ship was attacked unsuccessfully by German submarines in the North Atlantic. Kerouac described his experiences aboard ship in *Vanity of Duluoz,* but Norma Blickfeld never appeared in the book. There Kerouac wrote, "I'm not mentioning love affairs much in this book because I think acquiescing to the lovin whims of girls was the least of my Vanity."

Kerouac's wartime letter suggests the strength of his idealism and his passionate desire to become a writer before he grew up and became, as he wrote in *Vanity of Duluoz,* "eviscerated of 1930s innocent ambition."

August 25, 1942
Love letter written at sea

Dear Norma—

You must excuse the stationery (and the pencil), but aboard these ships one is not always able to procure monogrammed and perfumed writing paper—I borrowed this sheet from the Puerto Rican night cook, who presented me it for so graciously composing a love letter for him.

How are you, Norma? Will you forgive me for not writing sooner. . . . I can't tell you very much, nor where I am, but I *can* say that I'm in the Merchant Marine, and in a very beautiful and enchanted land. I would have written to you sooner, but since at times things around here take on the aspects of war, I was not able.

Let me confess that I wrote you a long and dramatic letter before I shipped out, but I never mailed it. Of course, I was not able to visit you this summer as I had planned (at the Poughkeepsie camp), since I sailed out quite some time ago. But as to that letter, I shall preserve it as a monument to my emotional 'teens. (As I write now, the little Morro cook sits beside me eating oatmeal and Spanish chicken rice . . . it is morning, a grey drizzling dawn prevails, etc. etc.) . . . and I am in a most poetic mood. I'm studying like mad on this ship—*Outline of History,*[1] the Roman writers, some classics, Thomas Mann (what a Humanist!), and *The Shadow*[2] Magazine. Anxious to get back to dear old Columbia, if I can, in January. I took this trip in order to make money for school, but I misjudged the length of the voyage, and will not be back in time for the Fall semester. But what romance! . . . to stand on a deck bare-chested at dawn, and to listen to the pulse-beats of the ship's great, idle engine—Wolfe's "morning and new lands . . ."[3] In the interim between this trip and January, I shall go down to New Orleans for a South American ship. As soon as I return from this run, I'm taking a room in the Village for a few weeks to write like mad (with Sebastian,

1. H. G. Wells's (1866–1946) *Outline of History* (1920). Kerouac wrote in *Vanity of Duluoz* that he went to sea "with a little black bag containing rags and a collection of classical literature weighing several ounces in small print."

2. *The Shadow* was a biweekly American pulp magazine.

3. Thomas Wolfe (1900–1938), American novelist, author of *Look Homeward Angel* (1929), *The Web and the Rock* (1939), and *You Can't Go Home Again* (1940). Like most aspiring American novelists of his generation, Kerouac admired Wolfe above all others and took his autobiographical fiction as a literary prototype.

of course), and take in the theatrical season. I'll call you up as soon as
I arrive, and if Saroyan's on Broadway and the Russian restaurants go
on tinkling songs of home while Russians weep into their vodka, we'll
take that in together.

(Perceive—I have another sheet!)

How's Barnard? (You see, I don't know when you'll receive this
note.) If not so, how's the camp? Did you succeed in being assigned to
the care of blind children? Can there be such a thing as a female Humanist? (As Budd Schulberg[4] said, when a man finds a woman who can
think, he blithely allows that she has the "body and heart of a woman,
and the mind of a man.") Naive or not, that is you all over.

We did have a wonderful time last April, didn't we! Third Avenue
(our penthouse, our little song), the Bowery, Chinatown, Union Square,
the Harbor and your engaging little German singing, and the G.A. with
its orgiastic Joe Colleges . . . (Shades of Elliott Nugent . . .)[5] Twelve
hours together, twelve hours after almost two years, and now, months
since April. I must make up for this when I return . . . after I left N.Y.
last Spring, I went on South and wandered about in my own lonely
way, from city to city, village to village, listening to the Negroes sing
the blues, eating and working in lunchcarts, hopping freights and listening to the great American music of a train whistle. But I never did
hit Asheville, N.C., Wolfe's hometown. I will next time. Suffice it to say
I enjoyed myself, but the next time I wander America, I'll have money
to do it more freely. And stories—I've millions of them, all ready to
pop out. Now, more than ever, do I want to write. I've left aimlessness
and paradoxical chaos behind me. . . . I'm developing an understanding
of relations, which I believe is true knowledge, and I find the particular
Genius of poetry (as Thoreau would have put it) quite redundant in
myself . . . (entrez l'ego). I am either frank, or egotistical & vain, or all
three. I don't remember Whitman having been self-depreciating, nor
Wolfe with his long hours at the mirror, nor Saroyan indeed, nor Joyce,
etc.[6] If anybody tells me I'm disillusioning myself, or harboring "pre-

4. Budd Schulberg was the author of the bestselling Hollywood novel *What
Makes Sammy Run?* (1941).

5. Elliott Nugent was a popular stage and film actor, playwright, and director.

6. William Saroyan (1908–1981) was the Armenian-American author of the
popular book of short stories *My Name Is Aram* (1940), which Kerouac had taken
as a model when he started to write a book of short stories the previous fall in
Hartford. James Joyce's *Ulysses* (1922) was another literary influence on him at this
time. See *Vanity of Duluoz*, Book Six, II.

tenses to a higher mentality," or even "trying to rise from the 'people'," as my father claims,[7] I'll tell them they're damned fools and will go on writing, studying, travelling, singing, loving, seeing, smelling, hearing, and feeling. . . . Write to me, Norma; I miss you. Address: JACK KEROUAC A.P.O. 858 c/o Postmaster, N.Y. City. Forwarded Air Mail to us. Yours ever, Jack.

EDITOR'S NOTE

In February 1951, soon after Kerouac and his second wife, Joan, had moved into their apartment on West 20th Street, Cassady made a brief trip to New York to see the infant son he had conceived with Diana Hansen the previous year. He couldn't supply transportation for Jack and Joan to come back with him to San Francisco, and Kerouac described their last sad encounter in the final pages of On the Road, *watching as Cassady's counterpart, Dean Moriarty, "ragged in a moth-eaten overcoat he brought specially for the freezing temperatures of the East, walked off alone." The next month John Clellon Holmes brought Kerouac the manuscript of his completed novel* Go, *a fictionalized account of the lives of Ginsberg, Cassady, and others in their circle. On April 2, 1951, Kerouac began the three-week stint of marathon typing of a new version of* On the Road *on ten-foot sheets of paper that he had found in the apartment. The novel nearly completed, Kerouac learned that Ginsberg had immediately told Cassady about it. "Worried you might get wrong impression of what I was writing," Jack wrote to Neal that he'd just about finished a story that "deals with you and me and the road." There was relief as well as apology in Kerouac's tone when he confessed to his friend that he'd "telled all the road now. Went fast because road is fast. . . ."*

TO NEAL CASSADY

May 22 1951
[Richmond Hill]

Dear Neal,

7. In *Vanity of Duluoz,* Kerouac dramatized the arguments between his parents about him after he dropped out of Columbia and came back to live at home. Gabrielle always took Jack's side in his quarrels with his father, telling her son, "Listen to me, dont listen to him, if you do, you'll be the same thing he is, he never did anything himself . . . he's jealous that you'll go out and make something of yourself. . . ."

Want you to know I didn't ask Allen to write you a letter about "your doom" and that in fact my book about you is not about your doom but about your life and I know your life in many respects better than Allen does . . . not sluffing Allen but I was worried you might get wrong impression of what I was writing. From Apr. 2 to Apr. 22 I wrote 125,000 [word] full-length novel averaging 6 thous. a day, 12 thous. first day, 15,000 thous. last day.—10,000 thous. devoted to Victoria, Gregor, girls, weed, etc. Story deals with you and me and the road . . . how we first met 1947, early days; Denver 47 etc.; 1949 trip in Hudson; that summer in queer Plymouth and 110-mi-an-hour Caddy and Chi and Detroit; and final trip to Mexcity with Jeffries—last part dealing with your last trip to N.Y. and how I saw you cuttin around corner of 7th Ave. last time. (Night of Henri Cru and concert.) Plot, if any, is devoted to your development from young jailkid of early days to later (present) W.C. Fields saintliness . . . step by step in all I saw. Book marks complete departure from Town & City and in fact from previous American Lit. I don't know how it will be received. If it goes over (Giroux waiting to see it) then you'll know yourself what to do with your own work . . . blow and tell all. I've told all the road now. Went fast because road is fast . . . wrote whole thing on strip of paper 120 foot long (tracing paper that belonged to Cannastra.)—just rolled it through typewriter and in fact no paragraphs . . . rolled it out on floor and it looks like a road. Now Neal I want to tell you—your doom is of no concern to me simply because I don't think you're doomed at all and in fact I expect your soul to get wilder and wilder as you grow older till at ninety you will be a great white-haired saint even if a "blank" brakeman (Allen's wds.)[1] Fuck it, in fact you know you will wind up in Mexico with your family if you have any sense . . . but even if you don't . . . It's not your doom; I been worrying all day that Allen

---

1. Ginsberg had written Cassady that Kerouac had nearly finished a book about him but needed help with the ending of the story: "Jack needs, however, an ending. Write him a serious self-prophetic letter foretelling your fortune in fate, so he can have courage to finish his paean in a proper apotheosis or grinding of brakes."

Cassady got into the spirit of things by supplying a few alternative endings for *On the Road*: "Tell Jack I become ulcerated old color-blind RR conductor who never writes anything good and dies a painful lingering death from prostate gland trouble (cancer from excessive masturbation) at 45. Unless I get sent to San Quentin for rape of teenager and drown after slipping into slimy cesspool that workgang is unclogging. Of course I might fall under freight train, but that's too good. . . ."

made you sad; made you say about blind-spots cock cancers and what not. Another thing: pay no attention, partially [sic], to material of last January dealing with Virgin Mary girls . . . cunt is all and I know it. I don't harken back to Black Christ Cunt at all . . . I know cunt is all, I live cunt and always will and always have . . . saying this to assure you I don't renounce the one thing you hold dear but hold it as dear. To forestall, therefore, this psychological development in your brain possibly . . . "Jack wrote about Virgin girls . . . now he has turned on me and spells my doom." All Allen's own mind. I believe in your energy, your loves, your greatness, your final and magnificent grandness like Whitman's and I believe in your LIVING and not your DYING (I'm not a Cannastra, a Ginsberg, a Carr). I believe in everything about you except you dying and if you die I won't know what to do with myself in this world, in the special compartment which is reserved for you, the other reserved for Joan. I love you as ever and not only that I don't want you to die. Clear? And I love Carolyn and I love your children and I love women and I love life and celebrate and believe and let's hear no more and this is the way I'll be till ninety.

If book sells, I get advance immediately, June, and take off at once for Mexico, bus, things slow freight, arriving Mexcity, look for cheap pad, settling down temporarily till other developments and other books (will now write all my books in twenty days.) Of course since Apr. 22 I've been typing and revising. Thirty days on that. Will be my routine . . . starting with my own life, pure aspects, no fiction, till I can invent like a Dostoevsky and of course I know how and can and will. As for you, don't wanta hear another word about your inability to decide whether to say "although" or "till" or "rather" or such shit in front of a sentence . . . How many times do I have to tell you the letter about Joan Anderson is an American masterpiece and so are you leaving it to ME to sweat to publish it. Now you also know why I haven't written lately—novelwork—and soon as I finish I write you huge letter telling EVERYTHING about N.Y. Jerry Newman[2] gossip, etc. All. Don't have to write back—let me write all our letters.

Jack

P.S. I was waiting to finish my book to write to you & surprise you.

2. Jerry Newman was a New York friend and jazz enthusiast who founded Esoteric Records.

EDITOR'S NOTE
*In a letter to the writer John Clellon Holmes in the summer of 1952,
Kerouac described the euphoria he felt living in William Burroughs'
apartment in Mexico City. Midway through the composition of Doctor
Sax, Kerouac felt himself at the height of his creative powers, on the
verge of discovering "something beyond the novel and beyond the arbitrary confines of the story . . . into the realms of revealed Picture
. . . wild form . . . my mind is exploding to say something about every
image and every memory. . . ."*

TO JOHN CLELLON HOLMES

June 3 [1952]
[Mexico City]

Dear John,

Dig this, PEOTL EATERS OF THE HIP GENERATION: It was
only a customary (I'm writing this as I go along) week in the life of Bill
and I when all of a sudden, to break the calm or paralysis of our long
after-dinner conversations dominated by his massively informed and
never-endingly sour and severe pedantry full of richnesses and prizes
and unspeakable sophistications of speech, comes along a gang of young
American hipsters: first young tall blond B. in Levis and bohemian sad-
dlestrap shoes and strange little yachting cap on head, once owned a
motorcycle, once fished his own boat in Key West—a kid of the crazy
generation of the Fifties, anxious to find his way through the maze with
a string of hip signs, with little hip wife . . . seven year old kid, two
others . . . 28 . . . and real nice, good smile, nice kid, sweet boy in fact,
that's your thought, he's a sweet boy, he's hip, he's all right, he's real
cool, and his wife too, and they have some peotl and give us some so
Bill and I are settling down mashing up our peotl buttons into a green
little dish [. . . .] so Bill and I eat the peotl and get the usual results:
first you feel within minutes the wild toxicity of the poison . . . "these
green apples have a toxin in their tree" . . . "old peotl cactus grooking
in the desert to eat our hearts alive" . . . a charge like a high Benny
drive . . . then nausea, and finally the desire to vomit but you can't
without great difficulty and if you do anyway you will lose yr high at
great cost, and for two hours absolute, absolute misery. So Bill gets
going on some miserable line . . . of something, anything, to keep alive
. . . he begins with . . . "Ah, I feel awful, I feel worse than if I was
suddenly a prisoner in the High Andes, a penalist in a town like Quito

up on the High Andes all dark and windy and cloudy all day with
incredibly dirty old Indian women sitting by a wall huddled in their
robes against the cold wind and across the street you see an old man
with his hands in his cape, nothing to do but sit and already night is
coming if that's what you're waiting for, sort of an unpleasant cold
wind coming up, you know it'll be a cold night, and as I step off the
bus to enter the Penal House I'm strapping my leather belt of the leather
jacket because of the cold wind that's just swooped down from the
Andes and I look at my leather belt buckle with a feeling of complete
and irrevocable hopelessness. The Penalists are allowed to sit around
the stone square all day, the Landlady of the Penalists won't have them
hanging around the room, besides she only wants them around for
meals and Sunday afternoon's one tea . . . Penalists can buy one candy
bar a week, in the one store in town, and can stand around looking at
the candy they're going to buy on Sunday but have to stand behind the
Customer's Line. I am treated with greater contempt by the old bitch
in the Penal House because she has some paranoid idea I'm a privileged
snob on account of my brown leather jacket and gray felt hat. So I sit
all day huddled in my jacket and hat in the cold dirty winds of the High
Andes. None of the Penalists know how they got to the Penal Town,
they only know one thing: that they can never leave. This is because of
an impassible mountainpass, can only be attempted with guides, and
anyway there is an Escape Consultant for the Penalists who wish to
escape but he is an old fumbler and doogler Major Hoople[1] idiot boast-
ing about the past, filling out endless papers, works his hobby in the
evening, by day has a regular weatherbeaten indoor bench placed outdoors under the Square tree and the Penalists wait for their turns in the
other benches as the endless interview drags on. Finally some of the old
Penalists become dotty and yell out at night, 'Well, boys—got the guide
all bought for Monday morning . . . wish me luck,' " and a great silence
permeates the gloomy halls of the Penalists, and Bill is dismally surveying the floor and realizes he is not in Hell which is at least hot, but in
Eternity which is so cold . . . He told that story to prevent himself from
vomiting. Isn't it great?

So we got high on the peotl and I went out and walked around
feebly in the moonlight of the park with no coat on wanting to sit in
the grass and stay near the ground all night by moonlight, with the
lights of the show and the houses all flashing, flashing in my eyeballs

1. A popular comic-strip character.

not in technicolor riot but in a great flapping of light that clapped over
my eyes in intervals, as if, and I knew, light was a throb, and is. Bill
got on a talking kick. The next morning Wig arrived from San Francisco, a bop bass player I'd known vaguely there, but he came to Bill's
for stuff and so I met him, he played with Shorty Rogers and the new
group out there. Shorty Rogers trumpet, arranger; Jimmy Guiffre on
tenor and the great Art Pepper on alto, Hampton Hawes on piano and
get his piano, and the one and only "Haw!" Shelley Manne on drums
(with a French horn and a tuba also), and bass, a group that Wig says
is the "First indication that California can do something the East can
do; Shorty Rogers doesn't blow like Miles [Davis] at all, he blows entirely different, for my money better" (with which statement I find hard
to agree, I heard the entire new album on 33 by Shorty Rogers and his
Giants and he doesn't blow like Miles, but his own way (of course, as
Wig himself says, you can't compare these things) . . . So Wig's in town,
has a big car, and suddenly says to entire assemblage gathered in a
hipster possessed afternoon in Bill's pad and my pad, B. the blond hipster, his wife, Don, Dave, an Indian girl his wife, and pick up his
speaker, 33 modern sleek machine and a whole case of longplayed bop
albums mind you, and come back, hook up in bedroom, set up music,
and first Wig plays Stan Getz and the Swedish group with Bengt Halberg
on piano, the marvelous Lars Gullin on baritone, great rhythm section
—first music I'd heard in months . . . months . . . then that night Wig
wigs and goes to sleep and leaves machine to me, by now we're in stone
cottage out in woods and got fire going and outside is raining and got
weed, peotl highs again, Bill high, and I play everything in albums and
for the first time in months contemplate the music of bop . . . also play
Bartok, Walton quartet, Villa Lobos . . . till late next day, play all the
Bird albums including the marvelous blues he blows and the choruses
he interchanges with Miles on an album called Modern Sounds in Jazz,
featuring its Creator Charley Parker, name of album, a blue album, a
must, Miles plays a solo in there as pure as wood.

  [. . . .]Someday I'm going to write a huge Dostoevskyan novel
about all of us. If I could only stick to novels long enough to tell a few
good big stories, what I am beginning to discover now is something
beyond the novel and beyond the arbitrary confines of the story . . .
into the realms of revealed Picture . . . revealed whatever . . . revelated
prose . . . *wild form,* man, *wild form.* Wild form's the only form holds
what I have to say—my mind is exploding to say something about every
image and every memory in—I have now an irrational lust to set down

everything I know—in narrowing circles around the core of my last writing, very last writing, when I am an old man or ready to die, will be calm like the center of whirlpools and Beethoven's quartets—I love the world, and especially do I love the external eye and the shining heart of pure heart-to-heart mornings in a sane eternity, with love and security, but at this time in my life I'm making myself sick to find the wild form that can grow with my wild heart . . . because now I KNOW MY HEART DOES GROW . . . SALUD! HEALTH! JOY! WRITE TO ME SOON! LOOK FORWARD TO A HUGE JOY IN THE VERY NEAR FUTURE—I see it in yr cards, in the sky. Someday I am going to be a hermit in the woods . . . very soon now I'll visit my site.

Jack

EDITOR'S NOTE

Kerouac had come up from his home in Florida and was staying in Joyce Glassman's Manhattan apartment when On the Road *was reviewed by Gilbert Millstein in the* New York Times *(September 5, 1957). Millstein called it "an authentic work of art" whose publication marked "a historic occasion." After this auspicious beginning, reviews of the book appeared, as Kerouac said, "everyfuckingwhere." Most were unsympathetic, as when* Time *accused Kerouac of writing a novel that created "a rationale for the fevered young." In the swirl of controversy,* On the Road *moved onto the bestseller lists for a few weeks, and Kerouac was beseiged by interviewers wanting him to explain the Beat Generation. In the beginning of October 1957, he wrote a letter to Allen Ginsberg (then living and traveling abroad with his lover Peter Orlovsky and the poet Gregory Corso), describing the first month of "roaring parties," public appearances, movie offers, "nervous breakdowns," and the generally tumultuous experience of sudden literary fame in New York.*

TO ALLEN GINSBERG

Oct. 1 '57
[New York City]

Dear Allen,

Of course now in a position to send you your $225 sometime this Fall . . . Did you see Gregory in Amsterdam? I writing to him separately . . . First, you must tell Peter that I wrote him a long beautiful letter about the Russian Soul but mailed it c/o Orlovsky instead of c/o Ansen, Venice, so it's probably still there and he must send for that letter for sure . . . it was to you too . . . important you shd. read it. Everything's been happening here, including this last satori weekend[1] with Lucien and Cessa and kids and Joyce at his upstate country haunted New England house with birds peeking in the holy windows, a big blurred Dostoevskyan party with socialites where I was the Idiot, etc. so mad in fact I could write a novel about just this last weekend, Lucien and I went mad in moonlight haunted house yelling coyote cries and gibbering and seriously insane sitting in our shorts in the old parlor as girls tried to sleep . . . then when all sleep I played 4 hours massive musical suck-out of everything in pump-organ incredibly long sonatas, thundering oratorios, shoulda heard . . . A guy called Leo Garen (who you better meet, 20, hepcat) will produce a play about Neal if I write it, offers me a weekend in Taft Hotel in room overlooking Broadway with free sandwiches and typewriter if I knock it off, which I might (big play about Neal, horses, the night of the Bishop etc., with you and Peter in it)— But another guy called Joe Lustig backed by money also wants a play about Neal—Meanwhile Hollywood somewhat active on *Road,* Marlon Brando's manager (his Dad) I heard was interested—Italian publishers bought *Road*—Grove Press bought *Subterraneans* on new hard cover bigtime basis—*Esquire* bought casual baseball story for $400 (all spent now)—*Pageant* bought article on Beat for $300—I wrote intro to a book of photos by Robt Frank, to be trans[lated] into French for the English edition (Delpire publishers)—Ferlinghetti getting my *Blues* by mail—Letter from Charles Olson[2] saying I am a poet, he says, from reading Ontario stuff and "3 Stooges" (by the way, I sent you a copy of the "3 Stooges" *New Edition* to Venice, did you get it?)—[. . . .]— Unbelievable number of events almost impossible to remember, including earlier big Viking Press hotel room with thousands of screaming interviewers and *Road* roll original 100 mile ms. rolled out on carpet, bottles of Old Granddad, big articles in *Sat. Review,* in *World Telly,* everyfuckingwhere, everybody mad, Brooklyn College wanted me to lec-

1. Kerouac and Joyce Glassman had gone to upstate New York to stay with Lucien and Cessa Carr and their children. When Kerouac became so obstreperously drunk that he interrupted a doctor who was prescribing flu shots for the children, Cessa Carr told Jack, "Shut your big mouth!" and he was shocked into what he called a "satori," or moment of sudden awakening, what he regarded as a "kick in the eye."

2. Charles Olson, the rector of the experimental arts school Black Mountain College, was an American avant garde poet who wrote epic poetry about Gloucester, Massachusetts, in the tradition of Ezra Pound.

ture to eager students and big geek questions to answer . . . Of course I was on television big Interview bit, John Wingate show, mad night, I answered angelic to evil questions, big letters poured in saying I was beloved, finally a phonecall from Little Jack Melody[3] . . . I had nervous breakdowns, 2, now I got piles and I lay up read *The Idiot*[4] and rest mind . . . I had final evil flips of evil spirits and most insane dreams of all time where I end up in leading big parades of screaming laughing children (wearing my white headband) down Victory Street Lowell and finally into Asia . . . (parade is intended to cover me up from cops, when they look kids surround me hide me singing, finally cops join parade happy and it ends big blur of robes in Asia) . . . I been preaching Peterism, on TV too, about love, preaching Nealism, everything, I have just made big final preachment in American that wd. flip you if you knew details . . . big roaring parties finally where I see old enemies in a blur, shouting round me . . . news that Norman Mailer pleased with me, telegram from Nelson Algren praising me, etc. etc. in short we dont need press agents any more (I told Sterling[5] to leave minor details of our poetry & Burroughs to us, he is busy with contracts and $$$ and bewildered by yr. innocent demands, you being poet do not realize the madness of NY)—You will when you get back—NOW LISTEN VIKING WANTS TO PUBLISH HOWL AND YOUR OTHERS AND ALSO GROVE. THEY RACING TO REACH YOU FIRST. TAKE YOUR CHOICE. I THINK HOWL NEEDS DISTRIBUTION. IT HAS NOT EVEN BEGUN TO BE READ.

EDITOR'S NOTE

The next two letters to Allen Ginsberg and Kerouac's literary agent, Sterling Lord, in 1960–1961 give a sense of Kerouac's dedication to his writing, despite the distractions of being what he called "King of the Beats." He wrote to Ginsberg in September 1960, shortly after coming home to Northport, New York, after staying in Lawrence Ferlinghetti's cabin at Bixby Canyon, an experience described in Big Sur. *Kerouac passed on the news about their old friend Neal Cassady's current life in Los Gatos, California, after Neal had served time in prison for possession of marijuana. Writing to Sterling Lord in May 1961 from a new*

---

3. Little Jack Melody was one of Burroughs's drug connections in New York City in the 1940s.

4. Fydor Dostoevsky's novel *The Idiot* (1868).

5. Sterling Lord, Kerouac's literary agent.

home in Florida, in which he lived with his mother, Kerouac outlined
his plans for the Duluoz Legend, or "Jack's" Lifetime.

TO ALLEN GINSBERG

Sept. 22, 1960
[Northport, N.Y.]

Dear Allen,

Yes, just got back, big TWA Ambassador flight, tax deductible,
with wine and champagne and filet mignon and Chinese Tapei ambassador's wife in front of me etc.—New York seems cowed and nasty
after anarchistic crazy freewheeling Frisco—Saw everybody—Neal
greater than ever, sweeter by far, looking good, healthy—Walks to
work in Los Gatos now as tire recapper—would be willing to play Dean
in ON THE ROAD movie, anything better than tire recapping—SP
railroad won't take him back but want ME back (Al Hinkle reports)
(because all read "Railroad Earth," forgetting what a lousy brakeman
I was)—Much to tell you about Neal and everybody—Gave Neal
money in crisis, he very glad now, crisis was solved and he got fine new
rubywine Jeepster with good motor—gave him 100—(for rent) (he was
fired)—He got new job he walks to—Had love affair (I did) and almost
got married with his mistress but I was drunk—Prior to drunkenness I
was alone 3 weeks in woods in fine quiet fog with animals only and
learned a lot—Have changed, in fact—Am quieter, don't drink as much,
or so often at least, and have started new quiet home reading habits.
For instance had 11th edition of Encyclopedia Brittanica mailed to me
(35 bucks whole price) 29 volumes containing 30,000 pages with exactly 65,000,000 words of scholarly Oxford and Cambridge prose (65
million that is) and last night stayed up till 5 a.m. amazed in that sea
of prose—looked up Logia where Jesus is reported to have said (on old
Egyptian papyri dating to 2nd century) that one must not cease seeking
for the kingdom & WILL WAKE UP "A S T O N I S H E D" in the
kingdom! (just like my bliss-astonishment of golden eternity faint)—
Apocrypha, Shmapocrypha!—Thought I'd also look up bats as there
was a bat in Big Sur kept circling my sleepingbag every night til dawn,
was referred to Chiroptera (Chirop is Greek for "hand," tera "wing")
—found what amounts to a small volume of complete technical explanation with pictures and diagrams—This is the prize of prizes! I've been
waiting for this 29 volume edition since I first saw it age 16 in Lowell
High library—It's possible to make complete studies in Theology of

ALL religions, for instance, or study of all Tribes in the World, or all Zoology, all History to 1909, all Campaigns till then in detail, all biography till then, all Mysticism, all Kabbalas and Shmabbalas, all rare scholarly treatises on Old and New Testaments, all about Buddha, Hindus, rare exotic Malayan religions, visions, all Ornithology, Optometry, Pastometry, Futureometry and in other woids ALL—I simply can't believe such an ocean as the Pacific any more'n this encyclopedia—so my new reading habits: studying now, writing new book (started anyway) —doing exercise (headstands, snake pushups, bent bow and knee bend and breathing)—feeling fine—lost 10 or 15 pounds—only got drunk once since home 2 weeks. Wanted to get new novel in or underway before calling you but made a false start. Had to keep H.C. away who went and got himself job as electrician in Northport (!) and wanted to inundate my life as usual with all the ridiculous trivialities of his fancy —so he mad. But I can't worry about every Tom Dick and Harry who used to leave me alone to write VISIONS OF NEAL at my lonely happy rolltop desk in the early fifties.

Meanwhile, at Big Sur, I sat by sea every day, sometimes in dismal foggy roraring dark of cliffs and huge waves, and wrote SEA, first part, SEA: the Pacific Ocean at Big Sur, California. All sound of waves, like James Joyce was going to do. Wrote mostly with eyes closed, as if blind Homer. Read it to gang by oil lamp. McClure, etc. Neal, etc. all listened but it's just like OLD ANGEL, only more wave-plop kerplosh sounds, the sea don't talk in long sentences but comes in pieces, as like this:

> No human words bespeak
> the token sorrow older
> than old this wave
> becrashing smarts the
> sand with plosh
> of twirled sandy
> thought—Ah change
> the world? Ah set
> the fee? Are rope the
> angels in all the sea?
> Ah ropey otter
> barnacle d be—

(barnacle d be), rather, with the "d" all alone—Anyway this, and what Logia Jesus said about astonishment of paradise, seems to me much more on the right tracks of world peace and joy than all the recent communist and general political hysteria rioting and false screaming. Cuba Shmuba—I will come New York, open yr lock with key you gave me, wait if you not there, am buying rucksack etc., will see Lucien etc. so see you & Petey soon. Okay. Will come around the 28th—meanwhile please drop another line and enclose *Mescaline Notes* & *Gregory Letters* for the Cream File.

Jean

TO STERLING LORD

May 5, 1961
[Orlando, Florida]

Dear Sterling,

It was great to get out of NY and suddenly as if "coming back to America." All's set here. We have a guest room which we got to call "Sterling's Room" so don't miss it! Two twin beds. Patio screened, soon. A private park a quarter mile away for residents of this "exclusive" tract, with tennis courts! And I already lined up a good player for you [. . . .]

And now that I'm out of N.Y. I don't feel so hounded by that court case, forget all about it, and am ready to return to N.Y. to clear it up anytime. I hope to go to Mexico City first, however, for 2 months, to think, walk, write, alone, in a lil apt. Because that's one thing I haven't done in 3 years, is sit alone & think for months and work out the next novel. It will work out like this, probably: the Duluoz Legend: ("Jack's" Lifetime):—

1922–26	VISIONS OF GERARD	
1926–37	MEMORY BABE	(to be written)
1932–37	DOCTOR SAX	
1937–39	MAGGIE CASSIDY	
1939–43	VANITY OF DULUOZ	(to be written)
1943–48	VISIONS OF JULIEN	(to be written)
1948–50	ON THE ROAD	
1948–51	VISIONS OF CODY	(partially published)
1952–53	RAILROAD EARTH	
1955–56	TRISTESSA	
1955–56	DHARMA BUMS	
1956–57	DESOLATION ANGELS	

1957–61 UNTITLED NEW NOVEL   (to be written)
(and the non-story fill-ins like

> MEXICO CITY BLUES
> SOME OF THE DHARMA
> OLD ANGEL MIDNIGHT
> > etc.

So you see what the plan is. Now, more travel, more adventures, and future "chapters" of the legend in novel form.

If I can, I'd like to go to Mexico in a month or so, so let me know your plans. It's already hot down here but our air conditioning sends coolness from vents in every room of the house.

> As ever,
> Love,
> Jack

P.S. I got the checks.

EDITOR'S NOTE

Shortly after completing my doctorate at Columbia University, I was asked by the Phoenix Bookshop in New York to compile a bibliography of Kerouac's writing. I wrote to Gabrielle Kerouac, telling her of my project, and Jack replied on August 5, 1966, inviting me to look at the material in his collection. In my next letter I set up a date, and a few days later he sent me directions to his house, telling me he looked forward "to meeting a scholar and a gentlewoman." Then he closed by saying that I should "throw these instructions away, rather, that is, bring 'em with you—'Beatniks' look like Spooks in my mother's poor door at midnight—you understand."

TO ANN CHARTERS

> Box 809
> Hyannis, Mass.
> Aug. 5, 1966

Dear Doctor Charters:

I'm willing to go through my collection of editions at my home providing only you don't give my home address to anyone or any groups. I'm trying to work in the privacy of my own thoughts and domicile.

Also, I think my complete bibliography would come to a hundred pages or so. I think I have here, in my study, something like 99.5% information for the entire bibliography: I think the rest I can direct you to. (I've kept the neatest records you ever saw.)

So, if that's not too long, and you keep my address a secret, write and tell me the date you want to come: I'm sure we can get the whole thing done in one afternoon. I'll just pull everything out one by one, hand them to you at the desk, return the things back where they were (innumerable poetry pamphlets, broadsides, sheets from magazine publications, etc.) (and also all the 16 foreign translations of novels are either here or recorded in my pile of contracts and in foreign publishers' announcements)—Anyway, to make a long story short, write, give date, and I'll immediately send you my Hyannis street address and wait for you.

I'm going to Italy (invite of Mondadori publishers) on Sept. 26, so come long before then, please. So come on down.

Sincerely,

Jack
    Kerouac

IDENTITY KEY

Name	The Town and the City	Vanity of Duluoz	On the Road	The Subterraneans
Jack Kerouac	Peter Martin et al.	Jack Duluoz	Sal Paradise	Leo Percepied
Allen Ginsberg	Leon Levinsky	Irwin Garden	Carlo Marx	Adam Moorad
Neal Cassady			Dean Moriarty	
William Burroughs	Will Dennison	Will Hubbard	Old Bull Lee	Frank Carmody
Gary Snyder				
Gregory Corso				Yuri Gligoric
Philip Whalen				
Michael McClure				
Lawrence Ferlinghetti				Larry O'Hara
John Clellon Holmes			Tom Saybrook	Balliol MacJones
Kenneth Rexroth				
Herbert Huncke	Junky		Elmo Hassel	
Philip Lamantia				
Lew Welch				
Lenore Kandel				
John Montgomery				
Randall Jarrell				
Gore Vidal				Arial Lavalina
Peter Orlovsky				
Carolyn Cassady			Camille	

Name	The Dharma Bums	Desolation Angels	Big Sur	Book of Dreams
Jack Kerouac	Ray Smith	Jack Duluoz	Jack Duluoz	Jack
Allen Ginsberg	Alvah Goldbook	Irwin Garden	Irwin Garden	Irwin Garden
Neal Cassady	Cody Pomeray	Cody Pomeray	Cody Pomeray	Cody Pomeray
William Burroughs		Bull Hubbard		Bull Hubbard
Gary Snyder	Japhy Ryder		Jarry Wagner	
Gregory Corso		Raphael Urso		Raphael Urso
Philip Whalen	Warren Coughlin	Ben Fagan	Ben Fagan	
Michael McClure	Ike O'Shay	Patrick McLear	Pat McLear	
Lawrence Ferlinghetti			Lorenzo Monsanto	Danny Richman
John Clellon Holmes				James Watson
Kenneth Rexroth	Rheinhold Cacoethes			
Herbert Huncke				Huck
Philip Lamantia	Francis DaPavia	David D'Angeli		
Lew Welch			David Wain	
Lenore Kandel			Romona Swartz	
John Montgomery	Henry Morley	Alex Fairbrother		
Randall Jarrell		Varnum Random		
Gore Vidal				
Peter Orlovsky	George	Simon Darlovsky		Simon Darlovsky
Carolyn Cassady			Evelyn	Evelyn

BOOKS BY JACK KEROUAC

1950   *The Town and the City*. New York: Harcourt, Brace and Company.
1957   *On the Road*. New York: Viking Press.
1958   *The Subterraneans*. New York: Grove Press.
        The Dharma Bums. New York: Viking Press.
1959   *Doctor Sax*. New York: Grove Press.
        Maggie Cassidy. New York: Avon Books.
        Mexico City Blues. New York: Grove Press.
        Visions of Cody. New York: New Directions.
1960   *The Scripture of the Golden Eternity*. New York: Corinth Books.
        Tristessa. New York: Avon Books.
        Lonesome Traveler. New York: McGraw-Hill Book Company.
1961   *Book of Dreams*. San Francisco: City Lights Books.
        Pull My Daisy. New York: Grove Press.
1962   *Big Sur*. New York: Farrar, Straus and Cudahy.
1963   *Visions of Gerard*. New York: Farrar, Straus and Cudahy.
1965   *Desolation Angels*. New York: Coward-McCann.
1966   *Satori in Paris*. New York: Grove Press.
1968   *Vanity of Duluoz*. New York: Coward-McCann.
1971   *Scattered Poems*. San Francisco: City Lights Books.
        Pic. New York: Grove Press.
1973   *Visions of Cody*. New York: McGraw-Hill Book Company.
1992   *Pomes All Sizes*. San Francisco: City Lights Books.
1993   *Old Angel Midnight*. San Francisco: Grey Fox Press.
        Good Blonde & Others. San Francisco: Grey Fox Press.

FOR THE BEST IN PAPERBACKS, LOOK FOR THE

In every corner of the world, on every subject under the sun, Penguin represents quality and variety—the very best in publishing today.

For complete information about books available from Penguin—including Puffins, Penguin Classics, and Arkana—and how to order them, write to us at the appropriate address below. Please note that for copyright reasons the selection of books varies from country to country.

In the United Kingdom: Please write to *Dept. JC, Penguin Books Ltd, FREEPOST, West Drayton, Middlesex UB7 0BR*.

If you have any difficulty in obtaining a title, please send your order with the correct money, plus ten percent for postage and packaging, to *P.O. Box No. 11, West Drayton, Middlesex UB7 0BR*

In the United States: Please write to *Consumer Sales, Penguin USA, P.O. Box 999, Dept. 17109, Bergenfield, New Jersey 07621-0120*. VISA and MasterCard holders call 1-800-253-6476 to order all Penguin titles

In Canada: Please write to *Penguin Books Canada Ltd, 10 Alcorn Avenue, Suite 300, Toronto, Ontario M4V 3B2*

In Australia: Please write to *Penguin Books Australia Ltd, P.O. Box 257, Ringwood, Victoria 3134*

In New Zealand: Please write to *Penguin Books (NZ) Ltd, Private Bag 102902, North Shore Mail Centre, Auckland 10*

In India: Please write to *Penguin Books India Pvt Ltd, 706 Eros Apartments, 56 Nehru Place, New Delhi 110 019*

In the Netherlands: Please write to *Penguin Books Netherlands bv, Postbus 3507, NL-1001 AH Amsterdam*

In Germany: Please write to *Penguin Books Deutschland GmbH, Metzlerstrasse 26, 60594 Frankfurt am Main*

In Spain: Please write to *Penguin Books S.A., Bravo Murillo 19, 1° B, 28015 Madrid*

In Italy: Please write to *Penguin Italia s.r.l., Via Felice Casati 20, I-20124 Milano*

In France: Please write to *Penguin France S.A., 17 rue Lejeune, F–31000 Toulouse*

In Japan: Please write to *Penguin Books Japan, Ishikiribashi Building, 2–5–4, Suido, Bunkyo-ku, Tokyo 112*

In Greece: Please write to *Penguin Hellas Ltd, Dimocritou 3, GR–106 71 Athens*

In South Africa: Please write to *Longman Penguin Southern Africa (Pty) Ltd, Private Bag X08, Bertsham 2013*